CIRCO DEL HERRERO

[THE BLACKSMITH'S CIRCUS]

Vol. 1 & 2
Combined Edition

Circo del Herrero

For those I lost,
Like Bulfinch.
You're found in these words.

Learn more at: <u>circodelherreroseries.com</u>
10th anniversary edition

This edition published 2024.

As based on the original publications.

Vol. 1 Copyright © 2010

Vol. 2 Copyright © 2014

Cover design by SOBpublishing.

Print Paperback:

ISBN-13: 979-8-9855449-4-7

Ebook:

ISBN-13: 979-8-9855449-5-4

[BLA and GB GABBLER are characters in this story.

This novel was written by one person, not two.

All other brackets are GABBLER's.]

For Your Reference: FAQ [Spoiler Edition]
Taken from work previously published at circodelherreroseries.com by Gabbler

What are your full names? Can't say, because it'd give away our genders. And that would give away several plot twists later in the series.

Why do the Editor and Narrator break the 4th wall so much? Because our work is a statement on the Author-as-God mindset (whether the Narrator realizes it or not). No one creates in a vacuum. There is no point to a story without an audience. Insert other excuses here.

Why have an Editor annotate the story? Because sometimes people need interpreters—not just on the language level, but on the reality level. Some say there are two sides to every story. We are living proof. Everything we do is a work in progress—we wanted you to KNOW more than one person has played their role in this.

Why do you guys use "s/he" or "he/she" at times when talking about each other? Why not use only gender-neutral pronouns such as "they/their"? That's a good point. The main reason was that the Narrator and I *are* cis-gendered. We didn't want to hijack a gender-neutral pronoun that wasn't ours but wanted keep it vague enough to retain the mystery. But they/their does that pretty well too. We do drop a few they/theirs in the series and newer editions. This was, originally, a plot decision. We were expressing that, on the gender spectrum, we do lean more in a certain direction—unlike some of our future characters who *will*/use a non-binary pronoun...

What is the REAL reason you guys collaborated on this series? Because we, like all couples, think each other are brilliant. That, and Gabbler doesn't want BLA to make a fool of themselves and therefore make Gabbler look bad by extension.

How'd the Narrator get the idea for this crap? Um, you clearly aren't paying attention here. BLA believes every word written.

Why is the story set in the U.S. — most of all, the SOUTH? Because natural gas? Subterranean fuel? F*ck if we know why Vulcan chose to stir sh*t up in the "melting pot." I mean, who knows why he even has a statue in Alabama? There's no volcanoes around there, yet something is clearly attracting him... [Because The Author of this series grew up in the Bible Belt and has a lot to say (sub-textually) in response to literature like *American Gods*, for instance.]

Why are there nine Automatons? Much like the nine Muses, it seems to work just fine.

But why doesn't this book mention Talos or any of the other automatons Hephaestus/Vulcan [may have] created? Why isn't there a greater use of pre-established mythology in this book? WHYYY? Slow down there, mythology expert. Just because Talos isn't mentioned doesn't mean the story rejects that he or the others exist. This story just focuses on one batch Vulcan whipped up. If you wanted "old established myth," we suggest you go back to Hesiod and Homer. Or, gods forbid, maybe *Percy Jackson* is more your style. Have fun feeling smart about spotting the archetypes in *that* story.

Why does every chapter end in a slanty-name and a character list? Yes, we'll be upfront about the weirdness of it. Every chapter ends in a name and a list. Think it's a bit much? We wouldn't blame you. See (despite my best efforts to "free up" the chapters), our Narrator insisted. Our Narrator said (something to the effect of), "Like stanzas of a poem, the names create *form* for the novel." I, Gabbler, replied, "If poetry is your intent, then *why not write in verse*?" "Because I don't have f*cking time to write poetry! Is my writing not anal enough?" That's when I realized the Narrator's chapter "formula" was a great compromise. I'd kill myself if I had to edit iambic pentameter.

You said BLA is mute. How can they TELL you anything? BLA is very good at typing. In fact, BLA typed most of this up and I, Gabbler, just edited it. And Annotated it. And censored it.

The Blacksmith's Circus

Circo del Herrero

The Annotated Manuscript: The Automation: BOOK ONE

Vol. 1 of the Circo del Herrero Series

By B.L.A., the Narrator, Storyteller, Omnipresent One

&

G.B. Gabbler, the Editor, Annotator, Reason This Is Seeing the Light of Day...

Circo del Herrero

Acknowledgments (more like admissions):

I, the author of this story (who prefers the title "The Narrator"), would like to thank my "Editor" for the revisions and annotations associated with this account—even though said Editor took the liberty of chopping up my work and was quite insistent on making things "less embarrassing" (my Editor finds me shameful on many levels—especially when I claim this story is true). Though sometimes overzealous, there's no one else I'd let touch this work but dearest *Gabbler*.[1]

---

[1] Yes, I'm the Editor—the fourth wall-breaker. You might even call me another character in this story. At the very least, I'd like to think I'm its muse. My name is G.B. Gabbler (gender unimportant). The footnotes are all mine. I mention it only because the Narrator thinks it necessary to constantly remind you whose story this is and that I've *edited* it. I've changed various names, locations, and facts within this story—for more than one reason.

Chapter the first,

Too many freaks, too few circuses:

Please share my umbrella?[2]

Gabbler told me to start my story in a more interesting place (where I *had* started it wasn't "entertaining enough"). So, *in medias res,* here you have it:

As Odys walked down the sidewalk he saw the man—the man standing at the crossroad. The man just stood there, even though he didn't have to. The light was green and he was free to walk across. But he didn't. He simply stared at the traffic flowing past him. He even waved on the car waiting for him. *Come along, motorcar. I'm in no hurry. Have a good day.*

Odys noticed the man carried the absolute *longest* black umbrella, the fascinating kind that adapts into a perfectly fine walking cane. But there wasn't a chance of rain today. Not even sprinkles. Mildly overcast, perhaps, but nothing to deserve something *that* drastic.

And goshwow was that a top hat the old man was patting on?

As far as Odys could tell from the man's backside, this giddily-suited gentleman had time travelled from the 1800s—give or take a hundred years (Odys was no good at history). Not that Odys judged people by their appearance. No, Odys didn't judge, though he was mature enough (as a twentysomething) to know that elders didn't usually go about playing dress-up. Not on days other than Halloween. And even then…

Odys avoided eye contact when he eventually caught up to the stranger. Normally, he would have given a curious grin to someone so done up, but not today. Today was different. Today Odys was one. Not two.

His broken-down car had not only forced him to walk but his runaway sister had forced him to walk *alone.* Okay—fine—she hadn't really run away but she *had* abandoned him this morning. Now Odys was forced to brood and sulk and not know what to do with himself.

The older fellow didn't bother to glance at our aimless-Odys, who arrived just as the light turned red. The orange hand. That's no high-five it's asking for. Don't walk. Don't talk.

As he waited for the next green light, Odys stared straight ahead—watched his wakeful downtown settle into its afternoon place—refused to gawk at the probably-charming old chap. Gawking was rude anyway, right? Right.

---

[2] An obligatory epigraph for you: "There were golden handmaids also who worked for him, and were like real young women, with sense and reason, voice also and strength, and all the learning of the immortals; these busied themselves as the king [Vulcan] bade them, while he drew near…' —Homer's *The Iliad.* Book XVIII (Samuel Butler's 1925 prose translation).

Odys was much too depressed to spark a civil greeting. Or smile. Or even acknowledge the fellow's existence, for that matter. *I don't see this*, Odys thought to himself.

Yes, just stand still, Odys. You can't see him, he can't see you.

He'd just ignore the man until that light turned green. *Green, green, green. Turn green already, damn it.*

"You look like you've lost something, Odys Odelyn."

Odys made eye contact.

The old man adjusted his white-gloved hands on the umbrella's handle. *A swanky circus ringmaster, this man!* No, scratch that. Odys had always pictured a ringmaster with elaborate facial hair—a curled handle-bar mustache and devilish beard. This man was too clean-shaven to be a ringmaster, though he reminded Odys of one nonetheless.

LADIES AND GENTLEMEN, BOYS AND GIRLS, CHILDREN OF ALL AGES...

"Pardon?" Odys said with a frown (he refused to enjoy this unwelcome human interaction). And had he heard his name? What had the old man said? In his resentfulness, Odys had already forgotten. But *we* haven't, have we, Reader?

The man smiled—a warm and sophisticated grin. His jauntily-angled top hat half-amused Odys, who tried to hate it (he would enjoy nothing today).

...Was he some sort of immaculate butler?

"I said," (no longer lending Odys his eyes), "you seem lost."

...Was he on his way to a steampunk convention?

Odys realized he should respond. "Do I know you?" Hadn't the man said his name? Hadn't he? Hadn't he?

"Afraid not." The older fellow cracked another knowing smile. The man's confidence made Odys's eyes shift.

Odys gave himself a shake. Maybe he'd misunderstood.

The light turned green. Walk. Walk faster.

As they walked, the old man swung his umbrella—tapped it on the ground between his paces. These two characters fell into step, neither one walking too fast or too slow. Odys kept his hands in his pockets (defensively) while he tried to out-walk the man. But the man kept up with Odys's stride, his fancy coattails floating behind him. The tap, tap, tap of the umbrella's metal tip echoed off the cement. It reverberated in Odys's feet.

The sound annoyed Odys—so much he couldn't help but count the times it hit the ground— *eleven, twelve, thirteen...*

The tapping stopped and Odys sighed with relief. They both stepped up onto the sidewalk. A few more steps, then: "So, where *are* you headed this morning?" The man turned to Odys at last.

Blue eyes. Tiny little dots of sky. They peered at Odys as if looking at an old friend...an old friend he had dirt on.

"Just walking." Odys shrugged off the man's interest.

"Ah, me too." The man nodded. He tucked the umbrella under his arm.

Odys didn't know how to respond, so he didn't.

The traffic light turned red. Don't walk.[3]

"Have you a *reason*, boy? For walking, that is?"

Odys wanted to yell, *YES, MY STUPID CAR WOULDN'T START.* But it's a story full of curse words and violence (we'll save it for another chapter).

"Well, it's not really any of your business is it?" He felt bad instantly, so tacked on a nervous laugh.

"I suppose you're right, yes!" The man tapped his umbrella point on the ground—too jovially. "Forgive me for prying. I get carried away."

Odys cut his eyes at the man. Had this man escaped from some loony bin, and did Odys need to alert someone? He seemed harmless enough, yet there was a mischievous purposefulness behind his every action.

"...I see you're admiring my outfit?"

No, actually. Odys had just blotted it from memory, looked ahead, prepared to forget everything so he could concentrate on the important matter: his traitorous sister.

"Yes, you *are* dressed up," Odys forced a smile. All the man needed was a monkey on his shoulder or a few pins to juggle.

"I'd like to tell you I don't normally dress like this, but I do. I look nice, don't I?"

That statement deserved a chuckle. "Yes, you do," Odys consented. He frowned at his own laughter.

...Was this some candid camera prank?

"I met my wife, you see, wearing a suit like this. She's dead now. I made a promise that when I met her again, I'd be wearing a fancy suit." No chuckle from Odys this time. Had the man met his wife at some historical reenactment? Had he expected to die for a while now if he dressed like this all the time?

---

[3] Can I suggest jaywalking at this point, Odys?

5

"As they say," the man continued, rocking to and fro until the light turned green, "you never know when you're going to go. You can't plan for it. Unless, of course, you commit suicide. Then you *know* to dress for the worst."

Wait. What?

Odys was about to be confused when (ohthankgod): Green. Walk.

WALK QUICKLY, ODYS.

The man turned left as they stepped onto the curb; Odys went straight. One, two, three four, five uneven steps before: "Oh, Odys Odelyn!" he heard the man call. He made a half-trumpet with one hand, "You dropped this."

This?

Odys paused and turned in the alleyway's threshold, right beside a giant green waste bin and a loading-dock. Another chill ran down his spine. That was definitely his name. He wasn't mistaken, was he? He *had* heard his name, hadn't he?

Oh, hadn't he!

Like a magician performing slight-of-hand, the old man concealed something in the palm of his glove. His fingers opened like a magical bloom. He presented a shiny, round...quarter?

Well, it was the about the same *size* as a quarter, anyway. It reflected a spectacular amount of light—amber light. The showy presentation enchanted Odys. He had to *force* himself say, "No, it's not mine."

(Once again, he'd already forgotten the man said his name).

"Oh, but I'm sure it is, *Odys Odelyn*," the man insisted with slim bantering flair, a twinkle in his blue-blue eyes.

Third time's a charm. Odys Odelyn. No mistake.

"How'd you know my name?" Odys demanded, jaw clenching. Who'd want to harass him like this? He didn't have the energy or the time—

"Are you so sure it's *your* name?" the old man said, walking forward and seizing Odys's hand from his pocket. He inserted the warm coin in Odys's hand. "There's bound to be more than *one* Odys around. The name's not *that* original. After all, every time someone says Odysseus, they're saying *part* of your name—"

"My name's not Odysseus—"

"No one said it was." The man gestured with a nod to the coin.

Odys couldn't help but look at it. He realized its tarnished spots didn't stop it from shining.

"It's a penny," the old man said. "Penny for your thoughts." He tapped the ground with the umbrella again. He tucked in his chin and stared at the cement as if wishing he had kept his findings.

Odys examined the coin to appease him (Odys was in no *real* hurry this morning and perhaps this would lead somewhere).

"The date, there, says 1793," the man pointed, although Odys had already read it. "They only minted them that year. A collectable, for sure. Only seven known in existence, and that *isn't* one of them. You'll not want to give her away or sell her—no matter the price!" His polished voice was unexpectedly grave, more warning than advice.

Odys rotated the side that read "One Cent"—the side with the intricate wreath. He turned it over to the head: the profile of a woman with flowing hair.

Odys looked up. The man removed his hat. Odys felt like Frodo taking on the burden of Bilbo's ring, though he had no idea why. (But don't get ahead of yourself, Odys. Who said you're the hero of this story?).

"Why're you giving this to me?" His cold lips could barely form the words.

"Giving it? My boy, you dropped it!" *Silly young man!* "Did you know, Odys Odelyn, that many would like to do away with the penny altogether? They say they cost the government more to make than what they're worth. Many would rather have us round to the nearest nickel and be done with it. A disappointing thought, for sure. I always *did* like picking homeless ones up from the ground. In fact, that's how I discovered that one, there. People drop them like trash and simply let them be—as if it costs more to bend down than to leave it. But for me, I liked to save money. I valued little nothings, you see." He nodded, trying to make himself believe his memory. He smoothed back his hair one more time, tapped his hat down. "As they say, 'Find a penny, pick it up, and all your days you'll have great luck.' Don't forget that, Odys Odelyn. Today's your lucky day."

Before Odys could question that statement—

"Many would say that the girl on that coin is Lady Liberty. To a point, they're right. But that specific girl, there, is *not* the lovely lady Libertas! Not really. You may call her that, but ironically...that penny is anything but *free*. Not only is she *trapped* in that metal, but *bound* to be spent. That woman, there, is just the right sum for the ferryman."

What the hell was this, his catechism?

7

The old man lifted his umbrella and swished it toward Odys, tip inches from his face. Odys jumped back, almost bumping into a tiny woman with her dog. The dog didn't mind, but the woman glared.

"Let's just say, Mr. Odelyn, that the penny is my debt—my *obligation*—paid in full. I'll owe nothing else to you since you now have the funds. The rest is up to you."

Enough with the money puns, man.

Odys put up his hands. "Er—all right, then." Anything to shut this man up. People were staring as they tried to make their way into one of the building's entrances. *Is this man putting on a street show? Why's he dressed up? Is this a film production? Are we on camera?*

The man lowered his umbrella, fixed the hat on his head, smoothed down his breast. "Will you hold this, Odelyn?" The man presented the umbrella's curved handle.

"*How* do you know my name?"

"Take the umbrella and maybe I'll tell you." The man raised a brow.

To move this show along, "Fine."

Hands free, the old man reached into his suit pocket. Odys froze in place when he heard the click and saw the barrel—the barrel pointed *directly* at his face.

Holyshit.

"Sorry to do this, here and now, but I'm crunched for time. You walk very slowly, Odys." The mad man's voice was so rushed it whispered—Odys could barely hear it. The onlookers (debating whether or not to record this on their phones) were too preoccupied to hear.

"I'm being followed, you see. I'll need you to put that coin in your pocket. Quickly, now, boy! Don't spend my time—I've paid enough, dealing with you. That's it. Put it away. Don't you drop her either, boy. She's small enough to fall through that drain, there. Or even an unsuspecting pocket hole. She's very important. Now, open the umbrella."

"What?"

"I said open the umbrella!"

Obediently, Odys fumbled with the binding strap's button, hands shaking.

The black webbing popped out like a monstrous bat wing.

"Hold it up. That's it, yes." The man's eyes darted about. The few in the area were clearing out, ducking and rushing from this antiquated man with his antiquated gun.

Odys rested the umbrella on his shoulder, noticing the man was going to speak once more. Odys swallowed hard, bracing himself.

"Now, Odys Odelyn, that's my last cent, there. I've spent the rest. It's up to you to buy more time. Spend wisely."

The man drew back the gun and held the nose upward, as if finished with his prestigious show. But no. That wasn't the end of his haywire session:

The man shoved the gun in his mouth and gave an encouraging wink—a wink!—right before Odys heard the echoing BANG.

The pigeons flapped up.

As the blood, hat, and brains showered from the sky, Odys half-noticed the shiny name carved on the umbrella's handle: *Pepin J. Found.*

PEPIN: Willing to share his umbrella.

WALKING: Because he knew Odys would be walking.

HOW DID HE KNOW?: Because he's the reason Odys's car didn't start.

CHARM: 100%[4]

Chapter the second,

A penny for a pound:

Is this story just a Trojan horse?

Bang/boom/splat. Odys hadn't just witnessed a suicide. He'd witnessed an obliteration of unearthly proportions.

Pellets of warm fluid and gooey chunks fell from the heavens—Odys stooped and shielded himself with the umbrella.

...Could *that* little gun have caused *that* much damage?

When the blood-rain finally stopped (not that it was *excessively* gory—PG-13, I would say. Nothing *Kill Bill*), Odys straightened from his cowering stance and lowered the umbrella. The decapitated corpse was mostly-neckless. The (practically) toy gun hadn't done *that* to *this* corpse. Hell, no.

...Had it—had the head—*exploded?*[5]

Odys covered his mouth with the back of his sleeve. His eyes darted around—*Maybe someone else had actually shot him with a—a—a freaking bazooka or something?*

---

[4] Our chapters will always end in lists. Why? What do lists have to do with this story? I asked that same question. Our Narrator replied that, because this is a "Prose Epic" paralleling Epic Poetry (supposedly), these lists are a transmuted throwback to the "Epic Catalogue." I guess I liked the excuse, so kept them. After all, lists are one of the essential elements of an Epic, no matter the content of said lists. And, yes, this does mean you should expect other elements of the Epic to appear in this novel, actual poetry excluded. Invocation of the Muse to appear momentarily.
[5] A bit of a messy finish, but it certainly wasn't anti-climactic...

When the cops arrived Odys was still standing there. Odys dropped the nasty umbrella eventually, because a policeman led him to a warm car.

He was shaking. Shaking. Shaking as he noticed the shocked onlookers off in the distance, giving their various testimonies to surrounding officers. The news reporters would be here soon. There was a man in one of those trash-sack suits—the poncho kind that keep the gooey evidence off your clean clothes. He held a writing tablet. Someone called in more assistance.

Odys tried to read the other witnesses' lips as they gestured to the scene. He looked to his right where they were bagging the headless body and scraping off the remains from brick walls.

"A bullet did *this*?" The question full of doubt.

"Yep, we found it. There's no other weapon, no traces of anything else…"

No wallet, no ID, no nothing. Have fun identifying THAT decapitated body.

"He never met the man before?"

"Said he didn't."

"Where'd he get the umbrella?"

"Haven't asked, sir."

"Where did you get the umbrella, kid? Kid?"

Odys felt eyes on him from above. He had looked up—up at the sky as if expecting to see God pointing and laughing. Instead, he noticed a man watching from the rooftop on the building across the street. Odys touched his pocket to make sure he wasn't going mad—yes, the coin was still there.

The man was crouched low, like a monkey. His hair could have been red or orange or…

And he was tossing something—flipping it up in the air with his thumb and catching it. Maybe a rock? No. It was a coin—an omen. Each time was a perfect catch, even though he wasn't looking at the coin and his eyes were *most definitely* on Odys.

The man was mocking him. Flip, flip. A coin for a coin. He had *wanted* Odys to see him. He dashed off before the officer tried to see what Odys saw.

"Sir? Sir, can you hear me?"

The question registered. Odys gave a languid nod, eyes flickering back to the roof-spot. He was just being paranoid. The man was only some curious roofer who had heard the commotion. That's all. God, *please*, let that be all. No more of this, *please*.

"Is this his umbrella?"

Another nod.

"Why do you have it?"

"He gave it to me," Odys answered.

"Do you know his name?"

Odys shook his head.

They examined the umbrella, asked someone on the other end of their cop-radio to punch in "Pepin J. Pound," to search under aliases. Nothing came up. "Might be the brand," the officer said. "Or his stage name?" They all chuckled at the thought. "Is there anything else you should tell us? Did he give you anything else, Mr. Odelyn?"

How did *they* know his name? Is there no such thing as *anonymous* anymore? Oh, that's right—he'd given them his driver's license, his information. "Yes," Odys answered. He reached into his pocket, dug for the coin, watched their expectant faces.

He hadn't had his hands in his pockets for a while, so they were chilled—numb. He felt the coin—but what was that? His fumbling fingers cornered something sharp and jerked back.

He shook his hand, putting his finger to his mouth, expecting it to bleed. But nothing.

Perhaps it was all in his head. His fingers were just cold. Too cold. Everything felt like a bite or a sting when cold.

But no. The coin he had reached for felt heavier—it weighed down his pocket. He was becoming lighter than the coin. He leaned to the side, inclining like a catatonic drunkard. The *coin* was drawing him down.

Falling out of the open car, an officer caught him. Odys realized he couldn't feel his feet or hands—was he having a heart attack? Hardly. He's much too in-shape and good looking to be killed off just yet. Sorry, Odys, you'll live through this.

"The hell's the matter with him?"

"The sight must be getting to him. Put him back in the car, will you?"

But blood hardly bothered Odys—he wasn't squeamish. He could watch whole episodes of documentary surgical procedures and never have to look away! He wasn't some wimp!! He loved gore—blood and guts!!!

"Goddamnit, the kid threw up on me…" The man grumbled, jumping back too late, a look of pity upon his ugly face.

Odys mumbled a sincere apology, resting on his knees.

A female officer bent down, examining him. A concerned interest haunted her expression. "Mr. Odelyn, you all right?"

No, actually. He's just about to black out. And you, lady, are about to load him onto the parked ambulance that, after having seen the scene, hadn't planned on taking anyone *alive* to the hospital. So let's get this over with:

An agonizing pain pulsated though Odys's torso; they saw his blue-web veins push to their pale surface. He crumpled to the grey pavement. Over and out.

Stanza: Even a "Prose Epic" needs a break every now and then.

He woke up in a hospital bed.

He touched the blanket, looked at his hands. He wasn't hooked up to anything—no IV, no heart monitor. So why was he here? There were smears of brown on his arms—places the nurses hadn't given their all in cleaning off the blood. He touched his nose, realizing he didn't have his glasses. Deep in thought, he let his fingers slide down his bare face. It was times like this when it would suit to have a beard to stroke—something for his long fingers to do.

But what he lacked in facial hair he made up for in ponytail.

An attendant noticed him fretting with his messy hair and called someone—someone wanted to talk with him, so just sit tight.

More like sleep tight. He wasn't sure he could stay awake.

A few minutes ticked by. The other person was taking their time. As Odys waited for the doctor or officer or *whoever* who needed to talk with him, he replayed the morning through his mind—he replayed every second to be sure he wasn't going mad:

Why did he meet Pepin? *Because I was walking.* But why was he walking? *Because my car didn't start.* But where was he going? *Fuck.*

That's something he couldn't tell the cops if they asked.

Stanza: We interrupt your normal programming to...

...Deflate the tension I've worked so hard to build and flood you with back story.

And what that means is this next part *should* have been Chapter One. But, because Gabbler said I had to *kill* someone first to get your attention, we moved it. Beware the lengths Gabbler goes to, to keep you interested.[6]

Stanza: On the same morning Pepin offed himself.[7]

---

[6] Says the one who asked for my help! I may be the one who cut and pasted this here, but the Narrator *did* approve it. But, to justify my action: this coming section is no flashback. I know we all hate them in novels—so tedious to break from the structural narrative! No, no, it's not a flashback. It's an *insert*. The Narrator would want me to be very clear about this. Yet, in defense of flashbacks, all novels have them (it seems). So it's only fair that this Prose Epic doesn't escape the same treatment.

[7] In other words:
Chapter the first,

The cat was heave-hiccupping on the rug, tongue out as it tried to oust the thing gagging it. Vomit, you see, is the proper way to start this story. Vomit is the metaphor.[8]

Though you may cringe now, do remember, the cat—the stupid cat—is a main character. Not only had this stupid cat upchucked a slimy landmine, but Odys had just stepped in it.

"Odissa!" he shouted. "Can't you clean this crap up?"

"It's not crap. It's vomit!" she shouted from the kitchen.

He mumbled under his breath. Then, "So you *know* it's here?"

No response.

"Your stupid cat hairball'd the freaking hallway, Odissa. Don't just leave it!"

"If you don't want it there, then clean it!" his sister snapped back. Her "stupid cat" had started a new diet recently; he was having some trouble adjusting.

"You're disgusting." Odys grouched.

"You're the one who won't clean it!"

(Even if she *did* clean it, it wouldn't be good enough. Odys had a very specific method for cleaning such things).

Odys rolled his eyes. Then rubbed them. Where were his glasses? Everything in the apartment was a blur. Speaking of their apartment:

Though they could have afforded something bigger—much bigger—the quaintness suited their tastes. The bigger the place, the more stuff you'd need to fill it. And they already had *enough* stuff. They wanted to escape it—escape the *stuff* they could so easily acquire.

They had money. They'd always had money. And money had them.

In rejection of their privileged backgrounds, they'd embraced minimalism—though it could never minimize their past. That was something they could not escape. Even if they gave away all their savings, the act couldn't rewrite history.

They've been written down in ink. Not pencil. (Cue serious music).

He put his still-dirty foot on the carpet reluctantly. When he reached the kitchen counter, he took out a clean mug. "I'm not going to clean it," he lied. He'd clean up the hairball eventually. They both knew this. Even though it wasn't his cat, he'd clean up after it (hell, he'd likely deep-clean the entire apartment because of it).

A mad alchemist:
Not a mad scientist?
(As cut by me)
[8] Vomit of the Epic genre, that is. Word-vomit, on the other hand, s why B.L.A. needed an Editor.

It had always been *her* cat. Never his. The very second they'd moved into this apartment, she'd picked up the stray. God, that was a while ago, their "freedom" (as he called it). Now he was in his twenties and had a young-old face. The smoking didn't help with that.

He cut his eyes at his sister. Odissa took a humble sip from her coffee, flicked open their morning newspaper. She tossed away the green rubber band and headed straight for the arts section (where the book reviews are). Such a pretentious nerd she is.

He poured his own cup of instant-life, watching her. Her brown eyes rolled over the words behind her glasses, those old-school frames.[9]

Odys thought the style suited her, but that they were ridiculous. She was often outrageous to scare people away. They needed no one else…

BUT SO ANYWAY.

Done staring at her glasses, he soon realized she was already dressed—ready for the day. But it wasn't even noon yet. She was never dressed (let alone fully awake) this time on Fridays. Usually they were freewheeling slobs together. She would stay in her pajamas, not put on makeup, not do her hair. They looked even more like twins that way (he smiled at the thought). But now she was dressed, all prim and proper—makeup, hair, outfit.

He took a swig from his mug, a little dribbling down his chin.

Hot, hot! How the hell can she stand it this hot? Dabbing his face, he pretended it didn't faze him. He put down his mug and cleared his throat, about to interrupt her concentration. "You're dressed early."

"Yep," she replied, walking over to their wooden table. She plopped the paper down with a soft smack. She didn't look up from her news.

Odys took up his mug and followed her restlessly, a little puppy. He pulled at his junkyard-worthy undershirt to dry the coffee stain. He gave up and reached for a half-empty cigarette carton.

Just as he lit one, she was holding two fingers out, expectant. Her precocious eyes never left the crisp newspaper. Impatient, her fingers cut the air like scissors. *Chop, chop!* He removed the cigarette from his lips—which he hardly ever did unless the "drag was dragged," but Odissa was the exception. He placed it between her slender fingers. "Thanks," she said, bringing it to her lips. Doing so, "We *really* should consider using matches only."

He raised an eyebrow. "Yeah?"

---

[9] This, Dear Reader, is what we millennials called a "fucking hipster." But, I love her despite this.

"Yes. It'd not only facilitate our toxic habit's bio-degradable nature, but it's also more stylish." (There's probably a more pompous way of saying it).

"I told you that last week. Those _exact_ words."

Plagiarism! And what next? Would she say they should roll their own too? She'd become so snooty.

"But now I agree with you." And she just kept smoking, as if this hackneyed tangent never happened.

She was actually too much of a "good girl" to look like a professional smoker. But don't let appearances deceive you. She could drag harder than...well, she could drag, anyway. Nothing more than that. She's a modest girl.

After lighting a cigarette for himself, Odys could _now_ have his "breakfast," as he called it.

He drummed the table with his restless fingers. His cigarette burned away like a horizontal chimneystack. His right hand flicked on and off his Zippo lighter. He hoped the annoying sounds would redirect her attention. But her eyes kept reading. She was so austere. Was a book review more interesting than him?

Puff, puff, puff from the corner of his mouth.

The warm cigarette never left his lips. Once it was lit, it was permanent. Not even when he talked would he take it out. He would speak through the sides of his mouth rather than wave it between his willowy fingers for attention. Besides, he didn't talk much anyway. Not when he was smoking—which usually meant he was alone or with others who didn't talk much either (case in point: his sister).

Only when he was eating or drinking or didn't want the ash to fall on him would he _occasionally_ remove it. Most times, however, he cared very little. His smoking habit wasn't for looks, no. Cigarettes were a purpose—a means of shortening/enlivening his dull existence. So no, he wouldn't remove it.

His fingers drummed faster on the wooden table. He snapped the metal lighter shut. Aha! There were his glasses. He reached across the table, past the fancy ashtray. Ah, he could see.

But sight was his foe.

The apartment overwhelmed him. Now that he could see it properly, he felt the need to "tidy up." But he resisted the urge and settled for fidgeting in his seat.

He would clean things and count things and align things and straighten things and smooth out that rug when Odissa wasn't looking.

(I bet you thought they were slobs, right, because of the remaining cat hairball? No, no. Don't jump to conclusions!)

Odissa was lucky to live with Odys. That meant the only place she had to clean was her own room (which she still didn't clean regardless). What's more, she made it a point to give her brother more work—like the time she bought that hideous silver lamp with five bendable fixtures for the living room. *He* had to drive all the way back into town, return it, and pick out a style with an even number of bulb-holders. His eyes flickered to that very lamp. With six bendable heads, it looked like a fucking hydra. Almost gave him a heart attack the first few nights they had it.

He tore his eyes from it.

Some might say those eyes, fairly sunken in their molds, were too detached—and that just might be true. They were brown. Just like his hair. Brown. It may or may not be his favorite color; his preferences shifted. Brown like his sister's.

And why was she dressed, again?

Her brown eyes, however, were nearly black—black like that cup of non-froufroued coffee she was just about to finish. Though so dark, they made her ordinary face yieldingly simpler.

And since we're comparing them, notice his face is bolder. Everything about his sister is nothing more than a softer and more ordinary version of himself. Softer eyes, softer complexion, softer smile, softer voice, softer…

Identical twins look alike, but fraternal can be yin and yang. Contrasting similarities. Distorted effigies of each other. But by now you get the picture. MOVING ON.

He brushed sterile ash off the table to the floor he'd sweep later. "You look very nice in that outfit." (He wasn't going to let it go).

She exhaled before answering, "Why, thank you, Odys." Her eyes froze under their lids. Wait for it…wait for it…

"But you only have three rings. You need another."

"I know, Odys. Did it just to piss you off." She smirked up at him, folding her paper. She rested her hands atop each other, that cigarette burning in the right. Her spare fingers fiddled with the ring on her left hand—the ring-finger's ring—a silver band—a wedding ring to those who didn't know better.

"You know what Travis told me yesterday? 'Librarians should devour books, not smokes.'" She marveled at her burning leaves. She'd meant to change the subject.

He took the bait. He corrected her, "We aren't librarians, just library assistants."

"Same thing," she shrugged, waving him off with her smoking hand; don't be nit-picky. That's that.

It was pleasurably hard to breathe (which was Odys's only mindless action for the time being). The room was full of tantalizing smoke—wonderful, lingering, suffocating smoke. The smoke swirled around them like dancing phantoms. They were soon on their third round of cigarettes (insisting on advancing their inevitable lung cancer), before he realized he *still* had a cup of coffee. Ah, it was nice and cool, too. He wouldn't have to nurse it. Yes, sir.

His square-framed glasses slid down his nose. He didn't push them up. The glasses are deceptive, they make him seem placid and introverted. He's not. Not really. He doesn't hide behind them as some do, but he does use them to mislead. If either of them hid behind spectacles, it was his sister—but it was hardly a disguise upon her dainty face. Or maybe it was. Bookish by nature, she fit the librarian stereotype perfectly. Except the smoker bit, perhaps.

She was elegant when she smoked, unlike him—though not on purpose. He liked to watch her smoke; it comforted him. He enjoyed her tapering hand bringing it up to those lace-thin lips. Every interval between intakes was unique, and he observed each with revived curiosity.

She'd pretend not to notice his overly entertained eyes tracing from (one) the whirling smoke to (two) white cigarette to (three) pale face to (four) curved neck to...One, two, three, four. He would count her. On and on in an infinite sum that somehow always ended in an even number. She was even. Always even. Always balanced.

...Their mutually parasitic nature was (for lack of a better explanation) the reason I wanted to start my story here. Don't feel uncomfortable, my prudish readers; don't convict them just yet. Yes, you might already suspect an unorthodox sibling relationship, but don't let me prick your conservative bubbles. I haven't earned that power yet. Just ignore this erotic needle as I wave it in your face. It's not going to hurt. Much.

Honestly, you're just like everyone else familiar with the pair—guessing, predicting, and judging right from the start. Strangers often mistook them for a married couple; or, for those more familiar with the pair, to assume incest. Sometimes Odys even introduced her as his missus to ward off the curious stares and sly questions. *Just who was that girl he brought with him, and—more importantly—what was she to him?* Dear Odissa would play along buoyantly, bless her heart, and together they'd make a grand time of it. It was easier to pretend.

Thus, at parties (Odys was unusually popular despite his efforts; Odissa usually came off as the reclusive sort who scared away inviters), they would say things like, "Let me introduce you to my wife," or, "Have you met my husband?" when speaking about each other.

Odd phrasing of that nature.

It not only kept things (such as their clinginess) smooth and simple, but it also kept them from, as they say nowadays, being "hit on." And the plain rings they both wore on their fingers added to the effective repelling. Their make-believe marriage proved they needed no one else. They *wanted* no one else. So please go away.

To Odissa, they were Cleopatra and Ptolemy. Their solitude was their Egyptian throne. They were gods among men. No Caesar would overthrow them. But historical parallels aside:

He couldn't stand not knowing what the special occasion was—the reason she was dressed. "What would you like to do today, Odissa?" he asked, leaning towards her.

"Have you, dear brother," she said in her most pompous (and fake) British accent, "forgotten what today is?"

His eyes narrowed.

She rested her head in her palm. "Well, you must've suppressed it. I'm going to see him today. Our *father*."

"Oh." Odys mouthed the sound. "It's *that* time of year."

"Hm," she answered, no emotion in her sound.

He evened out her newspaper, putting the pages in a nice stack parallel to the table's dull edge. He liked even lines. He counted to an even number before taking his next step. One, two, three, four, five, six, seven, eight:

"Don't."

"Don't?"

"Don't go." It was almost a command. "Please."

She laughed, a feigned noise, and put out her unfinished cigarette. He counted the number of times she smashed the tip into the tray. Onetwothreefour…five. He hated odd numbers!

She saw him cringe. She knew *exactly* what he counted.

"I have to, Odys. We need the money. That's how it works." She slouched back in her chair, waiting for his unavoidable reaction. She always used tender unpleasantness to control him.

"You don't have to go anymore, you know." Quietly, "We don't need *him*."

"Yes, we do. If I didn't go, we wouldn't live comfortably. Gourmet coffee has its price tag." She attempted a smile at her own humor.

He put out his own cigarette—onetwothreefourfivesix (see, Odissa? *That's* how it's done)— and proceeded to space out the butts in a symmetrical arrangement. Just as he liked it. There was nothing else on the table to perfect. Nothing else to distract him. His brow wrinkled once more, the corners of his mouth declining. Though he had a naturally somber semblance, it was even more depressing with the topic of *their father* on the table.

"This will be the last of it, I promise. I'm going to ask him for more than usual. He won't mind. We're almost done with school anyway, and so I might—"

"If you ask for more, he'll ask more from you," Odys interrupted.

She frowned, disapproving. He could be so childish when it came to her. He didn't like others stealing her attention—attention that was his. She answered him, "Then I'll do more."

He didn't like that answer. One, two, three, four. The seconds ticked by like a clock in his mind. "C-can I go with you?" He faltered the question. He didn't want to go, but he wished to express his willingness to suffer. "I don't even have to show my face—"

"You know he wouldn't like that, and I'm not supposed to ask. And if he found out—"

"Then how long will you be this time? You have work Monday."

"Tuesday, actually. You've got Monday by yourself, babe. However, I should be back by Monday. That's his estimate."

Odys's jaw clenched. That was too long. Longer than usual.

"I'm also going to ask him about it." She was trying to justify her visit.

"It?"

"Well," her voice lowered, "who our mother was. Or *is*, whatever. I think he's willing to tell me now. Now that we're about to graduate. I can get *something* from him."

"I don't care to know. Any woman insane enough to—"

"Maybe we're adopted, then," she admonished him.

"That's likely," he laughed. It was too much to hope for.

"Maybe we killed her at birth," Odissa stated, as if this was normal breakfast conversation. "Maybe that's *why*."

That shut Odys up. He never thought she'd speak her mind so flippantly. Or that she'd speak that theory aloud. Sure, even he'd wondered about it, but...

"Never mind," Odissa said, waving her hand.

Truth be told, she had very little interest in mothers. Which was why they had never spoken about this before. At least, not like this.

Odissa stood up. "I'm already packed. See me out?"

He walked her to her car. He shook off the cold and his thought about dragging her back to their apartment and tying her to a chair.

He tossed her bags in her trunk and slammed the lid. She waited for him to come back and face her. He didn't meet her eyes as she stood there in her cute little scarf and jacket and mittens. Her petite, tip-tilted nose was pink. Her breath turned to fog. "Don't do anything stupid, Odys, okay?"

He nodded, lying. As soon as he returned to the apartment, he'd have his fit.

"And don't forget to feed—"

"I won't, I won't." he grumbled. "I won't forget to feed your stupid cat."

She put on a prepared smile and reached up to pat his cheek with her mitten. *Good boy, Odys.* He leaned away from her, a scowl on his poignant face. She expected this reaction. She could deal with his melancholia now, just as he'd deal with hers upon her return. She was always *affected* after "seeing their father." Odys always had to fix her afterwards.

Sighing, she entered her silver car, closed the door and drove out of the apartment lot. When he could no longer see her down the street, the separation had begun.

Our maverick stood still in the cold. All alone. One. He hated that number. He wished he hadn't shrugged off her touch. She hardly ever offered affection. And when she did, it was only to him. How dare he deny her that?

Blowing through his nose like a provoked bull, he cocked his head. He debated something:

See, he might have gotten dressed in a rush to walk her down here, but he was *still* dressed. He shouldn't waste his reasonable effort. He tapped his pocket—yup, wallet and keys. In a solid beeline, he went to his car. He'd go driving; he might even follow her (just a little ways). Nothing weird about that. Nothing that would surprise her.

He shut his car door and put the key in the ignition.

But wait.

…What the hell? Car won't start. Won't start. Start. START!

He must have tried ten times. Ten thousand fucking times.

As he hit the steering wheel—teaching it a lesson—he threatened to set it on fire. He settled for a dent in the car door, compliments of his foot.

He wasn't normally a violent person.[10]

Not about to pop the hood and let some know-it-all, car-savvy guy tell him he needed to do *this and that and that and this* to get it running, he decided just to walk. Just walk. Walk it off. Besides, he deserved this bad luck—to treat his sister like that. Walking was his punishment.

---

[10] Don't defend him, Narrator. He's actually very violent, in my opinion.

He rummaged through his deep pocket as he stepped onto the sidewalk. His shaky hand searched for his extra lighter as the other pulled out the cigarettes from his back pocket.

He smoked the fuck out of that cigarette.

His glasses glinted as he looked left and right before crossing. January was cold in these parts—though it doesn't matter *where* he is right now, so I'll not say the place. Locations are unsubstantial (as my Editor tells me). Just focus on the storyline. He'll not be staying here much longer anyway.

His feet made shuffle-sounds that helped him feel pathetic. It was a relatively dull walk, sparse traffic and people. A few morning joggers here and there, plugs in their ears. The genial cigarette smoke blew back in his bare face, thawing his sharp nose. He usually had those dark circles under his ever-scowling eyes, though today they were especially dark. Shady circles came with the complexion, you see. Oh, and that reminds me—I meant to mention that *complexion.*

It was rumored his father was Turkish or Russian or Armenian or Siberian or something. Something.

But Odys didn't care. Rumors concerning his father (interestingly enough) were often more entertaining than the man himself. Odys should know. He'd suffered them both. Rumors *and* the man.

His father—a hieratical-looking man in memory, but not in person—had sometimes spoken with a deliberately veiled burr that, at times, sounded like a sick blending of all Indo-European language branches—the kind of generalized accent that had broken down and only escaped accidentally. Or, as was also likely, his father had merely acquired it. How, though? Do not ask. He never answered.

So, despite my best efforts within this whitewashed genre, in sum we have two white rich kids. Trite upon trite. *But* who said Odys and Odissa were even the main characters? Not I![11]

…If anything, Odys often looked in the mirror and thought he looked nothing like his father. The fact he couldn't grow real facial-scruff led him to wonder…

Actually, forget I mentioned that..[12]

…The light had turned green. The pixilated man appeared in the light-box-thing. Walk. Walk. Walk. Don't walk. Run before that crazy driver hits you. Geez, what an asshole! A human can only walk so fast.

---

[11] Our Narrator tries very hard to be progressive—with the best of intentions. But it seems the story they need to tell won't "let" them. (What an excuse, am I right?).
[12] You should not.

In his rush, his hair fell in his face. He tucked it back. He wore it down to his shoulders and tied in a limp tail-knot creature. His tangled mane was always pulled back, though wavy-scribble strands somehow found their way over his forehead. Like an earthy curtain, today those loose locks helped veil his building insanity.

More ash fell onto his messy front—his shabby and somewhat-threadbare style was his only outward means of conveying his aforementioned minimalism (minimal use of the hairbrush and fashion sense). His unkempt air made him proud. He was good at being hygienically slovenly. "Hobo-grunge" might be the proper term, though I'm no authority on the matter. Odissa always held her tongue on this issue. He chuckled at the thought, smoke wafting from his lips. (He caught this sudden outburst and corrected the impropriety. He was, after all, supposed to be brooding).

As Odys walked up the sidewalk steps, not grabbing the frosty rail, he realized he was near his favorite used bookstore—ah, so that's where he was going. Subconsciously, of course. He rounded the corner, planning to pass it off. He knew it wasn't right to visit a place that isn't *solely* yours. Odissa's absence weighed him down...

He blew smoke out his nose, a deprived dragon.

All his depression might seem uncalled for—a very silly reaction to his sister visiting their father. But perhaps you don't know the half of it. Not yet. I haven't even told you *the man's* name—not that names tell you much about a person, really.[13]

When Odys and Odissa were children, they imagined what their father must be doing all those days, weeks, months he would disappear. They wished he would never reappear. "Business trips," he'd called them.

As slightly older children, they envisaged the man as possibly a con artist, a spy handler, or government mercenary—his black market character surely fit the profile. Turns out, it was worse than they feared. He was none of those.

During their lax childhood, the twins had watched many a gangster film and noted that the mobsters had to go *somewhere* for their medical aid; they couldn't just check into a hospital every time they got in a gun fight. That's the first place the cops look. There had to be a doctor on hand—for special cases and such.

That's where their father would fit into their make-believe beliefs.

He did not *make* them believe otherwise.

---

[13] Oh, they tell you enough all right. Especially if the person chooses their own name—which is what their father did.

All they knew for sure was that his study was packed with medical textbooks—some in different languages. They doubted their father could read them all, but they took up slack on the shelf.

Many of their father's rooms were locked. The study was the only "secret" place they'd managed to enter. This was (most likely) because there were few secrets in that dusty room a child could understand. The eye-level volumes were the ones you were *supposed* to notice—the ones distracting you from the plain, more important books high up. Their little eyes couldn't see into the towering shelves where the good stuff (no doubt) was tucked away. They hadn't dared go up the winding staircase or use the rolling ladder; if they had, not only would it have been riskier, but they might have learned their father's true profession.

And they already knew too many secrets.

Their father, when at home, would lock himself in his rooms. He'd stay in there for days and leave the children to their aloof nannies—plural. Yes, they had several over the years.

Odys wondered why their father even bothered coming home. It's not as if the twins wanted to see his face—his face with that scraggily beard (their father's facial hair added to his sophistic undercurrent, and Odys hated it. If he could ever grow such a monstrosity, he wouldn't. He feared he might actually look like his father, then. One time, he took his sister's hair up to his chin as she tried to touch up her face in a mirror. It was no real comparison). But why are we talking about beards? Let's get back to our hero twins' upbringing.[14]

They were very well off, and it seemed likely their father acquired the wealth from somewhere—or, possibly, *someone*. Little did they know how close their guesses came. A pomegranate isn't a carrot, but it's still just as edible—and Mr. Odelyn Sr. enjoyed the company of many a *delectable* character.

Perhaps the yummiest of his contemporaries was Mr. Augury, a man who had made frequent visits.[15] As the family's lawyer and oldest friend, every time his derby shoe stepped through their childhood threshold, their father would drop what he was doing and leave his off-limit rooms. No one could delight their father quite like Mr. Augury.

And no one consumed more of his time.

---

[14] "Receive your guest the bearded men" —*Chilam Balam*, Mayan book. It is a supposed prophecy and relates to Cortés and his welcoming. The beard, in my opinion, eerily foreshadows something about Odys. The beard (or lack thereof) is most important. The Narrator wants you to notice this…And then quickly forget it.

[15] And yes, I (the Editor) changed Augury's name (as I have changed/edited others) to OBVIOUSLY represent someone of ominous importance. Our Narrator had a laugh at the name I picked. An approving laugh.

Mr. Augury had a much older air and frame than their father, though he wasn't *ancient*. Only distinguished. Odissa called him Guglielmo Marconi. Her father, on the other hand, was Grigori Rasputin. "Though I think that's only when he's around us," she had added. She could be so forgiving.

Odys didn't know why she always compared people historically, but she usually got it right. Like Hegel with his spiritual manifestations in history, Odissa pursued this timeless principal in her own life. She was a sibyl who knew the past foretold the future.

But back to *Marconi* and *Rasputin*:

The twins didn't know how the two had met and never cared to learn. Why learn about a subject you hate? Such knowledge was useless to them even if they knew it. It could never rid them of their father. Even though their father had died, Mr. Augury was still alive. Thriving. Doing their father's will beyond the grave.

That's right, kiddos, their father is *dead*. You didn't read that wrong. I never said he was alive, did I? Go back and check, if you don't believe me (even Gabbler, my Editor, called this twist "mindfuckery." I disagreed.). I'll admit I meant to mislead you a little, but I never said he still lived.

See, to the twins, their father and Mr. Augury are as one. Their father had been a regal man and Augury preserved his regal wishes.

Their father no longer had a voice of his own.

Augury was that voice.

Though Odissa had gone to "see their father," the stone monument he'd become was hardly the worst part of her ritual reverence. Mr. Augury was sure to stick to the will and its *multifarious* rules for their inheritance. He did control it, after all. That's why Odys couldn't go with Odissa. It was against the rules. Their father hadn't wanted it—and still didn't. That's what Mr. Augury said. His words might as well be their father's. His word was law.

Even though their father was nothing but a skeleton in the closet, Augury could still hear him. Mr. Augury, in more ways than one, was *Odi Odelyn*.

ODYS ODELYN: Son of a trickster; named after him too.

SEASON: Winter—perfect for brooding.

ADDICTIONS: Cigarettes, coffee, and maintaining even numbers—not in that order. He's actually on the lookout for a fourth addiction, to make the number even.

TYPE: Byronic hero, theoretically.

Chapter the third,[16]

Alchemic principals:

What's the *matter*?

Odi Odelyn. Yes, that was their father's name. Odi, short for Odysseus. A heroic name.

Odys hated that name—he couldn't read Homer because of it. The twins strongly suspected it wasn't their father's birth name, because if it was one thing they *did* know about their father, it was his profound adoration of pagan myths. And if there was another, they knew people rarely liked their parent-bestowed birth-names. They were evidence of this (teachers always spelled Odys's name as Otis, and Odissa's as Odessa).

…Not that Odys cared about his stupid name.

Odys flicked his finished cigarette at the pavement and stepped on it. When he looked back up, he noticed someone stopped at the far-off crosswalk—the crosswalk he was headed towards.

It was a blurred silhouette in the morning glow. The figure just stood there…even though the light was green and he was free to walk. The man simply stared at the traffic flowing past him. He even waved on the car waiting for him to cross.

Come along, motorcar. He was in no hurry. *Have a good day.*

Stanza: And that's where we began, didn't we?

Yes. Yes, it is. We've come full circle.

"Fucking shit, it really happened," Odys muttered to himself in his hospital bed.

Stanza: Ch. 1 insert is DONE—let's get back to the real Ch. 3.

The officers asked him more questions—questions after questions. He signed his witness statement after recounting the whole ordeal and refused further conversations with social workers (who were very concerned about his mental stability). Cup after cup of coffee was proffered, because he looked so "terrible." Coffee was the only thing his nauseated body desired, though it was hard to take in.

The doctor had told him they didn't know what was *exactly* amiss with him, but his heart rate was low—below average—probably just nerves—here, take some of this.

The doctor had told the officers (who were surprised Odys wasn't on drugs): he should be fine—nothing in his system—shock manifests in different ways.

---

[16] Or, **Chapter the second**, if our Narrator had their way.

A cop who had just arrived wanted to know why the suicide had been so messy. A nosey nurse (who had overheard other doctors and nurses from the morgue) explained that if the bullet hits the right vein—the right angle—maybe—case closed.

The cops told Odys an officer would drive him home—thanks for cooperating.

"Whu-whaat time is it?" Odys asked as someone helped him into his coat. It was irritating how *slurred* his voice came out, how much energy it cost to emanate only four words, how they looked on him with concern and then skepticism.

"Just now ten."

"A.M.?"

"P.M. You were out quite a while."

Thanks, Pepin, for ruining my day and making me look like a weakling—if Pepin's who you really were. He put on his glasses, took back his wallet. His fingers also felt the coin. It was still there, eerily warm.

He fell asleep on the way home. The driving officer woke him up.

"I think we're here, kid." Pause. "You need help getting out?" No, thanks. "Call if you need anything, right? Not that you will, but." Pause. "People kill themselves every day. You just got lucky enough to be part of their attention-seeking. Don't let it get to you."

More like, *don't be such a little girl.*

"We'll send someone tomorrow to check up on you, likely." Shouting before the car door closed, "Just be glad you slept through the news crew. They had a fucking field day."

Stanza: Lady Liberty isn't so Greco-Roman.

Odys made his way up the apartment building, holding the rail for dear life. The yellow streetlights let him see his breath, though it felt more like his soul escaping than warm oxygen.

He rested his forehead on the doorframe and fumbled for the right key. He noticed his hands in the hall light. They bore a sickly, lavender tint—shades away from a bruise-colored plum. It was like his body knew he was alone now and, without the eyes of others, was willing to turn on him. His desperate, cadaverous fingers managed to turn the cold knob.

He found his bed. His face hit the inviting pillow…

A few hours later, he heard a thud from his twin sister's room—a drawer closing perhaps? A sniffle? A hum? Was Odissa home?!

He rallied himself out of bed, looking for his glasses. Where had he put them? They were probably in the covers. He realized he still wore his blood-splattered jacket. He was too unwell to bother removing it. Besides, it had nice pockets to rest his limp hands in. He always did appreciate pockets—never mind Pepin's blood.

He shuffled onward, hands nice and cozy. Wait, where was the coin, that ominous penny? *Must have fallen out as I tossed in bed*, he assumed. *Good riddance. May you be lost under the bed forever.*

…On his wobbly-way to greet Odissa (and beg her to care for him), he noticed the cat's hairball crime-scene from *THAT MORNING* had been cleansed of evidence. Odissa must have done it. But, uncharacteristically, it seemed clean *enough* (which was a rare feat for anyone— Odys had high standards). Was he sure he hadn't cleaned it?

He leaned on his sister's bedroom doorframe, flipped on the light. An exhausted smile spread across his too-white face—

But the sides of his expression quickly fell.

She wasn't there. Must've been the cat… "Merow?" He lifted his flickering eyes from mid-floor.

Thanks, cat, for waking him. He'd gotten up for nothing.

The cat looked back down and continued his operation—batting at something between his fuzzy mittens. Odys, about to swoop down and scoop it up (the cat was notorious for eating random artifacts from the carpet), drew back. It was the coin. *Howthefuck* did it get in here?

No doubt, it must have been the cat. That's the only logical way it could have traveled. The pesky creature was always helping himself to their stuff. Little thief.

Odys would have been angry if he hadn't become dizzy again. He could feel the blood rushing through his shriveling veins. The cat screamed at him. He'd forgotten to feed him dinner, but the beast was fat anyway and could miss a meal or two. Odys himself hadn't eaten all day. Even now he felt too weak to eat. The cat could suffer with him. So there.

…Never mind. That was mean. He'd go feed him.

He turned from the cat and coin with a glare, leaving it and heading to the cat food in the kitchen. But: *sniff, sniff.* Was that…*coffee*? He heard the pot begin to squirt out newly-hot contents.

Walking to the counter to inspect the pot, the rich scent flooded his shallow senses. He leaned down, watching the murky-brown droplets fall. He realized he was watching it like someone on LSD and adjusted his countenance accordingly. He blinked past his disheveled fringe, blowing the hair out of his way so he could inspect.

...This was no programmable machine set to a clock (they were still shopping for a fancier one), so *how* was it making coffee for him? He must be dreaming. Sleep walking. Yes, that was it.

He felt like a stranger in his own home...*alone*. He couldn't even trust himself anymore...*all alone*. The cat was there, yes, but the cat couldn't make coffee. No thumbs.

Perhaps he should take a stroll outside—to wake himself up? The crisp air might do him good. Or make it worse, whichever. He paused in the living room, deciding. It was a bad idea, but he thought about it anyway. If he was going insane, better to be *outside* where someone might stop him. He wanted to escape this unusual happenstance—this place where nothing was quite right—this place where he was *alone*.

The exhausting walk to the door had made it impossible to reach his bed again. He couldn't change his mind now (as if he could make it out the door) but he couldn't stand his own restlessness. He moaned, holding back the rippling, undulating soreness. He wanted to crumple over. But he stood for an eternity.

Stanza: The genie skulking in the bottle.

Eventually (thank God) that eternity ended. His unsteady hand was already turning the knob—twisting and wringing out his dubious fate. Odys was just about to pull when:

"Don't leave, Odys," a voice pleaded.

The hairs on the back of his neck stood on end. The voice was quaking bronze gongs—a song calling his body. Though his senses were dulled and fatigued, this metallic sound was sharp and clear. Had he died? Was this a heavenly undertaker sent to collect him?

Heaven or hell, he'd be saved from this tortuous weariness. He turned. He could see a girl's gleaming outline—a thin, polished delineation. He gave a sigh of relief; it was just a girl. Just a girl. A girl?

Not what he expected.

She was like syncopation—softer than predicted. Just from her few words, he had *almost* been sure she was anything but human. But now? Now he wasn't so sure.

She stood paces away from Odissa's room—had she just left it?

The dress she was wearing—Odys knew that dress. It was Odissa's. But this girl wasn't Odissa. "It isn't safe, Odys Odelyn," she told him, her voice like tiny brass bells now. "Not until we're both fully stable." Her posture was reserved yet poised.

"How—how'd you get in here?" Odys managed to say. Each hoarse word felt like slime leaving his tongue. She'd given him a heavy jolt, his senses galvanized—though he still wanted to puke and pass out simultaneously.

The dark apartment kept him from perceiving her face entirely, but he could sense she softly smiled—a smile like the glint of copper, quickly gone.

"How'd I get in? Well, now. You let me in." She spoke as if reminding a sleepy child.

He licked his lips in thought and tasted metal—metal in the air. Her body swayed in place—she was a sinuous cobra half-moving to the snake-charmer's tune in his head. "You let me in," she insisted. She tucked her hair behind her ear, waiting for response.

"Did I?" He almost didn't doubt it at this point.

She nodded.

Clearing the clot in his throat, "Why are you wearing my—my sister's dress?"

She strode up to him. Her every footstep consecrated the floor. "So two girls can't wear the same dress?" She stretched out her arm, flipped on the light with a kiss of her fingers. Those beckoning fingers took their time to coil back to her serpentine hand—the action exact, like a temple girl's ritual.

The simple fixture above them illuminated her once-suppressed face. Odys sunk back. She was *too* attractive. Like a human knows an android isn't real, he felt there was something unnatural about her "realness." Her auburn hair fell in docile coil-waves around her pointed features; those thick locks reflected too much light and compelled his barely-open eyes to squint. Her complexion was bronze-tinged. Her eyes—lids large as cloak hoods—crowded her face. If he had to guess, he'd call her Indian or Middle Eastern—no, let's compromise: Pakistani.[17]

In the light, she was a living sculpture—copper-casted. Any moment now she'd sprout multiple arms and assume a goddess's holy pose.

"You should be in bed, Odys," she suggested, at ease in coaxing him. He wished he could obey. But it wouldn't be that easy.

"You know my name too? How come everyone seems to know that? And *why* are you wearing my sister's clothes?" He actually wanted an answer to this one.

"Simple, Odys," she replied with a forced—almost malevolent—grin, "I needed something to wear." At least she was honest. She pulled up the falling strap from Odissa's oversized sundress.

---

[17] Gandhi wouldn't think it was a compromise.

His questions were getting him nowhere. He leaned against the door, closing her off from escape and helping support his drained body. "How the hell did you get into this apartment?"

She straightened her posture. He'd already asked that. The girl—almost angrily—bit her lip. "I told you, Odys. *You* let me in."

His brow furrowed. "Why don't I remember?"

She stared at him with those huge eyes—eyes with irises like tiny, glinting pennies at the bottom of two wide, clear wells. "I'm not lying to you. I can't lie—not to you. There's a difference, you know, between being *invited* in and being *let* in. I was let in, but *not* necessarily invited. Do listen, Odys, for I'm enervated too." She put a sensitive hand upon her chest—that bursting chest was the only thing the tiny girl-woman filled in Odissa's dress.

"How—how did I 'let' you in?"

"Well, plainly stated," she paused. "I was in your pocket."

He laughed. "What now?"

"The penny—the one that Pepin gave you. *I'm* the penny." She gestured to herself with her delicate hand—up and down. Ah, it's not every day someone tells you they're coinage. "Your cat tried to eat me, back there. Frisky little thing doesn't know to it play cool. I swear, I've nothing against cats, as long as they don't swallow. I've been swallowed before—by a dog, see. Not a very pretty way to pass the time, I tell you. Can't turn humanoid in a dog, no. Not unless you want the damn animal to explode."

Odys shook his head, trying to understand—a cold sweat formed upon his wrinkled brow— his hair stuck to his face—he couldn't keep up with her. So he decided to slow her down: "Who— who's Pepin?"

"Oh, come! I know you're smarter than that, Odys. He made it very obvious for you. Pepin! Pepin—the man with the umbrella. Pepin—the man whose head exploded. Pepin—the man who set all this"—she gestured to Odys and herself—"up. I suppose he arranged it very nicely, every detail perfect. I *should* know. He made me enact parts of it, no doubt. It's always hard to remember first off. I'm still getting used to you. I'm too busy to remember my own past—if I can remember it at all. Gods only know what Pepin made me do. And what he made me forget."

She rubbed her forehead. Her gaze didn't meet his, though the twinkling eyes noted his reaction.

Odys slouched lower on the door, legs about to give way. This young girl—probably somewhere between seventeen and twenty—was rambling on about things he'd rather not hear. The sad part was that he felt he could believe every word.

Odys looked up through his brown hair. "Why'd his head *explode*? Was it a bomb? It wasn't some sort of—of murder was it?"

"Oh, that's simple," she shrugged it off. She noticed the cat down at her feet. "Pepin's head exploded because *he* killed *himself*."

"What are you even saying?" *Of course he killed himself woman!*

She snapped her fingers—she had perfect nails—the kind of nails he saw on Asian salon windows, on posters with sun-washed color and feminine hands posing in awkward positions around hideous flowers or retro orbs. Everything about her was perfect—proportionate, symmetrical, idealized.[18]

"Pepin's head didn't explode *because* a bullet went through his brain. A normal shot wouldn't have bruised him. The bullet only worked because *he* was the one that shot it." She bent down to pet the cat. The cat usually hated visitors—just like his owners. "With a man like Pepin—a man with no soul to hold him back—anything he does to himself is amplified and injected into the action."

"*What?*" It was seriously hard to follow

"Never mind," she sighed. "I'm overwhelming you. Can you give me a cigarette? It'll make us both feel better."

"Excuse me?"

She didn't even wait for the OK. Reaching in his pocket for his pack and lighter, she was smoking away before Odys could count to five (which he wouldn't want to do, even if he could spare the energy).

She sucked on the paper so deeply that the tip transformed to ash in one robust inhalation. He could almost experience the sultry smoke entering her lungs, feel its exalted warmth, imagine its texture. Was she even old enough to smoke?

The smoke drifted from her tiny nostrils. She closed her eyes and sighed.

"Exactly what I needed to go with my coffee. Some say that your addictions stem from what your soul craves," she mused, examining the deteriorating cigarette. "Chocolate, I hear, can produce the feeling of being in love. Those with a jones for chocolate therefore crave love." She walked over and smothered it in the coffee table's ashtray. Now there were an odd number of butts.

---

[18] Idealized by who, though?

31

She rubbed her acute chin. Each time Odys blinked to clear his vision, her skin tone shifted into phosphorescent tints and hues, like dazzling tricks on the eye—just subtle enough to make you disbelieve.

She had a second cigarette going when she asked: "I wonder what coffee, cigarettes, and *even numbers* say about your soul, Odys?"

He found it hard to breathe, especially when she glanced at him with that too-knowledgeable visage. How did she know? The coffee and cigarettes were obvious; physical proof of those addictions were scattered through the apartment. But his compulsion? That was less palpable.

To provoke further confusion, she began an improvised list of metaphysical traits Odys carried: "You like paperback books because you can fold the cover around, making the book easier to hold with one hand. You've never smoked pot, nor had any desire to. You also hate the idea of alcohol—anything that can make your mind less guarded and allow someone to discover your inner secrets. And boy, you have a few, don't you? You hate board games—though you tolerate chess. You dress like a slob to counteract your regal upbringing. You hated gym class. In high school, most of the guys thought you were a homosexual, but you actually—never mind I won't go there. You also have a thing for Asian girls, though you've never truly pictured yourself with one."

She gestured to herself as if the situation were somehow ironic.[19]

Odys slid down the door—ass hitting the floor. He watched her brandish the smoke-trailing cigarette. The ash-air smothered him as it swirled around her, a sacred aura. He couldn't swallow his spit. His body couldn't process this cathartic assault—this looking-glass reflection of his innate self.

"Who the fuck are you? Did—did Pepin know all this? Did he—did he tell you?"

Taking out another cigarette, she silently snickered. It reminded Odys of his own smugness at things he knew better than others.

"No, Pepin didn't tell me. Granted, Pepin knew a lot about you, but he could never *know* you like I do. Oh, don't look at me like I'm crazy. You didn't tell the cops about me. You realized I was more than just a penny. Right after Pepin's brain scatter, when you touched me in your pocket, I *know* you felt it..."

Her voice trailed off, recalling the ordeal—as if she had been there.

---

[19] Isn't it, though?

She walked back over to him. "I *know* you felt me draining you." She bent down in front of him, balancing on her toes—her heels gracefully in the air! She placed the cigarette effects next to her. "I still am."

Still sucking the life out of him.

Cigarette smoke glided into his face. "I can tell you're going to like me, Odys. Eventually." She pointed at him with her pretty cigarette-clasping fingers. "I'm sorry I'm taking so much of your energy all at once to revive myself. It can't be helped." She frowned. "You do look like shit."

With unhurried approach, she reached out and touched his chin. Her white-hot touch agitated his tessellated brain. The world reversed into negative. He closed his eyes—drifting in and out.

He melted into her palm.

If you could see through the girl's eyes, you would see his face flush with color—healthy once more.

He realized her action and drew back, eyes sinking into his pallor skull, a shadow overtaking his attenuated body. "What'd you just do to me?"

She smiled—teeth so perfect. She withdrew her limb from him. "I cut the distance between us." She blew smoke in his face. It was almost as soothing as her touch. She cradled his chin and mantra-chanted, "*Nephesh, nephesh, nephesh.* The soul is breath. Your body's having a hard time adjusting to losing its soul. In fact, I don't think I've ever seen a Master look so godawful. Maybe it's because you haven't eaten in a while. Or perhaps it's because you're fighting against me."

"My soul? What do you mean I don't have a soul?"

She shook her head. "No, it's not that you *don't* have one. I have it now. I'm the shell that encases it—the lock and door that keeps the world from it. Your soul manifest, perhaps. I *am* you, Odys. An extension of your body. We're the same *person.* Your soul's my windup key."

She put a hand on his knee and leaned into him, looking him straight in the eyes. There it was again—that nervousness surfacing to her face. And there it went, tucked away. Her self-control scared Odys.

"Forgive me," she smiled broadly—never blinking. "It's usually the Master who has more control of their bodies—never as equal as this. You're letting your soul run itself. How strange. How scary."

She smoothed his hair. The caress belied his independence; it seemed inappropriate—someone so beautiful couldn't be alone with him. This was a dream. That's all. He'd wake up and find Odissa still at home. She never would have left. He never would have tried to start his car. He never would have met the suicidal stranger. And he certainly wouldn't have an anthropomorphic penny.

He gripped his stomach as nausea struck him. She quickly put her hand back on his face. "Whatever you're doing to me...stop it." *Reverse it. Make it all better. And then go away.*

"You have every right to be angry. But this is how it works."

"It?"

He saw through his half-shut eyes that she struggled.

"There's a name for what I am, Odys. I'm your Automaton. You're my new Master. When Pepin, my old Master, killed himself, he canceled the bond I shared with him. I became functionless—stagnant—inanimate. I couldn't change from my object-form until you touched me—until I took your soul. I need a soul to fuel me—to wind me up. We're like machines—your soul is the rechargeable battery. But I'm far from wires, gears, and bolts."

Her expression became sullen. She tore her attention from him. "I don't know why Pepin planned for you to 'reactivate' me,"—she flinched at her own word choice—"But I know he had his reasons." She paused. "In his last years, Pepin wore great unrest and would hardly let me see his thoughts—let alone remember them after his death. All his plans—all of them—were clandestine. He hid his true self from our shared brains. He was a good Master—one of my favorites—you already like him, you just don't know it." She began to smile, then her face dimmed. "Yet, it's unsettling that we don't know his plans for you."

With one free hand, she reached behind her, as if digging in a pant pocket. She retrieved something. "I'm as clueless as you," she said, unfolding his glasses (Oh, so that's where they were—but where did she pull them from? She was wearing a dress!). "Statistically speaking, I had to *happen* to someone. But the ratio's tweaked, since Pepin *chose* you. He meant for you to touch me before anyone else could. He cheated."

She placed his glasses on his nose and tucked them in. Her hands lingered. The frames were warm, as well as the glass. They fogged up, making the moment more awkward.

Odys blushed.

She cupped his cheeks like one does a puppy. "Admit it, you prude; it feels better when we're close."

Yes, yes, fine. It did. By her strange witchery, he no longer felt as if he might die. This time he embraced the rushing palliation.

"Don't worry, it won't always feel this taxing. You should be better in a few hours, *if* you get some rest. Now, promise me you won't try to leave, all right? Don't open this door." She pointed behind him.

"Why not?" He forced himself to acknowledge her request, even though he wanted nothing more than to evaporate through her hand.

"They'll know you're well again, and then they'll come."

"They?"

"No one to fear, Odys," she soothed, outlining his features with her fingertips until he closed his eyes once more. "Though we must be cautious. There are other humans with Automata out there—but only a few. They are a group. A family. Pepin wasn't part of it. But that doesn't mean you can't be. I can't remember why Pepin left them, but I don't think you'll have to avoid them like he did—oh, why was it that he left them? I can't remember!" She was talking to herself.

She remembered Odys and looked down at him. "Under my aegis, you are safe." She continued to brush his spectral face. Her touch became unnoticeable as he drifted farther away.

It was almost like she was Odissa, if he stared at the hem of the dress—*the dress!*—yes, of course, the dress. His eyes shot open—the girl felt the sudden tension. He wished she didn't wear it.

As if reading his thoughts, the girl said, "If that's what you want. But first take this." She forced her cigarette between his lips. Before he'd even attempted the first intake of smoke, the dress glided to the ground.

But she hadn't withdrawn her hands from him—her hands were there—right there! She hadn't taken *off* the dress—she hadn't *touched* her dress.

And that glint in her eyes—that proud glint.

The girl was clearly not intangible, though the dress had fallen through her like a coin in water. Even Odys, in his sickened state, could tell she was completely solid. Solid as something non-air could be. It had been her body—her limbs, torso, legs—that had reshaped itself around the falling dress. Like quicksilver, she had reformed around it as it reached the ground. It took Odys a moment—a long moment—to realize she was crouching before him *nude*. The dress wrinkled around her feet. Her bare legs pushed together. Her arms didn't even bother to cover anything—

Because she had no navel. No nipples. No...

Stanza: Faux skin of the golem of metals.

He quickly shut his eyes.

35

Careful what you ask for, Odys.

"It's okay, you can open them now. I'm covered."

What what what? *No longer naked?* Well, if she could take the dress off that quickly, she might be able to put it *back on* in the same amount of time.

Odys opened one eye and lowered his defensive hand. He swallowed hard, though nothing but mortification went down.

She smoothed out a tube-like dress as she stood and tugged at the hem—a snake pulling at her second layer of skin. The dress was a metallic material that complimented her complexion. It glinted like a newly-removed cicada husk.

"Took me longer than anticipated. Like I said, I'm tired too."

"Took you longer?" Odys questioned, his voice a little higher than usual.

"It's a part of me; it's my skin, if you will." She attempted to keep said "skin" down to her knees. "I can—to a point—shift my skin around a bit. It makes me use a lot of our energy, though—oh, forget it." She gave one last ineffectual tug at her hemline. "Anyway, didn't want to waste more of you, you see."

She bent back down and tried to keep her legs close together; the hem was rolling up despite her efforts. "It takes a lot of concentration just to create something this scanty. Later on, once you get more sleep, I can create something more modest, of course. Not that you should care about modesty." She took the cigarette back from his lips, just for one more good suck then, "I'm going to get us some coffee." She jostled the butt back between his lips.

"But I thought I was supposed to sleep?" His lids clamped down. This wasn't happening, this wasn't happening, this wasn't happening.

She patted his cheek. "Decaff, babe."

When she took a step back, he could feel an airy yank starting from the pit of his chest. Part of him departed with her. He knew it like a compass knows north.

"Come, up you go. On the couch." She gave him her hand; he clutched it like a blind man pleading to Christ. If it would make him feel better, he'd do anything she said—would believe anything she told him. Her arms lifted him like iron levers. She helped him to the couch and left him there like a rag doll.

She was back in a flash, handing him his mug. She removed the finished cigarette from his compliant lips. He no longer cared if there were an even number of butts—how many had she smoked again?

She crossed her legs. Her foot bobbed. She toasted the air with her own mug. "Your addictions are now mine."

Stanza: Pinocchio wants to be a real puppet.

Odys hadn't started drinking yet, he was too busy glaring at her and feeling exposed.

"You still don't believe your eyes, Odys?" she asked. "Not even my comforting touch has swayed you to belief? Not even my tricks?" She pinched her dress. "Jesus, you're still praying this is just a dream."

More like nightmare, but whatevs.

"Well, what else can I do?" She placed her mug on a coaster. "I guess I could tell you that I have only two forms. Sorry to disappoint, but I'm far from a real shape-shifter. I'm more of a shape-*tweaker*. For example."

She elevated her left hand and, with her right, began to pull at each left finger as if removing a snug, veneer glove. "I have my coin state, which may come in handy when I need to be hidden from, say, your sister." Odys watched her peel something off her hand. "Then, I have my human-esque form, to make you feel more comfortable when talking to your soul."

Comfortable? Ha! It was much easier to talk to a soul he wasn't sure he had.

She gave one last tug on her middle finger and withdrew a diaphanous skin in the shape of her hand. As it left the hand, it turned to a golden gauze-glove. Between two fingers, she dangled the limp material—never letting go.

"Those are my only two forms, though they can be slightly manipulated."[20]

She rolled the material into a ball between her lithe hands and, like a magician, pulled her fists apart. Her upturned palms revealed empty hands.

"Notice, I didn't let go of the glove as it exchanged hands. That's because it was still a part of me, Odys. Just as you can add melted metal to melted metal, I can move my body parts—so long as they're always attached to me. Manipulation has its limits, as does hylomorphism. What else might I do to prove you're not dreaming?"

Her candor made him hide an anxious smile. He supposed if this didn't turn out to be a hallucination, he'd owe her some apology.

"You should drink your coffee, it's getting cold."

"I like it a bit cold."

---

[20] By "manipulation," she does not mean she can assume completely different human appearances (i.e. look like more than one person). There's a difference between dying your hair and having facial reconstruction surgery. She seems to carry consistent traits that cannot be entirely manipulated. It probably takes too much concentration and/or energy.

She surveyed him with a sidelong glance, self-assured. She'd already *known* how he took his coffee. She was just pretending she hadn't, to make him feel more comfortable…

He took an obligatory sip and observed her satisfied grin. Trying to swallow the hot liquid, "What's your name?"

"Thought you'd never ask, Odys." She pushed back her falling bangs; the glossy fringe grew longer as it left her fingers.

Freak, Odys thought. *I'm in a freak show.*

"If you don't know my name, I'm not as real as I could be, isn't that right?" She sighed. "Nevertheless, if you want to know what to call your newest, quintessential body part, it's *Maud*."

MAUD: The machine prosthetic.

CREATOR: A god.

SIBLINGS: Eight.

GASOLINE: The soul.

Chapter the fourth,

The jinn in the coin:

Can you trust the Midas touch?[21]

"Maud," Odys repeated. He liked that name—as if he'd known it all along. "No last name?"

"You really think something like *me* has a last name? Sometimes I don't have a first." She helped herself to yet another cigarette. "Want one?" she offered (his own pack, no less).

He shook his head.

She ensconced herself in the seat. "Masters call me what they want. Maud's the default name. You *can* change it. Though Masters never really do. Not entirely. They're afraid of offending The One who made me." She pointed up and blew the smoke through her nose like a divine bull—a bull misplaced in a matador's arena. "Maud's a strange name for me, isn't it? When someone says 'Maud,' no one pictures, well, this." She motioned to herself. "If *you'd* made me, you would've gone with a more *exotic* name. Or the complete opposite—something simple and clever. Like 'Penny.'" She snorted. "But then again, that's the point. I'm not supposed to make sense or be clever. I break stereotypes. I'm an *American* coin after all—yet I wasn't crafted here. My creator gave me traits that were to *His* fancy—not anyone else's. But I'll stop talking about

---

[21] "Yet which of our gowned masters will give a tempered hearing to a man trained in their own schools who cries out and says: 'These were Homer's fictions; he transfers things human to the gods. I could have wished that he would transfer divine things to us.' But it would have been more true if he said, 'These are, indeed, his fictions, but he attributed divine attributes to sinful men, that crimes, and that whoever committed such crimes might appear to imitate the celestial gods and not abandoned men.'" —Saint Augustine, *The Confessions*. Beware of the traits gods give *you*.

myself—even though it's the only thing we *should* be talking about because, let's face it, I already know everything about *you*."

"...I get the feeling I'm supposed to ask more questions now?"

"Well, it would be better than me monologue-ing all the time."

Stanza: The dialogue is quite the monologue—in more ways than ONE.

He said the first thing that came to mind, "What are you? I mean, how do you exist?"

She raised an eyebrow—as if she could ask *him* the same question. "A god made me. The blacksmith one—the god of metallurgy—sometimes associated with volcanoes—yes, *that* one. Ah, I see that light bulb going off. I make more sense now, don't I?" She gave another condescending arch to her eyebrows and sipped her coffee.

"Vulcan?" he asked—as if to be sure he was getting his mythology right. He wasn't about to say *Hephaestus*, because he wasn't sure how to pronounce it.

She nodded.

"See, reading *The Iliad* in grade school wasn't a total waste of time, now, was it?"

Before thinking, he blurted, "Is there no way to—"

"Undo this? No. You can't take it back, Odys. There's no way to be rid of me. If I could, believe me, I'd give you back what's yours. This is no sweet cupcake for me, either. I feel what you feel. What's done is done. The only way Pepin could get rid of me was to die by his *own* hand. The only way to break it is for *you* to die. I can't."

"Then put me out of my fucking misery. I don't know what you're doing to me. But it hurts." He pressed his eyes under his glasses.

"I'm in pain too. You just can't tell because I'm an Automaton."

They observed each other for some time. Odys may have even dozed off. He wasn't sure. The cat jumped upon the armrest beside her with a sweet, ruffling cat-noise, starling him.

"He's too comfortable with you," Odys mentioned, eyes just open enough to notice.

"Ah, well, I did feed him these past few days, so I'm no stranger." She gave the cat a good chin-scratch.

"Past few what?" He was alert once more.

"Days, Odys," Maud repeated. "You've been asleep—off and on—for days. Even on the floor, there, was the span of hours."

"It was? What day is it, then?" He tried to glance at a clock but his hair fell in his eyes.

"Tomorrow—which is in a few minutes—will be Monday. But don't worry. No one but your boss has called, asking if you could work an extra shift on Saturday. And I quit for you."

39

"What? What do you mean?" Odys would have stood up (to further express his shock), but that little outburst cost him. He dabbed at the new coffee stain on his pants.

"I had to, Odys. It's not like you could work for them now. Not with what's going on."

"What're you saying? I need that job!" he shouted at her between pants-drying actions.

"No, you *don't* need it. Besides, why's Odissa going to see Old Money Bags if you really *need* a job? Yes. I know what you fought about that morning. I know where she went."

All he could do was glare at her in shock.

"Listen, Odys, if I say you don't need something, you don't. I can't lie to you. Let me show you *why* you don't need a job."

She retracted her hand and raised an inveigling forefinger. Her eyes searched around the room, pinpointing his hallowed ashtray. "Observe, please." She gestured to the somewhat-filthy thing. She placed her finger on the dimpled rim and traced it. When her finger left, it was no longer just a plastic, black ashtray. It was a *golden* ashtray.

"Solid as can be," she added, handing it to him for corroboration. He took it, his hand falling from the unexpected weight. His jaw dropped. He didn't even care about the butts falling to his lap.

She shrugged it off as if to say, *Meh, it pays the bills.* "Every atom—molecule—whatever-the-hell—equivalently changed. Don't ask me how it works. Moreover, don't expect me to *always* be able to do it. I have to use energy for this sort of thing—like forming clothes. Just look at me, panting. Also, when we pawn it they'll ask where you got it. If they don't the first time, they will the second. I can turn things into any metal you like, but selling the stuff can get tricky. But don't worry, we'll find ways. Welders love my work." She watched Odys place the tray back on the coffee table, as if it was an explosive device. "Just be thankful I didn't turn the couch solid gold, Odys. Would've fallen through the floor."

Odys leaned back in his seat and held his mug for comfort. "Okay. But what now? What am I supposed to do with you? You have to leave—you can't stay here."

"If I don't stay near you, you'll die. You can't live without a soul, Odys. Your body will shut down. You'll feel worse than you do now—"

"If that's what it takes to get rid of you."

"You'd leave Odissa here, without you?"

He pouted—no, *glowered*—at her.

Speaking of his sister: "She said she would be back on Monday. She—she didn't call?"

"No, she didn't call." Maud put her cigarette out in the now-gold ashtray. "The only other activity you've missed is the officer stopping by. He couldn't wake you. I pretended to be fifteen and without ID, just so I could convince him I was a family friend come to care for you. They mostly bought the lie, especially since I can flatten my chest if need be." She examined that bosom. "However, while we're on the topic of *Monday*, you have school, yes? I don't think you should be going to school any longer. Just as work would be unsafe, so will school. You have little reason to rush learning. While I have your soul, you're immune to so much as a paper cut— unless, of course, you wanted one. You have a few hundred years ahead of you, most likely— give or take the *internal* forces." She frowned at the ashtray. "I slow the aging process, but from the looks of things, lung cancer might've set in."

The cat curled himself in her lap. As she stroked its back, Odys felt envious, then ashamed.

"But how'll I explain this to my sister?"

Maud shrugged. That was the least of their worries. "I have a *feeling*, Odys, that your sister's just as symbiotic to you as I am. She won't question you if you play your cards right. However, I'm not saying you *should* tell her about me." He wasn't planning on it. "For the time being, I'll be the spare change in your pocket. Literally."

Odys leaned forward, face in his palms. He was feeling much more assured, yes. Assured that this was madness.

When would this hallucination end? And just what—what!—would his sister think? She'd probably be excited. She was all about the fantasy shit...

And speaking of his sister, he wondered why his sister hadn't come home yet. He was hoping for an arrival sooner than Monday. Why was it taking her so long?

"I would say you should call her, but..." Maud said, as if she knew he was thinking of Odissa. "She doesn't have a cell phone. Neither do you. You both hate them. You don't want them, because you don't need them."

"We're never apart," he defended himself.

"Save for these *visits* she goes on."

As if it justified his anti-cell phone behavior, "She said this would be the last time she'd go to him."

"Speaking of *him*—no cell phones means it's also one less way for *him* to find you—and to find Odissa. Let's not pretend your 'no cell phones' rule is about simplicity. As they say, the nose knows all." She tapped her nose.

Did they say that? If so, who was *they*?

41

"*Stop* talking about him," Odys said.

"If Odissa's not home tomorrow, we must do something. It's important we locate her." With her eyes averted in thought, "If Masters like Pepin are out there blowing their heads off, you can be sure something bad is going on. We don't know why you've been involved. Your sister's unsafe until we do. They no doubt know you have liabilities."

"What does my sister have to do with this? Are we in danger?"

"I don't know, Odys," she responded, leaning forward. "But there's certainly the possibility. Other Masters might feel threatened by you. They're watching. They'll know you have a sister. Remember that your sister's more mortal than you, therefore making her life much more precious, correct? No doubt others like us will realize this."

He didn't like the connotations. "Should we find her? Right now?"

"No, Odys. That's not what I meant." She rested her elbows on her bare knees. "I'm not going to pretend we're entirely safe. The others won't like that they had no say in Pepin's plans. They didn't choose you. And they don't know why Pepin broke the rules for you..."

She talked as if Odys now held some position or title in a council of other "rare coin collectors"—if you will.

"These others with—" *whatever you are.*

"Automatons, yes. Or Automata—however you want to pluralize it."[22]

"They were watching—from the roof. Weren't they?"

"Yes. And they always will be. They tend to keep tabs on one another. For personal safety and so forth. We aren't coeternal, Masters and Automatons. Precautions are necessary."

"Precautions?" Odys repeated.

"Don't worry. If they didn't want you in the picture, you'd be dead already. They'll want to know why Pepin killed himself for you. They'll not waste his death. Oh, don't look as if we should be hiding in bunkers, Odys. You're not dead yet. They're only making sure they've nothing to fear from you."

He glowered again.

"Tomorrow. We'll talk more about this tomorrow. Let's get some sleep. You're already looking better than you did on Friday night." She took away his mug.

He wanted to offer her Odissa's bed, though he wasn't fond of the idea.

"No, thank you," she said, grasping his arm to pull him to his feet. "I won't need it."

---

[22] We're inconsistent ourselves.

"You don't sleep?"

"That's not what I said," she replied, her face unreadable as he straightened. "Automatons eat and drink and sleep. We need such things...to keep our Masters healthy, too. Not as much as Masters do but..." She shrugged. "Even the soul needs a sojourn from the physical world."

"Then where will you sleep?" He didn't budge.

"Why, with you, Odys. Ah, I hope that doesn't upset you."

Hope? But she knew it did! It was clear by her expression.

She snapped to obdurate. "It's not as if I haven't been next to you, these past days. You wanted it. How else do you think you're alive, if I hadn't been so near? If you're apart from me for too long, you—"

"Die?"

"You might. But let's not test it." She narrowed her eyes. "As I said, I've never experienced this type of slow recuperation from a Master. It's a slight rejection of me—you're strong-willed, Master." Her eyes snapped to him minatorially.

Master, Master, Master. She sounded like the actress from *I Dream of Jeannie*. She certainly looked more like a genie/jinn than the pale Barbara Eden.

Maud patted his arm with patronizing force, "Don't think that we can't make this nightmare easier on us both, Odys. Don't you remember I can turn into a penny?" She took his hand in hers—cold yet burning. Then, as if his own were a black hole sucking her entirely, her body was drawn into the crevice of his sweaty palm. In the blink of an eye, the woman was gone and the penny was there, inert.

Observing the tarnished coin, he wondered if it had all been a vision. What if he'd only dreamed this Lady Liberty had spoken to him?

"I'm going insane."

"I think you should go to bed, Odys. You're starting to doubt reality."

Damn.

He squeezed the talking coin (to muffle any further communication) and went to his bed. He kept her in his fist, pressed to his soul-hungry veins.

Stanza: Let's fast forward through sleepy-time, shall we?

So, because I hate dream sequences and respect you enough as a reader NOT to force you through someone else's incoherent, speculative thought, I'll tell it to you straight.

Odys got pretty comfy that night.[23]

Well, eventually anyway. Mostly, he was too sick to bother with being anxious/worried about the implications of owning a MOTHER. FUCKING. AUTOMATON. Let's just say that when you're in a coma-like state you tend to forget what made you so comatose.

Thus, against his will, he let himself carry out his "normal bedtime routine" under those flannel sheets all the way to morning. Which means he tossed and he turned and he reached out and—

Wait a second.

His eyes shot open. He realized what he clutched—and what clutched him back.

Releasing a spew of unrepeatable words, he jumped out of his rickety bed, mattress wobbling and making the girl stir with its quaking. The *naked* girl, I should add.

Shielding his eyes—while continuing to curse—Odys dashed from his room. The girl raised her head. What was wrong? She looked down. Oh. *That's* what's wrong.

"Shit, shit, shit," she hissed as a second-skin formed.

Opening the previously-slammed door, she followed him out, repentance consuming her.

Odys stopped his pacing and mumbling and slouched over the kitchen counter.

"Odys—"

"What. Fucking. Happened?" He didn't turn to her.

"Oh, come on! You remember. It wasn't a dream, last night." *Stop wishing for that.* "It's me, Maud. Your Automaton. Your penny. Nothing happened. We didn't do anything in there. Trust yourself."

She leaned against the kitchen doorframe. She was a guardian pillar-statue before some grand temple, supporting its structure with her celestial weight.

"Are you covered, then?" he snapped.

"Yes, I am. I'm so sorry—we Automatons dream too, you see. Sometimes I dream myself into my humanoid form. We all do it. I didn't *mean* to. Clothes take concentration. And how else would you get better, if we weren't touching?"

His hands formed bridling fists. "My life is some—some divine *porno* now? That what this is?"

(I agree with Odys, here, that the forced sexual tension is a bit cliché and caters to a specific sexual fantasy, but don't blame me. I'm not the one that made Maud as she is).[24]

---

[23] A reader's discretion is advised. (Cough, cough).
[24] Sure you're not.

"I didn't mean to do it," she continued. He could feel her take a step from the threshold. "*You* didn't mean to do it. You didn't *make* me do it. It's not our fault. I tried to stay a coin, I promise—"

"You should've warned me *that* could happen." He pointed to his room.

"Then you wouldn't have gotten any sleep. You'd be dead!"

That's right, Maud. Completely ignore the fact your boobs were pressed up against him, your bare leg wrapped around him, your hand tangled in his bed-head hair (that was still standing up, btw).

"Hey, now, you were quite clingy too, thank you very much," she chided his thoughts.

"Stop it!" he snapped over his shoulder. *Stop getting in my head.*

She walked past him. She now wore a less-than-chaste metallic tank-top and short-shorts—the best "clothes" she could manage. It came with the voluptuous territory.

"You'd better get used to me, Odys." Maud found a half-used pack of cigarettes in a drawer. "No need for modesty. It's not like you're *really* attracted to me, though I *know* I'm attractive. Gods know I'm not 'attracted' to you. We're the goddamned same person, Odys. Get that through your head."

He stepped toward her. "If you know so much about me, then you should know I don't like this conversation. *And* you should know it's not about you in my bed. It's about how the *fuck* am I going to hide a naked woman every night from Odissa? Huh? You're no fucking coin!" He gestured closer and closer to her face, hysteria pulling his lips. "What's the fucking point of being able to turn into a coin if you can't stay that way?"

She didn't bother to respond, because he paled and had to grip the kitchen counter, becoming dizzy and out of breath. He took a seat at the table, barely making it there before his legs started to shake.

Triumphant, she lit the cigarette. "You should have breakfast."

"How can you talk about *breakfast* at a time like this?"

"Um, maybe because you're fucking hungry? Eat something."

"No. I might throw it up."

"But you must eat, Odys. Just because you don't eat doesn't mean this isn't happening."

She went to feed the cat first.

"Give me coffee, if you must give me something." He put his head in his arms, needing a pillow.

"Make your own damn coffee. Show some initiative. I've been taking care of you enough. You're better than you were. You've gotten plenty of sleep, at least."

Moaning, "If something like you is possible, then why isn't it possible to undo you? To free you from me?"

"This is fate. Everyone falls victim to it one way or another—and other platitudes like that— blahblahblah." She picked off tobacco leaves from her tongue, watching the cat eat.

"This wasn't the Universe's fault. It's *Pepin's*." He realized he was drooling on his hand and grimaced. He was disgusting. But he was too lazy to wipe it off.

"This could've happened to someone else, yes. But it didn't. The gods planned for *you* to deal with Pepin's plans. Otherwise, they'd rearrange this situation. But they haven't. They obviously like where this is going. And speaking of *destiny*," she said as she put the cat food back up, "is that supposed to be blinking?"

Maud pointed to the answering machine. She knew—because Odys knew—that it shouldn't have that RED. BLINKING. LIGHT.

Odys forgot his sickness. He rushed over to the machine and hit the tiny play button. In its robotic voice it spoke, "Monday, 6:30 a.m."

He'd never even heard the phone ring. He glanced at the clock. He'd slept in late. He'd been out cold. He narrowed his eyes at Maud, as if maybe she had ignored the ringing. But something told him she was just as ill as he and had needed her sleep too.

"Odys, babe, I'm leaving the hotel now—using their phone. Probably will stop for food soon. Sorry I took longer than I'd hoped..." Blah, blah, blah. Odissa would see him soon and they could talk about *"what happened."*

Odys drooped. "I hate when it takes long. I'd hoped he'd let her leave sooner."

His rising panic made Maud shift her footing. "She's fine, Odys. She always is."

"Fine isn't good enough," he grumbled, rubbing his face. He looked around the apartment. He hated the emptiness.

"I need to get out." He paced a few steps this and that way. "Perhaps go to the store, or have breakfast out. I don't want to stay in here. I can't stay in here—not with you. I must get out."

(I applaud you myself, Reader, for being cooped up with him this long. You deserve an outing!)

"All right, then," Maud said, though hesitant. "But I must warn you. *They* will see us leave. When we get back, things may not be the same. An active Master is scariest of all to them. Activity always invites the chance for things to go wrong."

"What would you have me do, then? They're bound to barge in now—that's how you make it seem."

"I'm just telling you it's about to get more complicated. The only reason they haven't come in yet is because they're summing you up first. They don't know what's going on, either. They don't know why Pepin killed himself. That much I remember. That was his whole fucking point. But, certainly, leave if you need fresh air."

"Can—can you make yourself a penny?" He felt it rude to ask. "It would make things *less* complicated." He didn't want the neighbors to see this beautiful girl perambulating with him. They might get the wrong idea. They might tell Odissa.

She slipped a smile. "Of course." Her body fell to the ground, her second-form rolling in uneven circles until ringing to a stop. He scooped her up (with only slight hesitation) and was halfway through the apartment parking lot when:

He remembered his car wasn't working.

He cursed under his breath and looked down at Maud. "Why didn't you remind me?" As if it was her job.

"You were so excited, even I forgot. I'm not feeling too well myself, you know. You're a lot to keep up with. And I wanted out, too."

He spoke to void, "I guess we'll stay inside. I would walk, but I remember what happened to me last time I tried that. Unless, of course, you know what's wrong with my car?"

Do Automatons fix cars?

"I do know, actually. Let's just say you're going to need some new parts for her. And they could take weeks to get in. Pepin *wanted* you to walk, Odys."

"Home it is then."

Mrs. Firth-from-Down-the-Hall was coming out of her apartment, curlers in her hair, about to toss out a few trash bags. She caught Odys's last words to the coin in his palm. She did a double take.

Odys retrieved his keys, pretending he was sane, mumbling a song to make it seem like he'd been singing.

Stanza: No man is an island.

Closing the door behind him, he went to flip on the lights.

But they were already on.

Two unfamiliar heads peaked out from the kitchen.

47

Odys goggled. Maud fell from his hand and reshaped herself to stand in front of him. She placed a hand upon him, telling him not to move. "I told you, didn't I?" she hissed.

One of the two strangers was leaning against the kitchen counter. His head had rotated in their direction, unworried. His eyes were indiscernible behind dark sunglasses—the kind so dark you can see your own reflection; a reflection that distracts you with your own warped image. He had been blowing a huge, globular bubble from a piece of bright blue gum.

It popped.

He sucked it back in and continued chewing, indifferent.

The other man, however, had to step around the kitchen wall to espy what his overly-relaxed comrade had noticed; he was carrying Odys's carton of soy milk, wiping his chin clean of newly-slurped dribble.

Odys's heart shot to his ears. It was that one—the one helping himself—the one with red-red hair—the one with the scraggly beard—the one with the cavalier gawk—that looked familiar.

The man from the roof.

How the hell had they gotten in here? And so quickly too. Hadn't Odys locked the door behind him? It wasn't even damaged.

Though Odys froze, it wasn't out of fear. They weren't looking for a fight.

Odys's eyes flickered to Maud. Her posture was defensive, arms crossed but unafraid. "They wait for us to leave before they sneak in. Too afraid to knock, are we, boys?"

The redheaded one almost smiled. "Why knock when you have a key, Maud?" He raised a single finger; it turned into a key until it he tucked it back into his palm.

He twisted the cap back on the soymilk unhurriedly. He snapped the carton down upon the counter beside his friend, the man with shaggy jet-black hair.

That black hair was too long and too short. Too in-between. The black-haired man had an aloof and remote bearing, his jaw chewing away at the bubble gum, arms across his chest. It was hard to tell his expression, or the direction of his gaze, because those huge sunglasses covered a great portion of his drawn-out face. His blanketed eyes might as well be closed—taking a nap.

Both men looked about the same age. No more than thirty. Probably.

The redheaded one was in a suit—an abnormally close-fitting and flattering white suit.

If Odys hadn't been uncertain about their intentions, he would have found time to feel bland compared to these dandified hoodlums.

"We thought you were going out." The redhead gestured to the door. "You know the drill, Maud. We were just going to do a quick run-through before we came over for an *official* visit. Getting to know the territory, that's all." Like it was the most reasonable excuse in the world.

The man with glasses turned his head away, staring off into the kitchen as if Odys bored him. Like a cow, he kept chewing away on that too-bright, too-fruity gum.

Chomp, chomp, chomp.

Familiar-looking Ginger, however, walked forward. A too-wide smile pulled his lips like an exaggerated Greek theatre mask. His scraggly chin-strap beard helped embellish the lunatic expression all the more.

With each show-offy step he seemed to stand taller and taller. He was maybe two or three feet away from brushing the low ceiling. Maybe less. Yes, less. With cocky disapproval, "So. This is him, the other face of the coin?" His body seemed to shrink back down to their eye-level as he scrutinized Odys. "A bit grungy for a rich kid, no?"

He had asked the question of Maud, pointing at Odys as if Odys was her new pet fish— uninteresting and, well, a fish.

But she didn't answer him; her chilled silence was response enough. Her lips stiffened. She didn't like how the Automaton had asked *her* as if her Master wasn't there.

When Maud didn't respond, the apathetic sunglasses-man (still in the kitchen) finally began to emerge from ennui and act alive. There was a histrionic quality to his movement. Something told Odys the man had to *embellish* every action. Otherwise there was no point in moving. With a wave of his hand and a tilt of his body, "What's he look like, *Fletcher?*"

FLETCHER: someonething very tall.

MASTER: Likes fruity stuff.

GLITCH: He sometimes blacks out/passes out when he's bored or unneeded. But I wouldn't call it narcolepsy. It's more like a computer's screensaver going up. He knows how to tune out the world. He was designed that way. And his Master finds use of it.

SEEING EYE DOG: For Dorian (who's here to chew gum and keep bitches in line).

Chapter the fifth,

Metempsychosis:

A pair of eyes for a pair of twins?

The sedate-souled man (still in the kitchen) had not turned his head to inspect Odys himself when he had asked his question. His disinterested, drowsy speech was *almost* free of any accent—a Spanish cadence flamenco-danced behind those teeth (something I'll just point out but won't force you to read). *"What's he look like, Fletcher?"* he had asked. It echoed through Odys's skull.

Fletcher, as we can now call him, looked back at his Master. His thick, knotted dreadlocks clung about his shoulders as he did so. The red hair—hair such a deep blood-red it sparkled like the paint-job of a flashy red car—was tied off with a lock somewhere between his neck and lower back. They looked more like limp spikes than actual hair. His made Maud's hair look red-brown.[25]

Fletcher rubbed his fuzzy chin as he answered his Master, "What's he look like? Well, Dorian, darling, he's average, I guess. Very average."

"Wonderful. What's his *color*?" the black-haired man (ostensibly called Dorian) asked. He adjusted his sunglasses. "Tell him so he knows we know."

"Brown," Fletcher nodded, agreeing with himself. "A pale-brown nature. Brown hair, brown eyes. Just like we guessed from the photos."[26]

Fletcher cut his pinprick eyes at Odys, letting him know they already *knew* him. The Automaton chuckled at Odys's confusion, shoulders rolling. Speaking of those shoulders, Fletcher had a purposeful slouch. His slim body bent forward and back, slumped against an invisible wall. He was lanky—rather, willowy—reaching at least a head taller than the rest of them.

"Charming. And how is he taking to Maud?" Dorian asked.

Couldn't he see for himself?

"He seems—"

But Maud cut him off. "Stop pretending you can't see him through Fletcher, you blind bastard."

"Fantastic alliteration, Maud!" Fletcher smirked, wiggling in place. That smile showed off one hell of a jaw line.

"You can ask me these questions about *my* Master. Better yet, talk to him yourself."

Razzle-Dazzle Dorian raised his brows in disapproval. "Can I, Maud?" Straightening up, he was taller than he first appeared—though not so tall as his Automaton (no one was). He would

---

[25] I cut this bit from the actual text, but thought some of you might actually enjoy the Narrator's further description: "This new Automaton (as Odys had assumed because of its bare feet; not even Maud thought to wear shoes—too much effort) was far from freckled-fair. His complexion was one smooth surface of light olive, like some muted tin can—a man who should have owned black hair. For example, if this were a black and white noir film, that red hair would *translate* as black. Yes, yes, under the right circumstances, Automata can look completely natural. Completely normal. Completely no cause to stare. But the world is not always black and white, and Odys couldn't help but stare."

[26] At first I thought this little "color" bit was weird. But it is explained later. I won't ruin the buildup for once.

have looked better with height—less platitudinous—though he wasn't *exactly* short. Fletcher was just freakishly tall, which made everyone else wee-little afterthoughts.

Despite his height, Dorian was quite eye-catching in his worn jean jacket, the sleeve cuffs pulled back like stiff wings on his forearms, hands in the pockets of his tight pants. Underneath that jacket was a bright turquoise shirt, blinding Odys's feeble eyes as it contrasted with those loud—nay, *screaming*—bright-purple pants. He looked like a goddamned peacock. And seemed proud of it.

Dorian walked past them, as if to take a look around. But he did no looking.

He had a nonchalant and buoyant walk for a sightless man. With his hands in his pockets, he had no way of guarding himself from undetected objects.

"*Can* I ask you, Maud? Can I really? I mean," Dorian expounded, "he can make the puppet talk but can he make her tell the truth? *No se.* You've been in here for days. *Days.* Pepin's dead, and you don't even have the courtesy to call and tell us why he fucking killed himself—why he gave you to someone we didn't even know. If you *knew* something, then you'd tell us. *Por qué no* haven't you told us? You should've told your new Master the rules. He needs to understand the way we do things."

"Why, so you could just barge in anyway? I knew you were watching this whole time, Dorian."

"*Sí*, and he knew it too, didn't he? He should've made a peace offering to get on our good side if he wanted to be treated nicely. Now we can't treat him nicely, Maud."

"You weren't going to treat him nicely, Dorian."

"That's kind of true. See, even if Pepin erased things in your brain we'd like to know—which we all know he did—that doesn't necessarily make you innocent. What Odys doesn't know can hurt *us*. That's why we're here, after all."

"But does that automatically make us your enemy?" Maud snapped, her feral eyes darting from Dorian to Fletcher.

Dorian shook his head, hair ruffling. "No, Maud." He had an almost inconspicuous way of talking from the side of his mouth, probably because of all the gum stuffed in it. "But you certainly aren't in the clear. Odys Odelyn, you know who I am? Recognize me? Think long and hard. If Maud remembers me, so do you."

Odys didn't understand.

"Playing stupid, are we?" Dorian shrugged. "Not that we didn't see this coming."

"He doesn't know who you are!" Maud insisted. Her passion redirected their attention.

Fletcher stepped closer to her, lowering his face to meet hers. He took her chin like a doctor examining a patient—clinically. She didn't fuss.

Though he was perfectly clean, there was a rusty, grubby nature to Fletcher's fingernails. In fact, anything worth outlining on his person had a dark, tarnished discoloration. It reminded Odys of a corroded antique—no, no!—a relic or artifact—something you'd find in the bottom of the ocean or in an ancient burial chamber; old and sacred, something with character...

Odys noticed several silver-like rings on Fletcher's fingers. They pressed into Maud's skin. What's more were those six—maybe seven—earrings framing his ear. God only knows how many were on the other side. He had details. Maud didn't. She was too tired to create them—no ornamentation.

Fletcher leaned close—closer than Odys liked—and took a sniff of her. A long sniff. His upper lip lifted as his nostrils widened. He closed his eyes as if it helped mull over the scent. Fletcher concluded, "She's not well."

"As if she couldn't pretend," Dorian said, as if to himself. (Granted, Fletcher *was* his self).

"She's conserving energy," Fletcher supposed, frowning. He opened his eyes. "If I didn't know any better, I'd say they're not even synced yet." He was talking aloud for Odys's benefit. Dorian *wanted* Odys to hear.

"Conserving energy, Maud," Dorian tsked. "Just what've you two been up to, to waste so much of it? Why must you conserve?"

"He *hasn't* synced with me, actually," Maud admitted for Odys. She waited for Fletcher to release her—not about to make any quick movement.

Dorian snorted. "Impossible. He'd be dead by now."

"Maybe he'll do our job for us, then. All we have to do is give it time." Fletcher flashed his pearly teeth down at Maud.

Odys licked his lips, building up courage to speak.

"He's afraid of me," she insisted.

Fletcher opined, "If you wanted us to take you seriously, you wouldn't've hid in here for days." He released her from his examination.

"We weren't *hiding*," Maud corrected. "You knew where we were. He was ill—very ill— until today. What was he supposed to do? Just look at him, Fletcher."

"Oh, no doubt he *is* ill," Dorian put up a hand. He had many rings, too. "But *why* is he ill? Each human reacts differently to an Automaton. Every human has their personal weaknesses." He walked over to the couch, taking cautious steps. "Maybe this is just Odys's weakness. It's good to see you, by the way, Maud. Or," with a self-deprecating smirk, "at least it would be, if I could *really* see you."

He sat down on the couch with a laugh-sigh. As if he weren't blind, he put his scuff-free kicks on Odys's coffee table—like he'd known the table was there all along. "It *has* been a while." Dorian stared off into space, watching the blank TV screen in front of him. "I'm sorry for your loss, also. Pepin was a good man, despite everything he's put us through."

"Pepin was a shut-in," Fletcher grumbled, expressing how Dorian really felt.

Dorian smiled—at the TV. The blank TV. "No harm in that, as long as he wasn't planning something too upsetting for us. And just what *was* Pepin planning, Maud?"

Fletcher stared at Maud when his Master asked it, tongue in his cheek.

"She can't remember," Odys finally spoke.

"Yes, yes, Mr. Messyhair. I'm sure she can't. Pepin was no fool. It's all *muy* convenient to wipe a hard drive. But what about you? What do *you* know about Pepin?"

"You were there," Odys pointed to Fletcher. "That's the first time I'd ever seen him."

"No need for nervousness, Odys," Dorian said. "As long as you cooperate, we'll not kill you." He frowned, playing with his rings. "No sense in killing you before we assess your usefulness. But if you're not useful, well, we'll have to make something out of this shit pile."

"If you touch him, I will kill you," Maud said—all seriousness.

Dorian's head tilted to Maud's direction, a creepy smile on his face. "Ah, Maud. Pretty face, tiny frame, metallic aura. Automatons never change. Neither does their color. It's the Masters that change—that still grow old. *Elixir vitae!* You know what that means, Mr. Odelyn?"

He didn't turn to address Odys. The TV was Odys. "Of course you do. Maud knows what it is. Maud knows she's the elixir. But me, well, I'm the antidote to that poison. I'll put you out of your misery if you're not careful about your Automaton's threats, there. But I digress."

"He can't read my thoughts." Maud was begging him to play nice. "He doesn't know what's going on here, Dorian. We're not well."

"He's well enough to be a bother, Maud. More of a bother than he's already been..." He slapped his knee. "And you've absolutely *no* idea how boring it was, waiting for you two to come out. We've been waiting and waiting just to get inside here safely. But that plan was foiled." He gestured to the foilers. "Fletch, search the apartment. We've wasted enough time."

"What?" Odys burst out. "Wait a second, I don't—" Maud turned and put a hand on his forearm, drawing his attention.

"Just let them. They need to know they can trust you."

53

"Trust me? They're the ones who broke into my place!"

"Hey, now, we didn't *break* anything," Fletcher retorted. He paused from his movement toward Odys's bedroom.

Odys ignored Maud and moved to defend his territory. "You'll search this fucking apartment over my dead body."

...Perhaps that trite phrase *wasn't* the smartest thing say (but he wasn't feeling a hundred percent, so we won't judge him too harshly), because Fletcher faced him in an instant, one hand in his pocket, the other pointing two fingers at Odys's head like a gun.

"Gladly," Fletcher accepted, slouching into the word. His sickle-smile widened as his fingers morphed into a darker, more metallic matter. Right before his eyes, Odys saw Fletcher's hand produce—manifest!—a sleek handgun from its own fractions.

Handy, to have a body that could grow weapons faster than a human could grow hair.

Odys went cross-eyed just looking at it.

Fletcher stepped even closer. "Have something you don't want us to see?"

But Fletcher's eyes darted away from Odys, distracted. His Master was in pain—crumpled over. He saw Maud standing over Dorian—her eyes met his with a flint-like spark.

...Dorian sat back up as if Maud hadn't just given him a blow that could have knocked the lights off of San Francisco. He drew out a new pair of glasses to replace the ones she'd just cracked on his face. Somewhere between point A and B, she'd knocked Dorian silly.

"Don't you dare point a gun at him—I'm not pointing one at you!" she barked at Dorian.[27]

Dorian smoothed his hair, smiling. It wasn't often a Master got to experience pain unless another Master/Automaton gave it.

"Well, I can't say that's the first pair she's broken," Dorian forgave, not bothering to pick up the previous pair's pieces. Odys wished Dorian's hair hadn't been so disheveled from the impact. Maybe he would have seen the rest of his mysterious face.

"I didn't ask for her—for this," Odys stated, pointing at the ground. Apparently the ground represented "this."

It was the only defensive thing he could come up with. His eyes were still watching Fletcher's hand. Maud's reaction to the (literal) *hand*gun made him assume it *would* work.

Odys's statement seemed to upset the Automaton even more. "*He didn't ask for this?* Does he think *any* of them did?"

---

[27] Gun = Fletcher's fingers

Odys saw Fletcher's dreadlocks stiffen like angry snakes. Maud was quickly between them. Fletcher was so close it looked as if he might bite her. "Disrespectful little—"

But Maud pushed Fletcher back. Though it was nothing but a blockade, Odys sensed a rumbling in his chest when she shoved Fletcher—felt the two souls colliding.

Odys noticed Dorian's head perk up. He'd felt it too, maybe even more sharply. Maud had meant to *shock* him.

Fletcher took a few guarded paces back, out of respect for the other Automaton. The gun sunk back into his palm, leaving only five dangerous fingers. His hand wiggled its finger-limbs, itching an invisible irritant at his side.

"We're innocent until proven guilty." Maud reminded them. "Now do what your Master told you. Search the place. You won't find anything."

Fletcher walked off, entering Odys's room. He glanced over his shoulder before closing the door defiantly.

Odys found it odd Fletcher would leave his Master all alone. If they didn't trust Odys, why would Dorian leave himself unprotected? Something told him Dorian liked to play with fire, to test its warmth.

"Please, Odys, Maud, sit down," Dorian invited them.

"Odys wants to stand," Maud said, crossing her arms. It was then that Odys noticed what she'd chosen to "put on": basically little more than underwear. Conserving their energy didn't conserve her modesty. But Odys was too troubled with these intruders to care. Odys rubbed the back of his neck, trying to keep himself calm.

Dorian chuckled to himself, as if he were the scariest thing on the planet. "Odys, Odys. Don't act so scared. It's not like we've decided your fate yet. I see Maud's shown you her gilded finesse." He pointed to the golden ashtray.

How did he know it was there? How did he see it? Because Fletcher had noticed it, some time ago. "Be careful not to be too greedy too soon. Gold is costly, when you're tired. Also, it makes you look more suspicious. You're supposed to be sick, after all."

He crossed his legs and leaned forward on his elbows—a physical representation of his shift: "Now down to business, Odys. I may not respect you because you have no fashion sense, but you're still a pretty face I don't want to ruin. I also don't want the trouble of giving Maud to some other poor soul. She's already *happened* to you, so we'll try to deal with it."

He steepled his fingers under his slight chin. "You see our dilemma here, no? We aren't unreasonable people." He laughed as if that wasn't true. He leaned back on the sofa, spreading his arms wide. His wingspan almost reached the tips of the couch, just short of where Odys's fingers could wrap around. "I find it odd that it's taken you so long to stabilize, Odys. When, exactly, did you touch Maud?"

"Near the alleyway, like he told you," Fletcher mumbled from in the kitchen. They heard a squeaky cabinet door close—hadn't he been in Odys's room? They'd never seen him pass!

Dorian laughed, proud of the distraction he had been for his Automaton. *This kid really is sick—too sick to pay attention.* He pulled out another pair of glasses from his pocket (this pair aviator style). "Yes, Fletcher, I know what we *think* you saw." Dorian put the extra pair on his head, making it seem like he had two sets of eyes. Like a headband, it pushed back his straight bangs. "You were quite far away when you spotted Odys, Fletcher. And Maud *did* stay in his pocket the entire time...How good of an actor are you, Odys?"

Odys didn't dignify his question with a response.

"Just so you know, we received a call from Pepin—the evening before the incident. That's how we were able to locate you. Pepin told us how to find him. We had no fucking idea what the bastard was up to," Dorian laughed. "But, when you get a strange message from someone you haven't heard from in a while, you can expect *something* to happen. Especially from Pepin. But as I was saying. Wait, what was I saying? Oh, yes. Odys, you don't have a reason to be *pretending* now, do you?"

Dorian reached into the same pocket he'd retrieved the glasses from and pulled out a pack of gum—the way-too-fruity kind with the flavor that lasts maybe five good chews. It was the last piece. Before he took it out he offered, "Gum? Let me guess: no, thanks?"

Odys got them back on-topic, "You've already made it clear you don't trust me or anything I might say. Perhaps I—I touched her just now, before I left the apartment? Maybe that's why I'm still sick."

Geez, Odys, don't try to play mind games before you even know the rules.

Dorian chuckled as he put the fresh stick in his mouth. He used the remaining wrapper for the old piece. He needed a good gum-to-teeth ratio. "If that were so, you'd still be out cold. Plus, Fletcher's been watching you. Maud's walked by that kitchen window. She's been animated for some time now. It does take weeks to *fully* adapt, though most Masters don't have health problems as you still do. It's not every day you're forced to interact with your soul, comprendes?"

He continued with conversational air, "I'm concerned about you, Odys. Having an Automaton is draining. Some might say having one is like being pregnant for eternity,"—Dorian giggled to himself—"though it's hard to know, since there are few Masters who ever give birth, given our lifestyle…" Chew, chew, chew. "I only bring this up because I think it may be a small clue as to who you really are." He waited for a reaction.

"…Who I am? But I thought you already knew." Odys listened for Fletcher. Where was he now? He couldn't hear him ratting around.

"Well, we *know* you are Odys Odelyn, but that hardly tells us anything. We need to know why—of all people—Pepin chose you."

"Is he the evil twin or the good twin?" Fletcher asked with a gradient laugh.

Odys jolted. How *dare* they know Odys was a twin. "I don't see what my current sickness has to do with Pepin randomly picking me."

"I don't think it was random at all. You see, methinks there's a reason you don't want Maud. And I think I see that reason." That was ironic, coming from a blind man. "Ah, I *knew* there'd be a day when we'd have someone who didn't want their own soul. The masochistic sort. Though you know the key to your full recovery, you retain a considerable degree of detachment from your Automaton—from *yourself*. I find this odd on two accounts, Mr. Sickypoo. The first would be that, well, look at her. Why wouldn't you accept such a tempting gift—especially if you're a straight man? Second, Odys, the pills to cure you are right there,"—he pointed at Maud—"and you refuse to swallow. You like the pain. Tell me, Odys, you ever been suicidal?"

"That's hardly your business," Odys replied, somewhat distracted when Fletcher sprayed some of his sister's perfume in the bathroom. Liking the smell, he gave himself a squirt. *Must they touch everything?*

"Fair enough, then." Dorian lifted his hand in apology. Odys noticed his thumb ring. Odys would never wear a thumb ring. "But I'll speak my point. Pepin might have picked you because he knew you'd be a willing scapegoat—a scapegoat for his bigger plans. Tell me Odys, do you have a *cause* to die for?"

Odys was sure there was a clear difference between not wanting Maud and not wanting to live. "I don't want to die," Odys stated, just for future reference.

"But do you want to *live*?"

"Isn't that what I just said?"

"Whatever you say, boss." Dorian pushed the sunglasses up. "You don't want to die? Sure, sure. Me, though, I don't ever want to go to Singapore. They ban gum there." He flashed his gum between his teeth. "That's what I don't want."

"So your sister sleeps here?" Fletcher asked, motioning with his thumb to the room he left behind. He was a quick little bugger.

"Yes," Odys answered through clenched teeth.

"Then why's there stuff piled on her bed? Boxes, books, and shit—it's the biggest *shelf* in there. Where the hell does she sleep?"—as if she were a messy slob, which was slightly untrue. "Does she not sleep at all? Insomniac or something? We *know* she lives here."

"Just what exactly are you looking for? Why not search Pepin's house? Even *I* would like to know what you'd find there!"

"Oh, we've searched his place all right—more like *places*," Fletcher chuckled, picking up the small trash bin in the corner and turning it upside down. He prodded through their garbage with his monkey foot. It turned up disappointing.

Odys shivered, imagining what messes he'd made in the other rooms.

Fletcher dropped the bin. "We found exactly what we expected there: nothing."

Odys shifted his footing. "Just leave Odissa out of this. She doesn't know anything and she *won't* know anything. Your secrets are safe—I'm no threat to you."

"Oh, now, it's not so simple," Fletcher laughed as he walked up to his Master. He jumped up like a weightless sprite onto the couch's arm—squatted like some bony orangutan. The Automaton's "fabric" clung to him as he balanced, threatening to be re-absorbed into his well-sculpted frame. "You can't just shoo us away that easily. Even if we trust you, you aren't off the hook." He removed Dorian's extra pair of glasses and slid them on. He cocked his head and stared at Odys, a creepy fashion mannequin too real to overlook. "You're one of us now. We won't let you ruin everything we've worked so hard to keep secret."

"That's right, Fletcher. He has something of ours, doesn't he? He has Maud. We have to make sure he won't misuse her."

"I already told you I won't."

"Easier said than done, Mr. Browneyes." Dorian tucked his hair behind his ears, though it was too short to stay tucked for long. "You may not want your sister to find out about Maud, but humans are too curious for their own good. And speaking of your sister, we'd rather like to know where Odissa is at the moment, and why she hasn't been back since the incident. We know you two don't have cell phones, we've checked up on it. Otherwise we would have found her by now. It's odd to find someone this day and age without a cell phone, isn't it Fletcher?"

"Yes, Dorian, it is," Fletcher nodded. "Almost seems fishy." He tapped Dorian's cheek affectionately with the back of his hand. Dorian took out his piece of gum. Like a bird feeding from his hand, Fletcher peeled off the tacky blob and popped it in his own mouth.

Dorian re-tucked his hair behind his ear and re-crossed his legs. "No cell phone _is_ fishy." He itched his chin. He was clean-shaven, though the faintest shadow threatened to darken his shy chin. "You see, Odys, we happen to know you and your sister have lived together for some time now. She usually _is_ here. Right here. Can you tell us why she _isn't_ she here?"

"Why do I get the feeling you already know where she went?"

"'Know' is such a precise term, Odys. We only have a _guess_. You going to confirm my guess or no?"

"Odissa left on Friday. For a business trip," Odys lied. Anything concerning their father and/or his lawyer was just business. Family business. "She's supposed to come home today."

"Should—should we send someone to look for her?" Maud asked. Her tone made Odys's ears perk—as if she were requesting.

Dorian to Maud, "You sound worried. Do we have a _reason_ to send someone out?"

"When common humans are involved—"

"I'll talk to Mother about it," Dorian raised a few fingers and turned back to stare at the television. "But, if _we're_ just learning about Odissa, Leeland's bound to know zip. Unless—" His eyebrow shot up over his frames, "Leeland knew about Pepin's setup already?"

"Who the fuck is Leeland, and why do you have to ask your mother for permission to protect my sister?"

Fletcher rolled his eyes at Maud. "So he's going to pretend like he doesn't know who Mother and Leeland are?"

Dorian huffed. "My, how their names always come up together, though."

Fletcher glared at the other Automaton, waiting for her to say _how much_ Odys might know about them. But she only pursed her lips, allowing them to do the damage.

"I'll take Mother if you take dick-wad," Fletcher mumbled to his Master.

"Sure. Leave me with the hard part!"

"You know I can't talk about _that_ part It sounds too silly coming from me. I never do it justice. I'm not serious enough."

Dorian prompted Fletcher to get on with it.

Fletcher snarled at Odys. "Fine, I'll give you a fucking history lesson. Take notes. Mother's the one who sent us to watch you. _And_ the reason Dorian's accent keeps slipping to Spanish." He glanced down at Dorian. "You can tell how much they've talked by the times he reverts."

"And, my God, I've been slipping a lot lately," Dorian grumbled.

"She's the Big Boss. And, since Pepin blew himself up, she's the oldest of all Automaton Masters now. Runner up is Leeland. She's the one Leeland hates the most."

"And loves the most," Dorian said in aside.

"Can you not wait your turn?" Fletcher clucked at his Master.

"I think that's enough about Mother." Dorian shifted in his seat, suddenly uncomfortable. "This boy is suppressing things for a reason. And it's not because of Mother. Leeland, though." Dorian crossed his arms. "Leeland is an old Master—a Master of Coraza. His *second* Automaton."

Fletcher tilted his head, judging their reactions. In a sing-song voice, "Someone had to die for him to gain herrr..."

"This is why he doesn't talk about Leeland," Dorian waved to his Automaton, exhibit A. Dorian tucked away a bitter-looking smile behind his lips and tossed aside a pillow. "We Masters can't die very easily, Odys, but Leeland wants to change all that. He's succeeding in many ways. Leeland's first Automaton was Admund, the first-made of Automatons—the one who 'knows' the most—the Automaton who has lived a little longer than the rest. Maybe by a few seconds, maybe by a few years. Who fucking cares? The point is, he saw things his siblings didn't."[28]

Dorian was off-topic but didn't seem to care. He was trying to get comfortable on their damn couch once more—this topic made his sweetness sour. Made him squirm. Fletcher frowned at Dorian, knowing his Master was stalling. So he intervened.

"The fact of the matter is, Mr. I-don't-know-who-Leeland-is, we lost track of him."

"Pepin isn't the only one we couldn't keep tabs on," Dorian added.

"But what does Leeland have to do with me?" Odys demanded. "Or my sister?"

"Leeland, Leeland Lafayette," Dorian mouthed, a sadness invading his throat as he fought against melting into the couch.

"*Monsieur Lafayette*," Fletcher spat. "Name ring any bells?" He shot a dramatic glance at Maud. "Do *you* even remember, Maud? Or is that something Pepin erased too?"

"He's not ready to know who Leeland really is," she warned.

Odys might not be ready, but you are, Dear Reader. In fact, you've been (informally) introduced to him before.

Stanza: Allow me this moment to set up the Dramatic Irony.

---

[28] Admund the Automaton saw his siblings being made, for one.

Leeland Lafayette—double Ls—such alliterative flow! Gabbler chose it, as Gabbler chooses all names to replace the real ones.

Odys Odelyn. Odissa Odelyn. Odi Odelyn.

I can tell you Dorian's last name starts with a D, too, if you hadn't already guessed.[29]

Do note, Admund (Leeland's first Automaton), had no alliteration to his name. Automatons have no last names. They need no last names.

Need them? No. Have them? Sometimes.

And _what if_ we gave him—Admund—a last name? What would it be? Hmm...

How much more can I prompt you?

The alliteration gives them _anonymousness_. Yet it also gives them _identity_. What "A" last name has my Editor written in? What "A" name has been given? Come on, I know you haven't forgotten! Who, besides his father, does Odys hate?

I'm tapping my chin in thought.

Hmm...Doesn't "Admund Augury" have a nice _ring_ to it? Indeed it does. The first created of all Automata would certainly make for a very fine lawyer, I assume. For no reason in particular.

Stanza: Now that we know what Dorian and Fletcher know...

Dorian stretched—stretched away the tension this topic was giving him. "He's not ready to know who Leeland is? But, dear Maud, he already knows."

"I do?" Odys asked Maud.

"Fletcher, show him that he knows."

Fletcher whipped out his hand, fingers forming a sheet-like film. An image upon his paper-skin slowly formed. Like a photograph—a thin computer screen—Fletcher created an image between his fingertips. Easy as designs on fabric, Odys supposed. 2D not 3D. Like a tattoo to a human.

"You recognize him?" Fletcher asked.

Odys took a step back. Yes. Yes, in fact, he did recognize _him_—that image on the sheet.

"This, Mr. Odelyn," Fletcher stated flatly, "is Leeland. Your sister might be in danger if he is involved. Leeland has more than one Automaton. And, if we're not mistaken, he'll want yours as well—whether or not you had _arrangements_ with him. Understand? Best to confess right now if you made a deal with him and or Pepin so we can help you."

---

[29] Such like a comic book.

"Define help!" Maud spat.

Fletcher ignored her. "You'll be nothing but a device for his bigger plans. Don't play dumb, boy. No, don't look to her. She can't help you. She hasn't so far, has she?"

Maud waned, chin lowering.

Dorian grew impatient with Odys's silence. The boy continued to stare at the photo as if still confused. But how much simpler could they make it for him? "Is this Master your father?"

"My father is dead."

"Are you so sure about that? Because last I checked, Leeland is alive and well, and, quite frankly, pretty damn near immortal. Think about it. Didn't your father hang around another man—a strange man like Fletcher and Maud—he maybe couldn't be separated from him? That sounds *un poco* like a Master-Automaton bond, no? No? Maud, why is he not answering me? Odys, just say it. Is Leeland the man you knew as Odi Odelyn?"—angrier—"*Is* this man your father?"

"*No.*"

The tension snapped.

...Ah, Reader, I bet you thought Odys would say *yes?* Of course you would. I led you to it. But don't expect to be fucking clever, got it? Just because I let Gabbler edit the names to obscurity doesn't mean I'd let anyone fuck with my plot twists. Never.[30]

Fletcher's face fell. "He's not? But you recognize him."

"I know him." He shot a nervous glance to Maud. Why hadn't she told him? Why hadn't she *said* something? "I—I think my sister's in danger."

"Of course she is, you fucking idiot! Now who is he, Odelyn?" Dorian pressed. "Who's Leeland to you?"

"That's—that's *Mr. Augury.*"

DORIAN: In-between stagnant and transitioning.

FACT: He thought Leeland would turn out to be Odi Odelyn. Guess not.[31]

---

[30] Geez, Narrator. Lesson learned.

[31] Talk about a red herring! Yeah, so the Narrator misled you on that one. And, to a point, so did I (sorry). But this probably isn't surprising. The Narrator is trying too hard, I know—I know! But we can't let my "editing" get in the way of the story, you see. This is just how my Narrator reminds me who's boss. So petty.

    If it's any consolation to you, Reader, there will be no more hateful twists like this one (if you even care to call it a plot twist, pitiful as it is). This one was done for a point (a point directed toward me, not you). Our Narrator is the real god in the machine.

    Yet what a discovery! If Leeland isn't Odi Odelyn then that means Odys and Odissa were raised by an Automaton. Not Leeland himself. (Crisscross!). But, what's worse/interesting is...Odissa just visited Leeland, our story's quintessential bad guy.

    (Dun, dun, dun!).

BITTERNESS: Not caused by coffee.

SEXUAL ORIENATION?: About to be straightened out.

Chapter the sixth,

A curious case:

Isn't that what killed the cat?[32]

"Mr. Augury?" Dorian repeated, screwing up his face.

"Yes," Odys answered.

"And who is that?"

"So you *don't* know about my father?"

"You just said this *wasn't* your father, Odys. Seriously, get your stories straight."

"It's not. That's not my father. But—but what do you know about my father?"

"I know he's dead—supposedly—and that his name is Odysseus—Odi, for short. Other than that, our evidence suggests you didn't care much for him. After all, your sister handled everything with the lawyer, Mr. Augury—who's *also* just as hard to match a face to." He frowned at the picture Fletcher had concocted. "Granted, we had fifty percent chance."

"So you *do* know who he is?" Odys was exasperated.

"'Know' is such a precise term." Dorian repeated himself. He enjoyed confusing Odys. "Does this have something to do with why you're not afraid of me?" Odys asked. "You already know everything about me, don't you? Everything!"

Dorian shrugged. "We clearly don't know enough, because our first guess was that Leeland was your daddy dearest. But yeah, I'm not *afraid* of you. I pity you. It's not just Pepin who involved you in our mess. You've always been involved. Leeland had *plans* for you, Odys."

"Odys has a part in two plays." Fletcher studied Odys for his Master. "Pepin's and Leeland's."

"Sí, sí, you've got Pepin's destiny written all over you. We just can't read his handwriting. But Leeland's, well, his handwriting is very *neat*. Much more readable."

Fletcher "put away" his faux-photo, the image he'd conjured from memory—an unflattering image, at that. He crumpled it into his hand, the paper wad disappearing like a magician's trick, reabsorbed into his body.

---

[32] I've found another relevant quote for you: "My name is Nobody. My mother, father, friends, everyone calls me Nobody." —Odysseus to the Cyclops, Homer, *The Odyssey*, book IX.

"I must say, Dorian, this *is* unexpected," the Automaton stated to his Master, hands on his hips. "If Leeland isn't his father, then...who is?" His black eyebrows jumped up and down, inviting Odys to guess the secret.

Dorian frowned at his Automaton's eagerness—the same kind of frown you give when disappointed with your reflection in a mirror. "Well, Fletcher, since we opened the grave and no body was there ..."[33]

"You did something to his body?" Odys asked, slightly appalled.

"No!" Fletcher snapped. "Didn't you hear us? There wasn't a body TO do something to. Stupid boy—listen! Besides, it wasn't us—per se." He pointed between himself and his Master. "We were busy watching you."

Dorian sat back down. He thought aloud for their benefit, "It is nothing for an Automaton to fake a death. I mean, depending on how long the Master and Automaton stayed apart for their whole *act*, it might put a strain on the Master...But once the casket was closed, no problem; an Automaton needn't breathe. It's also nothing for an Automaton to break free from the ground— dirt, wood, cement. That's nothing. *Nada y nadie.* Your father—who wasn't your father—easily faked his death at his Master's behest—in whatever way. Obviously."

This all made perfect sense to Dorian.

The only unnerving thing about Dorian's acceptance was that he seemed to welcome it—as if this, perhaps, was the resolution he had wanted all along from this encounter. He even gracefully itched his groin, at home and so comfortable with his surroundings.

He clapped his hands together, the mystery solved. "Also, though you're putting on a good show, the fact Maud wouldn't recognize Leeland or Admund from your childhood memories— and therefore didn't *clue you in* before we mentioned it—makes this all seem *suspicious.*" He scrunched his nose and made circular motions with those same hands he had clapped.

Odys couldn't help but agree.

Maud huffed. "Of course I knew. But look at him! He didn't *want* me to say it. He didn't want me to *know.* Can't you see he doesn't want this? He doesn't understand what all this really means. I can't speak unless he *allows* me. Do you think I've been given the chance to tell him so much as the time of day, let alone everything I know? You think this is how he wanted to break it to himself? No. He wanted me to do it *gently.* Now I can't. Fuck you both for making this so hard on him!"

---

[33] Pun from epigraph-footnote intended. (I don't care if I'm the only one laughing here—I have to make this editing job fun SOMEHOW).

She stepped in front of Odys, as if defending him instead of herself.

Fletcher and Dorian shared a side-moment: "Do we believe her?" "Of course it's a logical excuse." "I'd suppress it to, if I were him." "I wouldn't want to be an orphan, either—to start from scratch."

"You know we can hear every word you're saying right?" Maud said.

Dorian shushed her. "Don't interrupt me while I'm talking with myself." A few more mumbled word with Fletcher, then: "Fine, Odys," Dorian announced. "We'll pretend you didn't know your 'father' was an Automaton."

"But I saw his body. He was dead." (Odys still refused to believe). "He *died.*"

Maud looked at Odys, as if she wished she could have told him sooner—in a different way. She made him feel like he'd been holding her back. Admittedly, he *didn't* want to know all this. He didn't want this to be happening at all.

"He couldn't die, Odys," Maud said, turning to him. "Automatons *don't* die. You only viewed the body once, didn't you? Leeland likely bought off the funeral home, the cemetery— to make things run smoothly. Leeland isn't stupid. He arranged everything. For about eighteen years he had to pretend as you grew up. With his Automaton no longer needing to stay away with you twins, it could be less stressful—less stressful on his body. And, less complicated in terms of keeping up the act. At least on one end. He's still pretending a little, though, isn't he?"

Odys's mind darted to Odissa and her *visit*. "I don't understand why he would fake his own death!" Odys shouted, denial oozing from his every twitchy movement. "It makes no sense. We were about to move out anyway when it happened. We wouldn't have been in his way—"

"He didn't want to give you the chance to come back to him and force the act on again. And he knew you hated him," Maud stressed.

"So you think he was doing me some sort of favor?" he barked at her.

She stepped closer to him, as if about to comfort him. But thought better of it. "Masters and Automatons can't be apart for long. That's why Augury was always there—*Leeland* was always there. Always visiting your father; your father always visiting him. He wanted to *insure* the act was over, Odys. But he also didn't want to ruin everything he'd built up. He kept ties to you and Odissa for a reason."

Dorian nodded as if things were adding up. "After his fake death, the distance was absolved. He could pull the strings from afar as Augury."

Odys shook his head, panic rising. Not only was his father non-human but was—worse still!—alive. "No. No," was all he could say.

"My God, he really *isn't* synced with Maud," Fletcher gaped. Fletcher cleared his throat. "Just look at his face."

Odys tried not to sound stupid but he just had to be sure: "Does that mean I'm—I'm potentially—I'm half—?"

"Automaton?" Fletcher sniggered. "Weren't you listening to us, boy? You hear him, Dori? He thinks he's half Automaton! Hell, no. If you were, that'd be a miracle. An *unnatural* miracle. Automatons can no more make babies than a…Well, we *can't*. You must have noticed Maud's unapparent, well, you know." He whistled and pointed between his nipple areas.

"*Everyone* has noticed, from time to time," Dorian stated through his pensive stance. He rubbed his chin roughly.

"We're not reproductive beings," Fletcher went on, wanting to be clear. "Though still very sexual." He gave a soft thrust.

Dorian ignored his Automaton's joke, realizing something. "This still doesn't make any sense. What's Pepin's motive?"

"Fuck Pepin's motive," Maud said, "I want to know why Leeland made an Automaton raise his 'adopted' kids." She used bunny ears when she said "adopted."

"This means I'm an orphan?" Odys said to himself.

Fletcher gave a laugh of pity. "Nothing gets past you, huh?"

"You know, don't you?" Odys realized. "You know who I am!"

"No, *you* know who you are but apparently you won't let *Maud* say!" Fletcher shouted at him. He realized his excitement and took a deep breath.

Dorian tried to explain himself, his Automaton, "I think we're almost on the same page."

"But the question now is, where in the world did Leeland find a pair of twins?" Fletcher asked.

"You're saying there's no way he adopted me legally?" Odys interrupted the conversation.

Fletcher chuckled. "Our kind can't do anything *legally*, dear. We're off the grid."

"Legal or not, you hated him anyway, right?" Dorian asked.

"What makes you say that?"

"As I've already implied, Odys, we have many sources. Most proved what kind of relationship you had with your father."

"And those sources would be?"

Fletcher tucked his hands into his armpits. "Your school records mentioned you had a father, but the little box you checked said never to contact him. Always a nanny or a 'guardian.' And the angsty blog you dabbled with for less than two weeks when you were sixteen?—that clued us in too. You do know how to leave a trail, Odys Odelyn. But don't worry, we can clean it up."

"Now, Odys." Dorian put a finger to his lips in thought, "Let's not beat around the bush any longer. We need to help your sister. Leeland wouldn't let go of something he's invested so much into, right? And that's just what you twins are—investments. Big investments. He has a lot of stock in all of us. He puts us on the shelf like a piggy bank until he needs some *change*." He shook the metaphorical piggy bank. "Now, this Mr. Augury. He's a secretive man, right? Just *how* does Odissa know where and when to meet him?"

Knowing it would sound cliché, "He contacts her."

"Of course he does," Dorian laughed. "And she believes, of course, that he's *retired*. So that's why he has no offices and work number? Plus, he's 'old school,' so he doesn't have a cell phone of his own, right? And because he lives in, perhaps, say, Guatemala, it's no use for him to give you a *real* working number because international calls are a bitch. Am I getting warmer?"

Odys's silence told him he was.

"I swear to the gods," Dorian chuckled. "He's played every trick in the book. And he's played them so well. No wonder you didn't see through it, Odys. I don't blame you."

"Don't patronize me."

"I wasn't. I sincerely pity you. I pity your sister more, because she's with him now, right? Is that why you wanted me to send someone to escort her safely home, Maud? Is that why Odys is so worried? Is this why you worry *for* him, Maud? Poor boy didn't realize *why* he was so worried. But it all makes sense now, doesn't it Odys?"

"She's on her way home." Maud reminded them. "Leeland *let her go*. Even you know that by now. I saw you tapping the wires when Odys was ill." She pointed out the window.

"Leeland probably doesn't know Pepin's dead yet," Dorian supposed. "He doesn't know he shouldn't have let her go."

Fletcher shrugged. "Maybe he forced her to call and give a fake update."

That sent a chill down Odys's spine.

"Or," Dorian mused, "if Leeland *does* know that Pepin's dead." He paused. "Maybe letting Odissa go will just be part of some *bigger* plan?"

"Oh my God! Enough with the conspiracy theories," Maud said. "Whatever the case, Odissa needs to be found."

Dorian straightened and walked to the door. "I doubt Leeland will be right at her heels when he finds out Pep is dead. Leeland has had his plans for the twins all along. Lee's never been chomping at the bit." He said it as if he *knew*. "It's not as simple as *helping* you, Odys. You've always needed help. After all, we would've helped you a long time ago had we known about you."

"Don't try to flatter him!" Maud barked. "You only help yourselves."

"Speaking of helping yourself," Fletcher noted, "Odys has done bang-up job of it already." He pointed to her. "Touching our things."

Maud glared up at him, body mimicking his crossed arms. Fletcher towered over her, twice her size. He seemed to delight in her attention—even though so negative. Dorian didn't move, letting his Automaton have this moment. "You really should get dressed, Maud." Eyes moving up and down on her barely-clothed body.

"Your chin-strap is hideous," she said.

"But you do like the dreads?" Fletcher peeked over Dorian's sunglasses.

"I can tolerate them," she told Fletcher, her bright eyes narrowing.

"I'll have to change them, then." Keeping his chin-strap beard, the dreads disappeared, his hair morphed into a spiky mohawk with spikes reaching *at least* six inches. Maud scoffed, turning away; she had known precisely what he was going to do.

...Odys grimaced at the playful tension and wondered if Dorian was trying to lighten the mood through Fletcher. Dorian needed Odys compliant, not defensive.

"Put it back, Fletcher." Dorian opened the door. "I liked the dreadlocks. But Maud's right, you're too pretty to cover that face with hair. Doesn't suit you." With a too-pleased smile, "Odys, our souls critique each other. That's a sign we're growing comfortable. Come, Fletcher, let's go."

Spikes falling and twisting back into their previously freakishly-long dreads, Fletcher put his sunglasses on his head like a tiara and followed Dorian, putting a gentle hand on his Master's back.

"You'll hear from us again soon, Odys Odelyn," Dorian said. His hand twisted the door knob excessively. "Very soon. Don't leave your apartment. We'll be observing. I'll tell you what Mother has to say in regards to your status among us *and* how we'll handle your sister. Adios."

"'Handle' my sister?"

Dorian ignored the question, about to step out. But he remembered something. "By the way, what is the cat's name?"

"The cat?" Odys repeated.

"Yes, the cat." Dorian turned around in Fletcher's protective arm. "Fletcher noticed him in Odissa's room. The fluffy brown tabby. Not very friendly."

"Not to strangers, no," Maud informed, her voice piqued.

Odys raised a hand, telling her *quiet.*

Fletcher's eyes widened, thrilled in their interaction—as if Odys had just told himself to shut up.

Odys asked, "What does the cat have to do with this?"

It was ludicrous to include the cat as some sort of problem to their operation.

"He's another liability to you—and, potentially, to us. We need to have inventory of our *valuables.* Any life can be worth something, depending on what you're willing to pay for it. Leeland picks only the *choicest* liabilities, to save time and effort. He knows you'll care nothing for the bum on the park bench compared to something you've invested in."

There was that word again. *Invested.*

"Your sister has a fucking photo of him on her dresser, man," Fletcher stated, creating a baggy sweater to make it look like he was ready to brace the outside air (barely-clothed people tend to stand out in winter). Imagine what metallic sheen the sweater had—be creative.[34] "He's a liability by default."

Fletcher propped the door open with his bum, waiting for Odys to tell them the cat's name so they could leave.

But Dorian would wait no more. "No matter, Fletcher. Not everything needs a proper name in order for us to take account. Besides, we don't want to get too attached. Although"—a smile came to his lips between gum-chews—"we already have a good guess from the vet records that his name is *Bulfinch.*"

BULFINCH: Named by Odissa (it was either that or Lancelyn Green).

FOOD: Canned food, dummy. What's with this dry shit?

BATH: What are tongues for?

PETS: Are a major plot device, so don't laugh because a cat gets his own list, stupid human. And stop wiping your muddy shoes on that rug! That's where he throws up. And sleeps in the afternoon.

Chapter the seventh,

The immortal Hand or Eye:

In what furnace was thy brain?

---

[34] The Narrator seems to already tire of describing the ever-changing outfits of Automatons. For future reference, if clothing is not described to your satisfaction, feel free to concoct your own fashion for the volatile characters. I do.

Fletcher bowed—*Adieu*.

As the door shut behind the unwelcome visitors, Odys turned on Maud.

"My cat's vet records? Seriously? What else do they know that they shouldn't?" (As if the cat needed such privacy).

Maud huff-sighed. "Don't underestimate what they *don't* know. They were more afraid of us before we found them in our kitchen."

"*My* kitchen. Not ours. I may need you like some sort of goddamned IV, but you're no welcomed guest, either!"

She ignored his shouting. "You haven't eaten in three days, you need some food. I can't eat for the two of us." She put up the soy milk carton Fletcher had left out, its sides moist with condensation. Odys hoped it was still good after being left out for so long.

"Don't change the subject."

"What subject, Odys?" She picked up a rag.

"They came into my home!"

"Look, under their 'rules,' I'm their property. They're only *letting* you 'rent' me. You're a storage unit for them. I have no say what the other Masters do with us. Neither do you. The gods give, but Mother can take away."

"They seriously take orders from someone they call 'Mother'? They're fucking freaks, Maud."

"And what does that make you?" She bit her lip and stopped her tidying—tidying for Odys. Like Master, like soul. "Mother has to protect what she's built up. You can't blame her for that."

"'Built up,' is it?"

Another huff-sigh. "She and Pepin set up the network—the group. A few decades later, Pepin wanted out. Mother took over. He left and we (more or less) retired. Until now."

"That the abridged version?"

"Any time I have to talk to my Master *aloud* is the abridged version."

"Yeah, like I want to read *your* thoughts. Who knows what's in that hard drive of yours? Viruses? Spyware?" He noticed his antagonizing didn't bother her. "If Mother and Leeland are the oldest Masters now, how old does that make Dorian? How old is he?" He looked twenty-five, no more than thirty.

"Dorian's about sixty—maybe sixty-five—if he didn't lie to us about his age."[35]

---

[35] Never ask a lady her age.

She saw he wanted more—more dirt on this Dorian fellow. Finally! He was interested. Dorian was the bridge Odys needed to bring himself across.

"He's the newest Master, after you. No longer the baby. He was [around twenty][36] when Fletcher came into the picture. He didn't know Pepin well."

"But he seems to know 'Leeland' well." He used finger quotations around the name—as if Leeland were somehow a phonier name than Augury.

"They could say the same about you."

"And they hate him because he wants to kill the other Masters?"

"Is that not a good enough reason?" She laughed. "But yes. That and the fact he doesn't play by their rules." She saw he didn't understand. "They try to keep tabs on each other so if a Master dies they can get the Automaton before an innocent civilian accidentally picks them up; also, that way they can choose who gets to reactivate the Automaton—someone they all like, of course. After all, they have to live with each other—for a long time, right?

"Off and on, Leeland's created quite a stir for the others His last attack—as they would call it—was on Dorian a few years after Dorian became a Master. Let's just say Leeland found some of Dorian's 'liabilities.' Other than that, Leeland's been quiet. That's scariest of all."

"Why does Leeland do it? I mean, why does he want to kill all the Masters?"

She wouldn't look at him. She knew he didn't want to know. "Not the other Masters, Odys, just Mother. If you want the simplest answer, you might just say that all the other Masters are Mother's liability. They all love her dearly and she loves them. That's why it's important they find out if you're worth the trouble of keeping. You'll need to love her, too." Maud found another cigarette. She'd found nothing she wanted to eat. "Everyone needs a mother."

"What's her real name?"

"You think anyone really knows that?" Maud laughed. "Nah, no one knows. Pepin wasn't even sure—and he knew her the longest. You and Dorian here are the only two Masters alive with real names—names that can be fact-checked. You didn't get the opportunity to hide yours; and Dorian, well, he didn't know to. Names are such strange things." She could tell he wasn't about to start calling Mother "Mother," though. "When we aren't calling her 'Mother,' we're calling her 'Gwen.'"[37]

---

[36] I am also responsible for the brackets/omitting clear identifiers. Think of them as me turning up the music whenever our Narrator starts to sound too insane. Pay no attention to the man/facts behind the curtain.

[37] "Then all went on their knees, and holding out their arms, cried, 'O Wendy lady, be our mother.' 'Ought I?' Wendy said, all shining. 'Of course it's frightfully fascinating, but you see I am only a little girl. I have no real experience.'" —J.M. Barrie, Peter Pan (novel). I was quite proud of the fake name I picked for Mother's fake name.

71

MOTHER: A.K.A. Gwendolyn Gwendy.

NEED-TO-KNOW: She has many children.

HER INTERNET MEME?: Pedo-Mother-Bear.

ALWAYS: In need of a good cry.

Chapter the eighth,

Occult Science:

Is it easier than Occult Mathematics?

"That's as real a name as we know for her." She gave a bitter smile. "Pepin had a few names of his own." She sucked her cigarette to stop smiling.

"…You want to know what Fletcher's inanimate form is?"

"Is it not some sort of coin like you?"

"No. A rusty, red paperclip. The kind you see in college parking lots. You know they could have been useful at one point, but you walked over them too late and it's already rained and the red-brown will look unattractive on your crisp homework papers, so they're not worth picking up."

"Why would a god make him a paperclip? It's too simple. And modern."

"Why am *I* a U.S. coin? I certainly wasn't minted the year my coin says. I was modern once. Vulcan knew our forms would eventually fit into a time frame. He *planned* for it." Maud tapped her nose.

"But your timeframe has passed."

She shook her head. "No. What I'm saying is the Automaton forms are all starting to catch up with the present. All our forms have proper context now. *Now* is the time Vulcan planned for us to be relevant most of all—"

Before she could properly punctuate her sentence, the apartment door opened. Waltzing in, Fletcher threw down a large duffle bag near the couch. Dorian floated in behind him.

"You're back sooner than expected," Maud stated.

"Mother does have a phone, you know. All we had to do was call to give her our update," Fletcher said.

"Well, then, I retract my statement. You took your time."

"Had to collect our things from the car, Maud," Dorian said, leaning against the back of the couch. "Besides, we weren't sure we were going to let Odys live, on our first visit. We didn't know if luggage was—how do I put it?—necessary. Plus, we had to get a fresh pack of gum, see?" He held it up.

"Excuse me?" Odys questioned.

"Well, we do like gum," Dorian grinned—his fake grin reaching the bottom of his glasses and exposing his wad.

"He doesn't care about your gum!" Maud snapped. "Just what do you think you're doing?"

"Sorry, chap," Dorian said, turning his head in Odys's direction—a courtesy for Odys, "but we're moving in."

Stanza: Are they at least paying rent?

"House arrest," Dorian expounded. "To protect our interests as much as yours."

Fletcher waltzed into the kitchen. Opening the fridge, he took out the milk Maud had just put back. He grimaced, noticing its warmth. "Don't you people ever put back your spoilables?"

"I have a sister, you know," Odys stated, wondering how they planned to hide from her. How would he hide Maud, let alone two more strangers?

"Your sister is all the more reason to have us around," Dorian gesticulated. "Without us, this place'll be a hotspot for hell."

"So you expect Augury to pull something?"

"Leeland, you mean. And eventually, yes."

"And what about Odissa? What are Mother's orders?" Maud asked. "Odissa may have left Leeland, but Leeland still knows her whereabouts. Send someone to her area. Then if something bad happens, someone will be able to reach her quickly."

Dorian raised a hand. "Yes, yes, I talked to her; Mother's willing to send scouts out for your sister, though that doesn't mean they'll find her. She drives a silver Honda, right?"

No answer from Odys. He knew he didn't *have* to answer.

So Dorian went on: "If you can inform us where she's heading from, we'll update them."

"From the cemetery-mausoleum park in [redacted]."

"Well, yes, but how *far in* do you suppose?" Dorian leaned forward, as if talking to a little child.

Odys guesstimated her location.

"Very well, then. Fletcher, please make the phone call before Odys has a panic attack."

"Why do I have to do it?" He said, still rummaging through Odys's fridge. He picked up a log of cheese and sniffed it. He put it back and checked out their yogurt selection. If they'd had whipped cream, it would have already been swirled in his wide mouth. *Blah! These people eat too healthy.*

"You must make the call because you have my phone."

73

"That's no good reason," Fletcher grumbled as he closed the fridge door and pulled out a phone from his back "pocket." "Can I also order a pizza? These kids got nothin'."

"If you must."

"And Chinese for dinner?" Fletcher turned to Odys, eyebrows asking if he was interested in takeout.

"Whatever gets you to make the goddamned phone call," Odys growled.

Fletcher glared at him, his fingers punching away at the cell phone as he glided to the bathroom for quiet.

"I suppose," Dorian stated, standing up from his leaning position, "when your sister arrives, we'll need to get our stories straight." No duh. "Mother has asked we not tell her anything. Understood?"

Of course that was understood. But did Dorian *understand*? "I wonder how we'll do that, since you probably won't let her go to school, work, or out of the apartment?" Odys pointed out.

Dorian chuckled, taking off his jacket. He was well built for a blind man (who should have found it hard to walk straight, let alone work out). He tossed his jacket perfectly on the back of the couch, as if he could see it. Fletcher not only saw for him but reminded him where everything was, didn't even have to be in the same room for the whereabouts of things to be clear, if he tried.

"You've gotten crankier, Odys." Dorian said, tucking his straight hair behind his ear. He seemed genuinely concerned. "Something the matter?"

Yes, being a prisoner in his own home is *exactly* how Odys wanted this day to play out, Dorian. "I don't see what good can come of this, even if this makes things safer."

"Sorry, can you repeat that?" Dorian put a hand to his ear. It was hard for him to concentrate on two conversations going at once (for he could "hear" Fletcher's current one in the bathroom as well as his own). Dorian didn't like his distance and so walked over to the table to sit with them.

Odys saw his hand reach out—for the first time—to guard against unexpected collision with its edge. With Fletcher away, it was more dangerous for him.

"He said get the fuck out, Dorian," Maud mumbled.

Dorian crossed his arms and legs. He sighed despite pushing a smile. "So, Maud, what's this new Master's addiction, hm? Anything we should worry about?"

He "looked" at Maud when he asked it. Well, in her direction, anyway. Dorian remembered facial cues were important, even if they landed like a bad joke.

"Why do you care?" Odys asked, a bit nastily. It was, after all, *his* addiction.

"Well, you may not realize it, but addictions—"

"I know, I know. She's given that speech already."

Maud glanced at Odys. "He's coffee and cigarettes."

"Ah, the two that blacken you from the inside," Dorian stated, tapping his chest. "But, speaking of coffee..." He motioned to the empty table. *Be a good host, Odys.*

Maud's lip twitched. "I'll put a fresh pot on."

Odys found nothing to resent there.

Dorian remained quiet for a time, probably retreating to his own thoughts that Fletcher's current phone conversation clouded. Odys took the opportunity to stare/glare at him (since Dorian would never know the difference).

Dorian raised a finger. "Mother just told Fletcher that you'll be meeting her tomorrow—and that she's sent out one Automaton and Master to try and track down Odissa."

(Because Odissa is the damsel in distress—something every story needs).[38]

"Tell her thank you for us, Dorian," Maud said.

"Don't thank her just yet. Your sister's vague whereabouts kind of make things pointless. But, if Leeland *does* make a move, we'll have someone on their way to clean up the mess."

"That's a nice way of putting it," Maud hissed, starting the coffee pot.

"Well, Maudy," Dorian defended, "when you have *all the time in the world,* you can waste it by looking for little girls." He frowned. "We're good at tracking people, but we're not omnipresent."

"But you and I both know that if fate wants you to find her, you will. We can all smell the gods on this one. Every domino falling into place."

Fletcher came out of the bathroom, wad of tissues in hand. "If I were you, I'd worry more about Bulfinch," he grumbled as he looked over his shoulder, dabbing his nose with the tissues. "If he pees on our bag, I swear I'll make his innards into violin strings."

Bulfinch was sniffing the unfamiliar bag cautiously, whiskers rowing with every new smell. He noticed their attention and became self-conscious, darting away when Fletcher blew his nose.

"Must you blow so hard?" Maud growled, annoyed.

"Gold?" Dorian asked him, curious.

"No. More coppery than anything," Fletcher replied, scrunching his nose and examining the goods. It hardened in the tissue.

---

[38] I wonder how Odissa would feel about that.

Maud rolled her eyes.

"Just be glad Automatons needn't use the restroom," Dorian chuckled. From the corner of his mouth, "Flushing metals. It's not good for pipes."

"Unless, of course, we want to," Fletcher added, dabbing his nose. The sticky coppery-stuff clung from his nostril to tissue.

"He *needn't* blow his nose, either," Maud stated, annoyed with their prattle.

"But it tickled. The cat hair got up my nose." He pointed to the non-existent cat (likely in Odissa's room now). "An Automaton must keep his bellow clean!"[39]

Maud took out some mugs, gave Dorian a handful of sugar packets (just as he liked it).

And they waited on the coffee.

Fletcher, who realized the sudden lull in this plot,[40] strutted into the living room and turned on the television, plopping himself on the couch.

"You don't mind do you?" Dorian asked, like a parent for a child.

"No," Odys answered, glad to be rid of Fletcher.

…

They listened to the hum of the television and drank their coffee. Every so often Fletcher would laugh, and so would Dorian. Maud and Odys exchanged uncomfortable glances, feeling trapped and in a dream. A bad dream.

Though Fletcher sat in the other room and Dorian's back was turned to the television, Dorian enjoyed the same scenes as Fletcher, laughing aloud as if his eyes were watching.

Fletcher began sniffing loudly—snorting as if he had something else stuck in his nose. He was doing everything but picking it.

"Fletcher, dear, you still remember the bathroom?" Dorian asked, standing up. He could tolerate his own sounds no longer.

"Yes, boss," Fletcher replied as his Master walked in. Dorian didn't shut the door behind him. Merely needed a tissue. He delivered it to Fletcher.

"Couldn't have gotten it himself, huh?" Maud said as she pulled at her shorts. She was having trouble keeping her always-metallic clothes at a suitable length.

"He's watching my show for me, isn't he?" Dorian stated, as if Maud weren't making sense. "It's not a *commercial.*"

---

[39] Fletcher seems to be comparing his nose to a bellow, which is quite interesting since blacksmiths and smelters use bellows—which fall under the reign of Vulcan himself.
[40] He's not the only one who noticed.

They heard Fletcher blow. It sounded like a faltering foghorn.

"Geezus, I told you, Dorian!" he exclaimed. "I told you Caffar put that pet tracker inside me when we were sleeping—back in June!" Fletcher shouted at the tissue, "I told you she was experimenting with me again! The fucking thing's all corroded too!" He tossed the wad away from him, appalled.

The pet ID tag had made its way through his body—rejected it through one of the few available Automata-openings. Fletcher shivered. "You *have* to tell Mother about this! It's unacceptable. We feel violated!"

"Who's Caffar?" Odys whispered to Maud.

"Another Automaton on 'Team Mother.' Her Master likes to *try* things."

Dorian sighed. "Who knows, Mother likely told her to put it in you. At least you know your body got rid of it."

"I'm not some cell phone Mother can bug whenever she wants to." Fletcher turned back to his TV show. "And you all made fun of me for sneezing!"

Speaking of noses—Maud had a tickle of her own, though it had nothing to do with cat hair. "Talking about noses makes it itch," she laughed for Odys's sake.

Odys noticed Dorian's ear turn toward her as if this talk of noses were too, too fateful.

With the same hand she had scratched with, Maud covered a gapping yawn. Her body seemed relaxed—too relaxed. Come to think of it, she looked as if she hadn't slept all night. Odys, however, felt better—better than last night, anyway. Maybe this was the stabilizing balance she'd mentioned—the synchronizing? He noticed that they were starting to look alike. (Like shit, in other words).

He realized she was wearing an even scantier outfit—had her shirt shrunk and her short shorts become...? Well never mind, he didn't want to look under the table to properly check.

"I wish you'd eat something, Odys. I'm getting weaker."

"Oh, yes, forgot to tell you that the pizza Fletcher ordered in the bathroom will be here in twenty minutes," Dorian said.

"Pizzas? As in...more than one?"

"He can eat a lot," Dorian elaborated.

"Doesn't mean he needs to," Maud added, just as Fletcher snorted yet again.

She rolled her eyes for Odys's benefit. He almost smiled. Odys observed these two intruders with curiosity and trepidation—to the point he forgot Maud was an intruder herself. She was his only ally now, and he found himself leaning toward her.

Fletcher flipped through the channels with the remote. "Boring, boring, beneath me, boring," he mumbled to himself each time he pressed the button. He only stopped when his (Dorian's, actually) cell phone vibrated. He whipped it out of his "pocket." Froze in place.

Dorian frowned as his Automaton read the text message. "Change of plans, Odys."

"What?" Maud said, itching her nose again.

"You're seeing Mother *today*. Waiting on more info."

Maud was about to scream, *"But Odissa could be here soon!"* but her words were interrupted by a spastic series of stress-related nose twitches.

Like someone gripping their chest during a heart attack, Maud covered her nose with great passion. Her face pinched—her head shook and made her copper curls quake. (Odys became aware that nose-issues were as contagious as yawning). Before she could clothespin it to a stop:

"Achoo!"

Maud's issue, however, was a bit more severe than Fletcher's nose blowing. Right when she sneezed, she disappeared.

Well, not *really*. She was just no longer in her human form. Odys bolted up, looking over the table corner, down into her seat. There, on the chair:

A pretty penny.

"What happened?" Dorian asked—acting truly blind.

Fletcher's head shot up. Leaping over the couch to get to them, he arrived in a matter of seconds. "She sneezed out."

They heard Maud release a soft moan—a sound from nowhere. Nowhere but the penny.

Fletcher leaned in, his long back hunched over. Extended out so, his loose dreads fell over his face, making him look like a weeping willow. "Pick her up, man!" he ordered Odys.

Odys obeyed. "What happened? I—I didn't make her do this."

"Of course you didn't, you anorexic Euro-grungie!" Fletcher snapped in the air, fingers sending (what looked like) sparks as he tried to redirect Odys's attention. "She's tired. No—that's the wrong way to put it. When tired, Automatons can sleep, but this is more along the lines of pooping-out. Exhaustion, stress, trauma!"

"It happens, sometimes," Dorian clarified, more calmly than his Automaton. "When a Master doesn't properly take care of his Automaton or body."

"He tuckered her out. Made her work too hard. Made her hard-drive crash!" Fletcher threw his hands in the air, as if Odys had just broken his new Christmas toy. *Why we can't have nice things!*

"She's unwillingly conserving energy—so she doesn't have to keep up the clothes-act," Dorian reported. "You haven't synced yet, Odys. That's what pushed her over the edge,"—too many programs running at once. "Sneezing out might be the equivalent of a catatonic fit. They vary in size and style, but they can *always* be prevented."

"The nose always warns you," Fletcher said. "Isn't that what I was saying? Nobody ever listens to me."

Odys glared at him. He'll check the nose all right, right after he punches this Automaton in the face.

"How can we not listen to you?" Dorian mumbled. "You never shut up." (Dorian sometimes hated himself, you see).

"This wouldn't have happened if you'd eaten something," Fletcher scolded. Speaking of eating, Dorian was hungry. His eyes darted to the fridge.

"But you told me there was pizza coming!" Odys got the feeling Dorian was playing good cop/bad cop with him all at the same time.

"Boys, boys!" Dorian raised two hands, a strange grin on his face. "It's not that big of a deal—this time. She'll be fine."

Fletcher scoffed and went into the kitchen.

Odys cradled Maud in his palm. "Maud—you okay?" Now that he thought about it, she was acting far different than the scandalously-confident Maud from last night.

"Yes, Odys. Was just a tickle."

"Can you turn back?"

"Best not to."

"Dumb question," Fletcher said, coming out of the kitchen (once again). He was licking a spoon full of coffee ice cream, the tub in his left hand. He made a face as if it tasted better than expected.

"Just hold on to me for now. Not sure how well I can keep clothes on."

Dorian laughed. "He'd best get used to that. If I weren't blind, I'd swear I'd have seen Fletcher naked more times than dressed. Odys, why don't you eat a little something, *sí?*"

"But not this." Fletcher babied the ice cream. "This is mine." His voice was muffled, because of the spoon.

Odys was about to obey but he remembered the cause of Maud's sneeze-out—the tipping point of her/their stress:

79

"Wait," he said. "You just said I was seeing Mother. *Today*. But when? I want to be here when Odissa returns—I don't want you two messing with her."

"Relax, dear," Dorian said, waving a hand. "That's part of why Mother will see you now. Your sister's at [such-and-such a place] having lunch."

"There? You mean you've found her?" Odys questioned. He looked at Fletcher who was going through the phone again—likely deleting any evidence of a text message in case Odys demanded to see it. "But that's—that's still *hours* away from here. I thought she left sooner than that. How did they get to her so fast?" Something told Odys they'd planned to spy on his sister since the beginning. "You're sure it's her?"

"Perhaps she made more stops along the way," Maud said from his hand. "She might be shopping. You hate shopping."

"She usually calls if she's going to do that," he said to the air, forgetting she was in his hand.

"Usually is not all the time," Dorian said, smacking his gum. "And with no cell phone, it'd be hard to find a payphone these days."

Odys ignored the condescending comment. "We've got a good three or—maybe—four hours ahead of us, depending on traffic. That's how long it will take if she's coming from there."

"Just enough time for an interview with Mother Dearest," Dorian supplemented, sitting down on the couch beside Fletcher. "Now quiet! I'm trying to watch this."

But Dorian wouldn't get to watch his show after all. There was a knock at the door. "Pizza!" Fletcher exclaimed. He rushed to it, looked through the peep-hole. He gasped, dropping the ice cream tub. Odys cringed at the mess it left. "Dorian, darling, is it just me or did Mother *really* change her plans?"

"Who's there?" Maud asked—a fear in her (muffled) tone.

"Not the pizza delivery man. Fucking hell," Dorian sighed. He put his forehead in his hand, cursing something in Spanish about *la Madre*.

Another forceful knock—

Fletcher put his back to the door, as if to barricade it. To Odys, "She sent the big dogs. Fucking Mother planned on changing her plans all along!" He didn't really seem surprised so much as entertained.

Another knock; Fletcher jumped.

His phone buzzed. He whipped it out.

"In fact," he said, "Mother's escort for Odys got here fast—even before her text to prep us!" He giggled and bit his nails, reading. His eyes danced.

The door shook again. It rattled the walls.

"Who is it?" Fletcher asked, his voice too high and too mischievous as he put away the phone.

"You should open the door before Mother's dog gets angry," Dorian said—as if he had no control over Fletcher whatsoever.

"Open up!" the commanding voice shouted between the *bang bang bangs*.

"Just a minute!" Fletcher said back, still chewing on his nails. To himself, "I—I have to think of something good, Dori. I wasn't prepared for this!" Fletcher flipped back around, peeking through the peep hole again (he had to stoop low to use it).

"Open the damn door, Fletcher!" the woman's voice demanded again. The voice sounded ready to invade. "You can't bide your time in there forever, coward!" She rattled the locked knob, seeing if it were locked. Mumbling, "Fuck's sake, I didn't die in Vietnam for this." (Not even I know what she means by that).

Odys felt his hand being forced open. Maud fell from it and reformed—though she probably shouldn't have. She wobbled in place and used his arm to steady herself.

She had formed because she wanted whoever was on the other side of that door to see her when they came in. "Don't be scared, Odys."

Odys raised a brow. Should he be?

"Prepare yourself, Odys," Dorian said, his ambivalent tone missing the same caution of his words. "You're going to meet *Bob*."

BOB: More like BYOB.

DOG: More like Mother's b*tch.

LAP DOG?: After she has a few beers.

ESCORT: More like SWAT raid.

Chapter the ninth,

Oh, did I say pizza? Because I meant kidnapping:

Who's fibbing the most?

"I've got it!" Fletcher exclaimed to Dorian—as if he'd just come up with some necessary solution. He had the perfect trick up his sleeve. (Fletcher hadn't seen Bob in quite a while, and he needed to make up for lost time). He cleared his throat. "Password?" he insisted, knowing it was the *worst* thing to say.

A muffled grunt and then, "You're dead!"

The knob twisted to no avail.

Fletcher jumped back from the door. Crouching low in the corner, he tensed with anticipation. He hadn't been given this much opportune fun in weeks.

Most likely, there was no password. And Fletcher was about to die. (Odys certainly wouldn't miss him).

That wicked grin on Fletcher's face met "death" with merry expectation.

Pew, pew.

A silenced gun blew off the knob. The metal parts dropped to the floor, smoking from the heat.

Dorian seemed blasé (as usual) with the commotion and went to top off his coffee (which he did not actually like). Odys was nervous the neighbors were going to hear—or worse, *see*—the hubbub.

"That's my fucking door!" Odys cried.

Maud ate her lips, signaling to shut up about it.

Assuming a butler outfit, Fletcher shooed them away with two hands—*don't mess this up for me*. Maud pulled Odys back.

There was one more shot—a shot to take out the bolt. *Peeeew.* The doorframe was busted, wood-splinters springing to the air. Someone tapped the door open.

The woman who owned the rough voice stepped forth, her hunky boots thudding against the floor. She looked behind her—left and right—to make sure no one had seen her. The curvy female tucked the huge, smoking gun back into her holster and paused in the door way. She crossed her arms, squishing a too-loose camouflage jacket against her chest.

Her Chola-esque aesthetic made it almost hard to tell she was Asian. She had the hard-core makeup: the outlined lips, over-shadowed eyes, packed-on foundation. All that was missing were the drawn-on eyebrows. *Ay caramba.*

Her icy-black hair was slicked back in a loose, low bun. That bun unintentionally exposed the tattoos trailing up her neck; but they weren't your normal, every-day hard-core tats. Not some cheesy dragon, Asian symbol, pinup girl, cameo, or girly rose. Nope. She was more interesting than that.

They were blobs. That's right, blobs. Blobs like spots on a cow, dog, or oil-stained driveway. Misshapen, tiny spots with waves, curves, varying sizes—green-black dots as if she were a document with retractions.

"Bob's blobs," as they were called in others' whispered conversations.

Though this drill-sergeant's hair was held down with a bandana, a large portion of her fringe fell over her right eye and trailed down to her full, prodigious lips. Her uncovered eye, however, darted to Fletcher—still in his butler suit.

"Still see you make *him* do all your childish bullshit," she chided Dorian.

Dorian sipped his coffee—as deaf as he was blind.

"I only open doors for ladies, sir," Fletcher said, giving the visitor a little bow.

Without giving so much as a second glance, she said, "You look like a damn Raggedy Anne doll, Fletcher, with that damn hideous hair."

In the blink of an eye, he had assumed a full fencing uniform (foil and all), just so he might use them as props while saying: "Touché! Why, thank you, Madame. And, my, my! Is that another spot? I can't wait until you finally decide to dot your face. God knows you should have covered the hideous thing ages ago." Swish, swish with his sword.

"Speaking of faces, might I borrow yours? My damn ass needs a break."

"Your Filipino ass? Or your American one? What ass-hat have you decided to wear today?"

"You want to talk about ass-hats? Let's go back to that hair of yours."

"I'll put that on my to-*don't* list, you crap-burper." He stood at attention.

"As if you even know how to write to *make* lists."

"At least I don't keep lists of all the people I killed in active duty."

"That's not a list, dumbass. It's a tally sheet. Like FUCK I want to know their names."[41]

"That's right, you have a thing about names. That's why yours is so short and simple."

"Your stupid red hair will go well with Dorian's stupid red blood when I spill it."

He rolled his eyes. "Honestly, calling you a bitch would be an insult to all female dogs!" He bit his lip to keep from laughing.

She caught his momentary weakness and began to circle her prey. "...So your butler and fencing suits are for me? Why didn't you slip into something more comfortable, like a freaking coma?"

"Seriously, I can always tell when you're bitchy. Your lips move."

"You don't know the damn meaning of bitchy—but then again, you don't know the meaning of most words."

"There was something about you I used to like...but then, you came through the door."

"I'm searching for a damn fuck to give—"

---

[41] Our Narrator said that it's also safe to assume she has a tally sheet for those killed in *inactive* duty.

"AHEM!" It was a voice from the apartment entrance—a polite but reprimanding sound that brought an unexpected end to the flying stichomythia.

This was when Odys realized Bob and Fletcher's engrossing "duel" had lasted only a matter of nanoseconds.

Bob bowed her head. "You barely giggled this time." She'd let Fletcher win this round—though she still had a *few* more feckless insults at the ready. (Little did she know Fletcher was on his last limbs, ready to pull out the weaker/default "I know you are but what am I?" insults. She could have pulled through). She cracked her neck.

Her Automaton—the one who'd just stopped the madness—followed her in. Ducking to make sure he missed the door frame, he glanced down at Fletcher.

Fletcher frowned, "He's a little tall right now, isn't he?" said Fletcher (usually the tallest one in the room).

"First impressions, Fletcher," Bob said. "First impressions."

"You can't just let him stomp around like that," Fletcher grumbled. "We're weird enough as it is."

And so the other Automaton (with a heavy sigh) began to shrink—shrink like someone lowering a car they had just jacked—until he stood just under Fletcher.

"Better?" Bob growled.

"More natural," Fletcher replied, examining him. "But then again, you two are usually so full of hot air, it's hard to tell."

What this new Automaton now lacked in height he made up for in weight. His vest half-covered nothing but pure, ripped manbod. That well-toned core had pecs the size of dinner plates—dinner plates for giants.

Fletcher made his shirt disappear into his skin and his muscles swell to slightly unnatural proportions, mocking the newcomer.

Bob and Maud rolled their eyes (well, Bob rolled her *eye*—singular. Who knows what the other one was doing underneath all that hair).

[Want to read this new Automaton's full profile? Read this footnote:[42] Or don't. It's your dime.]

---

[42] Our Narrator's description of Bob's Automaton got a little out of hand, so I cut it down—but didn't delete it. (I suspect there's a reason our Narrator went into full-description mode):
 "This Automaton held his head high, his back very straight, feet solid on the ground. Bob had dressed him in what Odys classified as 'Motorcycle Attire'—the kind worn by biker gangs for an extra notch of badassery. Like all

Bob waltzed up to Odys. "So you're the new one, huh? Guess Automatons are like assholes now, everybody has one. You're skinnier than I thought you would be. Grungier, too. Thought Pepin had more class. What're you supposed to be, some damn urban sub-hipster? At least you're not as fucking *prissy* as Dorian. Maud, slutty as ever, I see."

This woman was a cup full of sunshine. Damn fucking good sunshine. Odys tried to hide behind Maud.

Bob turned away to take in the room with her single eye, hands on her curvaceous hips. She didn't even bother to flick back her bangs to view the world properly. One eye showed too much anyway.

"She's in a good mood," Maud whispered to Odys, her expression shifting. She rested her arm on Odys's shoulder to relax and also hide the fact she was shaky. She couldn't fetter a toothy smile, "Good to see you too, Bob."

Automatons, he had a chameleonic appearance, though it stayed within the range of his six-foot framework and dense casing. But don't let my description deceive you.

See, if you could get past that bestial mustache that looked like a cross between an unintentional Fu Man Chu and a Hungarian (perhaps just a Hungarian that severely needed trimmed), past the huge, round nose (like a glob of clay), past the constantly-squinting eyes (narrowed in either anger or smile—the polar opposites not helping his case), past the huge arms that looked like they could snap you in two (bear arms with less hair), past the long tail of braided, hafnium-grey hair (though the color didn't age him), past the bushy furrowed brow (more like a unibrow), he actually had an adorable mug.

The only uncoordinated aspect of his otherwise symmetrical face was his minor under-bite. It made his mouth-line waver between German Cyborg and King Kong. If he were to smile, it would not only be the scariest thing but also the sweetest.

Oh, and had you not been so preoccupied with looking up (and feeling small), you would have noticed the Automaton's almost-bare feet. He, unlike other Automatons, *always* thought to 'wear' shoes (well, they were flip-flops that looked more like heavy getas, but he'd *still* thought to make them. He did, after all, have manners).

Speaking of manners, he was quite the clean-feen, you see. He usually did all of his Master's laundry, sweeping, dusting, cooking, grocery shopping, and etc.

And in a frilly apron most times.

And if this didn't temper him enough, he also liked knitting (though he sometimes miscounted), quilt making (though he was never satisfied with the finished product), and scrapbooking (though he had few moments worth documenting). He loved to exhibit his (quite presentable) creations for any poor soul willing to look—or, even better, he'd give his crafts to you.

The only thing he was positively excellent at (and therefore proud of) was *baking*. The man had a way with sugar and breads, I'll tell you! Vulcan had blessed him with the powers of the oven, some internal timer that got things *just* right.

...But it was Bob who completed Cestus's character.

Bob, who looked maybe thirty-five to (and don't tell her I said this) forty years old, seemed like the perfect, age-appropriate ~~wife~~ HUSBAND for Cestus. That was their IRL ploy—what they used in social situations as their excuse for being together.

...But enough of me telling and not showing. Back to the story."

"Bullshit," the prehistoric rockabilly snapped (this was actually one of her more cordial greetings). "You both ruined my evening. I had a pool game I was going to win. Everything last minute! Being a chaperone is *not* my idea of fun. Believe me, you're going to make up for it." She pointed at Odys; her leather gloves made a stretching sound.

"Another night of no drinking, Bob?" Dorian said from the couch. "Too bad you can't drown those voices out tonight."

"At least I don't *listen* to the voices like you, you sulky bastard," she said. She peeked into the kitchen. She peeled off her leather gloves as if they restrained her hands (they certainly make it harder to give someone the finger; she was an expert at it). She slapped the gloves in her hand, "You don't fucking see me moping around, do you? No. God knows I fucking get out. The only reason you're not fucking 'hermit-ing' right now is because Gwen made you come here."

Her curse-word collection was *fantastically* arranged. Odys was in awe.

"And just why are you here so early, Bob?" Dorian asked.

She took two sniffs of the air. "Holy Mother of Jesus Christ, how many packs a day are you up to? I'm suffocating in this smoke shop. You and your sister must be on respirators by now."

"I thought you were about to leave, Bob," Fletcher said. "No hurry or anything."

She turned away from Odys, her fringe waving to expose her second eye. That slight little thing glared at the world with continual bitterness and disapproval.

"Believe me, I can't wait to leave," Bob replied. "Let me just set some ground rules for this newbie, here, before we head out. Rumor has it he hasn't synced with Maud, so he'll need to be informed about how I do things." She glanced once at Odys. "I thought not syncing was impossible, but his fuckedup face is proof enough. Don't look at Dorian like he's betrayed you, boy. You want us to trust you, right? Then there can't be any secrets—no bullshit. Which is why you better listen to my rules." She paced to and fro with small range. "I'll give him a good orientation, Dorian, because, hell, I'll never speak to him again after this, God willing."

Fletcher snorted. "Leave no mystery between you that will keep him coming back for more."

"The most intelligent thing you've said all evening," she said over her shoulder. "Now, the ground rules. Odys, I'm the fourth oldest Automaton Master in this crap pile and plan to stay that way. If Pepin were still alive, I'd be number five. I've moved up in the line, though that doesn't mean much since you have, too. It's best for the newbies to know their status in this damn order, ain't that right, Dorian?" She clicked her heels.

"Sure is, Bob."

"So that means you do what I say. When I say it. No questions."

SIR YES SIR!

"In fact, it's better if you just don't say anything Keep it zipped." She leaned into her action of zipping up her mouth. "Number two, you may have noticed this jacket I'm wearing. Yes, I served this country. But don't you dare ask me about my pre-Automaton history. Don't ask me if I'm a veteran. Because that makes me sound old. Veterans are over and done with their shit, and I still wake up to it every fucking day. I wake up to shit. Just like what I'm doing now—cleaning up Mother's shit. You're the shit, Odys. Understood?"

Odys nodded, unsure if she knew the pun she'd just made.

"And yes, these are tattoos—not birth marks." She pointed to her neck. "But don't you dare let me catch you staring at them. Because staring is fucking rude and I will blind you. You want to be like Dorian over there? Keep staring."

Odys quickly looked at her lone eye, avoiding the spots. She huffed at his fearful face, turning away in disgust.

Odys thought, Is that how Dorian...?

"No!" Maud whispered back, disappointed he would think so.

"Oh, and number three, unless you want your balls chopped off, don't make fun of my name. Yes, goddamn it, it is my real name—as real as you'll ever need to know. It's Bob. Just Bob. Not Bobbie, Bobbers, and Godfuckinghelpyou if you call me Robyn."

Odys hadn't planned on it, but okay. In fact, Odys was kind of hoping there'd never be another instance when he'd need to address her at all.

"She likes long walks on the beach, classical music, and her favorite color is black—just like her heart," Dorian said, sliding in a new piece of gum. "What else is there to know?"

"So have we figured out if he's gay too?" Bob asked, her lone eyebrow rose in conflagrated curiosity for any revised intel.

"Why? I didn't think the closet was enemy territory for you," Maud spat.

"He's not gay, Bob," Dorian sighed.

"Then why's his hair so long?"

Something told Odys that Bob didn't really care about his hair or sexuality. It was all a test— a test in how you'd react.

"It's like no one knows what a haircut is anymore!" She pointed to Dorian's hair as well, as if it weren't always that length. "We could give you a haircut, you know."

"Does that mean this colossus is gay, you fag hag?" Fletcher gestured to her Automaton with the biker-braid nearly reaching the floor. Fletcher leaned over to Dorian, whispering, "She'll make him a drag queen yet, Dori. The ugliest one I've ever seen."

She cracked her neck. He had her there. "At least he brushes his."

Bob's Automaton glanced over at Fletcher, expecting a comeback—his poor head had been darting everywhichway as the group exchanged rude discourse. Quarreling was standard procedure with this lot, and he recorded every minute of it.[43]

"But, oh!" Bob cried, remembering she had an Automaton. "I forgot! I'm so sorry," she apologized to the Automaton (so sweetly it was shocking) and beckoned to him. Grabbing him by an arm like a gentleman displaying his arm-candy, "He does deserve a formal introduction." Her head snapped to Fletcher. "Fletcher? Where are your fucking manners?"

Fletcher rolled his eyes as he reclined on the back of the couch, knowing what she wanted (introductions were "standard procedure"). With a wave of his hand, "Odys, meet Bob, her royal bitchiness, and her wife, *Cestus*."[44]

CESTUS: Not Aphrodite's girdle.[45]

HOBBIES: What Bob *used* to do.

FAVORITE HARRY POTTER CHARACTER: Hagrid.

BAKES: A really mean cookie. Seriously. Dey da bomb.

Chapter the tenth,

Screams = curses:

We all curse for ice cream?

"Cestus and Bob, meet Mr. INeedAShower," Fletcher gestured to Odys. "No, no, wait. Our own Mr. *SNAFU*. That's a better one." He saw Bob's lip twitch and eye roll, the closest he could get to her impenetrable approval.

"And beside him," he went on, "is his version of Maud. Maud 2.0, if you will." He put his hand upon Dorian's head. Dorian didn't seem to care if the Automaton messed up his hair. Fletcher's long fingers pulled through it like a comb, as if considering for Dorian the haircut Bob offered.

---

[43] I'm assuming he "records" it for later analyzing. Bob must keep her skills in top shape, going up against an Automaton.
[44] Can I just applaud his *mold*? Finally! An Automaton that fits the notorious hype, right? After all, shouldn't this story's Automata live up to the connotation as something god-forged and mighty? Maud (a frail *femme fatale*) and Fletcher (a skinny telephone pole) do nothing at first glance to live up to any menacing bequest. I was getting worried this book was about sex toys rather than war machines... On second thought, that's not much better.
[45] Aphrodite had a girdle named Cestus that had the power to inspire love. This Cestus, on the other hand, inspires us to question who Bob really is inside (let's go ahead and look up the definition of "bipolar").

"Good to meet you, Cestus," Odys said, extending his hand to the ginormous being. In the middle of his action, he started to regret it.

The Herculean Automaton didn't take his hand, but frowned. Like some towering, sluggish, topiary creature, he held up a beefy finger (one moment, Odys) and retrieved something from his back pocket.

"Something for you," he stated in a rumbling voice. It took a lot of work for his big mouth to form that simple phrase—the sounds more like malapropisms. He handed Odys a knitted beanie cap—one with a giant poof on top. "A welcoming gift," Cestus added, "to start us out on the right foot."

Rather, to make up for his Master's *wrong* foot.

Without asking, he slipped it on Odys's head, a fashion designer making sure the clothes looked right. A finger to his lips, he nodded to himself. That would do.

"And Maud,"—he clomped over to her—"I thought we should make up for all the holidays we've missed. This is for you." And he plopped a too-baggy shawl over her head, arranging it on her tiny shoulders. "Made them myself, of course."

Bob: "We assumed it'd be hard for you to keep your clothes on."

"Thank you very much," Maud said, shifting in the giant blanket now restricting arm movement.

"At least you're decent now," Bob grumbled.

Cestus twirled the end of his mustache, pleased.

"Thank you," Odys remembered his thanks. He was sure he looked like an idiot with his poof.

"Odys is particularly fond of hats," Maud said to assure them.

"Good. But don't be a brown-noser, now." Bob cleared her throat.

"And where's *our* presents?" Fletcher whined has he adjusted a new bow-tie he'd just formed. This one was bigger and more Victorianly-frilled (he'd put on his butler suit once more). As he tugged on his sleeve ruffles, "You can't just give presents to total strangers and neglect the people you know, Cestus! You *know* Dorian needs socks."

Bob pursed her outlined lips. "Don't you have Fletcher to masturbate into?"

"I'd rather have a scarf," Dorian corrected.

"Don't give them *reasons* to call you a fag," Fletcher said. "At least not bad ones." He turned to Odys. "Don't feel special just because Santa here brings you presents. He does nothing but knit all day and can't find enough people to give them to. It's the only way Bob doesn't explode."

Bob changed the subject. "Let's get a move on. It will take us approximately thirty-six minutes to get to Mother's location, and heaven above knows how long we spent trying to open the damn door. Oh, and that brings me to my next damn point." Her eye narrowed at Odys as she put on her gloves. "In the event that you manage to pull something on us, I'm not afraid to pull you down with me—if you know what I mean? Mother may *think* we know enough about you to prove you're just an innocent little victim, but." She paused. "Even the Masters we personally approved started out as innocent and look where that's gotten us."

Bob started out the door, beckoning them with a curt wave.

Cestus waited for Maud and Odys to trickle out, making sure Odys grabbed his coat and scarf before out the door. With a nod, he bid Dorian and Fletcher, "Good evening, boys. Behave yourselves."

"Yessir, Mrs. Bob!" Fletcher saluted. "And for God's sake put a shirt on!" He went to assess the door's damage. To Dorian, "I think my insults are getting better." He examined the blown-off knob. Not much hope for the little thing.

"I'd say so," Dorian nodded. "As well as your composure. You used to giggle so much when she insulted you."

"I didn't giggle," Fletcher said, tossing the knob. "And if I did, it's because *you* couldn't control me well enough. Maybe if you did a bit more laughing around her yourself I wouldn't have to."

Stanza: You're a soul with a body; Masters, with two.

Walking through the parking lot, Odys felt like a prisoner being handed over for transfer.

The day was barely half over, but the sun was behind the clouds. Rain tried to form. It made it seem like evening. The car windows outside wouldn't see the remaining ice melt from their windows. The cold was doing nothing for Odys's health.

He kept glancing at Maud.

Odys didn't so much mind the fact he was having his day interrupted as he did being seen with an overly attractive female, some tattooed freak, and a conspicuous monster. At least Maud was wearing some shoes now, so she didn't look like some abducted prostitute.

Those shoes looked more like bare feet with dangerously tall spikes sprouting from the heals. The lace-up threads made them appear more legit. He didn't know how she walked in them. So poised.

He counted the times her heals tapped on the pavement.

Odissa never wore heals. She couldn't stand them—or stand *in* them. The poor girl could only wear pretty flats, which Odys liked anyway. His sister was already tall enough...

Walking, walking, walking. Just *where* had they parked? There weren't cars this far out. Only some driverless ice cream...truck.

Odys looked at Maud. *Are you kidding me?*

"That's it there. That's right, the damn piece of junk right there," Bob pointed, seeing Odys's expression. Her voice turned to white clouds in the winter air.

Odys thought they would have driven something, well, less *obvious.* "Standard procedure, boy, so don't give any lip. Standard fucking procedure." Putting her hands on her hips she mumbled, "I swear, this shitty eyesore's a metaphor for my life. Go on. Get in."

"The back opens like so," Cestus said, swinging the hind-end open with ease. The latch had an open lock dangling from it. "This isn't our first choice of transportation. We usually drive our motorcycle, of course."

"We?" Bob said. "You mean me, right?" She didn't want to give them the wrong impression. She wanted it perfectly clear who was *the man* around here.

Odys wondered if Cestus rode in the cramped sidecar or right behind her. Either way, it was an odd picture.

The truck, completely empty, had its serving-windows bolted down from the inside—not like Odys actually expected it to be full of frozen delights, but it was a bit...how shall I put it?

Like a cell.

"What'd you expect, first class armored truck? Hell, no," Bob said. "We only need a damn cage to keep *you* in and *directions* out. Not that you couldn't break out if you wanted to. But if you do, well, I'd *love* to shoot something today. And we can't have you knowing where we're headed, you see, so that's why the windows are bolted. Standard fucking procedure." She pointed into the truck again, telling them to get on in. Don't make her repeat herself.

With a sigh, Maud went up, taking Cestus's hand. Easy does it.

Odys climbed on in and watched Cestus roll down the door. In the darkness, he heard the latch shut and the lock click. A part of him wanted someone to have seen those two stuff him in here. Someone call the cops! Open the door! He'd suffocate!

"Don't be silly, Odys," Maud said, putting a hand on him. "If anyone did see, it's not like you were struggling, right? Besides, if anything bad happens, I can easily break us out of here. Don't freak out so much. We can trust them. Bob's bark is worse than her...well, no, it's not but... Just sit down."

91

She felt her way to the corner of the truck and sat down, next to the built-in (but empty) icebox. He followed her. He could just make out her outline because of a crack emerging from the bolted window.

It's so cold. Upon thinking that, Maud snuggled in closer to him, just as the modified ice cream truck started.

"Is it always an ice cream truck?"

"Could be. I've never had to be kept from knowing where Mother is before, though. Mother never hid from Pepin. It was Pepin who hid from her. Mother's hiding from Leeland now—as always."

"Well, at least they found my sister."

"Yes." Something in Maud's voice was doubtful.

"Must have hawk eyes if they could spot her while driving."

"That or they're lying to get you to cooperate."

"I wish you hadn't said that."

"I'm sorry," she said. "But you were also thinking it. I just don't want to lie to you."

Odys breathed uncomfortably as Maud took his hand. They were alone now, so he didn't complain about it. He needed her touch and didn't want her to sneeze out again (like an owner embarrassed by an untrained puppy, he didn't want Maud to act up).

The rickety ice cream truck turned. Was that a melody? Oh God, what would they do if a child shouted out "ICE CREAM!" Would they really stop? He prayed not. One look at Bob and any parent would call the cops.

Oh, wait, that's what he wanted, wasn't it?

Maud changed the subject. "I put some cigarettes in your pocket. They'll warm us up."

The lighter illuminated their faces.

"Maud?"

"Yes?"

The truck hit a bump. "Of all people, why me? Why would Pepin give me something that I don't want and that others don't want me to have?"

Cigarette bobbing between her lips, "You and I both know your fate's been tied to Vulcan's game since childhood."

"It's not fair. I'm part of Pepin's game within Vulcan's game. A game in a game—"

She laughed at his dramatics. "Whatever *Pepin's* game, Vulcan's going along with it. You don't see him here, taking me away from you, do you? You can't have made too much chaos for the gods by having me. Maybe you're more important than you think."

"I don't want to be important."

"Everyone can see that," Maud scolded him. "And you're not *that* important. If you were so *important* then you'd fix everything with the snap of your fingers. Don't start acting like a messiah just yet. Just because you have a role in this game doesn't mean yours is the biggest part. Don't let this go to your head. You're just another hand that makes up Vulcan's body. He has many hands—just like every other god."

"What're you talking about?" Odys sighed.

Stanza: Not that you'll have no other gods. [46]

Her eyebrows came together. "There've been many hands, in the past. Hands of hands. Hands always have a *hand* in doing what's meant to be done all along. Hands make up the body of the Universe—God. Whatever you want to call it."

He pursed his lips. "Is this the part where you deconstruct my religious beliefs and blow my mind?" He was willing to let her talk him into it, at the very least. Partly to keep himself from falling asleep.

She blew out some smoke. "Exactly. You're catching on. Of course you would. If you didn't, then you wouldn't have me. Pepin wouldn't leave me to a *complete* idiot."

"...Did I just insult myself?"

"You knew this was coming. You were just waiting for the right time to tell yourself. Not that you'll find it necessarily hard to believe what I'm about to say—"

"Vulcan is a god. There's more to it than that?"

"Be patient! I'm getting to my point—this is a point you've wanted all your life, Odys. A point most humans never get. Don't ruin the buildup. Now, where were we? Hands. Body parts. The Universe is everything, all that jazz."

[...] [47]

---

[46] Not that you'll have no other gods, but that you'll have no other gods *before* me.

[47] This part was omitted because it probably only makes sense to certain pseudo-intellectuals. Pseudos like Odys with too much reading time on their hands—like someone else I know (cough, cough). Besides, let's admit it, some of you aren't reading these footnotes anyway, and it's my job to edit things down:

"Maud waved a hand. 'Take Prometheus, for example. His limited-yet-significant role in man's creation story begins with clay—no matter if it was the Neanderthal, Denisovan, or Homo Sapien creation. Whatever. He shaped "man" from the ground—a clod of dirt, as the myth goes. Long story short, from dirt man was made and to dirt he shall return. The god that created man was part of the capital-G God. The gods make up the heavenly body—whatever that may be.'

Circo del Herrero

"In short," Maud said, "no matter who you are and what you do, life goes on. The gods don't give a fuck who you are, as long as you carry out Their will, you understand? Messiah or Hitler, you're unimportant. You're a tool—a device. Your plot in this story—this game—is all arranged. You might as well stop fighting it."

What a round-about way of belittling a person.

He blinked past her, taking in her gusty speech-making. What was he trying to tell himself? He looked back at her as he lit another cigarette. The light showed her well enough.

"That's—that's why Leeland's still alive, isn't it?" Odys asked her, his cigarette-rough voice hiccupped the question. He understood why she'd just ranted. She'd ranted because he needed her to. "Vulcan lets him play the 'game' only because he's using him; Vulcan let my father—no, I mean Augury or Leeland or *whoever*—kidnap me and my sister as children. But for what end?"

She shrugged, no inertia in her parlance: "What gives you the right to ask that question over anyone else?"

"But I'm being used like Augury—or Leeland, whatever. He and I are on the same fucking playing field. I don't like being compared to him—don't like that my life is being used against me. That's what this means, doesn't it? I mean, isn't this supposed to be some good guy versus bad guy shit? But how can that be when Vulcan's not choosing sides—when he's an asshole? He let Augury ruin my life—and now he's let Pepin."

There were too many Hands everywhere.

'The hand of God may or may not be a literal hand, just like the hand which molded the Biblical Adam may or may not have been a literal hand. It's all a metaphor. Doesn't God have a merely nominal body anyways?

'Not even the Muslims or Jews will depict Him, for that limits God to man-made characteristics, and God shouldn't be restricted. Jesus is okay to depict, for Christians, but do you think they ever got it right? There were no cameras, back then. I should know. I'm older than the church! Jews weren't blonde,' she laughed to herself, knowing Odys (on any other day) would be loving this conversation. 'And besides, do you really think God is Michelangelo's pull-my-finger Grandpa? Hell, no. But I digress. Prometheus and the like are the hand of the Universe—of God. Anyone can be the hand of God. Even Hitler.'

He narrowed his eyes. 'So you're calling me Vulcan's Hitler now?'

She huffed, rubbed her forehead. 'Good and bad guys play their part, Odys. Prometheus was *punished* for giving man fire—for sympathizing with man. How can the hand of God be punished for what it was meant to do? Why was Prometheus able to do it in the first place, if it wasn't meant to be done? Just think of His poor liver, pecked out every day! Perhaps Prometheus had, in the end, stepped out of line. Fire became the method to make weaponry and thus made way for atomic bombs and shit. It gave man too much power, some could say. But it also helped man survive. We can't really know if Zeus was justified for wanting to keep fire from man, but whatever *happened* was allowed to happen. The Universe still made use of it all. The world still spins on its axis, no? And men got to keep their fires. Same with Hitler. Even when Hitler was alive, the world kept on spinning. The Universe *allowed* him to be born in the first place, right? And It allowed poor Prometheus to be punished. The Universe is never fair. But It always allows you to play your part.'"**

* For an interesting Western hand-of-God reference, see Exodus 33:17-23.

**Look! A footnote in a footnote! It's a feetnote!

She reached out to him, offering her hand like a cold press to soothe his head. He was so exhausted that he tried to ignore what she was doing. "Maybe the way to feel free is to accept your cage. If your cage becomes your home, then the gods have no power, do They? Not if you like where They've put you."

He mumbled, "I'll never like where They put me."

They rode in silence for a minute or two or twenty.

"Did Pepin have a family?"

"Didn't he tell you about his wife, when he first spoke? He always dressed like that, you know. Wasn't an act," she laughed. "He had a wife, yes, but when I came along…things got weird. She left him, in the end. At first I was their 'maid,' who stayed in the guesthouse. Because of me, they became very rich. At first Mrs. Pound knew nothing about me. Pepin kept me hidden. Later, it became harder to hide me. Within two years of my bond with Pepin, she'd grown suspicious. She guessed an affair. Pepin tried pretending he was having trouble sleeping so he could lounge in the study with me. But of course I would dream and wake up naked beside him. It's only natural. The first time Mrs. Pound walked in on us…Pepin hated himself. Of course you know what it looked like. And yeah, it's only a matter of time before Odissa finds us like that…"

She took in a shaky breath as the truck made a large turn, pushing them against the wall. "After she left Pepin, she remarried and had children. Pepin was alone. With me. But he loved her until her dying day. But, with a face like his, he had a few affairs. Even with ex-Mrs. Pound a few times."

"And with you?"

"No. Pepin did not love me like that. He was too…racist to. At best I think I he thought of me as his daughter. He *wanted* to, anyway. That was the most elegant way to think of me."

"Maybe it's good he didn't have children, then," Odys said with disgust.

Maud just sucked on her paper.

"Even with all those affairs, he had no children?"

"I see what you're getting at. But he often checked up on that sort of thing. He and Mrs. Pound had been trying for, oh, say, a year before I came into the picture. Nothing happened, if you get my meaning. I think that was probably a good thing A blessing."[48]

"I see."

---

[48] And very convenient narratively, I might add.

"Besides, being a Master makes it hard to fit children in the picture. They're not something you want painted in. Everyone in your life becomes a liability. In fact, I wouldn't be surprised if you're the only Master *with* liabilities now."

"Without liabilities, though, what's there to live for? Masters obviously don't live for each other. Dorian and Fletcher don't seem to like Bob. If Masters can't tolerate their own, then what's the point?"

"They're *stuck* with each other. You also don't know what I know about them, so you are judging before you understand. They tolerate one another enough to reach their goals."

"Goals?"

"Yes. They've got nothing left to lose. Leeland took everything. They don't have to tolerate each other to still be family. They have no choice now."

Odys chuckled. "I'm surprised they didn't tie our hands. They must not be too afraid of us, you know?"

"You still look like shit, that's why. And it's no use tying mine." He could hear the smile in her voice. "No doubt Dorian's spread the word you're a fucking martyr for your innocence, trying to disown me and all. They know you're complacent. On top of it, they pretty much have your sister hostage—so of course we'll behave. But yeah, I have to give it to them. They are being nice—nicer than I expected…"

Stanza: Ice cream sandwiches.

Cestus and Bob rode in relative silence, the jingle of the truck the only sound they needed. Bob scowled a lot when she drove. Cestus had retrieved his knitting bag and was counting away. This was how Bob multitasked. This was how Bob survived.

"He seems like a nice boy. Nervous-like, but kind," Cestus said as he looped his yarn.

"I'd be nervous too, if I didn't know what the fuck was going on. At least we normal Masters got prepped beforehand. Pepin just trapped this boy into it," Bob grumbled. She turned her blinker on. "Goddamned maniac! Can't you read the sign on my ass? 'SLOW: CHILDREN!'" she pointed behind her. "Damn people, never caring for anything…"

"Well, I think he's a nice boy," Cestus added.

"You would, wouldn't you?"

"Yes, I would, Robyn."

"Sorry. I just have a lot on my mind, you know."

"Yes, I do." He knew best of all.

Silence.

Driving, driving, driving.

"Fletcher's getting pretty good at pissing you off," Cestus grinned down at his tiny Master.

"Yeah, but Dorian's still not reacting enough to me. He always uses that damned Fletcher."

"At least he still acknowledges you through Fletcher. He didn't always do that."

"It's not healthy for Dorian to hold it in. Fletcher can't be his only means of emotion. That stoic bastard isn't going to get better if he won't let us in."

"He'll come around with time."

"Time, ha!" Bob mock-laughed. "Time! All we have is time. How long has it been though? Twenty-plus years that bastard's been like this? So gloomy. He should be happier."

And you're such a ray of sunshine yourself, Bob.

Cestus sighed. "Maybe trying to *provoke* him isn't the way to bring him out of it."

"You always say that, but it's not like other methods have worked. Mother babies him and he just keeps growing more and more distant. Pepin, for a while there, tried to be a father figure. What other methods are left?" she grumbled, honking her horn at a little old lady in the car in front of them. "It's green!" Bob shouted at the windshield.

...

"But you have to admit, Dorian was quick to take on this assignment."

"No, Mother was quick to offer it to him."

"Yes, but Gwen knows what she's doing," Cestus gave a sly look.

Bob turned her head away from him to smile. She was attractive when she smiled. Even when she showed no teeth, the smallest upward lip-arch made all the difference. She only smiled for Cestus, though.

"But yes," she admitted, "Fletcher *was* pissing me off. He and Dorian are a nasty combination for me."

Too many bitches in one room.

"He knows just how to push my buttons. I was about to play dirty."

"And I knew you didn't want to do that."

"No, I didn't."

"Because Dorian—and Fletcher—would never play dirty."

"Though they *did* mention my spots." She squeezed the wheel and hunched forward.

Road rage was the least of Cestus's worries. "Have we not reclaimed the spots, though? Made them our own? Don't they know and respect that? They only make fun of things they respect."

"I know!" Bob growled. "But that was a first. It was mean. Not like that wasn't his point, but..." She cracked her neck.

Cestus said nothing, knowing that she needed to talk—to get things off her chest:

"It's not like him to acknowledge my spots. I just feel so sorry for the kid—for Dorian. He has it worse than me, you know?"

"More or less."

"No. Not more or less!" She snapped at him, swerving a little as she glared. "I get off with these—these tattooed 'scars' and what does Dorian get?"

Bob didn't cry. She just got angry. At herself.

"We lost loved ones too, though," Cestus reminded her. He had to recount his loops after watching the road for her.

"Yes," she huffed. "But I'm not blind on top of it."

Driving, Driving, Driving. SPEEDING. Honk! Honk! Get out of her way, motherfucker.

"...Can you hear that?" Cestus said, leaning in. He pointed with his thumb behind their torn leather seats. "I think they're chatting."

"Why does that make you so happy?"

(Happiness? NO! There'll be no happiness in Bob's ice cream truck).

He chuckled. "It's only that Odys seemed so, well, *removed* from her."

Bob rolled her eyes. "I bet some*thing* like Maud embarrasses him. It's the equivalent of having a porn magazine under your arm all the time. The world knows what you've been doing." WHAT YOU COULD BE DOING.

Stanza: All around the mulberry bush the monkey chased the weasel.

"Fletch, *must* you eat them out of house and home? We just ordered pizza," Dorian said, reluctantly opening his mouth so Fletcher could spoon-feed him.

"But it's coffee-flavored."

"As if I've never had coffee ice cream before." Licking his lips, "Not too terrible. Despite you dropping it on the floor earlier."

"I know, right?"

"You're going to feel bad for abusing their house if they turn out to be clean."

"No. Not really."

"It's so strange," Dorian said, recalling his interactions with Odys, "He only gets excited for news of his sister."

"You don't get excited about *anything* anymore," Fletcher mumbled under his breath as he gathered the last bit of expensive ice cream. He'd finish off the peanut butter next.

"This job's too boring to show excitement. I'm surprised you haven't blacked out from the boredom—you usually put your screensaver up."

"You make me seem like I'm narcoleptic."

"Aren't you? I swear, if you were a computer you'd have a screensaver up in two seconds of no activity. No other Masters have that problem with their Automatons."

"Other Masters have lives, that's why," Fletcher said, draping one of his long legs over Dorian's lap.

"Don't put the tub there. Throw it away. This isn't your house, is it?"

"Fine, I'll throw it away. But later. I'm too tired to get up." He gave a wide yawn and snuggled in. "Besides, if this isn't my house, means I don't have to clean it."

"See what I mean? The moment I let you run yourself, you sink like the *Titanic*." His soul could be so lazy.

"I'm just doing what you won't let yourself do." He put his head on his Master's shoulder, an awkward giraffe.

Dorian nudged him. "Keep your eyes open. I'm watching this show!"

"I can't help it if you're not even going to put an *effort* into helping me wake up. Just because the juke box is on, don't mean it'll play without a quarter."

"So you're a juke box now?"

"Better than the *Titanic*. Not as tragic."

"Well, how much more do you want me to take over, huh? You know I don't like turning you into a mind-controlled zombie."

"Ew, bad analogy. I hate brains."

"Funny you should say that, since you don't have one."

"Burn. However, doesn't hurt as much since you're practically joking with yourself and already know the punch lines."

"Ditto, then." Dorian said, itching his chin. He wanted to shave.

"How bored *are* we, if we have to keep talking to ourself like this?"

"I don't know. What's sadder: the fact we're babysitting a cat right now or the fact conversations with myself always turn out the way I want them to?"

"They're tantamount."

"Want to stop, then?"

"I think that'd save time, since we both know the ending."

They both gently nodded to themselves in unison.

…

Fletcher whispered in his ear, "I could wank you off in their shower. That would be fun."

Dorian cracked a half-smile. "Maybe once the show is over."

After the pizza came (and quickly went), Fletcher decided to fix the door. However, his idea of fixing the door was to take off the old and exchange it for someone else's. He was a very clever worker, Fletcher.

"Aren't you going to change the apartment numbers?"

"I'd like to see if Odys notices," Fletcher said, putting on his finishing touches. Duct tape stolen from the kitchen's miscellaneous drawer helped hold the splintered doorframe pieces in place.

"The *neighbors* are sure to notice."

Fletcher half-ignored him. "I'd say they'd need new keys, but it's not like they'll be here much longer."

And an Automaton needed no keys. They *were* keys.

Fletcher spotted Bulfinch sticking his nose out of Odissa's room, sniffing the pizza aroma. Fletcher hissed at him, scaring him back into his hiding spot.

"He hasn't had lunch, has he?" Dorian asked.

"Nope. But speaking of pests, do you think it's wise that Mother sent the you-know-whos to track down Odissa? When Odys finds out who we let near his sister…Well, let's just pray he *doesn't* sync with Maud anytime soon. He doesn't need to know what *she* knows about **them**."

"Was thinking that myself."

Of course you were, silly Dorian.

"…You really think **he** found Odissa?"

"I don't see why **he'd** lie—especially about something Mother told **him** to do. Besides, the stars are aligning far too well for me to doubt fate at this point."

Dorian put his feet down from the coffee table. "Mother knows what she's doing. Besides, she had to give **him** something to do. You know how **he** can't sit still. That's why you and I got the babysitting job. At least **he's** not bugging *us* for once."

Fletcher cringed. "Even so, I'm not going to be the one to tell Odys that Mother sent out our lecherous little *Mecca Makepeace*."

MECCA MAKEPEACE: A feral stray.

MUSLIM?: He *does* identify as a Trekkie.

AGE (ACTUAL, NOT PHYSICAL) AND TYPE: Middle-aged delinquent.

HEIGHT: Just short enough to suffer little-man syndrome, justifiably.

Chapter the eleventh,

The youngest are the elders:

This kinda has the whole *Interview with the Vampire* thing going on, doesn't it?

Mecca Makepeace and his Automaton, Q (short for Quarrel), had been sent on a mission. They were watching for a silver Honda in the opposite lane. Calm-Q swung her tiny feet. She could dangle said feet because she was far back in her seat and shorter than most beings. Cuteness was added when she twiddled her delicate, glove-covered thumbs...

Sigh! As if they were *actually* helping. Why did their information on Odissa have to be so vague? And *who* on this god-forsaken planet didn't have a cell phone these days? It was the twenty-first century, for crying out loud! They could have tracked her if she'd only had a phone! They were very good at tracking. They were the best at it.

Jesus Christmas, they'd never find her!

"Um," came Q's mild and pusillanimous voice from the passenger seat (her voice matched what she was wearing, as always). "Didn't they tell you the license plate number, Mecca?" Of course she knew they had. She could read her Master's thoughts—though not the ones he'd accidentally forgotten.

"Yeah," Mecca grumbled. Of course she would ask that.

"Then, um, what was it? I'm trying to help you look. Don't you *want* my help?" She put a tiny hand up to her lips, hoping her offer wouldn't offend him. Her voice was a high-pitched whisper—the kind of voice that comes from the most modest and gentle women. She was a delicate thing today.

She saw his face pinch, his eyes on the road. He could hardly see over the steering wheel. She was surprised that his feet reached the pedals. Perhaps he had grown recently.

"Don't you *want* me to help you?" she asked again.

"Mecca..." he started (yes, referring to himself in third-person—and no, it wasn't baby-talk), "...can't remember the plate numbers."

"Huh? Oh, Mecca, you're *always* forgetting," she cried. "I wish you would have told me, so I could have remembered for you. Or written it down. Why did you keep me from knowing? Now we'll never know for sure if it's the right car. Especially in this poor light."

The clouds wanted to rain/sleet.

"Well, we've got her picture, don't we?" he snapped. "Mecca knows what she looks like and what her car looks like, too. That's all Mecca needs!"

"Oh, I wish you weren't so proud and would call Mother to confirm," Q half-heartedly abnegated, smoothing out the wrinkles of her frilly Rococo dress. She looked even younger in that Alice-in-Wonderland garb—complete with self-formed lace, stockings, and bonnet.

Though it was nothing to brag about, Q was *at least* a head taller than her Master, and looked—maybe—five years older. But looking older than Mecca meant an iota.

Mecca Makepeace, you should know, had a ten-year-old's body. But a frat boy's carriage. For example, every time he sent Q into a liquor store for *the goods*, it backfired; they always had to steal their supplies. This made them very practiced at thievery.

"Mother could repeat the number for us. Or—or maybe you could call Dorian?"

"Com'on now, Q. He'd make fun of us. We can't screw this up!" he scolded her; her, the doubting voice in his head manifest. "Mecca doesn't want us to look bad. Mecca can do this *on his own*." No need for even an Automaton!

"Oh, dear," she sighed, her voice cracking. Her fingers sprouted a lacey fan and began to beat the air. "No wonder they never send us out. You can't even remember a license plate number. You should have let me help you remember. You usually do. They *expected* you to."

Mecca rolled his eyes as his Automaton fretted. She worried too much sometimes. She knew darn well that he was testing himself. HE WAS THE GREASTEST. He would prove it.

To himself, at the very least.

His Automaton went on, "And it doesn't help things that you lied and said you'd found her, back there." She snapped and re-absorbed her fan.

"Mecca has to make himself look good, Q." [49]

He turned up the radio. Its volume would have disrupted any normal tender-hearted girl's train of thought, but Q did not mind Gorillaz blasting through the speakers. She folded her hands in her lap, a life-size doll. She would match any in a display case. Today, anyway. Only today. Tomorrow she'd look different.

---

[49] Long story short, the (what I like to call) "non-baby-talk baby-talk" stems from Mecca's Q-given enlightenment. So much knowledge shoved into an underdeveloped brain manifests itself in different ways, including his speech. You could say his third-person references show how a child would conceptualize being more than one person—granted, he's not *exactly* a child in this present time. This is pretty much how our Narrator explained it to me. Just FYI.

Mecca thought about rolling his window down, but remembered Q. Her lengthy, straight hair threatened to lash out at you if the wind ever took it; it could coil round you like a whip. Plus, the air would make her cold. She wasn't *really* wearing clothes after all.

Mecca liked to keep her comfortable. He was very considerate of his second body. He paid great attention to detail. Well, *some* details.

At first glance, you would have mistaken that second body, Q, for a Japanese Lolita abducted straight from the sub-cultures at Harajuku. A second glance would have you questioning whether or not the vanadium-black haired girl was really Japanese at all.

Her nickel-kissed skin gave her a suspiciously indigenous-American appearance. Had our alleged Automaton-Creator molded that flawless face to exhibit that flat nose, full brow, brisk eyes, high cheeks, thick lips, and broad chin to fit within such an ethnicity?

Of course. Why wouldn't Vulcan want his bases covered? Especially since His designs would end up in the Americas one day. Why not?

She sighed—the absolute most adorable sound—knowing it was no use arguing with her compatriot about these issues. She was only helping him test himself.

Mecca Makepeace had a delightful and amusing face—a round orb balancing on his too-skinny body. He had alert little eyes, always narrowed (to help him think of something naughty).

His wide grin always seemed more like a gnashing—flashing those baby teeth. Once you got used to it, though, you could hear the boyish giggling that managed to escape the fangs. And if he smiled enough, you would see he was missing a tooth, the spot unfilled (for almost ten years now).

Mecca's dimpled cheeks were just the right temptation to squish or push a finger in (a trademark gesture of his, which Q's perspective helped him perfect to help him better get away with shit). His mother used to pinch those cheeks all the time. Or, at least he hoped that's what his mother would have done, if she had lived long enough to meet him. She'd died, just when he started living. But he didn't miss her. How could he? He never met her. For all he knew, he never really had a mother. He had little proof and was more apt to think he just appeared one day. Who needs a mother, anyway? That's what he'd been given the Automaton for.

Little Makepeace, you see, was the youngest person to ever get one. Most times, Mother and the others wouldn't have given their blessing for someone his age. In fact, he hadn't gotten an "OK." He'd gotten an "If you must."[50]

These past generations haven't let Mecca grow much. Q slowed it down.

Q was a mother to him. A mother, a sister, a friend, a toy.

Someday, he'd look older than her, he would. Then she couldn't look down at him anymore. Then—then!—he could finally be the one others first noticed (he hated how everyone addressed Q over him, thinking her more mature or his babysitter—which was true, but still). She was the one who couldn't grow. Mecca could grow. He kept track.

Now, you might get the idea to compare little Mecca to, say, Peter Pan. Very well, then, I won't stop you. The homage is certainly there, I won't deny it (the Muses do know how to recycle a concept, don't they?).[51] Just as Peter never matured, Mecca did much the same. His brain has also taken its time to ripen. But perhaps that somehow makes him all the wiser, unlike the decayed and decrepit minds of old folk (no offense, of course).

However, *unlike* Peter, Mecca felt no desire to *never grow up*. In fact, he wished he might somehow speed it along (but not too much, mind you). Ah, age is wasted on the old. But don't feel sorry for this young'un. He knew normal children had terrible lives.

For example:

Had Mecca ever gone to school, he would have had to study. Had he a mother, she would have made him eat his vegetables. Had he gone to an orphanage, he would have been given proper parents. Had he real parents, he would have had a strict bed time and missed out on all those crime-filled rumpuses.

What a miserable life to imagine!

He pushed back the sleeves of his too-big black shirt that he'd stolen (or borrowed, if you were to ask him) from Dorian. Poor Dorian often found his artifacts missing or gently abused upon re-discovery. Dorian was Mecca's favorite person to steal from because Dorian had excellent taste in *things*. In fact, this car was one of Dorian's. He had a garage full of fancy cars. He wouldn't miss one.

"Are you sure you don't want me to drive, Mecca? Of all the cars to pick, you chose this monster."

---

[50] Leeland seems to have made things more of a "must" in their decision making, I should mention. Mecca's childhood was tied to the Automata lifestyle long before he got one. Much like Odys, as you will find out.

[51] Sure, blame it on the Muses and not your lack of creativity, Narrator.

He didn't respond, because he didn't have to.

The streetlights turned on; it was just cloudy enough for them to be necessary. Under each passing light, the fair coloring of Q's lace and ruffles illuminated the car in sparkling flashes. Mecca scratched his head. His hair was naught but an afterthought—a mere darker shade than the rest of his baby-soft skin. Or, at least, it would have been if we could see it under his "Ninja mask"—which is where Dorian's shirt comes in. The shirt came with the car. Those too-big *sleeves* I mentioned earlier, well, they weren't on his arms.

It wasn't really a Ninja mask. It was more or less a black t-shirt craftily folded to LOOK like a ninja mask. An assassin must make do.

The shirt tag was sticking up on his forehead like some unshaven curl, because he forgot to fold it under. He still gets points for trying.

But as I was saying, Mecca didn't have hair. Anything but a buzz officiously interfered with his cosplay (he had a vast collection of wigs and hats, you see—none of which he had time to grab before this "mission").

"LOOK!" Mecca exclaimed, pointing to the opposite lane. Q lifted her submissive eyes, just as Odissa drove by; Q could tell Odissa was (embarrassingly enough) singing and wiggling in her car seat. "Mecca *told* Q we wouldn't need numbers. Mecca is the great-EST!"

Q's mouth hung wide. "This is all too convenient. Vulcan *meant* for us to find her. I can smell it. The nose knows." She rubbed her nose, keeping her eyes on Odissa.

Mecca grumbled. He didn't want to think that maybe (just maybe) Q's nose had led him to Odissa. Q mentally assured him that she was *just now* smelling such things and that he really *was* THE GREATEST.

And of course she was right—there was never any doubt about his greatness, really.

Tongue between his lips for concentration (making his mask protrude), the little boy swerved and drove across the grass divider. It left a tire trail in the moist grass. They sped on up to catch the silver car.

ILLEGAL U TURN.

Q's nose was tickling away. They were *meant* to be following this car…

You may find it hard to believe that two kiddos wouldn't be spotted driving, or, because of their raging recklessness, be pulled over. Not to worry. These two had planned for the worst. This car had tinted windows. Mecca utilized those windows to the fullest extent and would often pick his nose without feeling guilty.

And if a cop pulled them over? No problem there. The vast assortment of handguns Q could create would get our friends out of most situations. The guns were for intimidation…mostly. Mother would positively hate it if they *actually* killed someone. And besides, Mecca would out-speed a cop before he'd pull over for one. Because he was the greatest.

They bobbed between cars and lanes.

"Do you really need that?" Q asked him, in regards to his "mask." It was slipping off his head.

Adjusting it as he steered with one hand, he looked over at Q. "Humph! Look at what you're wearing. You should change your outfit to fit the assignment. Mother never gives us work, so you should have fun with it."

"But *you* told me to wear this."

"It's messing Mecca's concentration," he barked, pounding on the steering wheel. "Q will not ruin this fun for Mecca!"

Rolling her eyes at his pout, her frilly dress sunk back into her skin, re-surfacing to be a tight cat-burglar-like costume. She looked at him through her "mask." Her voice muffled by her own outer skin, "Better?"

"Mecca's satisfied, though Mecca wanted something more…ninja."

"You do know this is a *stalking* assignment, right? Not an *assassination.*"

"Mecca is ninja! When we get up to the car, Mecca will take off the mask and become a spy. That's what the sunglasses are for." He pointed to the dashboard (also a pair of Dorian's).

"Looks like she's turning left," she sighed, adjusting her mask. He was always dressing her up, like some doll or role-playing partner. "Also like her picture, yes," Q said, as she glanced at the driver beside them. They slowed down to tail her.

A few minutes later they would "re-confirm" spotting Odissa—Q would personally make the phone call. Gottah give those updates.

"…What did Mecca tell Q? When making a phone call, Q should wear a head-set!"

"I'm not a telemarketer! And the headset gets in the way of the real phone, you ass."

Now that she was out of the Lolita costume, she could act with less propriety.

"Then Q must think of a better costume for the occasion!"

(There was a costume for *every* occasion).

"If you can't think of one then how the hell am I supposed to?" she mumbled.

She thought about it and turned herself into a Beverly Hills-esque pre-teen: too much bling and too much sass. As she re-dialed the phone number, she said, "I can't believe we, like, actually found her. But, like, then again, I can't, like, believe half of the other things we've done either."

LIKE.

"It doesn't matter if we believe it, Q. *They're* the ones who have to."

They were very good at making people believe what they wanted them to believe.

"Oh, they will believe us. Right until Odissa walks through that door too early."

(Odys had been right to hope she'd leave as early as possible).

"Dorian's probably so bored he won't mind either way."

"Unless we walk in on him defiling yet another bathtub."

They both giggled.

Stanza: Orphans and the pathetic fallacy.

Meanwhile…

The ice cream truck screeched to a stop. Maybe at a red light? No. Bob killed the engine.

The door opened. The dim light made Maud and Odys's eyes squint. Cestus waved a hand in front of his nose. Their cigarette smoke wafted out with them.

"Did you *have* to smoke in my truck?" Bob caught Odys's deer-in-the-headlights look. "Don't look at me like I'm about to dump your body in a ditch, boy. I'm not going to kill you unless you deserve it. Besides, I don't like taking care of free Automatons once their Masters are dead. Too risky. You're not worth the post-*effort* of killing for no damn reason. Now, rule number one, don't talk about Leeland. It will make her cry. Two," Bob held up two fingers, "Don't drag this out. I've got somewhere to be. And so do you."

Odys stood up, but Bob held her hand higher, telling him to stay put, she wasn't done. "And three, Maud has to stay out here."

"Why can't she come with me?" For the first time since all *this* started, he wanted her more than anything.

"It's just standard procedure. Standard fucking procedure."

"You say 'standard' like this happens all the time. It's been—what?—over twenty years since something INTERESTING happened, right?" Maud chided as she hopped out of the truck.

Bob huffed, "She just can't go in."

"In where?" Odys stepped out of the truck, glancing around.

They were in a park. An RV park. Out in the middle of…

Jesus Christ, where was this place? Land of the abandoned, that's where. Odys never knew there was an RV park this close to them. Granted, all these trees kept the outside world pretty much invisible. Yup, this was a no-man's land. An isolated spot reserved for the junkiest of trailers, rusted cars, underfed hounds, and toothless folk.

Odys wanted to cry.

Cestus pointed to the right, to the closest trailer. It was a rusty, pill-shaped RV with pop-out sides and an extended canopy. A wicker table and chair set were neatly arranged underneath the too-huge canopy. Something told Odys the trailer hadn't originally come with all those bells and whistles—that it had been modified.

It was getting too dark and the poor streetlight in the middle of the lot did nothing to illuminate more details. Overall, Odys would have thought that people with gold-making Automatons could afford, um, something more accommodating.

There were maybe twenty or so filled spots scattered about the gravel. A few children had poked their heads out, spotting the ice cream truck but didn't approach. Even little kids could tell this rundown hunk-of-junk didn't have the good stuff.

"Cestus," Bob said as she locked up the truck up, "escort him, please."

"This way." Cestus yanked Odys from his safe-place.

Odys turned and gave Maud a weary look through his in-the-way hair. As they approached the trailer, Odys spotted a dainty tea set on the wicker table—but one saucer was missing its splendid tea cup. He heard someone take a nearby sip. Beyond the table was a boy walking from the curved nub of the RV's nose. He had obviously wished to go unnoticed until that very moment. He stepped away from the tangled brush and ungroomed trees—trees that converged with the trailer's front as if it had been purposefully pushed against the greenery to somehow make it blend in better. The trailer's oneness with the flora made a nice little niche to listen from and not be seen. He'd been waiting underneath the nose. Expecting them.

The boy held the cup in one hand, elfish fingers looped trough the tiny handle. An adult's hand could comfortably fit two. He had three—and could have squeezed in four. In his other hand, he grasped something worthy of hiding. Had it not been for the boy's relaxed face and attitude, Odys would have guessed the reason he'd been lurking was to conceal the pipe he'd been smoking—but not just any pipe. A pipe that suited him quite nicely. A kiseru pipe.

He walked up to them, sucking on the kiseru—his dainty face shameless. He held the pipe blatantly—for the entire white-trash world to see.

He was the most riveting child Odys had ever seen. But that was, of course, because this child was not a child. The boy was so striking that Odys found himself staring, making sure it wasn't an alien. Or a wee spirit.

But he was none of the above.

This Automaton was a god toting his customary symbols—the tea cup and pipe in his hands—hands that sported clean but too-long nails. They were claws—sharp points just like the tips of his side-swept bangs. The fringe-hair grew to his eyes and would have annoyed a normal person. The rest of his hair framed his face, draped over his delicate shoulders, trailed down his lower back like a veil.

Mother's Automaton blew out his pipe smoke, a purposefully indiscreet and gauche exhalation reserved for the next. He put his teacup down and crossed his arms. His wrist and fingers supported his pipe like a branch for a bird. His every graceful action achieved a purpose— what purpose?

Cestus nodded and greeted the other Automaton, "*Anselm.*"

ANSELM: Automaton of Gwendolyn Gwendy.

ANSELM: The youngest-looking Automaton.

ANSELM: The Automaton with the oldest Master.

ANSELM: Gwendolyn Gwendy's Automaton.

Chapter the twelfth,

We all wear many faces:

Do some need a face lift?

Cestus, not stopping to chat (as if Anselm wouldn't want to be bothered), led Odys to the door. Cestus was about to knock when—

Anselm was next to them in an instant, an eerie smile on his face. His grin made his jaw-line protrude. It made him look like a man, only miniature. His oblong lids flashed those expressive eyes—eyes like newly-minted dimes. Without saying a word, the boy opened the door with a self-made finger-key. He opened it slightly.

No need to knock; Mother's Automaton welcomed them.

He was wearing only a vest on top—even in this cold!—like some sophisticated ragamuffin. He didn't even shiver or hold himself for warmth. Poor Maud shivered as if naked and gripped her new shawl for warmth. Cestus even gave "burr" sounds here or there.

"Thank you," Cestus said. The boy came just above his knee-cap and made no effort to push the door open fully.

Cestus thought Anselm's rude behavior was funny—Odys somehow missed the joke. They were fucking with him—trying to scare him—test his fight or flight.

Cestus entered after Odys. Anselm followed close behind—not shutting the door. He gave Cestus a wide-eyed look that said more than words. He'd take it from here. Cestus patted the little Automaton on his shoulder and left without words.

Maud watched it all from afar. She leaned against the ice cream truck, arms crossed. She thought about smoking a cigarette.

"Stay where we can see you," Bob grumbled at her as she walked over to the chairs under the canopy to sit. The tea was for her (Mother was always a good hostess).

Maud nodded, not going to move an inch. She was going to stand here. And wait. And prove her Master was good.

She looked up at the setting sun, then back down at Bob. She counted how many times Bob stirred her tea—one—two—three—four…

Stanza: A Prioress that is best dressed.

Odys was alone with the Automaton.

He tried to distract himself.

The trailer was a gypsy hollow—a cave, more like. The lackluster lamps cast entrancing shadows. Wooden beads hung as a door from the ceiling. Colorful-but-faded drapery covered every available surface. Hypnotic incense and candles burned, creating a sweaty and exotic aroma. Odys loved any kind of smoke; it was fire he feared.

The place was cramped—with books upon books—a large collection of Catholic works and Spanish titles. He recognized one, and only one: *Cien Años de Soledad.* He had read it in English and had taken enough Spanish classes to understand the title.

Funny, to see a book like *that* on a shelf owned by *these* people; hundreds of years had passed among the Automatons and their Masters. Perhaps only *they* could appreciate the repetitive nature and continual stream of isolation Marquez presented.

Anselm watched him reading the titles, making Odys self-conscious.

The sitting area brimmed with pillows bursting over their seats. Odys could see a welcoming, built-in bed at the butt of the trailer. Tiny potted plants decorated every crevice and surface: herbs, flowers, ferns, the like. It presented an earthy feel that contrasted with the cold weather he'd just retreated from.

Anselm set down his pipe (its smoke was dwindling) on a special stand atop a nearby ledge and went straight to the pillows, nesting himself among them. Just sitting there.

He stared at Odys like an alien examining an earthling—an amoral interest on his little face. His homogenized eyes, with slight, attractive folds underneath, made the Automaton seem wiser. He was as slender as he was tiny. His jewel-head of platinum-white hair (that Odys would have called "bleached," had he not known better) gave him a false sense of age—an old elf.

Whereas Q simply acted like a life-sized doll, Anselm *was* one. A creepy living doll.

The boy didn't blink. The boy didn't say a word. The boy didn't even breathe.

(Odys noticed this because he would have counted).

Instead, he tried to ignore Anselm and wait six seconds between each one of his own breaths. When that got old, he pretended to be interested in the dying pipe smoke. It had the most delicious flavor and lingered in his lungs. The faint etching on the pipe's tobacco-basin caught Odys's eye. Before, Anselm's long-nailed fingers had concealed it. Now, it danced behind the floating smoke. It was the symbol of the hanging snake. The snake on a pole. The bronze snake of Moses.

Or, as it was later adopted: the cross of Flamel.

The Automaton's gaze widened with delight when he noticed Odys strip his eyes from the alchemic symbol. Odys recognized it—of course Odys recognized it! This symbol was everywhere…in certain circles. Including his father's books.

This very symbol was part of what made Odys realize his "father" was infatuated with ancient myth. Myth was central to many alchemic concepts—alchemy being the precursor to the sciences. His father was obsessed with that unholy trinity—myth, alchemy, science. But now—just now—Odys realized his father's *obsession* had always been more. Odys's heart raced, mind jumping to his father—and to Mr. Augury. *More* made sense now. Too much sense.

Anselm could tell the image bothered him, so his fingertips reached out and brushed away the image, leaving a charred pipe basin behind. It was then that Odys understood Anselm had probably etched the symbol there to begin with—with those long, thin nails. *Are all Automatons obsessed?* Odys thought. *Do they make their Masters obsessed?*

Let's answer that later.

As the staffs of Asklepios and Hermes's presaged the crucified Christ, this snake-cross symbol predestined another divine shift: Mother, too, was a symbol—one for the Automaton Masters.[52]

---

[52]Fun fact: As the bronze serpent (see Numbers 21:4-9) is much like the rod of Hermes (the caduceus, with two entwined snakes) and the staff of Asclepius; the re-occurring image is further invoked by Jesus Christ (see John 3:14-15). The parallel to this story, however, would be that the cross of Nicholas Flamel, who has historical and legendary roots in alchemy, is slightly connected to the god Vulcan, who was and is seen as an alchemic and/or metallurgical god.

Because of her Automaton's mystical quality and the loyal hype, Odys expected Mother to be some wise Galadriel or *Matrix* Oracle.

However, his fanboy expectations are about to be WAY OFF.

A divider within the trailer pushed back. Odys looked to his left, into the now-exposed kitchen. At last he saw her. His eyes widened in fear, then narrowed in confusion.

Despite her attempt, she lacked a certain *mystery*.

The venerable-looking woman didn't give one glance to Odys. She walked to the window beside Anselm, her own teacup in hand. She peered through the blinds at Maud, Cestus, and Bob. One half of her lips pulled up.

Her age was ripe, though her complexion bore only smile-lines. She looked certainly old enough to be *a* mother—but not Bob's or Dorian's. She barely looked older than Bob. How did she get away with such reverence—such a title as "Mother"?

But even with apparent youthfulness, she was worn down with age. She moved as if stiff and sore from some invisible chain restricting her—an age-old chain of secrets passed down to her from previous generations. Though she could almost pass for in her late thirties, her oddities gave her away. She was old despite her youth; she was young despite her age.

She took a sip from her cup, slowly. Odys noticed her hands shake—a tremble.

Odys could barely make out Bob's figure through the blinds. Half of her body was cut off by the ledge. He did, however, notice she slipped a few jolts from a thin flask into her newly-poured tea. He smiled, though he didn't mean to. He saw Maud studying her nails. But back to Mother.

He wondered if he should say something first? Perhaps a hello? No, he didn't want to seem in a hurry.

"I suppose," Gwen finally began, "you'd like to know where you are?"

"You don't have to tell me, if it puts you in danger."

Still looking out the window, she said, "Dear boy, what makes you think we're in danger? Perhaps all this"—she waved her hand—"was to protect *you* more than me?" Odys doubted that, and hated the mind games.

"Oh, of course it isn't true. I tend to protect myself *to* protect my children." She sighed, wrapping both hands around her tea.

Odys noticed a silver wedding band on her ring finger. It made him conscious of the one on his own. He stuffed that hand in his pocket.

"Yet..." she said as she studied her tea. The steam rose to her face and she breathed it in like a priestess inhaling sacred smoke. "I do want to protect you, Odys." She adjusted her sweater.

Her draping, ruffled attire gave her the dearness of a Catholic nun, though the bright colors and Mesoamerican patterns gave her all the flair of a village _bruja_.

She compressed her grape-colored lips into a thoughtful frown. Her dark lids blinked more than was natural, batting things away, keeping tears locked behind those feathery lashes. Odys wished those eyes would land.

"Ansi says you smell like smoke. Automatons have good noses." She tapped her nose. "You smoke?"

"Cigarettes, yes," Odys nodded, overly enthusiastic.

"Ansi also says you like to stare at him," a laugh behind her voice—a laugh at an inside joke. "He appreciates the attention, I assure you." She leaned to her Automaton. Anselm reached up and covered her hand with his. She continued staring out the window. "He is a very vain man, I tell you."

Man?

Dear little Ansi kept his gaze on Odys. The tiny freak still hadn't blinked. Was he working hard at sending chills down Odys's spine? For some reason, Odys got the impression Gwen wasn't _making_ him do it. It just came naturally. Gwen didn't seem the type to toy with people in such drawn-out ways. Even if a ghost smiles at you, it's no less unnerving to know it's a ghost.[53]

"Anselm likes to be admired. And I like it when people admire him," Gwen added, more for herself. Though she faced one direction, her starry eyes never rested. They darted around their focus, never giving whole attention—as if parts of the foci were too bright and made her eyes water.

"And I am just as vain as he, if only in a different way. I am vain in the fact I flaunt my children—the Masters and Automatons I love. They are, perhaps, the only reason I haven't given up yet. Unlike Pepin. I'm selfish to want to stay with them. To fix this—this problem."

Which problem?

"I smoke a pipe," she confessed—her topic spurts didn't seem out of character, her speech as fluttery as her eyes. "Ansi introduced me to it. Our addictions used to be black tea with milk, warm baths, and…stew. Homemade, of course. Funny, how addictions can be replaced. I smoke only in the evenings, but I delight in it more than other habits now. My, Maud is covered more than usual. It's usually like trying to keep a hat on a cat with her and clothes. She just can't do it. It takes too much. That's how she was designed. But you like her modest, I hear?"

---

[53] Or, maybe an old woman in the body of a young child is just creepy in itself.

News got around too quickly—another reason Odys hated cell phones.

"I do hope Bob wasn't too rough with you." A subtle wrinkle appeared between her thick eyebrows. She put a hand on her chest. Skinny and far from well-endowed, Mother's flat chest made her appear younger.

She would have looked more refined with salty flecks in her great mass of fine-velvet hair; Odys suspected those lighter roots meant she dyed it. But despite her touch-ups, she was a dashing woman—gentle, reserved. Her thick hair lent the perfect equalizer to her prominent forehead and large eyes.

Let me repeat myself/paint the imagery thick:

While her overall appearance screamed loud octaves of bright Frida-Kahlo colors, she was also in tune with a symphony of muted Virgin-of-Guadalupe mildness. To be unoriginal: She was a woman who aged like wine. Yes, she could be summed up so easily—so *clichély*. It's what made her so approachable. So adored.[54]

"Dorian called before you arrived. Said Bob may have scared you. Cestus, I'm afraid, got all her tender spirit and she was left with the churning contempt. She wasn't always this way. None of us were. She's less spiteful when she's drunk, though." Mother's eyes glistened with dewy tears, about to weep. She quickly changed the subject, "Did Maud tell you how Automatons got their title? I ask because Dorian says you don't seem to know much."

"No," Odys answered, half curious and half reluctant. He put his hands deeper in his pockets. He still hadn't sat down/she still hadn't invited him to.

Mother sighed, looking up at the ceiling. She gestured to nothing. Her prayer to Vulcan a whisper, "You want me to tell him everything—the back story? You want me to do the work for You? Making him sync with Maud would be easier and quicker for everyone!"[55]

She mumbled in Spanish before sighing and accepting her duty.

"We gave them their name. Pepin and I. Calling them 'robots' or something else just didn't fit. 'Automaton' is somehow more respectful. And the term 'humanoid' makes them seem like— like aliens or scientific experiments…"

She paused to remember where she was going with this tangent—this monologue. She was putting on a play—something she'd often recited to herself. She had expected this moment. She knew exactly what she needed to say—if only she could remember.

---

[54] I don't particularly find her loveable. She cries too much and talks too much and touches Anselm/herself too much (ha, ha).
[55] But we, as readers, would be so left out!

"Hefesto—Vulcan, excuse me—had named them something else. 'Guarders.' That's what he called them—at least, in English. Though, that word itself is archaic and we'd now translate it to 'Guardians,' I guess. Even the Automatons found that title too silly for modern standards. Vulcan hasn't complained about our name change, so he must understand language's evolution." To herself, "At least he understands *that*."

She shook her head, clearing her thoughts. "'Automaton' proved suitable. These alloyed creatures cannot wield themselves, so *Automaton* just makes more sense. You only need to wind them up once for their gears to turn on their own."

Anselm stood up, knocking over a few pillows. He didn't care to pick them up. He stepped to the other side of Gwendolyn, eyes never leaving Odys. He brought her hand to his cheek, his lips almost brushing it.

"I do wish you'd stop, Anselm. Stop looking at him; it upsets me, you know," an instantaneous response to a provoked thought. "Stop staring at him, I don't want to see his face, not yet." So hard to block Odys out. She patted Anselm's face away, but he did not budge. "Stop tempting me."

Anselm blinked and turned his head away, as if Gwen finally agreed with herself that she didn't want to see Odys. The wall would now be Anselm's focus. Mother's soul would stifle her own bipolar curiosity.

"Sometimes I can't help myself," she choked out a laugh, eyes dancing at Odys's feet. Though she laughed, she dabbed her eye. "As you may or may not know, Odys, the Automatons have an expansive memory. They knew each other from their creation. Thankfully, that's something no Master has forced any of them to forget. I assume Vulcan gave them a memory because he wanted them to recognize each other. Vulcan, who has been known to stick his nose in our affairs, created nine Automatons. Yet, nine is not the perfect number, is it?"

Though the number was *odd*, Odys actually had nothing against it. Nine divided by three equaled three. Nine minus three equaled six. Turn six over and it would be nine. Nine was just an upside-down six. It wasn't the *worst* of the odd numbers. But yes, why nine? Why was that number important?[56]

---

[56] I don't really get why it's so important that there be an even number, unless our Narrator is just as OCD as Odys or assumes Vulcan is too. Or, maybe the point is really about the "holiness" of the number nine. I don't know. I leave it up to your interpretation (one more reason to release this story upon the world—to help me better understand BLA, if it can be done). However, I did find in my research that every year on the island of Lemnos fires were extinguished in Hephaestus's honor and would not be reignited for nine days. It takes nine to purify, I guess? But enough of my conspiracy theories.

"That's because there are actually ten—ten *creations*. Except the first was…"

"A failure." Anselm finished the sentence for her. His voice as haunting as his looks. Odys wasn't sure he'd really spoken.

"A god failed in their plans?" Odys asked. It sounded illogical. Impossible.

"No," Gwen corrected, "Vulcan himself didn't fail. The first *creation* failed. The very first Automaton was no Automaton at all. Granted, there have been many creations much like Automatons in the past—beings also made by Vulcan. But *these* automaton-Automatons were created for a specific reason." She gestured to Anselm. "As the Automatons will tell you, their First needed no human soul to function. And, since it needed nothing, it had free will. Vulcan created it for a purpose and *it* chose not to do it. It failed. Thus, he made nine more creations. Automatons. Beings that lacked the wind-up key."

Nine more problems, some might say.

He felt the urge to ask, "And what was the First creation's purpose?"

"To protect mankind. To be good. To…" Pause. "Well, perhaps I should no answer for de gods"—her old accent slipped through in her distress. "We still don't know whether or not Vulcan made *them* on his own volition or under higher orders. Either way, he did so willingly— he *did* it. The First's origination had no true evil intention behind it. Vulcan has always appeared—to me—to be the type to do *the will* of the Universe—to do 'good.'"

But she didn't seem at peace with Vulcan's harmony…

"The nine Automata were created to take down the First." Her eyes narrowed in thought exactly when Anselm's did too. "And the first re-cast—the first of the nine Automatons, not *the* First—was Admund—the creation you thought was your father, Odys. Vulcan designed him before the others. I want you to know this." She paused, biting her lip. "He was a first draft—the one with the most convoluted ideas behind him. Besides the First, of course. He was not yet simplified like the other Automata. Vulcan's idea was *grand*. That is why Admund is grand."[57]

She bowed her head, sickened to make excuses for Admund and his Master. "As El Herrero—the Blacksmith—went down the line, the Automata-idea became more *practical*. Practical as a paperclip or coin. Given to humans, they served their predestined purpose. The First was greater than a single Automaton, I hear. That's why Vulcan needed nine."

"Could the god not take down his creation himself?"

Anselm's head snapped in his direction. "Did he not?"

---

[57] Admund's inanimate form is an iron stylus. Cestus is a safety pin. Anselm's, a broken compact. Q's, a hat pin (or, "bobby" pin). I edited out mentions of this because it was so easily summed up here.

"What he means is," translated Gwen, "didn't he *solve* the problem by creating the others?" Maud's voice ran through Odys's head. *Hand of God, Hand of God, Hand of God.*

Gwen went on, "Who are you to question Vulcan's methods? A man has sex with a woman and creates a child, yet when the child grows up and becomes evil, can the parent simply kill their offspring? No, there are laws that bind the parent—moral and governmental. Who are we to even understand the laws that bind the gods?"

"Do we trust Vulcan blindly, then?" Odys laughed, to see how she'd react. He instantly regretted being so bold. *She didn't deserve that.*

"You are not blind, Odys Odelyn. You are yet to open your eyes." She moved away from the window to sit down on the built-in furniture. Anselm stood beside her, leaning against the seat, hand on her leg. He conducted himself like a man. He caressed her knee in a protective and almost controlling way, as if she were *his.*

"Speaking of opening eyes," Gwen went on "When will you open yourself to Maud? According to Dorian's updates, you're suicidal."

"I'm not," he said too quickly. He took in a deep breath. "I'm not suicidal."

"That's good, then." She took a sip of tea. "Dorian also said you were *brown.* Is that correct?" She waited. "Ah, I've confused you. Dorian can see people's favorite colors. I assumed he would have dropped that bomb by now. Dorian says my color is a red-purple. He wasn't blind before he gained Fletcher, yes? Some say when you lose one body part the others take over or adapt. He can now see colors—auras. We think Fletcher helped such an adaptation, but the fact remains he's *always* right."

Your color doesn't mix well with others.

"How did he go blind? Don't Automatons protect us from harm?"

Mother flinched. "Did you learn nothing from Pepin's suicide, Odys?" She waved it away. "Forget I said it. Let me finish with my other *historia*—the history of Automata. You've not heard it, correct?"

He shook his head. "I don't know any of this. Maud hasn't told me."

"She shouldn't have to."

So Mother was testing him—testing his acceptance of Maud—as if he should know everything Maud knew by now.

"Where was I? Ah, the nine. Yes, they took down the First. And that was that. I'm sure Maud can present you with the full details if you're still curious. Verbally, of course." She frowned in his direction. "But my point is, Odys, the Automatons served their purpose. It was up to humans to decide their new one. When the first Masters left with their Automatons, fate took its course. The Masters went on with their lives. The Automatons trickled down the timeline into the present era. The Automatons were scattered."

She took in a breath, remembering. "So many lives and ages. Just because a Master can live longer does not mean life is certain. Not only have Masters killed each other before—from the beginning—but Automatons can only protect your body from so much. You can still catch a cold, you know. Sometimes it's nice to be sick. It reminds you that you're still human. Many a Master has been killed by his own body. Cancer, obesity, disease, suicide. You are not immortal if you don't want to be. Sometimes sickness is suicide."

She glanced at him—at his *direction*, not him. She wondered how he would react to her last comment. She wanted to know *how* suicidal he was.

I'm NOT suicidal, he thought at her.

She adjusted Anselm's clothing—his skin. "You'd be surprised how many Masters Automatons have had. Long life should mean few Masters for an Automaton, yes? But no. Ah, enough of death. As I said, the Automatons were scattered. Not even *they* knew the whereabouts of their brothers and sisters. It's not like we could put out an ad in the paper. We've tracked down their history, of course—we know what Automaton has been where. If they ever forget—if they are ever *forced* to forget—they can relearn it and put their history back together by talking to another. Fill in the blanks."

She sipped her tea. Her eyes had been dancing around him, absorbing everything but his face. "I wasn't always the oldest Master, you know."

"Pepin, yes," Odys stated, glad he finally related to this speech somehow.

"No," Gwen killed his hope. "Not Pepin, dear. He and I might have stumbled across each other in [some Victorian-era date year here], but that hardly made us the oldest. We were the ones to track down everyone. Or to begin to, at least. Once we started, we had the help of the others. And no, it wasn't easy convincing everyone to rearrange their lifestyle. Automatons are hard enough to accommodate..."

"Yes, we found Masters older than ourselves. Of course, some died and we relocated the Automatons to suitable new Masters. Poor Cestus, when we first met him, his Master was two hundred and thirty nine years and—oh—" (her eyes went up in thought) "four months, two weeks and six days old, I believe—that's what *Ansi* believes. If that's wrong, I have the date written down somewhere, of course, but..."

She flashed her eyes in Odys's direction, quizzing him, wondering if he was doing the math (and, if he was, was he comparing it to something he *already* knew?).

How could he know? Why shouldn't he know? Why wouldn't he know?

What do you know, Odys?

Nothing, you idiot, because you haven't synced with Maud.

"But you see, when that Master had touched Cestus, he was in his eighties. He was already so old. The age we look now depends on when we first touched our Automatons. That, and several other factors." She looked at Anselm for a brief second. "There was also one Master, God bless her soul; she tuckered out when the cancer struck—well, we think the cancer was inside her before she touched her Automaton. She also caught a cold and it finished her off. We think she wanted it to. She wasn't alive when the whole group finally organized. Such a shame," she dabbed her eyes as Anselm soothed her. "Arranging Masters is emotional work. And it asks much of the Master—for they cannot *really* agree to what they're getting into. Not until they have the Automaton is it obvious what kind of burden they are. Thankfully,"—her voice cracked a little—"we don't have to do it often."

Especially when Pepin does it for you.

Gwen was staring at the floor now. "As you might have noticed, Odys, we have rules. And we're a family. Like it or not, you're figuratively married to Maud, now. And we don't like the fact it was done—how do you say it?—in Vegas."

"Shotgun wedding," Anselm whispered to her, cutting eyes at Odys.

"Yes, the worst kind of arrangements. The family wasn't there. The family didn't sanctify it—bless it."

"But I was forced to marry," Odys pleaded—as if he agreed with the allusion.

"An *arranged* marriage." Anselm nodded once in agreement. "And yet, still so much like a raping of our daughter."

Odys wondered if Anselm had ever talked so much.

Gwen shifted her legs, a physical manifestation of her mental shift. "I have decided an introduction to our founding ground-rules might be a good way to start off." So things hadn't really started, huh? "Also, your reaction to said rules will be a perfect way to judge your character, I think."

FIRST RULE ABOUT AUTOMATON CLUB.

"Rules: number one," Gwen began, as if reading from a piece of paper floating in the air. "One and only one Automaton. If you get more than one, we even you out. You see, we'd rather not learn what would happen if all Automatons were bonded to one soul—one Master. Two heads are better than one, they say—but more than that is reserved for the divine."

A picture of a many-armed and many-headed Vishnu or Shiva or So-on shuffled through Odys's mind like a deck of Hindu cards. *That's what Leeland will be if he keeps at it,* he thought to himself with a gulp.[58]

"As I'm sure you know," Mother went on, "Leeland broke this rule but is yet to be punished. Punishment is easier said than done, yes. But remember we do have leverage on *you.* You cannot become like Leeland. We won't let you. We've learned from our mistake.

"Rule number two: Let no outsider know about us. If Odissa finds out, that is one thing. It is another for her to know *too* much and for that knowledge to pervade the world. If we can trust her, fine. But we'll only trust her with so much. If she slips—even once—she will have to be quieted. You understand?"

He didn't delight in hearing those words, and she didn't delight in speaking them. He could almost see the water-works forming; she wore her heart outwardly.

He refused to answer her.

Unable to look in his direction, she glanced at her lap. Anselm kept eye contact for her. "Just think of what would happen, Odys, if the government found out. We've had to erase many things, in the past. We take no pleasure in it, and it gets harder each time."

"Then why not let the world know?" Maybe if she had left Odissa off her list he wouldn't be so defensive but…"Wouldn't it make this world better, if you did? People would—would flock to you. Who could—could interfere with you? Wouldn't it be *easier*? What do you risk, if you're found out? You can't die. You could do so much."

Gwen helped herself to a moment's breath; she was taking time to unburden herself. "Sí, I've wondered if the world had the right to know. Perhaps it does. However, we're not the only things hiding, are we? Ah, you don't know what I mean. But someday, you will. You will learn that Vulcan himself hides."

"But Vulcan has reason to."

Anselm chuckled behind his Master.

"What reason?" Gwen smiled a curious smile.

"The same as God's?"

---

[58] Personally, I thought of Lord Voldemort and the Horcruxes, with Leeland's soul split into so many parts.

"So you're saying He wants people to believe with faith? Where did you get that revelation, Odys?"

"I only thought—"

"I can see why you'd think it—as if all the gods want us to believe without seeing? Ah, Odys. That's not so. Even I've seen Vulcan and need no faith to believe in him. And he doesn't want or need my faith. Some gods, I assume, don't even want to be *believed* in. For sure, they conceal themselves for many reasons, but answer this. Odys, will you—right now—step into the light and show the world what you have? Would you *really* tell them you have an Automaton, even show them what Maud can do?"

"Probably not."

"Exactly. We don't want that attention. We don't know if it's right to expose ourselves and therefore the others like us by default. Once it's done, it can't be undone. Thus, as a general rule, we won't overstep our bounds. That's merely the first reason why. Number three," she held up three fingers. "Kill no one you don't have to. Even if Odissa finds out, we may let her live. We'll take great pains to keep people alive. But if it becomes more than pangs, we mustn't die for them. The gods have entrusted us with these secrets. And we will keep them."

She opened her mouth, about to explain those statements. "When—when I first gained Anselm, it—it wasn't easy. To hide him was easy, but to keep myself hidden wasn't. I could run from my family, but they could always catch up. They...*suspected*. You act differently when your soul's outside you—when there is *more* to you. It is not simply a matter of pretending. It's a matter of remembering which lie goes where. And sometimes you say things others don't understand. You know what your Automaton knows—things humans cannot comprehend."

Odys understood. For one, he knew that Augury was Leeland. His sister didn't know that. He understood how it'd be easy to slip up.

"The fourth rule is: spend wisely. Use fake names, cover your tracks, be seen as little as possible. Remember your every step lest it cost you later. For certain, the world would love—absolutely—your Automaton's ability to make gold, wouldn't it? Ah, to be adored for your ability to create national riches! But what would riches be, if gold became so available? What's gold, but one of the weakest metals? Even coal can be burned for warmth, but what can gold do?"

She pulled at her golden cross necklace, as if it cursed her for saying such things. "Rule number five: treat your Automaton fairly. Do not abuse them. However, I feel I needn't stress this point with you—someone who refuses to *use* your Automaton in the first place. Number six." She paused, trying to remember.

In part, these rules seemed arbitrary. This shocked Odys—and he wasn't sure why. Were they not handed down on stone tablets? Not inscribed by Vulcan himself?

"You must be ready to defend this family. We don't just sit around, enjoying long life. We sometimes meddle, when we can. Gold can go a long way, but it cannot solve this world's problems." She paused, trying to give an example. "Dorian, God bless him, walked into a burning house once—saved two children and a dog. Needless to say, everyone watching saw his face— and Fletcher's. They wished to make them heroes. Not a scratch on them, of course. When things like that happen, we try to pass as..." She blushed, as if she had just thought something religiously irreverent. "The Automatons are better at it, at passing for angels. They are so beautiful, aren't they?"

Angels? Hm. Anselm here was more like a creepy diablito.

"Angels! That brings back memories, doesn't it, Ansi?" She asked him as if he might help her remember.[59]

"For a time, I didn't accept Ansi. Though he told me what he was—*proved* his abilities—it was hard for me to believe he was also a *part* of me. He was like a genie to me. Just some slave and external facet bound to me, not my own *soul*. At first sight, I thought he was an angel, the way he reflected light..." She smiled to herself, reminiscing. "That's not to say I didn't—as we say today—*sync* with him. Oh, yes, I did that. I was much too young to realize I could choose *not* to."

Again, it seemed like she was scolding Odys.

She breathed in deeply, the fluttering gasp her prayer. "In *Nueva España*—New Spain— when I found Ansi, my family was fairly well off. For that time, we might be considered upper middle-class. We owned one of the largest ranchos in the area. My father had great plans and hoped I would help in reaching them. He wanted me to marry his—you might say—*business partner*, a man with large ties to those who would usher in the Mexican Empire. My mother just wanted me to marry *period*. Needless to say, I didn't delight in the arranged planning—I even begged to become a nun. I stole one of my father's horses and ran," she added with mirth.

Anselm watched him, making sure Maud hadn't told him any of this; Mother didn't want to re-tell old news.

---

[59] Prepare yourself, reader, you're about to get an origin story you didn't ask for. If you don't care how Gwen ended up with Anselm (because no one expects you to have a hard-on for Gwen's past like BLA), go ahead and skip to the stanza titled: BACK UP THE BACK STORY. Otherwise, my apologies for being unable to chop this obligatory info-dump out...But at least it's not a fucking flashback. We draw the line somewhere.

"I headed north with nothing but a bag of clothes and a gun. No money. I did not get too far that night. I couldn't see a damn thing—except for an old well overrun with weeds. I found it from memory. I slept there that night. That morning, I had let down the bucket to try and draw my horse a drink and I noticed something at the bottom—under the rocks of the well's crumbling wall. The sun hit it just right, otherwise I wouldn't have seen it. There was barely any water in the well. That's why it had been abandoned. The rope was too short—it wouldn't let the bucket scrape the bottom. Someone had dropped the object there purposefully—purposefully out of reach." She was looking at it now. She was re-observing her own history. Anselm had recorded every antique detail in their brain. "I knew I would need water—for me and my horse. But I also knew I needed money. Whatever was down there was precious metal—or worth a meal, at least. At first I thought it might be a pocket watch. I tore my dress and made the rope longer. It took me hours to fish him out of the murky bottom.

"Later, Ansi would tell me his previous Master had left him there, knowing he could come back for him. He'd hidden Ansi there, away from his fellows. Those fellows had started to question the horse-breaker's surprising vitality against the horses' bucking and bruising—and also the man's astounding collection of golden-cast objects."

"The man, of course, had refused to do rocks," Anselm chided. "To do so would make others think he'd struck gold somewhere—on someone else's land. Too much attention. If his objects had a shape, they were less likely to think he'd found it from the ground. Granted, people started thinking he had stolen the objects. He also had a terrible gambling problem. I was used to repay a hefty amount of debt."

"Needless to say, he wasn't the wisest Master Ansi's ever had. Automatons can only enlighten so much. Sometimes sin clouds the light."

"He rarely let me out of his pockets. Too drunk to remember where he'd even put me, sometimes."

"That's how he'd died, by the way," Gwen added. "He'd hidden Ansi from the eyes of others, only to swear off drinking and die of liver failure two days later. That's what we assume he died of, anyway. His distance from Ansi likely worsened the impact of withdrawal. He killed himself, basically, in that way."

"He wanted to die, though," Anselm stated. "He knew he wasn't smart enough to keep up his game with me.[60] The other ranch hands had planned on killing him, in fact. Of course, that would not have worked. *They* couldn't have killed him. But he was in love with one of the other men on the ranch. The fact that his friend actually hated him had caused much heartbreak. He didn't have me long at all."

Mother wished to distract Odys from Anselm's emotionless explanation: "Ansi's Master before him was—"

Odys guessed she'd say a bullfighter. He quickly told himself not to be a racist like Pepin.

"Well, perhaps I should start farther back."

Anselm, she explained, had been brought over with *los conquistadores*, and sailed on the [name redacted].

A passenger had kept the pocket mirror a secret, but the secret hadn't done him much good: He had struggled to keep Anselm in his inanimate form while with his comrades—never really sleeping on the ship or on land. One night, natives attacked. Anselm's conquistador-Master took it as an opportunity to abandon the others and create his ordained city of gold. He would use Anselm to not only record his name in history, but to raise it up: The natives would worship him as a god and the Spanish Empire would honor him with a title. He had no modest plans.

But the man soon became lost. He had lost all possible contact with his fellow explorers. Glory would mean nothing if no one recognized him. The heat and loneliness drove him mad. He fell ill and died in the forest, assuming he alone survived the natives' attack. He had *let* the fever take him—suicide.

Not even an Automaton is much good in a new world; Anselm hadn't known where they were. Anselm was no help. An Automaton only knows what it has been taught, what it has observed.

Thus, Anselm, in his inanimate form, rested beside the skeleton of his former Master for many years, waiting to be touched again. The forest flora had consumed him and the decaying body.

Anselm was inanimate until a native, who had been recently banished from his Aztec city for unmentionable reasons, tripped over the remains and landed on Anselm. The older Aztec had no real use for the gold Anselm could make, since it was the excrement of the gods. But nevertheless,

---

[60] And an Automaton is only as smart as the Master allows. If the Master is too stupid to realize what power they hold, of course there is not much hope for him.

he found a companion in him. Anselm had to calmly explain (in the man's own tongue) that no, he was not a god, though one made him, and so on and so forth.[61]

The man contemplated using Anselm as a weapon to re-enter his civilization by force, perhaps to even become king. However, on the long journey back to the man's homestead, he fell ill. And died.

"Most likely from previous tooth decay, poor nutrition, and a newly-touched Automaton sucking most of his energy." Anselm could remember the pain, as well as the location of the death. "He was already so pitiful—a reason he had been banished in the first place. Always complaining. Always begging. But at least he died with such new ideas and hope."

"The corn got them every time," Gwen added, mournful for those who came before her. She pointed to her teeth. "But that brings us back to square one. The horse-breaker discovered Ansi when he was running from a town he'd just robbed with his band. They were trying to make their way to Brazil—running from the law. They had hidden in the cave the Aztec had crawled into to die. The others left him behind when the horse-breaker fell ill after touching Anselm. They left him beside the Aztec's skeleton. He found his way to a Mexican rancho instead."

Anselm had terrible luck in Masters apparently.

"I had slept in that well for almost a week," Anselm went on, sitting beside Mother in the open seat, "as my Master had commanded. I waited for him to either return or call me to him. The strain of our distance *promoted* his unexpected death. Liver failure might not have been such an issue otherwise." He told his story with little sentiment.

"Thus, Ansi was mine. But I did not get past the well that day. As you know well, Odys, I fell ill instantly, my consciousness becoming aware of my soul—aware of my necessary need for the thing *taken* out of me. The workers of the land I was on eventually saw my horse and discovered me. Ansi hid. My parents were soon contacted, for my family was well-known. I was taken back home. The doctor examined me. I was bedridden with 'unknown sickness.' Privately, I heard the doctor whisper to my father that it could be the stress he was putting upon me. I could hear my mother begging him to change his mind..."

She paused, gathering her thoughts. "It was in the dead of night that I learned the truth of my illness—the first time I saw my Ansi. It had taken a lot out of us, for him to journey to me."

Too weak to stay formed for long, I might add.

---

[61] An Automaton, who knows the thoughts of his or her Master, also knows their language automatically, I would assume. This is how they collect languages.

125

"He had to be quiet—unseen. I was fifteen then.[62] Ansi told me of the others out there. He told me of things I'd never been taught. He opened my mind, as Maud could do for you. His memories—what he had of them—were given to me. I became changed, enlightened. My parents did not like me talking about my new dreams—the dreams Ansi had helped me acquire. Dreams of Spaniards and Aztecs and gods. When I was well again, they locked me in my room—my punishment for trying to running away…But, of course, Ansi could help me escape. Which is what happened." Her lips parted in merry smile. "They had kept me in there for over a month. They could hear me talking in my room, to Ansi. I wanted them to hear—to let them think I was talking to the divine. In a way, I was. He was my angel."

Anselm reached out and put a hand upon Gwen's. He didn't care if Odys noticed. "But, once I was free from my family, I made a life of my own—*our* own. We never needed anything. It was easier back then to do as you pleased—to drift and wonder. You think I would have stood out, coming to the United States with Ansi. But things could be stranger back then. Ah, back then. It was so much easier to cheat and lie and be forgotten. Now we need papers, cards, licenses, codes, passwords—so many things to dance around. Ay, just listen to me! I sound like a grandmother in her rocking chair."

Pause.

"Ansi convinced me to attend university. I assumed a fake name here or there. Never got a degree, of course. I moved too many times. But, oh, I tell you! To learn for the sake of learning, that's a gift. School, of course, is easy, since your Automaton can remember everything you forget. Also, to observe the evolution of the university has been a show…

Stanza: Origin stories are so unORIGINal.

"For a time, it was just Ansi and me, in the Americas. We took many travels. We never stayed in the same place for long. It was upon one of our travels, sojourning in France, that we visited a circus. Ansi had learned the new French just so we could know our way around."[63]

Or rather, you made him learn it so you didn't have to? Lazy Mother!

"It was a traveling circus. It was no grand thing, but it turned out to be a *very* special display. As we sat in the stands, Ansi noticed two Automatons—two performers in the chaotic show. In the three rings were two Masters. Turns out, an 'American' owned the circus with his fellow

---

[62] Math tip: I've calculated that for every 100 years a Master has an Automaton it seems to age them about 10 physically. It checks out.

[63] New French. Opposed to, say, Norman French, Old French, What-have-you (which, perhaps, Anselm knew before coming to the Americas) (?).

French comrade. The American, of course, was not really American at all. It was Pepin. Granted, he had lived in Louisiana for a time before he moved back to England—long enough to perfect an accent. See, when his wife had left him, he'd taken Maud and traveled the world. He eventually ended up in France. There, he had *also* watched a traveling circus, just like me. Except *that* circus he hadn't co-owned. From that crowd, Maud and Pepin had spotted Fletcher. And Pepin found his true calling. The circus was the perfect place for them."

Odys pictured Maud in her tight suit, riding a horse, swinging from the trapeze, or—even better—as the bearded lady. If she could grow clothes then why not facial hair?

"Pepin and Fletcher's Master went into business together—bought out many circuses for a great sum, let the owners retire. Pepin took over magic tricks, and Maurice (the other Master), he dealt with, well, everything else. In a matter of years, though, Pepin got bored with it all, for a Master needn't work. Hobbies should never be work, yes? Eventually Maurice left, too. They gave away their circus for free, to a trusted family. However, it didn't have as much prestige when the Automatons and Masters left. No one could do their tricks or dare-devil stunts. The new owners hated that they didn't share their 'secrets.' Even our best intentions are spoiled, Odys."

She looked down at her pretty feet. She had a dignified way of rearranging them periodically. "Thus, Pepin, Maurice, and I began our travels together, finding the others. That was un circo all on its own. As Maud herself will tell you, the Automatons did most of the work. They knew the signs. They'd finally been given the proper chance to find each other. Once everyone was tracked down, that was hardly the solution to our problems. The next step was to find inheritors of our legacy, to set up a systematic order to our chaos. We decided the States would be where we'd base ourselves. After all, it's easy for those who stand out to blend in here. The melting pot of the world, America!"

And what was Vulcan melting down?

"But back to rule number six"—story time was over—"we have to relocate, when we overstep, though overstepping is not always bad in itself—as long as it does a good. Not even Jesus stayed in the world to heal all the sick. We all do what we came to do. I'm sure there are more rules, but I can't think of them now. We don't need to address them all just yet."

She flipped her wrist to glance her watch. "The rules only seem to make me tell long stories, anyway." She reached out and Anselm clutched her hand. With that simple gesture, Odys realized that, at one time, there hadn't been such a drastic physical age difference between them.

127

Stanza: BACK UP THE BACK STORY.[64]

"You said you had to find inheritors—earlier." Odys wanted her to clarify. *Is that what I was to Pepin?*

"We composed a list of worthy candidates, people we could trust." It sounded like an organ donor list. "Some died before we could make them one of us. Others, well, they're still alive, but might not want an Automaton if offered one, since they're so old already. We have to make hard decisions, Odys. Sometimes we are not fair." She sighed. "Others are young and don't know we have chosen them. And others, well, are like you. In by default."

"Who's on the list?"

She crossed herself, asking for forgiveness from those she could not save. "Ah, it doesn't matter. It's best not to know. Most will never get an Automaton. We will lose them as friends. Plus, Leeland would love to know those names, so I can't tell them to you."

"How does someone get on it?"

"We make them kill each other in a gladiator arena and drink the blood of virgins."

JUST KIDDING MOTHER NEVER SAID THAT JUST SEEING IF YOU WERE PAYING ATTENTION AND YOU WERE GOOD FOR YOU.[65]

"We vote on them, agree on them." She shrugged.

"And that's how Leeland got in?"

"Yes, yes. Democracy. Two wolves and a lamb deciding on what's for dinner."

Odys was confused. Was Leeland the lamb?

"At first, he *was* good." She had trouble admitting it; her eyes became glossy. "You see, Odys, he was kind, once. We all loved him. And he loved us. He loved us *too* much. I wished to become a nun in my frivolous youth. Ansi saved me from that choice. Leeland didn't understand this until later."

She noticed his quizzical stance. "Don't overthink it, Odys. You know exactly what I mean." She went on with her history. "For a time, there was little for us to worry about, though the First World War didn't make things easy. We kept a low profile. Pepin, though, bless him, went to fight—in *both*. When the second war came around, I kept Anselm well hidden in case they thought he was Japanese. He looks very Asian, no? It was during those wars that Leeland appeared in our lives. Pepin wrote to me about a young, orphaned Jewish boy from France he

---

[64] "No man chooses evil because it is evil, he only mistakes if for happiness, the good that he seeks." —Mary Wollstonecraft.
[65] Mental eye-roll. See what I have to put up with?

had befriended. Leeland later fought with Pepin in the second World War. Leeland worshiped Pepin. Such a bright boy. In a way, Leeland was Pepin's son. He let the boy ripen a bit before proposing that we give Leeland the next available Automaton. Leeland was part of the family…we liked to keep Automatons in the family. We hated hiding the truth from him."

She looked at Odys's hands, trying to say more without words.

He put those hands back in his pockets. "Will Odissa be part of the family?"

"Odys," she shook her head, "*You* aren't even part yet. But I hope you will be. It only seems fair, that she'd get an Automaton, doesn't it?" She smiled, hopeful. "It's not all up to me. I have to think of others. We don't even know how she'll react towards this."

"And you don't want another Leeland."

She bit her lip in response.

Anselm was glaring at Odys now. STOP TALKING ABOUT LEELAND. Don't make Mother/me cry.

"You must understand, Odys. Leeland was like a son to me, too. I *could* have been his mother, though that is not why I…"

Refused his advances.

"Leeland hated them, after he found out."

"Them?"

"The Automatons," she snapped. "Because of me, he hates them. Part of me hates them, too. Just look at what they've done to *your* life, Odys. In a matter of days, everything's changed for you. For us all.

"Leeland plans to eliminate all Masters so Automata won't be a problem for him—or the world—any longer. When we gave him Admund, he thought I wanted to live with him forever." From the corner of her eye, she noted Odys's reaction. "Like I said, don't overthink it."

She could see that he was, through Anselm. "Because of me, Leeland killed a Master named Rhett—Rhett Bernice Rouben. He was known as Bernice in our circles. That's how Leeland gained Coraza." She calmed herself a little. "Leeland threatened Bernice's last surviving daughter and her family if he didn't give himself up. His daughter, middle aged at that time, already thought her father was dead. He had faked his own death to avoid explaining his agerasia. But Bernice was a good man. Of course he gave up willingly—his daughter had a family of her own. We had a mess to clean up afterwards, but it was otherwise a clean job.

"We others had a choice to make. Either give up the last remaining lives that mattered to us, or give ourselves up and let Leeland win. He had something on all of us." *Had.*

She closed her eyes and breathed in. She needed to get back on target. "When this group was founded, we agreed to certain rules—to make things fair. Even Pepin Pound agreed to them. Enforced them, also. But with you, Odys, he broke them." Her brown eyes flashed up at him.

Upon looking at him—*finally* looking at him—her eyes welled up with tears.

Oh, GAWD. Bob was gonna kill him.

What'd he do?—what'd he do?!

Mother turned her dear face away, fingers on her mouth. Anselm retrieved a handy kerchief from his pant pocket, as if this were expected. He glared at Odys.

Look what you did to me.

"Oh, don't keep looking at him, Ansi," Mother whimpered between hiccup sounds. "You see, I cry far too easily. That's why I can't look at you. *Ay, mi dios!* He is such a nice young man, Ansi! Do you not see his kind eyes, Ansi? Look at his fear. It makes me so angry!" She pounded her knee with a fist. "So angry this happened to *him!*"

Anselm smoothed back her hair as she tried to collect herself. She seemed more upset at the fact she couldn't control her emotions. "Yes, yes, Gwendolyn. I like him too."

Huh? He did? An how did he treat the people he *didn't* like?

Anselm lifted her chin with his long-nailed fingers. "He must be going home now, Gwen. We don't want to make him late for his sister." His face was inches from hers, too close for Odys's comfort. "Best get to it."

She nodded, stood up, dabbed her nose again, and faced Odys. Though her eyes filled with new tears, she stood her ground:

"To the final reason you're here, Odys. You must understand the situation I am in. Pepin, though not a foe, was not the closest friend either. He wasn't being a hermit for retirement. He didn't *just* want privacy for privacy's sake. You see, there was a vacant Automaton. A great bout of evidence suggests Pepin did something with it. Before we could give it to the next person we all agreed upon, we realized it was out of our reach. Though Maud may know little about it—or perhaps nothing at all—Pepin may have given the Automaton to someone else—someone like you. Or, he has hidden it so well we cannot find him—it."

Pepin was so willing to give away Maud, how much easier would it be to give away an inanimate Automaton with no Master to kill off?

"Maud's said nothing," he assured her.

"So you see our situation."

"No, not really. How could Pepin get away with something like that?"

Were they not more careful?

Mother's chest swelled. She hadn't wanted to get into this. "When we are deciding on our next choice for a Master, someone must guard the inactive Automaton. That someone was Pepin. Granted, he had it in his 'protection' for many, many years. But, he'd always done it before. We trusted him. Also, let's just say that the group takes its time in picking. We are very careful. We'd only just agreed on our next choice and tried to contact Pepin when...we realized he'd cut off all contact with us. He avoided us. He hid from us. *Years* later, when we finally tracked him down..."

Her eyes met his once more.

Oh.

"Thus, you can see why we don't trust him. Though we have no precise proof he's done anything *bad* with the missing Automaton, he never told us where it is. It's discomforting to think where our Automaton might end up—or *has* ended up. What if the Automaton is in the hands of someone who cannot handle it—who might misuse it? And did they even agree to accept the burden? They would be like you, Odys. It is so unfair what we all must suffer through. I have always wished there were some way to end our endless cycle."

She dabbed her nose and glanced at a small clock on the wall. Her eyes seemed hesitant to observe it. Time was no worry to their kind, but it also gave little comfort. She wanted him to leave now.

"Gwen?"

"Call me Mother, if you like. Everyone else does."

He fought to form the word. "Mother, then. Do you know who my real parents are? How did Leeland come to have us—my sister and I—if we aren't his? Raised by his Automaton or not, does that mean we *can't* be his children?" He already knew one of the answers.

Gwen moved her eyes from him then closed them to hold back the tears. Hadn't Bob told him not to bring up Leeland? Why couldn't he control himself?

Because he felt entitled to know. He had the right to his own past.

"Though there is quite a lot we do suspect, Odys, it wouldn't be right to give you the information when it isn't certain. Not from me. Besides, the fact you have Maud—who can tell you just as much as *we* suspect—makes us wonder if we should take away motivation for syncing with her. You are killing yourself, Odys Odelyn. Like rejecting food, you reject Maud."

His face fell—how dare she know so much about him.

"But we will tell you, if you end up more than just a trick."

131

Odys nodded. He noticed Anselm was playing with a cell phone now, the glow not helping his creepy face.

"It is time for you to go, Odys," she said, like some Ms. Havisham around her stopped clocks. "This meeting went well—better than expected. You will see me again. In the meantime, keep your sister uninformed of our secrets. For her protection as well as ours."

She showed him to the door, opening it, letting the cold air attack. Before Odys was entirely out the door, he turned. "Why didn't Dorian tell me about the missing Automaton?" The question seemed to surprise her. "Did you tell him not to tell me?"

"No." Her voice was soft yet coaxing. "But maybe if you stopped rejecting Maud and accepted her fully, you would have known without being told, Odys. If Dorian did not tell you, it was merely because it didn't matter at the time. Why does this matter now?" She narrowed her eyes, curious.

"Because..." He paused, waiting for the answer. "I don't think Maud knew about— remembered—the missing Automaton. She would have told me, had she known. And—and she is now upset about it." He looked to Maud at the Ice Cream truck. "She didn't remember Pepin did this. I can almost feel it."

"So you're not reading her thoughts?" Mother asked, disappointed.

"Did Pepin give you an—an alibi?" he asked, as if trying to sort out the discomfort Maud made him feel. "Any excuse or reason why he wouldn't give it back?"

Mother's eyes smiled as she spoke, proud of Odys and his cleverness. Her attention darted from Odys to Maud near the ice cream truck. "No, he did not. That's why we have mixed feelings on the matter. We had hoped that if Pepin was innocent, he would have told us who had taken it, or why he was hording it. Either he kept silent because he was the criminal, or he could not tell us because—"

"He knew something you didn't?"

She nodded slowly. "Leeland is always very—how should I say it?—perceptive. If Pepin's silence was so Leeland would not hear, then Pepin was wise. However, that means he remained silent for us as well. Why wouldn't he give us the Automaton?"

"Why would he not, at the least, tell us that he *couldn't* tell us?" Anselm reminded them as he rubbed his eyes with the tips of his fingers.

"Forgive us, Odys, but my Automaton is my skeptical nature. I am grateful he took it from me. It suits him better. He is also sleepy. He sneezes out easily when tired—because he worries for me. And that is never safe for us. We also do not want you to be late. You want to beat your sister home, don't you?"

"I was surprised they found her."

"Ah, well, Automatons are crafty things." She tapped her nose, as if he should know what the action meant.

As he left, Gwendolyn Gwendy looked out her trailer window once more, parting the blinds with the hook of her finger. "He's so ill, Ansi."

"He's not suicidal," Anselm said as he took up his pipe once more. "Dorian is wrong about that."

"He's too kind to want Maud. That's it."

Anselm nodded. "That's why he is refusing her."

"He doesn't understand that it's actually wrong to fight against the inevitable."

Lighting his newly-stuffed pipe with a match, Anselm sucked in. "But Maud isn't the winter season that he can ignore until spring."

"He has such a kind face. He must truly hate all of this."

"He'll get used to it. Or else." He continued to scroll through their phone as he smoked.

"I don't want to have to kill him, Ansi. I don't."

Anselm removed the pipe from his lips. "But I won't let him harm us, Gwendolyn. I won't let him disturb what must be done. I won't. Just pray he does what's right and we won't have to."

"I think Dorian wanted him to be suicidal for that very reason. So that we wouldn't have to."

Stanza: The immortal mortal.

When Odys had left the trailer, he'd realized just how out of breath he'd been. Like an asthmatic, each step closer to Maud was a loosening of the intangible noose around his neck— fish plopping back into his bowl, his lungs relished Maud's relief. He didn't even notice Bob bitching about not being able to tell if mother had cried.

Odys couldn't wait to be locked back up in the ice cream truck so he could touch Maud without shame. He grabbed and held her hand to his head, repeating "Fuck, fuck, fuck," to himself as the truck started.

When he no longer felt like all the blood was rushing to his head, they sat back and had a little in-the-dark conversation I think you'll find interesting:

[...][66]

---

[66]Omitted to speed things along:

'"Aren't you going to ask me?"

Odys kept his eyes closed and thumped the back of his head on the metal wall. "Ask you what?"

"The questions. The questions you had about Gwen and Anselm. The ones you couldn't ask Mother."

"Isn't the fact you're bringing it up some form of me asking?" he stated. He still didn't like she could read his mind—that she was his mind. "So, like, she's in love with—in some sort of love with—" He cleared his throat. "Herself?"

"You picked up on that did you?" Maud laughed, but it wasn't funny. "She said she wanted to be a nun, didn't she? What is the self, if not an image of God?" Another laugh.

"However she wants to justify it, I suppose." He frowned at the statement, in no position to judge. "I just don't understand how she's so forgiving of Leeland. When she talked about him, she teared up as if she felt sorry for him."

"You can't blame him for wanting to solve a problem"—Maud knew she was a problem—"I only wish he had a different solution."

"Is that what he thinks it is? That's why he's killing everyone? Because Gwen won't fuck him?"

"Masters have killed each other for far dumber reasons than that, Odys."

Stoplight; the velocity made them shift in place.

"Just what was Vulcan thinking when he created Automatons?"

"Well, as you now know, he made us to take down the first. We called her Alpha. Well, she wasn't exactly female. All Automatons are, in some way, androgynous."

"I still don't see why he had to create Automatons to stop her."

"Alpha was...different. She had no inanimate form, though she could take on any object's shape. She was, perhaps, an advanced Automaton—a rough draft so complex that she needed to be chiseled down to fit within her format. That's what Vulcan did when He created us. We were her editors—editors to a story He wrote."

"How did you stop her, then?"

"In Admund—your father—Vulcan instilled what you might call innate knowledge of Alchemic sciences—which is where Leeland, perhaps, finds his prolific knowledge and skill in many areas, taking it from his Automaton like someone downloading an application."

Sounded like jacking into the Matrix.

"Don't get me wrong, we all brought something to the table. But Admund led us. With the help of the others, Admund and his Master stripped many of Alpha's principles down. We took away the physical. Made her, in some ways, dependent on a human soul and body."

She recounted this history as if she did not remember it—and perhaps she didn't anymore—but had been told what she'd forgotten.

"A willing vessel—a young temple girl—accepted the burden of housing Alpha inside her. We trapped Alpha in human form. In all actuality, you might say we turned Alpha into a ghost-spirit. That's how we put her inside the girl. Like a demon possessing a body, she was within. However, unlike a demon, she couldn't leave her vessel and died with it. She also didn't control the girl. The girl was still aware. She still was. We were thankful for that." Maud paused. "Alpha's life was bound to the girl's—dependent upon it. There was nothing left of her when the girl died. Her—or their, rather—grave is in [somewhere in Italy], as Vulcan ordered."

"If we're the hands of Vulcan, then he should wash His hands more often. I mean, why do you still exist? You've served your purpose. Alpha's gone. Why do we still need you? Why can't Vulcan take you away from us?"

"What need of evil has man? Yet it exists, Odys. Doesn't man himself—at least once—contemplate his own purpose? Yes, I wish I knew what Vulcan had in mind. This is far from the best of all possible situations."

She sighed. He sighed.

"Let me illustrate my statement with something: Various cultures all have their flood myths—the one that wiped out humanity. Noah, Gilgamesh, the like. Yet the Universe, when it recreated the world after that flood, still saved parts from the previous to re-purpose things, right? It's not uncommon for gods to use scraps. Even humans are scraps, Odys. Not just Automatons."

Scrap metal.

"We're not easily disposable. We *can* be repurposed. But you take my point. I won't go on with my questionable theodicy. There is ditheism to every god."

Driving, driving, driving.

They were silent for many miles.

"...And no, actually," Maud said, a joking chide in her tone, "I *wasn't* the Bearded Lady, thank you very much. I was the magician's Lovely Apprentice. I was also the sideshow to draw them into the tent. I had many jobs in *El Circo*."'

Stanza: Chimeras of man and metal.

Since Odys (and you) got a shit-ton of backstory from Mother just now, why not a little more? This next part should've been at the very beginning of the novel (but we knew you wouldn't notice it otherwise)/Book Intermission/This is the Prologue-thing:

Narrator's (not the Editor's) preface (Gabbler wants nothing to do with this part),

Aztec gold:

What's the price of your soul?[67]

The Muses can kiss my ass. Inspiration's done too much damage already—Gabbler suspects I'm insane. Yet Gabbler's still so interested in my story. Gabbler hopes I'm joking—only putting on a show (Gabbler has always liked my eccentricities).

For sure, I'll put on a show! Right after I get off my soapbox. This "Preface" is all Gabbler allowed me in terms of my *opinion*.

(This is what the epic has become, people).

The subject I'm writing about is typically captured in verse, not prose, so I'm not so sure the Muses would even answer my call if I "invoked" Them (which is how my predecessors went about things). Their silence—just like the rest of the gods'—is all the inspiration I need.

(Again, this is what the epic has become, people).

Now, you have the right to stop reading. I can't stop you from putting this book down. Even if I could, I wouldn't try. You either read or you don't. It's already been decided.

I could go into a long tangent over fate and destiny—how you were predestined to notice this book. But I won't. You wouldn't take me seriously. Gabbler doesn't take me seriously. Gabbler doesn't see things like I do, yet Gabbler loves me.

Am I being unclear? Let me start again:

Freedom. The gods want you to think you have it. Freedom enslaves you to Them. The gods use our freedoms against us. They manipulate us into thinking we have choices, that freedom has intrinsic value. But you always end up picking what They wanted you to pick. They can always use your choices for Their will. Always.

That's what happened to me. And it's happened to you.

Now, I'm sure I sound like some holier-than-thou psycho at this point, and I'll not correct you. Even Gabbler cringes when I put things so frankly. Gabbler says I should just tell the story,

---

[67] I tried to get our Narrator to *not* include this part. But they insisted. A compromise was putting it (inconveniently) here. Overall, I suppose it will give Automata (as characters) more context as well as formally introduce ourselves.

not convince you of anything. But then I tell Gabbler, *Shouldn't they know what the gods are doing to them?*

Now, it's not my objective to teach you life's elementary paradoxes, but someone needs to break it down for you: out of so many options, Fate's brought us together. You chose this book, yes. But why?

Your eyes follow each line accordingly. You might even turn the page—if I'm entertaining enough. Yes, yes, the gods took care of everything for me. I didn't even have to try.

And *of course* the gods would help. This story's too much fun for them—my irreverent comments included. Of course they'd let this story *happen*. They allowed you to notice this book and, for some reason, They allowed me to write it. This was Their plan all along—even the prose format and Gabbler's footnotes and this brazenly-inserted preface.

(This is what the epic has become, people).

Now let me give some back story—best to get it over with.

Cortés and his kind shouldn't have searched for El Dorado. It had been in Europe all along—a city of gold manifest in a being—a divine tool capable of creating more gold than a ship could carry—an alchemical slave who knows its creator-god's metallurgical secrets.

An Automaton.

Of course, those Spaniards had no way of knowing what complex fortune hid on board their ship, tucked away. How *could* they know that Ponce de León's Fountain of Youth isn't a fountain? They could not. And they would not.

Not if the Automaton's human Master had a say.

It doesn't matter what ship—or where—or when. It's best for you not to know. Gabbler thinks it'd only cause trouble. You'd start to really believe me, then. And *then* I'd have your free will completely—you'd have no choice but to believe. Gabbler says that name-dropping would only hurt my purposes. Gabbler says I mustn't frighten readers away. Gabbler says that even my lies are *faithful to the spirit of truth.*

See, Gabbler wants them to be lies, and I understand. I must pretend this is just "a story." Otherwise, Gabbler becomes impatient and shifty-eyed.

But as I was saying, a Spaniard brought the first Automaton over.

The rest of the smithy-god's creations took their time in arriving to the West's west. They had nothing but time—TICK TOCK! In this *time* they drew the attention of other gods.

Not just the Greco-Roman ones, no.

The Automata were in a new land.

The humans, who use their free will, had started moving all over the world. To and fro. If humans move, then Automata move. The gods watched anxiously. The gods of one place counseled with the gods of another. The gods knew the Automata—beings enslaved to humans—could likely cause a lot of problems if not inhibited. Humans could misuse them. They *did* misuse them.

But Hephaestus-Vulcan assured the Holy Ones They need not worry—do not worry!—worry not, Universe, for Automata will help mankind carry out Our will.

Their will be done!

And it was.

That is how this story actually begins—where I, your Narrator, fit in.

As you might have guessed, I'm omnipresent (which is good for Narrators to be, I see all sides). I wasn't always so ubiquitous, though Like Cortés (unfortunately), I am a god created out of nothing and someone history will rightfully scorn—a metamorphosis! Yes, yes, this is my apotheosis.

Really, this quasi-immortality is *the least* the gods could do, considering everything I suffered for them.

…This is why Gabbler thinks I'm mad.

You'll find out soon enough—sooner than I'd like—that I'm a character in this story. I've changed a lot since *then*, though. Divinity aside, I hardly recognize myself. Maybe that's a good thing. It's easier for Gabbler to doubt me, then.

Oh, how Gabbler doubts. Gabbler loves me too much to believe entirely. Gabbler is free from the truth. It makes me hope Gabbler's here willingly, despite knowing so much…

Dear Mortal-Gabbler didn't exactly like my participation in this story. Gabbler said I could've been a better character. Gabbler's right. Yet, Gabbler didn't disown me. Gabbler's my editor.[68]

Gabbler says I should establish my intent—my purpose—with this story. As if I claim one! Should I claim one? Gabbler says *That's what prefaces are for.* I'm not so sure. But fine. What's one more lie? It somehow proves my point. .

Thus, my intent is to make you question blind men.

---

[68]Among other things. I'm also part of this story's frame, apparently (though some might say I'm nothing but a footnote). I didn't have such a major role in our Narrator's first typed drafts. And yes, they are typed before I see them. The Narrator is a mute and cannot verbally tell me anything, so this is not dictation. I thank God for computers, otherwise, I'd know so little about our Narrator—god complex and all

Homer was blind. Milton was blind. I am mute.

What good is poetry to me if I cannot recite it? It gives me no joy. I can scarcely eat, let alone speak. Prose is further punishment for my self-inflicted sins. Only Gabbler dulls the pain. Gabbler's blind to it, my pain.

Yet we make a poetic pair.

Gabbler thinks I secretly wish to embellish pre-established myth. So be it. After all, an epic is the least pretentious effort a writer can attempt, right? Sure. But do notice: there's more than one reason I wanted two names tacked to this story (i.e. let's move this secondary shitpile to a primary worth respecting!).[69]

Ah, what else should I mention? Words, words, words! So many to choose from, yet you only need one: Freedom. Do we have it or not?

Let that be prefatory for now, Reader. In the meantime, let's get back to the story. The twins' lives are about to change forever. And, more or less, so is mine.[70]

Stanza: Enough introduction!

Now then, that Prologue [Foreword(s) and Preface] wasn't *so* bad was it? And besides, this story wouldn't fit within its "genre" without it. Gabbler said we should sell this as an urban fantasy. Don't most have them? Was ours just as vague and mysterious? I'm nothing if not formulaic.

---

[69] As in Primary vs. Secondary Epics.
[70] **Editor's foreword(s),**
Please use your free will to choose one of the following notes (but do read both, thanks): Which is for you?

Dear Prone to Believe,
As you can tell, this isn't my story. I'm only its Editor. My footnotes should help you tolerate the Narrator—someone very dear to me. I've changed names, locations, and facts to make the Narrator's story a treatise—a parable—an allegory—a myth. Because that's what it is to me. The Narrator has (hesitantly) allowed me to do this. See, with my overt participation, this is a story within a story—a lie within the truth. This way, no one expects you to believe it—especially the Narrator's Preface (above). But you can if you like. For sure, I don't believe Homer's version of history, but I do believe in his storytelling abilities.
—G.B. Gabbler
P.S. Someone needs to tell you not all Automata are wind-up toys. Even you are a machine.

Dear Prone to Doubt,
Like me, you may not take the Narrator seriously, but some parts you should admire. At the risk of sounding defensive: even Homer sang an urban fantasy for his day, and Virgil's propaganda was the first of eminent fanfiction. This "tradition" is how I tolerate my part in my lover's imagination. So if I play along, don't judge me. I have my reasons; I openly undermine my own authority—all relationships need compromise. Besides, lies make truth much more entertaining... Also, if you can't properly suspend your disbelief, then it's good this book began at Chapter One—ornate introductions like these don't help Doubters stomach the fantasy anyway (and I hate prologues just like the rest of you).
—G.B. Gabbler
P.S. A cyborg metaphor has more to do with changing the human soul than the human body.

Oh, and by the way, I forgot to mention above that if you *do* happen to notice any plot holes or typos or whateverthehellticksyouoff in this manuscript BLAME IT ON GABBLER, NOT ME. I can hardly be held responsible for mistakes Gabbler failed to notice.[71]

Stanza: Automatons are a perfect excuse for soliloquy.

Back at the apartment:

Fletcher cleared his throat. "My legs're sore."

"Stand up, then."

He did. He faced Dorian. "I'm bored. I need something to do. And something to chew. Something new. Can I go to the gas station at the corner?"

"We shouldn't leave." Though Dorian actually liked the idea.

"But I'm bored! And you feel too ugly for me to give you a BJ."

"I can't help it if I'm bloated from all that pizza. Besides. We already had enough outdoor fun when we put on the new door for this apartment."

"Com'on! You'll be fine on your own. I'll be five minutes. You know how fast I can run."

Dorian frowned, fighting with himself. "Go make some coffee or something."

Fletcher straddled Dorian and pet his hair. Dorian's soul didn't want more coffee. Not unless it was sugary and packed with calories. He begged again, "You know, if Leeland's waiting for us, then why not present him with an opportunity? It's better than just sitting here. Me leaving isn't something Leeland would expect." He leaned in to whisper, "Why would we do something so stupid?"

"Fine, then." Dorian gave into himself—that nagging Automaton. There was something recalcitrant inside Dorian. Fletcher manifested it. "But you better make this trip count."

Fletcher kissed his Master, lips still touching when he said, "As you wish!" And he flew out the door, forgetting to lock it behind him (not that the broken doorframe would do much to support a lock regardless). He'd turned out the lights, though. Dorian didn't need those.

The television cast blue waves over him.

(Cue uneasy silence).

Just as Dorian was about to zone out and start listening to the TV again, his phone distracted him.

Perfect timing.

---

[71] Sigh. You see my work is cut out for me.

He wished Fletcher were here to see the number. He couldn't see it. But something told him he already knew who it was. A smile spread across his lips as he answered it. It was no happy expression.

"Yes?" he said.

"Hello, Dorian," came that familiar Baroque voice—the voice that sent chills of irrational hate down Dorian's spine. No other voice could cause his laid-back back to become so tense. "I see the group is all astir. Something the matter?"

Dorian took a moment to formulate a rational response. "The gods have a way of letting you time things so *precisely*, Leeland."

"They must be on my side, then. But answer my question. Your answer will be part of my transition. You know I don't call unless there's a point. *What* has the family in such a fluster? Everyone moving—here and there. I can hardly keep tabs on you all."

"I think you know, Leeland," Dorian growled. The hairs on the back of his neck stood up. Do you see his fingers balling into a fist? I do.

"I may or may not know," Leeland agreed, satisfaction ringing through his coyness. "However, Coraza just told me Fletcher stepped outside. Her eyes are watching. You are a poor babysitter, Dorian. Your soul can't sit still for long."

Dorian said nothing, his face composed as he listened, apprehensive.

"Anyway, how's that old dog, Pepin? I haven't heard from him in a while, you know. Have you? Ah, I guess he's not talking to you lot either, then? He can be a pompous prick at times can't he? Or, should I say, *couldn't* he?" Leeland chuckled, fond of his own joke; his French accent, which he had learned to suppress, often showed itself through such forced speeches. "What? Too soon? Pepin wouldn't want us to be so serious. He'd want us to—to remember him fondly with laughter and—"

"How did you find out?"

"The nose knows, Dorian. Vulcan let Admund smell it. Admund's been watching the stars, Dorian. Don't you know they're aligning? The gods are plotting *us*, dear boy. We're the stars of their production."

"What's this call about then? If you want to kill me, come on in. Do it."

"You know that won't be necessary. Coraza is fine in her place. But by the look of things, you've practically invited her in. I'm sorry to say that I'll have to turn down the invitation. I can't give you what you want, Dorian. I can't."

"Then why bother making your Automaton watch us?" *Keep him talking, keep him talking,* Fletcher reminded Dorian.

"Because I need to know what you are up to I must make sure everything is falling into place."

"Aren't you afraid you'll spoil the fun by telling me you're planning something, Leeland?"

"Who said I was planning anything? Can't I call to check up on things, Dori? Can't I? After all, you are babysitting my children. Well, they're not *my* children. They're my Automaton's children."

"What do I have to do to get you to show your face, Leeland? Even if it's your Coraza-face, I'd still like to see it."

"Funny you would say that, Dorian. You can't really see anything. You're blind. Don't you remember I took your sight from you?"

"You didn't take it from me. I gave it to you."

"I'm glad you put it that way. I did not enjoy accepting it, even if it did buy you more time."

"I know how you like to play fair."

"But your eyes didn't buy *enough* time, did they? They still died because you couldn't figure out how to stop me. Well, that's not to say you didn't *know* how to stop me. You could have given me what I really wanted. But I was kind enough to let you all try. Was it worth the price though? Do you still like living—living as a blind man?"

Dorian considered it for a moment, fighting to keep his calm. "Maybe, if it caused you to save the twins."

"That is not why I 'adopted' them. Just because you took out your eyes, like I asked, does not mean I felt indebted to you. Admittedly, I thought you'd demand to know who the twins *really* are—demand proof. Yes, they are *exactly* who you think they are. I know you're not stupid."

It was odd to see Dorian's normally-stoic face so shadowed with emotion. His face cringed as if about to weep, but his voice didn't mirror it. "So you really want me to believe they're *those* twins?" He rubbed his mouth, trying to rub away his expression. "I'll not fall for it."

"Well, I suppose you are right, Dorian. I need to clarify. So go on. Ask me. Don't you want to be sure? *Beg* me for proof. I could find twins anywhere. You need to be sure."

But Dorian didn't beg.

"Come now, ask. You know you can't do a DNA test on them. You weren't related by blood."

141

(And Leeland wasn't stupid enough to leave their real family's bodies available for such things).

Dorian remained silent.

"You won't play along? But I thought that's what this was for you, Dorian. A game. You always had such a fun time playing with others' lives—gambling your eyes away. But moving on. What I can't make out is why Pepin gave Maud to my son. Or, excuse me, my semi-adopted son, on my Automaton's side. Maybe you can help me, Dorian:

"Did Pepin give Maud to Odys because I wouldn't harm him, my quasi-child, and therefore be unable to complete my so-called 'goal' at collecting every Automaton from you purposeless Masters? That would put a lot of faith on children I forced my Automaton to raise, though. Admund—Odi Odelyn, that is—never cared much for his duties. But that only comes with being *my* Automaton—I'm not the fathering type. Yes, yes, that does make Pepin out to be stupid, doesn't it? So, either Pepin was stupid or...he was on my side. Could it be that my philosophies finally won him over? Did he become sympathetic with my plight? Pepin did, after all, love me as a son, didn't he? That's why they gave me Admund in the first place, isn't it?

"Maybe Odys will be smarter than you were, Dorian. He won't give up everything just so he can keep his cursed Automaton."

His disappointment in Dorian's choices could not be missed.

"Now, I do want you to notice that Odissa just left me and I had *every* opportunity to use her against Odys—against *all* of you, potentially—right then and there. But I didn't. I let her go. She came so willingly to me, too. Odys might do something stupid if I don't let her go next time."

The line went dead.

Dorian was too preoccupied in calming himself to turn off his phone. Once done with that, he'd think about calling Mother. Mother needed to know he had finally made contact.

Just as he had opened his mouth to call Gwen (voice activated calling, you see), he heard something out in the apartment entry hall. He paused, listening, trying not to breathe. The doorknob twisted.

The door swung open with a slow creak—its reaction to a cautious tap. The person on the other side wasn't in a hurry to enter.

But who was it?

Well.

I hate to ruin a surprise (yes, it was meant to be a surprise—meant to be dragged out and BOMB-DROPPED), but let's be sure to side-step any plot holes here and instead remember we were recently introduced to Mecca and his truth-berding ways. Yes, yes. We can therefore safely assume this is Odissa—even though we're just as blird as Dorian at the moment. But Dorian, the poor dear, cannot *assume*. That's *dramatic irony* for you, if you did not know.[72]

If you didn't, now you do. You're welcome.[73]

But, THE POINT is don't be fooled. I've shared some of my omnipotent power with you so you can just sit back and enjoy the shit about to hit Dorian's fan:

See, to Dorian it could not be Fletcher, no, because Fletcher, right then, was at the cash register, paying for his gum and worrying about what his Master had just sensed. *That* Dorian could see. It wasn't Maud or Odys, no, because Bob would call when they had arrived. *That* was standard fucking procedure. It wasn't a neighbor, either, because those people usually knocked. *That* was just common courtesy. And, of course, it couldn't be Odissa, no, because Mecca had said she was still on her way in his last update. *That* left only one relevant option.

He was about to see one of Leeland's faces.

Yet, part of him questioned such a conclusion—but he brushed it aside. *Who else could it be? The cat? Cats can't open doors. Not even broken ones.*

The person on the other side no doubt found the unlocked door strange. Even Leeland understood the human penchant of locking doors.

Maybe Leeland was just toying with him Leeland was fond of using psychological measures to prove his points. From the genesis, Leeland's agenda didn't include outright killing. In fact, they hadn't seen pleasure in his eyes when he took his second Automaton. To be fair, Leeland hadn't *killed* anyone. Ever. He got *others* to do it for him—he got them to give up their own lives.

Let me rephrase:

Leeland didn't *enjoy* killing people. He simply wanted them to kill themselves.

This tactic had helped level the playing field—a playing field for a holy war Leeland had discovered—a war that not only God would approve, but Vulcan too. After all, Vulcan had let things line up so perfectly for Leeland. Leeland was a finger on the Vulcan-hand of God. This was the will of the Universe. Otherwise, it would not be so.

Now, since I've decided to go into a back-story during an edgy scene, I won't interrupt it much-much more. I will only say this: Leeland was miserable. Mother had made him that way. Mother's unnatural love for her precious, disgusting Anselm-self had been the final proof needed

---

[72] No, that's Mecca for you.
[73] BLA is very didactic. BLA loves to teach *me* things too. BLA can't help it. The god complex makes for one huge, patronizing issue I struggle against on a daily basis—and *I'm* the one with the graduate degree.

to define Automatons as evil. If one Automaton made a single person unhappy (such as himself), they were not worth their price. Not to Leeland. Without much more reasoning than that (for what more did he need?), Leeland decided to spare all humans of their unhappiness. He took it upon himself to cleanse the world. He would take on the burden of bearing all Automatons, for he was the most logical of them (clearly).

Dorian's mind raced forward, not to and fro. Though he doubted Coraza had come in to kill him, he wondered why Leeland would change his mind. Perhaps she thought she might not be heard coming in. Perhaps she was just coming to leave something for him. Perhaps she wanted to watch him beg for a death she would not give.

The door fully opened and he heard a footstep. You would never expect a blind man to move so quickly—jumping and pinning the enterer to the wall. It was a girl, yes. That much was certain. His crushing arm felt subtle breasts. It *was* Coraza. By God, it could be no other (else there's a major plot hole a-ripping, ha, ha).[74]

Dorian had expected her to submit this easily. That was how Leeland toyed with him.

"Why're you here?" Dorian demanded as he smashed "Coraza" into the wall.

A whimper.

A pretending sound—no less! He knew Leeland's games. The craven noise gripped his heart, which began his fury. He hated when Leeland fucked with him—when Masters used their Automatons as emotional puppets. That's why he'd acted so promptly. He didn't have time to second-guess himself. Not now. "Answer me!"

A small, frightened cry.

He didn't believe the sound; it teased him. "Not even going to fight me? Too much of a saint to kill me outright? What's he going to take this time? Both hands? Both feet? Take them, then!" Dorian shouted through his teeth. He practically foamed at the mouth, his hands like steal traps clutching her clothes. He could almost see Coraza's steel-black skin, her glazed-over and Master-possessed eyes, her graceful frame, unfettered smile.

Any second now she would laugh in his face.

"Why bother coming in if you're not going to take what's yours?" (As docile as Dorian normally is, it's quite scary to see him like this. He was growling furiously—making sure to cram his opinion in swiftly. If she was going to let him be angry, then he'd take the opportunity).

---

[74] For Dorian's small world, maybe.

"This reaction what you wanted? Wanted to make sure you can get under my skin? You win, Coraza! What do you want me to say—to do—to make us even? You coward! I'll never give you peace—I'll never take my *real* anger out on you. Why do you think you're still alive, you miserable prick? You think this is *cathartic* for me?"

Well, Dorian, that's hard to answer, since you're choking her...

He realized she tried to speak but failed. Normally, an Automaton wouldn't have such trouble—even *if* a human could have closed off their throat...

Suddenly, the clothes he gripped felt too real. Her pain seemed too real. *She* was too real.

"Please, I—I don't know what you're talking about! I—I live here! I'm—I'm *Odissa!*"

ODISSA ODELYN: The girl coming through the plot hole (neatly re-stitched).

DISLIKES: Smudges on her glasses, because she has a hard enough time seeing as it is (thanks a lot, Dorian).

SIGN: Gemini (go figure).

WORD: Nympholepsy, because it sounds dirty.

Chapter the thirteenth,

Mecca's trickery:

Wasn't that dramatic? Wasn't that ironic?

"I'm Odissa Odelyn!" Not this Coraza-person he was talking about. "Please! Please, you're—you're hurting me."

It certainly wasn't Coraza's voice.

She could see herself in his sunglasses and was left to imagine the gruesome revelation behind them.

His body relaxed but not his grip. He didn't want her to run away screaming.

"If it's money you want, I'll give it to you," the girl pleaded, though he didn't look like a robber. His confused countenance confirmed that she had no need to fear him. Much.

To get him to speak through his muddle, she went on, "I swear, I don't know what's going on—I'm not trying to trick you! I—"

But he put a hand over her mouth. Well, it was more or less where he *guessed* her mouth to be. Close enough. She went a little cross-eyed, looking at his hand.

He didn't like that this girl—the one who had the right to be affronted—was actually trying to *sympathize* with him. No need for intervention mode.

"Shh!"

Her little heart was beating like a rabbit's.

145

"I—I—I thought you were someone else." (Clearly). "Please don't scream or call for someone or—or talk so loudly. Can you do that?" He tried to reason with her, but he sounded more like a criminal trying to hide. It didn't help his case.

He felt her head try to nod under his hand. She'd do anything as long as you didn't accuse her of being someone else again. It was scary to be so confused—was she being robbed or murdered or kidnapped or not?

Dorian stepped back, hands raised for calm. "Are you OK?"

"I don't know."

He used his ears to detect her next movement. But she didn't move. She was too afraid to. She kept herself pressed against the wall.

As he continued to step back, he almost tripped over her stray bag. He'd forced her to drop it when he'd pounced. He smoothed out his shirt as he closed the door, clearing his throat. "Well, I'm sure this all looks bad," he said, his voice shaking.

She said nothing to reassure him.

Stupid! This is why he's always so composed. Composed, composed, composed! In the heat of emotion—ANY EMOTION!—he exploded. When void of sentiment or passion, he'd found it helped him never be so *rash*. He'd worked hard at building up his flawless reputation; stripped himself of emotional expression; suppressed any feeling.

"How badly did I hurt you?"

"Why the fuck are you in my apartment?"

Oh, that.

She went on when he didn't answer quickly enough. "D-does this have to do with—"

"Odys, yes," he answered, trying to fill the silence. He pushed his fingers into his hair, other hand on his hip.

Odissa paled. How did they know her brother's name?!

"Yes, this involves your brother."

Dorian flipped on the nearest light switch, so she could see him clearly (Fletcher, who was on his way, had reminded him to do it). Odissa became panicky at the sight of him; this man was being hesitant for a reason. He moved so slowly and deliberately.

Her voice growing higher, "What did Odys do? Does he owe you money? I have money—I can—"

"This isn't about money!" He quickly quieted that. *Jesus, you'd think her brother was a cheating drug dealer or something, the way she talks!*

"Then—then what's this about? *Why* are you in my apartment? God, I knew he'd do something. He always does." She was rambling to herself, no longer even looking at him, as if he weren't there—as if she hadn't just been attacked.

Dorian turned to the side, hand rubbing his lower face as if he might crush himself.

Odissa noticed him once more. Was this man blushing? He didn't seem the type. He seemed too repressed to express such silly emotions. Even his earlier-conveyed fury far from befitted him...She wondered why on earth he would jump *her*. One look was enough to tell she needed no more than verbal threat to make her cower. The lights might have been off before, but it wasn't as if it had been too dark to see her mousiness. Was this man blind or something? No, he seemed to see well enough...despite the fact he was wearing sunglasses in the dark.

She rubbed the back of her head; it was sore to the touch. "Why is my apartment number wrong?"

Yes, about that. "It's a long story." Please don't ask him. Please stop talking.

"Did Odys do it? Did he switch the apartment numbers to hide from you? The idiot!"

"Why do you think Odys would do something *stupid* like that?" He put his hands on his hips, actually curious.

Her hand dropped from her neck. She had no answer. There was no answer for the stupid things Odys did when upset. For example: the first time after "seeing" her father and Mr. Augury, she'd come home to a re-arranged apartment. Her room was then in the living room, his in the dining area, and the kitchen had held the couch. His excuse had been, "I couldn't stand it, being in the apartment alone and knowing you wouldn't be back soon. The emptiness kept reminding me of it. So I changed it." He'd consented that it didn't make *normal* sense, yes. But if part of his life was irregular, then all of it should be too, so there. Every consecutive visit after that, she'd come home to something just as weird, unfortunate, or bothersome. (Odys isn't as normal as he'd like us to believe).[75]

Now, back to the present:

Fletcher burst through the open door, saving them from each other.

He no longer had the dreads and was wearing a snazzy cop uniform he'd just assumed on his way up—or, what he hoped looked very much like one.[76] He pretended he was surprised to see Odissa. Fletcher took on a deep, respectable, and official voice. "Oh! Odissa Odelyn. You're

---

[75] Can't say I did believe it.
[76] Just to be clear: I do not think Fletcher's natural state includes dreadlocks in the first place. Just so you know.

home earlier than expected. Hello, I'm Officer Fletcher." *Fletcher, Fletcher So-and-so.* He extended a hand.

"Sorry I'm panting, those stairs wear me out." As well as running half a block. "Just went for coffee. Nothing happened, did it?" He looked between them as if he could tell (of course he could tell! He was practically THERE when it happened—listening through his Master's ears). He waited for no answer. "Sorry to surprise you, Ms. Odelyn. We, um, thought you'd be a little longer...We're from the police, sector 69"—he cleared his throat, regretting his number choice— "3. Dorian, here, is on duty. Your brother should be home shortly."

Nice save, Fletcher. He even had a small cup of faux coffee in his hand. His outfit was complete with a large, quickly-formed badge on his breast. If only all uniforms looked so good. This outfit was going to cost Dorian in energy later.

Odissa found it easier to interact with Fletcher (she knew *what* he was: a cop—versus whatever Dorian claimed to be), "What is going on?"

"Dorian hasn't said yet?" Fletcher put on a frown (he was a very good thespian), "Miss, your brother was unintentionally involved in one of our cases—a suicide, two days ago. A man approached him and, well, threatened your brother before shooting himself. We have reason to believe Mr. Odelyn may be in further danger—as well as you. We've been assigned to remain with you at all times." He took a fake sip from his fake coffee.

He spun his lies with such dignity and grace Odissa wanted nothing more than to believe him. *OK, so he's done nothing wrong.*

"Your brother's coming home as we speak—from the station. Don't worry, he's fine. Though, if you forgive me," he said, hiding one side of his mouth from Dorian, "I'd say the stress has had its toll on him. He didn't take the scene very well. Threw up a little. Well, a lot actually. I mean, everywhere. He'll be a story we tell the newbies for the next decade, right Dorian? Blood and guts must upset him. He's not gotten much sleep these past few days. Clearly doesn't deal with stress well."

He could tell Odissa was starting to think things through as he rambled so he stepped up his pace, "He'll be another thirty minutes or so. If you'll just sit down at the table, here," he directed her with authority, "I'll show you the newspaper article and the file about the case. The article lists no names, for Odys's protection, but it'll prove my point." He leaned over and mentally whispered to Dorian as Odissa walked to the table, *We should kill Mecca.* "I think you probably need to make a call or two, detective?"

"You know I do." Dorian slipped out. Fletcher closed the door behind him. His Master was going to make a very important phone call. (Once he stopped rage-shaking, of course).

Odissa picked up her glasses along her way to the table. Dorian had somehow managed to shake them off her little nose upon impact.

Sitting down, she rubbed her shoulder. She was bound to bruise. Worse than a nectarine in a batting cage.

"Sorry about Dorian." Fletcher was almost too apologetic, catching her curiosity. "He was expecting someone else. Did he say anything that frightened you?"

Yeah, everything. She didn't want to overtly tattle on Dorian. She wasn't sure he deserved it; and, if he was a cop like Fletcher, hadn't he just been doing his job? "I can't—can't remember. I think I scared *him.*"

"This is a very serious situation, Ms. Odelyn. We all get a little antsy." He half-winked at her. Working his magic, Fletcher pulled out an official-looking manila envelope from their duffle bag. From the sheaf of important-looking papers, he showed her the article in the local section. When Dorian and Fletcher had been spying on Odys, they had clipped it out for later "scrapbooking."

It was a small, unimportant paragraph. Public suicide. Body unidentified. Many witnesses. No one else injured. Police would not disclose further details. Yada, yada. In other words, the *real* police had no idea what was going on. And nor would they.

"This is what the man looked like. You don't happen to recognize him do you?" He had pulled the picture from his "pocket." When she tried to take it from him he shook his head. "No, no. It's our only copy." *Don't touch.*

She shook her head, apologizing that she couldn't help.

Fletcher put the picture away. "Would the name Pepin Pound ring any bells?"

"Only the alliterative ones," she smiled past her nerves, scolding herself for trying to be witty at a time like this. *Maybe I have a concussion.*

"That's quite all right. We didn't expect you to recognize him, anyways."

A little bit more chatting and:

"Why, though," Odissa wondered, "do you have to stay with us, if it was a suicide? What did the man threaten?" She cleaned her glasses on her shirt compulsively. She put them back on to read the article one more time. She was glad it didn't mention names. She hated attention.

"Ms. Odelyn, this is a highly classified case. We're not allowed to talk about it, and Odys isn't necessarily allowed, either. In fact, he doesn't even know how valuable his information may be. Not even I do. I just do what I'm told," he said, trying to make it light. "We'll be staying here, until things are settled. Undercover, that sort of thing. For your safety. We'll try not to impose."

She narrowed her eyes. She disliked the thought of company. It was always a hassle to entertain or be civil. Though she had many questions (like who Dorian had thought she was) she thought it best not to ask. Her questions would likely sound stupid anyway. She didn't know a *thing* about how these situations worked. She didn't even watch cop shows, so all his bullcrap seemed believable.

"What about…" she began but stopped.

"Yes?" Fletcher said, acting concerned. Her timidity warmed his heart.

"My school and work. I have to go to them this week. I can leave the apartment, right?"

"Let's just say you have to stay here, Ms. Odelyn." He braced himself for her reaction.

With downcast eyes, a sound escaped her lips. At least she wouldn't have to go to work and pretend to like people. "This seems like the witness protection program." Her eyes flickered up. It wasn't was it?

He pursed his lips. "You will have to quit your job."

"You mean I can't go back—ever? It will take that long to sort this out?" Her voice teetered on shrill.

"We can talk about it once your brother arrives."

"But if I need to quit my job, shouldn't I do so?"

"Actually, we've arranged to have it done for you."

Gooddeal! She hated confrontation. She realized her relief and felt strange for accepting it so easily. "Can I make some coffee?"

She was asking to use her own stuff now?

"How about I make you some myself? I hear you've been driving all day." Plus, his Master still felt bad about assaulting her.

…She didn't like how comfortable they already were in her home.

Stanza: Mechanical syllogism is used.

Dorian, his fingers moving swiftly, had called up his little friend Mecca.

Dorian didn't think Mecca had shirked his duties. Mecca was too loyal for that. Little Mecca broke rules *just* enough to evade scorn. No, this little "mess up" was far from a breach in dependability; it was more targeted, most likely. And the target of his exploits? Dorian, of course, for he was easiest to hit.

Mecca did not lie (often). This was not a lie (most likely). This was his masterpiece (as was everything).

As Dorian expected, Mecca didn't pick up.

"Hello?" Q answered.

"Q!" Dorian greeted, a fake smile matching his too-merry voice, "Hand the phone to your Master there, now, please. I need to speak with the little tyke."

"Dorian, he's…he's busy at the moment."

The falter in her voice meant she'd covered for him. Not even his soul was a good liar after they'd been caught. "Busy? Doin' what exactly?"

Silence was the very answer he'd expected.

"Tell him to pick me out something to read, then, since you're both at a fucking comic book store."

He could hear Q's moan-of-dread—almost hear her guts churn. Dorian always knew where he could find his unreliable little *Pygmaeus.*[77]

"We—we haven't been here all day. We just arrived."

"Yes, because you are so very truthful all of the time."

"Dorian, you know we get bored. We *did* follow her, I swear. We watched her walk into the apartment too. We just didn't call. And we—we didn't *lie.* Not really. We just neglected to tell you everything. You see, after you tapped their phone line, Mother sent us as soon as Odissa left the message where she was."

"I know that."

Q was stalling. "And at first *Mother* told *us* to tell *you* to tell *Odys*"—Dorian tried to keep up—"that Odissa was actually going to be later, so Odys would come to Mother more willingly."

"We all knew that, now get to the point."

"But when Mecca actually gave his first real update, he lied to Mother about the time, because he hadn't *actually* found Odissa yet and wanted to impress you all with the short time it took to find her. He was trying to do things on his own, you see. He needed the self-motivation."

"So you *did* lie?"

---

[77] My Narrator has mentioned to me that Mecca also got his kicks out of going to the *actual* book store, finding a few hardbacks with sleeves, removing said sleeves, slipping them on upside down, and then squeezing the book back on the shelf. The simple satisfaction that the next browser would get upside down text was enough to fuel him for a few days. Q got the ones on the taller shelves. This was their purpose in life. Rather, one of them.

"Only so he could impress you all! He gave Mother a time estimate that *could* have been true if we'd found her *right then*. But we did find her eventually, though. It's like Vulcan *meant* for it to happen!"

"I seriously doubt He meant for you to lie."[78]

She made excuses for her Master, "He can't sit still long enough to read a *real* book, that's why we're here—in this comic book store. If he hadn't made it fun for himself, we wouldn't have done the job in the first place. Mecca knows when he's nothing more than a plot device to move a main character along."[79]

What. A. Clusterfuck.

Dorian had to give the guy credit. He'd managed to find a moving car all on his own—without the use of a helicopter. (Thank God no one gave him a helicopter).

"But you didn't follow procedure. You let everyone believe—multiple times—that she would be here later." All his updates were lies. LIES.

"Yes, but," Q interrupted. "It was almost as if Vulcan *meant* for us to keep lying. Vulcan knew Mecca needed this to look good. Mec deserved it. You won't tell Mother, will you? You're good for it, Dori."

"I fucking jumped her, Q! Fletcher wasn't there and—"

"Wut?" she giggled. This was better than expected. Vulcan could be so hilarious!

"So you're glad I scared the shit out of her?"

"Why the hell did you *jump* her?"

"I swear to God, Mecca!" He was talking to Mecca through her now—she was the phone. He cursed them out in Spanish. He was just grateful they didn't do anything *funny* to Odissa. Like make her crash her car or something (oh-ho, what fun!). "You could have jeopardized everything, Mecca! Do you *want* her to find out about us?"

"The fuck did you jump her for? Why wasn't Fletcher there? You should be glad we'll promise not to tell Mother you were playing with fire by letting Fletcher out. We're even now!"

Dorian held the phone down, swallowing rage. When he put the phone back to his ear Q was still talking. "…but honestly, do you always attack people coming into their homes? Were you scared, wittle Dorian?"

---

[78] …Or did He?

[79] His real purpose in this story is to annoy other characters and he would rather not break away from that, my Narrator tells me.

He was silent. He didn't want to tell Mecca about Leeland—how Leeland had called. The little bastard didn't have the right to know. So he changed the subject. Huffing, "Are the employees giving him dirty looks?"

She whispered into the cell. "Only a little, but he's already traded in a few and there's a life-size you-know-what for sale. He's bound to snatch it up. We've never been in this store before, so there's a whole new selection of collectables he's debating over. Really, he might as well buy the whole store." Dorian could tell she'd gone outside, by the sound of the cars zooming by. "He just doesn't know if he has enough storage for everything he wants."

"As long as he doesn't make you take pictures with the life size you-know-what, like he did with the *other* you-know-whats." Dorian remembered the albums upon albums Mecca had of his Automaton in unreasonable situations with all his fanboy memorabilia. Mecca forced her to assume specific costumes to fit the unholy scenes. God only knows what he really took them for. Probably sold them at high school campuses after school, though he didn't need the money. Likely passed them out for free. Maybe pasted them on telephone poles.

"He says you didn't have to look at the last ones, you know. It's not his fault you're a pedophile."

"I'M FUCKING BLIND, IT'S NOT LIKE I WAS LOOKING!" He shouted into the phone. Those pictures had scarred him through Fletcher—and had given Fletcher a nosebleed of liquid metal-blood as he tried to filter the images for Dorian, but failed. "You tell the little punk that he's going to get a spanking next time I see him."

As if she was embarrassed to say it out loud, "Mecca says that you can give me *two* spankings to make up for it, as long as he can take the pictures "

"And I'll break that fucking camera. Jesus Christ, little pervert. Anyways, Q, I've got to go. Tell Mecca this isn't over. Mother *will* hear about this."

"Yeah, sure," Q mocked him, "Go tell Mommy you let Fletcher leave the apartment. Mecca still managed to find a fucking moving car. Mecca is the greatest!"[80]

Still spewing muffled curses (in Spanish), Dorian hung up.

---

[80] I told our Narrator that Mecca is a very cartoonish character (not that the others aren't, but, when compared, Mecca is somewhat unrealistic in my opinion). In one second, he will be carrying on an intelligent conversation with another adult and in the next demanding something like a bratty five-year-old. He doesn't act his actual age or the age of his body. To this our Narrator replied: "Mecca wants to grow up, but he doesn't know what he's asking for. How could he? No one does. Yet he knows a little more than most, because he has an Automaton. However, it is that same Automaton that is slowing his brain development down too. I think poor Mecca himself is confused about how he should act." I would have told our Narrator to cut him as a character, but I learned he had a bigger role to play in the second volume, so I let this slide. He is a necessary evil. Just take my word for it.

It was most likely the group's fault for giving Mecca a virtually meaningless (and very dull) assignment. Mecca could smell a purposeless job a mile away. Might as well put a camera on a slug just to make sure it wouldn't recite the alphabet—that's what this job had been to him.

But then again, *they had found her.*

"Vulcan's paying attention again," he whispered to himself. He rubbed his forehead, trying to process his disbelief.

He needed to call Mother. Somebody needed to update the rest of them.

He waited for ten minutes—he even counted—before calling her. He had to make sure he was calm enough to talk about Leeland. The cold air helped freeze his emotions.

He listened to Fletcher and Odissa's awkward conversation in his head—a conversation Fletcher was managing well. *At least one of me knows what he's doing—even on autopilot.*

Counting, counting, counting. Waiting, waiting, waiting.

According to Mecca's previous (and false) calculations, Odissa would have been arriving right about...*now.*

On the phone with mother:

"He called me, Mother." Mecca was already in the back of his mind.

"...I suspected he would—that he'd call at least one of you. Oh, Dorian, I wish he'd have called someone else. I know how it affects you. I can still hear the rage in your voice."

They talked a little in Spanish—they drug it out from each other.

Mother would let him pause and she would listen to his silence. She knew he needed silence.

"Before you go, I must say I don't think Odys is suicidal. You're wrong about this one, Dorian."

"But you know I can see these things, Mother." He ran a finger along the wood panel wall. Calling Gwen "Mother" came so natural to him now. What started as a joke that they slowly let him in on now felt just as easy as calling to an Auntie or Grandma. What didn't feel right was why he didn't call her "Madre" to put his own spin on things. Albeit, it was too late to change now. "Did he make you cry?"

"Do not be silly, Dorian. I cry even when happy. But Bob, now, she's stressed because of this. I need to find something to distract her. I think I'll send her to the cabin. Should she prepare it? We need to be together. You know how these things get everyone worked up. We need a break."

"*Sì, sì,* yes," he rambled on in Spanish to her. When they spoke Spanish, they were being private. Sharing a private matter. I'll not intrude by jotting it down. "Ah, I have to let you go, Gwen. I'm getting another call. I think it might be Bob with Odys."

"All right. Goodnight. Keep me informed. I want texts every hour."

As he answered the phone, he could hear the ice cream truck's too-merry tune.

"Hello?"

"We're fucking ten minutes away."

That was all.

He continued to wait outside for them to come up, pacing. There were only two sets of footsteps. The mini biker gang had not come up with Odys and Maud. They'd done their job and that was it.

Though Dorian couldn't see it, Odys had allowed Maud to take his hand. Upon seeing Dorian outside his door, Odys drew it back. The anti-PDA was in his nature.

"Um, why do I have someone else's door?" Odys asked.

"Don't ask questions if you don't want to know." Dorian said. He had wanted this moment to be funnier.

Odys took off his hat Bob had given him and thrust it at Maud, tired of looking ridiculous. He made to open the door, but Dorian stopped him. "I must warn you. Your sister, she...she came earlier than expected."

"You lied to us, Dorian?" Maud accused. She tried to peak through the window to see what was going on in the apartment. "To make us go willingly? You know we should've been here when she arrived."

"Yes, well, believe me, it wasn't planned," he half-lied.

Maud severed her eyes, studying him. "Wait. You sent *Mecca,* didn't you?"

"I didn't. Mother did. Everyone else was tied up."

"So you aren't lying?" Odys asked, trying to work this out. *Who the hell is Mecca and why is he named after the most famous Islamic pilgrimage site?*[81]

"No. I—I'm not. In fact, when she came in I—I thought she was someone else, so I—I..." Dorian cringed. "I *frightened* her."

That's one way to put it.

---

[81] Is it offensive that he assumes Mecca is a boy name? I'm not sure.

Though Dorian seemed sorry, Odys was not in a forgiving mood and pushed past him. Dorian managed to grab hold of Maud and prep her. They needed to make sure their stories were straight. Maud took off her shawl and "put on" her own version of an officer-esque uniform. Sadly, she looked more like a stripper about to "arrest" someone who'd been a naughty boy.[82]

Odys walked in on Odissa sipping a cooling cup of coffee, awkwardly chatting with Fletcher about headlines in a newspaper they were sharing (Fletcher had numbed her further questions by saying things like, "But I'll save those details for when your brother gets home." And she had taken it as a hint to start up the small talk). Her head lifted when Odys burst into the room.

"Odys, they told me what happened…" she managed to get out before he'd knelt down beside her; she'd tried to stand up to greet him, but he'd gotten to her fast. He held her head and kissed her hair, as if to make sure his hands weren't deceiving him. She shied away from him. "Fletcher said you didn't know the man—"

His eyes landed on Fletcher. They'd get their lies straightened out later. Right now, let him inspect his sister. Odissa's eyes flickered to Maud, who closed the door quietly behind her. That Dorian fellow—the one out of uniform—still hadn't come back in.

Maud walked up to them, extending a hand and comforting smile. "Hello, I'm Maud. Good to meet you. I'm Odys's police escort for the time being."

Short and simple of it. She put a hand to her hip, where her formed gun rested.

"Escort" is one word for it. Odissa felt hideous with Maud in the room. She had worn her comfy traveling clothes and minimal makeup today.

Odys pressed his sister. "Dorian said he frightened you? What happened? What did he say to you?"

She found a cigarette. "I'm fine, Odys. But, God, you look like crap." She noticed he didn't want to talk about it. She changed subjects. "I almost wish I had a cell phone so I could have known what I was coming home to." She forced a laugh (she was the one who had always enforced the NO CELL PHONES rule).[83]

"We won't be in the way," Fletcher assured her. "Odissa and I were just getting to know each other, Odys. She's been very *cooperative*. Where were you again, Odissa? I know Odys told us, but I can't remember for the life of me." Fletcher asked, now drinking out of a REAL coffee mug (earlier, he had pretended to throw away the adjunct paper-like one away, very smooth-like).

---

[82] A potato sack on Maud would look good.
[83] If you don't have a cell phone, then it's certainly harder for Odys to stalk you when you go on a trip, for one.

Odissa shot Odys a look. "I was with my lawyer," she exhaled the smoke from her trembling lips, praying that her alibi (if she could even call it that) didn't drift off along with the exhalation. "My father's will allots us sporadic checks—which is in my purse by the way, Odys. Don't let me forget. Our lawyer, Mr. Augury, handles them. Writes in the numbers, even. I was gone to collect it." She could see Fletcher was about to ask more, so she saved him the trouble. "My father's will states we must meet at his [let's just say grave site]—an aggressive rule, but," she shrugged, "worth the money." She flicked her cigarette in the ashtray.

"You were gone a long while just for a *visit*, though," Fletcher stated—not caring if he was unceremonious.

"Well, I'm not going to drive all the way out there and not get other stuff done," Odissa answered matter-of-factly. "I mean, not only does Augury take his time, but..." She paused, noticing Fletcher watching her brother. Odys was glaring at the table. "I also take mine."

"We tried calling him," Fletcher continued the conversation, a cop once more. "Odys didn't seem to have any of his...working numbers." Fletcher let on a light air of suspicion.

Odissa looked down at the floor beside her. She realized she was already telling them things they knew. But she would play along.

"Where is Mr. Augury's firm?" Fletcher helped her. He took out a "pen" and writing "pad" from his "back pocket," ready to "scribble down" her answers.

"Well, I don't know where he's based. In fact, he said he'd just finished with a bit of traveling." Of course he had. "He's retired, if that clarifies the situation. He was one of our father's closest friends, so Odys and I are his special case. I'm not sure what number would be best to reach him. Most times, we either stick to previously arranged dates or he—he calls me." She looked at Odys, who had taken up a chair diagonal to her. With her every word he cringed.

"What did your father do for a living again, Odys?" Fletcher asked, as if Odys mentioned it before and he'd only forgotten.

"What does our father have to do with this?" Odissa asked, hoping to avoid a long conversation. Her eyes flicked to Odys and back. He, too, didn't like where this was going. "It's not like our father was here when it happened. Neither was I."

"All information's valuable," Fletcher stated, as if it had *merely* been a question. "I know no one expects to talk about this sort of thing to strangers, but it's routine." Aw, look at Fletcher, trying to sound all legit. "Like I said, we aren't allowed to talk about the finer details of this case. What you don't say may be the very key we need. Might as well tell us what you know, so it can be cleared." He said that last part sweetly.

Odissa sat still, averted her eyes. She gripped her coffee cup so tightly her knuckles whitened. Fletcher's eyes darted from the girl to Odys to Maud. Maud, who knew what the twins were experiencing, had turned away. She pretended to listen to the quiet television. She was only here because of protocol, don't mind her, tralalalala.

Odys's eyes flashed to Fletcher, jaw clenching. He glanced at the door, as if telling Fletcher to listen for Dorian, and listen well, because he'd only say this once. "Our father wasn't one for sharing details. We guessed that he was a doctor in another country, before he immigrated to America—and 'immigrant' may or may not be the proper term for him."

Fletcher's face pinched at Odys, reminding him to keep calm. "Where was your father from?" Fletcher wanted to know what lies Leeland had woven. He wanted to watch Odissa react to them. Her reactions could prove Odys's innocence.

Odissa shook her head. "He kept that from us."

Fletcher frowned. "You don't have a guess?"

"European."

She was playing this off as nothing. She *believed* it was nothing.

"And I'm sure," Odys went on for her, "you understand, Officer Fletcher, how licenses don't always neatly cross borders, so if he *were* a doctor, there may be no record of it here. That's what we always presumed. Even Mr. Augury handles most facts with that same *undertone.*"

Odissa looked at him funny, wondering why he'd stress that point. "We've no way of proving what he was or wasn't. But he *was* in the medical profession."

"And your relationship with him wasn't on the best terms, yes?"

"Why does that matter?" Odissa cut off her brother's hostile "Yes."

Fletcher was taken aback. Odissa had said it so accusingly, as if it weren't anybody's business—even if it could solve the case of the century.

"Why bother us about *that* detail? He's tortured us enough beyond the grave. Please, let the dead rest, and let that say enough of how we feel about him."

Her eyes begged Fletcher to not provoke Odys.

Odys turned to his sister. "It won't make me mad to tell them. Besides, they may stop the questioning for now, in front of you, but when I'm alone with them, they'll push it."

Her body tensed. Was this stranger not as polite as he put on?

Fletcher stared at her, watching her wheels turn.

Something clicked behind Odissa's eyes. *This isn't some protection program. This is house arrest.* Their father had really screwed up this time.

The topic boiled up in Odys's throat, ready to come out in heated, gurgling words: "You want to know why we hate him? Why *I* hate him"—for Odys could not speak for Odissa, not entirely. "My father performed tests and…" Odys struggled for the right word. "*Experiments.*"

Fletcher screwed up his face. Why was Odys starting with this point? Granted, that *sounded* like Admund™—his brand, his mark left on a Master.

"When she was a child, well, our *father* diagnosed her with a condition. Whether or not he came to that conclusion on his own or with a second opinion, he was correct. Our current doctors verified it."

Odissa cut in, as if her brother weren't explaining it right, "But it's not any illness, so don't look so concerned. We're dealing with a pre-existing—a born-with—issue. If you even want to call it an *issue.* My father was a bored rich man needing something to fix. Our lawyer, Augury, still swears by our father's contribution to the medical field. Augury has done a lot of legal work for others in the medical profession, you see…"

Yeah, yeah. Sure he has.

To his sister, "Augury defended him only because he—" But Odys stopped himself. Gentler, "You and I both know Augury defends those others wouldn't." He looked at Fletcher, "Apparently, as Mr. Augury has before implied, Odissa's a perfect match for what one of our father's studies needed and, well, she became his favorite guinea pig." Odys's face twitched. He was staring at the table, as if he might explode if he made eye contact.

Odissa felt the need to defend her brother's dramatics. "My father came very close to finding a cure. But he ultimately failed."

"But if you're twins, then…" Fletcher pointed between them, wanting to be clear. This Dr. Frankenstein story was jumbled enough as it was.

"No, it's not like that," she answered. "I'm what he needed only because I am, well, female. It has—or had—to do with my…reproductive organs. It's not life-threatening. It never was. And it probably shouldn't have been explored to begin with. It wasn't like I got to consent to such major decisions about my own body. How can a child consent?"

Odissa half-wished the female cop, there, would do the interrogation. It would be less embarrassing, and she had such a sympathetic face. She glanced at Maud, who was realigning the candles on the windowsill as she tried to blend in with the wall—*Odys isn't the only one fidgeting,* Odissa thought.

Odys shook his head, anger still simmering, "She's putting it too delicately."

Odissa tried to watch Odys balance out this conversation, but her eyes kept moving back to Maud and the expression on her face—an expression so much like Odys's. *She agrees with Odys. She already knows. Do they all know?*

"Before she hit puberty, he began his *tests*. Overall, she was a case study—maybe one of many. Don't ask about his research. He never let *her* ask."

Doctors making house calls only because they live there.

"Your answer's not telling me anything, Mr. Odelyn. What *harm* came from your father's medical tests? Why does this cause you so much trouble?" *Tell me why you hate him so much.*

Odissa leaned forward. "Because eventually he tried to get me pregnant. Then he succeeded. All of them miscarried within"—she searched her brain for a measurement—"weeks of conception. This all happened before I was even eighteen. And like hell I got to choose who the father was."

Fletcher didn't breathe as he digested Odissa's words. He could feel the goosebumps forming on his Master's arms outside—such bumps weren't there because of the winter cold. He didn't realize Leeland would go to such great lengths—or that his plans for the twins could expand so nefariously. "But *why* would your father—Odi Odelyn—do that?"

She clarified, "There was no sex involved, if that's why you look so shocked. It was all done by artificial means. Probably some castaway sperm from the sperm bank garbage." She forced a laugh, though her hand couldn't hide her trembling lips. "Did the man who killed himself know my father?"

"Yes," Fletcher answered.

Odys's nostrils flared, disagreeing with Fletcher's choice to admit it. He could tell it got his sister to think—think *inside* the box—think things like "Maybe the man who killed himself had illegal research of his own and wanted his secrets to die with him?" *This has nothing to do with real life, Odissa!*

Odys finally looked at Fletcher. His voice low, "If you think about it, Fletcher, children—grandchildren—are a lot of *leverage*, aren't they? They're *investments*."

Odissa's head turned, wondering what that meant. She was certain now—certain that Odys knew something he couldn't tell her—something they wouldn't let him tell. *Everyone knows what this is but me.*

Fletcher remembered to breathe. "If that's the case, then I can see why you have your reasons for hating him, Mr. Odelyn."

Odissa latched onto Fletcher's discomfort. "Since our father obviously has something to do with the suicide, why not ask direct questions about him?"

Fletcher offered her the edge of his smile, liking her bitterness. "Well, your perspective on things has given me much to think about. But all right. The cat's out of the bag, I guess. Your father has *a little* something to do with this case." He crossed his legs, his arms. "If you hated your father so much, why didn't you report him? Why didn't you let the authorities—even, say, a nanny or random adult—know what he'd done to you? It clearly bothered you—even as a child. It's stuck with Odys all these years."

"There's the fact we have, in the past, feared our income would cease if we spoke too loudly about him. We're dealing with a great deal of money, here. Money we don't know the root source of. We just..." She stopped herself, waning.

"What?" Fletcher coaxed. But the question was directed to Odys, as if he might allow his sister to speak more—might tell her it was alright. Was there something more to this?

"Is that not enough?" she asked Fletcher. Her expression seemed to both beg and scold him. "Don't get me wrong, I'm not ashamed of telling you the basic facts—even spurting off my medical history. But there are some things doctors simply shouldn't do. Most of all, there are things *fathers* shouldn't do."

Odys wanted to yell, HE WASN'T OUR FATHER. But he wouldn't jeopardize everything—including this innocence-test.

Fletcher bowed his head. "Your father seems just as mysterious to you as he still is to us, Odissa Odelyn."

"But he's not mysterious," Odissa said. "It's like we said before. He was a bored rich man."

"And now his lawyer is a bored rich man, isn't that right, Ms. Odelyn?" He pulled a picture of "Audell Augury" from his "pocket" and watched her reaction.

"Is this about *him* or my father?"

Fletcher sighed. "Both, really." And he put the picture away.

Dorian walked through the door. He didn't say a word.

Odys could tell these guys hadn't dealt with an outsider—a "regular" human—in a long while, at least not in this fashion. They weren't sure how to act around Odissa—a human girl they'd have to pretend around. Pretending took its toll. Maud's "outfit" was already weighing on Odys...

"Can you," Fletcher called back their attention, "possibly let us see the check you mentioned, then? For the account number."

161

Looking to Odys for permission, Odissa gave it to them. "It's not his name, you know. Augury doesn't put his name on them. I don't know who really signs them, though he said it goes through our father's account managers—whatever that means."

Fletcher, after studying it, passed it to Maud, who handed it to Dorian. After pretending to look at it, he stepped back outside to make a phone call about the numbers.

"Is this necessary?" Odissa asked, eyes searching Fletcher and Odys. She'd worked hard for that check, *nothing better happen to it.* "Why must you contact him? Tell me what you're looking for so I can help."

There was something too eager in that statement.

"If we knew that ourselves, we would ask, Ms. Odelyn. For the time being, there's no way to hurry this along."

"Can I have a word with Odissa, Fletcher?" Odys asked.

Odissa didn't like he had to ask.

"What about?"

"Is that a no?"

"It wouldn't be *appropriate*, Odys." He saw Odissa's stare. "This case is very important. We cannot let you endanger others by spreading what you know."

"You make it seem like *I'm* someone suspicious," Odissa said. "As if I'm a suspect that might have killed the man who shot *himself*. We have nothing valuable to hide."

"Then let's not hide, shall we?"

As they continued to wait for Dorian, Odissa grew restless. Someone needed to say something, to interrupt the clanging silence. "Where's Bulfinch?"

"Check your room," Odys suggested. The cat was always in her room. It was basically his.

Fletcher didn't protest her getting up from the table alone, so she smothered her latest cigarette and went. Flipping on the light, she noticed Bulfinch's tail sticking out from under the bed. He was never really good at hiding. "I see you've kept the room in order..." She glanced at the cluttered bed, her dresser, her shelves, her desk.

The only reason she ever used this room was for the sleek computer sitting atop it and to be alone sometimes. Odys had the laptop.

Since she was going to be stuck in here tonight, she could lock herself in and catch up on her web browsing. Yes, yes, she would have to entertain herself tonight. The computer would put her to sleep.

Staring at the computer, she noticed the modem.

Gasp!

It had been...crushed.

Smashed. Battered. *Murdered.*

"What the hell?" she whispered to herself as she rushed to examine it. Then, she saw the actual computer. It was bleeding frayed cables—gorged of circuits—drawn and quartered of all internet possibility.

She traced the cable to the landline. It looked like someone had taken scissors to it. Her outside-world connection was gone.[84]

She wasn't stupid. She knew her brother wouldn't destroy his own connection. This was something more. This had to do with the "police." But why would police destroy a computer? Internet connection was one thing. It was *another* to kill the computer.

It could all be replaced, yes. But until then, Odissa would be trapped in this room. Just as they had wanted.

She looked about. She could tell things had been touched—moved slightly. She set a picture frame back up. Someone had been snooping. *They* had been snooping. Not only had they destroyed her computer but they had invaded her privacy. That was worst of all.

After calming herself and reasoning out what this meant, she set the modem down. As normal as could be, she waltzed toward the kitchen, passing Maud, who seemed concerned about her reaction to the room.

"Anyone want more coffee?" Odissa asked.

Fletcher watched her as she moved about the kitchen. Even Odys could tell she was acting strangely. As she fumbled in the cabinet for a new mug (though she hadn't finished her last one) she intentionally dropped it, letting it fall onto the counter. As if she had been trying to catch it, she knocked over the phone and a paper stack. The mug cracked on the counter and smashed to a million pieces on the floor.

"My God," she said, nervously apologizing. She bent down to pick up the disjointed phone, listening carefully. No dial tone.

She set the phone back in its place. Odys had rushed over to clean up the broken pieces of the mug. He sensed the fear radiating off her.

"I'll clean it, Odys," she tried to shoo him away. *Act natural, Odys!*

"Odissa, you already have a mug over there," he told her quietly.

---

[84] Fletcher: Helping Odissa avoid carpel tunnel, if only for one more day.

"Oh, yes. I'm just so tired."

"It *is* getting late," Fletcher said, leaning back in his chair so he could better see what they were doing. "Maybe we should all get to bed."

He was *sending* them to bed.

"Should I make up the couch?" Odissa asked, taking the garbage basket from Odys and brushing the last of the mug's fragments into it.

"Won't be necessary," Fletcher said, standing. "We don't sleep on the job."

Dorian walked in, as if he had noticed some cue. He put the check back on the table.

To keep with their act, Maud said, "I'm calling it a night. Fletcher, show me out, please."

"Will do."

The Automatons stepped out. Dorian "watched" the twins finish cleaning up the mug. "Will the television bother you if we watch it tonight?" he asked them.

"No," Odissa answered for the both of them, studying the area they'd just cleaned. "Well, I'll go to bed then." She nodded to Odys.

The awkwardness of the "goodnight" was astounding. They never told each other goodnight. Never needed to.

She took her luggage and shut her door. The two human men in the apartment stood there. They could hear her clearing her bed. There were so many piles stacked atop it. It took her a great deal of time to tidy—maybe because she was taking her time. She had too much time. She wasn't going to sleep tonight. Not with strangers in her home.

"She's too accepting of this situation," Dorian noted, his voice hushed. Odys stared at her door. "I thought she'd have more resistance to this whole *thing*." Even Dorian didn't know what to call it.

"She suspects something," Odys told him quietly. He hoped she couldn't hear them talking. "But, since she knows this has something to do with our father, she's too defensive to break her cover. She thinks she's protecting us. She was always paranoid people would find out about him."

"Find out about him?"

"We always knew he didn't accomplish things in the most legal ways possible."

"She probably noticed what we did to her computer," Dorian noted. Even *he* thought the mug incident was weird—yet clever.

Odys guessed what he meant and picked up the phone. Listened. "Did you *have* to cut the wires?" He realized Fletcher had probably done it when he "searched the place."

Dorian stepped closer, to make sure his whisper got to him. "We can't have her doing anything rash, Odys."

"Now she *will* do something rash because she'll feel caged here," he hissed back at him. "She won't understand."

"She doesn't have to understand, Odys. That's the point."

"So you want her to find out, then? Mother would be *thrilled* if you lost control of this situation."

Dorian sunk back from the statement, considering a new thought. "Despite all the questions you both answered for us tonight, Odys, there's one that goes unanswered." Which is? "Why does your hate for your unnatural father lead you to love your sister so unnaturally? The whole Byblis thing, sure. But the other *strangeness* is so thick I could cut it with a knife."[85]

"What does that have to do with any of—of this?" He eyed the door, waiting for Fletcher to come back in with Maud so he could take her and go to bed, but Dorian clearly wanted a word— or two or three. He could see Fletcher's shadow underneath the door, waiting for Odys to answer his Master.

"Does Leeland know you fuck your sister?" He wasn't judging. He was simply wondering if Leeland ever cared to notice the two children his Automaton had raised were so symbiotic. "I mean, how could he have missed it?"

"You think he really cared enough to notice?" Odys's voice was low and sizzling. "And what if I *had* gotten her pregnant? Wouldn't more kids be like having more Bulfinches around? More *leverage?* Not that he doesn't control our lives enough already." He paused, looking back to Odissa's door. "We were finally going to be free of him, but then all of *this* happened."

"But he was hardly in your life. In fact, he had killed himself to be out of it. What more freedom do you mean?"

"Odi—I mean Leeland—Leeland's always been here—looming over. And I've watched what he's done to my sister for far too long."

"He still manipulates her. So what? She's the one that still lets *him* in her life. Or is that not what you mean? Tell me what all this horror-suspense about experiments and such actually means. We've let you build it up long enough."[86]

---

[85] Byblis, in myth, loved her twin brother.
[86] Indeed.

"There are some things more *vile* than two twins fucking, Dorian." Odys wondered if he really didn't know. Dorian seemed to know everything about him already.

"I never said you were vile." Dorian tried to keep Odys calm. "But I know there's something you're not telling me—a reason you hate Leeland more than she ever will."

"Because it's not my place to tell," Odys hissed.

Odys saw the pity in Dorian's expression. It unnerved him. Why would Dorian—out of so many emotions—choose pity? Odys didn't want his pity.

Fletcher walked back in, penny in hand. He looked left and right to make sure the coast was clear.

Odys went to retrieve Maud, but Fletcher held her over Odys's head. Leaning down, he commanded, "You best sleep with her tonight."

Odys cringed, not liking the way that sounded and praying to God Odissa hadn't heard it. "Would. You. Shut. Up?"

No, not yet.

"Hey, hey, now," he said. He raised his hand, too high for Odys to grab at. He rolled Maud over his supple fingertips—bump, bump, bump. Maud was bound to be dizzy. "She might have your soul, but you still have our property. Keep that in mind. We don't want any more of her sneezing-fits because of your self-sabotaging tendencies, m'kay? It not only puts you in danger, but all of us. Leeland called, while you were away. Your sister needs to've all the protection she can get, right? We'll all be handicapped if Maud sneezes out."

Fletcher, with the back of his thumb, tossed Maud in the air; Odys fumbled for her.

"Now off to bed with you." Fletcher shooed him away, nodding to his room like a dad.

When they heard his door lock, Fletcher turned to Dorian. "Should we tell him not to lock it? So petulant."

"We have his sister, don't we?" Dorian answered, as if it were nothing to celebrate. "He'll behave." He sat down at the table and picked up Fletcher's used coffee. He gripped it for comfort. He still felt bad about what he'd just put the girl through.

"Don't beat yourself up about it," Fletcher told, so softly Dorian could barely hear. Fletcher studied himself in a nearby wall mirror. He looked sofuckinggood in a uniform. "You can't avoid her from here on out and also do your job."

"Yes, yes, I know." Dorian was already past that.

Now his major worries were how he'd maneuver their glib charade to keep Odissa unaware of his blindness. As Fletcher had observed her, he could tell—as her eyes had followed Dorian for fleeting seconds—she didn't think Dorian fit the role of a cop. And he certainly wasn't as *aware of his surroundings* as other people.

Dorian didn't "see" as clearly when Fletcher was away. Though the surrounding's blueprint remained logged in the Automaton's mind like a file Dorian could retrieve for later use, it was much safer for him to move if the file was constantly updated.

"I don't think she's stupid," Fletcher admitted. He watched her door, as if it might open. "But I don't think she's brave enough to question authority."

"To question authority, no. But to question what is and is not authority? She fits the type."

"She's an odd little thing, you bet."

"She *is* interesting, isn't she? How she can control her brother." Dorian placed a stick of gum in his mouth. "Yet she's so gentle."

"You should stop trying to see things in them, Dorian. It only hurts you."

"Yes, but there's not much left to hurt, now, is there?"

"I wonder what her favorite color is?"

"She looks brown, like her brother," Dorian stated. "But I don't think she's brown."

"Maybe taupe?" Fletcher's lip pulled up at his guess.

"Or just grey."

"Oh. I see," Fletcher sated, his face becoming serious. "I get it."

"And what exactly do you get? What am I *allowing* you to get?" Dorian needed his soul to help him face the facts.

Fletcher sighed. Dorian could almost hear Fletcher's tall shoulders hunch over, feel his Automaton shove his long hands in his self-fabricated pockets. "The girl reminds me of her too, Dorian, but so have many other girls."

"But even Odys reminds me of her. It's not something they could fake—"

Fletcher reached out and put a hand on the back of his Master's neck, his manner shifting. Crouching over Dorian he kissed his forehead, his lips lingering to mouth, "Then maybe it really is them."

"That's exactly what Leeland would want me to think," Dorian mumbled, putting a hand on Fletcher's arm.

A few minutes later, they would go to bed—on the couch, of course. They would sleep, despite what they told Odissa. They always slept *lightly* anyway. Wakefulness was what was *heavy*.

Stanza: No man is an island, but a woman is her own continent.

167

Odys, after placing Maud upon his dresser, sat upon his bed, head in hands.

"At least she arrived home in one piece," Maud stated, folding her thin arms after reforming. She sat, shapely legs crossed, upon the dresser—as if still a weightless penny.

"I don't like how she's involved in this—her private life examined."

"I'm surprised they didn't press further. Take it as a sign they believe what you're telling them. They're sympathetic."

"I don't even know how I'm going to tell her that our father wasn't our father and that Mr. Augury is actually…" He squeezed his hands.

"Odys, your sister can stick up for herself. Vengeance isn't yours to take. If anyone's, it's hers. Any evil committed has been upon her."

"Anything done to her is done to me," Odys hissed. "Shouldn't you know that, by now? Shouldn't you, my *Automaton*,"—he mocked—"know that by now? Don't you know what that man has done to us? What *hell* our lives have been? And now it turns out it didn't have to be that way—it was all an—an *act*."

Odys stood up, his catharsis over. Walking over to the dresser, he pulled open the drawer below her bare toes. Rummaging for a second, he pulled out two articles.

"Here," he extended one of his shirts and shorts to her. "They're too big for you, yes, but it'll save you—or *us*—the trouble of 'concentration' tonight. No *accidents*."

Taking the outfit, she commented, "You make it sound like I'm a bed wetter."

She slipped on the clothes, bunching up the short's slack with one hand.

"You take the bed," Odys pointed.

"Take the bed? You aren't—?"

"No, I'm sleeping on the floor."

"But Odys! We're both tired. We'll be ill tomorrow, if we don't…you know."

Touch.

"Whatever. Now go to bed." He couldn't stand knowing she was right. Even now he wanted to snuggle up to her like a cold pillow.

Sticking to his original plan, he took a blanket from the bed, one of the pillows, turned off the lights, and flopped on the floor.

Maud breathed in deep. No good could come of this.

A few seconds passed as they tried to fall asleep, but Odys still had something on his mind. "Mother said Leeland has something on all of them. I want to know what their weaknesses were. They know mine."

"Yours is still alive though. Theirs was taken from them. It's no good to know them now."

"I still want to know who I'm dealing with."

Her voice almost too quiet, "For Bob he—Leeland took her husband.[87] And when that didn't work…" She paused. "He marked her body—with marks worse than scars."

"Her spots?"

"No," Maud whispered. "Those spots cover up his marks—the words he wrote on her—the words he engraved upon her skin to remind her of what he'd taken. Small words, big words. Even a few sentences."

When Odys didn't respond she went on: "Silly, isn't it? The extremes he goes to, to *avoid* killing people. It's almost comical. He wants them to agree with him—agree Automata should not exist. He wants Masters to kill themselves and surrender. He doesn't just take, he wants to feel *right*. Now each time Bob looks in the mirror, she remembers what he took from her."

She waited until his thoughts were ready to process more information.

"He hopes to continue to remind her, until she gives up hope. Until she can't bear herself any longer. But she didn't remove the marks he put. She only covered them. If she removed them then he would win. She owns her marks now. She hated tattoos—her old self is nothing like she is now. She gave her past to Cestus. That is the only way she remains strong against Leeland—she gave up her own *self* to fight him."

"No, she gave up her husband. She let him die."

Maud sighed, agreeing with him. "But not just that, Odys. It was Gwen's fault it happened to her—her 'branding.' Cestus was away on business for Gwen when Bob got her first round of marks. Leeland's done it to her more than once. Gwen feels guilty because she had sent Cestus to do the *business*—both times. They wouldn't have been able to get to Bob if Cestus had been there." She rolled over on her other side. "Leeland sent his Automatons to do it. She could not fight them on her own. She had no choice but to let them—let them go on with their *inquisition*. They beat her up pretty bad and she woke up with the words. Apparently, she had let it slip once that she hated tattoos."[88]

"And Dorian? How did Leeland hurt him? What did his eyes have to do with his weakness?"

---

[87] I previously erased a reference to Bob's birth year. She met her husband waaay after gaining her Automaton. Born around the start of the Philippine-American war.

[88] I find it interesting that Bob didn't have her tattoos removed. Granted, she would probably have to remove them herself because she is a Master and nothing but a Master can "harm" her. It might have just been easier to blot out the words.

She didn't answer immediately. "Do you trust me enough by now to know I have your best interests at hand? You don't want to know why Dorian gave up his eyes. Every fiber of your soul is keeping me from telling you, Odys. It's part of the reason why we haven't synced yet."

Odys stared into the darkness, fists clenching. "That's what I'm afraid of. I don't want to know but they'll find a way to force it on me, won't they?"

Stanza: Adam ate the apple so he could rule Eve.

Odissa, semi-regretting the phone-stunt she'd just pulled, had finished moving all the objects from her bed. The last item was a box full of school files. She plopped it next to the basket of dirty laundry she'd just put down.

She peeled off the first layer of covers and, a few pats here and there, the dust was off.

She hadn't seen this surface in…

Months? A year? More or less.

Falling back on the bed, Bulfinch accompanied her (he happened to like the new, comfy space). "Ah, Bulfinch," she whispered while rubbing his side, "I am too nervous to get ready for bed. Perhaps in a few hours I'll peek out."

She stared at her door.

In a faint voice, "I'll tell you what I think, Bulfinch. Hey, don't move. It's rude. I'm still talking." She dangled him over her face. "There's something strange about this. Why did that *one* think I was *Coraza?*"—she said it with the same flair Dorian had given it. "I think my father might have had some unfinished *business* before he died. I don't think these are clean cops."

They aren't cops at all, Bulfinch tried to correct her.

She let him go and propped herself on her elbows. "And tell me, dear, did Odys feed you well while I was away?"

The cat rubbed against her.

"Ah, I thought not. In all this chaos, though, I can't blame him. If you had seen someone blow their head off, you'd forget about things too, I bet."

The cat was not forgiving.

She plopped back down. The cat curled up beside her, under her arm. "This is all inconvenient, isn't it, Bul?"

He threw his head back and meowed, *No more inconvenient than when you forget to clean the litter box, Odissa.*

"And by the way, my trip went fine, thanks for asking…" She trailed off in thought. She snuggled closer to him. "It's just you and me now."

Bulfinch didn't think she knew how to count.

Over his loud purring, she listened through the paper-thin walls. She could hear the TV.

Stanza: Eve offered Adam knowledge.

A few more hours passed, and, as Odys rolled over to straighten out his stiff back (the floor was unkind) he rolled atop something other than spacious floor.

His body pressed against his Automaton, who, during the night, had rolled off the bed to be near him. She didn't even stir when he'd squished her.

"Well, that worked well," he grumbled to himself. He partially understood she wasn't to blame—though neither was he. It was some magnetic attraction (literally). Odys gave in, waking her up. "Come on, we'll share the fucking bed."

Letting her tuck in, he crawled under the covers. "Back to back," Odys added, for clarification. Maud smiled as she rolled over. It was a relief.

Stanza: Adam went down with Eve.

Dorian found himself half-asleep and half-aware of what was going on. That is why, when Odissa finally got up in the middle of the night to espy the premises, she not only saw Dorian lounged awkwardly across the couch, but a Fletcher lounged awkwardly atop his Master.

And by "awkwardly" I mean "nakedly."

In Dorian's momentary drowse, he'd allowed Fletcher to function on his own...resulting in the automatic form-shift as the Automaton, too, snoozed.

Very stiffly, very quietly, and very uncomfortably, Odissa closed the door and locked it. Upon hearing the door close, Dorian started. Assuming what had happened, he punched his Automaton awake and—

Her back still pressed against the door, Odissa found her bearings and looked down at Bulfinch. "I don't think cops wear their birthday suit to work, do you, Bulfinch?"

Bulfinch, being a cat, had little problems with that attire. After all, it's what he wore most often. God knows he'd be pissed if you tried to dress him in anything else.

Stanza: Adam didn't try to stop Eve.

That morning:

Odys woke up to utter beatitude—finally, he didn't feel like his body was fighting poison.

That sickness, if only for this moment, had been dulled. No, not dulled, taken away. He knew it would come back, yes, if he moved away from Maud. But right now he was whole again. On the plus side, he was much more at ease knowing that, even though he slept next to an unsought woman (or something very much like a woman), he wouldn't open his heavy eyelids to see her naked.

No. More. Surprises.

He even hoped Maud wouldn't notice if he snuggled in a little closer, pretending to still be asleep. Even if she did notice, though, he wouldn't be too embarrassed. Why should he feel embarrassed? Just like someone hugging their arms around themselves for warmth, your arms never tattled, and neither would Maud.

"Wakey, wakey. Eggs and bakey," came a soft whisper above them. The gentle sound was just enough to echo through Odys's eternal Zen-space.

"Geezus!" Odys gasped, putting his hands up. The weapon Q held looked more like a metal Nerf gun.

Maud and Odys quickly sat upright, scooting back as far as possible—back away from the gun invading their bubble.

Odys glanced at Maud, who, to his surprise, held a pair of her own weapons, ready to shoot—she'd formed them so quickly, hair in her face.

"Good morning, Maudy!" Mecca said, his head peaking around Q's. He was dangling off her back like a giant monkey, his limbs making Q look like she had six arms. He whipped out a camera, shooting away.

"Mecca shot some really great photos of you both sleeping. This shot is *also* fantastic." Clickclickclick.

Maud shot the camera out of his hand; the poor thing exploded and caught fire (Automaton bullets aren't so much *bullets* as they are metal bits hot with energy).[89]

Q created a second gun as her poor Master mourned his camera. "Those photos were on the *other* one!" she said, as if she had bested Maud. Mecca tucked his second camera under his arm like a football. Q shielded him like a mother.

It seemed someone as petite as Q might snap from Mecca's weight, but we're talking Automatons here, so this girl was just fine. She carried him around all the time. Mecca hated floors (his feet were too sacred for such things).

"Mind telling me what the hell's going on here?" Odys asked Maud, as if she should know.

"Odys, meet Mecca and Q. Master and Automaton."

"Mecca is here!" he proclaimed. Odys was finally getting to meet him!

---

[89] A type of booger, you might even say. [Correction: my Narrator tells me to make a lava analogy here. Fine, hot-ore analogy made].

"They let a *child* be a Master?" Odys said.

"Mecca is not a child! Mecca will use dirt on you if you don't mind your manners! Your whole graduating class will have these pictures of you and Maud in bed if you cross me again. You must obey Mecca!"

"If you put those online," Maud growled, "I'll break every single one of your little action figure dolls. The ones you had to steal from that museum in New Mexico. You hear me? The ones in the Colorado bunker. *I know about them!*"

Mecca stuck out his tongue, unafraid.

"Put down your guns, Q!" Maud said, growling.

"No. You're *our* captive now, act like one."

Play along, Maud, play along!

"And how does Dorian feel about that?" She tried to see out the open door, as if they might have had to fight Dorian over "warden rights."

"Dorian has no authority over this," Mecca said. "Mother sent us!"

"We received a call this morning," Q said. "Er. well, a call and a text and another call. Long story short, Mother wants you for brunch."

Mecca, the saggy backpack on his Automaton's shoulders, exclaimed, "Oh my God, Q, do you see what Maud's wearing? She's got on *real* clothes! Look, they're too big."

Maud made her guns disappear as she pulled the covers up. She saw Mecca itching to start up his camera to record the proof.

Dorian poked his head through the door, a sinister look upon his usually-composed face. "What'd I tell you? I told you to keep it down. There's a *normal* person in this apartment." The reprimand was muted as much as could be. "I don't want to clean up more messes."

Mecca cowered into Q, burrowing the camera further. When he'd arrived this morning, Dorian had confiscated his first one before he'd let him even come through the apartment door (good thing he'd brought his backups).

Q guarded Mecca from Dorian like a shepherdess, he her faun.

...More like rotten satyr.

"Why the hell are there little kids in here?" Odys demanded, remembering to keep his voice down mid-sentence.

"What'd I just say? Mecca's not a little kid!" Mecca pointed at the camera.

Q covered Mecca's mouth with a hand, reminding him to keep it down. Pushing her hand away, "Mecca—who is older than you!—has come to collect you—for your next appointment

173

with Mother. She has big news. Big news you won't hear if you keep forgetting your place, young man." He narrowed his don't-fuck-with-me eyes. Q raised her gun higher.

Chewing some of the gum Mecca had brought him (a peace offering), Dorian said, "Odys, meet the reason I scared the shit out of your sister last night."

"Mecca's not the one that made Dorian jump her, or why Fletcher wasn't there to see things *straight!*" He laughed. "Straight! Get it?"

Q shook her head; let's not bring that up. There wasn't enough gum in the world.

"You said you scared her last night, not jumped her!" Odys hissed. He was almost glad they'd done it. Maybe Odissa would stay afraid of them.

"She's fine, though, isn't she?" Dorian shrugged it off, smacking his gum, trying to pretend he didn't care.

"You shouldn't let Fletcher leave the apartment," Maud admonished, taking off Odys's shorts. Odys noticed Mecca tilt his head as he watched her. As she stripped, she only revealed another layer of clothes (even so, Odys didn't like how she'd simply change in front of them!). "Why would you let him leave?" She tossed Odys's clothes at Dorian's face.

"He's sorta handsome, though, ain't he, Q?" Mecca asked Q about Odys. "You think our top girl followers will fancy him?"

"Since when do you cater to girls?" Maud asked.

"Since forever," Q said, "You should see the numbers Fletcher and Dorian have."

"The ones of them in bed get quite a few hits. Granted, they might be queer-hits, not girls."

"All right, Mec," Dorian finished this conversation. "You've done your damage." Just as he had wanted. "Get out," he ordered. "Let Odys get dressed."

"Dressed?" Odys asked as the party trickled out (Mecca glowering at Dorian). "Don't I have a say in this? Why do I have to go this early?" *Doesn't Gwen know brunch is between breakfast and lunchtime?*

"Why's the sky blue? Why's the grass green?"

"Why am I going?"

Tired of his questions, "Have you forgotten, Odys, we have you outnumbered? Right now, Fletcher's outside Odissa's door, gun ready. I have to obey Mother's orders, just as you do. By all means, I'd rather be at home letting Fletcher tickle my balls, but you and I both know this is some serious shit. No time for sleeping. Look at these bags under my eyes!"

"You're an old bag!" Q shout-whispered to his back.

Dorian took in a deep breath and closed the door.

Odys turned to Maud, eyebrows raised.

"Mother probably just wants to see *how much* you'll tolerate her. I just can't believe she'd send Mecca. Why not Bob again? Bob must be busy. Busy doing something else. Something more important. But what's more important than us right now? Makes me wonder. Mecca's actually older than Dorian, if you can believe it." She was like some personal narrator for Odys. Too bad he can't hear me. I'd do a better job. I KNOW EVERYTHING.

"That's fucked up," he said, rubbing the back of his neck. "But if he's older than Dorian, shouldn't he *look* older than, what, a nine year old?" He hunted for clean clothes, miserably tired. "I mean, immortality or not, we're not fucking vampires, right?"

He paused and waited until she shook her head. She laughed. "If anyone's most like vampires, it's the Automatons, not the Masters." She redirected, "Automatons affect each Master differently, depending on what *stage* of human the Automaton enters into. From the very inception of the Automaton bond, the human's aging is slowed. Gravity cannot pull to form wrinkles so easily; the human cells cannot die so easily. The human state is somewhat suspended from decomposition, left less damaged by time. Age is a form of death, in a way. Entropy. We shield from even that, though we can't stop it completely. We can't go against nature."

Yes, yes, it all makes sense, thanks for the early morning lesson. He half-listened while checking himself in the mirror—he needed to make sure he looked sloppy enough. He didn't have to try hard.

"I assume Dorian likes the fact Mecca will take some of your hatred. Dorian doesn't like being hated."

Not hearing her, "Will it be the ice cream truck again?"

"Definitely not," she sighed. "Not if Mecca's driving."

Once Odys was ready, he stuck his head out the door. The coast was clear. Well, clear of any twin sister. Fletcher really was at her door, holding a handgun to get the message across. And to stop Odissa if she were to try to come out before Odys left.

Mecca was still in his Automaton's arms, tongue out as he went through the pictures saved on his camera. They were in the doorway, letting in the cold morning air. Q had her huge gun resting on her shoulder, observing reality for her Master while he curated his fantasies.

Odys was about to ask if he could tell Odissa he'd be back soon, but Fletcher shook his head as he pointed for them to go on. Maud gave him the finger as they redirected to the door. This wasn't fair.

As Q started out, she nodded her farewell, "Fletcher, Dorian." Her gun disappeared back into her skin.

They walked through the parking lot (to God only knew what kind of vehicle). Mecca bobbed up and down between Q's every step. He said, "Mecca wants to tell you that your sister's in good hands. Excellent hands. Mecca knows you're worried, yes. Mecca knows all about you. Mecca thinks he might like you a lot because Mecca got Big Mama to tell Mecca everything."

"By Big Mama, does he mean Mother?" Odys asked Maud.

"No," Q answered for her. "That's Cestus."

"Mecca names things whatever he wants to," Maud added, clarifying what Q had just clarified. "And changes them to suit his mood."

"Yeah, Big Mama said he liked you," Mecca went on, sticking out his scrawny legs and arms behind his Automaton like a double pair of wings. "Big Mama said you're a real nice boy, even though you look like a street beggar. And if Big Mama thinks so, that means Bobmation thinks so too."

Odys assumed: Bob + Dalmation - Dal = Bobmation.[90]

He figured it was nicer that the B-word.

Mecca continued his logic, "And if Bobmation thinks so, then you've passed level one. And if you pass level one, that means level two must be cleared. Level two would be Mecca and Q, here. Mecca and Q will let you know your score by the day's end. If you pass, then you'll move on to level three. That should be the final level. That's Mother's level, that is."

Odys looked around for the car. "Which one are we getting into?"

As if Odys should already know, "Mecca will let you pick." Mecca and Q grinned wickedly. "Mecca never drives the same car twice."

"Are you joking?"

"Mecca does joke sometimes, but Mecca's not joking right now, because stealing a car is a very serious crime."

"He's telling the truth," Q stated, as if her word was Mecca-law.

"They're not joking," Maud confirmed. "However," she said to them, a bit crossly, "to keep with your record, Mecca, how about you drive Odissa's car down there, and we drive it back? After all, if we're driving it back, that means Mother's let us *come* back, right?"

---

[90] Bob needs a Bobmation plantation, where all of her can roam (I need to shut up; we don't have Disney money). But deargod if I have to buffer one more cutesy Mecca quirk, I'm gonna barf.

Mecca and Q looked at each other. Odys could almost see the inner conversation shooting out their eyes like laser beams. Sticking out his tongue in thought, Mecca made Q answer them, "Mecca says that, for you, Maud, we'll make the exception. But only if you let us take a picture of you in your cop uniform."

Rolling her eyes, she agreed.

Mecca whipped out his camera, and Maud, like some natural pin-up, struck a pose.

"Fucking hell, can we go now?" she barked after the flash.

Stanza: Eve knew God was hiding something.

From the window, Fletcher had watched them leaving the apartment parking lot. Until they were out of sight, he and his Master waited patiently.

"All clear."

They sprang into action.

Dorian started pacing, hand upon chin (to help his thinking).

"You *know* we need to get this over with," Fletcher reasoned with him. "We have to or we'll go mad."

"Do it," Dorian nodded to her door. Fletcher had Odissa's door knob off in an instant. He dropped it as he turned into a paperclip. Dorian scooped him up and clipped him to his coat pocket. His eyes on his chest.

He swam into the room. "Good morning, Ms. Odelyn. Rise and shine."

But she was already awake, eyes wide. "You—you broke my door!"

"You and I suffer a lot of broken doors, don't we? Yes, I *should* have knocked. I should do a lot of things society tells me to do. But I don't. Now, what're you reading?"

"Can't you fucking see? What if I had been dressing? Jesus Christ, you can't just barge in here and—"

"No, actually, I can't see."

She jerked back. "What? You have eye problems or something?" She hoped he couldn't see, indeed; see her ratty hair, smudged face, wrinkled clothes. She pulled the blanket toward her chin.

She was usually very clean and proper. She never showed her bed-face to anyone except Odys. Never.

"Bingo," Dorian said. "I can't see *as well as most*."

"Then why do you have this job, if you can't see?" Is that why he'd attacked her last night? But he had seemed quite coordinated—even now, he...

177

"I see well enough." He knew that wasn't satisfying. "I'll not pretend otherwise, I'm not an *official* cop. But I do my work for them—a liaison. A freelancer. Auxiliary. Whatever. Fletcher's official, though, isn't he?"—as if he wanted her opinion. "So, what are you reading?"

"The dictionary," Odissa said, aghast. She tossed her book down. It wasn't really the dictionary, but she felt the need to lie—to test his sight.

He nodded and stuffed his hands in his pockets. Then, he pretended to glance around. Odissa wished she could see behind his reflective lenses. For a while, they both said nothing.

"You realize it's rude to be in here, don't you?"

"Oh, yes, no doubt about that." He sat in her desk chair. He nudged a box that had once cluttered her bed. "But I also think it's rude you're being such a bad hostess."

"Do you know how early it is?"

"I was hoping that, since your brother's gone, we might have a little chat."

"He's gone?" there was slight panic in her voice. He knew she heard him talking out there—but she never thought he'd leave her.

"Gone back to the station."

"Station 69?" she mocked.

"The very one."

"You realize you're making me uncomfortable in my own home, don't you?"

"And I attacked you in your own home as well, don't forget that. How are you by the way? Bruises?" He gestured to his own neck area.

She ignored his question. "What was your name again?" Though she remembered. She remembered because she'd liked his name. She just wanted to make sure it hadn't changed overnight.

"Dorian."

"Like Dorian Gray," she mused. On top of it, he was the perfect manifestation of Oscar Wildean ideals. That was his historical parallel. Odissa liked historical context. Odissa had decided it befit him. Odissa was never wrong in her decisions. It was her natural ability. Yet she couldn't historically place Fletcher or Maud—those other two. She found it impossible. It bothered her.

He chuckled at the irony. "Yes. Though, if my last name were his, I'd spell it with an 'e' instead of an 'a.' Sounds more achromatic."

"…I don't think the color spectrum depends on spelling."

"You'd be surprised. Grey happens to be my favorite color." He paused, waiting for her to say "I never would have guessed!" as most people did (based on his *gay rainbow* appearance). But she didn't. "If I had to guess, I'd say you had a particular fondness for that color?"[91] He lifted a lone shoe out of one of her many boxes. He loved shoes.

Narrowing her eyes, "Why'd you say that?"

Did she have a diary she didn't know about—a diary he'd read?

She watched him shrug. "Fate has a way of being clever, doesn't it?"

She ignored her goose bumps and said, "It's silver, actually." She swallowed. "How'd you know?"

"Well, I didn't, obviously. You like silver. Not *grey*."

"What's your last name then?" She needed it for future reference.

"Dandor. Dorian Dandor's the name. Babysitting's the game."

"Dador? As in, means 'giver'?"

"No, no, *Dan*dor. But how wonderful! You know Spanish."

"Not enough to know what you and that other cop were talking about late last night."

He grinned at her standoffishness. "Would you like some breakfast? Cup of tea? Coffee? To come out of the bedroom?"

"I'd rather take a shower, please."

"And close another door?" He gestured to the one he'd just broken.

"I have a feeling you aren't supposed to be breaking doors, Mr. Dandor."

"Dorian, please. What are you going to do, tattle on me?"

"Why are you really talking to me?"

"I need some company."

She moved her feet off the bed. "No one should have company this early. Where's your other half—Fletcher—if you're so bored?"

"He's out at the car, checking the grounds." Lie. "That's his job for now. Just you and me in here. All alone. No one to stop me from breaking doors. Tell, Odissa, are you always this reclusive? Don't you want something to eat?"

"It's too early for breakfast. I just woke up."

"Don't lie, Odissa. You've been awake. Trying to eavesdrop. Haven't you?"

She wanted control of the conversation. "You have a paperclip on your pocket."

---

[91] Is grey even a real color?

"My lucky charm." He patted it. He tried to smile—such a half-assed action.

She reached across the bed to the floor, for her purse. She pulled out a cigarette. Maybe it would make him leave her alone. SMOKE HIM OUT.

"So early?" he asked, frowning.

"Want one?"

"Not unless it's a bubble gum one."

Her lips half-smiled around the cigarette as she lit it. "This whole thing isn't for our protection is it?" she asked, blowing out a lung full of air-ash. "You're not really cops—none of you. Maybe you're dirty cops?"

He said nothing, merely smiled. This was exactly what he wanted. She could see it. "Your friends don't act like cops—or anything in between. You're all pretending in front of me. But you almost don't care if I notice or not."

"People notice things all the time. Doesn't mean they really know what's going on."

"Was someone else over this morning—a little kid? I heard a knock at the door."

"No need to worry about that."

"Who said I was worried? I was just curious." She was trying to sound confident.

"Sometimes curiosity can kill. Just ask the cat."

Deciding she wanted to test his limits, "Can I take a shower now?"

"I wasn't aware you had to ask."

"I wasn't aware I didn't have to."

"Well, if that's the case then, no. You may not take a shower." His smile was wider than we've ever seen it. She amused him.

He pushed up his incognito glasses. She pushed up her own. Mimicry.

Wanting to throw her off guard, "Did you ever want children?" He crossed his arms, as if her reply might take a while.

His partner Fletcher must have explained "it" clearly to him, so she quickly un-furrowed her brows. "You don't have to ask so politely. It's not a touchy subject for me. And the answer is no. Not really."

He itched his nose. "And do you have a boyfriend we should consider? No one poking their nose in to check up on you?"

"Why? Would you attack them too?"

"Probably. We need a clear coast, that's all. But seriously, is there anything you'd like to inform me about—when your brother isn't around?"

"And what about you? That Fletcher, last night. You two were working on the job. Real professional."

He didn't even blush. In fact, his grin grew wider. Wider and wilder. Wilde.

What an Oscar!

She wondered if she could cash in on this glee. "Odys knows what this is really about, doesn't he?" she pressed. "Did he try to find something out about my father? Did he get into trouble because of it?"

"Let's say that Odys didn't *have* to try to find information on your father. It found him."

"*Are* they dirty cops, then? Maud and Fletcher?"

"Very. Very dirty. Very naughty."

"Was it really a suicide? Or did Odys see something he wasn't supposed to see?"

"Yes and yes."

"Did Odys also do something he shouldn't have? Does he owe you something?"

"Yes and yes."

Stanza: Adam didn't have the balls to bite first.

Driving.

In the back of Odissa's car, Maud and Odys sat stiffly. Mecca and Q occupied the front seats. They didn't wear their seat belts.

Odys prayed Mecca knew what he was doing. Maud seemed at ease with his driving—even though he could hardly see over the wheel or reach the pedals—but Odys couldn't shake the fact a cop might see a little kid zooming past. Odys looked like the only adult in the car.

As Mecca sped down the highway, tongue sticking out, Odys asked, "Just wondering: why are you letting me have windows to see where we're going?"

"Mother has selected a meeting spot for brunch. A public place," Q responded over her shoulder. "Of course she's already moved from the last location. Mother can't be too cautious, since you could've calculated the turns and speed. Maud's very smart, we know. It's not even because we don't trust you. But someone could get the info out of you. No doubt we're being watched." She turned to Maud, "Leeland called Dorian. Just thought you should know. We just found out about it."

Maud asked, "So where are we meeting Mother?"

"It's a surprise."

181

To fill the silence, Q and Mecca rolled down their windows and proceeded to scream at anyone jogging, walking, sitting, jaywalking and so on in the chill morning air. The onlooker's faces were priceless, trying to find the scream's source as they whizzed by.

DOPPLER EFFECT.

Maud rolled her eyes. They always did this.

But soon—very soon, thankfully—their throats could not take the cold, and they found the radio a warmer entertainment.

Odys gazed out his window, not seeing.

"You think Odissa will be all right?" he asked Maud.

"Why wouldn't she be?" Maud replied.

He looked at her. She was already turned to face him, expecting him to turn his head. Her eyes widened, like a flash bulb going off. Her expression seemed to say: *But I do think she has the right to know—eventually—that Odi Odelyn wasn't your real father—whether or not they want you to mention it.*

Scratch that. It didn't *seem* like she was saying it. It was—WAS!—Maud saying it.

In his head.

Or, maybe it was in *her* head and *he* was just tapping into *it*.

But, still, he had HEARD it.

Without even trying.

She put a stabilizing hand on his arm, smiling, proud of him—delighted he had finally read her thoughts. Did this mean he wasn't fighting "it" anymore?

Nope. When her fingers touched his bare skin, he felt relief. Their non-verbal communication had drained them. This big step forward had cost him—in fact, it was an *over*step. He was panting.

Q turned the radio up, the undulating noise a wall of privacy. However, privacy was unnecessary. They were done talking, for now. He felt his pockets for his cigarettes. But Maud already held an open carton. "They were in your other jacket. I knew you'd forgotten."

"Thanks." He took the pack hesitantly, like some expensive gift he wasn't sure he should accept.

She touched the end of the cigarette to light it before he could even reach for a lighter. He held the cigarette limply between his lips, not sure what just happened. His chin jutted out to steady it. But still it wavered just like his decision to start smoking it.

"Mecca wouldn't mind one as well, thank you very much," the little Master said over his shoulder, extending his little fingers.

Maud, speaking for Odys, "We don't give out smokes to minors."

"Mecca is no minor!"

"Minor in age, no; minor character, yes."[92]

"Gasp!" Q said, putting a hand over her mouth. "We take offense."

Maud scoffed. "The 'little man syndrome' is so overdone. Even 'little pervert.' Act normal for once."

"Bah!" Mecca said. "Mecca has worked years to perfect his image—qualities clichéd and new! Don't belittle Mecca's art."

"Pornography, more like," Odys said to himself. He wasn't sure why he'd said it, but he liked the bitter laughs the other pair gave.

Q turned down the radio, glad they were all conversing now. "Mother told you the extra Automaton's still missing, right? They say you don't know what Pepin did with it." Her bright eyes hoped for a secret or two. *You can trust me.*

"She doesn't remember."

"You mean *you* don't remember." Q's eyes danced. "Did Maud tell you how ironic it is, though?"

"How ironic what is?" Odys was supposed to guess, apparently.

"The missing Automaton is a twin, too. He and Maud are made from the same casting and materials. They're both coins—both pennies. The only two Automatons with dates on them. No need for carbon dating. They're very *specific* objects, compared to us others. In a way, Vulcan made them to be a pair, didn't he? They're his two cents. He first gave the twin-Automatons to a brother and sister. He made them to match each other."

Q's eyes cut to Odys, to see how curious he was about her little tangent. She turned in her seat, her little butt in the air. Her tiny hand clutched the headrest. "You didn't explain it, Maud? Oh, geez. I *do* think it's funny—that the *twin* would gain a *twin* Automaton. Don't you, Mecca?"

Of course he did.

Q giggled. "Perhaps the gods had something to do with this? Makes you wonder if Vulcan isn't laughing at the irony himself. Like two handguns, they were designed to work together—" she shot the air with her fingers "—but are still quite useful when apart, of course."

---

[92] See? Even the other characters feel the same way about Mecca as I do.

Odys looked at his Automaton, a tinge of fear flashing in his sepia eyes (the kind of eerie fear that makes your skin prickle—prickle at a plot that twists too much together). He wasn't sure why it unnerved him, but the stars had lined up too well for this. He didn't like being part of the line.

"It's not as dramatic as she makes it sound," Maud waved her away—though her eyes were wide. She'd been too preoccupied lately to ever realize the congruity.

Q went on despite Maud, "I think it's a good sign, Odys Odelyn. You're supposed to have Maud. It's a clear sign. We paired ones *see* the signs. And smell them too." She squished her nose. "That's why we're so interested in you—why we haven't killed you yet."

"One of the reasons," Mecca clarified himself.

As the car stopped (they'd barely driven as far as Odys thought they might), Odys didn't care to notice where they were parking. He was too busy feeling like the gods' pawn.

"You really don't remember what Pepin did with your brother, Maud?" Q pressed. "Not even a guess?"

Maud to Q, "I don't even remember if Pepin had him at all, at the end. I don't know what Pepin did with *Madus*."[93]

Q: Automaton of Mecca Makepeace, at your fan service!

WHAT NOT TO DO: Mock her Master by asking him if he's grown recently. Besides, he'll let you KNOW if he's grown. You'll never stop hearing about it.

CUTEST OUTFIT: A maid outfit.

FAVORITE POSE: Moe pose!

Chapter the fourteenth,

Internal corruption:

Which devices have malfunctioned?

Odissa wondered what was stopping her from dashing out of the room—out of the apartment. He admitted he was blind, didn't he? Well, partially.

Whatever that meant.

But then again, he had moved pretty fast last night, when he'd pounced on her. She decided to stay put. "I can offer you money…if it will make you leave us alone."

He chuckled. She was too cute. "You may take your shower now."

---

[93] Yes, I'll admit that I couldn't really come up with a good "M" name replacement for Madus and so I just rearranged the letters of Maud's name and added an "S." All the other Automata names have interesting meanings or connotations. Poor Madus's doesn't.

She couldn't help but wane. He was done with her. He'd wadded her up and thrown her away. He just sat there, in her room, watching her collect clean clothes for after. Didn't say a word.

As she closed the swollen door to her bathroom, she saw his grooming bags—the ones he'd shoved in the huge duffle bag he'd brought. Locking the door behind her, she told herself it would be safe to peek.

He used more products than she did. Or, maybe it was some of Fletcher's stuff too (she didn't know Automata needed no beauty products). She noticed a polka-dotted straightening iron.

She frowned. What had she expected to find—drugs?

She turned on the shower.

She looked over her shoulder at the bathroom's locked door. Surely, two *gay* men wouldn't care to see her naked. She was safe.

Stanza: *Dorian Gray* and his picture.

Dorian removed the paperclip perched on his pocket and let him fall to the ground.

"Jesus Christos," Fletcher whistled. He appeared beside Dorian, wearing his cop uniform in case Odissa came out. A smile lit his face as he glanced around for his Master. "You sure know how to carry a conversation."

"Yes, well, I wanted her to talk—talk more about Leeland."

"Then why didn't you try harder?"

"Because I think I already know why Leeland 'adopted' these twins."

"Psh. You knew that from the beginning."

"Yes, but." He stopped.

Fletcher finished for him. "Now we know why he was able to hide it from us. He liked having them believe he was in the mob or…whatever." He waved his hand. "Even this seems normal to her. Makes you wonder who Lee's been socializing with these past years, doesn't it? We're not the worst she's seen," he snorted.

Obeying Dorian's thoughts, he pulled out his Master's phone and punched in some numbers. As it rang, he handed it to Dorian. "Ah, Dorian!" Mother's voice sounded from the phone. "I was just about to call you. I just saw Mecca's car, but there's still a little time. You call for something?"

"Yes, Gwen. It'll be done soon. She's up and everything. Taking a shower now. I'll call you when it's done."

"Ah, *bien, bien.* You didn't have to start so soon. I told you I'd call when we needed her out."

185

"I thought I'd let her take one good shower before doing it."

"Ah, that is very kind. And early means we have more wiggle room."

"Also, I…"

"Yes?"

"Um." He sighed, not knowing what to say. "Er—fair warning, Mecca's picture-happy today. He has more than one camera."

"Nothing new," she mumbled in Spanish. "Oh, and Dorian—"

"Sí?"

"I know you think you know for sure, Dori. Even I do. But—but Leeland is clever. Don't get too attached. Leeland's been planning to do something with these twins for a long while now. It might not be them."

The line went dead.

The bitch has us tapped Dorian laughed, calmly putting away the phone. He patted it with his hand. Mother was always listening.

"She should trust us more," Fletcher said, watching his Master.

"No, it's comforting to know we scare her a little." Dorian smiled. "I don't blame her. She's right. She's always right." He put his hand on his hip. "They may not even *be* twins. Odissa looks younger, anyway. Leeland could have found two children who looked alike and—"

"But why'd he go to that trouble?"

Dorian sat down beside his Automaton. "Why'd he go to the trouble of raising two children at all?"

"These rhetorical questions aren't settling anything." Fletcher leaned into his Master's hair, to whisper in his ear. "Maybe we should believe and fall into the trap. We'll let it close in on us this time." Fletcher put a hand on his Master's arm. "Maybe if we play along, Leeland'll take me away from you. And you'll be free from needing answers."

"My thoughts sound scary when said aloud." Dorian rolled away.

"All the better to make Mother worry. She needs to listen. We can't be doing anything stupid now, can we?"

Stanza: The self-made man.

Fletcher and Dorian had hovered like vultures waiting to swoop—floating in this and that room, hardly lighting. Odissa took long showers, indeed. At least now she was blow-drying her hair. They could hear it.

Dorian walked to Odissa's bookcase. Fletcher turned his head in the bookcase's direction, so Dorian could better inspect. Dorian ran his fingers along the spines, as if they could read the titles.

"You think Pepin could have died for *me*, Fletcher? You think Pepin was trying to lessen the leverage Leeland potentially has on me?"

"I don't know about *lessen*. Now you and Odys share the same leverage, don't you? A leverage you didn't even know still existed until recently."

"If correct, Pepin had a lot riding on how much I'd care about Odissa. I mean, I let her die once already. Along with her brother and parents."

Fletcher sighed. He assured him once again, "You didn't know she existed back then, though. You thought Leeland was lying to you. And even then you gave up your eyes to buy time—time to try and verify if Dory[94] really did have twins..." Fletcher stopped himself, looking past his Master. He could remember Coraza off in the distance, verifying for Leeland that Dorian had ruined his eyes. That was the first thing he saw for Dorian—the first thing his Master could not see himself.

"But it didn't buy enough time." He pushed up his glasses. "I just hoped it'd be that simple— why Pepin died."

"Pepin wasn't simple."

"I want to tell the twins who I think they are." Dorian pulled out one of Odissa's books. He put it back in the wrong place, wondering if she'd notice when she came back in. "Be a dear and step closer, I want to see these titles properly."

"It might confuse them, if you told them " Fletcher put a hand on his Master's lower back. His Master was tired. Best to stay close. "Besides, Odys will eventually sync with Maud and there'll be no more hiding it."

"Exactly. Why not fess up to it now? I don't want them to hate me even more."

"The only reason Maud hasn't told him yet is (likely) because she knows we did the right thing; Odys doesn't want to hate you yet. He's trying to make a way to accept you and what you did. And even so, not even *Maud* can verify if Odys is or is not of the right set of twins, so we might want their forgiveness for nothing." He frowned. "Well, not *nothing*, but at least not *everything*. And can I just say that I don't think it's wise for Mecca to be handling the cat?" He narrowed his eyes at Bulfinch, who was watching with headlight eyes from under the bed.

---

[94] That's Dory with a "Y," not an "I." Not to be confused with Dorian's nickname of "Dori."

187

"At least we don't have to do it. Bulfinch hates us. He's on to us. Besides," Dorian went on. "Mecca could use something other than Q to play with."

"He does play with himself a lot, doesn't he?"

They both sniggered. Dorian said, "We're going to have to teach him a lesson, for what he did last night. I think some of his storage units might need to burn down. The ones in Arkansas, too."

"The film props? That's an assault to history, though! Those things are priceless."

"Perhaps you're right. It wasn't *entirely* his fault I jumped her. Maybe just sell everything in them. At the lowest price. Call [name redacted]'s bar friend." Dorian snapped his fingers. "What's-his-name."

Fletcher nodded. He'd get to it later. "Odd titles, aren't they?" Fletcher asked once their grins had become straight lines again.

"She's well-read. Too well-read, almost."

"It's eerie, Dorian. It's too eerie—even for genetics—that their reading tastes should be—"

"So alike? Yes, I agree. Fate has a way of being obvious, no? I miss reading. Though, it's easier now that you've done—and do—it for me."

Fletcher had a plethora of editions stored up before Dorian got him. "I made you smarter, I did." He tapped his head.

Dorian dusted off a book's cover. "No quicker way to read than to 'download' it from your Automaton."

"I wouldn't say *download*."

"No, I wouldn't; not in public. Ah, *The Wizard of Oz*. Like I said, fate, right? My, my. This is an old copy."

"The American version of *Alice in Wonderland*. Geez, I remember when this first came out. And *Alice*, for that matter."

"And the movies."

"Makes me feel old."

"We *are* old."

Fletcher's ears perked, but his eyes remained focused on what Dorian was "looking" at.

"Did you find anything incriminating?" Odissa asked from the doorway. She'd finally come out. She was clean, done up, dressed.

"For someone who works at a library, shouldn't you believe in borrowing books?" Dorian stated, gesturing with the book to her unmanageable collection.

She glared. "Well, they come in handy when the internet's down."

"I wouldn't unpack, dear." She had opened a suitcase. "Fletcher and I have somewhere to go, and you must *come with*."

"I thought I couldn't leave the apartment?"

"This is standard procedure." Dorian cleared the clot in his throat, hating that he sounded like Bob.

"Will Odys know I'm leaving?"

"He'll know." Eventually.

Panic in her voice, "How long will it take? He'd like to know where I am."

Dorian took out another piece of gum. "Or is it that *you'd* like him to know?" he said, feeding the gum in like a vending machine dollar slot.

"Where are we going?"

"It's a surprise."

"You really want me out of this room, don't you?"

The boys just grinned at her. It made her skin prickle.

"Please, let me call him."

"Please? As if I wouldn't let you?"

"Would you, then?"

"Well, since I have the choice, then, no Get your coat, Ms. Odelyn. We're going down the yellow brick road." He tossed the *Oz* book on her bed and led her out.

Fletcher tapped his nose at the book as he left. He could *smell* what Vulcan was up to.

Stanza: A triplet of twins.

Mecca had parked the car in a large, empty lot. A few quiet buildings lined it.

"Where are we going?" Odys had said before opening his door

"That pub there," Q had pointed. "But first, that pawn shop, just up the way."

Mecca nodded. "Best in this area. Haven't hit it for a few months now. Mecca needs cash."

"We aren't driving there?" Odys squeaked, in no health condition to walk.

"Walking is safer. We won't have to steal another car after. Mecca has his rules."

"Can't you go there on your own time?"

"And waste gas to drive up there when we're so close?"

"It's not your gas, is it?"

Mecca shrugged. "Mecca is green."

Stealing cars = environmentally friendly.

"Not how that works."

"Stop whining, Beans!" Mecca shouted downhill to them as Q picked up her pace.

Odys turned to Maud, aghast at his new nickname. She cringed. "My translation is because they're associating you with coffee beans. They *were* just in your apartment…"

Odys huffed. "Has no one ever taught him manners?"

"You'd think they'd come preloaded in an Automaton. Wouldn't need to be taught." Maud pushed him into a starting pace to catch up with them.

The pawn shop was, however, not entirely just "up the way." In fact, it was almost five blocks later when they finally reached it.

"Where the hell were they pointing to?" Odys was exasperated. He was jealous of the man relaxing on the metal bench outside the shop—a man very interested in why these four youngsters were entering the underground market—er, I mean *pawn* shop.

Q set Mecca on his feet (pretending that he had become too heavy for her). He looked strange on the ground—a baby gazelle taking first steps.

"You sure this is a pawn shop?" Maud asked Q. The sign was written in another language.

"Yes. The owner is Hmong. That's why the sign," Q answered.

Maud explained to Odys, "It doesn't even say 'Pawn Shop' in Hmong! How was I to know?"—as if Odys were judging her foreign language abilities.

"Come on," Mecca ordered. "You both have to come in, too."

Inside, the small shop with garage-sale flair had posters with Asian faces, advertisements in Asian words (both calligraphy and typeface), and heavenly high-pitched music playing overhead. A man came from the back, pushing past the curtain of red wooden beads. He remembered Mecca and Q (who could forget them?). Q began to speak (in what I can tell you is a Hmong dialect), gesturing to Mecca. He retrieved a few objects from his cargo pockets: a golden doorknob (that had once been brass), a golden ring (that had once been plastic), a golden clothes pin (that had once been wood).

The man smiled.

Mecca took the first price he offered, though it wasn't a high number. But what was money to Mecca when he'd gotten these objects for free? At least he hadn't stolen them—never mind, he *might* have. He had to find some way to make it "fun."

Q thanked the man and they left, passing by the man on the outside bench again (he shuffled his papers at them).

Mecca counted out the money. He licked his thumb more than once to help him count. He handed Odys some cash. "Here. Mother wants you to have a safety net."

"What? What for?"

Maud nodded. *Take it, Odys.* He took it.

Mecca tossed Odys the keys on their way back to the pub. "Q will blow up your car if you try to leave before Mother dismisses you," Mecca warned him.

They finally arrived at Splinky's so-called tavern. Odys reached for Maud's hand, feeling sick from all the walking. Too woozy to be apologetic about it.

The pub was a shabby little excuse for a drinking spot but cheery nonetheless.

"Bob knows the owners. Technically helped them start up the place," Q informed them, their tour guide. "The couple was pretty much destitute when she found them. It's only open evenings. We can't go in then when there's people. And when the owners might see us."

She saw Odys's confusion.

"The owners don't know where they got the money from, but Bob earns it back. They think it's an angel. An angel of whiskey!"

"Like hell they do," Maud said. "They probably think it's a drug lord they don't want to piss off, especially since they're doing so well."

Q rambled on, "So they don't call the cops whenever they know she's been in. Funny, isn't it, how near we've always been to you, Odys? Your campus is only twenty miles that way. Granted, we stay in many places. But it's strange you were going to school where we do a lot of our *business*. Vulcan's been playing plot-twister, we're sure." Q stopped outside the door. "Maud must stay out here. With me."

Q handed Mecca to Odys. Take the baby, Odys.

Through the backdoor, Odys and Mecca made their way into the main lounge; complete with table, chairs, and plethora of available alcohol.

"They turned off the power so the cameras go out. That's why the candles," Mecca explained. Enough light seeped through the windows that candles were slightly unnecessary.

Bob was sitting at the table, booted feet crossed and resting atop it. Her fingers comforted a shot-glass, wetted. Her eyes—or eye, rather (the other behind that huge glob of curled bangs)—stared at the table as if it were saying the most frightening things.

Her free hand flicked the antique-looking compact on the table. "They're here, tell her," she ordered it, as if it was some walky-talky or baby monitor.

The antique compact sprang to life, stretching out into a boy figure. The metal rippled and stretched outward, taking its time. Slowly, it formed a place for facial features. For a brief second it reflected Odys's face like a mirror. Then, losing some of its sheen, it became less chrome-like. Anselm sat cross-legged on the table, dense once more, staring at Odys. The table his lotus bloom. He opened his translucent eyes.

Mecca (in his best Irish brogue), "Oy, Bob, pissed yet?" He giggled to himself, proud at his cleverness as he slid down Odys's body and dashed behind the bar.

Bob paid no more mind to them, her duty done. Instead, she poured herself another drink. Downing it, she sucked air through her teeth.

Anselm looked down upon her, his white hair sliding over his shoulder. "Gwen said she is coming. And to be hospitable."

Pouring another drink, Bob chortled. For Bob, that meant not doing a damn thing.

"No need to get up," Mecca stated, as if Bob had offered him a drink. "Mecca can help himself." And help himself he did. He found a paper bag and began filling it like a shopping cart.

"Please," Anselm said to Odys. "Sit down." He gestured to the seat across from Bob. Though Odys would rather have stood than come near Bob and the creepy child-thing, he obeyed. Anselm watched him—continued to stare at him. "Bob?"

"What?" she barked at the Automaton.

Anselm said, "When's Cestus going to arrive?"

"Well, since he can't fucking grow wings and fucking fly, however long it takes to drive here."

"Perhaps you should go outside and wait for him. And leave the bottle behind." He grabbed it before she finished reaching.

Plopping her feet down, she wobbled up. "Thought you'd never let me leave." Was she being held hostage? As she passed by Mecca she pointed at him. "What's my rule?" she barked. He took a few steps back, crooked smile on his lips. He obeyed the five-foot rule (Bob had a measurable circumference).

Mecca waddled his heavy bag beside Odys with a clank. Bottle-toasting Anselm with an unopened whiskey, "Sesshōmaru."[95]

Anselm cut his eyes as Mecca snatched Bob's remaining bottle—no need to waste it.

Anselm leaned forward, elbows on his knees. To Odys, "And how is Maud?"

---

[95] Name of a white-haired character in the anime and manga *Inuyasha*. This is probably only funny to Mecca. Or our geeky Narrator.

"Fine."

"He slept with her," Mecca stated. "I have pictures, want to see?"

Odys winced.

"No, that's all right, Mecca." Anselm to Odys, "Willingly?"

"Yep," Mecca answered, trying to stuff a smaller bottle in his coat pocket to make room.

"Let him answer, Mecca," the Automaton scolded, lifting a long-nailed finger. "We need to know his progress. It isn't progress if we do everything for him."

"I did," Odys replied, hoping to abolish this conversation.

"Well," Anselm said. "You do look better today. Not perfect, but better. Dorian thinks so, too. He sends us updates on you, you know."

"I know."

Mother walked through the storage door—what had she been doing behind a storage door? Odys was surprised to see her in a pantsuit, not some pollera or Puebla dress. It seemed topsy-turvy to even imagine her in something so modernized. Her hair, however, was the one thing modern custom hadn't tamed. It was plaited down in a mass of rolling, twisted, softly-entwined braids over braids—some thick, some thin. Had she not been in her neutral pantsuit, she'd have been a dark lady fortune teller, Anselm her crystal ball.

Her kind eyes smiled as they found Odys. "Hello, Odys. Forgive me, but I was chatting on the phone." With Dorian. With others.

"He slept with Maud," Mecca repeated; he liked telling everyone Odys's business.

"As you've said, Mecca. And do not need to say yet again." She took Bob's seat after rubbing Mecca's bare head. Anselm took himself off the table, to rest an arm on the back of Gwen's chair. He was watching Mecca now, as if Gwen had taken over the responsibility of watching Odys.

"I haven't *not* slept with her," Odys said. "I was too sick before to know I was even doing it."

"Well, I'm glad you did. It's the only reason you're still alive, Odys. Look, your energy wavers as we speak. So pale. Your lips are blue. But it will ameliorate—once you finally decide to sync with her. How's your sister?"

"Fine."

"So I hear." Mother tore her eyes away, something happy in her tone. "I have also heard *other* things recently."

Mecca picked up his sack, taking the hint. "Help me carry this!" He shouted for Q to meet him half way—as if he needed to shout. His bag was about to rip by the time Q took it from him. He still insisted on being held along with their alcohol.

"He never sits still, that one," Gwen mused, staring at the door they'd just slammed. "But then again, I don't blame him. He knows a bit of what I plan to talk about."

Odys wished Anselm would leave, too. It would be easier to go through this without some supernatural creeper distracting him. Anselm moved around his Master and reached for the bottle Mecca had left behind. He swished around the liquid, observing the lively air bubbles. He lifted his hand and a translucent glass formed between his budded fingertips. He poured the contents of the bottle into himself, to drink properly.

"Now, Odys," Mother said. "I know I disturbed your sleep. But I have important news. Something's come up. This isn't how I wanted our relationships to begin, but then again, we both never asked for this in the first place."

Anselm finished his drink, though not all of the contents had been drunk. Instead, the self-formed glass closed its lips inward and absorbed the liquid into his skin. Anselm was merely enjoying the act itself, not the drink. Did Automata even enjoy consuming things like humans did?

When the Automaton reopened his fist, a circular object had replaced the shrinking glass. He let it fall to the ground, attached to thread-like chord—a nerve, a vein, a hair for the yo-yo to coil about. Up and down. Up and down. Up and down.

Up.

And down.

"As you know," Mother went on, as if her Automaton wasn't being a terrible distraction, "Leeland adopted you for a reason. You know we probably know that reason—or we have a guess. I will tell you that guess—after you do something for me first."

At the mention of Leeland's name, Anselm snapped up the yo-yo. His palm crushed it back into himself. The Automaton's fun didn't distract Mother. Anselm did the fidgeting for her. Busying her from crying.

Why isn't she bursting into tears right now like last time? Odys stared at Gwen. Brown eyes meeting brown eyes.

Brown eyes so much like his…

"I met you here because there are other shops around—with employees opening and customers shopping. The people tend to ward off Leeland. He doesn't want to make a scene. Scenes are last resorts for him."

There was a loud boom outside.

"But not a last resort for us, apparently," Mother grimaced—as if the explosion had been louder than expected. Odys looked out the cloudy window. His car had just exploded. Q was putting down her arm just as Maud was bursting in. Bob was pointing, ordering Q to follow "that bitch" Maud. Bob had given the order for Mecca to murder the car.

"What the hell is going on?" Maud shouted at Mother.

Odys stood up, as if he might run out—but he knew better.

Q, Mecca, Bob, and Anselm were all pointing guns at Odys. The message was clear. Maud held up a hand—stay put, Odys.

Mother sat back in her chair. "We can't have you running away after what I'm about to tell you, Odys. Granted, there are other cars out there for the taking, but you've never stolen a car and I think you'll behave once I remind you we have your sister, Odys." She looked at Anselm's gun. "He doesn't have to really form this thing to shoot something at you. But, God, how it reminds us humans what they're capable of, no?" She pursed her lips, to stop them from trembling. She stood back, seeing Maud glow red-hot.

"You kill her, they kill Odissa," Anselm reminded Maud as he reabsorbed his gun. He tilted his head toward Odys. Mother paced to the door, closer to her followers, Anselm her bright shadow.

Anselm's hands were behind his back. Mother, too, kept her appendages close, rubbing her fingers as she fretted. She continued, "I'm surprised how trusting you were of me—to obey me to come here. I am sorry for it. So sorry. Odys, as we speak, Dorian is taking Odissa out of the apartment."

"*Kidnapping* her?" Maud shouted, stepping to the door as if Odys should too.

"DON'T!" Bob shouted, gesturing at Odys with her weapon.

"You can't stop Dorian," Anselm said to Maud. "You know as well as anyone how pointless that thought is. You don't know where they're taking her." He noticed Maud glared at the others—as if they might tell her if she *forced* them to. "And *they* don't know, either."

Odys didn't like how Maud relented. But he heard her whisper, "I could find them if Vulcan let me smell them out."

"But he didn't let you smell *this* out, did he? He didn't warn you we would do this," Anselm reminded her.

Mother didn't like the tension, so she soothed it, "I lied to you yesterday, Odys. Which leads me to my big news. Madus isn't lost." Her lowered lids begged for forgiveness.

Mecca and Q's eyes grew wide, as shocked as Odys. Bob, however, seemed unaffected by the news. It was clear she knew something Mecca didn't.

"I lied because I was testing you."

Mecca and Q's eyes narrowed, contemplating why they, too, had needed to be tested.

"I know where the Automaton is. We just learned of its location—very recently. And you, Odys, will recover it for us."

"He will?" Mecca said. If anyone should be recovering the Automaton it should be someone loyal to Mother. Someone great. Someone like Mecca.

"Mecca," Anselm said tersely, "You know what needs to be done. You may go now. Hurry."

Mecca lowered his gun hesitantly and, crawling up on Q's back (her gun still raised), backed out of the room. They would steal a car in the adjacent lot.

"What's he doing? Where's he going?" Maud demanded, panicked. But she could see it on their faces—she'd been through *this* before—or, she'd seen it done to others. Perhaps she'd even *done* it to others. "I know what this is. We don't need to live like you! Leeland already knows where they live. Why cover their tracks? Why ruin their lives more? You know we have a cat in that apartment!"

"He will save Bulfinch!" Anselm shouted back. "Calm yourself. You know this has to be done, Maud. You're only reacting this way because of *his* foolish denial to how things have to be."

"*What* has to be done?" Odys cried, so confused.

"They're erasing you," Maud said, her voice cracking.

"More like just blowing up your apartment," Bob laughed. "Don't be so damn dramatic, Maud."

"Odys," Mother pleaded. "You know we are good people. Otherwise you would have fought against us by now." She gestured to Maud, who hadn't even bothered to form a threatening gun. "We're your only means of survival now. You depend on us. This *has* to be done." She went over to the bar, where a manila envelope rested. She picked it up, hand wavering for a heartbeat. "You do this for me, and you are one of us. Officially."

She placed the heavy envelope on the table—a parcel she'd prepared ahead of time. She rubbed her hand on her sleeve, as if the package had left residue on her fingers. "That, there, contains a cell phone, cards, fake passport, and instructions." As she stared at the envelope, her face contorted. "I lied to you about Pepin. And now I've stolen your sister to get you to do what I want. You might never trust me again because of this, but I have no choice."

"No choice?" Odys asked, confused.

Her eyes met his for a half-second, as if it hadn't been the truth. For sure, Mother knew there were other, less effective ways her little errand might be done.

"It's the only option, Gwen," Bob assured Mother. "The only way. You don't *need* Odys to trust you."

She shook her head. "He needs someone to trust. I wanted to be that person. I really did. But the stars have aligned too perfectly for me to be kind." She dabbed her cheeks.

"He will learn to trust you, once he realizes *why* you lied. The others understand this. He'll be no different. But, if he is…"

"But I've never lied like this before."

"There's a first for everything. This has to be done, Gwen—for his own good."

Maud realized Bob had put her gun down. Bob was trying to maintain her serious composure. Bob no longer cared about Maud or Odys. Bob's focus was on Mother and her hesitant authority.

Mother straightened, as if Bob had reminded her of her power.

"Odys," Anselm said, trying to stay on target. "Leeland knows where Madus is as well. That is because *one of us* told him."

"Who?" Maud demanded, shocked at Mother's lack of control over the group. Her eyes darted to Bob, as if Bob had already foreshadowed everything leading up to this point—this point about Mother's crumbling empire.

"Who?" Mother said. "Who do you think, Maud? The only one of us you haven't seen yet."

Yes, yes, count on your fingers, Reader. How many Masters and Automata are you aware of? How many have you officially met?[96]

Her voice low, "Wasn't it strange that she wouldn't be here to welcome you after all these years, Maud? It's because she's ashamed of what she's about to do—what she's been planning to do for Leeland."

---

[96] Part of the answer is that there are nine Automatons: 1) Maud 2) Fletcher 3) Admund 4) Cestus 5) Anslem 6) Quarrel 7) Coraza 8) Madus 9) Caffar.

Maud could barely say it, *"Rosemund?"*

ROSEMUND: Caffar's Master (because you wouldn't know, unless I told you).

QUICK BACKSTORY: When she was six years old and trying to figure out how an electrical outlet worked: They didn't make the child-proof crap back then. She slapped on some gloves and went to experiment. Upon realizing that sticking a fork into the socket led to sparks, electrical shock, and the fork melting to the wall (causing more sparks), it was no surprise that her parent's apartment caught fire. Rosemund was very proud of her conclusions—she learned something new every day! Not only did the entire slum-building burn down, but the flames licked off half her skin. From then on, she hated fire. But she loved the power of electricity that could cause it. Rosemund told her parents to blame fire, *not* electricity, for their homelessness. They blamed neither.

QUIRK: If you asked Dorian, he'd say her brain was fried one too many times, making her senses senseless—her common sense too common.

RANDOM FACT GENERATOR: She has red hair, which she thinks is more suitable for a pyromaniac. But she can see where "G-d" might have made the mistake. Needless to say, she can't wait till her head turns white. But with an Automaton, that might be a while. Or never.

Chapter the fifteenth,

A rose is a rose is a rose:

But what is it by any other name?

"But why would Rosemund defect?"—Rosemund was one of them!—"How does *she* know where Madus is?" Maud's questions made Odys swallow hard—how had Mother lost her loyalist?

"Because Pepin sent Madus to her—before he died!" Anselm shouted, as if Maud wasn't paying attention to the real matter: "Who knows or cares *why* he did it—or what he wanted *her* to do with it. Rosemund is willing to give Madus to Leeland—freely. Seems she doesn't want another Master to suffer and eventually surrender their Automaton in death. Seems she thinks Leeland will end up with all the Automatons anyway."

Odys laughed. "And you think I can stop her?" Odys mocked.

"Not stop her, no." Anselm shook his head, his eyes clouded in thought. "But you could change her mind. She freely admitted to us what she was about to do. She knows we see her reasoning, and she is too much one of us to hide the truth. But she would not let *us* explain *our* reasoning on why she shouldn't give up Madus."

"As if it would ever be a good idea to give another Automaton to Leeland?" Maud said. "Oh my god. You don't think it's a bad idea, do you? You stupid woman!"

Anselm's lips twitched. A shadow fell over his inimical face. He took a step forward. Maud did the same, two cast statues confronting each other The Automata's figures seemed to harden and glimmer like layered armor, their faces blazing with molten anger. Their expressions were emotionless, except for their flickering eyes—radiating—locked in mutual threatening.

"You will lie and tell her Odissa needs the Automaton," Mother said loudly, to calm the entire room.

"Lie? As in Odissa *won't* get to have Madus if I do succeed?" Odys shouted. He was already coming to the conclusion that *if* he ever got his hands on an inanimate Automaton, he would give it to Odissa—whether or not she wanted one

Anselm noticed Odys's wheels turning. "Even if you do convince Rosemund, she won't be so stupid as to let you near the inanimate Automaton, boy."

"So it's completely out of the question?" Maud asked, studying the envelope with curious eyes.

"I cannot guarantee anything at this time," Mother side-stepped.

"Just like you can't guarantee you know who I really am?" Odys asked. "You *know* who my parents are—maybe *you're* even my mother?"

Bob rolled her eye, not even attempting to hide her huff.

"Any one of us—the Masters—*could* be your parent, yes. Maybe even Mecca. Your accusation is valid only in the light of our youth. But of our history? None of us parented you, Odys. I'm not your mother. Not in that way." She covered her mouth, as if to stop what she was about to say, "Maybe if you synced with Maud—maybe if you stopped telling her to keep quiet— you would be able to connect the dots—connect as many as *we* have connected. But you haven't earned the right to know our secrets yet—secrets we thought had died along with your poor parents when Leeland killed them."

Odys didn't like the way Maud looked confused—as if Pepin had erased a portion of her memory that caused her current glitch; she was busy connecting dots—but would he ever allow her to show him their completed picture?

Gwen to Odys: "Will you do this for me?"

"What will you do to Odissa if I don't?"

"I rather hoped you wouldn't make us come up with ideas, Odys."

Stanza: I'm getting my planets mixed up with my gods.

199

Let's fast forward. About an hour later, back at that so-called pawn shop, this will happen: A woman walked through the door. The bell above her rang.

The fluorescent lights reflected in her black sunglass lenses—lenses mere shades darker than her charcoal-black skin. Like the rainbows in crow feathers or the vibrant shine in oil, the flickering lights played off her form. Had you been there, in that grimy shop, you would have blinked. Several times.

The first round of blinking would settle your eyes—to persuade yourself that her skin was perhaps moist with fresh, glossy sweat or lotion—that her silky makeup gave her that ebon polish. Or that maybe its tone, like a polished mirror, was simply so dark it couldn't help but shine.

The second round of eye-fluttering would be to pretend your eyes hadn't lingered on her physicality. This newcomer was worth staring at.

Her angular features elaborated her gaunt-oval head—a bare head, without hat or hair. Her nose peaked brusquely from her trenchant profile. Her face found its beauty in length rather than the width. The protruding cheekbones of her otherworldly-face framed broad lips. Those broad lips detailed her face with elegance.

Finally, we meet a face of Leeland.

Ignoring the entranced human eyes, she walked to the store corner where the man who'd been pretending to read the newspaper on the bench was now looking at the silver collection. She stood stiff on the tile floor. Her stonewall posture mimicked her down-to-business countenance. Her focus was unbroken. The man at the *Silverware and Etc.* didn't know what to make of her. Her splendor and purpose made him shift in place.

"What happened?" Her voice was like steel—smooth, hard, cold. Her bursting lips formed the words as if they needn't move to articulate the resounding question.

"They were with a boy—a young man. A white young man with brown hair. He played with it a lot, the tips."

Coraza smiled. She knew Odys and Odissa fiddled with their long hair when their fingers had no cigarette to play with. That was one trait that made them identical.

"And a woman—a young girl was with him."

"Yes, but what *happened?*"

"I can't remember all the names. I—I didn't hear them very well." He pretended to be shopping still.

"What did they sell?"

"Odd objects. The little black boy gave the white one money, after."

"Which direction did they go?"

He told her. "I watched the youngest girl use a bomb or something on the car that's still on fire, there," he pointed out the window beside them, where cops and a fire truck were now, around Odys's old car—though their presence hadn't been needed. The fire was dwindling. "I didn't believe my eyes—but I swear it looked like it was coming from her hand, not a bomb. No one else even noticed here—only after the fact." He saw she wasn't interested in his vision. "After that, the people inside the pub started to disperse. Then, the white kid that was with the younger ones—he took a car with that fine lookin' Muslim girl—the young girl. It was over with quickly."

She didn't seem interested in the car fire or anything about Splinky's Tavern. "Did the kids say anything peculiar when they were here?"

"Look, lady, you told me to watch them, not listen. Mind my own business, like. What did you expect, with instructions like what you gave? I have nothing else for you."

Coraza's Nefertiti-profile pulled up in smile. She crossed her long arms and leaned forward. Her beautiful skin hypnotized his eyes. She was letting it shine for that purpose. "Are you so sure you *didn't* hear more?"

She had noticed the ear plug dangling from his pocket—an ear plug to a listening device small as an MP3 player. He likely heard everything, then. Everything. She mentally complimented him on being prepared. He was worth the money. She pulled on the bud. The cord tugged up its device. It was no iPod. "What did you hear?"

"Look, I don't know what this is about, but—but those kids said some really weird shit. I don't know what you think I normally do, but this ain't like no job I've ever done before—kids involved. *Kids.* The fact that they were saying such things out loud—even that little boy—talking about it in *public.* If they're smart enough to thieve then they should be smart enough to not admit their crimes out loud." He laughed, as if so wise and mature about these illegal matters.

Coraza's obsidian lips twitched, almost smiling. "What makes you think they didn't *know* you were listening?"

His eyes widened. This poor man had gotten more than he'd bargained for when he accepted a thousand now, a thousand once the job was done. "Which family *are* you working for again? The Qiblas? Lakotas? I swear, I'm a freelancer, I have no ties."

"Ah, don't be so afraid, Mr. Menes."

He didn't obey. All he could do was be afraid.

"I know the man you spoke with on the phone didn't brief you properly over who you'd be spying on today. Don't worry. Those you spied on won't be interested in what you overheard."

"Funny, if I don't believe you." His voice wavered. When he'd accepted this job, he'd gotten goosebumps. They'd never gone away. There was something strange about *these* people. Something unholy holy. Something not human. He didn't like people who would hunt children— even if they weren't the law-abiding kind. *Maybe they weren't kids at all.*

"I promise you, they won't care what you overheard. In fact, we had hoped they'd use you to deliver a *message* or two to us. Not that they didn't. But we had hoped they'd be more overt. They have been, in the past. They've let our spies hear *things*. You did a fine job, Mr. Menes. At the end of the day, they just needed to know they were being watched. Here, here's your sum." She pulled out an envelope from her tight-jacket pocket. "You may go now, Mr. Menes. Don't worry, we'll not be calling you again, especially since this seems to have disturbed you."

Was his fear so obvious?

She could smell it on him. "We appreciate your work."

Menes took his money. Didn't bother to count it—or to watch Coraza hand yet another envelope to the Hmong man behind the counter—*You didn't see anything.*

Menes couldn't get away fast enough. Too bad that, after Mr. Menes finally made it out alive, he didn't make it *in*:

He opened his car door—but before he'd even slammed it shut—

The bomb went off.

His left leg was still dangling out the door.

Leeland doesn't kill people. They kill themselves. They triggered their own fate.[97]

(Semantics can be so forgiving).

Coraza left when she heard the screaming, dashing behind the building to lay low— inanimately—for a while until this whole thing blew over.

On concrete as a bent nail—the kind that had been hammered and struck off-aim, the head warped, the point dulled—she could hear her Master's self-comforting thoughts: *Menes chose his fate; he chose to open the car door that third time* [the third time sets it off], *just as he'd chosen his job.*

Stanza: Finding a purpose purposefully.

---

[97] This whole "Leeland doesn't kill people" thing made me have a conversation once with our Narrator you may find funny: I said, "He's essentially claiming he's a peanut and everyone has a peanut allergy." Our mute Narrator snorted and typed out, "Put that in a fucking footnote!" So I did.

A bit before Odys had stolen his first car, Odissa had walked through the apartment complex's parking lot, between Fletcher and Dorian. Fletcher led the way. It had just started sprinkling. The cement was spotted. It would stop momentarily.

As they walked through the rows of parked cars, Odissa stopped mid-step. Dorian almost bumped into her (and would have, had Fletcher not turned around). "My car's gone."

"Mecca," Fletcher told Dorian briskly.

"Your brother must have taken your car," Dorian explained, "No need to worry."

He gestured for her to keep moving, putting a hand on her lower back. Though it wasn't a directive push, he kept his fingertips there so he'd not risk running her over her again. He could feel her spine stiffen. He liked the feeling. Better to have her diverted than clear-minded. The last thing they needed was for her to catch every detail.

"Just where did you park?" It was cold; she was already freezing.

"We didn't. The cab's coming to pick us up."

"You called a cab?" She was expecting a cop car—which the lot lacked.

"And there he is. Poor man, he's been driving around since morning when Mother sent for him," Fletcher stated. They had wanted him to be ready for them—in case anything happened.

"Mother?" Odissa asked, confused about their family tree. Were these men brothers now? They looked nothing alike. And they slept naked together!

…But let's not go *there*, Odissa.

"Never mind that," Dorian shushed her.

The cab driver pulled up, some old fellow with a checkered cap. "Been drivin' round for hours," he shouted as his window rolled down. "The lady said to be lookin' for a tall redheaded fellow alongside a man and girl. I'sume that's you? Hope you know how much she said you'd pay. I set the timer, y'know. It's been going since five this morning. Ya'll already have a bill."

"Yes, yes," Dorian assured the driver, wide smile on his face. He opened the door for Odissa. Fletcher went to the other side. "Just be glad we're actually leaving early, mate. Otherwise you'd be bored shitless for another half hour."

Odissa didn't like this. No, not at all. The expression on the cab driver's face told her even *he* was suspicious—he didn't know what he was getting into. His eyes darted between Dorian and Fletcher, then to Odissa as he turned on and off his windshield wiper. She looked away when their eyes met; his seemed concerned for her. This all looked very bad, indeed (ahem). Sex trafficking? Drug trafficking? Mafia escort? All of the above?

Odissa was starting to realize this had *everything* to do with her father.

Fletcher was still in his cop outfit, which made this situation even stranger. Why did a cop need a taxi?

Dorian reached in his coat pocket, pulled out his wallet, leaned over the front seat. "Here. This is for so far—to prove we're honest customers, all right?"

The man's eyes widened. Yeah, yeah. Honest. He took the money. "Still going to the dentist office, am I?"

"Yes," Dorian answered, tapping the seat. "And please, no more saying aloud where we plan on going."

Odissa cut her eyes. Why not? And why on earth the dentist?

The driver was wise, and stayed quiet…all the way to the dentist's.

Odissa's heart fluttered. This was *her* dentist. When they pulled into the parking garage, she could no longer hope otherwise.

As Fletcher unbuckled his seatbelt, she looked to him. Was she getting out too?

"No," Dorian answered, putting a hand on her arm. "You're staying here."

Her skin prickled. Why hadn't Fletcher answered her? Hadn't her eyes asked *him?* How did Dorian know her question?

Fletcher shut the car door. The cab driver's eyes watched this procession in his mirrors. He wouldn't say a word. If you knew little, you'd be blamed for little.

Dorian broke the awkward silence. "Tell me, Odissa, how many cars are on this level?"

What was this? Some poorly-timed version of I-Spy? "Pardon?"

"Count the cars, Odissa." It was gentle command but a command nonetheless. When she didn't obey he reminded her, "Don't make me ask you a third time, Odissa. Don't you want to see your brother again?"

"One, two…five…ten, eleven, fourteen. Yes, Fourteen."

He put his head back. "And how many gold cars are there?"

It was dark in the garage. Not easy to tell. "Four?"

"No, five," the cab driver corrected her, "One just pulled in."

The color of the car didn't actually matter. It was more or less an exercise to get Odissa prepared for the real test.

"Wonderful," Dorian false-complimented. "Now, how many blue?"

"None."

"White?"

"Three?"

"Good." He nodded to himself. Leaning towards her, he whispered, "Now, if anything looks odd to you, I want you to tell me—right? Remember I can't see very well."

Hesitantly, "All right."

"*Does* anything look out of place? Anything?"

She took a moment, trying to find something interesting—something to interrupt the silence. "In the **handicap** parking spot, there's an abandoned **walking cane**."

Dorian suppressed a grin. The real test had begun! "What are the words?"

"Words?" she regurgitated. Her heart was racing. He was starting to scare her.

"The words—anywhere, on anything. What do they say? Read to me, Odissa. Read!"

She doubted he really expected her to go so far as to read car tags. She ran her eyes around the lot. They stumbled upon a commercial vehicle, the kind with crappy advertising pasted on the side. "Professional **Welding** School," she said aloud, "Night classes, call—"

But Dorian cut her off. "That's good. Anything else?"

Odissa huffed. He was being demanding—making the driver nervous. She didn't know if Dorian was serious. Was he mocking her gullibility in some way?

She looked up when something fluttered past. She thought it was a bird, but it turned out to be a flier. "Local **heavy metal** festival—last weekend," she summarized. The winter wind had forced it against a car's tire.

"Splendid. Now, that's all I needed, thank you "

Good seeing-eye dog!

A few minutes later, Fletcher was back in the cab. As Fletcher situated himself, Odissa noticed his eyes checking for everything she had verified to Dorian—the cane, the commercial vehicle advertisement, the already-blown-away flier. He sniffed the air like a hound picking up a scent—the nose knows. "Let's go," he told the cab driver, thump-thumping the seat.

As he was empty handed, Odissa wondered what he'd done back at the dentist office. Surely he hadn't had an appointment. That was too fast.

(NO DUH).

Out of the parking garage, they drove up the street a little ways. Taking a right, they went up a tapering hill and turned into a church parking lot, some hideous white-painted building with "Kirk" in the name. The huge parking lot was vacant—it wasn't a Sunday.

Dorian handed the driver another cash wad. "Out," he ordered Odissa. The driver left them in the lot. "What time is it, Fletcher?" Dorian asked as he strutted to nowhere in particular.

"The perfect time. Not a car in the lot. The maintenance folks don't come in for another hour and a half. We can go in unnoticed. Cestus was right."

"That's right."

They walked through the lot, up the concrete stairs and around to a back door. Fletcher added, "By the way, kudos on your six-year run of no cavities."

He'd said it just so he could see Odissa's eyes widen. He'd snuck in, yes. Whipped the dentistry hard-drive clean, corrupted their networks, grabbed the "Odelyn, Odissa" file from the cabinet, thumbed through it quickly, tossed a few papers in *this* and *that* trashcan.[98]

Mecca and Q would take care of her previous dentist's dental records on their way into town, though most information had been transferred when Odissa had switched dentists.

No dental history means no dental identification.

Before coming up to the church door, Fletcher peaked under the lid of a black trashcan. He pulled out a huge bag stowed away among the trash sacks. "Ah, this is one of Cestus's, I'm positive. I thought Anselm would've done the actual delivery." He shook out the bodybag, sniffing it again. Cestus always found the nicest ones, the kind with the dark black tarp that melted quite well—like rubber.

Odissa's jaw dropped, "What the hell?"

"Don't worry, Ms. Odelyn," Dorian said, pushing her onward. "It's not for you. Well, not for the *real* you, anyways." He didn't lead her to the door, but behind one of the building's modernized buttresses.

"I'll be right back," Fletcher said.

"Make it quick, dear," Dorian said as Fletcher kicked in the door effortlessly. Dorian crossed his arms—*muy impaciente.*

She could hear the alarm sounding. "What the fuck are you guys doing?" Odissa demanded. "The cops will be here any minute—what the hell was that bag for?"

"The *cops* are already here, remember?" Dorian said, grabbing at her arm in case she tried to step away. Odissa saw him flounder for her appendage. His blindness seemed to come in waves. "Don't worry. There's no cameras. Or, there won't be."

"That's not what I—"

"Watch for the cars, Odissa. Watch for them." He pulled her back against the buttress, next to him. When he felt she wouldn't do anything stupid, he loosened his grip.

---

[98] I'm not sure why Fletcher didn't also grab Odys's folder. But I do know that if both went missing it might make authorities suspicious. Plus, they are "getting rid" of Odys a different way.

"There's a funeral tomorrow, you see. The church partners with the memorial service across the street. There was a young girl who was in a car accident a few days ago. She was about your height, yes. Closed casket service. Practically unidentifiable I'm sure Fletcher can rip her jaw right out"—he pop-clicked his tongue, gesturing—"No teeth, see? We [as in Q] had to go through a lot of obituaries to find one suitable for you. Seems Fate wanted you erased from the mainstream, Odissa. The gods made this work out too perfectly. Well, not for the dead girl, though. But her family'll never know she's been removed. They'll not want to see that body again."

His hand tightened as Odissa tried to step away. Horrified, she prayed—PRAYED—the police would be here quickly—quickly now! She'd scream, thrash, fight. And then, when the cops saw her struggle, she'd tell them what freaks these supposed cops were.

Fletcher came out, the bodybag full and over his shoulder. The corpse weightless—merely a sash. Into the bushes she went, to be picked back up later.

Dorian dragged Odissa back down the concrete steps, her thrashing and reprimands didn't affect him. The alarm was screaming in the background, but they seemed in no hurry to leave.

"Let go of me! Are you fucking insane?"

"Fletcher, handle this, please," Dorian said as they waited for the first cop car to pull into the lot. Fletcher had her hands behind her back before she even knew Dorian had let go. Click, click.

"What the fuck?" she spat, over her shoulder. Where'd he pull those cuffs from? If it hadn't happened behind her back, she would have seen his fingers sprout the shiny metal cop-chains. He held her there, in place; chained to him.

As the second cop car drove up, the first car emptied its officer.

"Hello, officer," Dorian said, raising his hands. "In my coat pocket, you'll find my badge and papers. This is a classified case; please do your homework. This girl here was just trying to hide, that's why the alarm."

Fletcher also let one of his hands leave Odissa's back and flashed them his "badge." Dorian stepped to the side of the cop car, as if he were helping them get at his pocket—hands still up. As a cop came to Fletcher, Fletcher flashed his "badge" again. When the officer reached for it, Fletcher's hand switched to a gun so fast the officer died with that honorable insignia as his last sight.

As Odissa screamed, the second cop went down.

Now, because this had all happened behind her back, she had no (positive) clue what she had just witnessed. The cops had been killed, yes, but how? What had Fletcher shot them with?

Fletcher threw her to Dorian, who quickly brought her down to the ground and covered her eyes with the inside of his jacket. She struggled a little, but was also afraid she might lose her life too if she got in the crossfire.

She would not see Fletcher blow up one cop car, enter the remaining one and disable its recording equipment and tracking systems, then go over to the dead officers and take apart their radios and cell phones. When done, he reached inside his "pockets," digging for supplies. Dorian uncovered her face just in time to show Fletcher scattering some money and pill bottles in the corner of the parking lot—right where the pavement met the trees.[99]

They'd think this was a failed drug bust, hopefully. As seen on TV. Kirk on the Pill.

"Get in the car," Dorian ordered Odissa. She was too much in shock to scream again. How had they been able to do this—all of *this*—in under a minute? Why did the cops look more burned than shot—their wounds sizzling? She couldn't stop staring.

Fletcher retrieved his dead body from behind the bushes, placed it in the trunk, and crawled into the driver's seat. Dorian accompanied Odissa in the back.

"You killed them," she said eventually. "They did nothing wrong." She realized there were little flicks of blood on her shirt. They were turning brown—they looked more like food stains.

"It was either you or them, Odissa. I happen to care more about you," Dorian smiled. It was no happy sight. "Besides, it will distract from the fact that things went on *inside* that church."

Dorian laid his head back against the seat, slouching downward, as if to sleep. Odissa noticed Fletcher's eyes flickering to her in the mirror, every once in a while.

"I'm hungry, Fletcher," Dorian stated. He took off his blood-splattered coat and looked positively clean.

"I could eat something," his Automaton agreed.

"How do you feel about a pit stop, Odissa? There's bound to be a gas station somewhere by the river."

They were going to the river. To dump the body.

"I'm not hungry," she said as Fletcher turned on the cop lights so they could speed.

"Ah, that's right. You and your brother sustain yourselves on air pollution and soggy dirt—or, excuse me, cigs and coffee. But if you don't mind, we normal people need food."

Yes, normal. Very normal.

Stanza: Snail mail is the best mail.

---

[99] It's funny to me how Fletcher keeps cash and random drugs stored inside him.

Odys and Maud were less than five minutes from the apartment, depending on those traffic lights that Odys wasn't paying attention to.

Odys was yet to leave for his Super-Dangercus-(That'sWhyMotherDidn'tWantToDoIt) Mission, though he had every intention on going to Canada (yes, that's where Mother was sending him). But, before he obeyed Mother, there was something he needed to do.

O Canada!

Maud leaned her head upon the cold window, her coppery curls scrunching against the glass. The grey clouds had decided to shake out a little bit of snow. She looked at the car's side mirror, watching as it started to collect like lint along the edge of the road. *The weather's giving us a little bit of everything today—so unpredictable.* The snow would not last long, for the ground was too warm. "She's not going to be there, Odys. They took her. Bulfinch won't be there either."

His hands gripped the steering wheel of his first stolen car. "I just want to see it." He wanted to see what they'd done to his apartment. "I just want to see it."

Maud held her tongue. She knew her Master had to see for himself. Maybe then he would start to believe what she told him. "They've erased you, Odys." She had told him again and again as they had driven.

"In such a short amount of time?"

"Don't underestimate Mecca. He loves to blow things up."

"I could stop him."

"Don't get caught. The cops will be looking for you. Odissa won't be there—"

But he had told her, "I don't care. I'm going to see it."

And they drove by—far enough that the neighbors standing outside of Odys's burnt apartment building couldn't see him but close enough that he could see Mecca had released a very controlled fire where Odys used to live. "Someone could have gotten hurt," Odys mumbled.

"But no one did." She watched the cleanup crew work away. "They don't fake peoples' deaths that often."

"Really? Because they seem really good at it."

"You're dead now, Odys. They've given you a gift, really. It shows they have faith in you." He scoffed at her forced words.

"You should check your mail," Maud said. "One last time."

"But the people—" Odys said. He studied the firemen cleaning up the area and keeping people calm. "The cameras, too." He pointed at the news crew about to start a second report on "the situation."

209

But Maud shook her head, telling him to think through what she'd just said. "I'll go. I'll go check your mail." And she was out of the car, running down the sidewalk before Odys could reconsider. He saw her dash around the corner of a building to the mailboxes.

He pulled over to the curb, waiting. But just as he had sighed—telling himself that he should never have driven by here—her door opened again. "You have a letter."

Maud was beaming.

"I do?"

"Your mail runs early," she smiled as she closed her door behind her. "I *knew* this would happen." She smelled the envelope, pushing it to her nose. *The nose knows.* She looked up at him, nodding. "Pepin, Odys!" She pushed it into Odys's hands. "He always knew when to keep in touch."

"And when to vacate." He took the envelope from her. No return address. "Why do I feel like I *knew* this was going to happen?"

She shrugged. "I'm your intuition. And no, I didn't know for sure I'd find this. But we *did* have a suspicion that Pepin knew when to send a letter. Or, *I* had one."

"I don't like that Pepin is still in your head," he frowned.

"Do you *know*, Odys, when's the best time to send a letter?" she mused. "When Mother thinks she's destroyed the address." She gestured to the charred building behind her. "Pepin must have known she'd kick you off the grid."

But he didn't open the letter. He tucked it into his coat and began to drive away.

"But Odys!" Maud scolded. "It's from Pepin. I know it."

"Not here." Odys said. He glared at Maud, wondering why she had been so happy. Was *he* also happy and he just didn't know it?

He tucked away the thought. He had to get out of here.

Maud leaned forward in her seat, inconspicuously shielding any view someone might have of his face.

"It seems too perfect," Odys whispered as they blended back into traffic. "Too coincidental. To be sent a letter!"

*Post*humously.

"You're not going to open it."

He frowned at her. "Of course not. To open it would mean there *are* reasons. I'm not sure I want to know what they are."

I REJECT YOU AND YOUR REASONS, PEPIN J. POUND.

"Don't reject the reasons like you're rejecting me," she said quietly, looking into his purple-mooned eyes. Hers didn't look much better. For every brief moment of relief they exchanged, they took two steps back. They weren't getting anywhere.

"I'm afraid there might be reasons I won't like. Or worse, I just might like them and have to respect the bastard for what he's done."

He turned on his blinker, about to turn right—heading toward their little *mission* Mother had given him—the mission in the manila envelope. The mission Maud would later burn and drop into the bus station's bathroom sink.

Odys's heart was pounding—pounding next to that letter in his coat's breast pocket. Maud could hear it. She could feel it.

"I already don't *like* this situation," Odys continued to justify his actions. "That means I won't *like* his reasons."

"You don't know if it's from him," she said, playing devil's advocate.

"You and I both know it's from him, Maud. It's like—what's the word?" He snapped his fingers, "—*Cryptomnesia*. He made you forget he sent that fucking letter and now you're remembering it." He refused to look at her. "This has all been arranged. My whole fucking *life* has been arranged, Maud. And anything the letter says can't be too helpful, right? He *meant* for me to be clueless. Otherwise Pepin would've told me everything in the first place. This is just to dangle his plan in front of me. To give me hope that this is going somewhere. I'll not be Pepin's puppet on a string. I'll not let him pull those strings only to cut them later. That's what my so-called *father* did—is *doing*. And I'm fucking tired of it."

She looked away from him, knowing he was right. This letter deserved to be rejected with the same neurosis he gave everything else. Rejecting this wasn't out of his character.

But then she realized something.

She suck-clicked her tongue, eyebrows lifting. "But you still *have* a letter, Odys. You have something the others don't."

He glanced at her for a brief second. She was right.

Stanza: God in the machine.

In the crappiest gas/rest station that they could find: Fletcher had popped out *another* cardboard drink holder. He'd already made himself four sugary drinks. He was on his fifth. "Aren't you getting anything?" He asked Odissa "Don't make us guess what you want."

"Pick out anything. Otherwise I'm going to have to buy one of each," Dorian warned. "You have to tell me what you want."

211

Odissa couldn't even find the courage to look directly at them. Not after what they'd just done. Keeping her pale face averted, her eyes darted to and fro. She was only being compliant in order to save other poor souls from getting murdered. She felt responsible for what had happened to those cops.

Dorian began to pick up one of everything from the racks. "Just tell me when to stop," he said, trying to get a reaction from her. He was showing off.

The too-young cashier was very interested in Fletcher. She'd actually put down her magazine to stare at him. It wasn't so much *sexual* attraction as it was the self-same curiosity people have when slowing down to glimpse a car wreck.

"No, don't get the chips. Get the pastries!" Fletcher whined, putting a lid on one of his drinks. He licked his fingers clean. He popped open another drink holder. Fletcher leaned forward to Odissa. "Don't look so glum. We look suspicious." His eyes gestured to the cashier.

Odissa glared at him. "Obviously not suspicious enough," she mumbled. Before leaving the car they'd warned her not to say a word. Now they expected her to play along? Why did they even let her out? To make is seem like they were good guys? What? "Besides, you're doing it just fine on your own. Just look at all this liquid."

Fletcher made the fountain squirt out sweet tea. Tasted it. It needed more sugar. "Get me some packets. No, more." Taking the six sugar packets from her, he ripped them all at once. Pouring, he said, "You should tell him to stop now. He's trying to hold everything."

Dorian was still gathering items.

"Stop, please." Odissa said. Whatever she ate she'd just wash down with a pack of cigarettes. "Dorian, stop it!" Dorian didn't seem to hear her. The gum selection distracted him.

The cashier wasn't sure they were serious when Dorian dumped everything on the counter. "Sweet tooth," he said, proud of his destined diabetes. "Fletcher, dear, cover this and I'll go to the shithouse. Can I have a key, Madame?" He pointed to the restroom keys behind her.

"Do be careful," Fletcher wished, taking out Dorian's wallet. He'd never been in that bathroom before, though he'd been sure to remember where it was when they'd walked in, as well as the rest of the place. He knew when his Master had to piss.

Dorian reached into his jacket pocket. "I'm prepared," he said, taking out his folded white cane. It confused Odissa just a little. Why suddenly so blind?

The poor girl at the register had to ring up each item. Someone new walked in. All they wanted were some cigarettes and lotto ticket, but they had to wait because of Dorian and Fletcher. Fletcher pointed at Odissa, as if to apologize for their wait. "She's hungry."

He paid, making Odissa take the sacks while he carried the drinks.

She couldn't stop herself, "Why didn't we stop at a gas station *after* we dumped the body?" They stood outside in the cold, waiting for Dorian. It had stopped snowing and the sun was actually trying to crawl out from the clouds.

"Why don't you say it a little louder, so everyone can hear?" Fletcher was very hard to talk with. There was something haunting about him, as if multiple beings were peering through those black eyes—more than one agenda. On top of that, his odd attractiveness made him intimidating. Too impossible to be real.

"I could scream, you know. I could have told the girl back there to call the cops and tell them you have a dead body in the trunk."

He set down one of his drink holders and picked out a soda. "Yes, but, you didn't," he explained, the straw between his teeth. "You have to comply, don't you? Don't you want to see your brother again?" He downed the drink. Picked up another.

"You're going to disgorge."

"I don't think so, babe." He sucked it dry. Tossed it in the bin beside him.

"Do you two always work together?"

"Yes." It was one of those automatic answers.

He continued to stare in the direction of the bathroom. He slouched against the building.

"Is that your *natural* hair color?"

"You want to make small talk now? That what this is?"

"You can tell me what's going on. I won't do anything stupid. Not if will hurt my brother." Fletcher said nothing.

"I've seen worse—worse than what you did, back there. I'm not afraid of you."

"You think we want you to be?"

"Just tell me what's going on!"

"What if our lips are sealed to protect you?"

"That the truth?"

He shrugged. "You're no damsel in distress. That's the truth."

Though she was glad to break stereotypes: "But isn't this so Odys will rescue me—so he'll *do* something for you?"

Fletcher's lips twitched. "You're safer than he is right now, babe. He's the one in distress."

"What's that supposed to mean?"

But the subject was fleeting. Fletcher whipped his head around, panicked expression on his face—as if he'd just seen someone he recognized. But his eyes were too distant to be seeing. "Shut up, be quiet!" The straw poked his face, missing his lips. He watched the far-off bathroom door. "I knew it!" he shouted, ignoring the stares of those trying to enter the store.

"Um, knew what?" Odissa squeaked.

Knew he *smelled* something.

He stretched out a hand and plopped it on her face—a giant sea-star latched to her features. "Didn't I say shut up? I'm listening!" Mumbling, "I have to help him remember—he's letting me listen—he needs me—shut up."

Odissa lurched back.

Fletcher laugh-talked. "Oh-ho! I *knew* I smelled him. I could smell that ashy smoke miles away."

Stanza: The bright bring none.[100]

Dorian had walked around the building, unfolding his stick. He'd effortlessly made the corner, passed the truckers filling up their tanks. When he'd opened the door, however, the mental-images went blank, and the walking stick went down; Fletcher hadn't seen into this room. He put the key in his back pocket, the lanyard-tag dangling out.

A smile had been on his face as he had listened to Fletcher and Odissa chat. Then he remembered he had to pee, and he tapped his way to the urinals.

"Right in front of you, my man," a husky voice directed. Another good guy having a piss.

"Thank you, sir," Dorian said, his stick running into the spare spot.

"Don't 'sir' me, Dorian," the man said. Dorian heard him zip up his pants. "Sir's too informal. I much prefer 'Your Highness' or 'Your Majesty.'"

"Don't be such a queen, *Vulcan*."

VULCAN: Has suddenly taken notice.

DORIAN IS: One of the first in a long line of visits he'll be making.

DORIAN IS: Blind but can still read the signs.

DORIAN IS: About to be tampered with.

Chapter the sixteenth,

Not even:

Uneven?

---

[100] A reference to John Bunyan's Author's Apology in the *Pilgrim's Progress*: "Dark Clouds bring Waters, when the bright bring none."

Dorian tucked his stick under his arm and unzipped. "How did I know you'd be in here?"

"Because I _told_ you. Besides. The water closet is where I was raised. Flushed out of Olympus, I was." Or flung out, whichever.

"True, true," Dorian said. He'd been expecting this—Fletcher's nose had been picking up the scent—a scent someone purposefully leaves behind like piss; it wafted through Fletcher's nostrils and into Dorian's brain. _The nose knows._

Dorian heard Vulcan go over to wash his hands and noted the sinks' location. He could hear one of the god's feet dragging as he made his way—a limp, for sure.

"You do that on purpose, I think. You make your composite selves just as distorted as myth would depict."

Too bad we can't see Vulcan, either. But don't worry; he'll just be different next time anyway. The gods never stay the same. Why would they be so dull?

"Yes, I could fix this lame leg—this lame leg known by all. But it takes more effort than I desire. It's how I was _fashioned_, and it got me where I am. It's one of my _characteristics_. Those aren't overturned overnight. How are you to know it's me, if I don't give you _some_ sort of sign?"

"As if other gods can't fake a limp?"

"As if other gods would bother to talk to you."

Dorian chuckled, zipping up. "Dear god, please help me to the sink so that I might gain clean hands." He held up his palms, walking stick still underarm.

"You'll not wash your hands of this yet, Dori."

The god turned the water on and Dorian followed the sound.

"I know you're not on my side of things but...If I ask, will you tell me who they are?"

"What, the twins?"

"Who else?" Dorian answered.

"I can't do everything for you, Dori." He led Dorian's hand to the soap dispenser. "Though I can't keep you from asking."

As Dorian lathered up, he frowned. Quietly, "Who are they, then?"

"They're Odys and Odissa. That's who they are. And that's who _they_ think they are."

"Why won't you tell me—for sure?"

"Humans see things they want to see, Dorian. Who am I to tamper with that?"

"I want to see, _period_." Dorian rinsed his hands. He was handed a wad of paper towels.

"Yes, yes. Everybody wants something. I'm glad my job's gotten less demanding, in this modern age. Don't have to tolerate as many prayers. Though, some gods see that as a negative.

But I see prayers as giving man false power. If you want to empower a human—to give him real potential—you teach him the Arts. You give him power he can control. Like Alchemy. People've forgotten my hand in Alchemy. Now they always relate me to volcanos and blacksmiths. I'm more." He took the towels from Dorian, to toss them. "Am I not an Arch-chemic, Dori?"

Dorian put his stick down. "I don't see you taking your own advice much, V. Even Automatons have limited knowledge of your so-called Alchemy. But they're good at making gold, I'll give you that. Artisanal junk."

The god chuckled. "I always liked you, Dorian. Every time we speak, you try to press my buttons."

"But you haven't killed me yet." He paused. "Yet you *did* let me gouge out my eyes."

"Like I said, I'm not answering prayers."

"Clearly."

"And don't exaggerate. You didn't *gouge* your eyes out. They're still in there."

"Might as well not be."

He heard the Smithy-god inhale, wanting to change the subject. "Odissa's not like other girls, is she? With her every word, she looks as if she might whimper *and* growl. Much like Wisdom. I tried to fuck Wisdom, once. She didn't appreciate it."[101]

Dorian didn't *appreciate* this conversation.

"But that was a long time ago, and we both aren't what we used to be—she and I. Anyways, you, my Oedipus, will be fucking her soon, your '*Wisdom.*'"

"Cómo?"

"You heard me. I know you're not as deaf as you are blind." That one-liner was getting old. "She's yours, that Odissa. Might as well obey it. Don't avoid the oracle. You can't escape fate, Dori. In fact, be grateful. It's rare humans ever find their truest soul-mate, let alone have them pointed out. Though, this all depends on what you call a 'soul-mate.' There's bound to be different kinds, you know. Well, perhaps you don't."

"And I should just believe your prophecy because?"

"I'm married to the goddess of love, aren't I?"

"Are you? I can never keep up with you lot." He actually knew too much about gods. "I thought that marriage was officially over by now."

---

[101] Most likely a reference to when Hephaestus tried to rape Athena. She escaped him.

"Hey, now, even my hammer is an expression of beating love," the god chuckled. "But yes, a god-marriage isn't easily undone. Our divorces are…messier. Consort, wife, lover. Never mind the definitions of them all. Once the bond is made you're forever associated. But I know where you're coming from—we are a confusing sort. Also, it all depends on what Face of mine you're talking to. Sometimes I love my wife. Sometimes I hate her. Different wife for each Face."[102]

Dorian knew all about Faces.

"As I was saying, my wife-lover-consort—*They*—have investments in my work as well."

"Investments?"

"When I score, she scores. She's taken an interest and has fine-tuned some of my blueprints. I may not like how she went about it, but hey. Happy wife, happy life. That's why you'll fall in love with Odissa. My wife informs me there's no point in Us tweaking Odissa's interests—because she's already *interested*. Besides, Jostaca couldn't escape her role in the prophecy, either."

"I don't like the way you're paralleling this situation to such a *complex*, thank you very much. That story had no happy ending."

"But, geez, it was sure cathartic, wasn't it?" [103]

"I'd rather be purged another way."

"Yes, Dori. I know. But even if the twins are who you think they are, this was always going to happen. Even if I didn't want it to. You see, *all* the gods are suddenly envious of my toys. But I'm willing to share. Dori, the gods are paying attention to me now. Don't disappoint."

"So you thought I was going to fight my fate, did you?"

"Don't ask questions. Questions only lead to truth. You already have the truth."

"I prefer boys, you know. Though I don't mind making females swoon, I've an image to uphold. I don't think this'll work."

"Yes, but a preference doesn't mean always. Like Dionysus, it's time to stop playing dress-up."

"Dionysus? Really? That's the best you could come up with? I prefer to be called, like, oh I don't know, Tiresias or something. You're changing my sexuality."

"You still have a dick a you want to keep, though, don't you?"

---

[102] Faces are like forms for gods. Look into Platonics if you want to get all "philosophical." This is a point to be elaborated later. You could even parallel this to the *Hand of God* Maud was talking about earlier, if you feel like it. / On His wife: different versions of the Vulcan/Hephaestus myth list varying wives/consorts. I would argue that for this story you are supposed to assume They are (sometimes) representative of the same being, or He had many "wives." Either way.
[103] He's still talking about *Oedipus Rex.*

217

"I suppose you're right, yeah."

This was a transformation of Woolfian proportions. *And Orlando herself showed no surprise at it,* Dorian thought.[104]

"Dorian, you may be a woman trapped in a man's body, but my wife wants to make you a trapped *lesbian*. Don't worry, though, I tried to stop her. I said to her, 'You're stealing one of the good ones from the gay community. Curse you, Aphrodite!!!' You can't see it, but I'm shaking my fist for you."

Not liking being mocked, "And what did She say to that?"

"She shrugged and said she probably just fulfilled every fag hag's wet dream, so what's one curse among so many devoted? Besides, Odissa'll be better than using Fletcher to masturbate, right?"

"At least I'm not trying to rape a goddess." Vulcan's simmering silence was reaction enough for Dorian. So he moved on. "And what will Odissa think when she finds out I'm under a love spell? It's not very fair to her, is it? It won't be real."

"You and I both know that 'real' is relative. I'm a fucking god, Dorian. I decide what's real."

"You can decide only if the other gods let you. Even if you are a Face of the same Universe, you're nothing without Them. Tell me, V. Do They *all* know what you're up to? Lately Fletcher's nose has been tickling. He smells the Others—and they smell *ashy*. You're cooking something in the oven. And it involves the whole Universe—including Those who aren't willing to let you recast things? Why this sudden interest in your kids?"

"Better that you leave, Dorian. Fletcher's making Odissa nervous. You shouldn't have let him drop into this conversation. Your soul's too curious."

"I wish you'd tell your Wife to be more kind, V. Remember what happened to my last romance? Remember what Leeland did to him? Don't you care?"

"Romance? Please! Dorian, the only person you've ever loved is yourself. Odissa will be a great beard to show otherwise, though. And you'll be hers as well. She needs to get away from her brother. *He* needs to get away from *her*. They've never been apart. This is a lesson I need them to learn. Odys is one of my concerns now."

"So if we all fucked our siblings, you'd care about us?"

"Exactly why I care about you. You really screwed your own sister over, didn't you, Dorian?"

A gruff hand pushed him out of the bathroom.

---

[104] Direct quote from *Orlando*. (Dorian is Orlando in this quote. When Orlando is transformed, he/she doesn't seem bothered by it).

Stanza: The Yellow Brick Road is symbolic and will only lead to more metaphors.

Odissa remained silent as they drove to the river. She didn't open her mouth. Words couldn't help her.

She'd remained silent when Dorian had come back from the bathroom. She'd remained silent as the two men stuffed their faces with sweets in the cop car. She'd remained silent when they'd arrived at the river front.

"Might I see your purse, Odissa?" Dorian asked, putting out his hand.

"What? Why?" she stammered, thrown off. Her fingers fell from the strand of hair she had been twirling.

"Let me see your purse. Please."

She scooted it to him. She watched as he dove into the bottomless thing. What did his fingers search for? He pulled out her cigarettes. "Here, you need one of these." He retrieved one, as well as her lighter.

With trembling hands, she smoked.

"No need to fret, dear," Dorian said. He turned his face to the window, as if he could see out of it. "We have to do this."

"What—what *exactly* are we doing?" the smoke trailed from her lips brokenly, just like her voice. "Why are you doing this to me?"

"We're saving your life by killing you off."

"Does Odys know this?"

"By now? Probably," he said, taking her wallet out. He'd pass it to Fletcher later, to plant at the "crime scene" they were about to half-ass.

The river was shallow, with little pebble island-patches. They'd been in want of a good rain. Fletcher had opened Dorian's door for him, in case he needed out. The back cop car doors don't open from the inside, you see. There weren't even handles to try.

Fletcher closed the trunk and walked into the wooded thicket, the body bag over his shoulder. A carton of the cop's for-emergencies gasoline swung at his side. They'd filled it before leaving the gas station.

Dorian propped his foot upon the door's bottom frame, resting his arm on his knee. You shall not pass, Odissa. Don't even think about it.

She finished her cigarette. "Can you toss this out, for me?" she asked. "It's my cigarette."

She placed it gently between his willing fingers.

She scolded herself after she passed it to him. She should have used it to burn him, distract him. Maybe she could have squeezed passed him. But she wasn't that creative or courageous.

Not knowing what came over her (but perhaps wanting to distract herself from what Fletcher was doing to the corpse in the woods), "So, are you two, like, together?"

"Together?"

"You and—and Fletcher."

"What makes you think so?"

"Well, I'm not so sure I think it at all, that's why I'm asking," there was a nervous quaver to her voice that tried to pass as wittiness. "Though it's not every day a man sleeps on top of another naked if they're not together."

"Ah, that's right. You did see that, didn't you?" He nodded to himself, but said no more.

"Well?"

"Well what?"

"Are you?"

"Am I what?"

"With him?"

"What would it matter to you?"

She built up all the meanness she could, and stated, "He sure fancied that female cop, last night. Kept staring at her. And the fact that you would fool around on a job—"

"Any other discrepancies in our sexuality you'd like to address?" Dorian said through his undaunted smirk.

"Are you gay or not?"

"I've sucked enough cocks to know it's not a simple yes or no, dear."

"Why's it such a hard question?"

He shrugged. "For a kiss, you can find out."

Her face turned paper-white. Perhaps she'd gone too far. "Excuse me?"

"Was it not a good enough offer? Well then, perhaps I'll make it worth your while." He scratched his chin, considering something outlandish. "How about a ten second head start, out the door? Real-time. For a kiss, we can see how far you get in this cop car when I step out to blindly chase you and *you* step back in to drive away. Notice, Fletcher left the keys."

Her eyes saw them.

"Yes, this is a set-up. You don't know what I'm planning when I give you this option. Will you even be safer in your own hands? Will we do something to your brother if you leave? What?

I'll outright admit it. Maybe I've started to feel sorry for you, Odissa. Maybe I want you to get away. But, like my sexuality, you won't know until you kiss me, right?"

No response. Odissa was horrified, frozen like a rabbit.

"Ah, hard to make up your mind, is it? Well, like my head start, my offer also has a ten-second expiration. One. Two. Three…"

Odissa snatched up her purse, scooted closer to him, put a hand on the chain wall blocking the front from the back seat, and paused.

"…Six."

He put his knee and arm higher, blocking her from the open door. She knew he was playing with her, but she was willing to let him believe she was stupid—maybe then they'd relax and slip up. Testing his rules, she began to climb over him.

He grabbed her arm and pulled her back down. He'd not simply let her go. PAY THE TROLL TOLL. He smiled, "Eight."

Sucking in a bracing breath, she forced her face into his. He stopped counting. He lowered his leg as she continued crawl over him in his seat, but he wouldn't release her. She tried to draw her mouth away from the bubble-gum flavored lips, but he dragged her back to him. He didn't fight for dominance—only for her to stay put.

She had half her body out of the car, one foot touched the ground—

With his other hand, he grabbed her neck—she was pushing against him now. He stood up with her when she was finally out of the car, grabbing her other arm—he was doing the kissing now. She dropped her purse as she tried to pull away—she didn't need it anyway.

He closed the car door with his foot gracelessly and led her backwards to the car. She pressed herself against it, to get away from him. He took the sides of her face, as if to kiss her again. But he didn't. He merely held her face before releasing her. He shrugged. "I'd let you fuck me." Before he stepped back, she gave him a good slap, to go along with that kiss. It knocked his glasses off.

"Fucking weirdo!"

Holding his face, eyes closed, he started counting. "One! Two!"

She dashed away and went to the driver's door, slamming it behind her. She started the car—cursing under her breath. She slammed on the gas to get away—but to where? She hadn't planned on getting this far. She thought Dorian would have wrapped up this game by now. But no, she was *winning*.

221

The tires screeched as the dirt flew up behind her. She was just yards away from the main road before—WAH-WHAM.

Something hit her diagonally—something that had pushed the car's nose into a nearby tree. And that something had been Fletcher.

Not sure if she believed her own eyes, the only thing she could reasonably assume was... She had hit Fletcher.

But how was he alive?!

She crawled out of the crumpled car, panting as heavily as Fletcher. He'd rushed from the woods just to stop her. In the blink of an eye, he had her wrist and was dragging her back to Dorian. Dorian was kicking rocks around with his foot, humming. Very pleased with himself.

Fletcher set the girl down on a camper's log (the area was a favorite public outdoor site). Odissa obeyed, studying Fletcher. She shook from shock, not from the cold. Had she, or had she not, just hit him with a car?

"What the fuck were you thinking?" the Automaton confronted his Master. "You had me run all the goddamn way for this?" He pointed at Odissa.

"Ah! You know very well I was *not* thinking."

"Obviously!"

"Yes, yes, Fletcher. It was certainly spur-of-the-moment, but how are they to find out? Do they even *have* to know that I slipped up accidentally?"

"*Accidentally?*" Fletcher repeated, hands on his non-existent hips. "What're we going to do? What if they ask how she found out about me?"

"Well, look on the bright side. Now she knows, and we don't have to pretend anymore. At least, not as much. But please, continue to scold me. It's helping us work out this scenario."

(It really was, actually. That's why Fletcher was doing it).

"Jesus Christ, Dorian, Mother's going to be pissed. She'll know we did it on purpose. She probably heard the whole thing on your phone!"

"Yes, yes—if she's not busy right now with Mr. Messyhair. *Pero*, even so, you must admit it was pretty cute." He walked over to Odissa, still wide-eyed with shock.

Bending down to her he said, "You won't tell anyone I gave you the idea now, will you? It was all *your* idea, right? You tried to get out when I offended you—nay, *scared* you, if anyone asks. And as I held you back, you assaulted me, you distracted me—with that kiss. That yummy kiss. That clear?"

Odissa didn't know if she nodded or not. She certainly didn't say anything aloud.

Ill do this

"By God, if you want to see your brother again, it should be. Now come here, you're on lock down." He presented his hand—so sweetly Odissa thought him bipolar.

She lurched back from it. "What the fuck are you people? Some type government experiments or something?" Is *that* why they'd been interested in her father's work?

It was now that she noticed Dorian's breath was turning to fog in the cold and Fletcher's wasn't.

"Fletcher, go finish up the job and then see if the car will still run. If not, maybe you can fix it." Dorian put his hands in his jacket pockets, chewing his gum.

"Are you—you some sort of mutant?" She felt so stupid asking it.

Mutant? Superhero? Alien?

Almost any answer would have satisfied, really—anything to make her feel less crazy.

"No," Dorian snorted. "I'm just the love-struck girl who wants to have your children, apparently."

"Stop playing with me. What does my brother have to do with you?"

"The better question is what do *you*—not your brother—have to do with me?" He let that sink in. "Perhaps I don't give a fuck about your brother?"

Dorian barely gave any fucks.

Fletcher eventually pulled up the accordion-nosed car. Only one headlight worked. It blazed through the cloudy day.

Dorian opened the door for her. "I'm going to state it plainly. A god—Vulcan himself—has given you to me. You're mine. That is who you are, Odissa. You read the signs yourself."

...What, was she dealing with two *demigods* now?

"You're mine and I have a mind to make you like it. We're going to be happy together. Now, if you don't mind,"—he gestured to the inside of the crumpled car—"Follow the yellow brick road, my *Dorothy*."

DORIC DIMITRI: Twin of Dorothy (their mother originally spelt it 'Dorothie') Dimitri.

PARENTS: Dory and Dominic (his father spelt it 'Dominick') Dimitri.

HIS MOTHER, DORY: At one time her last name was Dandor (spelt 'Dander' by many a school teacher).

HIS UNCLE WHO DIDN'T KNOW HIS STEP-SISTER HAD RECENTLY GIVEN BIRTH TO TWINS WHEN HE LET LEELAND KILL HER: Dorian Dandor (he spells it no other way).[105]

Chapter the seventeenth,

Wonkier windings:

Just another brick in the road?

Time for some much-needed voiceover in this story:

Dorian just called Odissa "Dorothy," yes. But, despite the fact we're now filming this novel in color, it has little to do with *The Wizard of Oz...*[106]

Stanza: Stockholm Syndrome; this is how it works.

"Don't call her that." Fletcher marched toward his side of the cop car. Fletcher had "pulled" a "gun" out from himself and pointed it at Odissa to coax her back into the car—otherwise she wouldn't have budged. "Don't confuse her more."

He slammed the door behind her and crawled into the driver's seat. He glanced at her once in the mirror.

Odissa didn't have the slightest idea what they were rambling about. Most of all, she didn't care. Goose bumps formed on her arms as she wavered between curiosity and fear about these supernatural *whatevers*.

"Ah, just look at her. Her expression's perfect. This, Fletcher, is the kind of babysitting I enjoy—the kind where you get to be nanny and the boogieman at the same time."

"She looks like she's having a heart attack," Fletcher mumbled.

"That's reality for you. Real as a stroke."

"Tell me what you are," she demanded, pressing herself against the closed car door. "And don't you dare say vampire, or I'll punch you in your face."

God knows she hated tweenage vampire novels, and her life was *not* about to be like that shit.[107]

Fletcher snorted at that one. "Don't expect to *know* what we are even if we do end up telling you. Besides, we're not *really* the same thing anyways." He pointed between himself and his Master.

---

[105] Step-sister. Whew. That's a relief. Was beginning to think our Narrator was completely obsessed with incestuous relationships and that was starting to make me worry...Not that I'm really comfortable with the whole thing, but still.
[106] Well, that wasn't a lot of voiceover...
[107] It's amazing how much vampire culture is showing up in this novel. Please forgive.

"Not the same thing?" What the fuck did that mean?

Stanza: But enough of me spraying apprehension in the air...(squirt, squirt).

So, I may have glazed over a few facts previously. Let me mention those "facts" now: Right after Odys and Maud had left the others at the pub way back in chapter fifteen, Maud had ripped open the manila envelope, scanned its contents, and known exactly what to do. Digging in Odys's coat pocket for a lighter, she had explained, "To burn the unimportant contents later."

"What does it say?" he had asked her as they had sped away to his apartment.

Tell him what to do, Maud! Tell him what! Tell him!

"It doesn't matter just now, does it? Because you have a quick plan of your own. You're going to stop by your apartment and see what they've done. You're going to make sure they're not liars. That they mean business. But I tell you, Odys, they do."

"I don't care."

And so they had driven by. And gotten the mail. And then Odys had said, "Now what?" as they had sped away from the scene.

"You already know, Odys," Maud had said as she watched him turn on the blinker one more time. "You've been driving there this entire time."

He had swallowed hard, a panic in him fizzing up as goose bumps on his arms. He had been thinking so much about his sister and his apartment and that stupidfucking letter that he hadn't even realized it. "Then give me all of it." *Give me all you know, Maud. Don't leave me in the dark. Tell me what we're doing.*

In an exchange no words could even describe, his thoughts were imbibed within hers. The anxiety forced their minds to connect. Or, at least, connect more than they ever had before. In a matter of seconds, it was as if he'd read the entire novella-length directives—well, more like a Sparknotes version.

With annotations *a la* Maud.

As Odys had tried not to black out, Maud helped him steer. "Fucking pull over for a second."

"No, I'm fine."

He was not. It felt like someone punched him in the balls.

Maud tucked the two plane tickets and other important papers into her "bra" and started tinkering with the burner phone Mother had also supplied. She pointed to a little square near the battery. "She's listening," she had whispered. And she put the phone back together.

Let her hear, then. Odys had grumbled in his mind.

But Maud put the phone inside herself deeply—to muffle any sound.

They ditched their car outside the airport. They were on the plane to Canada within an hour and a half. He placed Maud in the metal-detector tray with his new cell phone and keys. He retrieved her. "For good luck," he had said to the TSA agent who noticed the strange looking coin. Luckily, they were more concerned with his sweaty sick-face than his oversized pocket change. *What is she, a fucking numismatist?*

Once Odys was seated, buckled in, the plane preparing for takeoff...

The in-flight movie started to play. His mind organized the thoughts Maud had given him. And with those thoughts, he suddenly realized the prominence of what they'd just done—the massive exchange of information overloading his brain. The mere thought gave him a headache.

He reached for the vomit bag, not feeling well as the cabin pressure squeezed him. But he hadn't eaten anything, so there was no point.

"What if the contents of that letter contain something that can stop Rosemund from feeling she needs to turn her back on us?" Maud pressed. She was in his mind. He hit his chest pocket, where she was, grumbling at her to "Shuddup." The person sitting next to him watched him nervously.

He thought back at her (it was a struggle): *"If he was dumb enough to send her Madus, I seriously doubt he planned for the need to stop her from misusing him."*

...

"I can't figure it out, Odys. What would make Rosemund do this? I almost wonder if we're not part of a distraction for something—something else they plan for Rosemund."

"Well, whatever I am, I know I have no choice. As soon as she sees me begging for Madus— the twin for my twin—she's supposed to submit? I doubt her heart's so caring at this point."

"What other angle have they got?"

"For one, why don't they just fucking kill her? Why send me to draw things out? She's broken the rules. They should punish her."

"She hasn't broken the rules."

"She's willing to help Leeland break them."

"You don't know what I know, Odys. Rosemund is good. Too much so to kill her."

He sighed, resting his head back. He dug her out of his pocket and held her for comfort. He was beginning to appreciate her and what she could give. Hell, if she could scan Mother's 20-something pages of a honey-do list (that Anselm had typed out in a matter of minutes) and later store it like some USB port able to jack into his brain, he'd have Maud read the entire internet. He'd be the most fucking intelligent being in the world.

...But what good would any of that knowledge be if he was a nobody—if he was dead to the world and couldn't share it with anyone?

"I don't think I want Odissa to have him, your 'twin'—even if we can collect him." Even if Mother would let Odissa have him.

"You don't mean that. Stop fussing. Odissa will grow old without him. She'll need protection too. She will die before you. You cannot be one. You must be two. Always even—"

"The fact they're holding her as bait means they don't trust me still. I could have done this without ultimatum."

"Could have? Yes. But would have? No."

"They'll never know now, will they?"

"Let's get this over with and then we can decide if we even want Odissa to be a part of this—in that way."

"Yes. Let's just stick to the plan. And if that fails. I've got my letter to tempt them."

Speaking of the plan, Odys kept running it through his mind as if counting:

Land in Canada. Take a cab to the bus station. Take a bus to such-and-such a place, where Rosemund had been tracked. Beg for Madus. Simple.

"What if I fail at this?"

"We'll be fine. She probably doesn't think anyone will come after her. After all, they're sending you—not someone she knows. Then again, if Rosemund's mad enough to do this, I wonder what else she'll do."

"That's not comforting."

"You know what would make you feel better?" Maud asked him. *"If you COMPLETELY synced with me. There is so much you would know—and be able to do—if only you'd—"*

"If it's anything like what I just did with you—you flooding my brain—I don't know if I could handle it."

"It only hurts because you only allowed a slight portion. You can't open the door just a crack and expect the world to fit through."

"I'll take only what I need from you," he said aloud, forgetting himself.

He got a few head turns with that one.

Stanza: More cracks in the foundation.

After a few hours of driving, Fletcher parked the smashed-up cop car in a no-parking fire-lane (it would make it back to its owners more quickly if illegally parked). Dorian woke up from his nap as the car stopped. It was then that Odissa stopped watching him and remembered herself.

Fletcher emerged from his seat, junk food wrappers clinging to him and flying away with the chill wind before he could stuff them back into the car. "Damn static!" he hissed, cursing the dryness of winter. (Static is much worse if you are an Automaton, it is safe to assume).

Opening the car door for his Master and Odissa, Fletcher's eyes scanned the premises. The street lights had just come on—the too-early moon was trying to free herself from the grey clouds and invade what was left of the day. Odissa followed Fletcher's eyes and could tell they were about to walk across the street into a shoddy motel.

Dorian stretched his arms and cracked his back while Fletcher made sure no one was watching.

"This is one of our safe zones," Dorian informed, as if giving her a tour. "We have them all over the country."

There were a total of five cars in the parking lot. The concrete was cracked, and there were several pot holes they had to avoid.

"You own this place?"

"Own?" Dorian repeated, as if that were silly. "This shithole? No. However, we do have room 25B all to ourselves tonight; we always keep it rented."

As Fletcher walked up to the door, he hesitated, wondering if he should do *it* in front of her. "Might as well," Dorian said as Fletcher looked over his shoulder.

Odissa gasped as Fletcher's body mutated. Sinking into himself—through his clothes and into his chest—his hand rummaged as if searching through a deep pocket. He hadn't used the key in quite some time, so he wasn't sure where he had stowed it away. But he was sure it was *somewhere* in his chest—where he didn't need to get at often. Soon enough, he pulled out the hotel keycard.

"I can't do that," Dorian stated, as if explaining the new rules for some board game they were starting to play. Taking her by the arm, "Only Fletcher can. He's the Automaton, *I'm* the human."

Dorian pulled Odissa over the threshold and Fletcher flipped on the light.

"If hungry, please tell," Dorian said. Fletcher put the snack sacks in the fridge. "We can have something brought. Delivery and the like. Anything you please. Aren't you getting hungry?"

Odissa lingered by the door as Dorian closed it behind her, releasing her arm. He made sure to bolt it—no more door problems, please.

Stanza: As one door closes, another is busted open.

Around this time, Bob had found Mecca outside the comic book store. The only reason he'd confessed his location was because she'd wanted him to track Dorian's phone. She could do it herself—through Cestus—if she really cared to. But she'd needed the excuse. "You can do it so much damn faster anyway. You already have it set up and everything."

Mecca had eyed her suspiciously as Q typed away on his laptop. Q had passed Mecca, the large baby, to Cestus. He climbed up Cestus like a tree, to perch on his shoulders. He pulled at Cestus's long mustache like someone holding bike handlebars.

"Veroom!" He made sure everyone acknowledged his joke before settling down. He put his cheek on Cestus's head, resting.

"We were just about to spy on Odys," Q admitted as she clicked *here* and *there*. "I'm glad Mother finally updated us on her plans for him, but geez. She could have done it a lot sooner. It would have made our tapping less slapdash. Could have planned things better."

"You know she couldn't tell you what she was up to. It would have ruined the surprise."

"As if we couldn't play along?" Q said, offended (they were excellent at playing along). "*You* did, didn't you? You played along."

Bob didn't comment.

Q went on clicking and typing, "You want to stick around for the big show? Odys's plane just landed. We have his phone tapped—if Maud hasn't tampered with it. *Will Odys live or die? Find out tonight!*"

"I'm good, thanks."

"But look at this; this is a picture of what we did to his apartment. They'll never figure out what happened." Q gestured to her screen—a picture of Odys's meticulously controlled apartment fire. "The body we planted—"

"Don't want to know," Bob said. She'd had enough of dead bodies for a lifetime. For two lifetimes. "Get back to finding Dorian."

"Why you suspicious of Dorian, Bob?" Mecca asked.

"He's not where he's supposed to be, that's all."

"How do you know he's not? Where's he supposed to be?" Q studied her face as she showed her the screen in Mecca's newly-stolen car.

Bob leaned on the open door, squinting her old eyes. "Certainly not there. Why the hell does he have her in our southeast hotel room?"

"Mother didn't tell him not to," Q shrugged. Why was this important to Bob?

Cestus stuck his finger though Bulfinch's pet crate. The cat rubbed against it, as if he didn't mind him (yet he had put up quite the fight against Q and Mecca). "He just wants out," Cestus said, catching Mecca's jealousy.

"Well, kids," Bob huffed. "Now we know where Dorian's at. If Mother asks, tell her." She turned to leave.

"Why wouldn't she just ask you? You're her hunting dog, Bobmation!"

Cestus put Mecca back in Q's arms. "Stay safe now." He patted Mecca's head.

But the others didn't understand. "Why does this matter, Bob?" Mecca pressed.

"Dorian didn't have to take her that far out." Bob reinforced. "He's putting distance between us. He's planning something. These twins change everything."

"What makes you say that?"

"Someone told me."

"Who?"

"Can't you smell Him on me? Worse than Odys's damn apartment, the ash." She was turning to leave—to go back to her motorcycle.

"He came to you?" Q yelled after them. "What else did He tell you?" She could see it on Bob's passing face that there was more. "Does Mother know He came to you?"

But Bob merely raised her hand in goodbye—didn't even bother to wave it.

"She knows something we don't know," Q said over the motorcycle's roar.

"Why would Vulcan visit her and not us? We're the important ones," Mecca said back.

Bulfinch watched them watching Bob. *No, I'm the important one.*

Stanza: But they soon remembered they could spy on Odys.

Let me fill you in on what you missed while we were observing Bob and Mecca, over there: The plane landed. Odys (and Maud) took a shuttle and a taxi to Somewhereoranother, Canada. There, they waited for the next bus to take them a few mumble-mumble miles thisaway.

And so they sat and sat and sat at the waiting station in Canada. Maud had purchased the tickets with one of the credit cards left in the envelope (anything to avoid stealing). She even used the sleek smart-phone to text Mother—as the instructions had requested—to give her an update.

"She won't respond, but you can be sure she got it," Maud sighed, putting the phone away.

When they had arrived at the station via taxi, Odys had gone to the restroom and let Maud form up. They'd gotten a few stares when they'd both come out of the men's room. Of course it looked scandalous.

The chairs at the station were shaped like melting half-eggs. Not the most comfortable things to sit in. The place smelled like freshly-poured bleach, but other than that, it was quite respectable. There were twenty or so riders waiting on buses. The room wasn't small, so they didn't have to sit next to anyone. They could whisper quietly in their private row, over the old-school background music…if only that old guy hadn't sat right across from them.

Maud watched with heated curiosity, leaning into Odys. Her hands were like the metal rails leading up outdoor steps, both cold and jolting as they helped you keep your bearings. She had previously assumed a tight pea-jacket to blend in, but was still as cold as her surroundings.

She studied the newcomer, the one sitting too close to them. Odys's eyes flickered once to him, but he was otherwise unconcerned. Sure, this guy had about forty other egg-seats to choose from, but perhaps he just liked this spot. Maud certainly gave it a view.

Odys was more concerned with how *concerned* Maud was. She glared at the older man, the man who had used a cane to aid his slightly unbalanced gait.[108]

It was a fancy cane, at that. The arch ended in flourish-of-a-knob.

Maud's nose itched. Something was in the air. Something like ash.

The man had a short beard that covered his weathered skin. Though his clothes were clean, and he (on first glance) seemed well-groomed, they couldn't help but notice his grimy fingernails, his blistered hands. The man caught her staring out of the corner of his eye and smiled. Almost every tooth was lined in a frame of gold.

Nice grill.

Her eyes started to dance around the room, looking for the signs. The silent big-screen TV behind the man was showing the news. The closed captions read, "Hawaiian volcano shows slight signs of activity."

Some otaku kid sitting next to his mom was wearing a *Fullmetal Alchemist: Brotherhood* t-shirt.

His little brother, who had been blabbering on about Star Trek, mimicked the fanboy's live-long-and-prosper sign.[109]

"No need to look for more goddamn signs, Maud, dear," the man said. He put his bad leg across his knee—the manly sort of leg-cross. "It's me." He tucked his cane into the crevice of the egg-chairs, out of the way.

Odys's eyes slid to Maud. What'd he miss?

Only the lining up of the Alchemical universe, that's all.

"You could have come sooner, you know," Maud said.

---

[108] Clue.
[109] So many clues it's now evidence.

231

The man rolled his shoulders. "Is that any way to speak to your father?"

"Father," Maud snorted, rolling her eyes. But if so funny, why was she gripping Odys's arm like she might pull him under her protection? And, why was he allowing her?

"I admit it's been a damn-long while. Nevertheless, aren't you going to be a good girl and introduce me to your new Master, goddamnit?"

She scrunched her nose.

"Who is he?" Odys whispered. But he had a feeling he already knew.

"Odys, this is—this is my maker. Vulcan."

Stanza: The Goddamnit Face of Vulcan breaks the Maya.

Odys's spine stiffened, his eyes widening in awe. It was like spider webs had landed upon them, making Odys cringe—no, poor analogy. It was as if ash and soot were falling on them—making Odys dance from their tickling heat.

As if formal introductions were a bother, Vulcan glanced down and brushed forming ash from the fold of his shirt. As he lifted his head, his eyes glowed as if hot coals, flickering between Odys and Maud like sulfur reacting to elements.

"Don't overdo it, V," Maud huffed at his exhibition.

Odys wondered if he should run, because, let's face it, when you look divinity itself in the face you can no longer deny the divine exist.

Odys wanted to deny.

Odys wanted to reject.

Odys wanted to do as Odys does.

"*Maker*, Maud?" Vulcan said, frowning at his shirt, the ashes refused to leave the fabric's fibers. "Though, I suppose the goddamn word got the job done, right? Right. Of course I'm right. I'm a bloody god, for Christ's sake, goddamnit. I'm always right. Now, down to business—I wouldn't be here if it wasn't important. It's not like I can be *entirely* everywhere at once. I'm not the biggest god on the block, you know. That's not to say I didn't plan this goddamn part out, so don't think it sloppy. I do have my reasons.

"Oh, speaking of reasons, there's a process to this." He coughed out a breath like smoke. "I'm supposed to tell you to not be afraid—fear not—and all that jazz, to keep you from running with your tail between your legs. Your goddamn Miranda rights. So, don't be so uptight, son. I'm not here to smite you. That's not my job. Relax a little, goddamnit, you're making a scene. Yeah, I've got dirt on you—but it's not my style to use it.

"Oho, what I know, though! But I'm no Automaton, am I? Nope. You can't keep my mouth shut, can you? Ah, not that I open it much. I'm not fond of playing with men. Or speaking with them. Granted, not many of Us speak anymore, goddamnit. But it's even worse with me. I don't get out much. When I do, I always dress for the part—I can't help myself," he wiggled his dirty, gout-ridden fingers as he gestured to his care. "It's not because I *have* to, but because, well, I feel the *need* to. It's my signature, certain traits. My Maker's Mark. My trademark. Limp and all, I'm not ashamed of what I am, or what I look like *manifest*. But anyways, I'll say what I've come to say—"

"Verily." Maud got a word in edge-wise.

Something told Odys that Vulcan was a man of many masks. Or various bodies, that is. The fact Maud took her time in recognizing him made him realize this.

Odys tried not to tremble—he wasn't sure what trembling would mean. Would he be trembling out of fear or awe? Or would that be the same thing, really?

Vulcan settled into himself once more, lacing his fingers across his distended belly. "Ah, Maud, dear, you've always had better fashion-sense than me. I don't know where you got it, but you did come out the perfect, hard-boiled vixen. I wonder which Muse inspired me to shape you. Not a one has yet claimed to be your mother.[110]

"Not that I blame them of course, goddamnit. We're all very much concerned with our own fates at the moment, rather than our spawns'. But I'm not like them. I invest in my children's future. Ah, this is fun, making him squirm, Maud. They always squirm at first, don't they? Later, when I'm gone, they wish I was here all the time, to hold their hand. Maud will tell you, Odys— just ask her—won't you, Maud?"

She didn't respond.

"Maud. You hate that name don't you, Odys? It was all the rage in London there for a while, though, wasn't it? I knew it would be, goddamnit. That's why I gave it to her. I knew you'd grow into it someday. Any of you got a light?"

He pulled out a pipe, from a non-existent pocket.

"You don't need a lighter," Maud said "Besides, you can't smoke in here."

"I can if I want, goddamnit! Besides, it's not like they can see me. Well, they *can*, some of them. But the others won't remember a single aspect of me. Not at all. It's all been arranged." He waved it off as his pipe began to smoke—on its own.

---

110 Not to say Maud has a mother. He means solely the inspiration for her.

Odys stared at the pipe as if he'd just witnessed a miracle.

"Yes, I'm a god of fire too—not just smiths and limps—because that's what's going on in the back of your mind, right? You're trying to classify me, and modernize me, and pin me down. Howsoever, you shouldn't, goddamnit. Depending on who and what you're talking to, I'm the god of many things. It's not like all gods can't have overlapping areas, goddamnit. We're always changing. That's how things work. Give and take. Everybody—even you, Odelyn—give and take." He pointed to Maud. "Some creations take more than others. Those that take too much will incur quite a bit of debt to society. That's how my first *model* ended up.[111]

"Sure, I'd made Automaton-esque things before. But I went with a new design, that time. And the rough draft—Maud's oldest 'sister,' if you will—was just that. Rough. That one—the Monster, as they call her—I named her Alpha. A good name, though it didn't fit her, really. Not that there's much to goddamn names anyways." He gestured to Maud. "*Maud.* No one's named Maud now. But the name fit once. It had a time and place. Everything has a time and a place, Odys Odelyn."

He tapped his pipe on the side of his seat. "That reminds me of a story, goddamnit. A really good one. I think you'll like it, Odys." He pointed to him with his pipe. "Once upon a time," he mused, staring off into bygone-space, "there were two wind-up toys that needed a good, goddamn winding. The toy maker, you see, usually saw to that sort of thing. And they—the toys—were happy. But one day, they took the key the toy maker used to wind them, so that they could wind themselves. And so the toy maker learned that his toys did not love *him*, but only what he could *give* them. His creations were willing to *steal* from him. His purpose in making the toys in the first place was so that he might be able to give—give all that he had. He wanted to give and to be cheerful in doing so. So he turned the wind-up toys into marionettes. They could keep their precious key, yes, yes. But now there were *strings* attached."

He chuckled at his parable, as if it applied to their situation here and now.

"I can tell you worked hard on that story, so I'll not tell you what a load of shit it is," Maud said.

Odys cringed, appalled she would insult a god like that. But Maud was suddenly much more comfortable around her maker since it didn't seem like he wanted something from them.

"Thank you, I came up with it just now. It's my current philosophy on creations, goddamnit. The puppets will always need *some* strings. That's the point. The hinges, the joints, the bolts that

---

[111] He's talking about Alpha, the being he made before the nine Automatons.

you can't control, however, can't be blamed on the maker when you hand free will over to them. There are bad eggs in every carton, but how's that the goddamn chicken's fault? A scientist does many a failed experiment before coming up with the finished product."

He gestured to Maud. *The finished product.*

"You need not go on," Maud sighed. "We get the point."

"We do?" Odys noticed the clock overhead. They'd have to be leaving soon.

"Don't worry," Vulcan assured them. "You'll get there safe and sound. I know how important it is to you that you go. Your sister's fate depends on it. *Or so they say.*"

"So you know what's going on?" Odys asked him.

"Know? Dear boy, why wouldn't I *know?*"

"Will they hurt her if I fail?"

"If you fail, that means you'll be dead. Mother'll have no use for your sister, then, goddamnit. If I were you, I'd be asking about your own life-thread, boy. Rosemund's an insane motherfucker." He laughed. "Well, she'd *like* to be, anyways, goddamnit!"

When Maud frowned he went on (the closest thing to acknowledgment of his inside joke).

"Let me give you an example of what I mean: I was chatting with Rosemund just this morning and we were revisiting her latest accidental explosion. Nearly took out an entire block. Only fourteen were severely injured, thank *me*. They'll be out of hospital in a couple of months. Except one little snot who visited Rome last year with his parents. He took a leak on one of my friend's favorite resting spots. I simply can't forgive that. He won't recover so nicely. He could have held it in."

"You mean you were there, with Rosemund, and you didn't take the extra Automaton away from her? You didn't do anything to stop her?" Odys questioned.

"Whoa, whoa, now. Before you start telling me when to blink, I'll stop you right there. You should be glad you're not worse off now, as is, goddamnit. I could have teleported her ass right in front of you and dealt her the upper hand. Where's the gratitude for that?"

"So you're on Leeland's side, then?" Odys was beginning to lose heart—no, *faith.*

"Hey, what makes you think I pick sides at all, goddamnit? Who says this is even good versus evil, eh?[112] Just take a look at yourself, friend. You're no saint. I mean, have you ever stopped for a minute and asked yourself *why* they're so anti-Leeland? Do they even really hate him? If they wanted to be rid of him, they could have done it a long time ago—even you've thought that.

---

[112] "...eh?" This is funny because they're in Canada right now. You have permission to laugh (please laugh).

"You most of all, Odys, know what a sick fuck he is. Hell, Leeland—Augury—virtually *was* your father, just masked. My oh my, what else does Leeland have his hands in?" The god wiggled his fingers. "If he can direct the lives of two twins by extension, who else is under his sway? And riddle me this: they're *just now* finding out about you? Honestly, Pepin had to off himself before they realized you existed—let alone that you're Leeland's Automaton's kids. It makes it seem like they didn't know because they didn't *want* to know. They didn't *want to know* about all the freakish things he's doing—all the freakish things he's done. And why don't they want to know? Well, I think I've said enough—just enough to evade the Higher Up's reprimanding. Thus, before you start making me pick sides, you'd best make sure you're on the right one, bucko."

Odys realized Vulcan had been leaning forward—into them—when the god finally sat back. With a sigh he did away with his pipe; it disappeared into his jacket pocket, still smoking.

"Also, there's a reason I never told them—Mother—you existed, Odys. There are reasons I keep certain secrets. There's a reason I've kept your *father's* secrets. In fact, I particularly like Leeland, the goddamn bastard."

"Why would you keep his secrets?" Odys growled. "You could solve all of this—fix everything! Why don't you?"

"Honestly, can you believe this boy, Maud? Tells me what I should do! These goddamn humans. They can't figure out their own lives, but they can *sure* tell the gods how to act."

"Maybe if you acted at all…"

Ignoring Maud, his lava-hot eyes flashed to Odys. With his thumb, he gestured in Maud's direction. "You know, I'm surprised you haven't fucked her brains out yet."

The statement was so profanely ribald Odys didn't catch on.

"Ah. Not that you let her use them anyways, her brains. Truthfully, most men would've found it justified ages ago. Even Pepin did, a few times. He made her forget that, though."

"You're lying. Trying to test him."

"He was ashamed. I can't blame him, no. She breaks down even the most chaste. I purposefully designed her as the prettiest of the species, a perfect vessel to tangibly exhibit my flirtatious qualities."

Was this a conversation with Pygmalion or what?

"I put part of myself in her, as all creators do to their best pieces. They're a type of homunculus—a form of me. Maud's the paragon of my—Well, just look at her. She doesn't even have to be *trying*, for her body to *scream* desirability—among other things. Ah, but what can I say? I did it unconsciously."

"Did you make Alpha unconsciously too?" Maud reprimanded him—the one who also made *the mistake.*

"Hubris is never acceptable, boy, even in the guise of your Automaton. Don't think I can't see you in her. I know the means and measures of my creations. You may not have your hand up her ass, but you still make the puppet talk. She's not just a fancy toy. Gods know you lot don't deserve them. But here I am,"—he tapped his chest—"the instruction manual, son. Mark my words: just because you're a rare case, Odys Odelyn, doesn't mean you are special. You goddamn, self-righteous prick. Yes, yes, you haven't fucked her yet. Not all of them do, but you haven't even wanted to look at her from the start. It's your whole *twincest* thing, I guess." He turned to stare out the window.

A cold sleet-spit was pattering.

"If you think about it, it would be an entirely less disturbing relationship than the one with your sister. No offense."

Hostilely: "None taken."

Their bus number was called. Maud forced Odys to stand with her.

"You really should get to know yourself, Odys," Vulcan said as the number was repeated. He looked up at them. "You're even without Odissa now. You're two."

Odys glared at him—almost snarling. "No. I'm odd now. Uneven. Because of you and your games. I'm three." *And I will not forgive you for it*

"One more thing before you go, dears. I have an announcement to make—a foreshadowing sort-of-thing. It's in my contracts to get the memo out. We're making a comeback, We gods. Can't you see the excitement on my face? I do have a spring in my limp, don't I? My dull complexion is brighter. Exactly, Maud, exactly. I'm finally getting some recognition—a role where I'm on top, goddamnit! You might call it a promotion."

"And?" Maud said, impatient.

"I'm just letting you know there's a big project in the works, and I've been elected as head-honcho. They like my ideas, upstairs," he pointed with a wink, "We've struck gold this time, Maud, baby. Gold."

"We? You mean you're going to involve us?"

Vulcan stood, taking up his cane. "You know, I've noticed a new fad—everyone on earth seems to be 'going green.' Have you noticed? It's a sort of salvaging of the goddamn planet, I guess. I suppose you might say the same for We transcendent beings. Fair warning: the gods are very interested in my resources. We're starting a recycling gig. It's going to make human efforts seem like baby steps."

The end.

No more chitchat.

Now, you might think he would have just disappeared, which would have been the *stylistic* thing to do. Also, it would have allowed them to catch their bus and make it to their destination on time. However, that is *not* how it happened.

Instead of the Smithy-god leaving...

They were the ones who disappeared.

In the blink of an eye, they were standing on a street corner—no wheels-on-the-bus necessary. With a heavy sigh, Maud said, "This is so like him, to be more malicious in play than helpful. He's not always so frank, though." She took in their surroundings, factoring in their exact location like some well-endowed GPS. "He has many Faces. This one wasn't comforting. He was too—too—pleased with himself."

"Yeah. If I'd known he'd do this, we wouldn't have had to buy these *goddamned* tickets."

Stanza: No tickets to paradise.

After they had ditched their car (for it was time to steal a new one), Gwen and Anselm had walked hand in hand down the street, the yellow street lights haloing them here and there as they passed. Anselm kept looking over his shoulder.

Anselm and Gwendolyn made sure to walk very slowly, to take their time. Every few steps they would pause and look around. Or sit on a bench. Or backtrack to look at some peculiar whatnot. They were killing time. Time was all they had left.

Gwen put one of her phones away. "Shall we get some coffee, then, Ansi? We won't be sleeping tonight."

"I'd like to be warmer, yes."

When there: "I'll have a [such and such] with an extra shot of espresso, and..."

Anselm: "The same."

The elderly barista-lady smiled down at him. "A bit young, aren't we, for coffee?" She made small talk as she punched in the buttons. "And so late at night!"

She waited for Gwen to tell him no and to pick something else.

Anselm donned his best shy-baby face and snuggled closer to Gwen.

"Yes, but just this once," Gwen insisted, handing her the cash. She wasn't a bad mother. *Don't tell me how to raise my kid.*

They stood to the side as they waited for their expensive, earth-friendly beverages. Anselm glared at the barista as she made the drinks, but each time she felt his wicked glare and looked up, he'd flash a wide grin to make up for it.

"You two related?" she asked, a sweet chit-chat baby-talk undertone in her high voice. Just being friendly.

"Y-yes," Gwen replied, off guard. She'd been watching the young flirting couple at the corner. Yes, yes. This was her son. Adopted. Whatever. Just make the coffee, if you don't mind.

"The youth are so hip these days. Even your little guy here has the crazy hair. Did your mom put up a fight, for that hair?" She winked at him while snapping on their coffee lids.

"Yes," Gwen said, rolling her eyes as if her son's (clearly bleached-white) hair was some sort of thing she had to put up with. Gwen pretended very well.

An elderly couple walked in. Anselm eyed them—how they acted, how they saw him, how they saw Gwen.

"I'll be with you in a moment," the barista said to them, her countenance suddenly rushed. Handing Gwen their coffee, "Ah, at least it's just hair, right? That's what I told myself when my grandson shaved his head. You'll get through it too, though—us grandmothers have to stick together, right?"

Grandmothers.

Gwen's heart sank.

The lady quickly turned to the new customers, not seeing Gwen's reaction. "Right," Gwen replied, taking the cups. Handing Anselm his, they turned to go. They weren't staying to drink them after all.

As they turned, Anselm flashed his brimstone eyes at the sleepy toddler who had been staring, making it cry from fear. It was enough of a distraction to make everyone forget about the strange old woman with the white-haired youth....

Gwendolyn found a bus-stop bench to sit on. Hands shaking, she gripped her coffee. Anselm put a hand on her knee.

She bit her lip as she straightened her back. "I never thought the day would come when they thought I was your _grandmother_."

People were usually kind enough to assume he was adopted. Even old ladies can adopt, see. People would at least beat around the bush. Even when he adjusted his skin tone and facial features to look more like her, there was still something that people would stare at them for (of course there was); and then they would brush it off as *he's not really hers, that's why I keep staring.* Usually it was so simple for Gwen to avoid the truth.

"This is the south—full of hillbillies, Gwen," Anselm said, standing up and facing her. He set his coffee on the pavement. "They have children when they're fifteen and are grandmothers by thirty. You know that. It was only one person."

"It was only one person when they started thinking I was your *mother*, Ansi. But that number grew."

A winter-chill swept over them, whipping Anselm's hair out from his face like sprouting icicles. His voice sharp and clear, "And so what if that number grows? Do you think numbers matter to me? Will they make me love you any less? *Have* they made me love you less?"

Could Automatons love at all, would be the better question.

Leaning into her, his white hair falling past those child-sized shoulders, he took her delicate chin. He forced her mascara-smudged eyes to look into his polished pools. He shook his head. He could see her thoughts, they were his own. She was thinking about how wonderful it would be if she could never grow old, if he could grow old.

At this rate, when would she become Anselm's great-grandmother? Great-great-grandmother? Was just a matter of time. There was never enough time. Even when you had so much of it.

Mother closed her eyes. "Of course the Fates would make this happen at a time like now. They know my hate for Vulcan and so the Fates provoke me. They mean to make me emotional!" She was angry-crying now. They were usually sadder tears.

"Don't," he ordered her. He looked about before putting his forehead upon hers. "Don't waver now. There'll be plenty of tears when this is all over. We've others to save them for. Come, Gwen," he whispered in her ear, "don't cry for us."

Stanza: Should you make yourself accept yourself?

For a few minutes, Maud and Odys had stood on the street corner, letting Maud take in her surroundings. She paced to and fro, heals clicking on the sidewalk.

"I know where we are," she finally said.

"You do?" Odys asked, surprised. Vulcan had transported them without so much as a commentary on *why* or *where*.

"Yes. This way."

He took her hand, because he was cold. Not that her touch warmed, but it did help him focus. "Where are we going?"

"That's the thing, isn't Odys? You don't know. But you *could*." There was something bitter in her voice. She was panicked—just as much as he.

He was showing up in her.

"This is going to take a lot out of us, for us to find them. And by us, I mean *me*. I might sneeze out, Odys, and then I'll be no help to you. We haven't eaten well in a while—or slept well. If Odissa is depending on us…" She huffed as they walked across the street, her eyes darting here and there, searching for something. "Well, *we* can't even depend on *us*."

When they stepped up on the curb, Odys pulled her back. He was sure the party standing on the deck of that snazzy nightclub thought they were a couple. But at this point he didn't care. He only cared about getting this over. "Do it, then. I mean, *let's* do it."

Maud sighed, impatient. "If you were willing, then it would have happened already. You have to accept the reality of this situation. It's not some switch I can flip. Not when I'm the switch."

He stared at her for a moment. She was no help. Cursing under his breath, he wrenched himself away. A grubby trash bin felt the wrath of his foot. One, two, three, four, five, six times. He didn't know how to let go of his control—after all, that's what he WAS. Control.

Panting a little, he looked back at her—back at *Maud*. Maud, with her cruel stare, a stare he was making her give, *Maud*. Maud, the voice of reason he was finally letting speak, *Maud*. Maud, the thing he wanted most to touch yet recoiled from, *Maud*.

Maud, Maud, Maud.

"Fine," he growled.

He stepped toward her. He was going to do it. He was going to let go.

He came at her, grabbing her up by the arm and dragging her in front of store-front window. Had anyone been watching, they would have thought Maud should look afraid, as if she'd just angered some jealous lover who was about to beat the living shit out of her. But her subtle grin said otherwise.

See, Odys was nothing to fear. Not only because he didn't intend to hurt her, but because he toppled over at her feet. "You really needed that running start huh? You should have seen yourself. You looked ridiculous."

"I know—" he moaned as he fought back his stomach juices.

Looking down at him with a this-was-expected glance, Maud crossed her arms. This could take a second.

Her nose scrunched at him. "Ah, geez, really? But you didn't eat anything! You *never* eat anything! The hell's that coming from?"

Heaving while resting his shaky hands on his shaky knees, Odys held back a second up-chuck. She danced around his slimy vomit with her pretty feet.

"Go on, let it all out." Finally, pity in her voice. She patted his back.

"Holy fuck," he managed to utter through his heaving spasms, as if he'd just run a marathon. His palsied face looked almost as bad as when he'd first touched her. "Holyfuckingshit. I thought this was supposed to make us feel *better*."

He squeezed his eyes shut. His brain threatened to pour out his eyes. The world wouldn't stop spinning.

"Best keep that mouth closed, babe," she said as more came up. "Geez, that slimy shit must be coffee. You'll be okay, just wait for your equilibrium to settle back down." She looked about, making sure no one was offended by his sidewalk decorating.

"Give me your hand, goddamnit," he cursed—not at her, but at the world.

Gathering him up, she leaned him against the store window. She cleaned him up with the cuff of her skin-coat. Then, she leaned into him, tucked her head under his chin. She leaned into him as if finally free, finally free to relax. Unstiffen. No more holding back. She breathed in with him. They flowed as a charged, syncretic unity.

"Gah, it feels better, doesn't it, to get it all *out*—get it all *in*?" She held him up by his coat collar as he started to slip. "Revelation does this to people—unsteadies them."

He still wasn't fond of the scene they were making, but he had never felt more aware of its necessity in his life. He *understood*. He understood what it was to *be* her. He *was* her. And he could no longer be ashamed of it.

He held the back of her head and pressed her to his chest, gasping. His hot breath steamed in the cold air. He could still smell his stomach-juices beside them.

"You now know what I know, Odys Odelyn. We're finally one."

Bleary-eyed, he looked down at her. "We know too much."

Maud laughed, though he hadn't been joking—not really. Her laugh made him smile. To catch your own cleverness!

"I particularly like the part where Pepin made you read every encyclopedia edition at his favorite library. I never have to Google a big word again."

"Yeah, well, the thing about encyclopedias is they become outdated."

"Geez, George," the old lady of an elderly couple said as they walked back into their car. They were just leaving the diner across the street, "Prostitutes everywhere. I told you not to take me here."

Maud flipped them off.

Stanza: As the sun sets, something rises.

"I wasn't aware we weren't going back to the apartment," Odissa finally forced herself to say, though it was a lie. She knew this was a kidnapping (of some sort).

"Don't worry," Fletcher muttered, sitting on the bed—the *one* bed—the *only one bed*, "Bulfinch will be taken care of."

"Taken care of?" she cried.

"He means looked after."

Fletcher chuckled as he found the remote. He'd *meant* to sound menacing. He liked making people fret. That was Dorian in him.

Odissa remembered to exhale. "But I need my things—"

"Believe me, you'll be taken care of too."

"Just to clarify," Odissa swallowed hard, "This *is* a kidnapping, right? I mean, *why* did you have to fake my death? I still don't understand—" As if logic could excuse Dorian for killing two innocent cops.

Dorian waved that off. "If anything, we're protecting you."

"Protecting you from your father's sins."

Odissa sat down in the sole chair. She clutched her purse, her only comfort.

"Oh look, we're scaring her, Fletcher," Dorian reared back.

"What do you mean, my father's sins?"

"Should we tell her, Fletch?"

"Don't ask me, it's not as if I have a say in what we're doing," Fletcher grumbled.

Dorian sighed. "We could, perhaps, let her know she's adopted."

"What?" she gasped.

"Oh, how smooth," Fletcher said, no emotion in his voice.

"I know! Did it on purpose," Dorian grinned, gum flashing. "Odissa, dear, the man you know as your father wasn't your father. In fact, *no es un hombre*—he wasn't even *a man*."

"What was he then? One of *you?*" She pointed gracelessly.

Dorian's lips spread into toothy grin—smacked his gum. "He's what Fletcher is, yes."

"And, for godsake, what *is* he?" She pointed to *it*—Fletcher.

243

"I already told you. An Automaton. Don't you know the definition of the word? Can't you guess the connotations?"

"An Automaton?" What a ridiculous word. "So, a *toy*? A *robot*?" Somebody bring her a dictionary!

"No, no. Not in a literal sense, girl!" Fletcher said, turning the channel. "Is an Eagle Scout really an eagle? No. It's *titular*. We're really called Guarders."

"Don't confuse her. Words never do you justice anyways."

"Fuck you."

"I stand corrected." Dorian grin-giggled.

"You make that joke a lot, don't you?"

Dorian knelt down beside her. She scooted back, wondering what he might do. He was too smart, too clever.

"Your father was an Automaton controlled by a Master who was human—like me. He's not dead."

Her eyes narrowed in suspicion, brows coming together. "Alive?"

"Fletcher's immortal. He can't die. Neither could your so-called father," Dorian tried to assure her.

"I've seen my birth certificate!" She was starting to panic.

Dorian licked his bottom lip. "Don't kid yourself. You saw what Fletcher did to your car. Automatons aren't human. They can't have children. But they can fake papers."

"Best not to tell her that Odys is now one of you."

"Hush you!" But Dorian had meant him to say it. She could tell by that stupid smile.

"Like you." Odissa reinforced.

"He has an Automaton now, sí."

"But maybe not for long," Fletcher finished.

"Quieres to become un paperclip?" Dorian threatened. He was enjoying his show—his act for her. He liked spilling beans at more than one angle.

"Better twisted metal in your pocket than a humanoid who has to suffer watching you ruin everything Mother's built up. Even Odys would be pissed! Just because Vulcan tells you she's your soulmate in some gross bathroom does *not* mean you should tell her the secrets of our universe. But I congratulate you, my friend, on yet another perfect segue."

"Couldn't have done it without you, dear. Now, Odissa, this is a perfect chance to ask me about Vulcan, since I set it up so nicely. Don't let me down, dear, I worked very hard on it—this build-up."

"Vulcan? As—as in the Greek god?" *You've got to be kidding me.*

"Roman, too, technically," he corrected.

"You're serious?"

"So serious I'm breaking rules for you," Dorian said with half-energy. "Right, Fletcher?" But Fletcher was asleep, smoothly snoring. "That's right."

"Is he all right?"

"Agh, yes, he's fine," Dorian waved a hand. "He's only somewhat narcoleptic. We haven't gotten a good night's sleep in a while. He's not well. At least it's not a sneezing fit." He walked over to his Automaton.

"A fit?"

"Well, it's better than crashing, I mean. He's just bored. He's just about the only Automaton that can do this—go into sleep mode so easily. Vulcan designed him that way. That, or I make the most use of that function." He patted his Automaton like a car. "He knows when he's a third wheel. This is him saving energy. I'm bored with trying to lead you on, you see. This is me telling myself outright and doing something productive."

Like listening to a schizophrenic ramble, she nodded.

"Plus, he's pissed at me. I'm pissed *at myself.* This was probably one of our bigger screw ups, telling you what we are. But we'll suffer the consequences."

Dorian walked over to the smoke alarm on the wall. Taking it down, he removed the battery. "This thing goes off for the slightest bit of smoke. Believe me, I know." Anselm had been in here with his pipe once. The beeping was outrageous. "Now you can smoke carefree, m'dear."

It was like he was *ordering* her to smoke. She complied with his expectations and pulled one out.

Though she wasn't sure this was even real, her hands still shook. She blew out the smoke in shaky puffs, each one a prayer that this was some elaborate joke.

Dorian leaned against the wooden television stand.

Several seconds passed before she realized Dorian wasn't listening to the TV—he was listening to *her.* The equivalent of staring at her. "What?" she demanded, perhaps too rudely.

"I need to use the restroom."

"Um...OK?" Thanks for the update.

"No, you misunderstand. I'm not about to leave you out here, unsupervised, with Fletcher."

"As if you can 'watch' me any better? I'm starting to think that he's your eyes."

"How astute of you. Most don't usually notice it."

"Or could it be you wanted me to notice, like everything else?"

"Oh, that's likely too. But, as I was saying, I'm going to need you to follow me in here, thanks."

"What, to watch you piss?"

"You can close your eyes." What is it with Dorian and the *restroom*? Did he have a weak bladder? "Please don't make me force you. Because I *will* do it. Don't make me wake up Fletcher. He needs his sleep. Think of someone other than yourself."

She understood the need to keep her close. She was, after all, half-considering running away (only half). "I promise I won't try to run. I know what Fletcher can do."

"And I promise I won't do anything to you in the bathroom. Not even to the image of you in my head. But I *will* do something to you *here* if you don't do as I ask." He smiled and presented the bathroom.

She left her purse beside her, taking only her cigarette. Funny, though, when she came in, he told her to shut the door as he set the toilet lid down. "Have a sit."

"I—I thought you had to go?"

"No, I said '*use* the restroom.' The tub is in the restroom, isn't it?"

Technicality.

Dorian hadn't bathed in days (he'd been too busy babysitting).

She took a seat. But she quickly stood back up. "What the hell?"

He had turned off the lights. "Not like I need them anyways. Besides, you don't want to get embarrassed, do you? So please, sit down."

Even though the lights were off, she closed her eyes. Then, crossed her arms, crossed her legs, crossed the fine line between discomfort and comfort zone. She could feel her cigarette's ash fall to her lap. The darkness didn't make this any easier.

A discarded article of clothing brushed against her dangling foot, startling her. The light that streamed under the door showed where it landed. She could hear him take of his glasses, the ear-rests clicked together.

As he ran the water she could hear him fumbling, his hands brushing over the knob and the shower wall. She observed her cigarette's glowing tip. It illuminated her fingers, little else.

"Sorry to put you through this," he added, stepping in—no honesty in his statement.

"I'm sure you are." She watched as her cigarette burned out. Nothing more but a filter left.

"I know I'm being speedy. I guess you could say I'm making up for lost time."

"Do you want me to ask what *that* means, just so you can tell me?"

"I'll go on ahead, thank you. I'm very old, you see. Not as old as Fletcher, who is immortal, but I'm well past my mid-twenties."[113]

"Again, if you say you're a vampire, I'll punch you."

"Didn't I tell you I was human, though?"

"Vampires were humans once, too."

"I get your reasoning, but no. I swear, I won't even say that word." He sank into the tub, the spout-water still spilling. "Fletcher rubs off on me, you see. That's why I'm quasi-immortal."

"Like pixie dust?"

"No, not really."

...

"Aren't you going to add to that?"

"Nope."

"Why not? Why are you holding back now? I thought you wanted me to know everything."

"Eventually, yes. But I also want to keep the mystery alive, Odissa. Don't want you to like me just because I've got my hand in divine matters and the like. I also have dashing good looks, money, and excellent taste."

He turned off the water.

She could hear the shallow water rippling off him. She could also tell he'd placed his hand on the side of the tub, his rings clanked against it. Over a minute passed in dead silence. Odissa's butt was getting numb. She had to hunch over on the stiff seat. "How much longer are you going to sit there? Are you even using the soap?"

"I don't know where it is, can't see it."

"Did you even try to find it?"

"Who says I'm taking a bath to wash? Don't some just like to soak?"

"What would you do if I just walked out and sat in the main room?"

"Probably tackle you. However, I'd be wet. And naked. And I would enjoy it more. I encourage you to do it. It would be fun."

"I'm uncomfortable."

---

[113] He's robbing the cradle.

"Well, you asked the question."

"No, I mean, this seat. I need to move. Can I—can I stand?"

"Sure. So long as I don't hear that knob."

"I won't," she said, standing and stretching.

"Of course, you could always sit here, in the tub, with me. Help me find the soap."

"Wow," she said, stretching her legs. "That was the cheesiest of the queso right there."

Dorian chuckled. "Prepare for more, until you use your chip to dip."

She'd taken a few back steps to the door. She remembered her cigarette butt. "I'm going to put my cigarette out in the sink, okay?"—but it had died long ago—"That's what you'll hear."

"I think I can tell what a running faucet sounds like, and all the sounds therein."

"I'm sure," she said, fondling the area. Making sure to knock over the extra complimentary stack of paper cups and—oh, there they were—bath soaps, she slowly turned the faucet knobs…and flicked on the light switch nearby.

She was careful—her hand flat on the wall—to use her other fingers to stifle the noise.

She turned the faucet off, her scared eyes still looking down.

It was when she heard him sink back down—into the clear water—that she looked at him. She'd wanted to see his face. All of it.

His eyes were grey. Grey eyes. Cloudy eyes—once brown, maybe. They were ringed with pink-red scars as if said clouds had eclipsed two burning suns. Those eyes were painfully private, as well as the nothingness they saw. But let's leave these soul-windows, lest they become overwritten.

Suddenly, he shot higher in the tub. "You're clumsy," he stated, letting the drain up, the water swirling downward. "Now we can't use those cups. They're dirty." He rose from the water, as if a four-minute bath were all that was necessary.

Cringing and panicking, she turned from his nakedness to face the door. She realized she had gasped—but quickly turned it into a clearing-of-the-throat. "You just wasted water."

She heard him reach for the towels neatly folded above the toilet "Nah, it wasn't a waste if I got to be naked in front of you."

Her hand reached for the light, but she was afraid he'd hear the click.

"You like baths, Odissa?"

"Sometimes," she said over her shoulder. "But only to relax." She had answered too rapidly. She could hear him getting dressed—putting on the same clothes.

"Ah, same here. I don't find bathing in your own filth to be very clean." He seemed disappointed. Had he really expected something *romantic* to happen?

"Me too." Nervousness radiated within her statement. Her fingers waited for the next time he would speak so she could flip off the light without him hearing. She had to time it right; she could sense he was suspicious.

But a hand reached past her. And turned it off for her.

She had been too caught up to realize he'd stepped so close. She whipped around, willing to push him away, if need be.

"You think I couldn't hear the light's buzzing?"

She heard the I'm-not-so-stupid smile in his voice. She slowly inched backwards to the door. Her heel was upon it.

"For someone so scared, you do very brave things, Odissa. Why were you so curious? You wanted to see me without the glasses? Why didn't you just ask?"

"Who says it was the eyes?"

He leaned forward—a drip from his hair-tips fell on her arm. "When you kissed me, there was fear. Fear that I might do something to you. Not inflict pain or bodily harm or death but something metaphysical. A psychological reaction. But—you liked the kiss, yet you were afraid. Why was that?"

If he could hear the light buzzing, she wondered if she could hear the angry stroke her heart was having. "I don't trust you."

"It was if you expected no less from me; though, that thought wasn't just directed towards *me*, but what I *am* in general. And what am I? A male." He paused, for effect. "Even now, you freeze up. This morning you were sharp and somewhat enjoyed my pestering. Now you're defensive."

"Can—can you blame me?" she struggled to keep up with his smartness. "This morning you hadn't stolen a dead girl's body, killed two cops, or—"

"Taken a bath in front of you?" He laughed. "You're not in control, here—not even a little. You're vulnerable. Why not take control?"

He moved one electric-inch closer, a serene snake that could taste her fear; or, a gardener who wanted a smell so he might recognize the flower.

The doorknob jabbed into her spine, preventing her from becoming one with the wood. As she squirmed forward from the cold knob, it allowed him to brush noses with her.

"What control can I take, when *you* have it?" she snapped at him.

He took a step back. He could feel her relax. In a very *serious* tone (a *grey* sound uncharacteristic of his normal rainbow-vomit), "I think you misunderstand me, Odissa. I'm not in control here."

She saw his outline kneel down, the light from under the door making him clearer. He reached for her pants button.

"What are you doing?" She snapped at him, pushing his hand away.

He did not persist. "This—you and me—certainly isn't how I thought things would play out," He said up to her. "I was just doing a job, but then *you* came into the picture. You have more control than you think. And here I am, losing all of it." He let that settle in.

She tried to turn the knob but he fortified it with his arm.

"Tell me, Odissa, why your brother really hated your father—*still* hates your father."

"Is that why you're making fun of me? You just want to know more about my father?"

"You think I'm making fun of you? Jesus, do I really seem that fake?"

"Yes! You're fucking *gay*. You know so much about me already, Mr. Dorian. What more could I add?"

"That's probably true, but I still want you to *talk* to me."

"You tell *me* more and I'll tell *you* more."

"Ah! Getting to know each other!" He said, popping back up to her level. "Like a first date." His voice was once more the monotonous, spinning disco-ball. He leaned against the sink, making his body a diagonal blockade, the space just tight enough so she couldn't open the door.

"Usually there's no taking baths together on the first date," she mumbled.

"Together? That was in no way *together*. I may have been out of the dating scene for a few decades, but I know the difference. I can show you what *together* is like."

She said nothing.

"Well, I suppose we've done a few things most couples wouldn't *think* of doing on first dates. Chatting in a lightless bathroom one of them."

"I wouldn't know. I've never dated." She had hoped that would stop this conversation's flow—bring his elated tone down a notch. But it didn't. Only made him worse.

"Well, then! We'll have to amend that, my señorita."

She gave a little jolt, his excitement unexpected

"How about tomorrow? We can spend the day together. The whole day."—as if that wasn't the plan already. "Your literal blind date."

"Didn't we already do that?"

"So we'll call it date number two. No matter. Now, I suppose it's bedtime for you? It is for me, since I haven't gotten a proper rest in days. I know you didn't sleep so well last night either. Especially since you were so busy watching me and Fletcher, you little pervert, you. What must you do to get ready?"

"Since I don't have any of my things, I guess I'm *already* ready for bed."

Her main issue was where she was supposed to sleep.

"Ah, me too."

She heard him pick up his glasses. "I'll not wear these then, if I don't have to. You already know what my eyes look like. I'd say the same goes for my pants, but if you wear them so will I. I'm nothing if not fair."

"You do know I wear glasses, technically, right?"

"You can open the door now, if you want."

She did.

"Where did he go?" she asked, looking for Fletcher.

"What do you mean?" Dorian asked, though it wasn't a question at all. "He's right here." Dorian picked him up and pinned him on his unbuttoned shirt collar. "He'll take up less bed-space, this way."

Realizing what he meant, "But—but—but that paperclip isn't even the same *mass* as Fletcher."

"Ah, look at you, trying to bring science into religion." He pulled back the covers.

"Is he your eyes?" Odissa asked. He arranged the pillows more evenly. "Even as a paperclip?"

Dorian plopped himself on the bed and wiggled his toes. "I swear, I needn't tell you anything more, because you'd figure it all out on your own. But yes. He's my eyes—even when his eyes are shut, sometimes. Granted, he still has to be paying *attention*—which is often a challenge for us both."

He sat up, his smile dimming. "The main thing you need to know is that he *is* me. An extension *of* me. Now, enough of this chatter. Bed time." He patted the space beside him.

But he knew it wouldn't be so effortless. That's what made this so enjoyable.

Odissa sat down in the chair—her main method of rebellion.

"You think you're going to sleep there?"

"Give me a blanket."

251

"No. And, on top of it, I'll turn off the heater and freeze you out. We'll be snuggling in a matter of minutes."

She pulled out another cigarette. "Do it," she said, holding it between her lips.

"I *can* break the chair."

"Do it," dangling her cigarette-arm off the chair and blowing smoke out her mouth's corner.

"And I don't mind the floor either, if you decide to stretch out."

"Then. Do. It."

Dorian's countenance turned somber. With a sigh, he rolled out of bed. Turning the droning television off, he said, "I didn't think I'd have to pull it out, but…" He drew out a tiny little hand gun from his pants. It looked more like a toy than a real weapon. She froze in her chair as he pointed it at her. "Come, Odissa. In the bed." He sloppily gestured with it.

Odissa got over the gun very quickly and suppressed a smile. "You won't shoot me."

"I won't?"

"You just said I was your—your 'soul-mate' less than thirty minutes ago. Now you're willing to kill me?"

"Who said I'd shoot to kill?"

She grew very still.

"After all," Dorian shrugged, "I'm willing to steal dead bodies to make it look like you've died. I'm the one who made Fletcher kill those cops. And, what's more, I clearly have a fucking gun pointed at you. What makes you so sure you know *anything* that I'd do, Odissa?"

"Then do it already."

"I just might." For a few seconds there, he let the silence build up and raised his gun a little higher. "Plus, I'm blind, so I might not *mean* to kill you, but miss my target. Best not to make me so much as *demonstrate* it's loaded. I do, however, know you're somewhere about…*here*." He waved the gun in a circular motion about the vicinity.

"They'll hear you—they'll hear it go off."

"What? The people in the motel? Oh, Odissa, they've heard *many* things before—many of my loud noises, believe me. That's why we pay them so much. Now, in the bed, please."

With his other hand, he presented it.

"I won't."

He half cocked it.

Nothing.

He cocked it all the way.

Nothing.

He raised it higher.

Nothing.

He let gravity take the nose, the trigger guard swinging around his finger. "This, dear Odissa, is a metaphor for my dick." Limp. "And oh, how it goes off for you." He let out a series of *hee, hee, hees*—very pleased with himself.

Her skin prickled when he laughed—his *true* laughter. He was usually so void of true expression and had to pretend normal emotions. She could tell the sound also startled him—felt unnatural to his throat.

He walked over to her, put the gun on the table. "I give you the dick." He scooted it to her. "You're the man now."

She eyed it but knew better. All his talk about being *immortal* had ruined any hope that she could hurt them. His bravery enforced this.

"For Christ's sake, you're full of shit." She jabbed out her cigarette on a complimentary plastic coaster. "I'd crawl into bed just so you'd shut up."

His ears perked. "Really?"

"Yeahno," she spat.

"Fine then, have it for yourself. You win. You've limped the dick." He gestured to his own. "Fletch and I have to keep watch anyway."

"I can't sleep if I know you'll be *watching*."

Dorian's face went uber-stoic once more. "Here." He raised the paperclip up in demonstration and tucked him under her purse on the table. "Now I can't see a thing. I'll trade you places." He pointed at her chair.

She stood up. "Leave the lights on," she commanded just as he reached for the nearby switch. As she took the bed, "So I can see you."

Giving a promissory bow, he lighted the chair, next to the gun.

She faced Dorian. He stared at nothing with his vacant eyes. For a brief moment, she wanted to slap the strange grin off his face—the triumphant grin.

Because of the gauche arrangement, she felt like she was actually lying on the floor, so uncomfortable! She was so uptight she didn't even remove her glasses, though they put pressure on her nose and ears.

Dorian's hair was still damp. He smoothed it back while resting his head. She watched him put his legs on the table. An hour ticked by. He kept his eyes closed, though:

"I know you're not asleep," she said eventually.

He lifted his head. "Look, I promise I won't move from this spot. Please get some sleep, Odissa. Please." He was begging her. "Don't waste a good bed. You might not get one tomorrow."

After a few minutes of silence, she stuck her tongue out at him—waved her arm—gave him the finger. When he didn't react she knew *for sure* he couldn't see her.

Despite her best efforts, she dozed—but was startled awake when Fletcher knocked over her purse as he reformed. The noise didn't disturb Dorian, though, who was just as sleepy as Fletcher. Fletcher, in all his nude glory, sleepwalked onto Dorian's lap. Dorian shifted his position to prop up Fletcher like a giant baby—as if he knew Fletcher was coming. Together they made a perfect pietà.

Odissa watched with wide eyes. It was in this moment she realized they needed to touch—to be near. *This is what happened last night.*

Fletcher wove his fingers through his Master's hair and nestled in. His toes reached the carpet. Dorian rested his head upon Fletcher's chest as if it were a pillow. Fletcher's leg eventually slid off and exposed his junk to Odissa—rather, what there was of it. She tried not to stare, but failed. He lacked nothing but testicles. He had no use for those. His dick could harden through sheer will.

Something told Odissa that Fletcher's genital situation was a statement on his reproductive ability rather than his gender(?).[114] Her eyes darted to their faces. They looked so uncomfortable it made her feel bad for hogging the bed—but only for a brief moment. Her eyes peeled from them and landed on the far door, trying to avoid any further thoughts about them and their body parts.

As if her eyes had predicted it, the motel door shook.

She gasped, waking the boys. Fletcher's puffy eyes noted hers and he whipped his head in the door's direction. Odissa saw—*saw!*—the bottom of the door lift as if it were a flimsy curtain—just enough for someone to slide a letter under it.

Dorian sighed, knowing what Fletcher and Odissa were seeing. "Put some clothes on, Fletcher." He slapped his Automaton's thigh as Fletcher slid off him. "Don't want to show Odissa the goods just yet."

Odissa was panting—concerned that they were *un*concerned about what they had just seen.

---

[114] "Sex" didn't seem the right word, here.

"Speaking of perverts," Fletcher muttered as he approached the letter. He gave a morning stretch as he looked down upon the letter. He sniffed the air before touching it. "You smell that, Dori? That's not Daddy."

"That's his Wife."

Fletcher ripped open the letter, a small key sliding out. He read the parchment, "'Dear Dorian-Fletcher: My husband has made me aware you're having trouble getting Odissa on your good side. I know what it's like to be trapped in a relationship, but that's no excuse for *her*. Since my husband won't allow me to tweak Odissa's interests as I've done to yours, I hope this helps. Please use this key to go to [Such-and-such a mall] to take her shopping. You girls could use a shopping trip. It's small—no security guards at this hour. You'll find all alarms and cameras disabled. This will get you through the doors. If I'm going to make you want her, I can at least help you get what you want.' Signed 'V.'"—Fletcher looked up—"And that doesn't mean Vulcan."

Odissa drew herself further into the corner. Gods really *were* involved.

Dorian stood up. "Get ready Odissa, we're going shopping."

Fletcher gathered their scattered things (including Odissa's). "I'll go start the car."

"Car? What car?" Odissa said, remembering the cop car. *Surely not that car!*

"Whichever one you like."

"Go on ahead, you two. I've a phone call to make and some shoes to put on." Dorian pushed back his hair.

They left, but Dorian didn't make a phone call. Instead, he just held the phone in his hand. Why was he so hesitant to tell Mother what he was up to?—not that he wanted to hide from her. It was impossible to do that anyway. But for the first time in a long while he wanted privacy.

Stanza: Gods in the machines—plurals.

Fletcher led Odissa out to the parking lot, his hand on the back of her neck. She was too dazed to disagree with its placement.

"Who does he have to call?" she asked—her voice too curious and excited. "Is it about Aphrodite? The gods don't normally poke their noses in your business, do they? That's why he's scared?"

"The gods are the least of his worries. Now, which car shall we take?"

"You mean you were serious?" Odissa stopped her pace.

"If you aren't going to pick, I'll do it for you."

"But why can't we call a cab?"

255

"Because they don't accept gold, and we haven't much cash on us."

"What?"

He touched her purse and it fell to the ground with a clanking *thud*. "Gold," he repeated himself. "Now tell me which car."

But she simply stared at her golden purse she had struggled to pick up. "All my stuff—"

"Never mind. I like this one," he pointed to the jalopy far from the parking lot lights, "Nice and crappy—and probably doesn't have a car alarm." He circled the car and slipped his mutating fingers down the thin window slot to pop the door open. Opening it for her, "Mademoiselle," he said. She watched as he shifted his attire, putting on his best chauffer suit and cap.

She cautiously curled into the car, eyes wondering if anyone else saw his costume change. It was so dark though even *she* doubted her eyes. "It looks so real, your clothes."

"That's the point," he said, noticing her hand draw back. She had wanted to touch him. Dorian climbed into the back with Odissa. "Out of all the cars, you picked this one?"

Odissa didn't reply.

Leaning forward to his Automaton. "How's it coming, darling?"

The car started, and Fletcher responded, "Fine, dear, just fine."

WIRED.

"Then let's get going!"

"We're really going shopping because a god told us to?" Fletcher grumbled as he backed out of their spot.

"They have a game plan. And we are the chesspeices."

Fletcher rolled his eyes. "You Masters are His Automatons."

Dorian waved himself off. "Besides, what else is there to do?" To Odissa, "Are you hungry yet? Would you like some coffee, Odissa?"

"I'm fine."

"Indeed you are, but I was asking if you wanted some coffee."

With a mental eye-roll, Odissa turned away from him to stare at the fast-moving night. She could hardly remember her name, let alone keep up with his chattiness. She rested her head on the window.

Driving, driving, driving.

"Is Vulcan going to be at the mall?" She really, really hoped not. Her brain had handled enough for one night. She was in no state to visit a god.

"Why would you think that, Odissa?" Dorian asked.

"Well, did you expect Venus to show up at the hotel?"

"She has a point," Fletcher mumbled.

"No one should ever expect anything from a god."

Stanza: Meanwhile...

Bobmation had sniffed Dorian out. But she wasn't quick enough to catch him.

Bob parked her motorcycle and Cestus squeezed himself out of the sidecar, pulling up faux-goggles that disappeared back into his skull. No one with normal eyes would have noticed the goggles vanish as they passed under the awning.

Ignoring the DO NOT DISTURB sign Fletcher had left behind, Cestus rooted for his own copy of the key card. Bob unzipped her leather jacket upon entering. She placed her helmet on the table as Cestus bolted the door behind them.

"They *were* here," he said, tossing a pillow back on the messy bed. "How did they know we were coming? Wait. You smell that?"

Bob frowned away as she studied the room with her one eye. "Cigarettes."

Cestus snorted at the smell. "Venus. She's been here. She must have warned them we were coming. Didn't Vulcan tell us His plans wouldn't be disrupted? She's helping Him!"

"But why would They think we'd mess up Their plans?"

"We wanted to see Odissa, didn't we? We wanted to see her before things went"—he chose his words carefully—"bad. Maybe They knew we'd spread secrets—secrets They don't want them to know yet. Hell, we already have. We told Mecca about Vulcan."

"But it was the least They could do for us!" Bob huffed. "I only wanted to see her with my own eyes. I promised Him I'd go along with the plan, didn't I? I gave Vulcan my word. I only wanted a *glimpse*. I wanted to know what I'd be dying for." She found her flask as she peaked into the bathroom. She saw Odissa's cigarette butt in the sink and frowned at it. Under her breath, "Dorian and his damn baths!"

"You already know *what* you're dying for, Bob."

"Yes, I know *what*. But poor Gwen will think it's for –for other reasons." She stared at the wall as if reading her thoughts from it. "Not selfish ones. I know more than she does; I know what Vulcan plans to do—what he plans to do with her plans. Vulcan flat out told me, didn't he? The bastard. But I'm not dying for Gwen. I'm dying for myself. But cheers to me if I can help Gwen out while doing it." She raised her flask.

"What if Vulcan's lying? Lying about what Mother's secretly up to? What if He only wants you out of the picture—period."

"Either way, I don't want myself in this goddamned picture. And like you disbelieve Him! You saw Mecca's reaction back at the pub this morning. I'm the only one Gwen had told about the little *Madus* mission—and even then you know she was lying about it to cover something else. She only tells us her plans *after* stage one has begun. I wouldn't know that at all if Vulcan hadn't showed me—proven it to me. And why would Vulcan lie? He's never lied before. If He wants me dead, might as well not fight it. Not as if I could. He at least respects me enough to let me do it on my own terms. Not that natural events could kill me otherwise. He kind of has to respect me, doesn't he? He can't just wave his goddamn arm and BOOM I'm dead. He's got to play by his own rules. Automata are his rules. He has to show the Others that he's in control. And he fucking is. Nah, I won't fucking fight it."

She opened the mini fridge, delighted when she found they were quite stocked up—not just with Dorian's leftover snacks. The sweets tumbled out as she reached for the mini alcoholic drinks.

"Speaking of not fighting it…" Cestus gestured to the room, the motion hesitant. She looked up at him, her bangs falling back and showing her second eye.

Her brows came together as she studied her Automaton's panicked face. Her voice breaking, "You don't think…"

But no, she *did* think. "The gods did this on purpose. They want me to do it here—now." She stood up. "Why else would They arrange this private room? Vulcan's not going to *give* me a chance to mess this up is he?" She laughed in disbelief.

She found herself sitting on the bed because her legs trembled. Cestus sat beside her. She downed the tiny bottle.

"He could have let me say goodbye to everyone."

"You and I both know you aren't good at goodbyes."

"I'm too much of a coward to say goodbye. That's why I'm about to kill myself, isn't it?" she spat.

She looked up at the ceiling fan above them. Then at the sash on the curtains. These would be useful. She sighed. "My suicide in this room will leave quite the message for Dorian. Vulcan probably means for it to. Death follows in his path." She gestured as if she could see the writing on the wall. She chuckled to herself, witty even on her deathbed.

Cestus took something out of his jacket—out of himself. "But how sad, you won't get to give her the scarf."

"I'm giving her so much more than that." She scoffed, wishing her flask wasn't half empty. Not about to get all sentimental, she swished her drink around. "Text them, then. Tell them what I'm about to do. We don't want a poor little cleaning maid to touch you first."

Stanza: Great expectations…

The mall building was antiquated—filled with dying businesses. Each store had an outside and inside entrance. They waltzed up to the front. Dorian didn't even bother to be subtle with a back door. As they opened the entrance with the key…no alarm went off.

This proved the goddess's narrative.

Dorian walked up to the nearest store. Fletcher used his own "key" to open the trellis-bar gate. Again, no alarms.

"But the camera's—" Odissa started to say as she looked up.

"Have a bit more faith, Odissa," Dorian assured her. "It's not every day a goddess tells you to go shopping. YOUR WILL BE DONE, VENUS!" He shouted it into the building.

"Venus has outdone herself this time," Fletcher mumbled, crossing his arms. "The gods really want you two together. Just have sex already and be done with it."

Odissa glared at him.

They found themselves in a department store—one trying to get rid of unwanted Halloween costumes. ALL COSTUMES ON SALE!

Dorian and Fletcher darted about. "Take anything you might need, Odissa," Dorian said. "A new purse—socks—undies. Here's your chance " He'd already picked up a purse and was stuffing things into it.

Even Fletcher had on a scarf—a scarf he (an Automaton) didn't need.

"Why are we in the costume section, again?" She felt like she was sleepwalking.

"Oh, look. She's so tired she can't remember I've already told her three times. You need something to wear for our date."

"Yes, that. But seriously."

"I *am* serious! This is a very serious occasion our first real date. I'm thinking something with frills, aren't you, Fletcher?" He gestured to a sloppily-made Victorian dress.

Fletcher shrugged. Dorian spared little energy for him and he was fading fast. "I wish this place had a home interiors department. So that I could find a bed. Don't care if it's the small kind."

"He just doesn't understand, really," Dorian explained to Odissa. "He can wear whatever he wants. It's not often humans get to change their character." (To Dorian, clothes were character). "How about a Marie Antoinette costume?" he said pointing to a far rack. "We'd go out for *cake*."

"I'm not putting these on," Odissa said. She crossed her arms for emphasis.

"At least pick out a hat."

"Can we go if I do? I don't like this, Dorian. What if the cops show up?"

"You're forgetting our last run-in with the cops? Didn't we handle that nicely enough? What do you have to worry about?" He took a bright pink feather boa from Fletcher and draped it around his neck. "Here, if you don't put on these cat ears, I'll dress in drag."

"You say it like a threat—as if I'd care." But she found herself putting them on anyway. *I will not face the fact I want to see him in a dress. No, not today.*

"Good, now we just need to find the matching tail…" he ripped open a nearby package.

"I thought it was just the ears!"

"Oh, com'on—have some fun!" he said as Fletcher plopped a huge leopard-print pimp hat on him. He was starting to look more and more like Elton John.

She grabbed the tail from him to put it on herself. She didn't want him near her ass. "I'd have more fun if I wasn't having a god—as they say—*pimp* me out." She pointed to his hat, for effect.

Dorian giggled.

She picked up a package of feathery fake eyelashes and lost herself in their shimmery glitter—glitter that would probably flake off into her eyes and were too long to wear with glasses. When she put down the box and looked back up at him, Fletcher was gone. "Where'd he go?"

"He's going to keep watch. Just enjoy the date."

"This isn't a date."

"Well, dahling" he said, flipping the dangling boa over his shoulder, "Call it whatever you like."

Stanza: No need for a note when Automata record the whole moment perfectly.

The parking lot lights leaked through the blinds and cast eerie bars on Cestus's profile—as if trapped—trapped in thought—trapped in Bob's thoughts. So Noir.

"It worries me to see you doing the worrying for us."

He walked over and sat next to her on the bed once more, keeping his arms firmly crossed, head low. "They haven't responded to our texts."

"Not as if they don't have a lot on their plate right now," Bob adjusted the "rope" she'd made out of the curtains. She tugged on it to make sure the fan wouldn't come down. "Besides. We've been dramatic before, haven't we? Plus, it will take them a little while to figure out where we are."

Cestus said nothing.

"Vulcan approved this. He said he'd make use of my death. He *assured* us." Vulcan had, indeed, come to them. As a dwarf, small as Ptah, he had made himself known at the bar of Bob's choosing—shared a drink with her. "He gave us peace about it. Accept the peace, Cest. What else can we do? We're here—in this empty room—everything's been pre-programmed to result in this exact moment. I'm done questioning it."

"He knew we would do it anyway. With or without his divine blessing." Cestus rubbed his eyes with his huge fingers. "Eventually."

She ignored his comment. She sighed and her leather-covered body creaked. "You know, I really liked that hot cocoa you made, before we left this morning. Would have been a good recipe to take to the cabin."

"Finally perfected it, yeah. But you poured enough vodka in it to inebriate a horse."

"Well, I promise you, after tonight, I'll never drink again!" she raised her flask in the air in toast. Her leather coat sleeve pulled with the action. It showed her wrist spots. She downed the last of her drink—it was all gone.

"That's some promise. Too easy to keep."

An unnatural smile spread across Bob's face, the irony conflicting her. "I'll stop trying to pump myself up."

"We were never the funny ones anyway."

"I guess I should be more prepared for this," Bob said. She screwed the cap back on her flask and tossed it on the floor. "Jesus Christ, I thought I was. No, I *am*. I've got nothing left. I'm just anxious about how much this will hurt. It's not fair—how long it'll take. I mean, Pepin used a real gun. And just look at the mess he made. I can't imagine what an Automaton's handgun would do. No, this is the cleanest way."

She eventually stepped up on the chair and put the noose around her neck. She reached out to Cestus, in the last minute. "I want you to know, Cestus, that you've done my soul wonders."

He kicked the chair out from under her. Her force pulled the fan, cracking the ceiling and exposing wires like an uprooted tree. He waited inanimately for her to struggle to death—though it wasn't much of a struggle. Not when you're willing to go.

Her last thoughts to Cestus—the last words she inscribed upon him—were meant for his new taker: *Promise me you won't erase the memories I gave him. You can have him, but just let me live on through him.*

And just like that, there was no more Bob.

Stanza: (Nobody kills Bob until she says so).

It was exactly one hour later that the bolted motel room door cracked open—prying the bolt right off. The newcomer cast shadows over Bob's dangling body. His shadow reached up like tentacles—snatching, grabbing, smothering. Of course you can't see his face. Not at first. So, let me tell you who it is:

Admund—Automaton of Leeland—finally showed up. Leeland himself was too busy driving (no, I'll not tell you to where). Admund was closest at the time.

Bob had expected one of Leeland's faces to come, just as Vulcan said he would. This was all part of His plan. Bob had surrendered to it.

As he drove, Leeland's lips moved; and, many miles away, so did Admund's. Their speech so synchronized:

"What made you do it?" Admund said up to her, he stroked his beard in Leeland's churning thought. "And with such timing, too. How did you know this would help so much? What will your Mother say?"

But Admund could smell it in the air—the reason Bob knew. So many smells! "The gods told you what we are up to?" He looked around the room, turning his dignified head. Leeland watched and spoke through him, "You wanted to finally help me? Or is it because you know I'm finally catching Gwen's attention? Helping me is helping Gwen. Yes, yes. You knew something." He shook his finger at her, then stuffed his hands in his "pockets."

He bit his lip.

He could not know that Vulcan had told her (in slight detail) He would make use of *all* their plans—including Leeland's. But only enough to get her to submit to His will (for a human could never understand, without getting a little upset, that the gods could never really please them all).

He sat on the corner of the bed, watching the still-Cestus. "In this wake, I will confess that letting your husband die was one of the hardest things I ever did. Your spots as well made me feel so cruel—crueler than when I forced Dorian to take out his own eyes. You were always so much *harder* to disturb, Robyn. But how can a father instruct without a rod? Fathers cannot be gentle. Your Mother is finally learning this as well."

Admund took a plastic bag out from himself and put his hand inside. Through the plastic, he picked up Cestus—for later usage. He zipped the bag and folded the lips over—tucked it away inside his Automaton body. Never touching it.

He dug Bob's cell phone out of her pocket and read her messages. He deleted the texts to his Master. The others could never know the conversation. But he left the phone so they could later track it back to this room...

He was about to leave, but had one last confession stored inside him. "Since I have you here, all to myself, I might as well say something that has always weighed on me, Robyn." He wanted to push back that veil of hair in front of her eye and tuck it behind her ear—to make her like she used to be. But he didn't. He could only touch her foot for one second.

He put a hand on his chest, to steady himself. "I want you to know I wasn't playing favorites when I didn't stop you from killing your husband and yet saved Dorian's niece and nephew. You both selfishly let your loved ones die to keep your Automata. Granted, Dorian didn't know his step-sister had recently given birth. So tragic of them, that they had wanted to surprise him with the news. But that's the cost when you choose an Automaton. You lose touch with your past life and are constantly surprised it goes on without you. That's what makes Automata so vile."

He waved his hand. "But you know that story well." And his Master hated to relive it—relive that day Admund had "shared" a taxi with Mr. and Mrs. Dimitri and their new twins.

"Dorian didn't know—not for sure—what he was letting die. But you did, Robyn. You knew who you were giving up for Cestus. But I want you to know I only saved the twins because I saw a way to get at you all. And so far, the twins have been the perfect bridge to you, haven't they? They _would_ have been perfect, anyway, if things—" He shook off the thought. "No matter. I'm nothing if not adaptable. Hell, I have more than one body—I can fit into any situation."

He pulled at the sides of his face and forced a heavy chuckle, jutting out his chin in thought for his Master. "No, Robyn. I wasn't playing favorites. In fact, I really only wanted to save one of them—one of the twins." He scratched his nose and sniffed. Venus's perfume clogged his large nostrils. "I only wanted Odissa. But you likely knew I wanted her to have a child—to make me (or Admund, really) a 'grandfather' and therefore give you lot more reasons to _reconsider_ your existence. It would have made all this,"—he gestured to their inherent situation—"so much easier."

He sighed. "Would have given me more to work with. I'm barely scraping by as it is. I could have convinced you all so _quickly_, with her children involved—you and Gwen hate to see children suffer, especially. But maybe my children are why you've done this? Do you feel guilty after all these years, finally?"

He shook his head, as if that didn't make sense.

"Speaking of guilt," he sighed. "Had I known at the time how infertile Odissa would be, well…" He put up his hands. "No, I still would have saved her. There was always the possibility I could have fixed her.[115] She's still paying off, despite it. Though I saw a use for her, I knew— no, *understood*—that she would need leverage to be controlled, at least until she was grown. See, I knew leverage needs leverage sometimes. And her *leverage* turned out to be more useful than I first imagined. He's kept her out of my everyday affairs in his obsessive attempts to avoid me. That's the only reason I saved and kept *Odys*."[116]

ADMUND: The undead father.

HIS MASTER: Didn't look at all like the twins.

THE PERSONA ODI ODELYN: Left specific instructions in his will.

INSTRUCTIONS: It wasn't just about visiting a grave site. More respects must be paid.

Chapter the eighteenth,

Deus ex machina:

But which machine?

"Come, Odissa, let's browse the next stop in our *costumes*," Dorian gestured to the exit, extending an open hand.

She ignored the hand. "I'd hardly call them costumes."

"Well, we must use our imagination then, my kitty. Please, take my hand. I really can't see."

"Will Fletcher know where we're going?"

"Of course, he's already opened the next place we're going."

"And where's that?"

"The inside dollar theater just down the strip—one that's apparently been closed for some time."

"I don't want to watch a movie."

"Who said anything about a movie? I'm hoping we'll be too busy to pay attention to anything like that."

---

[115] I'm offended he thought Odissa was broken.
[116] Notice he didn't say "let Odys live." Then again, it would have thrown off the Proper Noun ending our Narrator is so attached to.

And so she found herself in a dimly lit theater before a huge and tattered screen, in a row with vandalized seats, beside a wanna-be Elton John.

Oh, and for some reason, she had a suspicion that Fletcher was watching from above in the projector stand—probably chugging away at some drink he'd stolen. She knew he was watching from somewhere—Dorian was too *aware* of his surroundings.

"Isn't this nice?" Dorian said, putting his feet on the back of the seats.

"Sure," Odissa lied. She eyed the flickering exit sign. Below it, the door was boarded up. No escape.

"I wonder if they've left a popcorn machine behind? Should I send Fletcher to look for one? Granted, he might not find any popcorn to go with it—"

"I don't really like popcorn." She adjusted her tail. It was very uncomfortable to sit with.

"So, what movie is playing?"

"There isn't one."

"Imagination, Odissa. Use it."

"I feel like I'm in someone else's movie right now. Aphrodite's."

"Well, let's not talk through the movie then. Let's play our part." Dorian laughed. "You want the gods to get their money's worth."

She hated that she wanted to laugh, so changed the subject. "It feels shallow—the fact you're in love with me because a goddess forced you. It undermines the real thing, doesn't it?"

"Does it now? Define 'real love.' I doubt everyone has the same definition. I've learned to accept fate. It takes less effort if you know the gods will handle everything. Even if I have no control, I'm still enjoying myself."

"It seems you've enjoyed a lot of things in your life time—on both ends of the spectrum."

"Believe it or not, I've always gone both ways. Well, okay, maybe more bisexual with a heavy emphasis on the male form. But there is a *minor* attraction to a select few women..."

"Sounds like a college degree."

"Ah, but I'm not the one with a complicated love life, am I? You think I can't see it?" He retrieved a fresh pack of gum. He must have stolen a new one when she wasn't looking. He tossed the wrapper behind him. "Why do you share his bed? I mean, it wouldn't be so obvious if we hadn't *seen* your bed—a bed you didn't use. Otherwise, you hide the fact well, I'm sure. You shut everyone else out because you don't need them. Why would you when you've an opposite reflection of yourself?"

"You think everyone wants to fuck themselves, is that it?"

He shrugged. "I've fucked Fletcher. Plenty of times. Most times he opens his eyes when I do it, so it's like I'm seeing myself as I fuck him. It's wonderful."

"I don't know how to respond to that."

"That's what's great about this, isn't it? We don't *need* to respond. We just understand each other. That's the key to a good relationship. Ours will be perfect."

She snorted. "It will, will it?"

"Excuse me, not *will be*, but *is*. Already."

She felt the need to defend herself. "Just because we share a bed doesn't mean anything's happening."

"No, I guess it doesn't," he passively agreed. "But at least you admit you share his bed."

"We just...always have." She found herself crossing her arms.

"Why?"

"When growing up, I'd cry without him. I was afraid of the dark and being alone. Our father..."—she paused and started up again—"He—he let us have our way, if it would shut us up. So would the nannies. Ah, look, I've finally shut you up."

"Odissa," he turned to her, leaning on the chair arm, miscalculating the direction of her face by a hair (Fletcher wasn't paying enough attention)—"*have* you fucked him? I don't want secrets between us. I need you to admit it to me."

She laughed—laughed because there was nothing else to do.

"Why not just tell me you haven't, if you haven't?"

"Because why should I?"

"So you aren't even going to *lie* about it anymore? You're just going to keep the truth from me?"

Exhausted, "Yes, exactly."

"All right, all right. We can change the subject."

"Why don't we change company while we're at it?"

"Are you saying you don't like me?"

"Exactly."

"Ah, so you *love* me," he stated, proud of his cleverness.

"Why would I do that?"

"Why *wouldn't* you?"

She said nothing.

"What else should we talk about, then?" He tilted his head, slouching in his seat. "Haven't been on one in a while, but isn't this what couples do on dates, talk about their past love lives?"

"This isn't a date."

He gripped his knees—knees attached to those legs perched on the back of the seats. "What would you call it then?"

"A fucking kidnapping."

"Awww. Because I stole your heart? That's so sentimental, darling." He let his laughter settle. "So, since we're on a date—"

"Not a date—"

"—I need to know how many sexual partners you've had. I need to know what to expect in the STD range, you know? I can still catch those things, even with an Automaton."

"This isn't romantic conversation, just to let you know." She'd move down a seat if she knew he wouldn't follow her.

"Sure, I'd rather stop the chit-chat too and get right down to business, but I don't think we've come that far yet."

Before she could comment, his phone rang.

"Aren't you going to answer that?"

"Ah," he said tapping his coat's breast pocket, apparently where he'd put his phone. "Too bad Fletcher's eyes aren't here to tell me who's calling."

"I can tell you," she offered.

"Don't insult me. Just because I'm a girl doesn't mean you have to open doors for me and the jam jar too."

"Then make Fletcher come down and read them."

"No. I liked where our conversation was going. But where were we again? Oh, yes. *How many relationships have you been in?*"

She stared at his phone. Its screen lighted the fabric as it rang again.

"Just answer it."

"If you insist." He picked up. "Hello? Oh? Oh, really? I see. Okay. That was quicker than we expected—Oh, yes, I guess it's hard to plan these sort of things—Of course I want to hear what you recorded from his phone. Fletcher's bored out of my wits, send it over! Oh? Mm. Yeah, we can be there, in the morning. *Sí,* puedo. [More rambling in Spanish too fast for Odissa to keep up with]. No, I wasn't aware. Yes, I'm keeping her *entertained*." He smiled in Odissa's direction, wanting her to hear. "Oh, well, that's wonderful. Oh, all right then. *Sí, sí.* Buh-bye."

"Who was it?"

"Mother."

"Your mother?"

"No, not my *real* mother. Everyone just calls her that. Apparently your brother passed—a lot quicker than expected."

"Passed?"

"He did what we wanted him to." To himself, "And so quickly too."

"So you'll leave us alone now?"

He frowned at the hope in her voice. "No, no, dear. I'm sorry but this is your life now. Your brother's no free man. None of us are."

"What does that mean?'

"You're not stupid, Odissa. You met Maud. You know what she is. We can't let Odys just do as he likes with her now that he's one of us. Don't sigh like that. It shows your worry."

"How can I not worry? Why do you even have to test him? The gods can set up a *date* for you but not make you—you and your *mother*—trust my brother? Is that it?"

"Gods might meddle in our affairs, but they aren't going to solve our problems. They're *our* problems, after all. There's no need to worry about your brother. Not when he's on our good side...I thought he'd try and track me down and take you away from me. But he did things the right way. He's such an honest boy." *He will complicate things.*

"What?"

"Let's just get back to our date."

"No, not back to our date. This *isn't* a date, Dorian. I'm not here because I want to be."

"What'd make you *want* to be?"

"I need to know the—the truth. The facts."

"Facts?"

"Like the fact you have a fucking—what do you call him?"

"Fletcher?"

"No, what *is* he again?"

"Oh, an *Automaton*."

"Right. So hard to remember. How'd you even get one? How the hell did *Odys* get one?"

"I can't tell you that."

"Maybe if you'd talk more freely with *me*, I'd talk more freely with *you*."

"I need you to trust even when I *don't* tell you, Odissa. I'm risking a lot by telling you what Fletcher is to begin with."

She looked down at her feet, not liking his real face—a face that wasn't so pretend-happy. "I don't see how it can be that complicated."

"Oh it *is* complicated. However, Odissa,"—he sunk even lower in his seat, as if about to snooze—"what *isn't* complicated is the fact we're in this complication together." He sounded like a Facebook relationship status.

"You think that's all a relationship takes? Just being in the same room with someone?"

"I do," he flirted, resting his head in his hand, leaning away from her. "If two people are in the right place at the right time, then why not?" He lifted his hand. "And it might be easier for me to give information to you if only you'd realize that I do, indeed, have a phone. That phone can make calls to get you information. Granted, it has its price. I'm a payphone."

She watched him play with his rings. "And how much does it cost, this payphone? What's a dime worth to you?"

"I'm not going to do all the research for you, Odissa. You're going to have to find out."

For a long while she was silent.

How could he be so calm, when asking her to do this? She noticed one lone, expectant eyebrow rose above his glasses, expecting an answer.

"We can take it slow, you know. The first month can be free, with a contract, of course."

"How do I sign this phone contract?" She asked it mostly to fill the silence—to give her more time to process her decision.

"Well, as long as it's a long-term contract, it's simple. The terms and conditions apply, though. I'm most definitely the girl in this relationship. I think I'll just sit right here and take it." He put his hands behind his head.

Her skin prickled—prickled because even his blunt vulgarity charmed her. "Just tell me one thing," she said.

"Anything."

"Are we going to be OK? Is my *brother* going to be OK?"

Dorian inhaled deeply, knowing her angle. "Maybe if you tell me not to hurt him—maybe if you make it so I *can't* hurt him—you'll get what you want. *Take* what you want, Odissa."

"I won't let you hurt him," she said.

"Try and stop me then. Keep me in line. This isn't about using a phone. It's about using me. You can use me, Odissa. I'm vulnerable, impressionable. I just need attention. Don't you want to give me attention? Aren't I pretty? Won't you touch me? Dial the right buttons?" His fingers wiggled and landed on her warm leg.

"If this 'phone call' gets me nowhere, I'll stop being so complacent. I *will* start trying to run away. I *will* start screaming. I *will* start telling people you're not really cops."

"I promise I'll be a good girl. I promise." He presented his hand at her side.

She picked it up. It was no gentle action. She held on to it as she stood up—as if to let him know she wasn't about to make a dash for it.

"You know," she said down to him, "It's kind of sexist that you think being a female means being the dominated one. Not all females act like that."

"Then prove it."

He lowered his legs, the only mutual response to her first move. As she pushed them apart to stand between them, she considered how *this* was going to work (he offered no advice for the situation, so she was forced to improvise). Lifting the adjustable arms of the theater seats, she placed herself in his lap—facing him. He waited patiently for her to situate and smiled when he heard her take off her glasses. He let her remove his own—as well as the felt pimp hat. She tossed it far away so that he wouldn't be able to pick it up again.

With his eyes exposed, she felt safer to lean into him. He was more vulnerable. He suppressed a grin as she touched his face. He was enjoying this too much—as if proud his sales pitch had worked. After settling into his face, she let her lips brush his, but he didn't kiss back. He just sat there like a limp doll—a doll wanting to be played with.

Slightly offended, she held the sides of his neck as her body pressed down into him. His lack of *response* impressed her—never mind, there it was. *Took him long enough.*

But she felt him cringe a little, hesitant to proceed. "Odissa," he muttered as her hands pulled at her shirt.

"Yeah?" she said, pulling away.

"What are you doing?"

"I'm seducing you. If you couldn't tell."

"Don't you *want* this phone contract?"

"I was wondering the same for you."

"I mean, don't get me wrong, you're doing great for a new customer. But don't you want to enjoy the phone call itself? How can you enjoy dialing when you refuse to press the buttons with *purpose?*"

"Fuck you. I haven't even started. Besides, I've never been"—her voice only mouthed the words—"on top. This is strange."

"Be a man," he quietly commanded—as if such a statement were ridiculous. "You're in charge."

That's what scared her. She stiffened. "Have you ever fucked a girl before?"

"Is it really so obvious that I'm gay?" *That I still am despite wanting you?*

"So, no?"

He breathed in deep. Avoiding the true answer, he laughed and said, "I let Fletcher fuck a girl once. I watched it all through him. I didn't particularly enjoy it. But she sure did. She kept stalking him afterwards. Kept asking around for him. Couldn't let him form up from his inanimate form for weeks."

Angry he had just gone into full story-time mode, "But he doesn't have any balls. I saw him."

"I knew you were looking!"

Blushing, "You lying to me?"

"No. I'm serious. He can form them like clothes. He didn't freak her out, if that's what you're worried about." He frowned. "You like him more than me? Is that what this is?"

"No. I'm just not sure you can—"

"Stay hard? Well fuck, if you keep me jabbering on like this how *could* I make it last? Honestly." He pulled at her thighs, showing her how she should move them once more.

She ruined his smile with her own lips and he finally kissed her back. He kept his eyes open, as if he wanted to see her. She kept soft-humping him and kissing him, waiting for him to finally take himself out but it never happened. Her hands went to do it for him, but, for once, he guided them elsewhere as he leaned back into his seat. "It's okay, Odissa. Stop." He tried to hide the fact he was winded and his dick was still tight.

"What?"

"Not tonight." (He seems to have forgotten it was actually morning, technically).

"What? Why?" She had worked so hard! She felt used. Was this some joke to him?

"So you're saying you want to?" There was something sly in his voice.

"I thought that's what we were doing."

"Honestly, Odissa, the way you treat me!" He threw the back of his hand on his forehead—like the queen he was. "I don't sleep with people on the first date. No one would marry me if they could have the milk for free."

"I think I'm lactose intolerant now." She tried to play along but it came out too mean.

He chuckled. "Don't be such a dick." He sighed, enjoying her—even though he couldn't see her. "Your willingness to fuck a complete stranger amazes me—even if you *do* like me."

"You know why I did it." She tried to get her hands out of his grip. "I want to see my brother again."

He waited for her to calm down and he set her wrists free. The shadow-of-seriousness took him once more. "At first glance, Odissa, you're nothing but a bookworm in the corner hoping no one looks at her. That's what I thought at first. But then you slowly realize that this girl is fucking her brother for a reason, and it's probably a good one." He found her wrists again. He knew she would slap him around—she'd done it before. "I wonder what man made you retreat into your brother's arms?"

The ghost of a laugh escaped her. "You call it *retreat?* I don't call it that. I'm not escaping from misuse. You sound like him."

"You admit it? If not misuse then use; who uses you?"

She pulled back from him, but he kept her on his lap. Her frogged legs tried to stand.

He kept his face down, his grey eyes never blinking. "Who, Odissa?"

A chill trickled down her spine as his unseeing eyes then looked directly into hers, as if knowing where hers were. Timid once more, hers fluttered away. As she blushed, she noticed Fletcher standing a few rows from them near the entrance, watching them. Watching her. He loomed over the situation like a duplicate of Dorian—she was outnumbered.

"Stop looking at me," she hissed at Dorian, though looking at Fletcher. "Stop pretending you can see my face. I don't need you to look at me, Dorian. If you don't want me to lie to you, stop lying to me. I don't need it. You're the one lying—*pretending.*"

Lowering his gaze, a sliver-of-a-grin haunted his lips. "Fine. It takes a lot of concentration anyways to locate your face." He put a hand on her thigh. "I won't pretend if you won't pretend. Now tell me who else you've been fucking. Does Odys know this has been going on?"

She tried to slide off him and stand up, but he wouldn't let her go—not until she answered. "Only one other. Besides Odys."

"Who?"

She paused her struggle, confused he would ask. "Who the fuck do you think?" she spat.

"I don't follow."

"My husband, you idiot." *How dare that you mention it!*

His head shot back. "You're—you're married?"

"You mean you didn't know?" Odissa said, her suspicion ringing. "But you know everything about me—"

A redness took his grey eyes and a shock took his throat. "Your last name's Odelyn!"

"I *kept* my name. That wasn't what I wanted from him." *Like he doesn't already know.*

He shook his head. "We'd know about something like this. We found no marriage license when we checked up on you. Don't lie to me, Odissa. This isn't a game. It's not funny." *Please, no.*

"*I* don't even have a copy of the license. It's not something I'm proud of. I don't go around telling people." She suddenly felt the need to comfort him. "You really didn't know?" She wondered if Dorian was only pretending—toying with her again.

"Pero—Cómo—?" He wasn't sure how to ask it.

"You never thought to ask Odys why he wears a wedding ring? One just like mine?" She tried to show him her ring. "It's for him to pretend mine isn't real." And maybe it *wasn't* real—not all of it. In her heart it wasn't.

"Why didn't you *tell* us?" Dorian spat. "How the hell did you hide this from us?"—but he wasn't talking to her. He was cursing someone else…

The spell of Venus's harmony was broken. It was tainted. Not only did Vulcan give him Odys's sloppy seconds, but some Helen-of-Troy? MARRIED! He was more pissed at Vulcan than anything else—he could almost picture the god and His Wife chuckling.

"Why didn't you tell me from the beginning you were married, Odissa?" His voice revealed how hurt he was.

"Isn't it fucking obvious? Why do you think we hate our father so much? Didn't Odys tell you? I thought that's why you didn't ask me about it in the first place. He'd go into a rage!"

When she pulled her wrist from him he realized he'd been hurting her. "My God," he said, taking her face. "That's why he didn't want Odys to visit him—only you. He never wanted Odys. Maybe that's why Pepin gave him Maud? He knew Odys isn't as safe. Odys was never the reason, that's why Pepin chose him. It was always *you*—that's why Odys had to be involved."

"I don't understand." But oh, yes, she did. She was catching on.

"Odys is the leverage. The leverage of the leverage."

She wanted to remind him she was still there, "I'm the leverage?"

"And he knew just how to leverage you, because you're married to him. You're married to *Leeland.*"

ODI ODELYN: The 'father' who made arrangements for his arrangements.

273

ARRANGEMENTS: Arranged a marriage with Mr. Augury (quite easily too).

ARRANGED: Because Mr. Augury needed a wife to complete what he'd arranged (cough, cough).

ARRANGES: A win-win. The twins get their inheritance and Leeland gets a pawn for spawn...if only it had worked out more fertilely.

Chapter the nineteenth,

The conclusion:

To what, nothing at all?

"Not to Leeland. To Audell Augury," She corrected him.

"That's the same person!" he barked, fuming. He latched on to her as if she might run away— as if she might realize the potential of her *leverage*. "Why the fuck would you *marry* him?"

"Because he—he threatened to ruin us, Dorian—me and Odys. To cut us off. It was the only way we could get our inheritance." She paused, done defending herself. "You know so much about him, why didn't you *know* this? I thought that's why you were kidnapping me!"

(Well, *part* of the reason why).

"Don't act as if I'm not making sense. You're the one not making sense! He *can't* be married to you, he's—he's—"

"In love with someone else? You know, do you? Of course you do. You do know everything!" She studied his reaction. "I know he loves someone else. He's made sure to tell me every time he fucks me—every time! Sometimes I think he told my father to make me marry him so that he could get back at the woman he's in love with. You know, don't you?" She leaned into him, gripping his clothes. She was so close to the truth!

He turned his head away.

She pulled back. "You of all people can't hate me for having secrets, Dorian."

"You know why I'm hiding mine. I'm not fucking normal."

"I didn't realize I was hiding mine!" She calmed herself. Her voice a whisper, "I *tried* to get out of actually marrying him. But he's too *moral* for that. Why aren't you talking? Say something. *What did I do wrong?*"

"Leeland took everything away from me. He did this to hurt me, not Gwen."

"Gwen?" *Oh, the other woman.*

"Put your shirt back on. The mall will be opening soon and we need to make sure we can get out of here." He let her off his lap and stood up, straightening his clothes. Dorian started talking to himself as Fletcher approached: "He wanted her to get pregnant and he wanted control over the child—all would mean more control over *me*." If Dorian had had the space, he would be pacing. He settled for heavy breathing and pushing back his hair. "Marrying you meant what though? That he felt guilty for trying to impregnate you—virtually raping you?"

"What are you talking about? He never—"

"Your father was his Automaton! His Automaton was *him* trying to impregnate you." He started pacing again. "Of course being married to you kept Odys hating him, right? Meant Odys had to share you. Is that it? Kept Odys away and yet there. That's part of it too, isn't it?"

"That and the fact he wanted to fuck her to piss you off," Fletcher mumbled.

"Don't fucking say it out loud!" Dorian shouted at himself, putting a hand over his own mouth to hide his rage.

Odissa shrunk back from him. She felt the need to assure them, "I was going to ask for a divorce, once I graduated. I *never* loved him."

"That's exactly what scares us, Odissa," Fletcher added, hopping over the back of a theater seat to get a closer view. "The things you've done for money."

"Only to give us a life that would eventually free us of it!"

Instantly, the old Dorian snapped back. "Free you of it?" That earth-shattering smirk on his face miffed her. "You want a life that's free of him? Well, it looks like you've been given one." He gestured to the room. He meant himself.

"Why don't I feel like I'm free of him, then? *You're* not free of him. He seems to be the only reason we met!"

Fletcher put his head in his hand, watching them as if viewing a movie. He would have formed a self-made popcorn prop if the moment hadn't required *some* seriousness. Dorian was moving past his shock.

"I'll never be free of him," Dorian agreed. "But I can damn well make sure you are. You're my baggage now, do you understand that? Just to be clear, you better *act* like my baggage—not Odys's. Mine. If you want things to go peacefully, you'd best understand this. Odys has an Automaton and he's synced with her and that means he can no longer deny what your father did to you—or what you *let* your father do to you. He knows he is only alive because of you and you are only alive because of me. Odys can't help you now."—Quieter—"He's never been able to help you, really. You're the only reason he's still alive and, if you know what's good for the both of you, you'll remember that. I choose if Odys lives and dies because of *you*. Now, be a good boyfriend and give me back my gum."

As his lips came in, she was hesitant to kiss back. He did not kiss her nicely, but willfully—too determined—crazy psycho bitch with man strength. She took the sides of his face to restrain him.

Though her eyes were closed, her eyelids noticed a flash of red—like the flash of a camera when it catches you blinking. Pulling away, her eyebrows knit together.

Blinking past blindness, "Bulfinch?"

Fletcher was already watching the cat (who was quite fuzzed out, clinging to the back of a theater seat). Mecca popped up from behind that same seat. "Costumes! Had no idea you liked *pussies*, Dorian." (Har, har). He took a few more photos on the run.

Fletcher, who had smelled Mecca and Q seconds ago, had been waiting for them to show themselves. He lunged at Mecca (as Mecca lunged for the runaway cat). "Can't you call first?" the Automaton scolded as they dashed away.

"WHAT are you doing here Mecca?" Dorian shouted.

Q, scooping up Bulfinch, answered, "We got bored. Were you seriously just making out with a girl, Dorian?" There was something concerned in her voice, as if this wasn't how things were supposed to be.

Fletcher redirected them, "You got bored?"

"Mecca doesn't think Bulfinch is very fun. Bulfinch doesn't like to be dressed up as various things."

Snatching her cat from Q, Odissa exclaimed, "Why the fuck do they have my cat?" Bulfinch was very frizzed; she had to hold him by the scruff. She stared at Dorian, whose head turned away from her—giving no answer. This hadn't been how he wanted to tell her.

Odissa's heart raced—fast as Bulfinch's. She clutched him to her chest and steadied herself on the arch of a seat. But she didn't have time to panic about her home—

Mecca hopped up over to the seat next to her. "Mecca has decided to like you, Odissa. Mecca has decided that you shall tuck him in tonight when Mecca goes to bed."

"Like hell she will," Fletcher snapped, glowing with fury.

"Who is Mecca?" Odissa asked, turning to Fletcher, a confused arch to her brows.

"That little dingle berry right there," Fletcher pointed, frowning. (The third person always confuses people when said aloud—Mecca looks better on paper).

"At least Mecca's not a big one like you," Mecca mocked as Q picked him up.

"Why are you here, Mecca?" Dorian pressed, yet again.

"Mecca's here to follow you to the next spot."

"Were those *Mother's* orders?" Dorian doubted.

"Did Mother give you the okay to *molest* the captive?" he retorted. "Bob warned us we should keep an eye on you. This what she meant?"

"She's not a captive," Dorian defended himself. He was embarrassed he'd been caught. "And since when do you listen to that bitch? Tell Bob to keep her nose out of my ass!"

Mecca looked up to Q, ignoring Dorian. "Mecca's thinking a Princess Leia look would suit her. Dorian is Jaba. We'll photoshop those pics!"

"That's funny," Q whispered, "because she's a twin."

"Mecca is Han, come to rescue her from her own twincest!" He made his eyebrows jump, waiting for Odissa to react.

Fletcher explained, "His adolescent brain is kind of stuck in maturity limbo."

"Dorian, we brought some of the *stuff*," Q said, looking very serious, "in case you didn't have any. Mother, for sure, won't want her seeing the route to the cabin."

"Ah, you're right," Dorian said, putting a hand to his chin. "I completely forgot we'd need precautions."

Mecca laughed, leaning over the back of a theater seat. "Mecca would too, if Meca had boobs in front of Mecca's face." He pointed at Odissa. Well, more at her boobs than anything.

"This kid's a pervert," Odissa observed unnecessarily.

Mecca nodded, "But Mecca can't help it."

Fletcher rolled his eyes, thumbing at Q. "What are those, if not tits?"

"Who wants to play with your own, though? Never as much fun," Mecca said.

Odissa was slightly appalled Q just let the little boy squeeze and jiggle her tiny boob. She cradled Bulfinch away from the child.

Q handed Fletcher something in a small disposable box she'd dug from her bag.

"Are you serious?" Odissa said as Fletcher took out the LARGEST needle she'd ever seen. "What the fuck?"

Fletcher stuck it in the vial. She hated how he knew what he was doing, as if a nurse!

"You want to see your brother don't you?" he asked, squirting a little from the needle's tip. "There should be no side effects. We've used this hundreds of times. Funny, this drug was your father's recommendation, even—a long time ago. He's probably used it on you plenty, so chance has it you'll have no reaction to it." He gave a bitter smile. "Just sit back."

She saw Dorian step forward, as if he might restrain her if necessary.

"No, I'll let you." She gave Bulfinch back to Q, whose outstretched arm offered to take him.

As Fletcher gave her the dosage, he said, "We should have used some of this last night. Then we both could have gotten a good night's sleep."

She glared at Dorian as he finished. "Be nice to my cat."

"We saved him in the first place, didn't we?" he soothed, tucking her hair behind her ear. She was asleep in a matter of seconds.

"Sooo," Mecca filled the silence. "You wanna feel her up while you got the chance?"

"Finally want to know what boobs feel like, Dorian?" Q chimed. "I would have let you feel mine."

Dorian raised one of Odissa's eyelids for Fletcher to see. "It's actually good you showed up when you did, Mec. You saved me from being too heteronormative just then. I was being too 'stereotypical masculine,' if you will. I was scaring her. And myself. Odissa isn't like other girls."

Q raised a brow. "And you're not like other boys, which is why we're still confused."

Dorian thought to Fletcher, *I almost couldn't control my anger.*

She wasn't afraid of you, though.

Fletcher carried Odissa out to the car, sitting her nearly in his Master's lap and crawling in after. Dorian cradled her as Mecca started the car.

"I think this will work out, Dorian," Fletcher said as he adjusted Odissa's cat ears. He let his too-long fingers trail down her hair, arranging it into place.

Q looked over the backseat. "Stop molesting her, Fletcher!"

Fletcher ignored her as she giggled. He merely said, "She's the one, Q. Just look how happy my Master is." He patted Dorian's sleepy face.

"But if that's a good thing, who knows?" Q baby-talked. "You smell a bit different, Dorian. Everyone does these days." She turned back around, assuming the outfit of a cat as well, to match Odissa. "I like cats, too," she assured Bulfinch (who was in her lap). He braced himself as the car moved, his eyes dizzy as the world whizzed by.

As they drove, Dorian and Fletcher didn't touch. They normally would have. They would have held hands and nestled in together. Instead, Fletcher placed his willowy hand on Odissa's knee and watched the sleeping girl for his Master. There was no need to touch Dorian. She was the conduit. "It's nice to be taken care of, isn't it, Fletcher?" Dorian kissed the top of Odissa's head before he leaned his own back.

In private thought, the two exchanged Dorian's personal plans: *Will we give Odissa an Automaton? Yes, I cannot live without her. Whether or not she wants one? Yes, whether or not she wants one—we can't lose her again. We will give her Madus. It just seems right, doesn't it?*

Even when we kill Leeland—oho, the plans we have for him!—we will not give her an Automaton of that man. He has tarnished her enough already. No, she will never have Admund or Coraza.

CORAZA: The third face of Leeland.

WAS: Sometimes a nurse or nanny to the twins, though they can barely remember her.

IS: Not used very often, for Leeland is not sure how he feels about being so *feminine.*

WILL BE: A match for the screw, Caffar.

Endnote/Chapter the twentieth (depending on what you'd rather call it),

To be continued:

Who doesn't love a good cliffhanger?[117]

This story nears its end. I've been told to keep it short and sweet—not that I followed those directions (word count is such a bitch).

Read book #2 (if there *is* a book number two, publishers willing)[118] to find out what awful things Odys had to go through on his little Mission Impossible; to find out why Vulcan wanted Bob out of the picture; to find out what Leeland plans on doing with Cestus; to find out how Dorian will avenge Odissa; etc., etc., etc. I need not go on.

But, while we're still pushing past 100,000+ words, let's analyze what this fast-approaching, half-assed ending means.

Even if this novel *was* tied up with a pretty bow, let's not kid ourselves. We all knew this was going to be a "series"—this story's self-awareness didn't exactly promise you something stand-alone in the first place.

No, this closing isn't even a real cliffhanger and it's not trying to be. This is my biggest twist. Most novels, even in a series, can stand alone. This one can't. No Epic can stand alone without the context of the others. Isn't that right, Gabbler?[119]

Do remember, even Homer got more than one volume (and *how* did he end his first tale again? Exactly. You have no right to be pissed at me. This unfinished finish is the art!). At the least, this non-ending will give you something to complain about to your friends.[120]

The worst of you will actually try to decipher this part as if it really has some meaning. *What does it mean?!* It means move on to the next damn volume. Need I convince you?

Fine. Here it goes.

---

[117]Me.

[118] If you're reading this edition then you know there is!

[119] Well, yes, all of the Epic poets kind of influenced each other by default. They were, after all, working in the same genre.

[120] See, Reader, you've gotten your money's worth. *Cringes*

Ahem.

I mean, I guess I *could* just give you a teaser for Volume 2? Say something along the lines of *"Vulcan will admit the Masters are all part of his major plan to make the gods notice his handiworks and skills—humans are just beta testers for something much more sinister."* But I won't. That's not enough of a cliff to hang. That's more like a window ledge. A clear view of the street. A street that leads somewhere. The possibility of the earth to catch us if we decide to jump.

No, I need the river rushing down below. Perhaps we won't die if we fall. But where does the river lead? The rock is crumbling under our fingers. There's no one to catch us.

So, instead, I'll tell you who I am—the character who I am/will be in this story—give you a reason to hang on tight because, good lord, are those alligators?!

(Drum roll, please).

Stanza: The end ends a mystery.

They say that cats have nine lives. I've used up quite a few.

See, I used to be a cat—in a past life.[121]

I'm not anymore. Vulcan made me change all that.

What? Don't believe me? Well. You just read a whole story about how inanimate objects can become humanoid. How much easier to believe an organic creature can become a human, then?

Yes, yes. A cat becomes human.[122]

Vulcan's divine plan—to be enacted in the next volume(s)—created heavenly cyborgs of more than just humans. All animals must bow to the machine (as I, the cat, did). This book was the thesis for my own humanity. The next will be the body and conclusion to that divine claim.

Ovid and Kafka wrote of metamorphosis, but I merely mention it in passing. Just how did I become a human? Well, that's for another time—later I'll detail how Bulfinch became *me*.[123]

ME: Anonymous.

ME: Divine in my own right.

ME: A perfect example of the Author-as-God.

ME: Yet nothing without Gabbler.

End Vol. 1[124]

---

[121] I am looking at our Narrator now and can promise you they are no such animal. Completely human. As you can tell, our Narrator has quite the imagination.

[122] Or vice versa, depending on your need to work out some issues through writing this story, Narrator. But, at least there's a little more of that *dramatic irony* for you.

[123] And now you know why we wanted two names supporting this story. Or, rather, just my name.

[124] Another bonus footnote! This is where you would have to buy Vol. 2 if this weren't the combined edition. Lucky you.

Circo del Herrero

The Annotated Manuscript: The Pre-programming: BOOK TWO & THREE

Vol. 2 of the Blacksmith's Circus Series

By B.L.A., the Narrator, Storyteller, Feline

&

G.B. Gabbler, the Editor, Annotator, Enabler...

The Annotated Manuscript: The Pre-programming: BOOK TWO

Preface,

Freedom isn't free, but neither is slavery:

Is it OK if we put our prologue in the right place this time?[125]

So, the last book dealt with Freedom, if you care to remember (not that you should, because that's my job, *remembering*—I'm the one recounting *my* history, after all). Gabbler will probably edit that part out, but I don't care.[126]

The Freedom therein implied—if you even picked up on it (and of course you did, because I wasn't too subtle)—was the lack thereof. Automatons have the least of it, don't they? Not that they really *know* to want it. They cannot want. Not for themselves. Their Masters might want freedom for them—might want them to want. But it doesn't work like that.

I could go on and on about how unjust, complex, and depressing the whole issue is—even for humans (poor humans, always mulling over such mortal-minded dilemmas as if it helps). However, I think you already get the point. Which leads me to my *next* point.

Slavery.

Freedom creates slaves. We are slaves to free will. We're all slaves to our choices. Just like I'm choosing to write this book, here, despite the fact Gabbler thinks I'm insane for *believing* in it—believing this book is my own history.[127]

Speaking of books, where'd I leave off in my last one? Gabbler pried it from this dilettante's grasp before I could put any real finishing touches to it. Gabbler's always in such a hurry. Mortals usually are. But back to that ending, here. You may wonder how a person like me—a person who claims to be not only divine but a cat—can be typing this out now? I've been getting many

---

[125] **Editor's foreword,**
Not that it will do much good:
How much is too much setup?

Dear Doubters and Believers,
All footnotes are the Editor's (I'm the Editor, G. B. Gabbler). This is to help the reader better grasp the Narrator (who is not me, because, once again, I am the Editor). Also, for the sake of prudence, some names, certain locations, and various details have been purposefully made as vague as I please (or perhaps haven't) to keep the story unbogged with "unimportant" details. This is volume two in our series. Enjoy the continued storyline, picking up right where it left off. Also, hello again. Glad you're still here.
-G. B. Gabbler

[126] No, I won't completely edit out our Narrator's madness. I won't hide it for our Narrator anymore. I *will* make my presence known. I would never leave you alone—wouldn't abandon you like that.

[127] Like I've said before, this is a work of fiction. I believe this fantastic *story* is actually helping our Narrator work out some issues. Beyond that, I think it is a brilliant piece of literature (and of course I would, after I've helped make it what it is).

questioning letters from readers, trying to make sense of it all. The smarter of you will guess that maybe Bulfinch was—will be—given an Automaton; that this is how I, Bulfinch, am able to type out these memories and interact on such a human level. Perhaps this is even, say, why I am mute? Like Mecca, it could be that my "language" is a bit off...

But I tell you it is much weirder than that. Though, what fanfiction could be done with it! I'd terribly love to read it—how it *could* have happened. I do think Vulcan Himself would have enjoyed such a twist. Perhaps He even entertained the idea once and that's how I ended up here? For sure, you see, He lost control over His story. It stopped clicking and chiming and ticking so well. His shiny toys caught the attention of other gods. He had to share. They tarnished a few things, including His intentions.

I do not have an Automaton. Not in that sense. A cat soul is different.

Though I doubt it had been properly tested, the only soul-key to fit into an Automaton is a human one. That's the only way they were wound. Can you imagine the design flaw in that—if any an inanimate had been dropped on the floor and a stray cat or dog's paw happened to grace over it—kick it?[128] Well, I do wonder. Perhaps I'm a novelist after all, Gabbler? How creative I'm being now—branching out from the truth like this.

No, my reader, no.

You try too hard to make sense of chaos. You must let the primordial soup sprout its fungus on its own terms according to what rotten ingredients were brewed...

Gabbler, more than most, tries too hard also. Gabbler does not know that, no matter how hard we try, the gods have already decided to make use of this work—of what happened. I could type out a single word over and over again—*shit, shit, shit, shit*—and He would still find SOME way to use it.

He, of course, being The Blacksmith—our patron god *Hephaestus*.

Chapter the first,

Split personality:

Who are you when you're more than one?[129]

Way back in book one, Odys had synced with his Automaton Maud. It went a little something like this:[130] (see the footnote I'm having Gabbler insert).

---

[128] Or squirrel or raccoon or...
[129] "[The Novelist] does not write books to confound philosophers, perhaps because she is able to write books that delight them. In conversation she is the least formidable of women, because she understands you, without wanting to make you aware that you *can't* understand her." —George Eliot, "Silly Novels by Lady Novelists."
[130] From book one (edited out in case you don't need the refresher):

OK. Well, I think all that is enough of me doing the whole "Previously on the *Circo del Herrero* series" thing. We're all caught up. Let's get to it.

Stanza: "This one was not one working to have anything come out of him..."[131]

Maud had dragged Odys to the nearest gas station. After flirting with the high school kid behind the counter to distract from Odys's disgusting sick-face, they were out in no time with some painkillers, energy drinks, and food. Oh, and let's not forget cigarettes.

"These are for you," Maud said, handing him the pills. "And this is for me." She popped the tab of a too-hardcore energy drink. "I'm NOT going to sneeze out because of you." But she didn't chug it. Instead, she shoved the can into his face. "Drink up."

"I'll throw up!" He shoved her hand away, spitting out the drink. More dribbled down his front as she tried again.

"No, you won't. Not if you eat these."

"How much shit did you buy?" He'd been too dizzy to notice. The fluorescent lights messed with his eyes. Walking, he did as she prescribed. Having trouble opening the pill bottle, he hardly noticed they were walking to a parked car. The next thing he knew Maud was shoving him into the driver's seat, hissing at him to "Scoot the fuck over" before someone noticed them.

Odys had just let her steal a car, yes. Upon realizing what he'd just let her do, well...it was a very frightening moment. It came so naturally. He hadn't thought twice about it this time.

"Fuck, Odys, you can't reconsider something after you've already *done* it." Maud barked as they sped down the street.

Driving driving driving.

'Odys had stepped toward Maud—he was going to do it—he was going to let go.
But wanting it wasn't enough.
Wanting wasn't working.
Otherwise, it'd be done.
Maybe it was a limitation on his mental ability, but he found hands-on so much more effective.
He came at her, snatching her up by the arm and bringing her in front of the store-front window. He wanted to *be* her—be able to find Rosemund and stop this fucking madness—so he *took* her. Had anyone been watching, they would have thought Maud should look afraid—as if she'd just angered some jealous lover who was about to beat the living shit out of her. But her subtle grin said otherwise.
See, Odys was nothing to fear. Not only because he didn't intend to hurt her, but because he toppled over at her feet. "You really needed that running start huh? You should have seen yourself. You looked ridiculous." *It looked like you were going to kill me. Maybe even kiss me.*
And that was how it was done.
That is how cloned personalities become one again.
...
Odys threw up.'
Also, in case you've forgotten, Odys is on a mission for Mother to stop Rosemund from giving the inanimate Automaton, Madus, to Leeland.
[131] Gertrude Stein. From her work "Picasso."

285

He stared out the windshield as if viewing a photograph that seemed hauntingly familiar. This street was familiar to Maud. He recognized it from her memory. He rubbed at the goosebumps it gave him—who had put that memory in her head?

After some silence, and after Odys had finished off all his goodies, he wanted to fill the quiet. He wanted to distract himself from how stupid he had been not to sync with her before—how it felt like he had just taken a giant shit after being constipated for days. His stomach hurt but he was *better*. He wanted to admit it, but his lips would not move. Look, his lips try.

"You *can* still talk to me, you know," Maud said. She had just obeyed his unspoken command. She spoke. Because he'd wanted her to. "After all, it's nice to talk. Even if you don't need to anymore..."

"I feel like crap. But it's a different crap than before."

"Like the crap feeling you get after you just ran a marathon? The kind of crap that's good for you?" (Odys didn't want her to talk about "the constipation," so she chose a different comparison).

"I wouldn't know. I refuse to exercise." Talking to her was easy now—a joke with yourself. "But yeah, just like that."

The cell phone rang—they jumped at the unfamiliar jingle. Odys dug it out of his pocket, handling it as if he were a natural with them—even though he'd hardly ever used one (he's a grandpa, remember?). Maud was making him do things he wouldn't have before. "Hel-hello?"

"Odys!" Mecca's voice shouted from the other line. "Mecca's just calling to tell you that everything will be fine, and that Bullybird is fine too."

"You mean Bulfinch?" He was starting to catch on to Mecca's thought process.

"If you say so. Anyway, Odys, Mecca also wants your CD collection."

"What?"

"Mecca stole it from your apartment before Mecca blew it up. Because Mecca wanted it. Mecca doesn't just let things go to waste."

"Excuse me?"

"Mecca means, when you die, can Mecca have the CD collection?"

"When I *die*?"

"Well, it's not a matter of when. Mecca's really asking if he can have them now. Because Mecca already knows when you're going to die."

"*What?*"

"Rosemund's gonna to kill you. She may be an old lady, but she's still one crazy bitch, and Mecca's *pretty sure* he's the only kid in the world that's still willing to listen to CDs."

Maud grabbed the phone from Odys, "Listen here, you little shit. You can have the damn CDs, but if you so much as hurt a hair on Bulfinch, I'll fuck you up. I know where you keep your first edition Batman comics and I'm not afraid to use them as coffee filters!"

She hung up the phone and her tone softened: "He's only trying to scare you. Take it as a compliment. This means he's paying attention to what we're doing. And he's worried about us."

"Worried Rosemund won't finish the job."

Stanza: Let's speed this process up.

Drive, drive, drive, and: "Odys, we're here. I think." She slowed down the car. "This looks like what Mother said."

He woke up. Her hand was on his shoulder. Now it was shaking him awake. "You sure?"

They came to a stop outside a gated community. One of those fancy gates that blocks off an entire ritzy neighborhood—the kind that normally employ a security guard to push a button. But there was no one in the little attendant booth. The gate opened on its own.

"Well, I heard that people in Canada don't lock their doors..."

"Yeah, but this is a gate. Someone should be in there. What if she killed the security guard that's supposed to be in that box? What if we drive over and set off some signal and then we both explode?"

"That's not how she works, and you know that."

No, he didn't know that. Rosemund was supposed to be a good guy. The others thought they'd known her before. But they clearly didn't know shit. To top it all off, all the things she was capable of were worse now that she was, well, *rogue*. For example: Odys (drawing on Maud's memory, here) recalled the time Rosemund had almost (accidentally) killed Mecca with her "improved" Tesla coils (though Mecca had volunteered to hold "this," so it could have been prevented) and then blew up one of Mother's motor homes (also on accident). The authorities blamed the power outage on a lightning storm.

That's what they were dealing with now.

"Look, there's a hiring sign in the widow of the box. Maybe she didn't kill them. They just don't have anyone working it. Set to automatic or something."

"Is that part of the appeal of meeting here? No security guard? That's ridiculous. I just don't get it."

"She didn't necessarily pick this spot. This is just where Mother's tracked her. Her cell phone usage is from this area. So is her internet history."

"Yeah, but we could kill someone! The houses are so close together."

"That's the point. It keeps you from pulling out the big guns, doesn't it?"

They drove through the gate.

"Why don't they have street lights on in this place? For a fancier part of town they sure don't splurge," Maud muttered. Canada was weird. Their headlights showed a few cars parked on the curb and in driveways, but other than that the place looked like bedtime. Maud tried to spot lighted windows as she drove. "Maybe there was a power outage..."

"With Rosemund, that's a possibility. Wonder what she blew up this time—Maud, slow down!"

"What the—" She slammed on the breaks. "The hell?"

As they turned the corner into a cul-de-sac, the car's headlights flickered over something circling around.

Upon hitting the breaks, the circling thing in the distance noticed the lights…and had stopped. Right in the middle of the cul-de-sac's loop.

It was no deer in the headlights look. The headlights flashed over her white windbreaker, her red hair sticking up in untamed, frizzy curls—as if she'd just stuck her finger in a light socket. The big granny glasses flickered like a nocturnal eyes, making Odys stiffen. She looked like some caged animal that had been pacing—pacing, pacing, pacing—her cage. Waiting to be fed.

Except this cul-de-sac wasn't a cage. It was an open range.

"Oh—oh God! She's got the electric powerchair!!!" Odys gasped (with just the right amount of exclamation). "You know what she keeps in that thing—"

Yes, Dear Reader, he's afraid of a lady in a pimped up wheelchair. Or, excuse me, powerchair.

"Shush!" Maud observed Rosemund.

Rosemund looked like she *could* have been attractive—outside of that jumpsuit, wannabe afro, and scarred epidermis. Well, at the very least, most would call women her size and stature "cute" or "petite." But don't let the cuteness manipulate you. Seriously. Be prepared. Save yourself. That sort of shit.

"Stay calm, Odys. I've got the brights on. She—she can't tell who we are."

Hopefully.

Indeed, Rosemund scrunched up her tiny face.

"Yes, but Caffar can!" he hissed, looking about for Rosemund's other half.

Maud put the car in park. "She might think we're just normal people. If she wanted to kill us, we'd—we'd already be dead. After all, it's not like she's expecting *us*, of all people. That's *why* they sent us." Maud was trying to rationalize it, her body held tense and tight—ready to run—to fight if need be.

"Then why is she out rollin' around tonight? She's expecting something!" His voice was a bit too panicked. There were over a billion reasons why Rosemund Rosemary would be *rolling*. And those reasons ranged anywhere from *expecting something* to *wanting to burn battery power*. They watched Rosemund jerk her head like a wolf sniffing the air for scent.

"Maybe she's keeping guard?"

"For what? Another one of her experiments? For Leeland?"

"There's no way he's here—is there?"

"It's like she can hear us!"

"We look suspicious."

That was fucking obvious.

"Should we back up?"

"I don't know!"

They watched Rosemund for a few more seconds. And she watched them. She stared into the headlights like a mesmerized moth—her face whited out by the contrasting light.

"Honk the horn," Odys said. "Honk it loud. Get the whole neighborhood's attention. So she won't do anything stupid."

Maud did so, loud and obnoxiously. Over and over again.

Not unbuckling his seatbelt (because he didn't have it buckled) he shot out the passenger's side—Maud doing the same in symmetrical fashion. A handgun quickly formed into her hand.

With the headlights lighting their path, Odys scanned the houses as they walked toward the cul-de-sac. He told himself if he was noisy about this, the neighbors just might wake up. He needed the neighborhood to see this, if things grew violent. Surely—surely!—Rosemund wouldn't cause too much trouble if people were watching. *Too many people to kill.*

Maud's high-heeled feet clicked like tap shoes upon the concrete. When Rosemund noticed Maud's figure, Odys could see a wicked smile spark in her eyes under those glowing granny glasses. She recognized *them*.

Pressing a button on her handlebars, the woman—who, up close, looked too young for a wheelchair—backed up. The loud beep-beep-beep unnecessarily alerted no one behind her.

239

Now facing them head-on, Rosemund moved forward a few wheel-turns. Odys wondered if those new lines in her face were finally wrinkles, or just her scars deepening. Maybe both. If Odissa could see her, she'd say this woman was too hip for this world. And then Odys remembered that, oh yeah, he's not concentrating. Back to the story!

But speaking of stories…

A story, as you know, can be delivered in many different formats. To properly introduce Rosemund, it might be best to shake things up a bit. We must do her justice. The meta is calling us to bring her out of the closet. Yes, yes this should add a bit of flavor to this baked fruitcake (if you don't get this joke then your gaydar is broken. Come back when it's fully functional)…

Mobility, A Play[132]

The Persons of the Play:

Odys Odelyn, a man who's just been connected

Maud, Odys's Automaton

Rosemund Rosemary, a woman who has something Odys needs

Caffar, Rosemund's Automaton

Narrator, me, of course

Gabbler, shut the fuck up for once in your life, baby

Act I

[Setting: somewhere in Canada. In some strange neighborhood where the only light is only Odys's car headlights (well, it's not really his car, because Maud just stole it—but you know what I mean). Odys and Maud are approaching Rosemund.]

MAUD: [To Rosemund, a woman who looks older than Mother but isn't. Rosemund has slight hints of scars on her face and hands. The scars are burn marks. Rosemund is a tiny woman, barely taller than Mecca. She is wearing an AC/DC shirt (though she most likely isn't a fan of the band)[133] under her windbreaker jacket. Every time she moves she swooshes. Other notable

---

[132] A closet drama in four acts. Our Narrator is obviously bored with the story format and wants to try a hand at Goethe's medium (let's not mention how it falls short—we don't want to offend). Warning: This play involves Rosemund. You will notice she speaks very repetitively and tritely. She even maddens me. Our Narrator has said that "All characters have glitches. This one is hers."
[133] Before you think our Narrator cares less and less about subtly and is shooting straight for caricature, consider why these overt symbols trim the characters. My semiotics call them a clue to the truth—truth so piled on it reads as

attire is: the limp surgeon's mask dangling under her chin, the high-top shoes, and the too-big glasses.[134]] What's with the surgeon's mask?

ROSEMUND: [Pulls up the surgeon's mask before speaking] Masks are used to mask things, no? [Rosemund gives a slight shrug].

MAUD: No one thought otherwise.

ROSEMUND: They didn't? Well, how am I to knowknowknow what an Automaton thinks— if at all? [When she "glitches," she bobs her head to the side a little.] Thoughts are needed to think. [To Odys] AND YOU! You, young man! I've been expecting you, Odys Odelyn. You are looking well, as someone who is well should look.

ODYS: [Eyes narrowing] How is it that you knew we were coming? Do you know why we're here?

ROSEMUND: But of course I do. Mother *told* me. She tells me everyeveryeverything. I tell *her* everything. Just because we disagree doesn't mean we can't talk. That, and I *do* know how to track a phone. [She looks at her watch.] But you're here earlier than expected. I was surprised how quick your signal jumped around. How did you get here sososo fast? Did you catch a different flight? A flight *without* a plane?

MAUD: You could say that. Vulcan airlines.

ODYS: So you know what we're here for. [It wasn't a question.]

ROSEMUND: But of course, of course. She wants the coin. She wants Madus. She sent you like some ASPCA commercial—to beg me to save your poor sister from the pound. So gogogo on. Give us your thirty-second spiel. Sell me your sell!

MAUD: Tell us where the Automaton is, Rosemund.

ROSEMUND: [She puts her hands up slightly] It's simply not so simple.

ODYS: You haven't touched him, have you?

ROSEMUND: [Pushing up her full-moon glasses and observing him] Why would I want to touch Madus? Mother'd not likely like that. I need Mother to like me, in the end. I have no need for *two* Automatons. I still wantwantwant peace. [Rosemund waves her hands as if to settle the situation. Her nails are long and fake and painted an outrageous color. On every one of her fingers she has rings.]

---

ridiculous and, therefore, lies. The fact the Narrator doesn't want to be taken seriously only drives my suspicions. There is a meaning in here. A meaning I want the Narrator to see once I find it.

[134] Which she probably needs because she's damaged her sight so many times from overexposure to bright light.

ODYS: If you want Mother to like you, you shouldn't have kept him in the first place. You can't give him to Leeland, Rose.

ROSEMUND: Rose? Just because you sync with Maud doesn't mean you get to call me that, boy. Don't be so familiarly familiar. [She shakes a finger at him] If you want to call me that, then show somesomesome manners. Don't come to me demanding—

MAUD: [Over the hum of their car engine] You can't give into him! Madus is needed elsewhere. A twin for a twin! The fate is too perfect, Rosemund. You *have* to see it, don't you? Hell, forget seeing it. I can smell it. You know this is meant to be! Odissa *will* have Madus.

ROSEMUND: Meant to be? [Rosemund leans back in her chair] Don't tell me what's meant to bebebe, boy. I was meant to die a long time ago and look at me! Still kicking. And what's one more Automaton to Leeland? It'll save us from watching him torture another poor soul. He'll get to you as well, you know. Eventually. Mother may think she'll weaken my heart by sending you—a boy she's threatened—but it won'twon'twon't work.

ODYS: You don't care that you're forcing Mother to play the part of Leeland in this? She'll kill my sister! Don't you love Mother more than that?

ROSEMUND: Oh, listen to you—pulling that card! But Mother forgivingly forgives. [As if talking to herself] She hasn't killed me yet, has she? After all, she only sent *you*. She'll come to terms with it. She'll forget what I've done with Madus—eventually. I break no laws bybyby giving Madus away. Leeland will do the breaking—he'll break them only by touching him. That sinful sin will be upon his head. Not mine. What is best is for the best.

NARRATOR: [A voice from the sky that the other characters do not react to. In fact, they pause, as if time itself has stopped so that I might contextualize] Rosemund's platitudes never say much more than what they say—ha, ha!

MAUD: I wouldn't be so sure, Rosemund. Even if Mother forgives you, we can't. We'll kill you if we have to. We want Odissa back. You know who Odys is—how he's connected to Leeland. Mother's told you, I'm sure. [Rosemund crosses her arms, her windbreaker crinkling] Pepin didn't hide Madus this long just to have you give him to Leeland. Don't ruin everything he's built up—you wouldn't betray him like that. You were always on his side. He was like a brother to you.

ROSEMUND: You just threatened to kill me. [Leaning forward on her electrical wheelchair and resting her head in her hand] But just how do you intend to find out where Madus is if I'm dead? The dead are dead! What's your planplanplan, anyway? I thought you were going to beg. I expected a good begging! You're bad at begging. [A light down the block turns on in an upstairs window, her eyes make theirs flicker to it. With urgency in her voice] I've made up my mind, boy. Go home. I have things to do.

MAUD: Things to do? [Maud steps forward as if to follow her as she starts to roll away] Like what? You seemed bored out of your wits seconds ago, going in circles. I say you've got too much time on your hands! [Rosemund stops in her act of turning around, blocked by Maud]

ROSEMUND: [Defensively] Well, if you must know, I got a call from a new customer who would like me to restore and rewire a sixteenth-century automaton[135] for a museum. They want me to fix it so they don't have to wind a key. Make a robot turn the robot. Ironic, right? Have I ever told you the story behind my interesting interest ininin automata? How I think that's why I caught Vulcan's eye in the first placeplacepiace?

NARRATOR: [The characters freeze-frame]. Time to interrupt, here. Rosemund is what we might call a *tinkerer*. She is very much interested in converting anything and everything into an *electrical* contraption. But of course Odys knew this. Because Maud knew this. [Characters unfreeze]

ODYS: Of course you haven't told me. You just *met* me.

ROSEMUND: Oh, that's rightrightright. But, Maud is you and you are Maud. If I've told her—or any other parts that *were* once her—then I've told you.

ODYS: [Smiling down at his feet in frustration] If that's the case, then I do know your story. And I also know this...*behavior* is not like you, Rosemund. What would make you betray Mother—who I thought you loved?

ROSEMUND: [In a low voice, resting a hand in one of her jacket pockets] What is one more Automaton in Leeland's possession? It's one less person to suffer. We can't seem to kill him, so why not pacify him? It's less trouble for us all. No one will missmissmiss an Automaton they've never had. It is also one less Master to make Gwendolyn cry.

ODYS: But your actions will cause more harm than help. It is *you* who make Mother cry!

Act II

[Setting: The three houses at the end of the cul-de-sac are suddenly illuminated by porch lights, bringing them to the audience's attention]

---

[135] That's right, not capitalized.

ROSEMUND: [Pulling something out of her pocket, making Maud and Odys tense] Mother cries no matter the occasion. But this is the lesser of two evil evils. Now, because we are standing at a standstill and it is in my nature to make sparks, I will make a proposed proposition. If you can guess which house, out of the three at the endendend of this cul-de-sac [pointing]—one, two, three—that Madus is NOT hidden in, then you'll know where he is.

ODYS: What?

MAUD: He's—he's in one of these houses?

ROSEMUND: I didn't say that. I said you'll know where he is. Knowing is only knowing. [A light turns on in one of the houses]

ODYS: There's people inside those houses!

ROSEMUND: Houses are sometimes homes, yes. They are grand homes, aren't they? Very upper-middle class. Middle class is not so middle anymore these days. [With a sigh] I need to know how much you want Madus.

ODYS: Rosemund, this isn't like you. You don't kill innocent people.

MAUD: On a regular basis.

ROSEMUND: You can always turn around and go home, Odys. We don't have to play this game.

ODYS: But I can't. Mother has my sister. I can't have her back until I retrieve Madus. Don't you even care, woman?

ROSEMUND: Well then, I'd pick a house if I were you. Pick a house, any house—any house that's a house! What'll it be? [Odys gapes] One? Two? Three? I give you three seconds—no more than three. One...two...three! Ah. I guess I get to choose for you. [She presses a button on her remote, house number three explodes].

MAUD: [Screaming, trying to get the neighbors to hear] HELP! FIRE! [No one responds, but a few lights down the street come on]

ODYS: [Shouting at Rosemund, panicked, eyes wide, coming at her] STOP IT! This makes no sense! There are people in there! How do I know that wasn't the house Madus was in? How's this beneficial to anyone? [Rosemund backs up her scooter to get away from him]

ROSEMUND: [Matter-of-factly] Who said my game was to benefit anyone? Get back from me or I'll blow them all up! [She shoos them away as she continues to roll, holding up the remote] Which house is next?

ODYS: I'm not picking a number! Stop this! FUCK! [Running to the middle house, shaking its large gate, screaming when the gate is locked]. Wake up! You have to get out!

ROSEMUND: [Shouting over the crackling fire] Funny how people don't care their neighborhood's being blown upupup. [She shrugs and presses another button, house number one explodes].

ODYS: [When no one answers the door, he starts looking around the dark neighborhood. Slowly, he realizes...] They're empty [Quietly]. They're all empty! [He watches as Rosemund pushes more buttons and lights flicker on in various windows down the street]

ROSEMUND: [Turning her wheelchair around and noticing his expression] That's rightly right, Odys. [She raises her remote, making him jolt from the house. She pushes a button. Number two goes up in flames]. They're vacantly vacant. All of them. [She pushes another button and a speaker in the distance starts playing Eddy Grant's "Electric Avenue." The lights in the houses flicker in unison.]

NARRATOR: Rosemund wired this whole neighborhood up quite nicely, though. She bought out this neighborhood a while back, decorated it herself. Picked out the cars and everything. Soon they'll be donated to homeless urchins of her choosing. Except the ones she blew up.[136] "Burnt houses are burnt," as she would say.

ROSEMUND: Oh, don't look so shocked, Odys. [Odys studies the buildings around him, panting. He now notices how much like a ghost town it looks, with the fires and flickering lights illuminating everything]. That's right, I wired all these houses. I control their lights. Planned to scare the shit out of this whole 'hood come Halloween. Didn't really care for these three architectural atrocities, though. There's no one in them. Welcome to my light show! [She starts pushing buttons and the neighborhood houses' lights flicker madly—offbeat to "Electric Avenue"].

ODYS: [The heat and light make him squint] Fuck you, Rosemund! [He flips her off, with both hands and paces as if he wants to go].

ROSEMUND: [Laughing] Cruel tricks are so cruel. [She continues to laugh, then starts coughing, from the smoke]

MAUD: [Her fingertips forming a gun again] It's not funny, Rosemund! Tell us where Madus is. [She points the gun at her, stepping forward].

ROSEMUND: [Giving a deep sigh, turns off the music] Oh yes, about that. Now that the funfunfun is over I guess it's time you knew. I don't even have what Mother told you I had. Lies are lies. I never even had him to begin with. We still don't know where he is—what Pepin did

---

[136] The houses, not the urchins.

with him. This was all just to test you. [She pulls out a phone from her pocket] Mother lied about her lie, see. She lied about a lie to get you to come here.

MAUD: What? [Maud takes the phone, scrolls] Are you fucking kidding—

ROSEMUND: [As if she didn't hear her] Also, they now know that you've synced with her [She nods in Maud's direction]. Couldn't have asked for more. Mother's been listening to the course of this eventful event.

NARRATOR: More like uneventfully uneventful.

ROSEMUND: Not only has Gwendolyn been tuning into your progress, but I can see it right now. I can see you're *aware*, Odys Odelyn. [Going on quite proudly, rolling between them as if pacing in her electric scooter] This idea was all my idea, really. [She gestures to the houses, the setup] I suggested to Gwendolyn what we might do, to get you to show some realrealreal colors.

ODYS: I don't believe you—*how* can I believe you aren't lying to get us to leave?

ROSEMUND: If you don't believe me, then you should call Mother. For sure, we hoped you would react this way to the exploding houses. You're a good boy, Odys Odelyn. I sure didn't want to waste all my wired wiring. Now if *only* I could remember the buttons for the sprinklers. [Squinting at the remote, pressing odd button combinations]

ODYS: [In disbelief] Gwen had me believe— [the sprinklers come on—helping to exterminate the fires]

ROSEMUND: [Looking up from her remote and rolling forward] Yesyesyes, she had you believe what she wanted you to believe. But we had to. We had to know your loyalty. [Smoke is wafting around them. Odys's phone chimes.]

MAUD: [Checking Odys's phone] Mother sent us a text. It just says, "She's innocent. You're free." [Turning to Rosemund, her nostrils flaring] Are you trying to give us emotional whiplash?

ODYS: [Cursing under his breath and kicking the car] This is ridiculous! All this. For WHAT?

MAUD: I should kill you right now for this fucking trouble, woman!

ODYS: [Apologizing for Maud] Sorry, I didn't mean that. [He rubs his face]

ROSEMUND: [Not bothered by his outburst] We wanted to be sure you're innocent. Even saints cause a lot of troubling trouble—and scream just as loudly as they're being burned. We can't have screamers here—screaming away our secrets.

ODYS: So did I pass your goddamn test?

ROSEMUND: You did shout a lot. But you did it for Gwen. For Madus. You obeyed her, so we know where your priorities are.

ODYS: [Mockingly] I believe you when you threaten to harm my sister. What a discovery for you!

ROSEMUND: [Scolding him] You're not dumb enough to disobey us. Now we know. [More nicely] Now, if you don't mind, I've been staying at 1606 Ernest Street, which is where my bags are. You can give me a ride there, so I don't wearwearwear out my powerchair. [She stands up, preparing to collapse her chair] Walking takes a toll on my lungs—but you likely remember that. [She uses air quotes around the word "remember"]

ODYS: [Still in disbelief] I'm not taking you anywhere. Not until you tell me where Madus is.

MAUD: You know where he is, don't you? I can see it on your face! You might not have him, but you know something. Does Mother have him or not?

ROSEMUND: [Swooshing over to them. She has a slight hunch as she shuffles] I told you, boy, I don't have him! We don't know where Madus is. You can't have something you don't have *because you don't have it.* God only knows what Pepin intended for thatthatthat penny. You really think I'd give that damned Leeland another? No. [Mumbling] Just one more Automaton to have to find when we kill him.

NARRATOR: Damned Leeland is damned!

ROSEMUND: You know me. [Her eyes flash to Maud, then back at Odys] You knew it was odd for me to threaten such a thing. Reasonable, but oddoddodd. Of course I might do it, if circumstances were different but… [She shrugs with her round shoulders] But you know I would never make Gwendolyn cry. Never. Now be a gentlemanly gentleman and open the car door for me. [She holds up her long nails]

ODYS: [Still skeptical that this was so anti-climatic] I'm not doing anything until you show me where Caffar is.

ACT III

ROSEMUND: All right then, if you're that paranoid about it. [Digging through her pocket and pulling out a few batteries, a few fuses, and one teeny-tiny screw. She scrunches up her face as she looks at them. Picking out the screw with her nails and tossing it into the air—] Caffar, he wants to know you're not hiding in the bushes.

CAFFAR: [After falling to the ground and twisting upward into life, appears to be a very average-height, white-coded Automaton, with dark brown hair, the color of corroded alloys. Her skin parallels the off-white glint of metal in the sun. She is "wearing" a skin-tight body suit and has too many piercings to count. She crosses her arms, defensively, yet her face is expressionless.] ...Not hiding in the bushes [she repeats].[137]

NARRATOR: And now you are introduced to Rosemund's second tongue. Her Echo.

MAUD: Clearly. You're hiding behind all that jewelry. Since when did you become a freak show attraction, Caff?

ROSEMUND: Do you hear her, Caffar? As if she wasn't a circus show herself!

CAFFAR: [Serious, without expression] Circus show!

ODYS: [Huffing at first, gesturing once aggressively. Then, toning down what he was about to say, to be respectful] I come all the way out here, and all of a sudden you're the good guy again? [He goes to open the car door for her] I don't understand why it had to be so much trouble.

ROSEMUND: [A smile underneath her surgeon's mask] Good guy? Good guys are good, Odys. And if good guys are good, then why are you so upset?

ODYS: Does this mean I get my sister back?

NARRATOR: If Dorian lets him.

ROSEMUND: Does this mean you ever lost her? [Noticing his gruff face] I know, I know, Odys. We're liars. Liars are liars. But look, we're bad ones. [She gestures to the area, as if he should have seen through this ruse] Granted, it did make you piss yourself. [She laughs. Odys turns away, thinking, hands on hips] You know as well as I it was the only way to test you. You had to go through this hazing, if you're to be one of us.

ODYS: [Scoffs]

MAUD: [Turning her other hand into a gun] Fine. Get in the car. Both of you. [Caffar picks up her Master's chair with ease and unlocks the trunk with her mutating finger, stows the chair away. Then, climbs into the car].

ROSEMUND: [Stuffing the batteries and fuses back into her pocket, she accidentally hits the remote. Suddenly, nearby sprinklers turn on, misting Odys, who had just come over to the driver's side to drive] Curse these curses! [Rosemund tries to turn them off. She quickly slams her door to avoid the water].

ODYS: [Taking off his coat] Jesus, Rosemund, who put up the sprinklers to water the fucking pavement? Honestly! [He dabs himself off]

ROSEMUND: Didn't know who'd be on firefirefire. [Using her sleeve to wipe off her glasses] Must you point that gun in my face, Maud? Not pointing one at you.

---

[137] Caffar repeats. She always repeats.

MAUD: [Who still has her gun pointed at them lazily, notices the letter she retrieved from the mail earlier. It's inside the breast pocket as Odys drops the wet coat over her lap] Best take this out, so it can dry. [She flicks it, as if to dry it] Might as well open it too, to make sure no ink is running. [She tries to hand it to him].

ROSEMUND: [She and Caffar looking over their shoulders to see what has caught their captor's attention, says to Caffar] And he thinks we're the ones with secrets!

ODYS: [Trying to dab off his own glasses, he says to Maud] What? Oh. [He grudgingly opens the letter, shaking it.]

ACT IV

ROSEMUND: [Peering over the back seat, her huge glasses sliding down her nose] I dare say, that letter is a letter. I know that stationary. I know that typeface! [She points]

MAUD: [glancing down] What's it say?

[They all start to read it]

CAFFAR: What's it say?

The End

Of the play, anyway.

Stanza: Mail Delivery.

The posthumous spam-letter from Pepin read thusly:

Dear Odys, I gave Maud to you for a reason, but I am sure you have figured that much out by now. If anyone asks, Madus is safe. I have a plan for him as well. Also, though it might not matter (depending on how you take to her), tell Maud I am sorry I had to make her forget. I know it sounds silly, because an Automaton does not have personal feelings, but I left a part of me in her that will understand why I erased so much of her—rather, me. At least, I hope part of me is still in her. I plan to leave myself there. I apologize to myself, then. Just in case.

The real reason I am sending this message is to tell you no one is safe. Leeland may think— may even tell you—that my actions speak for him, but they are entirely my own. Do not trust Leeland, and certainly don't trust Mother. I will not go into detail as to why but—

Well, why do you think I have avoided them both all this time? Hell, I should probably tell you to not even trust me, because I have played my part in this. I have known for a while what Leeland had done to you and your sister. I am just now getting around to doing something about it. I hope you will forgive me—though hope is of little help to you. What help is a dead man?

I am sending this letter—well, my <u>friend</u>[138] is sending this letter for me, <u>I</u> will be dead by the time it needs to be sent—in a way that will hopefully keep them from finding it in your mail— Vulcan willing. I know they will check everything on you until they "trust" you. And even then they will not give you peace. Only when you are dead can you rest. I have learned that the hard way.

    -Pepin J. Pound.

    Odys threw the damp letter on the dashboard, the paper rustling and sticking. "Pointless!" he hissed at Maud. "Your Master was pointless!"

    "Is there a P.S.?" Rosemund asked, leaning forward. Maud reminded her with the flick of a wrist that she still had a gun. *Don't be nosey.* Rosemund leaned back. "Well, there you have it. When Pepin hides something you're not going to find it. It has to let itself be found."

    "Thank you for the obvious," Maud snapped.

    Rosemund chuckled. "It's from his typewriter. That's his signature. It's really real."

    Odys, "No one doubted that. Of course it's real. Far too real!"

    "Real!" Caffar shouted back.

    "Why would someone even fake a letter from Pepin, Rosemund?" Maud asked, narrowing her eyes.

    Rosemund shrugged. "Weren't you just ranting about how you can't trust us anymore?"

    "But Mother would hardly fake a letter to us warning us to distrust her. Why would she even do that?"

    Rosemund shrugged and Caffar mimicked the gesture—just seconds off.

    "Well," Rosemund said, "Are we going to mull over this worthless plot device or are we going to go and see your sister?"

    Maud shoved her gun in their direction. "You want to talk pointless? Everything with *you people* is pointless! At least Pepin had the decency to mail his pointlessness. You make us go all the way to fucking Canada."

    "If being pointless is the point then it's not pointless." Rosemund tapped her forehead with her knuckles,[139] telling them to think about it—as if it made sense. Her skull echoed from its metal plate (put in after one too many explosions). "Now, let's go get my things in that house, there, 1606. We can't be late for our plane. It leaves in two hours."

---

[138] Our Narrator did not seem to know who his "friend" was and said it was "likely a hotel clerk or someone else who could be paid to do such things on a specific date."
[139] To use a finger might hurt her nails.

"You were so sure we were coming with you, weren't you?" Odys grumbled.

Stanza: This would not be the last of her beautiful creations that were beautiful.

"The house there, 1606," Rosemund pointed out for the hundredth time. The car stopped. She led them inside a very spacious house and up the stairs. Caffar helped Rosemund like Vulcan's own female automata walking sticks.

"Don't touch anything. It's probably booby trapped," Maud whispered to Odys.

"No, not booby trapped," Rosemund said as she climbed her way up the stairs. Her rings and nails clicked against the wooden rail every other second. She paused for a breather and looked down at them as if in a trappy music video. "Just a few cameras here and there if I wanted to check up on things." She pointed left, and right and sighed. "My lungs might not be able to kill me"—breath—"but they can sure remind me they're perfectly imperfect." She continued up the stairs, all but wheezing.[140]

They entered a room with a door decorated in cartoonish robot patterns. Rosemund flipped on the light and gestured as if she had brought them there just to see it. "This house is for a family with twins. Like you and Odissa, Odys. Because you're a twin. The boy of a twin pair."

"A twin pair," Caffar repeated as she grabbed two suitcases from the corner. Apparently they'd slept in this room. Not the main bedroom.[141]

"Yeah, I know the definition of 'twin,'" Odys said, looking up as an electric train ran about their heads. He was very distracted with the busyness of the room—flickering string lights and spinning galaxy lamps, a bookshelf shaped like a robot with arms that moved every ten or so seconds and with a muted TV in its painted stomach, a child-sized merry-go-round with frozen-posed horses spinning about. It was a less like a *Blade Runner* toymaker scene and more like Willy Wonka—sans candy. "Where are you getting these families, anyway? Syrian refugees or something, Rosemund?"

Rosemund paused in her journey to the center of the room, avoiding a Roomba and panting. Her poor lungs had always been weak—weak from that original discovery of electricity and the fire it caused. She shrugged to him. She didn't want to elaborate.

"So you're putting up entire neighborhoods now, Rosemund?" Maud pushed her. "And decorating them on top of it?"

---

[140] This may be a good time to remind you, Reader, that Automatons do not heal retroactively. They preserve and extend the life and function of the human body they inherit.
[141] That's not weird at all.

301

"I didn't build this neighborhood. I bought it out. Will give these houses to people I like. People of my choosing—the choicest people. I'll keep a few for myself, of course. Need places to store my things and things to store in my places." She shrugged, stuffing a laptop in a bag.

"You have some sort of list of people like Mother has for new Automaton Masters?" He didn't know why he was asking, for this did not surprise him.

"Yes, but my list is much more ininintricate than that."

"How so?" Maud laughed.

Rosemund's glasses flashed when she turned. Her surgeon's mask bobbed over her lips as she said, "Because I'm dealing with people who will never end upupup on Mother's so-called list. These people are much more important, because their lives will go *unprolonged*." She zipped up her handbag and handed it to Caffar. Then, she began to straighten up the bed they had slept in. "Every detail countscountscounts."

"You've decorated to match your own interests, Rosemund." Maud avoided the robot's moving arm as she turned off the TV (to grace Odys's thought to save electricity).

"What? All the automata? Nah, automata are everywhere." Her red eyebrows were waving over the too-big glasses. "People just don't notice. But children, well. Children notice. They can be taught to notice." She gestured to the room's bells and whistles. Her eyes traced her designs. "Ceiling fans, spinning trays in microwaves, printers—all automata in some way, Maud. This room just givegivegives those concepts a more friendly interface. Some collectors say that electricity has no value in automata—that we should keep the windup keys and not have them run constantly. But energy is energy, no matter if sporadic or constant. So why not *automate* the automata? On and on and on."

"And on and on," Caffar said as she nodded for them to leave.

Before moving to the door, Rosemund picked up one last toy as if she couldn't resist a demonstration—a fuzzy rabbit. Rosemund wound the rabbit and put it on the ground. It hopped in its pre-programmed fashion until it missed its last leap, kicking on its side. "You tell me whether or not that rabbit would like to live and die constantly like this? Electricity is the cure."

"It has no brain," Odys said, entertaining her point—a point that might help him understand her if only he could get her to keep talking.

"But if it did?" Rosemund's eyes sparkled up at him.

"Electricity only works for stationary automatons," Maud said, picking up the rabbit and placing it on the shelf. "Wires would just hold him back."

"But batteries, my dear!" Rosemund pointed to the air. "That's what we humans are for you. *Batteries.*"

Maud laughed. "I'm sure museum curators would love for you to strap battery packs on the back of priceless antiques, Rosemund, but is it really worth your while?"

Rosemund tilted her head and huffed at Odys "Exactly why I focus on this room instead. *Worth my while.* You're just jealous this wasn't your childhood room."

A shadow overtook his face, sucking him back to the reason he was here. "I had plenty of toys, thanks to you people. I never wanted for a damn thing." He pointed for her to get a move on.

But Rosemund didn't budge. "We would have given you a room like this, had we known about you, Odys. You do realize that, don't you?"

He noticed a tone of guilt in her words. "You wouldn't have given me back to my real parents? Or the orphanage?"

Rosemund narrowed her eyes and thought for a moment. "No," she said in that scratchy, high-pitched Eartha Kitt voice.[142] "Your real parents would have always died. That couldn't have been prevented. That's the only way we—" But she redirected. "If Leeland wanted you, we would've known you were worth something. We would have saved you from him, had we known."

"Rosemund, who do you think that he is?" Maud demanded, stepping forward as if trying to catch what Rosemund had just said. "Did Pepin tell you anything—mention anything—before he died? Did he know who Odys was—*really* was?"

As if Maud had shaken the floor with her divine weight and somehow jiggled the gears in the wooden rabbit to make its notches click, the toy kicked again, startling them all. Rosemund watched the rabbit tick to a complete stop—she, the seer who foresaw the rabbit's life winding down and the real reason it had jumped. Rosemund looked to Maud. "Vulcan says no. Not yet." She pointed to the cursed toy.

"Not yet, not yet," Caffar said to herself as she checked the time on the too-colorful clock above them.

"But you know *who I am*, don't you? You know. Tell me my real name. The others know too, but they pretend they don't—as if I mean their worst fears are true."

---

[142] So Rosemund dresses like a black woman and even talks ike one? Why not make her one? Couldn't seem to convince our Narrator of this because "Well, she wasn't black." Apparently she just wants to distract in any way possible from those scars? I'm also getting mobster wife vibes so I'll let t slide.

"Not *all* of them think it would be a badbadbad thing, Odys, if you really were Dorian's nephew."

"Who of them?"

Rosemund adjusted the threads of her mask. "I ever tell you the time I met Dorian?"

"You mean did you tell Pepin and do I remember for Odys?" Maud asked, rolling her eyes. Of course Odys didn't remember.

Rosemund didn't seem to hear her. She sat down on the bed with the spaceship sheets, crossed her legs. She flicked her fake nails as if adjusting her settings—fine-tuning the channel she was about to broadcast: "He was such an ugly little duckling. It was Bob who introduced us to him—when we were finally introduced to him. Bob and her husband had fallen in love with him his charm. Never seen anything like him ever before because there was never anything like him before. You know whywhywhy we picked him? Because *he* knew *we* were different and so we had to pick him. You could see it in his eyes—his eyes could tell and you could see it there—there in his bulging, droopy eyes. The second we were in the same room we knew we couldn't live without this boy and this boy knew that we couldn't live without him. He knew we had chosen him—for whatever mysterious thing we had picked him for. Him, this rebellious college dropout who won us over with his bug-eyed stare. He had such huge eyes that were huge! And now he covers them."

Odys remembered those eyes—eyes that Maud remembered. It sent a shiver down his spine.

Rosemund clacked her nails together like a teacup dog on wood floors, added soundtrack to the story her words painted. "We wavered and debated over him, even though we had already made up ourourour minds and there was no need to waver and debate. There were others—more worthy and older—who we had wanted to give an Automaton to. Out of respect, that is why we wavered and debated. We at least wavered. That, and Dorian hadhadhad a family. Although a small one. Well, really he only had a sister. A step-sister. No blood relation whatsoever, but still. We knew he loved his step sister. We eventually settled on it *not being a big deal.* But you know this now, right? You know it was a *big deal.* You're synced with Maud. So you know *the deal.*" It was almost a question.

Odys knew, but he wanted to hear her go on. "But Pepin wasn't there when you chose him."

She pointed with her long, sparkly nail. "He knew what we were doing, though. By then he had given us the finger and told Gwendolyn, 'Do whatever the fuck you like.' He didn't give a shit—though he hadn't left us completely. He was only *removed*—but still part of us. He was there, but wasn't. He wasn't there to choose Dorian, but Maud was there. Maud was watching for him because he wasn't there. But even though Maud was there, he had no opinion in the matter." She pointed at Maud. "But when Pepin saw him with Maud's eyes, he actually came outoutout of his shell. We were graced with few visits here and there. No one could make Pepin laugh like Dorian. Pepin had always been the clever one. But Dorian surpassed him in that cleverness. And then Leeland rose from his silence. His ears perked up with our laughter and he roused himself from exile and was no longer silent. It was then that his crusade hit a new height. When he went on the rampage, Pepin retreated for good. Twenty years later, here we are."

She stopped playing with her nails and fanned them out in presentation. She looked like a manicurist waiting for her client to take a seat with those claws and that mask—ready to inhale fumes.

"Pepin left you all to your own mistakes," Odys said, watching the toy train coming back around.

"We're all apart. Every single oneoneone of us. I've been held up here, staying away from it all."

"But you talk to Mother every day. She can't help but cry to you. You and Bob," Maud scoffed. "She calls and demands you help her do this or that, and you just do it."

Rosemund's eyes smiled up at them as she re-tucked the comforter into the bed corners. "What can I say? I can't refuse her."

"Just like you couldn't refuse her when she got arrested on suspicion of kidnapping and you had to take out three cops just to bail her ass out of jail?" Maud had meant it to sting.

Bail is not meant in the literal sense here.[143]

"I admit she should have lied better about who Anselm was to her."

"She could have gotten out on her own! And you people wonder why Pepin avoided you."

"If I hadn't helped her, many more would have died. They had Anselm. Cameras on him! What did you want him to do? Kill everyone who would have seen him break Mother out of jail? She needed back up. Someone to turn the lights out and help her leave unnoticed…" She went on smoothing out the bed—as if it didn't look tidy enough.

"You people never care about who you hurt to keep on living," Odys muttered.

Rosemund stood with a groan. "Be careful, there, Odys, you sound just like your father."

"He wasn't my father. And Dorian isn't my uncle."

---

[143] Maybe all of Rosemund's Habitat for Humanity projects were her way of making up for her sins—sins Mother made her commit.

Rosemund's head turned to him. "You can't blame Dorian for what happened. Hasn't he been punished enough?"

"Blindness isn't a punishment if he has a second pair of eyes in Fletcher. But don't worry, I don't blame him. I blame *all* of you."

"I know you don't trust anyone, but your want for control won't get you control. I'm on your side, Odys. Just why do you thinkthinkthink I contrived all this, if not to finally meet you? Don't punish us for the past."

"You people let Leeland live because you agree with him," Odys growled to the air. "Deep down, you *agree* with him. You think he might have the right idea. You're so unsure and afraid that he *may* be right that you passively let this—this *chaos* churn."

"No. We passively let the chaos *settle*. And for Christ's sake, put Maud's gun away, Odys. You know you don't scare me."

Maud's eyes narrowed. "Only if you tell me what's with the surgeon's mask. Why do you need it? I know it's not to breathe—"

Rosemund unhooked one of the thin strings from behind her ear. Grinning, she flashed them her braces. "Didn't want to lead with them is all."

"Why the fuck do you have braces?" Maud asked, knowing Rosemund never needed them before. But these didn't look quite right. More bolts and wires than what you typically see.

"Either I, one, got into an accident restoring a carnival carousel or two, wanted to be a better electrical conductor."

"Why do I feel like it's both and that you injured yourself accidentally on purpose?" Odys screwed up his face, cocked his head.

Rosemund shrugged, taking her mask completely off. "They were so worried about me suing them that they didn't notice I stole somesomesome original parts."

"Why hide it from us?"

"Because who can take an adult seriously serious when they have braces?"

"You think *that's* why we can't take you seriously?" Maud clapped for them to get a move on.

She already talked like Gertrude Stein, but now, with those bolts and wires in her mouth, she was a Frankenstein.

Stanza: Pepin left them to assemble them.

Now, let's see what Odissa's been up to, shall we? In the last book she had just been given a heavy dose of mega sleepy-time in the theater and was about to be driven to an undisclosed location…

Odissa woke up in a bed. A very comfy bed.

But that's not what surprised her. Neither was Dorian lying next to her surprising. And neither was his nakedness. What *did* surprise her, however, was the fact *she* was still fully clothed—shocked he hadn't taken *the liberty*.

"Where are we?" Her voice cracked.

"Oh, you're awake? You've been out for a while. But so have I. It took hours to get here. We did need sleep, didn't we?" He adjusted the sheets which covered both of them. "We're in the cabin—our cabin. I can't tell you where, though. But it's a cabin."

"That little boy—Mecca. Where's he?" (A bit concerned and paranoid).

"In his room. With Bulfinch too. Bul will stay in Mecca's bathroom." He fingered her hair— hair fanned out on her pillow—hair he had placed there. "With the litter box. Cat litter makes Fletcher sneeze, you see—makes him not function well. Sensitive nose, sometimes, and I hate to push his snivels when things are tense right now. Otherwise I wouldn't mind. I wouldn't let that come between us. Bulfinch got a saucer of warm milk and a whole can of tuna. Which he did not eat."

"He doesn't like tuna. Only canned food. He'll only lick the juices."

"We've made a store run, don't worry."

"Can I see him? Why isn't he with us?" She saw multiple doors. One must be a bathroom. Why couldn't Bulfinch be held in theirs?

"Gotta give Mecca *something* to do. Otherwise we'll not be left alone." He stroked her arm lightly, as if wanting to tickle her. It didn't. It only made her more afraid. *They're holding Bulfinch hostage.*

"Where's Fletcher?" Her cloudy eyes searched for him, though she hadn't lifted her head.

"He's over there—the table. Are you done filling in the gaps now?"

She yawned, noticing her cheek had crusty drool stuck to it. She blotted the rest away with the back of her hand. She saw the rusty paperclip was next to a pile of books no one had likely ever opened. Fletcher was too well angled to spring up and block her. She wouldn't be looking out without his permission. She noticed the little lock-button was pressed in. No one (especially Mecca) would be getting in.

"Can we go outside?" She wanted to judge how trapped she should feel.

"We're still on our date." *You're stuck with me until I say so.*

Rubbing her eyes, "Why are we here?"

"Because this is where Mother wanted us to meet. It was all arranged. She likes to make us feel like family every once in a while. She probably has something important to drop on us too. Probably something about your brother. That's what these family *vacations* are usually for."

"You mean you don't know why we're here? You came because you were told?" One minute he was kidnapping her from a kidnapping and the next he was bringing her back.

"I know *some* reasons why I'm here. Your brother is coming too. Don't worry."

"I wasn't. I wasn't worrying about that part."

"You should. I'm still wondering whether or not I will even let you see him—if I should let you out of this room at all. I have mixed feelings, now, about your relationship. I don't want to *promote* anything."

It was like Dorian didn't have control over the words slipping from his mouth—but that he didn't mind they weren't his. Love was making him do such crazy things.

"I would never—we would never—not here…" She rubbed her forehead.

"Even so. I'm mad at your brother."

"Reasons?" She closed her eyes as she waited for his answer.

"He knew damn well you were married and never told us. It changes a lot of things. It changes everything—how I view it all. It changes the motives of everything."

"I don't know what you're talking about, but I know he didn't do it to anger you. You know he hates Augury."

"Leeland. That's his real name."

"Whoever. It doesn't matter. It's not *real*."

"It *is* real, Odissa." *Even if Leeland destroyed the documents to prove it.* "And there's a reason Leeland did it. There's a reason he married you. There's even a reason he'd be willing to fuck you, despite everything we know about him."

"You're making me feel ugly. He didn't mind me *that* much."

"I'm sorry. That's not what I meant."

"What *did* you mean?"

He paused, running his fingers over her skin in thought. "You may not understand it all, but you *must* understand that Odys should've told us. That was part of his—his *duty*. To help us stop what's going on."

She closed her eyes again like someone about to admit things to their therapist—why did she feel like she could speak to him? "He pretends I'm not married," she said simply.

"I'm not stupid, Odissa. He may pretend to himself that you aren't married so he can forget about his father. He may pretend to himself that you aren't his sister so he can fuck you. But he's not going to be able to pretend that I'm out of the picture now, you understand? I lost you once—I lost everything once." He said it so casually—an announcement of no more importance than favorite color or food (which was grey and pizza, by the way). "Though Odys is important to me too, I can't protect him if he lies to me. I can't protect him if he treats me like an enemy. You understand?"

"No. I don't understand anything." There was a tremble in her voice. Her hand near his arm threatened to pull back. She wanted to sleep and forget this was happening. To sleep alone.

"Don't be so afraid of me." His voice almost begged her. "You have to realize, Odissa, I only say these things because I'm not the one in control, here. Everything depends—so much—on you." He sunk lower on the bed and pouted. "Don't make me go to extremes."

Her eyes darted across him, calculating what response he wanted. "You're a manipulative little cunt."

He took off his sunglasses. Set them aside. "Manipulative? Yes. Cunt? Yes. Little? No." He stroked his dick over the covers.

She studied him and his size for a moment. "Then get it over with." She was quite irritated now. Not only did he have the opportunity to molest her while she was out cold, but he hadn't even taken her clothes off. He really *did* make her do all the work here.

He scratched his bare chest, as if considering it. "You know that's not my style."

Leaning toward him, she nodded. "It might be mine, though."

"Already got you pussy whipped." He flicked his wrist as if he had the world's smallest whip and went back to caressing his groin.

She laughed and brushed back his hair—testing what it was like to touch him. "You might be able to keep me from my brother, but I wonder how you intend to keep him from me."

"He's outnumbered here. Plus, he wouldn't want to jeopardize everything he's just earned with us. We own him."

"And who owns you?"

"You do, Odissa. Or are you just making sure?" His brows came together. "I'd do anything—anything, Odissa—to make you love me." He made sure every word came out clearly.

Frowning, she looked around the lodge-style room. At the moose-patterned curtains. Slowly, she removed her cat ears and studied them, thinking. "And even if I never fuck you, you'll still love me?"

"I have no choice in the matter." The tips of his fingers tried to find her skin under her clothes.

She let him explore, pretending to be lost in thought. "That's a very disappointing answer. Feels fake. Like I've given you a love potion to make you like me." Or, rather, shot CUPID'S ARROW.[144]

"All biology is a love potion. We never *really* get to choose what we're attracted to. It's in our genes. Our DNA. We never have a choice."

"Don't know if I believe that." She felt the obligation to draw him from his new isolated expression. In a whisper, "I will tell you something, Dorian. Listen to me, all right?" She put an inartful hand on his hairless chest and grabbed at his searching fingers with her other.

"Yes?"

"You can let me see him. Nothing bad will happen."

"He'll want to take you from me. The others might let him."

"Where? Where will he take me?" She whispered back to him. "You've killed me off. You have my cat. I've nothing to go back to. Plus, you all are so interesting here. Why would I leave?"

He laughed at her attempt to soothe him. "But he still might take you away. I can't let him do that. I'll have to stop him if he tries. He won't get far. They may not stop him but they won't stop me either. You understand? I see you do."

His laughter and threats sent a chill across her skin. She didn't know which to believe—his expression or his words. She was starting to believe both. "I won't go with him. If he needs to stay here, he'll stay here. Wherever here is. I won't let you hurt him. I can handle him."

"…Handle him?" He smiled at the thought. "You're yet to convince me of your *abilities*."

"If I recall, I'm not the one who stopped the sex last time."

"You should stop flirting with me, Odissa. Take it if you want it." He tipped his chin up, making himself easy to kiss.

But she wouldn't fall into him so readily.

She pushed the covers off of her legs, prepared to do as he wanted. "You *are* going to let me see my brother," she hissed at him.

"That all depends on you." He picked at the sheet's hem.

---

[144] Talk about insta-love, am I right?

"And I'm telling you, Dorian, that *you* need to let it depend on me, then. You're *going* to let me see him. You're going to trust me." She grabbed his chin. "And that will be all. I will only *see* him." He tried to move his chin away from her but she grabbed it again. "No. Dorian, if you want me to like you—to *love* you—you have to let me see my brother. You have to let me keep him calm. The minute he thinks you have me is the minute he causes trouble. The minute he causes trouble is the minute I have to choose sides. Let me make this easy for us, Dorian."

She could see the wheels in his head turning. She had never felt so influential before—so powerful.

"That's all I needed to hear," he said, putting a hand on her wrist. "Now are you going to fuck me or not?"

But as the smile faded from her face, she realized he was too serious to be funny. She knew this person before her was the perfect excuse to save her brother from himself—to save her from herself. Odys and Odissa could never go back to what they once were. Not after this—not after having your whole life ripped open and examined, the festering let open to breathe.

She studied Dorian, watched his chest move up and down. She could almost hear the blood in his ears.

Better to kill the past quickly than to draw death out with suffering, she thought to herself.

She started undressing. Fletcher must have been on screen-saver mode, because Dorian had a confused expression on his face, wondering if his ears were deceiving him. He put his arms behind his head, very pleased. He waited for her to come to him.

His smile was too wide for her liking. "Hard and slow, baby," he said as she helped him ease into her, "make it last."

"You'll get what I give you," she said through her teeth as she arranged herself.

And just like that, she had turned her back on the past in order to preserve what it once had been.

She jumped when he actually touched her face—making her pause and open her eyes. The act was a little off, but he still found her cheek.

"Look at me," he said through his breaths. "Look at me."

She looked at Fletcher, who was clearly paying attention now.

"No, at *me*," Dorian said. She looked at him for a half-second, his own eyes closed.

She covered his mouth as she kissed his forehead. She didn't need his help. She knew what she was doing. She buried her face in his neck—in the pillow.

Shall we give them some privacy now? Do we really need to know that Odissa hadn't expected to come, but, when she did, it fueled Dorian to use her crumpled body above him to latch onto her? Do we? No, we don't. We don't need to know that when he finished he groaned into her with such strength she felt she had stolen his ability to breathe. We don't need to know.

She needed a cigarette.

He rested his cheek on her chest. She stared down her nose at him with a frown, but let him anyway. "Are we really at this point? Cuddling?"

"Well, you aren't at a good angle to spoon..."

She heard the hurt in his voice. "Not here, but here." She pushed back his head to shoulder. "You're just heavier than you look. I can't breathe."

She realized she should probably show him affection, and so put her hand in his hair.

"You're so beautiful when naked." He cupped her breast and kissed it. "You should be this way more often."

"The one-liners need to stop. You're smart and funny and I know it already."

"Then what will it take to get you to smile?" He ran his hand between her legs—so eager to please.

She tried not to react. "How do you know I'm not smiling?" She glared over at Fletcher. *You don't have to show him everything, you know.*

Dorian laughed at her—laughed at how well she, a common human, understood him. But when his laughter died, he couldn't let the silence settle. "Why didn't you tell me you were *married*? I mean, from the get-go? All that flirting and you didn't mention it until the very last moment."

She rolled her eyes. "Because I liked you flirting with me." She pulled his chin up to kiss him.

He accepted her answer. His fingers—as his eyes—brushed her features. "If you break my heart, I will break him."

"You think he won't do the same when he finds out what I've done with you?"

"Don't even look at him."

She latched onto his chin. "Then poke out my eyes so I can't see him, you dick. You promised I could see him if I fucked you."

He licked his lips, slightly angry. "Did I?" He pulled away from her.

"You know that's what this was."

"Yeah, but don't phrase it like *that*."

She held back. "Look, I'm sorry. But you shouldn't say things like that either. You can't flip flop like that—"

"Just because I say something dramatic doesn't mean I actually mean it." He swallowed back the darkness in his voice.

"Well, I don't know that."

"Now you do." He sat up from her. "You want to take a bath?"

She thought about it for a moment. "I don't like having sex in the bathtub."

"Who said anything about having sex? I just want to give you a bath." He pulled the covers off and away from her.

"You saying I smell?"

"Your attitude does." He stood up.

Stanza: Mind your Mother.

Odys, Maud, Rosemund and Caffar got on the plane. They had boarded with the tickets Rosemund had already purchased. The already-purchased tickets were yet another sure sign Rosemund hadn't been *lying about the lie*—all this was planned out too well.

They sat together, despite being able to sit apart. There were so many open seats around them that Odys assumed Rosemund had bought out half the plane just so they wouldn't have to sit next to anyone. And that meant they could talk more freely. Rosemund wanted to talk. She was proving with her every gesture she had something to say—and in multiple ways.

As they drifted over America, Rosemund used Caffar to pick her nails. Screw-Caffar proved to be a bit less effective than a metal nail file, so she pulled one out of her hair.

Odys quickly snatched it away. "The fuck are you thinking? That's a weapon!"

The TSA agent clearly hadn't thought to pat down that massive mane of hair.[145] When Rosemund walked through the metal detector, her "medical papers" proved all the beeping was from the metal plate in her head. Never mind the nail file in her hair.

Rosemund didn't even demand her file back to hide, merely went on picking her bejeweled nails with Caffar as Odys hid it in his pocket.

How does she wipe her ass with those nails? Odys found himself thinking to Maud.

Probably has Caffar do it for her.

Rosemund flicked her nails and kept on picking.

A flight attendant walked by. Her eyes lingered on Rosemund's hands too long for comfort.

---

[145] Simpler times, man.

"Would you put her away? You're making people stare."

He wasn't sure if screws were on the no-fly list.

"Calm down—don't be so uptight. You almost gave us away back theretheretherethere in customs—with you needing to calm down. You really look suspicious when you are so uptight and need to calm down."

"I'm not the one that people are staring at!"

"With a face like mine, how can they not stare? My face is a giant scar and they would stare regardless. At least I give them something worthwhile to look at besides the scar which they can't help but stare atatat." She admired her nails and kept watching the silent in-flight sitcom.

At least she had stopped picking for a few seconds.

As Odys stared at the screw, he realized he thought Caffar was the most characterless Automaton. All else was kitschy paper doll dress-up. Her "characterless character" was most likely because Rosemund didn't need an Automaton to have a *character*. She was fine on her own. Caffar was so bland because Rosemund was *true*. True to her own soul.[146]

"You should sleep, Odys, while you have a chance," Rosemund told him. She turned off the overhead light. She studied it in its off state, as if she could see past the plastic and into the wiring.

"I'd like to, but I don't think I should sleep with you around. I might wake up to find I'm in some electric chair." Or find Maud naked on top of him—which would be much worse.

Rosemund turned back on the overhead light and cleaned her glasses, using the light to spot the smudges. Her scars around her eye wrinkled more as she squinted through the winged eyeliner. "So, about that letter. Why do you think Pepin doesn't want you to trust Mother? Besides the obvious fact that Mother likes to give a small fib here and there. But we all do that." *Mmhmm.* "Why just mistrust her and her alone? That's the question, isn't it?" She put her bottle rims back on.

Odys's lip twitched. "It's not so much a question as a fact. She's the biggest liar in the whole lot."

Rosemund laughed, rubbing her tongue against her braces. The peanuts on the plane always got stuck in them. "Did I ever tell you about the time I realized Mother killed her entire family?"

"What do you mean?" Odys ran through Maud's memories, not landing on anything.

---

[146] Plane Jane. That's how Rosemund liked her women.

"She killed them." Rosemund shrugged, digging out a toothpick from her hair. "Killed them dead when theytheythey started questioning her. That's how she got free from her past. A clean break is always clean."

She put the toothpick back in her hair. That's why she didn't carry a purse. Her hair held everything she needed.

Her voice grew softer as she said, "At first I thought I could never do what she did—kill my own family! Most of my family was dead or distant by the time I got Caffar. But then I realized I was a hypocritical hypocrite, Odys Odelyn. I realized that I've done many things to keep my Automaton, to keep my Caffar—even if I wasn't the one to finish offoffoff my own family. Leeland did that for me. But don't worry. They were just a few second cousins and a few great-great aunts. No one I liked. Most were dead by the time Leeland arrived anyway. But the thing is, I let them die. I let them die to keep this."

She held up Caffar between her witchy nails. Someone across the aisle narrowed their eyes. Rosemund looked strange enough, without waving screws about on a plane. She flicked off the overhead light once more, as if to take the spotlight off them.

She lowered her voice, leaning too close for comfort—those braces chomped at him. "There's a lesser of two evils always, but there is never a good to choose. That's my point. For example, I have a strange fascination with electricity"—her eyes darted to the overhead light— "But is electricity good in and of itself? Nonono. Electricity can be used for good. But it can also be used for evil. Electricity itself is neutrally neutral. It isn't ever a 'good' choice. There are no good choices. Choices are just choices." She adjusted a writing pen falling out of her hair.

Odys frowned, not wanting to argue with her comparison. "Part of me thinks that her family deserved it, from what I know about them."

"Yet you disagree with killing?"

He wanted to be clear: "I rejected Maud because I won't live for her—as all of you live for yours. I won't choose that. I think that's why."

Rosemund pushed up her bug-glasses. "You might not want others to diediedie for her, but *you* just might. There is chance for you to slip and give us cause to kill you still. You've been given a gift. You've finally unwrapped it, Odys. But will you get to keep it?"

"Since she's attached to my lifeline, I'd rather not exchange it," he replied.

"Pepin exchanged it," she told him gravely. "He returned her to the universe that gave her to him. He never asked for her, you never asked for her. Samesamesame thing. It's only strange

315

because we don't know the reasons he gave her up. You, though, Odys, you have reasons you might give her up. To protect Odissa, for instance. But back to my story about Gwendolyn."

She wasn't done?

"My point is, Odys, is that justjustjust because Pepin doesn't want you to believe Mother's tears doesn't mean they aren't real ones."

"You want me to trust her, then?'

As if she couldn't see his expression, she turned on the overhead light *once again.* "I want you to trust that she doesn't want to hurt you. After all, she's gone to suchsuchsuch great lengths to keep your ass around despite it being easier just to kill you. Yes, real tears are real, even if she does make a mistake. We all make mistakes. Pepin made mistakes too."

Am I one of those mistakes?

Rosemund leaned over and tapped Odys's pant pocket, where he had tucked away Maud. "You want to know what Pepin sent me for my birthday?"

"He sent you something?" Odys asked, moving away from her—not liking her that close to his junk.

"Of course he sent me something. Every year. I was his favfavfavorite. Just because he wouldn't speak to me didn't mean he didn't love me." She hovered over his pants again. "Don't you want to know, Maud?"

A stewardess walking by the parallel lane made a face at Rosemund, catching Odys's red face.

It's not what you think! Odys shot her a nervous smile as he pushed Rosemund away from his crotch. "Yes, yes, she wants to know," he hissed at her.

Rosemund sat back up, turning off the overhead light as she dug in her hair. When her fingers came back she turned on the light once again, for dramatic effect. She opened her hand and revealed: "Nothing," she said. "He sent me nothing. Nothing but an empty box. An empty box with a card that said, *'Keep him safe.'*"

Odys recoiled, eyes wide. Something inside him knew that was right—as if Maud remembered. "He did send you Madus? He tried to? Someone took him?"

"No," Rosemund flashed her braces. "He sent me you."

Odys narrowed his eyes. Her face was too smiley.

She leaned back in her chair and reached for her light once more with a long claw—but Odys beat her to it, blocked her button. "Let's just stay in the dark from now on, why don't we?"

Stanza: Who are you when there's more than one of you?

"Seriously," Dorian said, giving a good stretch. "You need to check out this bathtub. It's got jets. It might as well be a hot tub. Get your cigarettes, there, in your purse and let's go."

Already naked, Odissa simply got in with Dorian. Because he left Fletcher in the bedroom, she actually had to help Dorian up the steps to the giant bath and run it herself. He accepted her assistance willingly. "Help me, darling. I can't see," he had said, grabbing at her despite remembering exactly where everything was. Nothing about the cabin ever changed. There was nervousness in his voice that she simply couldn't refuse.

"Don't you just love baths?" He said across from her. They sat apart, rippling the water between them. "I do. I do my best thinking in the tub."

She did not answer, merely sunk lower in the too-hot water. She was sure she was flushed from its heat but didn't care. The man was blind.

He ran his toes against her leg, reminding her he was still there. "I was always going to let you see your brother, you know."

"Yeah, you say that now." She flicked her cigarette ashes in the water. She loved to hear them fizzle out as they hit the surface.

"You make the most interesting sounds," he smiled, just before sinking his head under. He came up, smoothing back his black hair. It made him look like a greaser. It made her snort.

"Marco?" He splashed, almost snuffing her cigarette.

"Fuck you," she laughed as he floated toward her. He took a dip and spit out the water. He spread her legs and rested on his knees in front of her, holding on to hers as if he might sink into the tub. He just hovered there, probably because he couldn't see where her face was and also because he didn't want to brush his face against her cigarette. She jabbed it out on the side of the tub. Making herself at home.

She studied him, floating there. He was listening to her every movement. She touched his face and wetted her hands. She watched water drip around his cloudy grey eyes—eyes with scarred sockets—eyes with little white bumps and webs covering whatever color they used to be. And then that smile—that scary smile she wanted to wipe off his triumphant face. She hoped he didn't realize he was more spectacular than his perfect Automaton—that she valued imperfection.

It was her brother who wanted everything nice and tidy and perfect.

Dorian, as if he knew her expression through her touch, said, "What is it?" She was being too gentle toward him. Too kind.

"Why did you call me Dorothy?" She seized the sides of his face, as if she had him trapped now.

317

"Why? Do you not like this yellow brick road I'm escorting you down?" He sunk lower into the tub, angling her grip on him. Her fingers slid a little on his wet skin. His hair touched the water and fanned out like an aura. He wanted to make sure her hands were still playing nicely.

"That's not a real answer, Dorian." She leaned into him.

He floated away from her. He spread out his arms along the tub. His grey eyes closed, readying himself. "I suppose you have a right to know. Odys will tell you eventually, I'm sure. Can't keep his mouth shut."

"About what?"

He rubbed a finger over his pink upper lip at a false itch. "I knew your real parents, Odissa. At least, I think I did. But I won't tell you more than that."

"Why not?"

"Not only would your brother hate me for it, but..." He trailed off.

"Since when do you care what my brother wants? I think he'll be too distracted about the other stuff we've done to care if you tell me. And does this mean he knows? Why does he know but I don't? It isn't fair."

"Your brother knows as much as I do. And believe me, that means he's not sure of anything."

"Not sure of what, Dorian?"

He huffed out his nose. "I'm going to make the others adore you, Odissa. Just you wait. I need to warn you that when they start arriving they might be a little suspicious about what we've been up to. They might not understand. Don't worry. I'll handle it. They'll love you. They'll let me save you."

"Save me?"

"When we find Madus, he'll be perfect for you. A twin for a twin."

She had no idea what he was talking about.

"Then Leeland will never get to you. No one will ever take you away from me again." He was smiling to himself once more, his finger back at that lip.

"Exactly how many times have I been taken away before?"

"Once, in the past. But an Automaton will keep you here with me forever. You understand? Maybe then—once you have one—you'll understand what happened to your parents, why I did what I had to. The Automaton will explain everything."

"What did you do to my parents, Dorian?" Her heart was making the water ripple despite her body remaining still. "I don't want an Automaton."

"Your brother wants you to have one too." To himself, "That's why he went so willingly to Rosemund."

Not sure what he meant, "He won't give me one if I do not want one."

"None of us were really given a *choice*, Odissa. You think you will be? And the others will want to make *me* happy. I will win them over. I will gain their votes. Why wouldn't you want an Automaton? You either become one of us or we get rid of you eventually. Why not finalize the deal? You have no life to go back to."

"You've made sure of that, haven't you?"

He chewed his lip, wondering why she was so obstinate. Could she not see what he meant? Surely—for she could see everything else.

"Why you won't tell me? Why can't you tell me why I'm Dorothy?"

His jaw clenched. He did not like her persistence. "You would hate me, that's why."

"What if I promised I wouldn't? Why would it change so much between us? Aren't we *destined* to be in love with each other?"

"No. *I'm* destined to be in love with you. The gods promised us nothing about *your* love."

"You were angry with me when I didn't say I was married. Now you're the one hiding the truth."

The water rippled as he huffed. "Leeland has leverage—family members, pets, friends. He uses leverage to try and get our Automatons. He *had* leverage on me, but...I still have an Automaton, Odissa. You understand what I'm saying?"

He heard her try to swallow.

"Do you understand, Odissa?"

"I—I think so."

"And do you hate me? Do you fear me?"

She was taking her time to answer when—

Fletcher opened the door. Dorian saved himself from her answer. Odissa sunk lower in the tub, self-conscious for a moment.

"They're here. In the drive." Fletcher cocked his head. He noticed her sinking in the tub and stared at her. He hadn't needed to barge in here, but his Master had wanted him to. He needed an excuse to look at Odissa. And he kept looking. Even when he said, "And you got a text from Rosie. She says he's very angry. He'll expect to see her..." he kept looking.

"Hand me a towel, Fletcher." Dorian stood up, water rippling off him.

319

Fletcher did so, never taking his eyes off Odissa. He loomed over the tub, a wicked smile on his tight lips. Dorian left her. But Fletcher told her to stay in the tub, as if guarding her.

"Who's here?" Odissa asked him.

He sat down on the edge of the tub, crossed his long legs. "Don't play stupid."

"Is he earlier than expected?"

Fletcher raised an eyebrow. "You're still ours for a little longer if you're indecent, now, aren't you?" He stuck his hand in the water, smiling when she didn't recoil from it.

"You think Odys hasn't seen me like this?"

Fletcher stopped smiling. "Don't be mean."

He swung his feet into the tub, the cloth of his pant legs not absorbing moisture. He hadn't cared to add that detail.

Stanza: Time zones and pinecones.

Odys barged into the cabin after Caffar and Rosemund. Maud was in his pocket, hidden from his sister. Rosemund had heard the good news that Odissa would be there—and had kindly shared it with Odys. And though his eyes searched for her, the first thing he noticed in the quaint-but-plush cabin was Dorian…in nothing but a towel. And some glasses. He was holding a steaming hot cup of cocoa.

"Ah, Odys!" he said, gently blowing on his drink. "Congratulations on your A plus plus. And your fully-functioning second brain."

Odys said nothing as he took in the surroundings, trying to find his sister in the cramped walls lined with doors. Dorian set his cup down, smoothing back his still-wet hair. "Rosie! Damn, look at those nails. "

They kissed on the cheek.

"Caffar's certainly looking gothic. What have you been reading lately? No, let me guess…*Girl with the Dragon Tattoo?* " (It had just become a best seller).

"I wear my heart on my Automaton's sleeve, what can I say?" Rosemund rummaged in the fridge, puffing up her hair as if it were an afro.

"Nice headgear, by the way," Dorian added. "You've got more metal than Caffie, here."

Rosemund gave him the finger. The scarred finger.

"Speaking of metal, you should have seen the junk Fletch sneezed out the other day. A fancy microchip of some sort. Wonder where that came from."

"I don't know what you're talktalktalking about."

"Mhmm. Sure you don't."

Odys's eyes landed on Mecca asleep on the couch—tongue slightly out. He was on top of Q—who was, quite clearly, nude under that scanty blanket someone had been kind enough to drape over them.

"He drove us all the way here," Dorian informed in a whisper (trying not to wake them),[147] itching his bare chest. "Wore him out, but thankfully we only had to steal one car."

Odys didn't care. "Where's Odissa? Is she here or isn't she?" He looked to Rosemund as if she'd been lying.

"I wondered when you were going to ask. She's getting dressed. In there." He pointed to *their* room—a room Odys knew Dorian always used when at this cabin. "I'll also let you know, Odys, that she knows everything, basically. Except where she is. We knocked her out so it wouldn't complicate things."

"But you didn't knock *me* out."

"No need, really. Leeland himself knows about this place." Dorian shrugged his bare shoulders and ran a finger over a dusty shelf, feeling the grime. *Cestus was supposed to clean.*

"Then why the hell did you knock her out?"

"Mostly for her own safety. The less she knows, the less she has to worry about."

"But I thought you said you told her everything."

"*Basically.*" He turned back to his hot cocoa.

"Why would you do that?" Odys's voice was low, trying to remain in control. "You know I didn't want her to know."

"Yeah, well, Mother didn't want her to know either, so I've not only disappointed you." He stuffed his face with a cookie. "Mother will be here soon. She's about twenty minutes away. Texted just before you came in."

"And Bob?" Rosemund asked as she rummaged through drawers.

Oh, yeah, Bob. Bob, if you care to remember, had just killed herself for mysterious reasons. Reasons I'm yet to properly illuminate.

"We can't seem to get in touch. She's likely passed out somewhere. Mother sent Ansi to go and check up on things. Mec said that she came to him right before we headed here. She had been looking for me."

Rosemund made a face at him. "I wonder why."

Odys narrowed his eyes at the conversation flow. "Yes, why?"

---

[147] Please don't wake them! I don't want to have to *reac* them.

"Honestly," Dorian moaned, "Bob freaks out when you break the rules just a little. Could be that."

"Well, your little excursions have caused us trouble in the past" Rosemund nodded to Caffar in answer to some unspoken question about the luggage.

"Excursions?" Odys repeated. But everyone ignored him.

Dorian shrugged it off. "But anyway, Rosie, to answer your question, Gwen's traveling alone. No Ansi until we find out where Bob's at. She probably forgot what day it is."

"It's not safe for Gwen to travel alone," Rosemund commented, concerned for her. She was already investigating the toaster, probably wondering how she could make it explode. "Why wouldn't she send one of us? She's the bigbigbiggest target."

"Mother can handle herself." Dorian assured (himself more than anyone else). He unplugged the toaster before Rosemund could push down the lever.

"I still don't like what you've done, Dorian," Odys lectured. "What—what did you do? How did you just—just tell her? Why would you even do that?"

Dorian frowned. "Vulcan complicated things."

Odys's brows merged. "How so?"

"I think what made things *most* complicated was that you didn't bother to tell us your sister was *married* to Leeland." Dorian was hissing now. "That was a major plot point you overlooked."

"Is that why you did it?" Odys brimmed, choking back volume. "Because I lied to you? It— it doesn't mean anything! I didn't even realize the full implications of *knowing* that fact until I synced with Maud."

"Yes, but you knew enough about Mother—sans Maud—to know your facts were valuable." His voice so low, Odys inched forward to hear: "It means he was willing to fuck her, doesn't it? Which is strange, since he killed *your* parents to get to *me* because *he* wants to fuck *Mother.*"

"You don't know if they were my parents! It's too much of a stretch." Odys felt defensive— defensive although he was the victim. "That's just what Leeland wants us to think."

"Good to know you haven't completely turned against our side of things." Dorian put another cookie in his mouth angrily. Chewing, "Look, be mad at me all you want. But you and I both know my punishment from Gwen'll be worse than any shit you can dish out."

Odys hesitated in place, wondering if he should be grateful that part was over. "And she knows what Maud is?"

"She's not stupid."

"You had no right to do that—to tell her," Odys huffed, looking at their door—the door Odissa was behind. He could feel her.

"That's not all he did to her," Rosemund said, sticking a knife in the toaster slots.

Dorian snapped at her, "Honestly, does Mother have to tell you everything? I miss the days when she didn't know how to text—"

"Wait," Odys said too loudly (making Mecca stir). "What does she mean?"

"You should tell him, Dori," Rosemund said, plugging the toaster back in—sure that it would work to her satisfaction within the tested outlet. She then began to look for the switches in the kitchen—the ones to the lights and the garbage disposal. This was her routine, to inspect for booby traps of others as well as test her own. "That's the only reason Mother lets us keep her anyway. It's not because Odys is actually oneoneone of us. Odys might even find a way to be grateful for it."

She turned on the garbage disposal and listened to it gurgle; they cringed and looked at Mecca—still asleep. Whew.

"For what, Dorian?" Odys said over the noise as it died.

"Vulcan, like I said." Dorian pushed up his glasses. "His wife got involved."

"You fucking with me now? Why do you speak in vague warnings?"

"Just go talk to your sister, Odys." Dorian waved him off and blew on his cocoa.

Odys scoffed, uneasy with the invitation to enter Dorian's room. But she was already standing there, in the doorframe when he turned around. Fletcher had just left the room. She had clearly tried to listen to this entire conversation.

Fletcher gave a mocking bow to Odys as they passed each other—a guard stepping aside for the peasant.

Odys fought back tears when he grabbed her. When Odys saw that the others were going to let them have a moment—a private moment—he jumped at the opportunity. He closed the door behind them, locking it, and not letting Odissa go. He was surprised they didn't shout at him to leave it open. "Fuck, I'm so sorry."

He pulled back to study her expression.

"Where the hell have you been?" She found his eyes too interested and too needy, so she looked away—at the messy bed that, thank God, had the sheets covering any proof of what she'd done.

"Why is your hair wet?"

323

Her skin prickled when he walked past her to inspect the room and Dorian's bathroom—how did he know it was the bathroom? Had he been here before?

"I haven't blow dried it yet," she answered quietly. It was the truth.

He paced back to her. "They told me you know what's going on. What I am. What I have." He expected her confirmation.

"Yes. An...an Automaton." She stuttered it out and beamed. She'd finally gotten it right.

"You know why you're here then?" He sat down on Dorian's bed—that unmade bed.

"It's OK, Odys." She touched his sleeved arm and sat down. "We'll be fine."

He just sat there, tired and wanting to sleep. Yet he also didn't want to take his eyes away from her. His voice dropping, "You know they *know*, right? About us." *What we've done.*

She swallowed and turned her head. "Of course they do. Half the people we know eventually let it cross their minds."

"At least we don't have to hide it, I guess." He tried to laugh, but the sound caught in his throat. It was muffled by his hands. "They know everything about us, Odissa. They've ruined us."

She didn't want to stay on that subject. "Where's Maud?" The name was foreign on her tongue.

Surprised by her question, he touched his coat pocket. Reluctantly, he took her out and placed her in Odissa's hand. It felt very exalting, to let Odissa hold his soul. He could feel her fingers tracing Maud's ridges—holding her until Maud warmed like flesh. He wanted to like it, but wasn't sure he should.

"I know what she is to you, Odys." She said it as if he'd better not deny it. "They talk about her enough. Can you make her form?"

He cringed at the use of her new vocabulary—how did she know to use these terms? *"Form."*

He took Maud from her hand and set her on the bed. Maud appeared before them, between them. Odissa stood up, as if to get away from her. Maud smiled—because Odys made her. It was a smile that said "Sorry." Sorry that she existed. Sorry in general.

"She looks different than when we first met. Not just what she's wearing—not just her skin."

He didn't like how Odissa talked about Maud as if she was an inanimate doll—normal humans shouldn't be able to tell. It was hard for *him* to remember she wasn't human, yet his sister regarded her with perfect skepticism. "It's because I'm controlling her now. I've finally—what's the word?—I've finally accepted her and we're...meshed together. She's me. I'm her."

"Like an avatar?" She was fascinated and horrified in her subject.

"Want me to make her go away?"

"No, let her be. And let her be herself."

"She doesn't have a self."

"Fletcher has a self."

"What do you mean?" *And why are you even mentioning Fletcher?*

"Even though he's Dorian's soul, right, Dorian still lets him be. She's you, right? That, there, is not acting like you. You're inhibiting her—inhibiting yourself. Aren't you?" She was staring at Maud as if watching a friendly ghost—recognizing the dead.

"How else would I act if I were an Automaton showing myself to my sister for the first time—the *real* first time?" He was sort of impressed by how he was handling her questions.

"I don't know. But she seems afraid of me. Are you afraid of me?" *I'm not judging you.*

He made Maud turn back to a coin and took her up—not only because he was embarrassed. He could no longer stand the smell Maud smelled—the scent of gods and secrets. "I don't know how you want me to make her act. I wish I didn't have her at all. Then I wouldn't have to act."

Odissa knew then that she would never see her brother again. Not as himself. He had to reestablish an identity—it was all still so up in the air. *He's a girl now too.*

She rifled for words to soothe him. "If Vulcan lets you keep her, you must be meant to have her, right?"

"What do you know of Vulcan? He lets even your goddamned *husband* keep one, doesn't he?" *She shouldn't know these words—these connotations! Vulcan, Automaton, Masters.* "What do you know about any of this, Odissa? You can't understand. I don't even understand!" He jabbed his chest with a finger, blood pressure rising.

She looked alarmed at his shaking but nodded. "I didn't mean—"

"I know you didn't." He brooded away from her. "Where did you sleep last night?"

"I'm not even sure how long I was asleep. But it wasn't just night. I woke up here."

"They gave you a room to sleep in?"

"Yes, this one." *That's what I meant by here.*

He looked around the room, seeing Dorian's suitcases scattered about. "Do you have a change of clothes? Where did you get those?"

"Dorian gave me these." She laughed, pulling at a blouse he had stolen.

Why was she laughing? Odys rubbed his face, knowing something was not right. But what? That smell burned into Maud's nostrils.

"Odys," her voice was low, "what else I should know?"

325

"Like what?" He found a smile—as if she were conspiring with him.

"The man who committed suicide? Who was he really?"

"Pepin? Pepin, gave me Maud. That's why I touched her, right after he killed himself. The first person to touch an inanimate Automaton is their Master." He went on.

"And this 'mother'—what is her name again?"

"Gwen. Gwendolyn. 'Mother' is her nickname. She's the one who had Dorian kidnap you."

"*Why* did they take me, by the way? Where were you?"

He didn't want to frighten her. "They wanted to make sure I got a job done. And they needed you out of the apartment. They destroyed it; you know that, right?"

She nodded. "Bulfinch is here too. I saw them destroy my dental records, Odys. We're 'dead.'" She used bunny ears.

"Dorian didn't do anything...bad to get you out of the apartment, did he?" He was trying to pull it out of her like a con artist. When had he gotten so clever?

She could tell Odys knew more than he could ever speak. It expressed itself outwardly. He couldn't look at Odissa the same—couldn't even see so much as a speck of dust without recalling an unfamiliar memory. He was FULL of memories. Memories that weren't his. He had to constantly remind himself that he wasn't dreaming—watching some home video—becoming someone else. And that mental reaction affected his expression. Maud affected everything. Odissa studied it.

"Dorian can be very frightening at times," Odissa assured him as she stood up. "But he didn't hurt me, if that's what you're thinking. I'm hungry. Is it OK to come out?" she asked as if he might know the rules. "Isn't there someone else out there? I heard her voice..."

Before he let her open the door, his hand still upon it: "Things will be different, now that I'm here—now that they trust me. But I don't know how different."

"No, you don't." She put a hand on his arm, telling him it was all right to open the door. "Honestly, Odys, I'm surprised they let you alone with me. Even if they can hear us. I think you have more sway than you realize." She looked at the door and gave a disappointed sigh. "This all should be more fun."

Her words sent a chill down his spine. "Fun?"

"Mythical Automatons and gods and shit. Odys I think I saw *Venus*. A fucking goddess lifted the door like in a—a hallucination or something! She was huge and yet not really there. I mean, am I making Her up?"

He frowned, not understanding and not wanting to—but *that* was the smell Maud had twitched at. "Should you blow dry your hair first?" He didn't want her out there yet.

She blushed, remembering her wet hair. And how it had *become* so wet. She touched it. She caught on. "Yeah, that's a good idea. There's one of those attached ones, on the bathroom wall. This place is a rental cabin or something, isn't it?"

"Or something." He didn't want to tell her.

She gave him a dutiful kiss on the cheek then backed away to the bathroom. "I'll be right out, then."

"And collect your things—if you have any. You'll…you'll stay with me."

She bit her lip. "I don't think I should, Odys." He could see her grow pale, could see her heart pounding in her chest. "They—they said this was my room. I don't know why. I don't want you to get in trouble." She was talking too fast.

She did know why.

"I'll talk to them. You'll at least get your own room, if I have a say."

She nodded obediently. *Oh fuck, he knows he knows he knows.*

Odys came out of the room into mid-conversation between Dorian and Rosemund, plowing over Fletcher who had been eavesdropping. They stopped their word-flow as he stood there, glaring at Dorian and flipping over a barstool.

They went quiet.

"What's the matter?" Dorian's long fingers set his cocoa mug down by the brim. He only reacted because Odys risked waking Mecca.

Odys's fist slid over the island counter, wavering between punching or breaking something. "Having Maud's memories, Dorian, lets me know a lot about you. Like how you always get the room with the best bathtub. I even seem to know the smell of your favorite cologne and soaps and lotions."

"As everyone should. What's your point?"

Odys had him against the fridge in an instant. Fletcher merely munched some cookies from a bag, continuing the conversation with Rosemund where his Master had left off. Caffar was busy staring at the ceiling bulbs. The lights had dimmed since Odissa started pulling wattage with the antique hairdryer.

"I thought you liked boys, Dorian." Odys growled. "But here she is, smelling like you and in the room with the tub. At first I thought, nah, this is just you wanting to be the gay BFF. Wanting to study up for when you finally get the nerve to chop that dick off. But that's not Odissa's style.

327

She doesn't do sleepovers. She *has no* friends. You better fucking tell me I'm wrong, Dorian. What are you playing at? You better fucking tell me this is just you wanting a fag hag, so help me—"

"I'm—I'm in love with her, Odys," Dorian replied, very honestly, very respectfully. He didn't even protest the arm choking him.

"What?"

Dorian shivered. "Vulcan told me to. Made me. Changed my—my very nature." He raised his hands to Odys's face, to his own nose. "There, you can still *smell* the gods on me. I don't want this either!"

Odys dodged his hands in repulsion.

"Perfumed ash—that's what it is." Dorian sniffed his hands as if he couldn't decide if he liked the scent, a dog fascinated with trash. "And I have no intention of chopping my dick off. I'm a femme he and always will be!"

"They have gender-neutral pronouns now, though," Rosemund mumbled, walking past them as if she could care less if Dorian lived or died.[148]

"We *transcend* gender," Fletcher snapped back, unable to resist defending how Dorian could still embrace his *he* at a time like this.

Odys shook his head, nostrils gaping like a bull's. "Do you know how sick this is? What if she *is* Dorothy, huh? What if she is?"

Dorian's face melted in sorrow. "You think I don't know how this looks? You think I wanted this to happen? It's not my fucking fault!" He jerked, rattling the fridge.

"Such an Eve!" Odys spat at him, hating how that shamed face made him feel—a face Odys made in the mirror far too often when looking at himself. "To blame someone else."

"Eve? Nah. He likes to think he's more like Paris claiming Helen because Aphrodite said he could have her," Fletcher said, licking his fingers. "Granted, both had apples involved."

Odys re-slammed Dorian into the fridge. A few magnets fell off. "What have you done?"

"I'm not the only one involved here, Odys," he warned quietly behind his wet hair. *Odissa played her part.* "And if you want to continue to be a welcomed guest, I suggest you recognize that."

Odys leaned in threateningly close. "I will not forgive you for this."

---

[148] I inserted this to acknowledge Dorian's decision to not use a they/them pronoun, but want to voice that historical accuracy is what we were shooting for. At the time, they were not as prevalent in our culture.

"I never asked for your forgiveness. Not in this." He breathed in deep when Odys let him go, controlling himself. "It's His Wife. The gods let His Wife to do this."

"*Why* would They do this? To what purpose?"

"Maybe He *really* wants to see you fuck Maud?" Dorian offered up.

Odys smacked the glasses off Dorian's face. They cracked on the floor. Odys chased Dorian's retreating visage. "Though you all fuck yours doesn't mean I'm going to. Why's He so concerned with us now, then? He's been silent all these years. How do I know you're not lying?"

Dorian uncurled. "Because, like you said, Odys. I used to fuck guys. Just look at my dick right now!" He chuckled. "I think it's proof enough when it does the same thing for her."

Odys looked down at Dorian's towel and cringed in disgust. He turned to Rosemund for input, but she was too busy taking apart the coffee maker now.

"You can join us in a threesome, if you want," Dorian gave a mad laugh—a laugh at the fact he couldn't believe what he was saying. "Might as well make sure we're incesty enough."

Odys pursued him around the kitchen island to kill him. Just as Odys was about to catch him, he jumped—the front door opened and Mother came in shouting. In Spanish, she asked Dorian *what the fucking hell was going on and why had he upset Odys?* Better yet, *why was he letting Odys beat him up?* Odys, because Maud was fluent in more than one language (do I even need to stress this point?), understood them. Picking his battles, he gave one more shove onto the ground and left Dorian.

Mother, who had just been bringing in some heavy grocery sacks, set them down and began removing her black leather gloves by each finger. Staring at her naughty children, her nostrils flared. "Odys, remember whose home you are in." She unbuttoned her black pea coat and removed her black cap. Her thick black hair was braided and re-braided down her back in one, lone mass. Her blackness distracted the puffy redness in her eyes. She looked like she'd just gotten back from a funeral.

"If I'm one of you now why can't you let us go?" *Why are we here?*

She smoothed down her skinny black dress, her hands trembling in fear that he would not forgive her. "Please, Odys, let's sit down. All of us. Let me explain."

It was like some galling "family meeting" invitation.

But Odys didn't move. "What more is there to explain? None of us are worthy of knowing what the fuck is going on in your world, Gwen. Not until it's over."

"But it *is* over, Odys," her eyes danced with happy tears. She came up to him, reaching out with that slender brown hand as if she might cup his cheek. "Don't you see? You're one of us now."

He backed away from her—from them all—in disgust.

"I'm not one of you. You didn't pick me."

Then, turning, he picked a random room (that he hoped was vacant) and locked himself in. He vowed to himself that if they tore down the door, he'd set Maud on them. *If I'm a captive, I'm a captive.*

He accepted his fate.

"No, let him go," he heard Mother say. "Give him some space. He's earned it."

Though he couldn't see it, and didn't care, Mother went back to her grocery sacks and took out some contents. "I got these for Cestus. He'll want to bake at a time like this."

"And where is Bob? Any news?" Dorian asked, rubbing his red throat.

Dead, of course, but that cover story hadn't broken the news just yet.

So let's get back to Odys:

He tossed Maud onto the queen-sized bed. "Let's talk this through, Odys." Maud's words were steely-but-faint whispers, so no one would hear though the walls—if they even cared to.

"Yes. Let's do," he almost growled the agreement, reaching out and expecting a pack of cigarettes. Maud pulled one out of her "bra," keeping a cigarette for herself. She had a whole carton in there, tucked away. They got it at their last pit stop. They may or may not have paid for it. "She was embarrassed. She couldn't look at me. She's always like that, when she…"

"Has sex with someone other than us." She snapped in front of his cigarette, making it catch fire.

He leaned forward, fingers in his hair, cigarette trembling in his lips. "This makes my skin crawl."[149]

"I know, that's why you made me say it." "At least if Dorian likes her then—" "She's twice as protected." "They can't threaten to kill her anymore. Dorian won't let them." "Maybe this is a good thing, Maud. The only reason she—she even…" "Perhaps it's necessary to give her a chance." "A chance to choose." "She's never had one of those." "Is that her?"

They stopped to listen to Odissa's genial voice through the door. She'd come out. And where was her brother?

---

[149] OK, so all this talk about Odys's face and hair yet there's no mention of his glasses lately? I find this strange but somehow forgivable. Maybe Maud makes him more confident that he doesn't need them, like Dorian?

They waited for her to come to the door—to ask to see him—to demand it—to bang on the door—to shout for him. But she didn't.

They lit up another round of cigarettes.

Stanza: Dry hair.

"You think I don't know that?" Dorian was saying to Gwen in Spanish. "Don't you see I couldn't help it?"

"There's always a choice, Dorian," Gwen admonished. "And now he'll be out of control."

Odissa's eyes flickered over the familiar and unfamiliar. Mother stood up to greet her, dabbing her eyes. They would never be dry. She glared at Dorian. *We'll finish this later.*

"I'm Gwen," Mother took her hand in both of hers, brought them to her chest. "I am very glad you're here and safe with us now. You don't know what danger you have been in. And this is Rosemund, and her Automaton, Caffar."

Rosemund waved from the table, but she didn't look up. She was too busy searching for a lost part to the dissected blender (the coffee maker had checked out).

Odissa found it hard not to stare at Rosemund's scars. And the blazing red hair, the brace-face, that goth-punk next to her.

"Rosie," Fletcher said, "Make Caffar change, you're scaring Odissa. First impressions and all."

The countless piercings disappeared back into the Automaton's head. Rosemund grumbled under her breath.

The introductions continued. "My Automaton should be here later," Mother said. "He went to pick up Bob and Cestus, who were supposed to beat me here." She looked at her watch, one last time. "Did you at least get some rest? I'm so sorry for the way we did this. Do you need anything? Has Dorian taken good care of you?"

Odissa looked to Dorian and nodded. She quite liked how calming Mother was. Even though it looked like she'd been crying, she made the room feel orderly—like she could control everything like an axis. "I'm afraid your brother was tired, so he went to bed." She leaned in to whisper, "Let's not disturb him."

Odissa's stomach tightened. Why had he abandoned her? What had she missed? Dorian sensed her questions and shook his head. *Don't ask questions, Odissa, it won't go well for anyone.*

"The long flight was long," Rosemund said—the first to come up with an excuse. "Jet lag."

"The food will be here soon, too. Pizza," Gwen said, quickly changing the subject. "Hope that's all right? What kind do you like?"

331

Odissa couldn't remember what she said. It was probably "Any."—anything to get them to stop looking at her so that she could look at them.

As if Rosemund could tell Odissa wanted free from this alien probing, she cleared her throat. Taking a deck of cards out of her pocket, Rosemund shuffled them all the way to the couch. Most were surprised she didn't take them out of her hair. "Who wants to play poker?"

Mecca sat up from his seat beside her and rubbed his eyes, fully awake now but refusing to look at them like a lazy cat considering another nap. "Poker lost its fun when Mecca lost his favorite machine gun to Dorian last time."

"Which you stole back anyway," Dorian mumbled.

"You weren't using it!" Q shouted, as if Dorian were wasteful.

Caffar, her body hardly moving as she picked something out of her Master's back pockets, unrolled two tickets as her Master said, "But money can't buy the sold-out [BIG CITY] Anime Con tickets, can it?" Rosemund sat smugly.

Mecca and Q were moving the coffee table toward them in an instant (Q wearing a fancy black-jack dealer costume and shuffling some self-formed cards that disappeared back into her palms). ANTE UP.

"You play?" Mother asked Odissa as she dabbed her nose with a handkerchief. She chose a chair in the living room, moving it forward. Caffar brought the wooden dining room chairs in, considered dragging in the actual table, left the rustic benches.

Odissa found it hard to answer Mother's question when she had so many of her own. "Not really," was the kindest response she could muster under her current frustration.

"We need a diversion, believe me. I will encourage you to wake up your brother when he's had rest. Come, you'll like it." Mother put a hand on her arm and tugged her in—a perfect hostess.

"Odissa is my partner," Dorian declared, just as Mecca had opened his mouth to. No one dared question him. Odissa found it odd that Rosemund was dealing out to Automatons as well.

"I can have my own hand," Odissa said, thinking this was awkward enough as it was.

"Yeah!" Mecca said, still moving chairs. "Give her a hand."

"No, no," Rosemund shook her head. "Mortals never have anything we want. We play for real tonight!"

Mecca grumbled, making Odissa wonder what he could possibly want from her losing hand. A boob squeeze?

Everyone settled in except Odissa, unsure where she might sit—no vacant chairs—no real space on the floor. They all looked up to her, waiting for her to sit. But Dorian patted his towel-

The Blacksmith's Circus

covered lap from the love seat beside Fletcher. "No thanks," Odissa declined, wanting to slap him.[150]

"Don't worry, my love. If you haven't caught on, they already know I'm fucking you." He said it in his toneless manner, waving his fingers just how Odissa thought Oscar Wilde might.

Mother tsked at him for saying it that way. "Your manners, boy."

Odissa turned bright red—more at the fact they hadn't ignored him.

"Here," Rosemund made Caffar give up her tight seat beside her. The Automaton could sit on the arm. But Dorian snapped his fingers.

"No, she already has a seat." He waved for Caffar to keep her ass planted.

And Caffar sat back down, glaring. *The fuck are you doing, Dorian?*

"Best show them that you like me, Odissa." The bright smile on his face did not match his dark words.

"Don't be silly, Dorian—" Gwen lifted her hand—there was a stool just there.

But Dorian cut her off. "Do I have to make you sit, Odissa? Your brother's not making you act up now, is he?" He took some gum Fletcher offered him. He chewed it under those new glasses Fletcher had supplied as well.

She looked to Mother and Rosemund. Would they say nothing about *that* comment? No, they would not. She saw where they drew the line. He showed her clearly: she was there only because she made Dorian happy. *And she best keep him happy.*

"I'm not a child, Dorian. I want a chair."

The silence deepened. Fletcher moved half an inch, daring her to sit between them. It was enough for a leg.

When she hesitantly sat down across Dorian's lap (leaning away from him toward the arm as if they shared two heads to one body), Mecca made it a point to switch places with Q. So he could sit closer to her in a wooden dining chair.

It was not normal to see a woman on Dorian's lap. It did not suit him. Even he knew this, but he carried on with the performance. The others watched the show with all the curiosity of an anthropologist interpreting a new cultural artifact they could not make sense of. Odissa wasn't being infantilized, she was being enthroned; they, her Hephaestus chair.

---

[150] Thankfully this wasn't strip poker, or we'd ALL see Dorian.

33

"You get to be my eyes, love," Dorian said kissing the back of her tense neck. It prickled her skin. "Now, let's keep Mecca from going to that con, shall we?" Dorian adjusted his towel under her.

"I will burn those tickets, if I keep them," Rosemund stated, fanning out her cards. Her glasses flashed as she studied them.

"Even though you spent money on them?" Mother asked, taking account of her own, reordering them.

"Who said anything about money? Stole them off a prick teenager."

"Sure you did," Fletcher rolled his eyes, adjusting his cards (playing with Automata increased the odds of winning, apparently, and switching out cards between a Master and Automata pair was freely done since "they know each other's cards anyway," as Gwen would say, despite her odds being currently halved).

And so Odissa watched them play poker—Texas Hold 'Em, Five Card Draw, or some variation she'd never heard of. She would put Dorian's cards down for him, for she could reach the table better, but Fletcher always double-checked her play—not because he didn't trust her, but because they had too much to lose.

And so it went.

Fletcher lost Dorian's David Bowie vinyl collection he kept in climate-controlled storage in Nebraska (to Mecca); Rosemund, not only the convention tickets, but her right to plug anything in for a week (to Mecca); Mother lost a kiss on the cheek to Mecca (which she would have given him anyway); and Dorian lost Fletcher's right to eat ice cream (which didn't bother Fletcher because he'd already eaten all of it) (to Q, and therefore Mecca).

Are they letting him win? Odissa wondered. *Or are these things worthless to them?*

"Mecca cheats," Dorian whispered to her. Which seemed true enough to Odissa, who caught all of them attempting to at one point or another. But faking cards and sleight of hand only got Automata so far when someone else was also cheating.

Still the games continued.

Their IOUs were written on scraps of paper from the notes section of Rosemund's pocket calendar. Those that didn't require a rain check seemed more like the results of Truth or Dare.

Suggestions for what the others should bet were unwelcomed, but offered and sometimes obliged. When it wasn't equal to the other raises, some refused to play a round. "No one cares about your passwords to the bank accounts, Rosemund. We can hack those anyway," Q announced. "I want to know what you did to our undeveloped Judy Garland negatives."

"You mean *my* Judy Garland negatives," Dorian grumbled.

"I won them fair and square last year!"

"Yeah, fair," Gwen snorted.

The pizza came and they kept on playing.

Mecca was most pleased with his winnings and had only once lost the right to take pictures all night (which they knew he wouldn't stick to) and had even gotten Rosemund to ante-up an experiment demonstration:

Caffar (though she had to plug her finger in the light socket, which was against their recent losses) demonstrated Rosemund's latest technological advance (for their Automaton world). "It only works if your Automaton has enveloped a rechargeable power supply inside them—car battery or something else they can hook their inner parts up to."

"She has a car battery inside her right now?" Fletcher raised and eyebrow and crossed his arms.

"She has two," Rosemund corrected. "And some...other stuff. Now, Caffar, if you will..." And she did. The lights in the house dimmed. "Look how easily the energy increases the pull of her skin," Rosemund had said as Caffar's head had split into two sparking masses like an amoeba. Apparently, with the right focus, Caffar could *almost* split. It wasn't exactly the most pleasant thing to watch (and Rosemund discouraged other Automatons from doing it) but Rosemund claimed, "It's the start to replicating an Automaton. Like asexual creatures, it's possibly possible. But it takes too much out of mymymy concentration." Her scarred lips frowned as she remembered something, making Caffar fizzle out of her hydra state. "Though it's not as if one could *actually* become two different beings. It's cloning." She looked at Q. "Not unless the Alchemy and electricity combined seamlessly, which I haven't figured outoutout how to do. I don't know enough Alchemy. Admund might know what to look for but the Words don't come to Caffar..."

Caffar wobbled in place, holding her nose as if it might bleed. But Automatons do not bleed. They sneeze out. Rosemund reached for her other hand to recharge, her own nose bleeding.

Fletcher cringed and grabbed them a hand towel.

"Is this you asking me to look into it?" Q wondered, taking out a lollipop she'd been working on for some time. What she lacked in knowledge she made up for in connections.

"If you're interested," Rosemund shrugged. "But that doesn't mean I'll give you the inner secrets to how Caffar does it."

"Another game, perhaps?"

This is how they govern themselves, Odissa observed. *This is their legislation. This is their justice.*

"Why are you trying to create a second Automaton anyway, Rose?" Dorian asked. "Not like we need more of them around."

Rosemund was not one to share reasons; that would take another card game.

But Mother checked her watch. They were running out of good material. "Odissa, maybe you should see if your brother's doing OK? I know he needs his sleep, but..." Her eyes darted to Dorian. "He also needs his supper."

Odissa jumped at the chance to get off Dorian's lap—well, it had really morphed into a position that was between his legs, the towel threatening to untuck itself at any moment.

Odissa could smell the smoke behind the closed door and the humid air of a shower. She knocked. Softly called his name. No answer. She tried the knob, just for grins and giggles. He hadn't locked it. The others weren't paying attention. Fletcher was watching from the corner of his eye, but otherwise they didn't seem to care she had been able to open it.

"No, Mecca," Fletcher squabbled, "We won't gamble our hair products on the next round. Out of the question."

Odissa let in a crack of light in the dark, smoky room. Odys really was in bed. With Maud. Fast asleep. They had used a candle as an ashtray and it barely held the butts.

At first it took her breath away—that he would even fall asleep when she was here, when he hadn't seen her for so long, when she had worried so much about him. *How dare he. He really had been sleeping.*

She knew her brother well enough. She knew this hadn't meant to hurt her, this accidental sight. Even though the naked woman in his bed—so beautiful and sweet—shocked her at first, she reasoned it out. Even her brother, there, holding the naked woman could be reasoned out.

Maud's eyes flickered open, startled. But Odys didn't stir. At first Maud's reaction was sad. Then shocked. Odissa saw her brother in Maud's eyes. A flash of anger—an anger directed at Odissa—and then a pleading apology. Odys woke up when he sensed Maud's emotions. He almost said her name but stopped.

The only thing frightening about this situation was that Odys didn't try to cover Maud's half-exposed body—the body touching him. There suddenly was no shame or grace to this intimate scene. He was letting his sister see what he had become. He *wanted* this chintzy image to impair her—as she had impaired him.

Backing out, she closed the door and pretended she hadn't been thrown off. She smoothed down her hair as if patting thoughts back down.

"He's asleep still," she told them as she came back to Dorian. But no one seemed to care. They were all too distracted by Mother, who was holding back a sob, crumpled over in a living room seat, everyone asking her what was wrong. They had noticed her get up from the table—listening to the voice in her head like someone answering a phone call—watching the images inside. Anselm, like a ghost, was speaking to her—from such a great distance—from such a horrific scene—from such an unwanted moment:

"Oh my god," Mother answered them. "He's just…" Tears welled up in her vacant eyes, as if watching something they couldn't see. "They're there."

"Who? Bob?" Rosemund pressed.

"Oh god," Mother gasped. "I see them. They're there."

Rosemund limped to her and grabbed her hand. "Who, dear?"

"He got to them!" Mother screamed, looking up as if she, too, could see Bob dangling from the ceiling. "Leeland got to them!"

Odissa recoiled at the painful sounds. She wasn't sure she should continue to enter the room. She was caught between two private worlds—caught where she didn't fit.

"What?" Fletcher pressed, his voice strained. His Master, on the other hand, had no words at all.

Rosemund pat Gwen's back—tried to get her to speak. "What does he see, my dove? What does he see?"

Mother clutched Rosemund's arm. "She—she did it, Rose. She finally did it. She killed herself."

Yes, Mother could see Bob. Anselm was standing below her in the hotel room, looking up with tears in his eyes at her swaying body.

Mother's eyes closed. Anselm's eyes closed.

Gwen did not want to see this site.

Odissa noticed a hush fall over the room. She watched it with unwilling eyes, not knowing what this really meant.

"Can Ansi find Cestus?" Mecca asked, almost panicked.

Mother looked about her, as if searching the hotel room. "No," Mother sobbed. "He's gone. Cestus is gone. He's not there. She wouldn't have hidden him, would she? She would have made it obvious—"

337

Rosemund turned to Caffar. "Go find Ansi. Help him."

"No!" Mother shouted. "Don't leave me. Don't leave me. All of you must stay here, Rosemund. Don't go." She pleaded with Rosemund, clutching her face. "I can't lose another one of you."

"Yes, Gwen. I'm right here. I won't leave. All of me isisis here."

"Has she texted anyone?" Fletcher asked the room, as if accusing them of hiding something. *Who did she tell?*

No one answered.

"Mecca saw her last," Mecca said, guilt rising in his throat.

Gwen rushed to him, leaving Rosemund behind. She picked him up in her arms and they wept together. "Hush now, it's not your fault. It wasn't you." She stroked his head.

"Can Ansi handle the cleanup?" Dorian asked, a bit too controlled.

Mother nodded, taking Q's hand as the Automaton tried to soothe her. Silver tears trickled down Q's pretty cheeks...

I'll admit this scene is melodramatic.

"I can't believe she did it." Fletcher pushed at his mouth. "She actually gave in."

"That's three he has now," Rosemund whispered. "That's *three*."

"Maybe even four if we count Madus," Dorian said.

In Spanish, Mother wept, begging God to forgive her for leaving Bob alone. Of course it would be Bob who Leeland would target next. She was the most vulnerable.

"But what did he have on her that he didn't before?" Odys said from the door frame. He had gotten up when he heard the crying.

Everyone stopped to consider, even though it wasn't pleasant. Finally Rosemund said, "Nothing." And maybe there really was nothing. No reason Bob had finally let Leeland have Cestus. Maybe *no* reason was the *best* reason, if it would make their guessing stop.

"She told Mecca that Vulcan came to her," Mecca said.

"What?" Fletcher growled. "And you're just telling us this now?"

"Vulcan came to you too," Q said, drying her eyes on the hem of Mecca's shirt. "Why would V coming to Bob be a big deal?"

"Because Vulcan *told* her something," Dorian said—growled at the Master-Automaton pair. "He told her something, and we should have known about it, Mec. Why didn't you *tell* us she knew something?" His fingers twitched to strangle the boy's neck.

"She was trying to find you. She could have told you herself," Q defended her Master. "But she didn't find you, did she?"

"You found me, though. *You* could have said."

"Long after we thought Bob had found you and gone on with her business!"

"You didn't think *to ask* why Bob wanted to find me?"

"Don't you yell at him!" Mother scolded Dorian. "It's not his fault. If Bob wanted to find you, she could have. But it...it must have been too late. She must have arranged it—" Her voice cracked. *There had been a timeline.*

And the tears started up again.

Rosemund held Gwen tighter, kissed her hair, hushed her.

They sat for some hours around the fire. Just thinking. Just waiting for Ansi. Just waiting for Ansi. Just waiting for Ansi. That's all they could do.

When Mother finally said, "He's here," they began to move again—to remember they were still alive. Odissa woke up with her head on the arm of the couch. Dorian had let Odys sit beside her, apparently. He had not fallen asleep. He had pretended to, though.

Dorian was suddenly wearing clothes.

Their eyes watched the door. Q rushed to the window. When Ansi walked in, Odys stood up from Odissa. Maud had been in his pocket since he'd left his room. That was probably for the best. It was very crowded in the house as it was.

As the Automaton walked in, Odissa guessed who it was—this small being with his head hanging low and doll-sized hand wringing the doorknob—and didn't expect a proper introduction.

They watched Ansi and Mother, expecting closure: Ansi moved his lips as if he weren't used to talking. "It's taken care of." The sound hit their ears only after he stopped speaking.

"What did you find?" Rosemund asked him—as if he might know something Gwen did not—knew things Gwen might suppress.

"I couldn't find any *reason*." His eyes flickered over the group, defeated in his study of their faces—hoping they might have a guess. "No reason."

"We knew she would break eventually," Dorian said, his voice barely audible. He uncrossed his legs and leaned forward. *We knew she was suicidal*

"How dare you," Ansi scolded him, letting the door slam behind him.

"But we didn't know she would break for Leeland. He'd never brokebrokebroken her before," Rosemund said, her hand squeezing the fancy hook of a metal cane.

339

Dorian shook his head. "She knew Odissa would be his next target to get to us. She didn't want to live through it all again."

"She didn't even know Odissa!" Odys barked.

"You think we know half the people who've died because of us?" Dorian laughed.

"Shush now." Rosemund shook a long nail at him. *Not in front of Gwen.*

"She was the only one with guts to do it," Mecca said to himself—a lonely little ball on the loveseat. Q put a hand over his mouth, realizing he had spoken it aloud. They both blushed and withdrew like an armadillo with two heads.

"I think the time is time for bed," Rosemund took over the leadership position, since Mother was avoiding eyes. She poofed up her hair nervously, waiting for obedience.

"Don't leave me, Rose," Mother sobbed, reaching out to her. Rosemund followed Mother to her bedroom. Anselm's phone dinged inside him—a muted sound and vibration. He reached for it but thought better of it. There was only one person it could be—he who was not here—and he could wait.

Everyone trickled out except Fletcher, Dorian, Odissa (who didn't know where to go), and Odys. They glared at each other's feet, unwilling to meet eyes. Odissa watched Caffar close the door behind her and her Master, those blank bead-eyes *knew* why the others lingered. Caffar never blinked. Never. Odissa's eyes blinked and begged for them not to go—don't leave her in the middle of this.

But there was a reason Rosemund wanted Mother alone.

"Odissa," Dorian spoke, crossing his arms over his sweatered chest. "Sit down." She sat back down. "Odys," Dorian addressed him, "this is a very difficult time for us. For you too, I'm sure. Maud hasn't forgotten Bob; you've lost someone as well. However, until we figure out what exactly is going on, I'm going accompany your sister. Do you understand? Let's not beat around the bush any longer. She's safer with me. Leeland won't guess that I have her. You're the more obvious choice. ¿Lo entiendes?"

"I do," Odys answered, crossing his own arms. His jaw clenched as he took a step toward Dorian. "I do understand. But I want *you* to understand I'm only comfortable with it because I know there's very little dirt Leeland *has* on you. Because you've already gotten rid of the dirt yourself, right? What little grime is left is now *part of the family*." He looked at Odissa as he said it. To be clear. To scare her. "And I'm weaker than you are. Leeland knows I'll break for her. If he comes looking for me, I don't want Odissa to be there."

"I'm going to ignore the fact you're correct but also give you my promise that—"

"Save it." Odys held up a hand. "However, I wanted to share this with you." Odys handed him the water-rippled letter from Pepin. *So you don't bitch at me like you did Mecca.*

Fletcher read it over Dorian's shoulder for him. Odissa didn't like the fact she had NO FUCKING CLUE what was going on.

"When did you get this?" Dorian whispered up at him.

"Before I left on Mother's wild goose chase, I stopped by my apartment to see the damage. Something inside me—inside Maud—told us to. Pepin meant for us to check the mail."

Dorian handed it to Fletcher, who calmly examined it—smelled it—tasted it. And then threw it in the fire.

Odissa expected Odys to react, but he didn't.

The orange fire light glowed over Dorian's body as if a demon.

"Mother already knows. Rosemund sent a text to her. Mother forwarded it to us. Secrets drift like ash. It's nothing surprising, Odys. But I do thank you for sharing it with me. I see you trust me, despite everything."

Odys wasn't surprised by Dorian's reaction. He leaned in closer, as if Caffar might be spying. "Vulcan also visited me."

Odissa's ears perked up.

"And?" Fletcher asked, tense with questions.

Odys shrugged. "And I'll see you in the morning." He kissed Odissa's head before leaving— his body pausing too long before tearing itself away. He didn't care if Dorian saw. "You know where I am if you need me. But tell him where you're going first. Don't want to *upset* him."

She glared at him—at both of them. She didn't like feeling like the placeholder.

Dorian led Odissa to their rooms. Once inside: "My brother's not as angry as I thought he would be."

"Why? You want him to be jealous?" Dorian asked, going into the bathroom to brush his teeth.

"I just don't understand."

"Well, if it makes you feel any better he did try to kill me earlier when you weren't looking. Come and brush your teeth." She watched him brush as she squeezed out toothpaste on her new tooth brush.

"Who just died?"

He did not answer immediately. "Someone named Bob. She was older than me. I was friends with her husband. She's the reason I have an Automaton, really. Her Automaton was named Cestus."

Those were the only facts that came to mind.

"Why aren't you more upset?" She began to do her own nightly ritual.

Dorian spat out the rest of his toothpaste and rinsed off his toothbrush. "Who says that I am not?"

Toothbrush impairing her speech, "I can't tell what you're feeling right now."

He was stoic once more. He waited for her to finish and then said, "I can't see. Help me find a cup. I know one's here somewhere. Fletcher's already asleep."

When they got to the bed, "Get in the middle, please."

"Between you both? But that's weird."

"Not only is it safer that way, but you'll be warmer."

"No."

"I know it's weird, but you'll get over it. Do it before I *make* you do it."

Obeying him, "So bossy."

He made her inch up close to Fletcher (who scooted in to sandwich her) and he put his arms over her in the blanket, his fingers brushing Fletcher's arm. Odissa kept on her back, hoping she might take up more room that way (which would allow her to turn sideways later and not have to touch both of them).

"I have to touch him," Dorian said as he snuggled against her. "I haven't in a while. We get sick if we don't."

"...Is he naked?"

"Why? You want me to be too?" He tried to say it jokingly, but it didn't lighten the mood. He buried his face in her neck. She felt something wet hit her skin. Dorian was crying.

So she let them have their Odissa-sandwich. She held his head grudgingly.

"Do you believe in hell, Odissa?" he whispered after choking down a sob.

"Why are you asking?" she responded quietly—as if she might wake Fletcher.

"Despite that you know there are gods walking around, do you still believe in hell—after everything you've seen?"

"Why wouldn't I believe in an afterlife?"

"No, *hell*. A place of torture."

"Why not, then?"

"Because how can so many versions of religion co-exist? Hell has little to do with the Greco-Roman gods, right? How can a normal person like you still believe in heaven?"

"I don't know what you mean. But if you think I'm so stupid, why don't you tell me what to believe?"

"There *is* hell, Odissa." He sniffed—though it was an emotionless sound. "If there's a hell then there's a heaven."

"Are you sure?" He didn't sound sure.

"No."

Fletcher started snoring softly. Something told her that the Automaton was sleeping for Dorian. He could force his Automaton to sleep but his own body was harder.

"Some say the absence of God is hell," she suggested.

"But there's nowhere God can't be. God is existence—the *gods* are everywhere. That means the condemned stop existing."

"So you think Bob stopped existing? You think she went to hell—to non-existence?"

"This isn't about Bob's fate. She sinned less than me." He reached from the covers to rub his eyes. "Even if I believed suicide was a sin, she wouldn't be damned. Where's her forgiveness? She sinned against no one. She did her gods-given job till then end."

"Then why are we talking about hell, Dorian?"

"Because I'm going there, Odissa."

"Who says? Why would you say that?"

"Because I left Bob. I've abandoned them all for you. Vulcan only makes sense to the person He directly speaks to, but Bob was going to warn me. That's why she was hunting me down. I know it. You've changed everything, Odissa."

"What's changed?"

"Who I am. I'm revenge. Leeland is the gods' leverage. I'll kill him because They allow him to live. I'll take vengeance into my own hands, because the gods owe *me*. The gods will damn me for this, Odissa. It's not justice. There's no justice from the gods."

She shrank away from his cruel face, back into Fletcher. "They won't damn you Dorian. You have every right to kill him. I wouldn't mind him dead myself."

"But your wants are nothing, Odissa—not to Them. You don't have the right to say who lives and dies. I've killed many people, Odissa. To protect my Automaton. I have let many people live as well to protect Fletcher. One of them is Leeland. The gods gave Fletcher to me and I've given my life to him. But the gods need to be punished now. And They will punish me in return. I can smell it."

She didn't know what he meant by that, but knew better than to correct a grieving man. "You've already been punished. You won't be punished more."

"How would you know?"

She held his face—thumbs too close to his blank eyes. "You're my Dorian Gray. Fletcher's your painting in the attic. You won't die. You're too beautiful. They've too much stock in you to take everything away."

He kissed her neck, lips trembling against her skin. He knew she hadn't understood his tangent. "To think I let you die once..." He sobbed.

The words sent a chill down her spine, but she found herself holding him anyway.

Stanza: Fairness and squareness.

Odys didn't brush his teeth before going to bed. He actually didn't have a tooth brush. If he'd rummaged through the cabinets, he would have found a fresh one, but he was never one to snoop. He sat on the edge of the bed, counting the cash left over from Mecca's generous donation. His feet were very cold. But he didn't want to wear his dirty socks. Tomorrow he'd ask if he could drive into town and buy new clothes. *Fucking permission.*

"It's not like the old days," Maud said sitting down beside him, crossing her legs and leaning in like a devil on his shoulder, "when you could just trade gold for anything. Now you have to have paper. Plastic."

"We should ask Dorian. He owes us. And he knows it."

"At least we have him wrapped around our finger." Maud studied hers.

"I just wish it could have been a with string less precious." Odys stared up at the ceiling, continuing his plan—his long-term plan and short-term plan—to kill Leeland.

It seemed so doable and worthwhile now.

"She likes him."

"How can you tell?"

He wanted to hear himself say it. "Never seen her have so much *fun*."

There was a silence just long enough to feel endless. "It's not Dorian's fault—"

"Never mind, I don't want to hear you say it, Maud."

Maud fell back on the bed, curls tossed about. Odys found himself lying parallel. They watched the ceiling. Maud turned to him, his impatience expressed through her. "You always knew your paradise would be lost eventually. Nothing stays the same."

"It was never Eden," he huffed. "In a way, I always knew what we were doing was selfish. Lazy. Like we were characters in a novel written in to defend masturbation—fucking yourself.[151] Loving her was loving me." He turned his head to the side, to look at her. He was reaching a point—a turning point—he'd never considered reaching before. "Funny," he mumbled, his eyes studied her face, as if seeing it differently. "Funny how much she's like…" he paused. "How much you're like her."

"You're making me act like her, that's why." Maud rolled over on her side, intent. "Get it out of the way, Odys. Let her go. She can be a part of you *apart* from you. Has she ever really been yours? She's not even fully Dorian's right now. Stop splitting her so many ways." Maud reached out and tapped Odys's ring-finger band. "Leeland could make her run to him. You never had that power."

Odys shook out that thought. "Am I trying to make myself hate her right now?"

"Leeland could make her run to him," Maud repeated, leaning into his face.

"But only because she thought we were dependent upon him."

"But were you?"

"She could always find excuses. She needed breathing room from me."

"Venus and the gods are a pretty good excuse this time, though."

"Leeland was always available as a backup plan for her. That's how she sees it."

"And we're her new backup plan?"

"I don't want to be backup."

"I don't think she wants you to be, either." Her lips pulled down. "I think by fucking her you were prolonging the inevitable, Odys. You were always meant to be alone. You've always felt that way. That's what made it so easy. You were alone with her. She was you—a version of you. You were two. But you're still two." She pointed. "One, two."

He nodded and rubbed his face. "I can see the signs, same as you."

"This is what the universe wants so there's not a lot of use fighting what you are."

Alone.

Odys, as he rammed his face into her to kiss her in a disaster of teeth and skin, accepted the fact that he'd always been cut off from Odissa, no matter how much they were from the same thread. The thread had been cut. Long ago. Only knots kept bringing them back together. And that's just what this entire life was. A Gordian knot.

---

[151] I'm not going to psychoanalyze this.

Maud took his face in his hands and he kissed her mouth hard, carelessly. As he found himself on top of her—and yes, let's not pretend this wasn't going to happen eventually—he delighted in the fact how easy it was—how easy it was to fuck her, himself. She could disband her clothes in an instant. He had no need to please her. He enjoyed, however, her pretend reactions—though he didn't make her do many. Why make such an effort? Her noises expressed his own delight. When he closed his eyes, her soundless responses made it feel real—though he liked that it wasn't. It wasn't real. Somehow the falsity of the act made it all the more acceptable.

With only one party, there was less shame.

He opened his eyes at the ironic thought. He stared down at her in her warmth as their rhythms became faster. Or, as he thought about it, *his* rhythms became faster. Maud grinned up at him—an expression he willed for her. It made her easier to fuck, if her expression provoked. As he pressed against her, he got even with his sister. He never fully had her and now she'd never fully have him. He was as self-reliant as he had always wanted to be. He let Odissa go, freed her from his over-bearing, lonely nature.

When done (so efficiently too), he made Maud lay next to him in her exposed state. "That gets rid of some of the frustration, at least…"

"…Did we just jerk off on the night of Bob's death?" He remembered. He felt no shame for what he'd just done.

"But we were quiet about it."

Odys's eyes reddened, fighting back tears at his pathetic lot in in this story. Maud held him. Odys choked into her hair. "This is why we didn't sync, isn't it? Not because of what I was repressing. But because I knew it would come to this."

"There's nothing wrong with this." With masturbating. "It's not like you did anything weird with me."

Automatons can do some weird sex stuff, believe me.

Stanza: Wash your hands after Petting the Dog.

Rosemund had finally gotten Mother to sleep and decided to take a shower before bed. Caffar sat at the bottom of the tub, bony and angled, looking up, rememorizing her Master's scars. Rosemund scrubbed and absent-mindedly thought aloud. "Bob wanted to see Odissa. That's why she was hunting down Dorian. That's what I think."

Caffar squinted past the water sprays. "I think."

Rosemund stopped scrubbing her pits and listened for a moment, as if she could hear something between the walls. No—she *did* hear something.

Maybe it was the fried wires in her brain picking up the radio-omen signals; maybe it was Caffar with her sound-magnetic ears—the only Automaton not asleep or preoccupied; maybe it was both of these beings who noticed the intruder. "Company is company—even if it's unwanted company."

"Unwanted company."

Stanza: A stranger visits strangely.

Maud and Odys had been lying on the bed for some time—hours. Dozing in and out. Not sleeping. Unable to rest. "I want a cigarette."

"Me too."

They sat up, Maud assuming a new outfit and shorter hair—the strands retracting from her face so they wouldn't disturb the future said cigarette.

"Next time I will be kinder," he told her, zipping up his pants.

"I know." He didn't have to apologize. Not to himself.

There was a soft knock on the door. Well, it wasn't even a knock. It was more like a brush on the wood before the doorknob fell off. Odys and Maud stood to their feet...as Coraza walked in.

The gun in Maud's hand wasn't matched with another's. Coraza paid no mind to it. "Answers won't be given from dead lips, Odys," Coraza warned them with a frown. "We'll make this worth your time."

Odys recognized her, of course. Maud knew who she was. Seeing her, now, he remembered her face in his own memories—not just from Pepir. Faces are easily forgotten over the years; but the fact he now realized she'd been there through part of his life, well, it sent chills down his spine. A babysitter here, a maid there.

Her face was expressionless—robotically void of awareness. She held the door opened for two others. First came in Leeland. The man who had married his sister. Following his Master was the other Automaton—the once-father.

"Hello, Odys," Leeland said—he looked about like a dad entering his son's room for "a talk." "How Maud has changed you. Aren't you going to frown at me like you used to?"

He didn't even care that there was a gun in his face, merely studied Odys for a second—searching for a reflection of himself in the boy he had made his own.

Keep staring. You made me what I am, old man.

He was clean-shaven. He wore a mid-length coat with a dark scarf bulging out of the collar. He looked so refined, especially in his unsoiled boots (Odys was sure there was mud outside, with the snow—yet he always managed to stay so *clean*). Leeland kept his bare hands in his pockets, relaxed and unworried. He'd not need to use them.

The wrinkles of his face did not age him. They added to the intensity of his look—the large nose—the ambivalent eyes—the wide-lipped mouth. But his voice was the most interesting— like crisp book pages scratching against your hand.

Maud was torn between shooting him there and now and wanting to know why he would offer himself up like this.

"I was hoping this was the right room. Rosemund usually takes the one to the right"—he pointed—"and Gwen, the one behind. I could hear Mecca snoring, and Dorian always picks the room with the biggest tub, so I figured this *must* be your room. Bob usually takes this room. But she's dead."

"Is that why you're here? To pay your respects?" Odys wasn't afraid for his life. He knew Leeland didn't kill. The only thing Odys feared was letting this asshole get away.

Maud's copper eyes flickered between the two Automatons. They stood as god-like pillars beside their Master. Today, Coraza had a slight inch of hair with shaved sides. Had Odys cared to study her, he would have noticed the designs cut into the hair—little waves like wires from machinery. Leeland had given her intricate details. Even Admund had them. Admund—Odi Odelyn—was never so fancy in his pretend life. Perhaps this was because he had always been so distant from his Master when playing the role of "the father." It took too much out of them.

"I'm sure you're wondering, Odys, if I have Cestus on me." Leeland turned out his pockets. "I don't. But of course that doesn't mean you'll believe me."

"I'm more interested in why you're here."

"I was about to ask the same of you, Odys. Why haven't you just run off—run away while you still have the chance? You really think you're safe here?"

Odys said nothing for a few seconds, staring at each part of Leeland in turn. *Is this really happening?*

Leeland chose the chair by the closet door, his Automatons framing him. "Here I am, Odys. In your grasp. My time is almost up. Take this last chance for closure, son. Go on."

Odys boiled, Maud's hand restraining itself from firing. "There's one thing I can't quite sort out in all of this, Leeland. Why make the Automaton the father instead of doing the job yourself?"

"Isn't that part obvious, Odys? No, that's not the question you really want to ask me, is it? But fine. For one, he can make himself look more like you than I can. Also, it was *always* in the books the father would die. And it would be very hard for _me_ to fake death. I can't hold my breath very long, you see."

"But why? Why did you make him"—he pointed to his once-father—"die?"

"Because you needed freedom. And I needed space. It was hard, with him being away from me for long periods of time. And I was getting so tired. Over nineteen years I acted! That, and it was very important I marry your sister. That was the most important part of all. I needed a _reason_ to get her to marry me. His death was the very thing. Ah, look, you are still so angry about it. Believe me, I never did it to hurt you, Odys. I did it to hurt others."

"Who, exactly? You think Mother gives a fuck about who you sleep with?"

"Shh. Keep your voice down," Leeland soothed. "Believe me, Mother cares. I freed two birds with one key by fucking your sister."

"Why did you?" Maud asked. "Why _marry_ her?"

"Yes, yes, get everything off your chest, boy. But look at me, not him. He's not your father. I was." He tapped at his chest. "You really want me to tell you why, Odys? Look at me. I'd be an old virgin without her. There were passions within me needing to be released. I am a pathetic man and I chose pathetic, convenient means."

"You love Gwen. If you wanted to hurt her you could have had anyone else—"

"But like Dante to his Beatrice, I could not have _her_. Having the idea of her is so much more...poetic. So I chose your sister. Like prose, it was easier to read. Isn't that what you _want_ me to say, Odys?" He gripped the knobs of the chair, his face snarling in some sort of pain. He composed himself. "No, you _know_. Maud lets you know. Without being married, I wouldn't fuck her otherwise. I'm a devout man—a _good_ man. I gave her a choice. It worked well for all of us. I thought it might even save you both from yourselves but it did not. That, and a marriage really is the ball and chain. Keeps the participants in place. I couldn't have her moving around—and I _knew_ Odissa wouldn't move around because divorce is messy. Makes people afraid of losing everything. Especially if they think they've signed prenups. Especially if they think it will bring to light all their darkness." He frowned, not proud of what he'd done. "The marriage made for a cleaner tie between us. It made the situation ideal; you couldn't stand the thought, so you would stay away. My marriage to Odissa put the perfect distance between us, Odys. Not too close and not too far. She agreed because she loved money. It made her feel secure. She can't make gold on her own. She needed me."

"Because she wanted to take care of _me_. Don't forget that. Everything she did was because of _me_." Odys glared at him over Maud's shoulder.

349

"Yes, *you you you*. It was always about you, wasn't it?" Leeland nodded. "I don't understand it. I suppose it comes from some form of guilt, why she attached herself to you. It wasn't my intention to torture you, Odys. You were just in the wrong place at the right time. I do love you as a son, Odys—as much as I can. It may seem untruthful, but I—I never expected to have a family. Not in this way. It all fell in my lap. I do not hate you.

"You see," Leeland leaned forward in his chair, "Dorian wasn't alone when he became one of us. They're supposed to be, though. He had a sister. Well, a *step*sister. She was married, too. They tried to get them to safety when I, as they will call it, 'went rogue'"—he used air quotation marks—"Dorian had invited them to his 'new place'—a diversion to get them out of their current location. The Dimitris were living in [redacted] at the time. I tracked them down quite easily. Put the bomb on the taxi. Admund was in the car, to make sure I knew what happened. Do you remember how it played out?"[152]

His question seemed to be asking something more than what was in Maud's storage space. Leeland waited for an answer, running the back of his finger over his lip. He pointed up with that finger. "I'm sorry it was all too easy. All too like fate. See, Dorian hadn't talked to his sister, or his best friend—whom she'd married—for quite some time. They'd lost touch. He avoided them because, as you know, being a Master means you have a lot of secrets. It is best to avoid people in general, to keep stories straight. And, because they wanted to surprise Dorian, they had kept a secret of their own. Dorian's stepsister had had twins. I even called Mother, to tell them the good news—to tell Dorian he was an uncle!"

Leeland spread his arms, eyes growing red. "I had hoped it would make him change his mind. But he didn't believe me. Do you know why? Because his sister was declared infertile many years before this. I found the letters of her confessing and complaining about it to him. The twins were completely unexpected. Didn't seem like they'd even been *trying*. Dorian's sister had been tested because her own mother had trouble conceiving, back in the day. A genetic thing that runs in the family, as you well know. They hadn't expected to have kids. Maybe adopt. That's what they'd told Dorian. So, as you can see, Dorian didn't believe me. He also thought his sister would

---

[152] Something that comes to mind—and sorry if this actually conflicts with what is known—is that perhaps Leeland uses bombs on non-Masters is because, if he were to use bombs on a Master, they might not work? If Masters can only kill Masters, I wonder if delayed bombs would still count? If slow poisonings would count? If intention counts? There's definitely a time delay that gives opportunity for the murderer to change his mind about what he wants the outcome for the victim to be (death or survival). And *this* leads me to wonder if that's why he could put distance between himself and the act of murder in scenarios with mortals like above? I also wonder if part of the reason why he didn't try these bombs on Masters was actually because he didn't want anyone to die, so his bombs would never work on them (thus he wants them to kill themselves)?

have told him. But she didn't. Wanted to surprise him. I was sad to spoil it. I told him when he had about, oh, thirty minutes before the bomb was set to go off. I thought that would be enough time for them to figure out if I was lying about the children or not. But it wasn't. And so Dorian started to panic. He didn't expect children. Children changed everything. Dorian had cut off ties with a lot of friends. They refused to speak with him or he couldn't reach them any longer. He had run out of ways to know the truth, you see. That's what Automatons do. They cut you off from everyone."

Leeland pulled his coat around himself, remembering. In a lowered, tearful tone, "So I said Admund could take the long way around with the taxi for a price—that Admund could get lost and slow the bomb down. I really thought Dorian would find more information about the twins in that time. Back then, though, there wasn't texting or the internet—not a lot to verify if I was lying. And even then there was the possibility I had faked their existence. I am good at faking, as you know. But as I was saying, Dorian ran out of time. Coraza watched it all—all the others helping Dorian as he suffered through the pain of burning out his eyes. I still remember it. It wasn't like a normal human wounding themselves. He healed so *gracefully*. That's what made it so...unworthy."

He rubbed his own eye as if the memory made it hurt.

"You know what he used to take out his eyes? Fletcher. Fletcher touched his eyes so exactly. They bled and then healed white. White. Not red or some other unfortunate color but pure *white*. Then Fletcher and the others tried to make phone calls in Dorian's place but they had no luck. They had some leads but it was too inconvenient to follow through. Dorian begged Coraza— begged me. But I think we all know what he let happen. He didn't buy enough time with his eyes."

He shook his head, blinking back tears that Odys wanted to crush out of his face. Leeland wouldn't be held responsible for their deaths. He would, however, have taken responsibility for saving them if Dorian had done what he wanted. *If only Dorian had done the selfless thing and killed himself.*

"Dorian wouldn't let me save them. He *refused* to do the right thing." Leeland frowned. "I sometimes think Dorian had already forsaken them and giving up his eyes was his penance for such abandonment. Not that there was much hope anyway. I destroyed the records of the twins after, you see. I also knew extra minutes wouldn't solve his problems—Masters have so many. However, before the bomb blew up, I saw something that made me reconsider my Trolley Problem. I was given an idea." Leeland paused, smiling and biting his trembling lip. He was censoring something. "Before it went off, I stole the children from their parents. At gunpoint, sadly. Well, Admund did. Your mother was screaming. I want you to know she cared about you, Odys. She didn't deserve what Dorian did to her. Admund was able to shield you both as the car exploded. But Dorian thought you were dead too. Later on, they were able to track down the loose ends and verify that his sister had, yes, had twins. He connected what dots I hadn't destroyed. He realized what he'd done."

Odys shoved aside his own personal ethics to Leeland's *Trolley Problem*. "Do you swear I *am* one of those twins?" It seemed like the more important issue.

His eyes lit up with an eagerness that scared Odys. "I can see how you'd think I might lie about that. But yes, you are. I really have no reason to lie. In fact, I've been wanting to tell you for some time. Just look at your sister, for example. Has she gotten pregnant? Even though we've been fucking her? No. She's just like her mother. I really hope you'll forgive me—forgive me for doing what had to be done with her."

"I won't forgive you," Odys laughed. "Perhaps Dorian didn't believe you'd do it. Perhaps he thought you had the wrong couple. Still does, really."

"Even so, he let them die. Here, look at these pictures I have of them, your parents." He pulled two photos from his pocket. "Look at how you resemble your father. Your mother was Cherokee. Enrolled citizen. Did Pepin let Maud remember? Your father's name was Dominic Dimitri. Your mother—her name was Doris. They called her Dory. At least, Dorian did." He noticed Odys wasn't entirely interested in the photos, so he put them on the nightstand. "They called their twins Dorothy and *Doric*."

MAUD: Automaton of Doric Dimitri

MONEY: It changes you. She'll change you. She's change.

CHANGE: She's not the same Automaton Pepin once had.

TWIN: Your two cents is worth something. Be careful how you spend it.

Chapter the second,

It was always so simple:

But does that make it less complex?

Leeland raised a brow. "But you knew that, didn't you? You knew. I know you can't forgive me. I don't expect you to. I can't forgive myself, either. I hate that I have them, these Automatons. No one should have them, Odys. No one."

But Leeland will be their willing burden. A martyr. A saint.

"Someone will always have them," Odys said, straightening up. His mouth twisted to keep from matching Leeland's frown.

Leeland's old eyes danced over Odys's face, searching for interpretation to the words. "So you know it can't be helped. That's why someone—and only *one* someone—needs to have them all. So that no one else suffers. Someone needs the burden all to themselves."

Odys stepped forward from his half-crouch by the bed, threatening as best he could. But he could not bring himself closer. "You created the burden, though, Leeland. You did. It would be easier to bear if you didn't kill everyone."

"Would it?" He scratched his graying hair, oiled back and parted with precision. Odys noticed the wedding ring on his left hand. It made the fury boil up inside him. "Are you so sure that everyone agrees with you? After all, Bob saw the light, didn't she?"

Maud raised her gun, ready to get this over with. Her eyes burned like fiery coals.

But something deep inside Odys told him to stop—a ghost's voice saying *No—not yet. We must know.* "What did you have on her? What did you threaten her with?"

Leeland's eyes reddened with tears. He covered the bottom half of his face to hide his weakness. "The funny thing is, Odys, I didn't. I didn't threaten her with anything. She had nothing I wanted—except for Cestus. She had nothing *anyone* wanted." No leverage. No life. "It was her time to go. She wasn't happy. It's not suicide, you see, when it's the only way out. It's only reversing immortality—our curse. Our souls are damned if we stay. Vulcan, our devil."

Maud, the only part of Odys that could push through the rage caused by this pathetic display, demanded: "Why did Pepin give me to Odys? Do you know where Madus is?"

Leeland pursed his lips and calmed his face. "I think Pepin thought I wouldn't harm you. I think he knows how fond I am of you and your sister. Perhaps that. Or perhaps he knows I've nothing to threaten you with, since your sister is something I'm using to threaten someone *else* with." He watched Odys's expression, wondering if he believed him. "But Madus? No. I'm not the one who has him."

"Just like you don't have Cestus."

Leeland smiled at that, laugh sounding through closed lips like a muted cicada. "You've never spoken like this before. It's strange, to have you *aware* of what's going on. Your sister was always better at it than you."

"What do you mean you can't threaten me with my sister?"

Leeland averted his gaze, his Automatons becoming uneasy. He lifted a hand the way you lift your shoulders to shrug, searching for words. "Gwendolyn, of course, boy. How could I kill my wife when she's doing exactly what I meant for her to?" He stood, eyes daring Odys to shoot him—go ahead. He did not care.

Why didn't he care?

"I have been trying to show Gwen her selfish ways. The most I got were penitent tears. But now? Now that she knows she is finally listening to me. And Bob overheard, it seems."

"The fuck do you mean?"

Leeland turned to leave—as if he were allowed—but stopped. He remembered something worth saying. "I tried to get her pregnant, your sister. I really tried. Admund's sciences failed. It might have made things a lot easier for all of us—given us more time. Things would have been different. You wouldn't have had to be involved for so long. But, thankfully, I can work with what I have. Good bye, my boy."

Wait, wait, wait.

Something needed to happen. And that something was Leeland's death, for sure. As the Automatons escorted Leeland out like human shields, Odys briskly followed. And Maud was even faster. "Stop!" Maud shot at him, aiming to miss. "Don't move." She needed to know where Madus and Cestus were first, before she finished him.

The funny thing is, though, that Coraza and Admund didn't try and protect their Master. In fact, they didn't need to. He was protected by Anselm—who had come out of nowhere.

"Do not!" Anselm ordered Maud. Once and only once. Odys, through his focus, realized that everyone was watching—out of their rooms. They had been listening. Mecca from Q's arms, Rosemund and Caffar from bath towels, Mother from the center of the room.[153] Dorian was just opening his door. Fletcher and Odissa popped out their heads. Odys noticed Odissa's eyes growing wide. Fletcher was shielding Odissa—telling her to get back.

Rosemund was a good, welcoming hostess: Caffar assumed a nice cattle gun. "Nice of you to stop by, Lee. And I mean that sarcastically."

"As if I couldn't tell," Leeland laughed at her. He walked around the coffee table, taking them all in like a proud grandparent. He jerked when Maud went for him again.

Maud glared at Mother as Anselm's hands caught hers from the floor, causing her to spark. Anslem had gotten to her in a matter of seconds. His long white hair twisted like snakes around him. His hand was alight with radiating soul—it clicked with a scraping, ratcheting sound.

---

[153] Why is Caffar in a bath towel???????

Maud's own skin continued to glow where Anslem touched her, yet the two would not submit. Admund and Coraza seemed well at ease.

Leeland's eyes landed on Mother. His eyes lit up at the sight of her. Just as he had wanted.

"Don't, Odys," Mother said, raising a hand as he took a step forward.

"What the fuck?" Q shouted at Mother, her gun ready to shoot. Mecca's brows knit together as he peered from behind her.

"Put the gun down." There was a strain in Gwen's voice. She didn't look well. It threw them all off, upon considering it. It was Maud who was finally able to look past it—able to do the math.

Maud shot at Leeland again, but Anslem blocked it with his shoulder, shoving into her. His skin boiled back into flesh, ringing and popping their ears. The wall where Maud's "bullet" hit did not catch fire, but it smoked behind Admund, his face blank and unbothered.

"Why?" Maud demanded, not relenting so easily. Leeland was so close—right *there*. She tried to push past Anselm, but Caffar jumped forward to hold her back.

"We need what he knows."

She sizzled and rang. "If he does have the Automatons, then he's not telling. Killing him wouldn't be any less than the leads we have now!"

Mother stumbled over to the back of the nearby couch. "You will do what I say or we will have reason to disown you, Odys."

"I won't let him walk away from this. I don't care where Cestus is—"

"Don't let anger from what he's done to you and your sister dictate your reaction, Odys. I need him alive. We all do. He's not going anywhere." She was staring down Leeland now.

Maud thrashed against Caffar one more time and Anselm stepped back. They stood in silence as Leeland observed Mother. When he finally spoke it was: "You are not well, Gwendolyn."

"You've seen what you came to see, Leeland. Don't make this more complicated. I can't control their hate for you. This wasn't what we agreed on!" Her words caught their attention—the tension snapped through the room.

"You look beautiful, though. Despite that he's draining you."

She flinched as if his words had made her heart stop. *Don't say it where they can hear.*

"But it's easier, the second time, isn't it? The soul's already been split once. The body has been through it before and knows how to cope—it remembers."

The Automatons drew to their Masters, recoiling from a traitorous Gwen and Anselm. Dorian stepped back to his door, where Fletcher was making sure there was something between Leeland

355

and Odissa. Guns formed in the hands of the Automatons. Caffar's fingertips buzzed with soul-light.

"How dare you—in front of them!" Mother spat. She could barely keep her eyes open from the pain. "You've betrayed me."

"No, my love. I've given you a reason to actually carry out what you promised me." The others were too caught on his tangled words to kill him yet. "I had to make sure you weren't lying to me. But I see that you weren't." His eyes gestured to her form. She looked as if she might pass out any moment—just as Odys had looked only nights ago.

"Forgive me," Leeland continued to Gwen, reaching into his coat. "It felt too good to be real. But at least I'm sure you have enemies now. A picture over text isn't proof enough. Images are faked—your hand, holding him." He looked around the room, noting their reactions. "These reactions are not faked. And apparently neither was Bob's when I sent her the screenshots of our conversations—even though she accused them of being fake; she *reacted* against her words. At least I'm sure you'll be worth it now."

"Worth what now?" Gwen hissed through her red, wetting face. "You have ruined everything—" *This wasn't how I was going to tell them.*

"Don't blame me for this, Gwen." *This is for your own good.* "I love you, Gwen. Don't worry, I'll keep my end."

He'll stop toying with them now. He'll stop fantasizing about eternity with her. He'll stop.

Her body buckled over, his words shaking her. Her fists turned white. "I know. I'm sorry. I'm so sorry." *I'm sorry I don't love you.*

But the others could not see her face; was she acting? Was this really happening?

He stopped looking at her—at them. "Don't be sorry. What's wrong has been made right." He checked his handgun they hadn't seen him pull out, cocking it. His hand was shaking but his flow was steady. Everyone's eyes grew wide. "I know we didn't plan it for tonight, Gwen, but I'm ready now. I've been ready, you see, for a very long time. I don't want to die by an Automaton either," he said, exhibiting the gun. "I wasn't born by them and I won't die by them." He pointed it to his head—just like Pepin had done. "May we finish what He started."

The blood rippled through the room. His Automatons fell down, inanimate.

They let the guts settle before breathing again.

"Jesus fucking Christ," Dorian cursed, turning back around. The blood had sprinkled even in their direction.

Rosemund's eyes darted to Odys. She took off her glasses, to wipe the blood on the clean side of her bath towel. "Well, I think we're owed an explanation, Gwen."

Mother, whose legs sagged a little at the knees, left her perch and found a blood-splattered chair. Anselm helped her into it. She was not crying now. Her eyes were wide with shock—with fear. She looked at Dorian—at Odys. She noticed Odys still had Maud's gun at the ready. She shook her head, "I didn't mean for him to do this."

She waved a trembling hand over the mess.

"How did you get him to do it?" Dorian pressed, though the deep sound in his voice let everyone know he already guessed the answer.

"I—I lied to him," she looked at her clenched fists, splattered with small dots of his blood. She wiped them on her knees, smearing and staining more. She looked once to the corpse but focused on the dripping ceiling instead. "It was the only way to get him to do it—to get him here." *On the floor.*

"But what was the lie you lied?" Rosemund asked, using her towel corner to smear the blood off her arms.

"I—I had him all along. Madus," she looked at Odys—but not at his face. Never his face. "Even before Pepin killed himself."

A lie of a lie of a lie of a lie!

"You knew about this?" Dorian snapped at Rosemund.

"I know about things *about* it." Rosemund used Caffar's towel corner on Mecca's pouting face. He backed away from her—no longer sure who to trust.

"But don't think I know why Pepin killed himself," Mother begged. "I don't know why Pepin chose—of all people—Odys. I know it was wrong to lie to you—all of you—all this time. But I saw an opportunity. I took it. Just now. I took it. Oh, Dios mío, I took it."

"And where is he then? Where's Madus?" Dorian pressed, stalking her. Gwen could see the effects of her betrayal on his face. "How did you get him?"[154]

---

[154] At this point, I flipped backward and reread Pepin's letter. I'll copy and paste it here for you as well:
Dear Odys,
I gave Maud to you for a reason, but I am sure you have figured that much out by now. If anyone asks, Madus is safe. I have a plan for him as well. Also, though it might not matter (depending on how you take to her), tell Maud I am sorry I had to make her forget. I know it sounds silly, because an Automaton does not have personal feelings, but I left a part of me in her that will understand why I erased so much of her—rather, me. At least, I hope part of me is still in her. I plan to leave myself there. I apologize to myself, then. Just in case.

"How should I know why Pepin finally gave him back?" she snapped. She rocked slightly in place. "I don't know anything about that damn circus man! But I used him. I used Madus, Dorian. I knew Leeland would have so much on us now that Odissa and Odys were here, and so I took him. I took Madus. I *lied* and said I would give myself up, Dorian. I lied to Leeland and said I saw the goodness in his plight and Leeland believed me! He gave himself up instead. He told me to take over his role. Because he loved *me*." Her face contorted, disgusted with herself. "He believed me too," she gestured to the floor, where the blood was pooling around the headless body. "You know he wouldn't have stopped. I finally stopped him, Dorian. Lo hice parecer *real*."

"Too real," Rosemund said gently. "Too real is too real, Gwendolyn."

But Gwen did not need to beg for Rosemund's clemency. Rosemund would love Gwen no matter what.

"How the fuck was this the best way to stop him, Gwen?" Maud shouted at her—at them all—her mad eyes demanded the others agree with her.

"I had to make him believe me, Dorian," Mother tried to explain herself to him, as if he held her fate. She held out her fist—and whatever was in it. "I don't know why Pepin killed himself but I know he wanted to keep Leeland away from Madus." Her fingers opened to show Madus—that modern-day penny.

"He didn't send him to you," Odys said, realizing that his first guess about Pepin's birthday gift to Rosemund had been correct. "You stole him from Rosemund's mail."

"And even if I did?" Gwen tried to shrug—too weak for forcefulness. "Rosemund didn't care. She didn't stop me. Tell them, Rosie! Dígales…"

Rosemund sighed, her eyes closing for a half-second. "This is me telling you, Dorian." She came to Gwendolyn and cupped her head. "Shh, shh, now. I know."

\

The real reason I am sending this message is to tell you no one is safe. Leeland may think—may even tell you—that my actions speak for him, but they are entirely my own. Do not trust Leeland, and certainly don't trust Mother. I will not go into detail as to why but—

Well, why do you think I have avoided them both all this time? Hell, I should probably tell you to not even trust me, because I have played my part in this. I have known for a while what Leeland had done to you and your sister. I am just now getting around to doing something about it. I hope you will forgive me—though hope is of little help to you. What help is a dead man?

I am sending this letter—well, my friend is sending this letter for me, I will be dead by the time it needs to be sent—in a way that will hopefully keep them from finding it in your mail—Vulcan willing. I know they will check everything on you until they "trust" you. And even then they will not give you peace. Only when you are dead can you rest. I have learned that the hard way.
-Pepin J. Pound.

"If Pepin didn't want me to have Madus he wouldn't have been so stupid as to send him in the mail!" Gwen cried up to Rosemund, her voice reaching hysterics. All her gasping made her start to heave. She leaned over the arm of the chair and vomited, not caring where.

"Now, nownownow," Rosemund grimaced. She kneeled down and threatened to flash everyone with what was under her bath towel.

Anselm glared at them all, studying their reactions. He noted Odys's own glare.

"I broke the rules to fix the rules," Gwen confessed, gripping the sides of her nightgown. She was pleading to Rosemund for forgiveness. Forgiveness was easy to come by, but not easy for her to accept. "I didn't think it would be so simple. But it was. I don't know if this is what Pepin expected me to do, but when Bob died, I knew Leeland was in action. I touched Madus tonight."

"No shit," Odys said, waving an arm at the floor—her vomit.

"And where does Bob fit into this? Do you know where Cestus is?" Dorian demanded, gesturing to the untouched Automatons on the floor.

"I don't know." Gwen shook her head. "But I had wanted to find out. That's why I had to touch Madus. I knew Leeland was skeptical. I knew it! He was testing my reaction to her death. I don't know why she gave into him. He was there, ready to take Cestus—like he knew she was going to do it. Maybe Leeland told Robyn my lie and she believed my lie? She believed I was taking over Leeland's plight? She died thinking *this* was what I wanted…"

And Mother began to weep into her hands.

"No," Odys shook his head, his face falling. "Vulcan let her believe it too." *He didn't stop it.*

They watched Mother weep.

"He wanted us to hate Mother?" Mecca squealed, wiping his tears away on the back of his sleeve. "He wanted Bob to die?"

Dorian rubbed his face, trying to hide his own tears. He had never hated Vulcan so much.

"We don't know where Cestus is," Anselm told them, his own eyes were cloudy and weary. Mother could talk no more, so he would. "This wasn't part of the plan. We thought Leeland would tell us if we did this. We know we broke the rules. We wait your judgment accordingly."

"There is no judgment," Dorian whispered down to Mother. "Not tonight."

"Are you kidding me?" Odys growled, every inch of him objecting.

Dorian's voice deepened, as if to match Odys: "We know what Leeland would have done if he hadn't been stopped. He would have…" Fletcher's eyes flickered to Odissa, who was lingering in the doorway. "She saved us from him. We are too tired to make decisions tonight."

"To bed, then," Rosemund said. "Clean yourselves up. Fletcher, you'll tidy this mess. You too, Odys, Maud. You helphelphelp me." By mess, she meant body. Caffar glared at everyone until they started moving—especially Mecca who had eyes that asked to stay. But Mecca was too upset for such work. He never worked well when upset. Rosemund sent him to shower and bed—one of them needed full rest, at least.

Dorian told Odissa to go back to sleep. She wanted to obey him, but she would find she could not sleep. Even though her life was no longer seemingly in danger (*That's what this meant, right?*), this greyness bleeding into what was once black and white made rest unthinkable. She would spy on them through the door; she would filter out the contrasts.

Fletcher was already putting on Dorian's leather gloves (strange for an Automaton to do) and placing the inanimate Coraza and Admund on the coffee table. Maud pulled off some bed sheets and used them to wrap up the body after they had stripped it. They'd turned out his pockets—to make sure Cestus wasn't in there.

"I don't want to say Mother is lying to us, but I think Gwen is lying to us," Maud whispered, hands on her hips. Or perhaps her arms were crossed. Whatever sounds best, so long as you know she was skeptical.

Dorian brushed off the comment. "Even if she is, she has good reason to. I'm sure."

"Are you *fucking* kidding me? You're going to side with that psycho in there? She got Bob killed!" Odys hissed at him. "And now what Automaton is Odissa gonna get?"

"I guess we already know your vote then, huh?"

"Oh, I *get* a vote, do I? Is this why Gwen made us come here? So she could break this news to us like some mom telling us she has cancer? She *is* cancer!"

"Less yapping more cleaning," Rosemund barked, tossing a paper towel roll at them.

"Should I make a store run?" Dorian offered. They were going to have to do a lot of cleaning.

"No. We'll just burn the place in the morning." Her eyes looked up at the brain-decorated ceiling. Those eyes were sad behind the magnifying lenses. "We won't want to vacation here again. Vacations are to escape the past, not be haunted bybyby it. Just clean what we want to keep."

Odys studied her little body, the bath towel engulfing it. He could make out her scars so easily now—a whole map covering her. Caffar held the door open as the other Automatons took out the body to the garages. "Whose car are we taking?" Fletcher asked as they exited.

"I'm done for tonight," Dorian said and he went to his rooms. Part of him should try and get some sleep.

Before the door was shut, Odys glanced into those rooms, the rooms with his sister trapped inside. She was sitting on the bed—and then the door closed.

"If you don't mind me saying so," Rosemund said, "I think Leeland wantwantwanted this."

"What do you mean?" Odys asked, wadding up a paper towel. *Of course he wanted chaos.*

"He wanted to say goodbye to you. He wanted a way out. Could you live with yourself, Odys, if you were him? He'd tried so hard these past decades to break us. He finally thought he had. But he wasn't willing to carry out the work after he broke us, was he? Even though Mother made him believe he was always right, he didn't actually want to be the oneoneone to carry out his justice. As long as he had—in his mind—been proven right, then he did not care to live. He had life figured out. He didn't want to be the only one with all the Automatons. He'd let Mother do that."

"He loved her."

"Yes, but he loved the thought that she'd given into his logic all thethethe more," Rosemund frowned. Her damp curls made her look all the sadder.

Fletcher came back in, "Forgot a lighter," he explained, eyeing them. He waited for Odys to fork one over.

Rosemund called after him. "Don't forget to mark the spot. It will look different when the snow is gone. We need to be able to find it come spring. Forgotten grave sites are forgotten." Fletcher saluted Rosemund sloppily and went on with his business.

"You going to decorate that bastard's grave?" Odys frowned at her.

"Odissa might. She has before, I hear. Come have some milk with me, Odys."

Realizing she wanted to talk to him way from doors, he didn't protest.

"I won't leave you alone with your lonely thoughts just yet. Being alone is lonely." She sat down the carton of milk in front of him as she found two glasses. She poured him a drink and downed the rest from the carton. Such a strange woman.

She noticed his eyes looking out the window over her shoulder. The sun was rising, making the winter sky an off-orange pink. Through the trees and across the street she could see the neighbors. "That van of theirs, in the driveway. It would fit all of us nicely. I'm going to steal it in the morning. If I can. I would call a taxi, but wewewe need to keep people from coming here. Can't have people knocking on doors and seeing blood splattered everywhere. And it's too much trouble to gogogo and rent one. They always want to see identification. I'd rather not go through that if we can work around a taxi. That van's always there. Begging to be taken. Room is room and we'll need more of it."

361

"Are we going someplace?"

"That depends on how many stick around after the vote."

The vote to keep Gwen alive.

Not drinking yet, "You knew all along that Mother had Madus."

"I am her oldest friend. Of course I knew."

"She didn't care if you knew or not?"

"She knew I wouldn't do anything about it. Because she knowknowknows I trust her. It's that very trust which makes me valuable, Odys Odelyn."

He scoffed, not only at the statement but at how she always glitched *in threes*. He mumbled "Know" one more time for her to make it an even number and pressed, "Don't you get tired of the—the lies?"

"If lies protect us, then why would I tire of them?"

"They didn't protect Pepin. They didn't protect Leeland."

"That's because they knew the truth, Odys. They knew too much of it." She picked up her unused glass. "They *believed* in too much of it. Do you want to know why it was so easy for Leeland to believe Mother's lies? Because her heart was in it. She believes herherher own lie. Only partially, but she still believes in it. You know as well as I that she's always thought Automatons shouldn't exist. She may not want them all under one Master, but she doesn't want any human to suffer with them. Part of the lie is only part of it, but she still believes that part."

"Bob was willing to die for her even if she was planning to take them all." Odys downed his milk as if it were alcohol. Anything to get the taste of those words out of his mouth.

"Bob had been willing to die for a long time. If she thought Mother had plans of her own, why's it so hard to think she believed Mother might do good?"

She's trying to sway my vote, Odys thought. "Because Mother's 'good' isn't any *more good* than Leeland's." He looked over her shoulder, out the window. The sky was brightening now—he could see it. The Automatons had better hurry.

"You think it's not, but how is it not? Your sister's life isn't in danger anyanyanymore. Neither is anyone else's."

"We don't know where Cestus is, do we? What good does that do us?"

Rosemund didn't say anything for a moment. Just looked at the wall behind him. "Funny, isn't it, that Anselm showed up after Mother last night? She was running late herself." He eyed her suspiciously. She picked up her unused glass and turned it over and used the concave bottom to better examine her bright nails. "Bob wanted out. She found something that justified her outing—just as Leeland found something to justify his."

"After all these years, why did Mother *just now* decide to lie to Leeland?"

"I think we all know the answer to that question, Odys, that question that we're asking. *You're* in the picture now. We were making up forfor sins. All of us let you die once before. Now you are free to live your life. We all are."

"What life?"

"You have a goose that lays golden eggs, and you're acting like there's something that inhibits you? The world is youryouryours, Odys, because you already have it. You have something everyone wants and that the world revolves around—gold."

"It can't buy my old life back, can it?"

Rosemund licked her braces in thought. "No, but you could always kill Dorian. Then she'd have no choice but to come back to you."

"I wouldn't."

"I'm glad to hear it. We just got rid of one Leeland. We don't need another."

"Mother's the new Leeland, Rose," he said without inflection.

"Then tell them so. Don't vote for her. Leave us. We have a new Leeland and we need a new Pepin. That seems to be the onlyonlyonly way this damn lot can function."

"You call this functioning?"

"I meant when we had two of them—when we had a Leeland and a Pepin—we were fine, fine, fine"—she gave herself a tick, noticing him counting and rounding her up under his breath. He restrained himself this time and she smiled a scarred, knowing smile. "Now we're all astir."

"Not Dorian. Dorian's happy."

"You think he's happy, do you?" She pulled out a pen from her drying hair. "No. Love does not equal happiness. Odissa will make him happily miserable. I can already seeseesee it. Not only is she free to reject him, but you're still in the picture, Odys. It's not veryveryvery fair on him to constantly fret on whether or not she still loves you and could come back to you." She finally stopped waving the pen around and wrote something on her hand.

Is there anything to come back to? He sighed and brooded.

She finished writing *STEAL VAN* on the back of her hand and said, "Come now. There must be *something* to live for besides Odissa, because you haven't diediedied yet, have you?"

He nodded, agreeing. "Vulcan. He's using us, and I will find out how and why and kill every damn thing He plans."

"You think that's possible?" she laughed. "He probably means for you to say such a thing as what you've just said!"

"If I can't dictate my own purpose in life, then I'll accept it blindly. Vulcan means for me to hate Him, so I will." He leaned forward on his elbows, as if threatening *her*.

"You really want to accept your fate that you think you want to accept, Odys?" Rosemund leaned in to match him. "Then take this advice." She paused for effect. "Become Pepin. Leave us. Pepin gave you Maud. The gods let him do it. You're his replacement in this game. Like I said, we were doing just fine with a Pepin and a Leeland. Now look at us. At each other's throatthroatthroats."

Stanza: After the deleted scenes there's still a story.

The three Automatons who had just "gotten rid of" Leeland came in from the cold, their job done. They stomped the snow off their feet-boots. The blood-splattered living room could wait until tomorrow. It was time to recharge with their Masters.

But before doing so, the three Automata bent over the two inanimate Automata. They would begin the second round debate for their Masters:

"How will we keep these safe?" Maud asked. "Who will watch them?"

"Caffar and I will each take one," Fletcher said. He gestured to them in their new plastic bags.

"How's that fair? Rose knew Mother had Madus. We can't trust her. No offense, Caffar."

"No offense, no offense."

"We have seniority. End of discussion," Fletcher said, reaching down to pick the bags up.

But Caffar caught his hand. She shook her head. Rosemund didn't want this to be decided tonight. Leave them there. She pushed them away from the coffee table where the inanimate Automata slept and went to her Master's room.

Stanza: The author's Hand Wave.

That morning at brunch (everyone slept in late), Dorian pulled out a chair for Odissa so that she might sit next to her brother. Between them. Maud and Odys were both drinking coffee, Odys smoking his last available cigarette, Maud holding a frazzled ~~me~~ Bulfinch. Maud passed ~~me~~ Bulfinch to an overeager Odissa, who squeezed ~~me~~ him in her arms.[155] *Thanks so much for your concern up until now, Odissa.*

---

[155] I leave these edits in there to remind you what I have to deal with on a daily basis—I have to deal with someone who thinks they are a cat! Or, excuse me, someone who thinks they *were* a cat.

"I have more if you want them—in my purse," Odissa told Odys quietly, about the cigarettes. She seemed nervous—embarrassed, even—to see him. She used Bulfinch as a distraction, trying to feed him toast crust Maud had just offered.

"I'll be just fine, Odissa," he replied. _Don't make them notice me._

She ran her fingers into Bulfinch's scruff, keeping herself from doing something stupid. ~~I just wanted to go back to my bathroom. It was safer there and less stuffed with weirdos.~~

"We're out of milk," Fletcher informed. "That means only orange juice or coffee." He stood up, going to get the coffee. Odissa didn't even have to place her order. He presented her a full mug.

Dorian turned to Odys. "Yes, Mecca was very upset about the lack of milk. He bought that specifically for Bulfinch. Some must have been _spilt_ last night."

When Odys didn't bite, Fletcher added. "Must have some giant babies in this house. They should apologize to Bulfinch."

Odissa was about to forgive all and announce milk usually made him throw up when—

"Not giant babies. Giant liars." Odys stuffed his face with some bread, as if more words might come out if he didn't stopper them.

"That's your final vote, huh? Mec's already said he's in if we're in. Rosemund's in of course. That leaves our vote," Dorian said. _And we already know how I'll vote._

"I swear to God, Dorian," Odys snarled at him, "You worship the ground that bitch walks on."

"If it weren't for 'that bitch,' we'd still be at a stalemate with Leeland."

"She used the one Automaton we had that would keep Odissa safe."

The raised voices made Bulfinch hide under the table in Odissa's lap (this conversation was beneath me and I was afraid to be associated with it, you see).

"She—we were never going to be safe with him. I'll not kill Mother over this."

Odys glared at Dorian. "Fine. Vote to keep Mother in. Fuck your democracy. You vote on rules just to break them anyway. But think on this, Dorian, she could have admitted to us—all along—what her plans were. God only knows how Rosemund figured them out. Maybe we would've _let_ her touch Madus then. But no. She has you—and everyone else—believe from the beginning that _I_ know something about Madus's whereabouts and that _I_ know where Pepin hid him. Fuck you and your Mother." He stood up and plopped his cigarette butt into Fletcher's glass of half-drunk orange juice. Stormed off to his room.

Crickets.

365

"That's how you decide if someone lives or dies?" Odissa asked, horrified. "You vote on it over breakfast?"

This was why Bulfinch preferred the bathroom.

Stanza: Mother knows best.

A few minutes later...

Rosemund peeped her head in the kitchen. "I told Gwen."

"Are you packed yet?" Dorian asked her.

"Yes and no. Caffar went for a gas run for the living room a fewfewfew hours ago, but she's back now. She's packing for me. I'm going to go hijack the neighbor's van. Spacious vans are spacious, you know. We'll all fit in it."

"Don't bother, I'll do it," Fletcher said as if it was ridiculous for a human to go to the trouble of stealing vans.

"No, no. I need out of this place. And don't insult me. I know how to wirewirewire a van."

She loved a challenge.

"All right then," Dorian waved her off. "But if you get caught don't expect me to come bail you out."

To Odissa, "Don't let him fool you. I've saved his ass from needing saving more than he's ever saved mine." Rosemund shuffled out of the room, her windbreaker swooshing.

Odissa leaned in, "I want to like her, but she's a bit insane, isn't she?"

"No more than you or I."

Fletcher got up for a new glass to replace the one Odys had tainted. He took his time in the fridge, debating on what drink he wanted. As he straightened up to pour, his eyes looked out the kitchen window. Fletcher paused. "Oh my God..."

Odissa noticed Dorian pause as well, as if inclining his head to the radio. He was watching what Fletcher was seeing through the window. Fletcher dropped his juice and ran to the living room.

Odissa stood up to see what he was looking at—Odys driving with Maud—away—driving away! I struggled in her grip, not caring what they saw.

They chased after Fletcher to the living room.

"He took them." Fletcher picked up the note Odys had left in their place. "'You know I will not touch what he has touched,'" Fletcher read for their/our benefit. "'And I won't let you give one of *his* to Odissa. Call me when you want to discuss how they're used.'"

They stood there for a while.

Mecca and Q came running into the house from the back (where they had been wiring the house, readying it for explosion). "We saw one of the cars was gone—who left?" And then Q saw the bare coffee table. "Where are they?"

"Odys. He took them," Dorian barked at her.

Bulfinch tried to leap from Odissa's arms, scratching her.

"You want Mecca to go after him?" Mecca asked. already headed to the door.

"No," Gwen said, coming out of her room with her bags. She still looked sickly and unbalanced. She had yet to show them Madus fully formed, as if she was ashamed of her new face. "He is one of us now. He is the safest place for them. I think this is a fair trade, all things considered."

At that moment, Rosemund walked in through the back door. "Why is everyone standing around and just standing? Are we leaving or not? It won't be long before thethethe neighbors realize their van's gone. We need to hurry—"

"Odys took the Automatons, Rosemund." Fletcher said.

"He took both, right?" She squinted and wheezed at the coffee table.

"You knew he was going to?" Mecca's brows lowered.

"He had every right," Gwen said. "Now, let's stop talking about this and get going."

Dorian recoiled. "We're not going with you."

Anselm narrowed his eyes. "Why not?"

"If Odys has a right to steal the inanimates, then I have a right to solitude!" Dorian proclaimed.

"Fine," Mother said, tears welling up. "We go our separate ways." Family vacay was over. "But we go them together. Mecca, you'll go with them."

"What? No!" Dorian protested.

"*Why* does Mecca have to go with him?" Mecca crossed his arms.

"Because Vulcan is planning something—killing off Bob and making Dorian fall in love— it is safer for us to be together. He's tweaking the gears. Adjustments have been made and we must make our own counter adjustments. That's why Mecca goes with you. Buddy system."

"And who goes with Odys, then?" Dorian buttressed his argument. "Who keeps him in line?"

Gwen looked at Odissa. "I think he has a direct *line* at all times. A direct reason to behave."

"If you haven't noticed, he just fucking left her, Mother." Fletcher pointed to the direction he supposed Odys to be going.

367

"He's going to come back, Dorian," Gwen said, putting a hand on Anselm to steady herself. "He's going to want to make contact. What's more, he's going to want to know where Cestus is when we find him. Cestus is perhaps the only Automaton he'd let Odissa have. The only one you'd let her touch, too. Isn't that right, Dorian?"

"And just where is Cestus, Gwen?" His accusatory tone shifted even their footing.

Rosemund laughed. "You don't care that she has broken the rules for Madus but you care that she might be lying about Cestus? You do have a funny way of loving your Mother, the lot ofofof you."

Dorian put a hand on his hip and huffed. "I don't care if you have Cestus or not, Gwen. I trust you with my life. But I need to know why you suddenly trust Odys more than me. I could have kept them safe. It's like you *wanted* him to take them."

Mother sighed. "Dorian, I love you. But Mecca will go with you, and that's final."

"We don't get a say?" Q asked, glaring at Dorian and Fletcher's shared expression.

Dorian denied them an answer from Mother: "Fine. But if Odys so much as hints where he is, I'm tracking him down and taking them back."

"Why bother?" Rosemund asked.

"You know why." *In case we never find Cestus.*

"Dorian, you wouldn't," Gwen begged him. "Have you even asked her about this?" She gestured to Odissa.

Odissa was surprised they remembered she was still there.

Oh yes, she was there. Because Odys had left her. He'd never left *her* before. She cocked her head as the fact flooded her, filling her up to her eyes.

Mother studied Odissa's reaction, pitying her as they spoke about her.

"I would give her Coraza," Dorian said, speaking theoretically—as if it to justify what he meant. "I don't want her to have *him*, though," Dorian said. "She shouldn't have to deal with *him*."

"And you think Coraza wouldn't have those same memories? I understand you, Dorian, I do. But—" Gwen paused, barely able to say it—"it would be unnatural."

"As if they aren't already!" Fletcher laughed in mockery for his Master. Dorian was unable to control himself, so consumed by his need for Odissa's lifespan to match his own.

"We are all unnaturally unnatural." Rosemund picked up her bags as if to remind them to *get a move on.*

Mother walked over to Dorian and patted his cheek. "She will have all you want for her and more, I swear. I'll make sure of it."

Dorian pulled away from her. *I wanted Madus for her.* "Is this another lie, Gwen?" Dorian said to her in Spanish.

Mother tightened her lips, unable to come up with more assurances and left them.

"Another reason to split up, Dorian," Rosemund stated as she went to the door. "We're not going to have you huffhuffhuffing all the time—breathing down our necks, thinking we know more than we do about Cestus."

"But tell me why I get stuck with the kid again? I would rather have you babysit them."

Rosemund and Caffar snorted. "You're not the one babysitting this time." In a whisper only Dorian could hear, "And because, Dorian, we all know what Mecca does when he doesn't have job to do—what he does when he can't handle something—**who** he runs to." She squeezed his arm as he inched closer to listen. "If you don't want to deal with that *who* then let him keepkeepkeep an eye on you." She let go of his arm and smiled at Mecca, who was queuing up his bomb with a tablet, making sure he had not heard. At little louder, "And besides, if we asked him who he'd want to go with—"

"Mecca wants to go with Odissa," Mecca said, ears perking up. Mecca didn't get a fresh audience every day and he wasn't about to waste it.

Rosemund's eyebrows raised—*There you have it*—matching the opposite arch of her frowning lips. Mecca grinned wickedly, though there was a twitch in the grin.

As the door closed behind Caffar and Rosemund, Dorian went to collect their bags. Fletcher followed, pushing Odissa along. "Call a cab, Mecca," Dorian shouted over his shoulder, "for the house down at the neighborhood entrance. Tell them your car broke down. Anything. Take your bags. We'll catch up to you there. Just go."

"But that's so far away!" he cried, gesturing to his heavy bags Q would have to carry.

"Then don't take as much shit next time you travel!" Dorian countered.

Dorian's shout made Bulfinch scratch free from Odissa. Q quickly scooped him up (fast as a cat), gesturing to Odissa, *It's OK. He's safe. Don't piss Dorian off. Go.*

Q and Mecca lingered in the living room, standing still, comforting Bulfinch. They'd call the cab in just one minute. Just one minute. Just one minute after they figured out why Dorian had hurried Odissa away from them:

"Tell me something," Dorian asked Odissa as he moved a bag to get his footing.

"Yes?" she whispered back, stopping as she went for a different bag.

369

"Do you think your brother will come back for you?"

Odissa straightened. "He just left me. Why would he come back just for me?"

"But would you go with him if he came for you?"

Her mouth twisted.

Fletcher was staring at her—watching her every reaction. She avoided looking back, lest she give too much away. She was so preoccupied with avoiding Fletcher's eyes that she didn't notice Dorian coming at her. When she finally realized his exact location, he had pushed her against the wall—too harshly to be playing. "Do you sympathize with him?"

"I don't sympathize with any of you. You all seem like such *great* people." She tried to cross her arms but he inched too close to let her. "You trying to be intimidating, Dorian? That what this is?"

"Hard to control a girlfriend that big, huh?" Fletcher mumbled as he picked up a few bags.

"I think enough is going on without your commentary, Fletcher," Odissa said over Dorian's shoulder—a shoulder too tense. She didn't know if Dorian was about to beat her or kiss her. "Stop making jokes, Dorian." She lowered her tone, "I can't read you.'"

He caged her against the wall with his arms on either side of her. "If I gave you the chance to run, would you?" He pushed back her hair with his hand so his face could better press against her skin. "Would you just leave me if I gave you the choice?"

"Why would anyone leave you?" She grit her teeth, grabbed onto his arm—his shirt. "How could I leave someone the gods speak to? You're too interesting. I don't seem to have a choice. It's what They want for me."

"They speak to your brother, too." He paused in his invasion of her. "What if he's in the right? What if They like him más que yo?"

She pushed her face into his, so that he could feel her words as her lips formed them. "I'm not interested in the gods' favorites. I can't stop them from talking to Odys. But I can stop Odys from disobeying you."

He gave her face a centimeter.

"You think I want him to obey me? No. I want him to not exist. There's a part of me so jealous of him—"

"Odys loves me because he sees himself in me. You love me because you have no choice." She had taken the sides of his face, ran a thumb over his lips. "You can't even control what you're doing now. I see it. You don't like what you're doing. But I do." He leaned into her fingers. "You think I would give that up? Give up someone so devoted to me?"

Fletcher noticed Mecca and Q out in the living room attempting to get in a glance. "Didn't we give you something to do? Go do it!" He shooed them away, going to slam the door. As they turned, he noticed a fear in their eyes. A fear for Odissa.

"Let me go, Dorian."

"I can't let you go." He pushed his whole bodyweight into her like a koala bear to a tree. He pressed his forehead to the wall, face in her neck.

"Am I fucking trying to run away? Am I struggling? I'm not going anywhere." She latched onto the back of his neck with a hand, gave it a squeeze the equivalent of shaking.

"That's all I wanted," Dorian said, releasing her and giving her a kiss.

"Fucking hell, Dorian," she said as she pushed him out of the way and smoothed down her hair. "Don't you ever do that again."

"Or what?" Dorian said, putting on his glasses. There was no humor in his voice. He wanted to hear her make a threat.

Her eyes were threatening enough and they fell into silence.

Fletcher began to hand Dorian some bags, too embarrassed to look at her.

Stanza: This is just another silly novel, I would like you to think.[156]

"I hope it's a yellow cab," Dorian said, adjusting the strap of his backpack—the one with all his hair products. He wobbled in the snow-covered road, trying not to slip.

Fletcher watched over his shoulder as they heard the fire trucks—the fire trucks that were coming to put out the house that smoked above the trees in the background. They'd gone out the back door—into the woods—and rounded out to the road.

"Why wouldn't it be yellow?" Odissa asked softly, wondering if they looked suspicious coming out of the woods like well-dressed campers.

"Well, you'd think so. But it's not like it used to be. Lately I've seen many a variety of colors for the cabs."

"Rather," Fletcher added, his voice a subtitle, "*I've* seen them. Green. White. Maroon."

"I *mean*," Dorian continued, pinning back some black hair with his many-ringed fingers, "as long as there's those little box-signs that say 'Taxi' on them, then they think they can get away with it. And I don't think it's fair. If I pay for a taxi, then I want to pay for the original experience. I didn't order a town car or limousine, you see. Besides, I take my colors seriously, sí?"

---

[156] "For all this, [the Heroine] as often as not marries the wrong person to begin with, and she suffers terribly from the plots and intrigues of the vicious baronet; but even death has a soft place in his heart for such a paragon, and remedies all mistakes for her just at the right moment." —*Silly Novels by Lady Novelists*, by George Eliot.

371

As the snow crunched under their feet, they could see the taxi cab just at the corner. But only one face—the driver's face—in the window. Fletcher looked at Dorian, and Dorian sighed. "Fuck." He knew what this meant.

As they neared, the driver rolled down his window. "Are you Fletcher?" He directed the question to the one who had fit the description.

"Why, yes I am, sir," Fletcher said, leaning down. Way down. He had his hands in his faux-skinny jeans pockets, balancing luggage off his arms.

"The kid, man," the driver said. "He told me to give this to you."

It was a neatly folded piece of paper, which Fletcher took.

As Fletcher prepared to read said paper, his eyes squinting because of the too-white snow, Dorian asked the cabbie, "Which way did he go?"

"He had a car," the man shrugged. "Was that girl with him even old enough to drive?"

"I don't know who you're talking about, friend."

The money Mecca had given him was reason enough to not see the age.

Odissa noticed Bulfinch in the back seat, freaking out as usual (I associated cars with trips to the vet). She quickly opened the cab door to soothe him through the bars. Her fingers were no comfort to me.

Fletcher crumpled the paper and tossed it over his shoulder.

"Where'd he go, though?" Odissa asked, concerned. She was clutching her coat collar in motherly anxiety.

As Dorian slid in beside her—knowing what Fletcher had just read—he mumbled, "To fucking *Maurice*."

MAURICE MAKEPEACE: The undead.

WAS: Once a Master.

PURPOSE: Vulcan's.

LIKES: "Ethnic" women. That's how he got his "ethnic" baby.

Chapter the third,

Éclaircissement:[157]

Is the past making more sense?

Odys stood in line next to Maud. He liked how the other men around them eyed her body. She was the curtain he could hide behind. Like a puppet, he made her cut her eyes in targeted

---

[157] French word. Look it up. Too hard to explain à la English.

directions, flip her hair at certain times, smile here and there. Flirting with every man. He had made her change her nose a bit, and sink in her eyes, darken her skin. Just a tad. Didn't want her face to be recognized later, should later ever come.

"How can I help you today?" inquired the frumpy Post Office lady. She didn't like the way Maud was dressed, clearly, or the fact that there were so many people in line. Busy day.

"I'd like to mail this package; first class, please."

She punched in the addresses, lowered her eyebrows. "Any liquids or perishables?"

"No."

Will that be all? Yes, it would.

Mailing back Mother's broken cell phone, cut up credit cards, and fake identifications was only the first step, but, yes, that was all for now. He even made the return address quite obvious for Gwen—inviting her to look for him *thereabouts*.

He didn't need her *things* anyway. Did he ever? He was free. He finally accepted the fact he DIDN'T need her help. No, not when he had Maud. After making her memorize every number in the cell phone and the details of the passports, he had methods of reduplicating anything he'd need.

The only things he didn't put in the package were the inanimates.

They were one thing he wouldn't give back.

When they left the Post Office, he had Maud drive. And scan for a new car to jack. His eyes barely saw out the foggy window.

"What about that piece of shit there? Easy alarm system to disable."

"Go for it."

And Maud went. [158]

Stanza: Of drug lords and landlords.

Dorian, Fletcher, Odissa, and Bulfinch got out of the cab. Paid the man. Unloaded their bags. And cat.

"A house," Odissa said—it was more of a question. She wasn't sure this was really their final stop.

"Dorian, she's not as stupid as she looks," Fletcher commented, practically lugging everything but the cat for them (Odissa clutched his carrier like a swaddled baby).

---

[158] About stealing cars: I cut a piece in book one, I think, about how, when going through a toll with possible cameras, Automata sometimes stick a hand out the window and let their skin trail down the car like a film to cover the license plate or give it a fake number. Chameleon-like, if you will.

"I don't like that you're mean to me through him, Dorian. It's cowardly."

"Get in the house, Odissa." Mecca left him in no mood to explain.

She followed Fletcher up the steps. Dorian took his time. He pulled up the mailboxes' flag. *Was there even mail in it?* Odissa wondered. No. It was a symbol. A signal.

The door was open. No key needed. It was a shabby place, on the outskirts of downtown. The houses squeezed together as if little monopoly pieces. No real lawns, just a patch of grass here and there—the road lined with cars because, back when these houses were built, garages weren't a big thing. Every other house seemed for sale for foreclosed...or like it should be. This neighborhood was so close to the highway it was a wonder anyone still lived here. The roaring of the cars echoed off the concrete.

Odissa stepped into the furniture-less house, the scuffed wood floors squeaking.

"We paid off the neighbor's drug debt if they'd keep out the squatters," Fletcher informed. He plopped the bags right down. "I'll see if they left the cot in the attic space. They seem to have sold everything else."

Dorian shut the door behind her. "We've property scattered here and there. This was the closest. Haven't been here since, well...since your parents died, Odissa."

"When you said the address to him, I thought—I thought we were just going to stop at a friend's house or something. We're staying here?"

"If you don't like it, we'll leave."

"No. It's not that." *Though why couldn't they just get a hotel?* "But you could have told me where we were going." She put Bulfinch's carrier down by the window. *Did you not trust me?*

"I'll turn the heat on."

Fletcher brought back a cot covered in dust—dust that danced about when he pulled it open. "I'll go to the store and bring back some necessities. Like sheets and sleeping bags. And cat litter."

"But you don't have a car," Odissa said. "You can't steal one in broad daylight!"

"The neighbors, clearly, hawked all our stuff—or *have* it. So, I think we'll be fine. Their car is as good as ours anyway."

He left.

"He's going to just take their car?" She watched him walk across the street. He barged in as if the door were unlocked.

"Oh, no," Dorian said. "He'll let them know he's doing it. They won't have a problem with it. And, well, if they do then he can explain why *he* has a problem with their problem."

Dorian sat down on the cot and invited her next to him. "I need to be honest with you, Odissa. I picked this house because it's also safest. Pepin didn't know about this house, and so neither will Odys. You understand? Maud doesn't know about this house." He fumbled to find her leg—to make sure she was there. "The fact Mecca bailed on me will also have Mother on my back. Mecca will be free to come here, though. He can, no doubt, find me."

She bit her lip, watching him. "I've never had a house before."

"Don't get too attached. We won't be here long."

"How long will we be?"

"We will be here until someone else makes a move. We all know something is about to happen, Odissa. The Automatons can smell it."

"You mean until a human makes a move—or a god?"

"That's what I don't know."

"Might as well let Bulfinch out until Fletcher brings back a litter box."

Bulfinch stayed in his carrier for a long while, rather than venture out. He had stopped meowing, settling on quiet judgment instead.

"This has traumatized him," Odissa commented, feeling guilty.

She had nooo idea.

She took out a cigarette to smoke. "I think it's colder in here than it is outside," she said, sitting back down on the squeaky cot.

"Give the heater time."

"How does this abandoned place have electricity anyway?"

"You don't know by now that we know how to wire and rewire things?"

"Sorry, I forget I'm not with normal human beings who are above the law."

"The neighbors pay for our usage. We steal from them. We've got a wire that runs from here to that house, there." He pointed at the houses, off a hair without Fletcher. "And one from there to there, if that one fails. Underground. That sort of thing. Rosemund taught us well. Has Bulfinch come out yet?"

"Yeah, but he went back in when he saw you."

"Smart cat. He knows when we need a moment alone." He smiled. Something in her was glad to see that smile.

She found herself reaching for his cold hand. She balled his into a fist and held it for a second until it was as warm as her own. Ran her fingers across it. Stuck her finger inside.

"You flirting with me now?" he asked.

375

She leaned back from him. "No. I'm trying to woo you. I'm trying to get that wrinkle, just there, off your face."

He blushed because he couldn't see where she was pointing.

"I've not run away yet, have I?" She touched his arm—she wasn't sure why.

He leaned back. "No, you haven't..."

To fill his silence she assumed the role of narrator. "Bul's not more than two feet away from the carrier now. He doesn't want to go back in there, though. He's about to have a panic attack. Doesn't know where to go—especially since there's no furniture to hide under."

"What was it like, being fucked by Leeland? Fucking him?"

"That had no lead-in."

"Doesn't need one."

"Haven't we talked about this?" She stared outside at the bright snow, visualizing kicking at it, crunching it beneath her shoe.

Bulfinch started to meow, nervous. Odissa calmed him, calling to him. But he settled for dashing under the cot, wide-eyed. He curled his tail around himself by her feet and waited.

When the wrinkle in Dorian's forehead grew deeper, Odissa leaned back on the cot and said, "I think you know what it was like having sex with Augury."

"Odissa, I need to tell you something. I know who your parents were."

Long story short, he explained it.

"...So, you really are my uncle?"

"Step-uncle." He wanted to be very clear. "Your brother knows, too."[159]

"I can't keep from fucking family members, it seems." She watched his expression, wondering how he'd react. She didn't know if she meant to be funny or not.

"Sometimes I half-think Admund put it in his head—Leeland's head. He gave him the idea to try and get you pregnant. I mean, all his medical experiments. He already had a foundation with them—previous Masters were all these mad scientist types. Not all of them were medically inclined, but Admund does give them a way with the sciences. Seems only natural he'd give those foundations to Leeland and he'd take off with it. Automatons. They do strange things to Masters. But, Jesus, this has been strangest of all."

And he went into a tangent about *why* Admund might be the most fucked up—the whole "he's the oldest" spiel.

---

[159] Now that I think about it, I wonder if Odys took the photos of his parents that Leeland left, or if he let them burn up in the house?

Odissa was having trouble keeping up. "I'm grateful you told me."

"I'm grateful you're still here. Not running away."

"You keep saying that, but do you know how convenient it is to—to have a slave? Someone so completely devoted to you? Of course you do. You have an Automaton. But see, I don't need one. I have you, I guess."

Dorian kept her hand and brought it to his face, overlooking her ignorance.

Bulfinch cautiously came up to them and arched his back as Odissa reached out. "Why do you think I wouldn't want one of Leeland's Automatons, exactly?"

"He's practically your father. It'd just be too weird. And I wouldn't want you to fuck me with him looming over us, sorry."

"But Coraza would be different? Aw—Bul's looking out the window!"

Standing on his back paws cautiously.

"Coraza hasn't had a history of psycho Masters is all I'm saying. It's like Vulcan cursed Admund to only be picked up by abnormals."

Odissa didn't press it.

Dorian asked her, "This store Fletcher's at doesn't have a great wet food selection, but we'll get one of each if that's OK?"

"We're giving each other play-by-plays for what we can't see." Odissa added a smile to her voice. "It's as good as watching TV, I guess. That we don't have."

"Want to move this show to the bath? A warm bath as the house heats up."

Stanza: Chekhov's now anti-guns.

"Now he's found the clothing aisle." Dorian had begun, just after he'd turned the water off. She had closed her eyes as he leaned back into her. She hadn't had proper sleep in a while.

"Need anything?"

"Some different gloves. Maybe a shirt or two?"

"You'll let me dress you, or do you want a say in what he picks out?"

Not wanting him to have to describe every shirt available, "I trust your judgment. I'm a small top. Size seven or eight in pants." *But you probably know that.*

He continued his narration as the steam of the tub floated into the cold air. "He's coming down the block now," Dorian finally announced, squeezing her hand a bit tighter.

Bulfinch had peeked in and watched them for a few minutes, wondering where his litter box was. He had settled for peeing on some newspaper that didn't make the lone garbage bin. Odissa cooed at him, but he would not be tricked into coming near.

377

"I'm glad you made him get the eco-friendly cat litter," she told Dorian as she pulled on the black hairs on his arm. They'd been soaking for almost an hour at this point.

"Nothing but the best for Bulfinch." He gave her leg a little stroke. His hand lingered there for a moment. "Oh, wouldn't it be nice if we could live here forever? Just us."

His hand slid down her leg.

"I feel like outlaws here. There's no furniture," she said, putting a hand on his. She had only agreed to take the bath because she'd been so cold. At least, that's what she'd told herself.

"Yes, but theoretically we could always get *more* furniture. Fletcher's bringing some folding chairs, by the way."

"Those will certainly complete the room."

"I can't see them anyway."

After their moment, he finally let Fletcher come in with their bath products and necessities (read: towels).

Setting a few grocery sacks down before going back outside for the rest, he looked down at them. "Are you guys going to stay in here all day or shall I join you?"

Odissa said, "I'm not sure where he'd fit, Dorian."

"You forget, dear," Fletcher said. "I can become small enough to slip through that drain. And I'm tired of going out in the cold."

"Yes, well, your nerve endings aren't as delicate as ours, so suck it up."

Dorian laughed. "Now who's the one being mean?"

Stanza: Spousal abuse works both ways.

Once the sheets were placed on the dusty cot mattress, the chairs arranged and the goods spread here and there, Dorian told her to get ready. They were going out!

"Bulfinch has his litter box, now we can go out—without you worrying about him."

"Nothing fancy, right? I can't go dressed like this."

Fletcher hadn't exactly gone to a clothing store.

"Don't worry. I'm a bit too depressed for something grand just yet."

Fletcher drove them (in the neighbor's smelly car) to a local diner. Seat yourself.

"This one," Fletcher said, pointing. Someone had left a day-old newspaper on the seat. He took his pleasure in reading it rather than the greasy menu.

"What will you be having?" Dorian asked Odissa. He had sat next to her, trapping her in the booth. Or, as he might have called it, *tucking her in.*

"Milkshake sounds nice," she said.

The waitress came up.

The place was just loud enough for her to raise her voice. The mod-country music playing above them clashed with the 50's diner ambiance. It made it hard for Odissa to concentrate as she placed her order. Dorian said, "Same thing, please."

Fletcher, through his newspaper, said, "The same thing for me, too."

"Same things, coming right up," the woman repeated, amused.

"She probably thinks you two can't read or something."

"Well, I can't, actually," Dorian stated, pushing up his glasses with a grin. She was joking with him. They were having fun.

"And besides," Fletcher said, "I've got the news. It's obvious I can't read the menu at the same time." He shuffled his local section.

The drinks in front of them, Odissa poked with her straw. "I hate cherries. Anyone want mine?"

"You hate them?"

"Well, no. Not *real* cherries. These all have the weird sauce on them." She offered it to them with a tip.

No one took it from her.

Offended that no one even bothered to reject the damn red dot, she changed the subject. "You think Vulcan is insulted that *Star Trek* used His name for an alien race?"

"Why would He be?" Fletcher said, looking over his paper. He had assumed fake glasses for his reading—big John Lennon ones (or Harry Potter depending on the generation).

"Because, well, certain seasons weren't as...good as others. I don't know. There's bound to be *something* that would piss Him off. And it's not like they asked His permission."

"Most humans don't ask permission. But then again," Dorian mused, "I don't know that they should have to. Spock is, likely, the least of His worries."

"Live long and fuck Vulcan," Fletcher mumbled behind his paper.

"Even so," Odissa said. "I still wonder His opinion on the matter."

"Maybe you'll meet Him someday. You can ask yourself."

They all took a sip (or two) of their drinks.

Odissa spotted someone far away. A handicapped man with even older parents. He could barely swallow the food his mother fed him. It was hard for Odissa to watch—not because she was disgusted, but because it hurt her heart. Staring at the family, "I think I'd ask Him *why*. If I met Him."

"Why what?" Dorian said, taking his lips off the straw.

"Why the gods would let something like that happen." She nodded once and Fletcher's eyes glanced. "Mistakes."

"Ah," Dorian said, his voice lowering. "Well, first of all, it's not like He's the one in charge of those issues. Second, people aren't mistakes."

"For sure. But, I mean in general...*why* does it happen? It's so unfair. Oh, never mind. I don't know what I'm saying. Well, let me rephrase. I'm just glad I can't have children,"—her tone was hushed. "So that can't happen to someone else. My children won't have that problem. Or me. God knows if I had kids what kind of monsters they'd be..."

She paled, realizing what she'd just said. She stared at her glass, unable to look at her boys. *Shut up, Odissa!*

"We all have our handicaps, Odissa," Fletcher said, a bit surprised she'd call disabled people monstrous. Especially now that she was fucking one. But something told him that wasn't what she'd meant.

"Fitting, though," Dorian forced a laugh, "given that Vulcan is, well..."

Disabled.

"He has a limp right?" she asked them, as if she didn't know. She was really leaning into the stupidity. "I'm not getting Him confused with Someone else?"

"No, you're right," Fletcher said, watching her grow redder and more embarrassed. "Most of the time, He does. What does it say about us if even our gods are disabled?"

She took her spoon, watching her face materialize in the warped metal. She noticed her sad expression. Was the glimmer of this outing melting just as her image in the spoon?

She caught Fletcher staring at her—spying for Dorian. She glared at him—THEM. Dorian inched closer to her, pressing his leg against hers. "What would you be doing right now if none of this had happened?" he asked, his voice hushed (as if anyone could hear them—in fact, the older folks in the restaurant seemed appalled by the look of this threesome).

"I'd be doing something with Odys."

"Like what?"

"Anything. We'd probably have just gotten off of work. We might do homework together for the next day."

"Are you going to miss school?"

"So I can *never* go back or anything?"

"Maybe we can both go back. Isn't that an idea, Fletcher? What would we study?"

"I pick for you, is that it? No, tell me what you like," Odissa encouraged.

"I would study only what you studied—so I could get to know you better. I never really did well in college, you see. I was too preoccupied with sucking all the dicks I never got to in high school."

Dot. Dot. Dot.

"I need to use the restroom," Odissa half-lied. She could go, but it wasn't a need.

Dorian replied, "Hold it until we get home. I'm not getting arrested for going into a girl's room."

"Even though no one could tell the difference," Fletcher commented.

"I love how you can make fun of yourself, Dorian. But that still doesn't relieve my bladder."

Chit chat chit chat chit chat.

The food came out.

They ate, as they were supposed to do.

Then, as they were halfway through the meal:

Lily Allen ringtone.

Fletcher pulled out the phone (yes, from his "pocket"), and looked at the CID. "Where the hell did he find a payphone?" he said as he passed the phone to Dorian. "They still make those?"

"Hello, Odys," Dorian greeted, his mouth half-full. "You know I let Mother have this phone tapped, so why are you stupid enough to call me?"

Odissa dropped her fork to eavesdrop.

She could hear her brother's faint voice: "How'd you know it was me? Never mind, stupid question, I guess."

"Let me speak to him!" Odissa begged, her voice a loud whisper.

Fletcher put his paper down and grabbed her wrist—warning her. She'd not be touching that phone.

"Why are you calling?"

"Don't you mean from where?"

"Get to your point, Odys."

"All right then, I want to know where you went."

"And you thought I'd tell you, Odys?"

"You haven't cussed me out yet."

"That comes later."

"Fine." He hadn't expected him to answer. "But you at least asked me why I was calling. You're still interested."

"Think what you must. It's true, Odys, I wish I could trust you"—Dorian put a hand up to Odissa, who was leaning a bit too close—"But, given the circumstances…"

"Ask me what I want again."

"I'll not be redundant, Odys."

Odissa was calmer now, listening—trying to imbibe it. They all sat very still in the booth. Odissa held her breath so she could hear over the *damn stupid music.*

"I want Mother to fork up Cestus. That's what I fucking want. I want a plan to get her to admit she has him. To prove once and for all she's beyond forgiveness."[160]

"And you have this plan, do you? You think you can't trust Mother, and that may be true. But her pros outweigh her cons. I'll not go against her."

"Pepin said—"

"FUCK WHAT PEPIN SAID!" Dorian shouted. The restaurant quieted. Fletcher waved them off, mouthing an apology. "You think I trust him over Mother?" He was hunched over, leaning into the phone as if he might get close enough through the cell-waves to punch him.

For a second or two Odys didn't respond. But Dorian didn't hang up the phone either.

"Pepin was willing to die for something, Dorian."

"So was Leeland and we're all grateful he did."

"Pepin didn't die because of Gwen, though."

"When you find out why Pepin killed himself, let me know, boy. Then we'll talk. Otherwise, you're just his puppet. Maybe you shouldn't have synced with Maud."

"Tell me where you are so I can tell you in person."

"I'm not letting you get near her, and you know that."

"Let me speak to him, at least." Odissa touched Dorian's arm. She knew she could get him to talk, and Dorian knew it too. But he'd not involve her with this. He ignored her.

"Let me talk to her, Dorian," Odys said.

"You are in no position to be asking for things, Odys."

"Then tell me how to earn your trust. You know this was the best way to keep Mother's hands off them."—the inanimate Automatons.

---

[160] Wait, what? He thinks she has Cestus?

Odissa could tell the conversation was ending so she had begun to beg. "Please, Dorian." She put a hand on his leg.

But Dorian shut her up. His hand went to her pants and grabbed her genitals, making her softly gasp from his horrific public display. He was doing it to express not only his jealousy but to finalize his stance on the matter. She was cornered against the booth's wall, trying to get away from him. She tried not to squirm—to draw attention to herself.

Fletcher kept hold of her wrist on the table, staring her down, keeping her still. His eyes cut to those around them—none had caught on yet.

Dorian continued on with his phone-convo, "I want an Automaton, Odys. I want the inanimates to be evenly distributed. You shouldn't have both of them. Give one to me and maybe you'll get to see Odissa again."

"Done. Set the terms."

"Get a cell phone. Text me the number. I'll text you the number to my backup cell."

How many phones can a person have? Odissa wondered.

"But do it tomorrow," Dorian clarified. "You understand? We're done for today."

The waitress, aware of the peace-disturbing threesome, came to ask if everything was all right. Were they done with their plates? Ready for the check?

But then she noticed Dorian's hand placement—the way Odissa was hunched over the table—the way Fletcher held her wrist. And before Odissa could pretend she wasn't embarrassed, it was too late. The lady's eyes widened—and seemed to ask Odissa if she needed her to call the police. Where these men bothering her? Fletcher calmly followed Odissa's eyes to the waitress's face.

Dorian's hand lifted as he cleared his throat. The conversation with Odys was over. He hung up the phone. Before the lady could turn away—Odissa had assumed a rebellious face and, with a rebellious hand, had rebelliously cupped Dorian. It was all just a game, waitress. No need to be concerned. Call the cops if you want, but not for _those_ reasons. With her left hand, she squeezed Dorian gently, between the legs, and stared the lady in the eye. "There's no problem."

The waitress's face shifted from concern to disgust. "You need to leave."

"We'll be leaving now, yes, dear." Fletcher opened a wallet—pulled from somewhere quickly. "This ought to cover it. Keep the change."

The waitress blushed. Maybe from embarrassment Maybe because she'd never been tipped so much. Maybe because she'd actually thought Fletcher was attractive (because he was).

And they were out.

"Remind me never to take you two out again," Fletcher grumbled, holding the door. "You're too expensive."

When the car started, Odissa slapped Dorian. "Don't you ever embarrass me in public like that again!" When he didn't respond, she slapped him again. Though a normal human couldn't hurt him, she could tell her actions pained him. And she kept hurting. She kept at it because she knew he'd still love her in the end: "You think I won't scream the next time you pull something like that? I swear to God I will!"

He grabbed her hand. "I'm sorry."

"A manipulative little—little bitch!" She put her seatbelt on with passion.

"I'm sorry," he said again. And he really was. "And thank you for—for saving face back there—"

"You're not welcome!"

"Oh, but I think I am." He crossed his legs, put a hand on her own. Fletcher drove faster and faster. "I think I'm very welcome."

Stanza: A sexless marriage and a sexful of divorce.

Odissa smoked in the bed-cot-thing, the covers pulled over her naked torso.

It was raining outside and she watched the water roll down through the cracks in the blinds. Dorian had his arm placed around her, propping both of them up as he leaned against the corner wall. He twiddled paperclip-Fletcher with his right hand.

"What do you think my brother's doing right now?"

"I just fucked you and you're talking about him?" He gave a wounded sound and kissed her hair. He was always kissing her—always begging her for affection. She pulled her head away from his lips.

"No, I just fucked *you*," she growled.

"I can fix that," he said reaching down the covers.

She squirmed away from him. When the laughter stopped, "Funny, isn't it, how I trust him and you trust Gwen?"

He stopped when she wouldn't let him kiss her.

"I don't think it's funny at all," he said with a craggy voice, shrinking from her.

"Hand me the ashtray."

The ashtray was a plastic cup. She blew smoke out the corner of her mouth.

"If I gave you an Automaton—any Automaton—would you use it to stay with me forever?"

She settled in under the covers. "So you're afraid that if I get one, I'll ditch you? That the new drama you're going to stir up?"

"Can't you just reassure me?"

"No. I'm using you. I'm using you to get an Automaton," she said, flicking an imaginary spec of ash off her lap (so nervous around him, even though he had the least invasive eyes of anyone she knew). "I'm using you because I have no one else in the world I could use to get one. I mean, even if I begged, Odys wouldn't give me one of the two he has. That's why he has them and I have to be here with you. You who have none to give."

"You don't have to be so cruel."

"You don't have to be so worried."

Blahblahblah, they fuck a lot and play twenty questions on repeat. Maybe they even ordered food at one point. Eventually, though, night came and they fell asleep.

Stanza: And as they slumbered...

From the floor in the opposite corner, the cell phone vibrated. It lit up the darkness like a holy candle.

Dorian unconsciously dropped the paperclip in his hand. The paperclip twisted upwards, becoming a man. Fletcher scooped up the phone next to the bags and went outside. He stole a quick peek at his Master and Odissa before he closed the door behind him. Dorian might want to know what this moment looked like in the morning: his Master, mouth wide open for flies, was quietly snoring, one foot peeping outside the covers. His head was on Odissa's chest, crushing her and keeping her lungs from rising fully.

Fletcher looked at the phone—a face floating in the darkness.

He moved to the door, texting back. He put that phone in his "pocket" and pulled out another from his chest. He counted to ten seconds before it rang.

Answering the phone with a hiss, "Do you know what fucking time it is?"

"My clock says 12:06," Maud replied from the other end. He could imagine her lips against the receiver.

"We said call tomorrow!"

"Tomorrow is today. And I'm just doing as you told Odys."

"This isn't what we meant."

He walked up past the house porch and grabbed onto the gutter. It creaked, but not enough to discourage him from pulling on it. He used it to swing himself to the roof with one arm. He looked like a skeleton creeping up the house. He climbed up to the peak with ease and crouched near the crumbling chimney—a pale, gangly gargoyle with a slump.

"You're being terribly brave about all this, Odys. How do you know I'm not with Mother, right now? Letting her hear aaall the plans we're about to make?"

"I'm pretty sure our bases are covered, Dorian. If you wanted Gwen to hear, you would have gone with her. But you didn't. You split up."

"How'd you know that?"

"Mother's not the only one with spies."

"Given Dorian's history, Maud, we deserve the spying. On the other hand, we have every reason to trust her. It's going to take a lot for you to turn me against her."

"I don't care about your stance toward Mother. I care whether or not things are fair."

"If Odys cared so much, then why did he make you do this phone call?"

"Odys is asleep. He'll know all about this in the morning. And don't be so hypocritical. Dorian isn't talking right now. You are. Your Master's a lazy ass, too."

Fletcher laughed. Dorian thought it was funny. "Tell me why—honestly, why—this couldn't wait until the sun came up?"

"Because I know you smell it too. Something is happening. The ash is in the air. It's thicker. It's all too coincidental."

"It's just people burning fires for the cold." He itched his nose, becoming more aware of the fact he *could* smell it. He couldn't stop smelling it. *The nose knows.*

"No. Being a Master isn't what it used to be, Dorian.[161] The gods are planning something— something big. It's all coming to a close. All of our plans will be for nothing. So will Mother's."

"And what was Gwen's plan, exactly, Odys?"

"She said Automatons shouldn't exist. She didn't want them damaging more lives. She's taking the burden on herself. She'll likely launch the Automatons she's got into fucking space and then shoot her brains out so that she doesn't have to feel guilty about dying. She wouldn't make new Masters *suffer.*"

"Look. In one week we'll give you a call. We'll arrange a meeting place. You'll deliver Coraza to me and then maybe we'll let you see Odissa. Clear?"

---

[161] We are well aware that it is Maud talking to Fletcher here. But do realize the proper nouns don't really mean much when they both recognize each other as Odys and Dorian.

"No. I'll only give you Admund. Can't have you tempted to give her Coraza just because you think she'll have less of Leeland in her. I won't do it. I don't want him near her. I've only just gotten rid of him."

Fletcher rolled his eyes. "We'll call you in a week."

"We don't have a week! You know it."

"Don't bother us again. You understand? You left us—you accepted this fate when you took the inanimates. This is how it works."

"Vulcan won't give us a week, Dorian. He's smothering us. I called you, now keep the ball rolling. If you don't, They'll roll it for you."

Fletcher removed the phone from his ear and hung up. "I'll drop the ball every fucking chance I get if it will fuck up Their game."

The phone convo ended, but Fletcher's wakefulness would not. Instead of sleeping, he perched on the roof, brooding for Dorian.

Stanza: The metal gargoyle.

Dorian woke up. He felt Odissa lift her head and push back her hair.

"Good morning," Dorian told her, smiling through his stubble-shadowed face.

"Morning," she mumbled, turning her head away from him (as not to breathe morning breath on him).

He fumbled under his pillow for the pack of gum Fletcher had put there upon making the cot-bed. "Chewy for yah?"

"Sí, gracias," she said. She wadded up the wrapper but wasn't sure what to do with it. She rolled it between her fingers. "Why the fruity gum instead of minty, again?"

"Because I don't like my gum the same flavor as my toothpaste? Does it matter?" He tried to kiss her, but was off target. He hit the side of her lips, instead.

This made her realize Fletcher wasn't in the room. "Where's Fletcher?"

"He went to get you coffee and cigarettes. Let's get dressed so we can go out to brunch, huh? I'll make up for the outing we had yesterday."

He was up out of bed in an instant. However, he was back down again, almost falling to the floor. "That's what happens, you see, when I don't sleep with Fletcher. Going to be a bumpy morning," he laughed as she helped him right himself.

"What do you mean you didn't sleep with Fletcher? He wasn't here last night? When did he leave?"

He started to answer, but paused—like someone trying to recall a foggy dream.

"I'm afraid he was up all night being anxious for me. But it'll get better as soon as I have breakfast." He leaned against the wall all the way to the bathroom.

Following him in her own sleepy daze, she asked, "What does he have to worry about?"

"Instead of a bath, let's take a shower. You want to try fucking standing up?"

"Can you even stand on your own?"

"Best we save the shower experiment for another time, then," he said with diluted confidence. He gave a stretch as he pulled back the grimy shower curtain for her.

"I'm just going to wash my face and fix my hair…" No need for a shower.

"I was so looking forward to doing yours today," he sighed, rubbing his puffy eyes. "But I can't see without Fletcher. I didn't think this through. I suppose you can just put a hat on me or something."

Odissa glared at him. It really wasn't fair that he *could* pull off "just a hat." It was she who had to make adjustments just to feel comfortable in her own skin. She stared into the mirror at him, there, wondering what "comfortable" and "skin" meant to Dorian.

As Odissa finished her hair and started on her makeup, she glanced at Dorian, who was dozing off on the closed toilet lid. She chose her foundation, noticing that it matched her skin tone perfectly; she marveled at how good Fletcher was at buying products. Not just because he was the Automaton of Dorian Dandor, but because his divine database knew much too much about everything.

"Were you always such a—a femme? Is that the right way of phrasing it?" she asked Dorian. "I mean, like, with my grandparents? Did they have a problem with it?"

The question rebooted him. "Yes and no. Your mother used to dress me up in girl clothes for fun. And by fun I mean I was the one who was having it. She always thought she might get in trouble for making me her living doll." He smiled in his fond remembrance. "How come you haven't ever asked about her? I mean, maybe you have, but you still don't seem entirely interested."

"What should I ask, then?"

"I suppose you're right. Where to start?" He ran a hand through his hair, thinking. "She was much like you. Or, rather, you're much like her. Except she took longer to warm up to me—and to others. She was very quiet—at first. We were the three amigos—her, your father, me. She was so loyal to us, she didn't even have a girl best friend. Well, maybe I count. She was always the type who was befriended, never the befriender. She wasn't the kind to fight for a place in, say, a circle. The circle had to come to her. If that makes any sense."

"It doesn't, but I like the way you talk about her. You talk about her as if you've..." She paused and tore her eyes from the mirror, choosing her next bit of makeup. "Thought a lot about her."

"She had this way of *reacting* to people. She would step back if you moved forward." He demonstrated, his movements sloppy and tired. "But it didn't feel as if she was avoiding you. She was drawing you into herself. Making you follow. She could do that. She could move you and control you if you came close enough. Reminds me of you, in a way. Our parents said that I started to mimic her when they moved in together I would say things she would say—the way she said it. I would move like she moved. Maybe because I wanted to be her. She was the most fascinating and beautiful human being on the planet..." He smiled at the memory—but it made him remember something else. "And then she and your father just moved away one year when I was in college. My parents didn't like your father—they caught me sleeping on him once. It bothered them, that he would let me. Your parents—they eventually stopped calling as frequently. I stopped wanting them to. And then I avoided them all together because making amends is—is hard. You want to know the last thing your mother said to me before she died?"

"Do I?" She had stopped putting on makeup completely now, frozen in place as she listened—not wanting to hear. He was only rambling on like this because he was so tired. She could hear the sadness in his voice and see the history in his face.

He fidgeted with his thumb ring.

"She wouldn't talk to me, you see, when I finally got them to agree to come and visit me. She was still pretending to be angry at what I had said to them the last time I'd seen them—that I didn't really have time, especially since *they'd* never had time for *me* before. That's how I'd phrased it, you see. I had just gotten Fletcher when they had finally tried to reconnect after all that time. Your father was the one I convinced to come out and see me—before it all happened. But on the phone before that, well, Dory had said 'Dorian, I don't know who you are anymore. We used to be like twins, but then we weren't enough for you. You became an alter-ego that isn't you.' That's what she said. I remember it perfectly because Fletcher burned it into my memory. I have two brains now—double the hauntings. And then she passed the phone to Dominic."

Dorian rubbed his forehead, massaging the memories back into place. "She could sum me up so easily. She made it so easy to—to be afraid of her. And she was right. But not entirely. She had rubbed off too much on me. She was the reason people loved me. I could amplify her. I would wear your mother like an outfit, Odissa, and I made her better than herself. She was my muse. But she didn't like looking into a mirror, I guess..."

"She should have taken it as a compliment," Odissa said, rinsing her hand. She didn't know why, but this topic made her feel guilty.

Fletcher came in through the door and handed them their coffee. He leaned on the bathroom doorframe, hair brushing the top. "You look fine, but he looks like shit. Why didn't you say something? I'll go get you some clean clothes." He left but turned back around. "Almost forgot." And he slapped down a box of new cigarettes. But he kept her from reaching for them. "Not yet!" he held up a finger.

And with his other hand he pulled a cigarette from "behind" his ear and stuck it in her mouth. He flicked the tip and away it smoked. He winked.

Odissa removed the cig and glared at Fletcher as he left the room. "I thought you said you were tired. He seems plenty full of spunk to me." And then she realized Dorian was asleep, head in his arm.

He started when she set the curling iron down. "What? What were we talking about?"

"You were talking about my father—" she tried to get him off the topic of her mother.

"Was I?" He laughed, trying to remember. "You know, your father shaved his head in the eleventh grade. Completely off. He liked it shaggy. But he also liked it cleanly. My hair would've been a bit much for him, too. He would disapprove of your brother's hair, *definitely*. Your mother wouldn't have minded, though. I think Dory—I mean, your mother…Gah, it sounds so strange, calling her that—'your mother.' It makes me feel like a pervert."

"If the shoe fits." Odissa smiled at him, but realized he couldn't see it. "I think this is the least of our sins."

"Well, yes. But the fact of the matter is that it would be wrong even if you weren't my by-marriage niece. I'm a hundred times your age"—he exaggerated. "I guess this makes me a cougar." He leaned back on the toilet seat, crossing his legs and clawing at her.

"Who do I look more like, my dad or my mom?"

Fletcher came in with a fresher pair of clothes and started to re-dress Dorian. Odissa stared for a moment, watching. Dorian and Fletcher were leaning on each other more than seemed right. Dorian almost fell over when putting a pant leg through.

"Odys looks more like your mom. You look like your dad when you smile. Your dad had a knee-buckling smile."

"It sounds like you had a thing for my dad."

"There's a reason I wanted to be your mother," he laughed, sitting back down.

She screwed on the lid to her mascara. "Get off the pot, I'm going to puke."

"I have digital copies of—of photos. Photos of your family. Digital records. I hate to bring them out. I never look at them. Maybe someday we can view them together?"

She could tell he didn't want to look at them in the near future, though. She wondered why he cared to even preserve them if he never looked at them.

"We don't have to talk about this, Dorian. We don't. I was doing fine without them—without a family."

"Yes, well, I wasn't."

"I couldn't miss what I never had."

Fletcher noted her expression for his Master, making him respond: "Ah, look at you, concerned. This is why I love you so much. I've been without someone who is mine for such a very long time."

"Is my brother family, though, to you?"

Again with the mouth twist. "You done getting ready?"

She turned away from him. "Let me fix this strand of hair."

Fletcher and Dorian waited. "You know, at first, when your brother gained Maud, I thought Pepin might be trying to help *me*. But then it became clear—no, *obvious*—that this all had to do with Leeland. Of course it would. Pepin was so…obsessed with Leeland. Always felt responsible because he's the one that *caused* Leeland. But now I see that Pepin only cared about Odys because Leeland cared. Not because *I* cared. Pepin didn't give a *fuck* about me. Hell, he probably liked your brother more than me. I'm really starting to question Pepin's motives."

Odissa suddenly wanted to keep him talking, so she pretended that strand of hair needed more than just a little work. "Pepin could have given Maud to me instead of Odys, couldn't he?"

"Sure," he shrugged. "He could have given Maud to you. You could have been just as worthwhile a person to catch our attention and get the same results. Why not?" He was too caught up in his anger to catch her meaning.

"But there had to be a specific reason. Why Odys and not me? And if Pepin did it, by some chance, to bring us back to you, Dorian, then why didn't Pepin just tell you we were still alive? Why not let you know who we were and bother someone else with Maud?"

He marveled at her understanding. But then the thought came to him. "And who else would he bother?"

"Someone already like you. Someone with an Automaton already. I don't know."

Fletcher responded more quickly than his Master, "He knew he needed to protect the twins from Leeland, and giving them an Automaton was the best shot for that."

"I *understand* that. But, and correct me if I'm wrong here because I'm still picking up on things, but Pepin didn't only have one Automaton, did he? He could have given away Madus—more easily than giving away Maud. Hell, he could have given *both* us twins an Automaton. But he didn't. He didn't want me to have an Automaton. But he wanted *Odys* to have Maud."

Fletcher narrowed his eyes at her.

Had Dorian been standing, he would have sagged at the knees at her insight—so shook was he in finding yet another reason to love her. "I see what you're saying," Dorian agreed. "Either Pepin wasn't able to give Madus to you or there's something *more* to how his gift was given."

Fletcher took off with it. "Yes, maybe something disrupted the major plan. What's happening is his plan B. Although, we're both assuming there's a plan A at all."

Odissa took it back. "Well, he could have just liked Odys and was tired of living, right? Why couldn't he have just randomly liked my brother over me?"

Dorian pursed his lips, disagreeing with her devil's advocate. He liked her original thought—as if he had come up with it himself. Pepin had chosen Odys for a reason. "That makes it all seem anti-climatic. Pepin did love a good show. Especially if it went on and on and on."

There were too many "what-ifs" now to keep the game fun. They dwindled into silence.

"...Dorian," Odissa asked hesitantly. The moment the name escaped her lips, she regretted it.

He heard the meekness in her voice. "Yes?"

"I don't want Admund or Coraza as my Automaton."

"Your options are not vast."

"I'll tell you which one I want."

"Well, go on."

"Madus." The name felt strange on her lips, but she knew it well enough. She liked how the name made Dorian stiffen angrily.

"Stop being cruel, Odissa. You can't have that one. By the time that one's available you'll be older than the pope." He crossed himself like someone waving off a terrible idea.

They walked out of the bathroom and into the living room, about to leave.

"Wait, Fletcher, go get my hat. And glasses!" Dorian touched his face.

Fletcher dashed away and returned, placing them on his Master. He preened a little for him, tucking some hair behind his ears. "I'm not sure I like this hat I bought you." It had a large puff ball on top. "It resembles a man bun too much. Maybe we should buy another one when we're out."

"After we eat, because I'm hungry," Odissa grouched when Fletcher adjusted the hat for the third time.

"Don't rush me," Dorian barked back. If he was going to be an unshowered slob, he might as well look good doing it.

"How many ways can you possibly wear a hat?" Odissa begged for a good answer.

Dorian huffed, seeing himself through Fletcher. "You're just saying that to get me to move, but fine—" and he opened the door quickly to appease his Odissa and started out.

And that was when he was stopped. He had bounced off a very broad chest covered in a black and white striped sweater.

Stanza: Stereotypes and archetypes.

Before Dorian could even recover from running into the pillowy-firm pecks, Maurice had caught him. Before Dorian could even slip through his fingers, Maurice's gun was already drawn. And, before Dorian/Fletcher could even notice Maurice point the gun in everyone's general directions (Nobody move!), he had already...

Turned the gun on himself.[162]

"You as my witness!" Maurice shouted, pulling Dorian's arm like a child would a doll.

Fletcher rolled his eyes and stepped in front of Odissa.

As the gun fired, Fletcher enveloped Odissa. The bullet ricocheted and hit the wood floor.

"You fucking idiot!" Dorian shouted when Fletcher was sure Odissa was OK. He ripped his body away from the intruder. "You could have killed her!"

Maurice hit the ground, fancy gun slipping from his fingers.

Odissa wanted to scream at the falling body but...

There wasn't any blood.

Taking her hand from her mouth (she felt stupid at being so dramatic), she stared between Fletcher and Dorian. They weren't concerned at all.

Dorian kicked the body. "Fucking Maurice! You can't pull shit like this."

"Is he—?" Odissa asked, wondering why they didn't seem to care.

Composing himself with a deep breath, Dorian pushed up his glasses. Fletcher took a cautious step toward Maurice, wondering if—just if...

---

[162] This scene seems so familiar. B.L.A. does love to wave a gun around

Well, it wasn't likely. Maurice had never been able to kill himself, so Fletcher didn't have high hopes (though there was still slight altitude—wishing every day that this thorn in their side would die for good).

Odissa jumped when Maurice's chest heaved and he opened one eye; the large thing rolled around the room, landing on Fletcher. "Am I dead?"

"Nope. Purgatory still," Fletcher said, leaning on his knees. His lips were a straight line, fighting against a twitch of annoyance.

Maurice sat up, moaning under his masculine weight. His shoulders slumped over, lip pouting. His legs were apart—like some little boy on the floor—a little boy with a waxed mustache. He frowned at his gun, cradled it in his palms. He began to blubber.

"Why must you do this in front of us? *Every* fucking time?" Dorian scolded, almost reaching down to shake Maurice but thinking better of touching something so pathetic. *Pathetic rubs off.* To Odissa, "He needs an audience—lo juro por Dios."

Maurice shook the gun in his hands—fighting against breaking it. "I was almost certain eet would work!" he spat, face turning red with frustration. "I had zee formula perfect—I vas sure!" He grit his teeth.

"You should have tested it beforehand," Dorian mumbled, gritting his own teeth.

"I may want to die, Dorian, but I do not want to die alone." He sniffed up his runny nose, staring at the floor.

"What witchcraft did you latch onto this time?" Dorian already regretted his interest.

Fletcher fought the gun away from Maurice and checked to see if there were more bullets. Empty.

Maurice looked up at him, sheepishly. His bottom lip quivered. "D'you know how hard eet iz to mine iron from Ethopia, get it blessed by priests of twenty different religions, and zen—and zen!—forge bullets from Italian volcanic coals?" He shook his head, tears squeezing out of his bulging red eyes.

"Isn't that like what you did last time?" Fletcher asked, picking up the bullet (that had bounced off Maurice's head) and sniffing it. A self-made one with—what was that?—ground *pearl*? He licked it to confirm again. He glanced at Maurice's gun. He couldn't classify what type it was. Probably a self-made contraption.

"OUI!" Maurice whimpered—on the verge of crying again. "But zis time I had it blessed by a shaman in the south of Maine, unlike last time. He is a favorite of Venus herself, so the witches said."

"Venus wouldn't come to them, you idiot. Was probably just some nymph or mermaid saying They were her!" Fletcher shouted, tossing the bullet behind him. "You know you can't trust the witches of Maine. They think they know but they don't."

"But eet was worth a shot!" He pounded his fists on his knees and kicked.

"Yes, but by now you ought to know your shots usually *miss*." Dorian hissed, gesturing for Fletcher to keep Odissa back, lest Maurice pull something else. "And why, again, must you do it in front of everyone? Some suicides are best done alone."

"Well, someone will need to clean up zee mess." Maurice gestured to the theoretical splatter that should have happened. Then, he seemed to notice Odissa. His ears—eyes—even his mustache perked up. "[Mumbling in French] So *zis* is the girl, eh? Zis must be her. [Mumbling more in French]."

His face turned into the most charming beam—as if he *handn't* just been weeping like a spoiled brat.

Dorian straightened, snapping his fingers. "You leave her alone. Don't speak to her. Stop it!"

Maurice was on his feet in an instant. He whipped his hands behind his back and leaned forward, turning one bulging eye toward her. Odissa swore his mustache's tips wiggled on their own—like a bug's antenna. "Ah! The infamous half of the infamous twins!"

Fletcher crossed his arms and rolled his eyes again. "Notice how the accent disappears when he's not being dramatic." Fletcher proceeded to scoff after Odissa almost smiled.

Indeed, I'm not fond of always catching his pronunciation and leave it to Gabbler to correct if I slip. However, feel free to imagine Maurice's accent as fading in and out.[163]

Odissa reared back—though he wasn't touching her, his every fiber intruded, forcing them to zoom in on each other. His hair was a dark brown, though his eyebrows and mustache were slightly black. Perhaps it was the wax. Even those bushy brows had a few curls.

He sent her mind into a vision—a vision of his zeitgeist. He reminded her (and I can feel you sighing now, for of course you've already called it) of an antique circus poster. A ringmaster—a mime—a strong man all at once. But there was another memory surfacing—a memory that made no sense—or perhaps not yet—of Mose the Bowery Boy.[164]

---

[163] Yeah, don't count on me to catch everything. The point is, after all, to leave the art bare and raw for the world.

[164] Mose. Legendary (and I do mean legendary—not real) volunteer firemar/street gang member in New York during the 19th century. Odissa is playing the historian again. I think I'm just going to start linking to Wikipedia articles instead of explaining things. Our Narrator assumes we're as knowledgeable as Odissa.

But this took her aback. She could always assign a historical figure (at least to humans) and it had never before been a fake one. A fictional folk hero could not count, no. Mose had no mustache. Wasn't Mose Irish? No wait—he was played by Frank Chanfrau. French enough—and mustachioed enough. Yes, yes, Frank Chanfrau—owner of the Bowery Theatre, first urban superhero, famed melodramatic actor—would do. And there it was—the mythos there—the rowdy immigrant yet to lose his European flair—the second-generation eccentric.

Yet he was no second-generation. He was a first. A very old original. A copy-and-paste of every French cliché I can think of. Let me stop there, lest I cram too much of him in and he become a lesser adaptation of the man he really was. Gods forbid I give him a beret.

An Antebellum French caricature—does that not clash nicely? But let me assure you, he's just what we needed to pick this gloomy story up.[165]

His finger came at Odissa's face. "*You* are the one Venus changed Dorian for." It was an announcement—as if for Odissa's benefit.

"Mecca knows better than to blab," Fletcher said, confiscating Maurice's gun for good by hiding it inside himself. He was busy trying to fend off Maurice and look out the far window—he could feel the neighbors' eyes because of the gunshot, but they weren't the type to invite the police. Poor Dorian was quite useless with Fletcher so torn between two tasks. He charged Maurice, but Maurice was always one step ahead—aside—around.

"No. It was Rosemund," Maurice said, never taking his eyes off Odissa as he dodged Dorian. Dorian was betrayed! "Why would Rose tell you my business?" He stopped his chase.

Still staring at Odissa, "We talk, we talk! After all, I'm her favorite guinea pig."

"Better you than me." Fletcher waved a hand, warning Maurice to keep his distance as he stepped to the window for a better look. He verified no one likely saw the commotion through the open door—it was at a good angle for privacy.

But Maurice did not heed Fletcher's warning. He took Odissa's hand, brushing it under his mustache. "I'm Maurice; enchanté. Mecca haz told me all about you. And his photography skills, well, zey did nothing to capture your true beauty!" He winked, enclosing her hand in his. He covered the side of his mouth to whisper, "My Mecca is a boy of many talents. Takes after hiz father. More ways zan one." Again with the wink and the wiggly mustache.

Fletcher pulled him back by his striped shirt.

---

[165] Yes, a suicidal character is the perfect pick-me-up.

Maurice turned to Dorian. "She is very pale, Dorian. But now that we know who she is you can tell there's a very *ethnic* streak about her. Her mother was Cherokee, no? And is she like you, Sorta Rican? Put her in a tanning bed and she'll look just très magnifique."

Odissa's eyes widened. *The fuck did he just say?*

Fletcher huffed in his face. "That's his favorite word, *ethnic*."

"Or was your mother only half Puerto Rican?" Maurice asked, as if that lessened her value. "No, that was your mother, Dorian. I got the Native American part right at least, oui?"

"I'm what?" Odissa asked Dorian, lighting up.

Dorian glowered at Maurice. He would threaten to kill him, but that would be no punishment...

Maurice turned back to Odissa, taking her hand once again despite Fletcher trying to slap it away. "And please don't worry, Odissa. I only want to kill myself because I have nothing left to live for. Nozing too dramatic."

Fletcher tugged him away again, Maurice's limbs flailing as he lifted him up like a puppy. "Touch her again, I'll break your nose."

Maurice pointed to Fletcher. "Odissa Odelyn, did you know zat Fletcher used to be *my* Automaton? *Oui*, I've been dead before—for a few seconds"—more like minutes—"But when I awoke, I couldn't control Fletcher. He was inanimate. I decided to live life without 'im. Zat's when our Dorian was brought into zee picture!" He slapped Dorian's back, making poor Dorian stumble forward.

Dorian was growing redder and redder. "Yes, all thanks to you, Maurice," Dorian mumbled. "We were just about to leave. Now, why don't you tell us where Mecca and Q are so I can kill them for bringing you here."

"Why *are* you here, Maurice?" Fletcher questioned.

Fletcher pulled Odissa away as Maurice kept inching closer to her (Odissa would be against the wall soon).

"Oh, Dorian. My son asked me to come. In times like zese, you know my boy needs his Papa."

"But *we* don't."

"I'm here to babysit the babysitters." He said it more like *baby-sit-airs*.

"You're just here because you want in on our hot Venus and Vulcan action," Fletcher scoffed.

"I brought him back to you didn't I? Give me some credit." Maurice's mustache twitched.

"Such a favor!"

"If you really think having him scampering about at a time like zis—when he is upset and looking for ways to cope—is a good idea, zen fine. Have fun bailing him out of an Ecuadorian prison again. I can't make that kind of money anymore. But you and I both know you could use someone like me—with no stake in zis feud—to keep *all* parties in line."

"Yes, but what's in this for you? We don't have the gods on speed dial—you know this. And we're not going to drive to Mexico to visit some curandero for a magic pendulum."

"Well, a simple invite for us to breakfast would be a start."

"Depends on who's 'us,'" Fletcher said to Maurice, looking outside the door for Mecca or Q—bound to be there! "We don't reward brats for their bad behavior."

Maurice upturned his nose, offended. "As if you should complain about my kids when you can't keep your own from fucking each ozer."

Odissa's jaw dropped. "How dare you—"

"I think I'm doing a fine job of it, actually," Dorian interrupted her and stepped toward Maurice.

"At the cost of the inanimates. They're no longer in your reach—"

"There it is!" Fletcher pointed. *The real reason he's here.*

"Q would be a safer storage place than Maud! How dare you all insult my son like this? He told me all about eet."

Fletcher laughed. "Not even Mother wanted to give your son the choice of handling an inanimate, Maurice. Wasn't just us."

"Q is more trustworthy zan Maud. Who knows what Maud is up to?"

Dorian shook a finger. "Automatons are not people. Maud has no *traits* outside of Odys. Why are you being so specific?"

About to be sorry he had asked: "Automatons can *make* the human!"

Fletcher squeezed the space between his eyes. "Not again with the Master Personality Transference Theory."

"You know eet happened!" Maurice pointed at Fletcher, brows merging.

Maurice remembered Odissa. "Perhaps she's even noticed it herself, zee transference!" His posture stiffened. "In her brozer."

Bros-air.

He realized he had her attention.

"Ah," he said with an esoteric crispness. "She *has* noticed."

"Don't, Maurice—" Dorian tried to inch to the door but it was too late. The show had begun.

Stanza: The Ringmaster's introduction.

His belly gravid with excited breath, "Odissa, have you noticed how Fletcher looks at Maud?"

Odissa's eyes went down in thought—how Fletcher had stared at Maud in the apartment when both had pretended to be cops.

"Ah, you have, haven't you? *Oui.* See, Odissa, I did zat."

"You did not!" Dorian snapped.

"Part of me is still inside Fletcher. And zat part is in Dorian too now. And zat part, no doubt, has been inside—"

Ooh la la!

"She gets the point—now get out of my house!"

But Maurice didn't budge when Dorian pushed at him. "I'm not ashamed to admit what I find attractive." From the side of his mouth, "(And that's a dark-skinned woman). Oh, how she could trick me into thinking she wasn't Pepin in disguise! That's the only reason I never touched her—" He mused, even though gadfly-Dorian was trying to shove him out the door to no avail. "If you're going to have an Automaton, *she* is the Automaton to have! Gods know I don't want Fletcher back. He's nothing to show off, you know."

"I resent that," Dorian said, crossing his arms.

"You would!" Maurice's eyes turned back to Odissa. "But the reason I mention Maud, Odissa, is because I have reason to believe that Masters transfer some of their *qualities* to their Automatons. I did it to Fletcher. Now, of course zis is what we believe happens with Automata memories—that their memories affect the new Master. *That* everyone seems to agree on. But what I'm saying is *personalities* affect them too. Like with computers: I reprogram the OS of one computer and zee next user has to deal with zee new settings. You leave your mark—not just your file-memories—on your Automaton. Zis is why Maud can't be trusted. She has turned your brother against us."

"There is no 'us,'" Fletcher said. "You stopped paying your dues a long time ago."

"He should never have been left alone with the inanimates. This would never have happened back in zee day."

Dorian buttoned up his coat. He was too angry to butt in so he had Fletcher do it: "Memories, personalities. Same thing for an Automaton."

399

Maurice's eyebrows and matching mustache rose, wondering if Odissa were catching on. "He doesn't like it, but Dorian has a zing for Maud! You see how he is pouting? Zat means it is true."

"No, it doesn't," Dorian denied.

"I am very zorry to zay, Odissa, but I do not think you were the first female Dorian fell in love with." He laughed a stereotypical French "huan-huan-haun."

"Love has nothing to do with how he looked at Maud," Odissa said, her brows coming together. *How the fuck did we get on this subject?*

Maurice shrugged in the French sweater-shirt I'm making him wear. "Perhaps so. Dorian can control it better," Maurice elaborated when he saw Odissa's curiosity. "But Fletcher is more obvious about it. Always looking."

"Everyone looks at Maud!" Dorian shouted, hand on the door knob. The cold was making him shiver—that or the rage.

"He makes excuses because he doesn't like zat I'm inside him. Making him notice her. Venus didn't have far to turn the dial, thanks to moi."

"Fuck you!" Dorian rambled on in Spanish—on why Maurice shouldn't be here, on why he better stop putting these thoughts in Odissa's head, on why he was such an asshole.

For a few seconds, the two men argued—each in their mother tongues. There was quite a bit of hand-gesturing—especially at Odissa. Then, finally:

"But eef zee girl iz going to have an Automaton, she 'as the right to know! You give her Coraza and the next thing you know she's Leeland. I say never use those Automatons again."

"This isn't your decision!" Dorian barked back.

Odissa walked to the door. "I may not have understood the multilingual [bilingual?] fight you just had, Maurice, but I think I understand why you *really* mentioned it. I can tell you right now I wouldn't accept Admund or Coraza. You don't have to worry about that. They will not be transferring anything to me."[166]

Dorian was boiling, his hat now askew. "Stop trying to frighten her into abstinence. Maybe if she did touch Admund, she'd understand your stupid theory then. She'd understand what it's like to have no control over what your Automaton makes you fucking notice!"

Maurice motioned to our frothing Dorian. "See, he admits eet."

---

[166] Are we really still on this will-she-or-won't-she subject? She's made it pretty clear she doesn't want them. Whyyy are we still talking about this?

"Let's go to breakfast," she said, feeling embarrassed for Dorian and like Maurice would not leave the house unless they did.

"Yes, let's!" Maurice clapped his huge, veiny hands.

"That wasn't an invitation," Dorian grumbled.

Maurice followed them out, just the same.

They saw Mecca and Q in Maurice's truck, their eyes peeking over the dash. Dorian went up to the nose of the car and shouted, "Get out of the truck!" He slapped the hood, threatening to dent it.

They locked the car doors, eyes wide. But Fletcher used his Automaton-ways to pop the lock and drag them out with his noodle-arms like puppies by the scruff. They didn't fight it.

"They're not getting breakfast," Dorian said flatly.

Fletcher plopped them in the snow. "Someone needs to watch Bulfinch anyway. It's your punishment for bringing this zombie along. Go, get in the house." Fletcher kicked Q's bum as she scurried away to Maurice.

"Oui, in zee house," Maurice shooed them away gently. "Order some food. Behave." He gave a wink to them no one but Odissa noticed, turned to get into his truck.

"Maybe it's good Maurice is here?" Odissa asked Dorian as they rounded their vehicle (clearly not riding with Maurice). "They seem to obey him."

They had gone so penitently it was almost suspicious.

"No." Dorian growled. He opened the door of Odissa. "Because there is no one for Maurice to obey."

"Why does Mecca obey him?"

"Because Maurice threatened to disinherit him of his antique circus equipment."

(Oh, the erotic things you can do with that!)

"Seriously?"

"Fuck if I know." He noticed he was being rude and corrected himself. "Mecca has daddy issues. Plus, who wouldn't be afraid of a spanking from someone you can't kill?"

"I'm surprised he didn't bring his clown car." Fletcher grumbled, watching Maurice back out and wait for them to start driving. "Mustn't be big enough for his ego anymore."

Dorian humphed and slammed the car door for Odissa.

Stanza: The first law of Metafictional Thermodynamics...

In his own car, Dorian released his angry tension...by *driving.*

I guess I forgot to mention that Odissa was a bit confused she'd been placed in the passenger's seat.

Fletcher leaned forward from the middle of the back, eyes on the road for Dorian. Dorian pressed pedal to the metal and sped through a yellow light. It made Odissa nervous to see him so mentally crowded. They had ignored her protests of "But he's blind…"

Odissa calmed down when she remembered Dorian wouldn't do anything to put her in danger. That was impossible. "Did you guys agree on where to meet? Did I—did I miss something?" They had lost Maurice in his truck minutes ago at a stoplight.

No part of Dorian responded.

Thinking of ways to distract him—to get his mind off the unwanted visitors: "Maybe I should drive," she glanced back at Fletcher, as if that part of Dorian might back her up. "I need to drive. It's—it's too *effeminate* for me to sit here."

"Not now, Odissa." *No gender-swapping jokes today!*

"Don't snap at me like that."

"He shouldn't know Odys has the inanimates. Mecca needs to keep his mouth shut."

"Why? Does it matter?"

"Yes, it matters! Especially since we can't kill him if we need to keep *him* quiet."

"And does he normally go about telling people your secrets or something?"

Fletcher gestured to Dorian. "My Master, here, is just looking for excuses to be angry. He's unhappy they were even able to find us so quickly. This means we have roommates."

"And," Dorian expounded his own expounding, "you're not even jealous. You're not even jealous I like Maud. Hell, you're not even jealous I like Fletcher. Makes me feel like I'm powerless. Like I have no control over this relationship."

"You want me to throw a fit like you? Is that it?" She leaned over the middle section of the car, blocking Fletcher's view for a few seconds. Dorian swerved a little on the road.

"Jesus—" Fletcher tried to look around her.

"You want me to be upset? I'll be upset!" She shouted at him. He frowned so she knew her abuse was working. "You knew he would find us. I can tell." She prodded him.

Dorian had Fletcher grab at her gloved hand. "Stop it, you'll make us crash."

"And if we do? I'll be hurt. You're the one playing a game with my life, Dorian. All for show!"

She sat forward in her seat once again. To herself, "You turn into my mother. You turn into Odys. Fuck."

The boys said nothing else. Fletcher's eyes glanced at her and back to the road. He adjusted his elbow on the back of their seats, not sure how to interpret her words.

"...And maybe I am a bit jealous," she said after a few seconds of silence.

His face still an unhappy slab, Dorian asked, "Really?"

"Sure," Odissa shrugged. "It makes me jealous that if it wasn't for Venus's intervention, I wouldn't have you. Not that that's new. That makes *me* feel powerless."

The window was foggy, so she pulled her fingers down on the glass. It was starting to snow in flurries again.

Odissa inclined her head against that window like someone trying to cool their fever. "So, like, is Maurice the only Master to not have had a *relationship* with his Automaton?" She waved a hand in the air, as if to make space for her words.

"Relationship?" Dorian asked. "You mean sex?"

She realized what she was doing and clutched the collar of her coat, embarrassed. Now she was going to have to annotate her statement—something she wished she had planned for better. "He seems to be the only one. All the vibes from the others ..."

"No, Maurice never fucked me if that's what you're asking," Fletcher said. "And I wouldn't call it sex, either. It's still very one-sided."

"But is it?" she asked. "That's not what I'd call masturbation—do you call sex with a sex doll masturbation? It's not like they're real, but there's no one else but you there, either. Then again, I don't do it, so I have nothing to compare."

Dorian, taken aback by her haphazard tone, still welcomed a verdant smirk, "You don't masturbate?"

Odissa thought about it. "I never had to." She enjoyed how her response bit at him.

Dorian swallowed her answer and upchucked one of his own: "Well, that's good. Because when you get an Automaton, I want the only one you're fucking to be me."

"That's not really fair."

"It's not fair you might just get a male Automaton."

"You didn't seem to mind yours."

"Yeah, well."

She cut her eyes at Dorian, liking how she had taken his mind off Maurice—so *powerful*. "Just think of the things I could make a male Automaton do to you, Dorian. What I could make Madus do to Fletcher."

She noted Fletcher's stoic eyes glance from her—as if his sight had brushed her shoulder like a hand.

"Don't say things like that," Fletcher said, though he wasn't sure why he said it.

"I would do whatever I wanted with my Automaton." She was pushing herself around by her elbows again. Her eyes narrowed—not at Fletcher, but at the Dorian who was looking *through* Fletcher.

As he tried to look past her—avoiding eye contact to keep his view on the road—he couldn't help but be distracted when—

She kissed him.

That's right. She kissed Dorian's Automaton. She could hear Dorian stiffen in the seat beside her—not only because he was having trouble seeing the road through Odissa's head, but, because, well, he could *feel* her.

Fletcher, trying to watch the road and find the right reaction, somehow remained very still for the whole experience—as if Dorian were taking his time in deciding whether or not this was...*OK*.

Dorian decided to pull over, bumping them apart. "Eyes on the road, man!" he huffed—at himself. "And *you*,"—he pointed a finger at Odissa—"that wasn't very nice. Don't touch me like that." He shifted in his seat, uncomfortable.

"What, like this?" She ran a hand across Fletcher's lips. Fletcher finally reared back from her.

"Now I've had a *relationship* with an Automaton. We're even, and now all we have to do is fuck each other without tally marks." She said it with a defeated tone, though she was quite smug with herself.

"You call that a relationship?" Fletcher forced a snort. "It was only a kiss." Fletcher stared at the road, an annoyed expression on his face, though the kiss itself had gained no reaction (for that, you must view the Master's face).

"Depends on how you define a relationship," Odissa watched the road as Dorian started driving again.

"You don't know what you're doing—what you're saying," Dorian said, gripping the steering wheel too tightly and shifting in his seat again. But he couldn't hide the fact his dick was hard. "You don't have a soul outside your body. You can't just intrude on mine like that."

"Yes, I can. I just did. And you liked it. You liked it a lot, as far as I can see. You liked it but the human part of you doesn't want to because it just looks *weird*. Is that why you don't like

Maurice, because he makes you feel *weird*, Dorian? He makes you remember wet dreams about Maud and 'ethnic' women?" She chuckled. "I like weird, Dorian. Haven't you figured that out by now?"

"I like weird too, and that's what fucking scares me."

"Where are we even going?" Odissa asked, pulling down the mirror to check her hair.

"To breakfast."

"But I'm sure there are a hundred different places that sell *breakfast*."

"But not all of them sell French toast."

"Yeah…that really narrows it down for me."

"Maurice has a very distinct compass, Odissa," Fletcher said as he tapped his nose. "He can follow us even if he doesn't see our damn car. He's fucking drawn to me because he's still inside me. Calling me. The pull is stronger at this proximity. And yes, that does mean we just admitted to his Transference Theory. But you don't have to tell him that."

She studied his angry expression—Fletcher looked angrier than Dorian now. Perhaps that's because Dorian was too busy trying to get rid of his boner.

Dorian parked the car. Before Odissa could unbuckle her seatbelt, Maurice's face was in her window, tapping the glass. He wore no coat, just that too-tight sweater. He opened the door for her, quite the gentleman.

"Stop opening doors for her!" Fletcher ordered, slamming his own. He wedged himself between them before Maurice could offer his arm.

Odissa opened the restaurant door for Dorian, to keep Maurice from doing it for her.

There were a few people in the diner, but most were over age fifty and surprised to see younger kiddos. At first they frowned at the fantastic four—so metro-sexual, that one—so hippie-ish, the other—so odd *she* was with them, that one. The older one was all right. His mustache was sublime.

But, these seniors seemed to realize they'd best not scare off new entertainment, and averted their eyes and their judgment. Yet they kept sneaking looks—unable to resist this group with men who reminded them so much of times gone by…

As they went to their far-off table.

"Don't you kids have some hot-happening place to be at?" A grey woman smiled up at them, clutching her black coffee cup. She knew her comment was random, but she couldn't resist. Old people have to create their kicks by poking at what's not theirs anymore.

Dorian took the opportunity to shine. "Why, this is where all the cool kids go!" His smile melted her heart, so charming and boyish.

They were in!

Dorian made Fletcher sit with Odissa. Simply because he didn't want Maurice near her or his Automaton now. *No touching my things.*

"What'll it be?"

The boys knew what they wanted and ordered—ordered too much.

Odissa, "Coffee."

Maurice, "Zat's it?"

Dorian, "If that's all she wants, then, yes."

(He latched on to any opportunity to snap at Maurice).

Waitress, "Alrighty, then. Just a few minutes." She picked up their menus.

"You already directed negative attention to us," Maurice scolded, his voice hushed.

"No, you did that!" Fletcher said, pointing and crossing his arms to match his Master.

"Stop it, both of you." Odissa hissed. "No more grouching until I get my fucking coffee."

"Yes, Madame," Maurice smirked and laced his fingers together.

They spent a few seconds lingering under the old-time radio music, oiling up their rusty etiquettes. Odissa wished an old person would talk to them again and break the tension.

"So," Maurice could stand the silence no longer, "has Odys made contact yet?"

"What makes you think he'd contact us?" Fletcher asked him, as if this family gathering had turned into a business meeting. The tone was shifting. Odissa pretended not to notice—she kept up her old-people-watching. But her ears tuned in.

"Mecca told me how you spoke to Mother, last you saw her."

"Oh?"

"Mecca said you weren't too pleased with her. Not zat you're pleased with Odys either."

Dorian decided to defend himself, "I was angry. I still am. I didn't like confronting her, but she could have done *all this* a lot differently."

"Mecca thinks you did like it. Mecca thinks you needed to get something off your chest, there."

"And I'm sure Mecca also told you what she did, so you know my anger is justified."

Maurice's mustache twitched and he spoke through the side of his mouth in Dorian's direction, never turning his head, instead addressing Fletcher. "Mecca said he had never seen you so angry."

Dorian added, "That little runt of yours shouldn't have brought you to me. Go and find Odys. Gwendolyn. Rose. Anyone but me."

"But you're the easiest to find," Maurice chuckled, gesturing to Fletcher. "No, Mother sent Mecca with you for a reason and I intended to figure out that reason."

This made Dorian prickle. They were getting off topic. "I've said before you need to put a stopper in him, Maurice. It was bad enough he was doing it"—all things in general— "when he was younger, but he's an adult now, technically. You can't keep making excuses for him. He's proving your hypothesis wrong. He hasn't matured. He won't. Everyone's thinking it. No one will say it. They don't want to hurt your feelings, but he's never stopped being a risk. And you're never around to suffer the danger or put a stop to it. You know he made me jump Odissa? I almost killed her because of his pranks!"

Odissa's eyebrows came together, putting the pieces in place.

Maurice just chuckled. "Can you blame him for being bored? Life iz so long and so dull. Let him have what little fun is left, Dorian."

The server brought out the drinks/Odissa's breakfast.

Dorian's jaw twitched. "If not for Gwen I would have put him down a long time ago."

Odissa gasped at his statement. "Dorian!" *To say such a thing.*

"You'll have to kill me first before you can get to zat point. You're so moody, Dorian. Is this because of the pictures he posted online of you and Odissa in the bathtub?"

"What?" Odissa blurted out, coffee going up her nose.

Dorian did not react. "This is exactly what I mean, Maurice. We can't manage with him."

"You think that is why you cannot manage? How has he held you back? He is your scapegoat!"

Dorian leaned into Maurice to growl: "She's supposed to be dead. What if those photos are found? It blows her cover!"

"Ah, but he iz so good at taking photos! Don't worry. Eet did not have your faces." He sighed, basking in his son's many talents. To Odissa with a wink, "I taught him everyzing he knows!"

"Though *why* is yet to be understood," Dorian grumbled. Fletcher took out his phone to see if he could find the site where the pictures were up. Hopefully they were a collection he could easily hack. He'd search Mecca's regular outlets.

Maurice, with winsome fashion, changed the subject, "Odissa, you want to know how Mecca got his name? Everyone does. Well, I say 'everyone' as if there *is* someone new to tell on a regular basis."

"You regularly remind us on a regular basis," Fletcher uttered, tapping his fingers on that smart phone.

The comment did not assuage Maurice. "I'll start from the beginning."

"Of course you would," sighed Fletcher.

"Look what you've done, Odissa," Dorian scolded her, as if she could put a stop to it.

But she didn't mind Dorian's irritation. She actually wanted to know. And she was starting to like Dorian's squirming.

"I'll give her the short version if you stick zis fork in my brain, Dorian," Maurice bargained, his eyes bulging toward the Master.

"No matter how much I'd enjoy it," Dorian replied with hum-drum airs, "I'm not even going to *consider* assisted suicide until after breakfast." He leaned back as if picturing himself doing it.

Maurice resumed his preface. "Perhaps a short version anyway, since I'm a tad depressed my bullet didn't work zis morning. That took me two years and fifty thousand dollars." He cleared his throat, the thought of wasted time choking him. "Now, Odissa, when I died, I had actually been in a very melancholy mood. Despite the fact I was very good at my job (I still am, you know), I was debating the purpose of it—of zee circus. Even today, I can still get a lot of money for my tricks. Hell, I'm even better at them now since I can't kill myself! But as I was zaying, I hadn't practiced the tightrope in many months, as I had been traveling in Rome on holiday."

He never walked the rope for shows. It had only been his personal hobby, to enjoy alone. He felt most would think him silly—a huge man on the rope. He'd rather stick an attractive Maud up there, to wow the crowd—someone the crowd would care about if she fell. Also, he'd rather see her up there himself. A spectacular view.

"What does this have to do with why you named Mecca 'Mecca'?" Dorian asked.

"To understand the name, she must understand the father!" Maurice insisted, as if Dorian were incredibly stupid rather than rude.

"But you died *after* Mecca became a Master."

"Which I will highlight in my story once I come to eet!" And he continued with his more-than-near-death experience.

See, when he practiced, he never secured the under-nets because he never had need of them. What need of nets has a Master? But as he fell from the rope, and before he hit the ground, life—as is expected—flashed before his French, French eyes. As he looked upon it (his life) he thought, well, he'd had a good run. It was only natural that a human would be afraid of a fall and therefore contemplate death during a major one. And as he fell, well, he had accepted the fact that if he _were_ to die, he wouldn't be too sad about it. It had been a full life, yes. Thus, in essence, he was willing to die. Very willing.

"Same as Pepin pulling that trigger," he said, pulling Odissa out of his flashback.

Fletcher looked up from the phone. "I still don't see what this has to do with Mecca, you self-involved—"

"You see, before I had died, my son had just celebrated his birthday. And we'd just given him his Automaton, the _beautiful_ Q."

"Pedophile," Dorian mumbled to the empty table.

"And so, I was content that my son was secure and safe. It was one more reason to accept death. Thus, some might say I was perfectly suicidal as I fell those somewhat-fifty feet. And, upon impact, I died." He clapped his hands together—splat. "For exactly [BLEEEEEEP] minutes.[167] I think I was able to be revived after so long only because I _was_ a Master. It was quite lucky, too, that Pepin happened to walk by and notice my death. One of my old dwarf assistants had begun to scream—violently, the poor dear. Zere was quite a lot of blood." He gestured with his hands—as if he had been gushing. "I landed on my legs. It protected my head, unfortunately."

"The only reason he didn't explode upon impact is because he didn't _want_ to die until his legs landed." Fletcher caught her eyes. "He didn't make use of the fall until the very last minute— didn't _try_ to die until it almost passed him by."

"And now I forever chase her—beautiful Death."

Odissa set her coffee back down, no longer finding an appetite.

"Anyway, before any of our relations could accidentally graze Fletcher (who had been sleeping in my pocket), Pepin used his scarf to pick him out and deliver him to Mother's care. Maud had been trying to revive me. She kept hitting my chest with her metal hands—hands charged with soul." He lifted his own up in demonstration. "They were able to revive me before the ambulance arrived. She could start a heart as well as stop it! They tried to pump me full of things. Pepin tried to do it for them at one point—thinking that it was just a normal human who couldn't puncture me. Pepin had to kill them later, because they asked so many questions. 'No, you're not doing it right,' Pepin kept saying, taking charge."

Maurice chuckled.

"Upon my hospital bed, we soon realized I no longer had any control over Fletcher. I was, at first thought, free of him. We didn't know the side effects would linger. I did not know I _didn't_

---

[167] The exact number is unimportant, and changes according to storyteller and listener.

have the option of death. When I came to, we all knew which option I'd eventually choose—*still* would like to choose, for that matter. It is a miserable existence, you see. With or without an Automaton. Mother said I could have Fletcher back if I wanted, but I didn't. I told them 'Give him to someone who needs him. I have no need!'"

"That's not exactly what you said," Fletcher said. "From what I hear it was more like, 'Fuck no. He's kept me from getting laid too many times. I'll share my bed no longer!'"

Maurice ignored Fletcher and sighed, still keeping up with his dramatic tone. "Of course they knew. They knew I had essentially done it—accepted death. It just hadn't worked. In the back of my mind, I even considered actually living a normal life—leaving all these fuckers behind. But zen zere was always the case of my son, Mecca—whom I had already trapped in this Automata-life with me..."

"No, you trapped *us* with him," Dorian growled.

Maurice gave a dramatic pause—staring off into space. "I did try to kill myself, later on. I was a liability to my son, after all, and Leeland was growing worse and worse. It was that attempt at death, however, that proved death impossible. Rosemund was all over me after that. She had so many things she wanted to 'test.'"

The breakfast was brought out, and Maurice sat back, the whole group eager to eat as if they hadn't just been discussing Maurice's blood and gore.

Thank you, no that will be all, yes, you can leave the check now.

Maurice watched Fletcher pour on his syrup so thick it ran over his plate (and proceeded to do the same for Dorian). He tucked his napkin in his collar. His voice very low, "As far as we can tell, I'm the first one to, well, *come back.* Also, the side-effects go against everyzing we know. Even Masters can kill themselves, but I can't now? In theory—"

"Ah, more of your theories!" Dorian shoveled waffle in his face.

"*In* theory," Maurice went on, "my soul must be stuck in a type of limbo. Still in Fletcher, maybe. Better yet—it's already in the afterlife while I'm just here, just my body. It's waiting to get its soul back. Zomezing like that."

"Yeah, *zomezing* like that," Dorian mocked.

"It was Vulcan!" Maurice said, waving his toast-covered fork. "He won't let me die. He meant for zis to happen. He has a purpose for me." He winked at Odissa. *And that purpose involves you.*

"Don't flatter yourself," Fletcher said, already done with his pancakes. He went back to his phone.

"Now," Maurice said to Odissa, "I only told you all this so that you'll understand what kind of a man I am—and why I named Mecca 'Mecca.' For sure, you wonder why—if I believe Vulcan has a purpose for me—I would still want to die? Well, Odissa, I don't like being controlled. Especially by a god zat isn't the highest up, if you know what I mean." He crossed himself the Catholic way. "He has no right to take away my free will." He adjusted his napkin like a tie. "I rebel in little ways: I stand in front of microwaves daily. I do not look both ways before crossing the street. I smoke, to blacken my lungs. Yet nothing works. Even my own body fails to destroy itself." He sighed a great sigh, staring into his food. "I *could* have died. But you damned lot revived me."

"I had no part in it, believe me," Dorian said. To Odissa, "They didn't even know I existed at that point."

"Before all that, I had traveled to Africa. Toured Egypt. That sort of thing."

"The *colonial* thing," Fletcher took a righteous drink from his orange juice.

"On my travels, I had a son."

"You can give birth now, can you?" Dorian asked, his lips covered in sticky syrup.

"No one knows the full story." Not even Mecca, for that matter. "And I like to keep it that way. As does everyone else, it seems, because they leave the DNA tests alone, well enough."

Fletcher snorted. He gestured with his fork to Maurice. "You wanna know why he doesn't want us to know if Mec's his real son? Because *he* doesn't want to know."

"He is my real son." Maurice's mustache ruffled. "They actually like Mecca, despite what they say." He cut into his breakfast angrily. "And it's not like Mecca lets them the chance to give a paternity test. Mecca wants to be mine and that's all that counts. Blood hardly matters beyond zat."

Odissa shook her head. "But why put so much effort into claiming he's your son if you're just going to undermine it with a speech like that?"

"Pardon?"

"You want to kill yourself. To leave him. That's not very fatherly."

"I can see you judge me. But even in death, I could still be a good father."

"And he really doesn't want to know if Mecca's mom slept with someone else before she died," Dorian added.

Odissa frowned. "Did I really need to know all of that, Maurice?"

"Oh, now you take our side!" Dorian huffed.

Maurice shrugged. With his mouth now full, "I think eet gives greater context, oui. See, after I learned zat 'is mother died, I brought him with me. And I eventually convinced Pepin and Mother to let someone so young have an Automaton. Zey knew he needed protection. The stars had aligned—Q was vacant at the time." He chewed a bit and washed it down. "Now, since we've gotten that bit out of the way, I can tell you about his name. For sure, you look at me—a devout Catholic!—and you find it strange that I named him *Mecca*."

MECCA: Not just a place anymore.

HOLY: Crap.

FATHER: Who cares if he's Maurice or not? No one else would claim him.

MOTHER: The reason Mecca needed his Papa.

Chapter the fourth,

Monotheism is the polytheism:

How many gods does it take to make monotheism?

"Yes, one good look at Maurice and you can tell he's Catholic." Fletcher rolled his eyes.

"I named him Mecca because we needed a little homesickness in our group. There was too much Greco-Roman talk, you see. There still is, frankly. Even we Catholics, with all our Latin! Abrahamic religions deserve their recognition. Zat and Mecca's mother never got to make her pilgrimage. Mecca came *to her*."

"That. That's the lead he buried," Fletcher jabbed at the disappearing words. "No self-involved tangent or rant about death needed."

"I wanted to remind Vulcan of his place in the religious order. That he is not so important anymore. Perhaps that's why I lived after my death." Maurice snorted. "He's punishing me for hubris!"

"And THAT," Dorian inserted, "is why Vulcan owes us all one for making us suffer eternity with this French asshole." He took a sip from Fletcher's orange juice (his apple was already gone).

They finished their meal—sat and stared at their empty plates while waiting for someone to make a decision. I'll make it now:

"Oh!" Maurice exclaimed cheerily, "Guess what!" (No one guessed). "Found a new wrinkle recently. Just here. Eet might mean I'm getting older!" He leaned in to whisper, "Older means death."

"No, it just means you're frowning more than usual," Fletcher noted, finally turning off the phone (Mecca's photos apparently taken down from the site—the hacktivist hacked).

"Speaking of frowning," Maurice said with a frown, "when's the last time you've spoken to Vulcan, zat worthless piece of *sheet*?"

"I'm sure Mecca has mentioned the mall excursion?"

Odissa blushed, recalling what Mecca had seen

"But zat smells more like Venus. Not Vulcan, Dorian."

"Same thing some days," Fletcher hissed—like a machine releasing steam.

"If you must know, He came to me to warn me His Wife was meddling. Which a lot of good that did us," Dorian crossed his legs under the table. Its brushed Odissa's knee.

She looked at him as if it were code for something she could not translate.

"The gods have been silent lately, but silence is golden," Maurice explained for Odissa's benefit. "It's the other *senses* that can speak. Gods still have a stench. My nose isn't what eet used to be, but I can feel His ash. It lands on me. Won't brush off." He shivered.

Dorian took out his wallet. "I'm ready to leave. See you back at the house, Maurice."

Fletcher pulled him back down with an outstretched arm. "Not yet. Do you smell that?"

Maurice's eyes rolled across the room. He pointed to a man leaving the bathroom. He was a huge sort. The poor man was balding, his white rolls of all-American fat jiggling as he limped over to them. The leg brace supported his entire calf—from ankle to knee. That leg threatened to buckle under the man's massive weight. Though the face seemed jolly enough, it was also tired.

The man stopped and looked down at them, heaving—as if he'd just walked twenty miles. Sweat was moistening the underarms of his shirt. The man sniffed, keeping his nose from running.

Maurice's mustache twitched. Fletcher's nose itched. Dorian's head tilted to hear. Odissa's eyes widened.

Could it be?

Maurice was the first to glower and speak. "Speak of zee devil."

They all looked up at the towering mountain-man—except Odissa, who looked at her captors because she didn't understand why they were frozen in place. There was hardly a tint of fear in Maurice's eyes, though Odissa swore his mustache twitched in anxiety. Maurice, you see, hadn't seen Vulcan in quite some time.

Maurice was about to speak (speak some angry, well-rehearsed words) when—he found he couldn't. Couldn't even open his lips.

"I hate the French," Vulcan said, like one might to an inbred dog. "They're always much more interested in my wife than me. Love language—*ha!*"

413

Thankfully, Vulcan's colossal size blocked the view of others who might otherwise catch a glimpse of what was going on.

"Actions speak louder than words, Maurice. All talk and no action."

Maurice's upper lip spasmed as he stopped trying to speak. He even struggled to leave his seat but found his ass glued down. Odissa was mortified. Maurice settled on the one thing he could do: give Him the finger.

But Vulcan was done with Maurice and turned his Moai-shaped head to Fletcher. "Heard my name in conversation. Thought I'd trudge by." The god wheezed in a few breaths—a very good act that went well with his costume. "I'd take Maurice's advice, if I were you."

"Advice? What advice."

"The advice he came to give. To bestow upon you're unwilling ears—one of the few senses you have left, Dori." He pulled at his lobes.

"So his plans fit yours, that it? Your plans haven't always been for my best interest, V. Your will be done, but what about ours?" Dorian tucked his wallet away.

"And just what do you plan to do about it? Stand in front of microwaves like him? You think that pisses me off? No. It's fucking good entertainment."

"Was Bob's death entertaining? Did you sell tickets?"

A few people were starting to stare, their old ears trying to listen. But don't worry, Vulcan wouldn't let them—no matter how many times they adjusted their hearing aids.

"Listen here, Dorian. I came because I wanted to give you an update on Odys. He's about to text you again."

The phone gave a little jingle under Fletcher's hand.

"Speak of the devil," Vulcan panted, a smugness on his lips.

Fletcher opened the text. Odissa read over his shoulder: "Tell me when we can meet and where."

"Take Maurice's advice and respond to Odys. That's what Maurice would suggest. Isn't that right, Maurice? He wants you to set up a time and a date. You should do that. But you won't will you? You're mad at me and doing the opposite of what I want. But you're the one suffering for it. The longer you drag it out, the longer you two have to stay under the same roof." He pointed between the two Fletcher-Masters. "You need Maurice, Dorian." Vulcan's saggy eyes cut over to Maurice. "But don't think you've served a purpose yet."

Vulcan lingered over them for a few seconds, looking right through them. Then, His eyes rolled over to Odissa for a few seconds. It was an indifferent stare. Dorian had hoped her first Vulcan-sighting would be more impressive. But that was usually asking too much from the god.

"Also note, I don't give a fuck if you think I smell or not, Fletcher. Now, if you'll excuse me, I actually intend on having coffee with these old farts back behind me. You may leave now."

Standing up, "Is that what you told Bob? That she could just 'leave' us?" Dorian demanded an answer with his waiting. "What did you tell her? What were your last words to her?"

The man turned back around. "Who?" The bodies in the diner paused. Then, "Don't make a scene, Dorian. She made her choice. I'll make use of all choices. Now go before I start a gas leak in this joint to teach you a lesson."

He must have pressed his magical play button, for the world started moving once more.

Odissa looked over her shoulder as they left the diner, the little bell on the door ringing. "He really *is* having coffee with them!" *But He wouldn't say one word to me.*

Was it odd to think He should have?

Dorian took her by the forearm and stuffed her in the back seat with him. This time Fletcher would drive. And he'd take the long way home. "He's not really having coffee with them. He's probably just possessed some poor bastard who was already here. Easier than creating a completely new look, likely. Hell if I know."

Stanza: Living dead boy.

Maurice and Fletcher parked their cars…behind the delivery truck.

"What the fuck did you do?" Fletcher-with-his-hands-on-his-hips asked the little boy inside.

"Mecca bought us lots of stuff yesterday. Mecca didn't shop too hard, though. Click here, click there. All from one place. Nothing fancy," Mecca said, browsing the web on one of his tablets. His little bare feet dangled down from Q's arms. Her eyes were supervising the men's delivery going on around them.

"Nothing fancy?" Fletcher shouted as an HD television the size of a car was squeezed through the door. "We're gonna get robbed!"

Indeed, the neighbors were staring.

"Mecca paid for convenience, not quality, this time. Besides, we're not staying here long. Papa already told Mecca *everything*."

(So that's why Maurice had been on the phone when driving).

Fletcher snatched the tablet from Mecca's hand. He followed it up with, "You know credit cards can be traced and addresses hacked. We're supposed to be hiding. You—you can't just redecorate someone's house."

Q rolled her eyes. "Like we really threw off the feng shui."

Dorian spun to Maurice. "He can't redecorate. *I'm* the gay one!"

"It's not redecorating if it's never been decorated," Odissa mumbled.

Maurice laughed. "Oh come, Dorian! You know he's safe about these things. And it's not like Odys couldn't find us if he really tried."

"That's not the point," Fletcher said, moving Odissa out of the way of a very nice mattress being brought in.

One gentleman told Q, "The bedrooms are all set."

She replied with a "Thank you so much. And the kitchen?"

Fletcher tossed the tablet back to Q. "He should have asked."

"But we wanted to surprise you," Q said, gently handing the tablet to her Master. His hands grabbed at it as if a baby blanket. "To make up for…things." Her eyes cut to Maurice. "If we're going to be uncomfortable here together, might as well make it less so."

Odissa grabbed Dorian's hand and, with a cheerio-tone said, "Well, there's no use standing when there's empty seats." And she sat him down.

It was much cozier, and Q had the TV programmed in a matter of seconds. "Stealing cable from the neighbors, but no biggie. The company will never know the difference."

Maurice had taken to a solemn rocking chair in the corner and, after crossing his legs, had pulled a pipe from his pants' pockets and a small tin of tobacco. "I'd ask if you mind, but I can smell a like-kind," he said to Odissa with a wink.

She had made herself comfortable on the new sofa, facing the television. Dorian had ensconced grudgingly as Fletcher had gone to inspect the house for any eccentricities. He suppressed a smile when he noticed a coffee maker for Odissa. "Good boy, Mecca," he said as he pat it. He would make some for Odissa.

Mecca had taken to the overstuffed chair, still busy on his phone and tablet. Odissa wondered if, perhaps, Fletcher had hacked something too noticeable (in regard to the cabin photos)? Mecca was engrossed.

"Can I use the restroom?" Odissa quietly asked, leaning over to Dorian.

His ears perked, alert. "Yeah, sure."

Maurice, puffing away, "You make her ask?" His bushy eyebrows danced.

Odissa, standing up, laughed. She'd let Dorian handle that one.

When Odissa got back, they were watching a Russian channel. And seeming to understand/enjoy it. Maurice's foot bobbed as Odissa sat back down, though his eyes were on the TV. She glanced out the window, at their reflection. The cramped coziness made it feel as though it should be Thanksgiving or Christmas—what Odissa assumed such holidays would feel like, based on movies and books. It looked as though it might snow again. There was light, but no sun. But she could tell the day was almost over. Their breakfast had been more of a lunch. Time was moving quicker and there was nothing they could do to tell the gods to slow it down.[168]

Maurice noticed it too. "They're growing impatient"—as if he'd had the same thought.

"Damn right I am," Dorian grumbled. "I want you out of my house."

Maurice pulled out his pocket watch, checked the time, his bold chin wrinkling into his neck. "Mecca, what time is eet?"

Mecca looked at his phone, confirming their fears. "Never enough time in the day for Mecca to get everything done," he sighed, shaking his head.

"The fuck have you got going on then?" Dorian said. *By all means, leave and do it.* "So far it seems like we're the only agenda item."

…

Odissa savored this moment with these amusing creatures who felt like coming home, despite Odys not being there.

"…Odissa," Maurice stated over the television's mumble and Odissa's vision.

"Yes?" She looked at him, confused that he'd address her suddenly.

"Do you think Odys would give you an Automaton if you asked for it?"

"What kind of a question is that?" Dorian thusly interjected, putting a hand on her back as if to remind Maurice he needed to go through him.

Odissa rolled her eyes at him, knowing he couldn't see. Mecca and Q stifled giggles at Odissa's expression. Eventually she answered Maurice, "No. I don't think he'd give me any Automaton I asked for. He spent his whole life hating my father and anyone involved with him. He finally has a chance to keep me away from Augury, and he'll do it. Even if that means staying away from me himself."

---

[168] Yeah, sure, the gods. In no way is it the fact you have too many characters in the pot now and not enough plot yet to get the stew boiling.

Maurice raised an eyebrow, his mustache smiling with it—devilishly. The lines of his face were sharp—even the wrinkles. And when he grinned—or spoke—his skin would pull or ripple over the well-molded bones. Wide bones. Yet still very sleek.

"And how convenient it is!" Maurice burst. His one eye popped toward her as he spoke. "How convenient that eet keeps Odys away from you. Odys's sacrifice has allowed Dorian to get closer to you. Isn't zat right?"

"Sacrifice?" Odissa repeated, as if she found the term appealing.

"The gods clearly don't want us to get closer because you three shits are here," Dorian snapped, pointing with three fingers.

Odissa crossed her arms, staring at the rug (it looked like a wannabe-Persian rug). Bulfinch was even lying on the corner fringe, as if on any other day he might play with the tassels (but not today—not when strangers were watching). Bulfinch always loved a good rug. He loved to throw up on them. This rug looked too old to be new. Had Mecca ordered some antique things as well? How did it get here? She hadn't seen it delivered. But no one else had commented on the rug so perhaps she was the one going mad...[169]

Maurice cleared his throat and tended his pipe. "Odys's little thievery gave quite an excuse for me to come into the picture, didn't it, Dorian? The gods want me to see you with Odissa. And I'm starting to see the whole picture. The gods needed me to see you two together."

Dorian laughed. "Mecca's here too, yet I don't see him whipping out his divine purpose like it's bigger than everybody else's."

Mecca and Q would have latched onto the entendre if only the joke hadn't been about their Papa. Their Papa was speaking. They must remain silent and let Papa defend himself. They bit their lips.

"I'm just saying, I 'ave eyes."

Fletcher came in and handed Odissa some coffee—he hadn't bothered to make any for anyone else. "I knew I smelled coffee!" Odissa exclaimed. She looked over at Q and Mecca with heart eyes. "You bought a coffee maker for me?"

Mecca shrugged. *No biggie.* "Also bought a cat bed, but Bullygoat doesn't seem to like it." He did not look up from his screen.

"Because you shoved him in it," Q sighed (Mecca clearly felt guilty about it).

---

[169] Mind the rug. Seriously, don't trip.

With that, Maurice stood up and announced, "Well, I'm going to adjust the temperature in here." Bulfinch was startled and dashed away.

"I think it's warm enough," Dorian said, glancing in the direction of the thermostat.

"Not zat kind of temperature adjustment." He pointed to the fireplace. "I will chop the wood."

"I think it's gas..." Odissa said as he as he passed by. She examined it from afar, seeing the button.

"Not anymore eet's not," Maurice replied.

"Chop wood from what?" Fletcher demanded a source.

Maurice looked out the frosted window. "There's a tree, over there."

"That's the neighbor's tree."

"I doubt zey'll notice." He winked at her.

"It's the only tree on this corner!"

He was out on the snow-covered lawn in seconds, shirt off. They watched him in their seats as he passed over the window. No one seemed as concerned as Odissa.

"Where'd he find an ax, even?" Odissa asked, craning her neck to try and see him once more. But he was shortly out of view.

"You don't have to stare so hard at him," Dorian snapped like and old housewife. "That's exactly what he wants. Attention."

"How's he not freezing?" she asked. "I mean, immortality is one thing but not *feeling* is another."

"Mecca thinks that's the point. He's trying to freeze to death," Mecca said, typing away on his tablet. His eyebrows had risen and fallen with each sentence.

Fletcher watched Odissa cradle her cup and stare at Mecca. Mecca was sad and she knew it. Too well behaved. Something had deflated his overactive bubble. And no one was bothered by the chopping going on outside. *They must know something I don't.*

"You think Odys is sacrificing himself for you?" Dorian asked Odissa, after making sure the 'kiddos' were pretty much tied into the cultural dances of southern Russia. He tucked some hair behind her ears. "I think he's just trying to control the one thing he has left."

"You really want to talk about controlling?" She reared back from his petting—his playing with her hair. Batted his hand away.

"Is what he's doing any different than what he's always done, when you were presented with a connection to your father-husband?"

She wanted to answer him honestly but remembered Mecca and Q. She'd not have this conversation in front of them.

"They're not really children," Fletcher whispered, taking Maurice's seat. "And they'd eves drop on us even if they weren't in the room."

Q nodded, confirming.

She took a moment to savor her coffee. "Yes, Odys is sacrificing himself for me. I believe that. We both have daddy issues. Can't that be an answer?"

Curiosity sparked inside him. "But who did you hate more, your 'father' or your 'husband'?" Air quotes implied.

She snapped her head in his direction—in the same second as they heard Maurice's ax hit something. "When did I say I hated them?" *Had she said it?* "You want me to hate him? You want me to hate them like Odys did?"

Dorian shrugged, snuggling into the couch as if he might take a nap.

Odissa stared at him. And Fletcher stared at her. "I don't think I do hate them, Dorian. I had a deal with Augury—"

"Leeland," Fletcher corrected her. Dorian tried his best to keep her from reverting back to lies. *He* was the truth.

"I neither loved nor hated them."

"But you're the victim of—"

"Am I?" She laughed, staring past the television. "I'm the one that *allowed* it to go on with Leeland. I'm just as responsible. This isn't—wasn't—rape, Dorian."

Rather than bring up he disagreed with her definition, "Drink your coffee. It's getting cold."

She got up.

"Where are you going?"

With a huff, "To pour this down the drain. The fucking drain."

But she never went to the kitchens. Instead, she walked straight out the door to watch Maurice chop wood.

When he heard her approaching, he put down the ax, heaving breath turning to fog.

"The tree still stands," he smiled through his panting. "Mecca actually ordered me some wood. He knows I love zee *entire* winter experience. He gets the best deals. Mecca was born in the wrong time period, I zay. Zis one is perfect for him. Should have been a millennial."

Maurice gestured to an un-chopped woodpile that a truck had no doubt dumped in their front yard. It wasn't wet with snow.

"I think they figured that, since you started chopping so quickly. We could hear you." She squinted in the brightness—the sun whiting everything in the snow. "I thought French men were supposed to be more interested in fashion and philosophy and romance over...camping and manliness."

A bacon joke manifest.

"I came from a different time in France, my dear. Also, France is no longer my home. I have no home. I am quite—as zey zay—*Americanized*." His lips expressed amusement. He arranged his log on the chopping block. "Well, Odissa Odelyn, do you like the cold or are you simply fond of watching me and my wood?"

She resisted a laugh. She gripped her coffee tighter. She was starting to feel the cold now. Snowflakes were falling into her mug.

His bulging eye brought the truth out of her, "I couldn't stand it in there, being *alone* with him." Out of all of them, Maurice was most like her. Automata-less. Single. One.

His brow rose, as if saying *Ah*. "Is Mecca not in zere?" He arranged the log once more and picked up his ax.

"No, he is."

Maurice cut his eyes at her—as well as that mischievous smile. She saw Mecca in that smile.

"That's to be expected." The ax came down. "Venus didn't think this through. She made Dorian too in love. And he's driving you mad." The ax came down again. "Or maybe zat is her plan? To drive you mad."

"No, it's not that." *Dorian's not driving me mad.*

"But it's part of it." He said it with assurance and tossed some wood away. "Dorian doesn't know what to do with his new character trait—with playing the hetero. He's latching on to zee only thing he's sure of. You." He saw her face. "Believe me. I know Venus."

"I didn't come out here to talk about Dorian. I came out here to escape him."

"He's going to be pissed, you know. Miffed that you came out here to me." He picked up a half-log, looking toward the window as if Dorian could see them. "Running's not fair to him. He can't help what he is." Maurice panted, the cold stinging. He tossed a few logs here and there. "What Venus made him."

Odissa hugged herself and her mug, looked up at the white sky.

Maurice rolled his shoulders. "But look at me, I'm rambling when you clearly came out here to get something off your chest. Your magnificent chest by the way, so delicate." He cupped the air in front of his own. "Too bad eet's not my type."

421

"Yeah, I get it. You like dark meat." She didn't have the heat/time to spare on ripping apart his sexism so: "And I know I've just made him angry. I know that. That's—that's why I did it." Maurice stood back from his work and admired it—all his wood. He rubbed his cold hands together, looking at them. Not a single chafe or crack in sight—*oh how he wished the flesh would split open from the cold!*

"You came out here to get away from them too," Odissa said. "You don't really want to be here, do you? You're not normally with them—ever. That's why you weren't at the cabin. You're not one of them. Neither am I."

Maurice sucked the chill air through his teeth. "I admit I'm not used to being cooped up with humans." He put a leg up on his woodpile. "I am usually very busy with my own devices. But I come when I'm called. Help me carry this to the back. Then you will go inside and get warm and face him. And I will chop more wood."

He stacked some wood in her arms and took up a load of his own under one arm. She tried not to spill her coffee.

As they walked to the backyard, Odissa said, "You knew Leeland, didn't you? You knew him before all this? You knew him better than Dorian?"

The snow crunched beneath their feet.

"Yes."

"Was he always a religious man?"

An eyebrow raised. "Why do you ask?"

She didn't answer right away. What she wanted to say was *Before having sex with me, he would pray—in a language I couldn't understand. He would never look at me. He hated it. And I felt sorry for him. Even though he hated me, he would call me back to him. And I would go. Because I felt so obligated.* But what she actually said was: "How could he do this to me? How could I let him?"

Maurice dropped his wood next to the back door with loud clanking. He helped her unload her own pile, handfuls at a time. "I think Leeland only wanted to have a child with you. A child would have taunted them—made things harder. He was too pious to touch a woman he wasn't married to. He was of Saint Augustine's mind—is that what you're asking? He believed the angels and demons were gods, but zat God was still out there. Zat I'm sure you have guessed by now. But clearly, his morals still trouble you. And with good reason."

They walked back to the front of the house. "Would he have threatened to kill the child? I don't understand what the point was." She started shivering—unsure if it was from the cold or the thought.

He picked up the ax and put it over his bare shoulder. "No—I don't think he could have killed his own child. But it would have, say, made it harder for Dorian to want to live. Dorian was already having so much trouble at it—at living." He eyed the tree above them, considering it next. "Now go back inside and keep Dorian from doing something stupid. You heard what Vulcan said. I need to be here. Dorian can't kick me out just yet. Don't give 'im reason."

He swung the ax down on his foot.

It bounced—nay, *slid*—off his boot.

He cursed in French, walking away. "Now I must get new boots! I never think zese things through. But I find it best that way. Saves me the trouble of premeditation. You laugh at me, vixen?" He made a *Humph!* sound. "It is I who will have the last laugh—literally, because I will outlive you! Why have an immortal body if you can't abuse it, no? Be gone with you. Zis is no freakshow." He boomed out the monologue as if a magician directing a volunteer off his stage. *Zank you for your participation.*

She tried to find it funny, but there was a sadness to it—to him wanting to be alone.

He watched her enter the house through the back. "That girl is too wise and too curious. Feels like zis is all just one show for her, not gods." He arranged his wood. "Well, I will put on the best show zat zere is, oui. Indeed, Maurice, zat is so."

Stanza: Odissa's priest absolved her.

Odissa stomped the mud off her feet. Her eyes adjusted from the bright snow-light and noticed Mecca was now watching cartoons…and smoking one of her cigarettes.

"Where did you get those?" Odissa demanded, marching over to him as if she were his babysitter. She almost ripped it from his lips then realized—

"From your purse," Q said, daring her to say more.

Odissa turned to her. "I know I shouldn't ask *you*, but is it okay for him to do this?"—as if Q were his big sister.

"Of course," Q answered, a mischievous smile on her face. She adjusted the lace collar on her goody-goody dress she'd just formed to stress that point. Tapped her Mary Janes together.

"We're older than you, kiddo," Mecca said, blowing out some smoke.

"At least give me one of those. They *are* mine." She looked in the box. Last one. "I was saving these, you know."

Mecca snuggled closer to Q, flicking some ashes onto the floor. "Mecca will buy you new ones. Don't worry. Mecca treats his ladies right." He winked at her—just like his father would.

"They went to the bathroom together." Q pointed, meaning Dorian and Fletcher. She took up a phone from Mecca's lap as it started buzzing.

Was it an alarm, a call, a message? Why did they always look so busy, these two?

"The water just stopped running before you came in. They're angry you went to Papa."

"Yes, well," Odissa said, deciding not to light up. "Guess I get what I give."

Q smiled, apologetically. "Give them this," she said, pulling a pack of fruity gum from her insides. "We noticed they were running low. Always keep some handy, in times such as these."

"I noticed Fletcher's been chewing up a storm. Is it because Dorian's stressed?"

Q shrugged. "Probably."

Odissa lingered over them. Woman-to-woman, Odissa leaned down to Q and asked, "*Should I talk to them?*"

Q, realizing that Odissa had a strange way of addressing her over Mecca—as if she were appealing to Mecca's feminine or mature side—said, "Yes. But just so you know, we heard them talking about Fletcher's boogers before they started running the bath. They're both getting sick. The nose knows, you know."

"Knows what, exactly?" Her head cocked.

Were the kids being immature or were boogers really a big deal?

Q, quietly, (because Mecca was trying to listen to the TV suddenly), explained the due information on Automaton bile(s). "What goes in must come out eventually," she added. "Either though picking,"—she held up a finger—"popping"—she made a gesture of a gun—"or, well, you know. Pooping." She shrugged. "The three Ps."

"Right…"

Mecca exclaimed, "Ooh! [Random anime show] is on! You know what that means, Q. Bunny suit, please!"

"I'll be back later," Odissa said, backing out of the room and where this scene was going.

She meandered to the bathroom, looking over her shoulder once more—out that fogged window—to spot Maurice posing with his ax as if he'd just cleared a forest.

She softly tapped on the door. "Dorian? Can I come in? Please?"

No answer.

She tried the knob anyway—twisting it with exhausted anger.

"Dorian?"

[Insert silent treatment here]

"Fine. I'll play it your way."

She stormed away. Back outside. To Maurice.

"Can I borrow this? Thanks."

Hauling Maurice's ax, she plodded right past the couch (Mecca and Q never peeling their faces from the screen) and back to the bathroom door.

One—two—three. She began hacking away at the knob until it fell.

The door (knob on the floor and its latch dangling by a few splinters) cracked open. Her walk was calm as she returned the ax to its proper owner with a "Thank you." She dabbed her nose on her sleeve as her body adjusted to the hot-cold-hot-cold pattern.

She sniffed and tapped the door open with her foot.

Clouds of steam flew up around her, fogging up her glasses. She took them off to see. She half-wished Fletcher would scream "GET OUT!" like a little girl—to lighten the mood and give her something to shout back at.

But he was merely a paperclip between Dorian's spindly fingers. He squeezed the rusty metal into his fist as she attempted to close the damaged door behind her. He didn't want to see her.

She commandeered a nearby handtowel and stuffed it into the huge peep-hole she had created.

"So many baths. You'll become a raisin, Dorian, at this rate. I'm not very fond of raisins."

He tapped Fletcher against the bathtub edge. "You left me. Alone. With them."

"I came back, though."

"I can see that."

"I needed some air. I was about to slap you."

"I wish you would've just slapped me." He stopped tapping Fletcher against the tub.

"I don't know what to do with you—you and your clinginess. I've never—never had someone like you before, Dorian."

Well, I guess Odys is completely forgotten, then.

"I'm driving you nuts, am I?"

She sighed. "You don't know how to be—how to be *this*."

"What, straight?"

"You and I both know you're not straight. Venus didn't iron you out, for sure." *I wear you with glorious wrinkles.*

He laughed at that, tucking in his chin to keep her from seeing how humored he was.

425

"No, I mean someone who turns me against my brother." The faucet dripped. "Are you just going to sit there, in your bathwater? Baths aren't baptisms, Dorian. You aren't a new person every time."

"If you're going to come in here, then join me."

"I don't have to join you every time."

"Then leave."

She bit her lip and turned to go.

But Dorian threw his paperclip at the door.

Fletcher sprang up, blocking her.

She turned back around, watching his bathwater settle down around him; watching his angry face become stoic once more.

"I changed my mind. You can stay. It's enough to watch me bathe."

"Thank you for *allowing* me to watch you. Of my own free will."

"Do you think I should shave this stubble?" he asked her, as if picking up where they'd left off. He ran his fingers over his protruded chin.

"No. I'd like to see what you look like with a beard."

"Odys never had a beard, did he? But Leeland did. I think I'll shoot for something in between."

"If that's your goal, you've already reached it, Dorian."

His hands went back into the water.

"You like my hair?"

"No. It looks better than mine." She leaned against the sink.

"Sometimes I think about shaving it. All of it. Even the head."

She crossed her arms. "Like Britney Spears? Is this your 'leave her alone' moment?"

"No, I don't want to be left alone, Odissa."

It punched her in the gut.

Odissa ran her hand across the towel rack and laughed. "So, what's up with the boogers? Q said you were talking about them? Made me all worried."

"She heard us cussing did she? WELL, SHE SHOULDN'T BE EAVES DROPPING!" he shouted at the door. "I made Fletcher spend the night on the roof, you know. It's been rough because of it. I could have just been groggy all day, but no. I had to tap into my reserves to battle off the *Makepeaces.*"—He hissed their name—"Ironically, they make anything but peace! Fletcher's nose—it was clogged up. It's bad for Automatons. A bad sign."

He pointed to the trashcan, full of drying, coppery slime.

"*That* came out of him?" Odissa gasped.

"When it's gold we keep it. A trophy."

"That's disgusting."

"No, it's hard work to make gold that way. He doesn't control it. Collecting it is one of a Master and Automaton's few simple joys—our pearls."

"Maybe tonight you should relax. Besides, don't you feel a little safer with the others here?"

He frowned once more, pouting at how right she was.

She knelt down beside him. "You want to go to bed early, then?" She smoothed back his sticky hair. He closed his blank eyes at her touch.

Fletcher watched them as he leaned against the door—already smacking away at the gum she had set on the counter.

"I'm a little hungry."

"Lunch in bed, then."

"But I haven't washed my hair."

"I thought you were shaving it anyway."

When she finally got him out of the bath she asked him, "What do you want to eat, then?"

"Mecca's ordered pizza."

"He has? He didn't say so. Never saw him do it."

Fletcher, using a spare towel to dab his Master off, replied, "Believe us. Mecca *has* ordered pizza."

As they exited the bathroom, there were a few flashes of light.

Fletcher charged.

"Damn it!" Mecca cursed from behind the wall corner as Q held Fletcher off. "Out of memory."

"Does this mean you have to delete the ones of me in me my fairy costume?" Q asked, as if it were such a waste. "The lighting was so good that day. My fans will love those!"

But Maurice, already back inside, was taking care of it. "Not right now, boy." He picked both the Automaton and child up in his arms, the captives giggling.

"Keep them on tighter leashes, Maurice!"

Before dashing off to their room, Odissa asked, "You ordered lunch?"

"More like *linner*," Mecca said as he attached himself to his father's hip.

427

Maurice sighed heavily, as if this conversation brought back memories. "Remember the days before takeout?"

"God, yes!" Q replied, her limbs still dangling in his arms. "Don't remind us! Makes Mecca uncomfortable. He was never fond of cooking. And it's such a hassle to go out. We look too young to drive."

Odissa didn't want to remind them of the days before drive-thrus. God only knows how sad their faces would be.

DING-dong.

Knock knock knock.

"That was quick!" Q said. "By my calculations we still have about twenty more minutes." She looked at her self-made wristwatch. Something wasn't adding up.

"Maybe they had our types of pizzas already ready?" Mecca asked.

"All twenty-six?"

"Only twenty-six?" Maurice asked. "Don't you normally shoot for thirty, so we can have leftovers? Have I taught you nozing?"

"We didn't know what kind everyone would like. So we ordered all the main ones."

"There are twenty types of 'main' pizzas?" Dorian inquired.

"No, twenty-*six*," Mecca corrected.

Though Odissa was enjoying the conversation about pizza: "Is no one going to get that?" And so she went to answer it.

Just as Dorian said, "She shouldn't be answering doors—" and Fletcher had every intention of stopping her, the next thing they knew the door was already open and they could do nothing about it.

And there were no pizzas.

There was *Maud*.

CAFFAR: The screw.

SCREW: That screws.

THAT: Screws.

SCREWING: You.

Chapter the fifth,

THEY GONNA FIND YOU:

Hide your Odissas?

Odissa had just stood there, taken aback. Maud, as far as Odissa could tell, stared only at her—just as shocked. *They let her answer the door?*

Odissa's hand around the knob was so tight her knuckles turned a blue-white. Anxiety over the dilemma was enough to make her freeze there. Even when Maud had smiled and thrown herself around Odissa—had brought her head to her cheek—she didn't know how to react. Odissa hadn't even thought about hugging back because she was still stuck on Maud's initial expression—that expression that mimicked exactly how Odys would look at her at a time like this.

Of course it was Odys's expression—his expression on the Automaton's face. The thought was too uncanny to be sweet. *She's even touching me like him.*

Just as Maud drew back to study Odissa...Fletcher had swooped in and trapped Maud to the floor.

"Don't!" Odissa shouted—not sure at who.

The floor cracked as Maud hit it. Maud was on her back, arms raised in surrender and admission.

Maurice calmed Odissa, "Best let the Automatons deal with Automatons." He pulled Odissa behind him, just to be safe.

Fletcher had straddled Maud and was angrily gripping her 'shirt.'

From the side of his mouth, Maurice noted, "Just look how he's enjoying it, being on top of her! Oh, to be him right now."

Mecca snorted.

But it was drowned out by shouting: "The fuck are you doing here?" Fletcher growled. "You think you can just show up here? The fuck are you here? How'd you know where to find us?"

Q had also jumped to action. While free of Mecca (still in his Papa's arms), she slammed the front door and was crouched for the ready beside Fletcher—for whatever was to come.

Maud's coppery wrists struggled and writhed under Fletcher's shiny whiteness. As they wriggled, they meshed and melted into one another. Their bodies flickered in enigmatic stretches, flapping and waving over each other in semi-solid form. "If you're so afraid of me—of—of us," Maud corrected herself, "why the hell did you let her answer the door?" She grit her teeth as she tried to outflank him.

They caught each other's arms or slipped out of each other's grip—each trying to keep hold of the other while barely solid themselves. They looked as if they were floating in space—or submerged under water. Moving rapidly, yet not going anywhere. Their hair and 'clothing' seemed so weightless in the struggle.

"Don't make me ask you again!"

The fight seemed pointless—like oil mixing with water.

"Why the fuck do you think I'm here, Fletcher? What do you even mean?"

"What the fuck do *you* mean?"

"Why'd you invite us if you intended to be so unwelcoming?"

"When *the fuck* did I invite you, Odys?" Dorian shouted at Maud—knowing her Master listened.

"You don't know when you sent a goddamn text?"

"Text?"

By now, Fletcher had eased his hold on her, and she had realized there was a misunderstanding. They ALL had realized there was a misunderstanding.

"I did it," admitted *Q*.

VULCAN: Has been showing his face(s) a lot more lately.

TO DORIAN: 'Recycling is incestuous, but useful.'

TO MAURICE: 'Oh look, it's that zombie I let live for my own amusement. You'll kill yourself only when I'm done with you. Like I said, recycling.'

TO ODISSA: 'You're making things a lot more fun for them. And a lot easier for me.'

Chapter the sixth,

Mecca's mischief:

How shall it be managed?

"We"—as in Q and Mecca—"hacked your number. Made it seem like the text sent through your phone—that it was from you. I'm the one that sent it."

"No," Dorian corrected, holding up his towel. "Let's no put a cute face on it."

"Mecca is cute!" Mecca protested. "But Mecca didn't tell them to come *now*." He insisted, glaring at Maud and kicking his legs. "Mecca didn't know Maud would come before Mecca could properly *build up to it*."

"Fuck you, Mecca," Maud grumbled up at him. "Excuse me if I can't read the subtext of a text."

"Well," said Maurice after a long pause. He rolled his frazzled mustache's end and stared at her chest. "That's all very well, but I'd rather hoped you'd be the pizza delivery man, Maud."

Fletcher wasn't ready for a lighter mood. "Why the fuck did he send you, Maud? Too afraid to come himself?"

"Exactly!" Maud admitted as Fletcher let off her.

"Why?" Dorian demanded, pissed at her exactness—shoved in a single word, no less.

Odissa moved over to him, noticing his blood pressure rising. Dorian could barely form the words through his anger. She touched his bare forearm—the one holding up his towel—to show her loyalty.

"Quite frankly, Dorian," Maud said, caring for her wrists, "he hides himself from you to spare you." The skin where Fletcher had touched was still glowing. Same with Fletcher. They were burning.

"Oh, what a saint this Odys is. He cares sooo much for us," Dorian spat.

"Where is he, then?" Fletcher backed up to his Master. He'd just finished straightening his skins/clothes back out.

"He is here—in the area," Maud stated, tearing her eyes away from Odissa—who still refused to acknowledge her.

"How the hell did you get here so quickly? Where were you coming from?"

Maud didn't answer, merely glared up at them from the cold floor.

"Almost seems like you knew where we were this whole time! So why come here now when you could have been here all along?"

"I didn't know where you were."

"Like hell. You probably followed us." Dorian muttered, crossing his arms over his bare chest. "You fucking stalker. Odissa, this is abusive behavior. I'll not have it."

Odissa rolled her eyes at him—a movement between *this isn't the worst he's done* and *you're one to talk*. "And you expect me to do something about it?"

Maud caught Odissa's face. "We *didn't* follow you. Had too much to do besides."

Fletcher flashed his teeth at her. "There's two of you. Could be in more than one place."

"I haven't smelt her," Q said. "We would have. But maybe not you, Fletch, because you're about to sneeze out. Look at you."

Maud snarled. "Can Odys come here or not?" She was tired of the trial going on.

Maurice looked out the window. "Iz he not out there, hovering?"

"He's not stupid! He can't take a beating as well as me." She smoothed back her hair, as if it had been in her face.

"You want to see Odissa, Odys?" Fletcher said down to Maud. "You give us Coraza, then. I bet at least one of them is in there, inside you right now, Maud. For safe keeping. Pull them out." He pointed at her—threatening to poke her.

"We already said we'd give you one!" Maud pulled Coraza out of her side and dangled the plastic bag.

"Give it." Fletcher scooped Coraza up and tucked her inside his chest. "And you don't touch me, got it?" he said to Q, as if she had plans for rummaging through his orifices.

"Why the hell would Mecca want her?" Q hissed. Coraza wasn't their intent for drawing Odys out of hiding.

"So he can come now?" Maud made herself reasonably comfortable against the wall.

Dorian crouched down, not bothering to pull up his towel in the back. "Come and do what? See Odissa? Can't you do that for him, Maud? Isn't he *technically* here now?" He pretended to knock on her head "Your avatar is barely welcome, Odys. You stay in there."

"We were afraid you'd do this, Dorian," Maud said, rubbing her tired eyes. "But fair is fair." Calmly, "If you come in here, Odys, I *will* shoot you."

"Get your gun ready, then, Fletcher," Maud said, smirking. "You won't fucking shoot *me* Dorian. What would Odissa think of you then? Fair is fair, right Odissa?"

Odys was dragging her into it.

Dorian grabbed Maud's throat, but she didn't fight back. "Don't you realize she's chosen me?" Dorian hissed. "There's nothing for you to come to, Odys!" He tossed her away.

Maud merely rolled her eyes at him.

Dorian stood back up, expectant. They all saw the shadow as it passed over the window— the cloudy day making it barely perceptible.

The doorknob turned. "Don't let him come in, Q!" Dorian warned, pointing. His voice shook through them like a bang.

But Q wasn't in a mind to obey Dorian. "You're unreasonable, Dorian," Q shouted back. "Don't be like this."

Fletcher had one gun-hand pointed at Maud and another—even bigger—gun-hand pointed at the door. "I swear to fucking god, Mecca, make her back me up!"

The door slowly opened. A final push made it swing wide.

But, to their surprise, it wasn't Odys (and, to their disappointment, it *still* wasn't the pizza delivery man). To cut short their upmost shock, it was:

"*Rosemund?*"

ROSEMUND: Her Automaton is as redundant as she (but emphasis isn't necessarily a bad thing).

ART: Rosemund once wrote a poem (inspired by Bob) and it went like this: "Fuck up./ Already fucked up?/ I fuck up the fucked fuck!/ Fuck the fucked fuckers who fucking fuck./ Fuck." (As you can see her vocabulary is advanced). The poem pleased Bob.

COPIES: Caffar copies not only words, but whatever her Master is currently into.

WORD: Word.

Chapter the seventh,

I once was found but now I'm lost; could see but now I'm blind:

What amazing grace will sound?

"This shock must be shocking for you," were her first words. With a fancy new cane, she stepped into the house, glancing about. Her eyes landed on the puny light fixture above them in the fan; it was a worthless use of electricity. "To be honest, though, I told Odys wherewherewhere you were. He was waiting for your OK, Dorian—very patient."

"Why are *you* here?" Mecca asked, straining his neck to look past her. "Where's Mother, then?"

They all looked behind Rosemund but no one was there.

Rosemund adjusted her glasses and stopped staring at the light fixture. "Gwen left me. She left me at a restaurant when she left me. Said she had to use the restroom and never came back. See, I had a feeling she was about to—a feeling she was about to leave me. Found her cell phone in the toilet. We can't track her. She left me, and Odys contacted mememe and I told him where you were. Give the boy credit, Dorian. He respects boundaries."

Dorian didn't have the energy to weasel Gwen out of yet another heaping pile of guilty. "You knew she was going to leave? And you didn't stop her?"

Rosemund stepped forward once and tapped down her cane. The cane gave her good reasons to pause and catch her breath. "Well, I never really stop her, do I? I have no control over her." *I let her get away with murder, frankly.* "The better question to ask is why she left me, because I have no idea why she left me. That's the realrealreal mystery. Especially when I have no beef against her. But I have my assumptions as to why. Hello, Maurice. I am not surprised to see you at a time like this, so I'm unsurprised. Mecca can't seem to let the dead rest, now, can he?" She frowned in Mecca's direction, as if he had thrown off the *proper order of things*.

But they had been thrown off by Mother long before his Papa.

433

She gestured for Maud to get off the floor as she herself took a seat on the couch, uninvited. The others drew in despite themselves. Rosemund was in charge now. Her age and legacy demanded it. "Q, get me some tea, would you, darling?" But she asked it of Mecca, leaning forward on her cane. It's only that Q would be doing all the work.

"Yes, come on in," Dorian said. "Make yourself at home, Rose. Bring whoever you like! Mi casa has plenty of room for all you goddamn strays."

Rosemund gestured for Maud to sit—*stop hesitating, Odys!*—sit down on the couch. "You can't avoid Odys forever, Dorian, because you can't. You need Odys." She leaned her cane against her leg after jabbing it at him.

"First I need Maurice and now I need Odys. Who the fuck *don't* I need?" Dorian mumbled to himself.

"Vulcan is shifting things for a reason. He means for specific Automata to land in specific hands. We can't stop his plans, but we can certainly figure out what they are, even if we can't stop them. That's whywhywhy I'm here. We must put our heads together. That's why you need Odys, Dorian."

"He's not one of us, Rosemund."

"There is no *us* anymore, Dorian—we are not us. Gwendolyn has gone. We're orphans now. That's exactly whatwhatwhat Vulcan intends to prove."

"She abandoned you, not us," Dorian said. "She wanted us all to go with her."

"She wanted one last goodbye, you idiots," Rosemund pursed her lips over her braces. "Just what do you think the cabin was? That was the original goodbye. Then Leeland fucked it up." She scoffed and stared at that shitty light fixture again. "You lot don't unununderstand her."

"You sound so disappointed that we don't understand a psychopath." Maud took out a cigarette and offered one to Odissa. Fletcher slapped the cigarette right out of Maud's hand. Maud glared at him, picking it up. She touched the end of her cigarette, lighting it. She smoked it spitefully. "But then again, you *would* understand her, Rose. Like knows like."

Rosemund craned her neck to get a good view of Maud (whose eyes were just as fiery and mean as that cigarette). Rosemund pointed with the cane again. "You sound just like Pepin over there, Odys. You use his words, his actions. You have a big Automaton to fill, boy…Vulcan has drawn us together and pulled Gwendolyn out. We need to know what itititit means."

"What what means?" Dorian growled, re-tucking in his towel as he sat opposite Rosemund on the new coffee table, a foot of space between them.

"What it all means..." Rosemund rummaged through hair and pulled out a screw. She tossed Caffar on the ground. She swiveled upwards and stood over her Master. "...It means I have a prediction to predict, Dorian." She crossed her legs and crossed her arms, her windbreaker rustling. "Vulcan is making a statement of us all. Vulcan let Leeland die in a way that ultimately contradicted everything he believed in—and *that* only happened by letting Gwendolyn contradict everything *she* believed in. She broke her ownownown rules. There is a trend trending here. He wants us all to go off-brand."

They thought about it.

"Everyone's different," Maurice nodded to Dorian, eyes popping out at him. "Doing zee opposite of what they've always held true. The whole liking girls thing. Gwen breaking her rules. Pepin giving up Madus. Bob killing herself after holding out so long. Leeland giving up. Mecca...behaving."

"That last one's debatable..." Dorian grumbled.

"Yes," Rosemund said. "He is drawing the outside in—inside out."

"Outside in." Caffar repeated, observing her Master with her flat, passive indifference.

Dorian took in a deep, settling breath. He pointed at Maurice and Rosemund. "You all are here to watch it happen—you're here to watch Vulcan turn us all outside in. That's the only reason you're here—mere curiosity."

"Curiosity!"

"Shut up, Caffar," Fletcher shouted at her.

Caffar did not react.

Dorian pressed on, "I won't stand by and watch like you. I won't give in that easily. You come here because you know that's what He wants. Fine. But that doesn't mean *I* will stay. I won't make his plot easy on Him!"[170]

Rosemund shook her curly head. "We aren't here to watch each other suffer. I'm here to show you you've been used to drive thethethe narrative along. It's no reversal if it still moves us forward."

Dorian's ears perked, finally understanding what Rosemund was taking the long way to. "Where is Gwen moving?"

"Gwen can't stand to break her own rules." Rosemund went on. "She will punish herself. Because we didn't. She will stick to her own rules because they are her rules. I think that was her

---

[170] Talk about quarreling with your characters!

plan all along. She won't let Vulcan contradict herherher because she won't be contradicted by Vulcan. No."

Odissa saw Maud pale. Odys had never thought about this and it showed through Maud. Something inside him felt guilty for hating Gwen so much.

But then Maud's features shifted. "Vulcan *means* for Odissa to have Madus." There was something too bright in her voice.

Fletcher's skin buzzed as he flashed a dirty look. "Have you no shame? Must you gloat for getting what you wanted?"

Q brought forth the tea. She took back Mecca from Maurice. "You really think she would do it?" She held Mecca tight as if to protect him from Rosemund's answer.

"If Pepin and Leeland and Bob were willing to die, why is it so hard to think she would be too?" Rosemund answered, picking at her braces. "That seems to be the way Masters go these days—the way they go is by their own hand."

They spoke some more about the logistics of it all. How could they be sure this was what she was doing? How dare they suggest it?

"When will she do it, do you suppose?" Maurice asked Rosemund. "You think she will warn us when she's about to?"

"Are her actions not warning enough, Maurice? She'll do it whenever the time is right. Whenever the stars alignalignalign." She drew a line in the air with the side of her palm; they, the stars.

Speaking of stars aligning…

Knock, knock, knock.

"Pizza!" Mecca exclaimed, the heavy topic forgotten. Q rushed to the door. But, once again (and so disappointingly) it wasn't pizza. It was only *Odys*.

ODYS: Not as tasty as pizza.

HOWEVER: He needed to be reintroduced into the story somehow.

THOUGH: Still kind of a letdown.

BUT: At least we can move on.

Chapter the eighth,

The nose knows that you know:

No nose can't know?

"Oh, it's just you," Q frowned, disappointed.

"Damneet all!" Maurice cursed, eyes looking up. "Stop teasing us like zat. I am starving." He peeked through the blinds, hoping to see a delivery car looking for their house. But no. He only saw more wintery weather.

Odys lingered in the doorway, face pink and windblown. His hot breath expressed the steam of his racing heart. Clearly, he'd been waiting outside for some time now—waiting until he couldn't stand it any longer. His red eyes demanded acceptance as they scanned everyone in the room. And then they landed on Odissa's.

Odissa took a good look at him, noting her own reaction to seeing him—him, the only thing left of her old life besides Bulfinch. She looked on him with anger and forgiveness. _You left me with them._

She was just about to avert her eyes when Dorian's huffing caught her attention. He was huffing and clutching his chest and—

"ACHOO!" Both Dorian and Fletcher sneezed. At the same time. Dorian tried to steady himself on the floor—his face red with anger and embarrassment.

Fletcher collapsed on that floor beside him, bouncing to the ground as a rusty paperclip.

Automatons can sneeze out. But Masters can't. (No matter how hard they try).

Dorian straightened and showed the blood running from his nose. He tasted it as it ran over his lips. "The fuck?" He lost his balance and reached out for the nearest object—the coffee table.

Mecca and Q cringed, their eyes wide with concern.

"For a sneeze-out to affect a Master…" Mecca said, but stopped. That was one bad _achoo_.

Rosemund stood up and shooed Odys back outside. "I told you to wait, boy! We've moved too fast." Rosemund waved her cane. "Give him a minute."

"No!" Odys said, pushing in. "I refuse to be an outsider in this. I have earned my place."

"You don't understand," Q said, stepping in front of him. She put a hand on his chest, pushing him back as if Dorian were Superman and he were Kryptonite. Her eyes were red with panic— they didn't expect this. "It's Venus. You're interfering with what she's done to him, Odys. He can't help but resist this. Can't you smell it? You have to do this gently. You know what the gods are capable of."

Maurice's eyes cut to Dorian, who was trying to steady himself on the arm of the couch. "My god, zee girl is right."

"Please, boy!" Rosemund begged Odys. "You just might kill him."

"Maybe that's what the gods want," Maud said under her breath. She put her cigarette out and stood up.

"Bite your tongue!" Rosemund slapped Odys on the back of his head. "No, they don't want him dead. They want him to hatehatehate you, though." Her voice lowered as she observed Dorian—Dorian clutching his chest as Odissa examined his face. "Venus gave him a reason. And a reasonable reason to hate Odys means there's a reasonable reason the gods want them to fight."

Caffar sniffed the air. She could smell the cause. Odissa.

"The gods leave clues wherever their hands touch," Maurice said as if he understood Rosemund. He twisted his mustache and floated about the room like an inspector investigating a crime.

Odissa glared at them and picked up Fletcher, thinking perhaps Dorian couldn't see him— that Fletcher was too sick to show him. Her heart pounded in her ears. She wondered how bad this was—what she had helped to cause.

She pressed Fletcher into Dorian's hand as he continued to smear blood on his face, thinking he was cleaning it. "How bad is it?" he asked. He could barely pronounce the sentence.

Odissa scowled. "The gods want Odys here, yet they don't want Odys near me? Make up your minds."

"It's a delicate balance," Rosemund replied. Her Automaton was inching closer and closer to Dorian to sniff him. He shooed her off angrily, feeling her too near. "If they didn't want Odys here then he wouldn't be here. The same house? Maybe. The same room? Maybe not. The Automatons are an interesting variable as well… "

"If the gods don't want us in the same room, then fine," Odissa said. She noticed the way Rosemund and Maurice were inching closer and closer together as they observed Dorian like a specimen. "We're going to a different room. You all can work out your own sleeping arrangements. Tell us when your damn pizza is here."

And she ushered Dorian to the bedroom, his heart fluttering at her beloved words.

Mecca was pleased to inform, "The couch converts to a bed. And that's a futon."

His purchases were oh-so practical.

"Did you anticipate such a sleepover, zen?" Maurice asked, popping one eye at him.

Mecca shrugged. "Mecca plans for all scenarios. Mecca has decided that he will sleep in his fort tonight."—as if the tension in the room could all but affect him.

"How strange," Rosemund said. "That is what I decided too. And how strange it is already sososo close to bedtime. The gods have sped up time. Now, has this fort you speak of been built?"

Stanza: Tense attention.

Odissa tucked Dorian in. He was trembling. It made her stomach churn, to see him so scared of his own reaction. In a whisper, "What's happening to you? What is this thing?"

"I don't know," he wheezed, angry at the question.

"So this has this ever happened before? To any of you?"

"No. Not to me."

She used his towel to dab the blood from his face. "It is evil, that a goddess would do this to you. I'm so sorry. I didn't know this would happen—that you have no control."[171]

"Venus didn't cause this nosebleed. I did. I did by staying up too late last night. Wouldn't be as bad otherwise. I'm making myself sick just thinking about it. All this just came together too fast and all at once—couldn't control it. I thought you were finally mine and—"

He shivered. His nose started leaking again.

"It's so cold in this damn house. I'll get those extra blankets." As she moved to leave, his hands grabbed her arm.

"No, I'm fine. Just...come to bed with me. I'll be very stressed if I don't know where you are. Fletcher's asleep right now. He can't see you. I need to see you."

He latched onto her and didn't let go until she said "Of course. I'm right here. But won't you let me properly clean your face?"

"No," he said. "Later."

She crawled into bed against all hesitancies. "At least the bed is nice. Mecca chose well."

"Humph."

"He bought all this to please you." She watched him cautiously—as if he might drown in another nosebleed. "He likes you. I think he likes you more than Maurice. He's scared of Maurice."

"I'm scared of Maurice."

"That's why he brought him, I think." She laughed and rubbed his cold shoulder. "Stop being so angry, Dorian. I'm here. I'm not leaving."

Her hand withdrew from his arm and traced the lines of bloody stubble.

"Just give me a moment to believe you. I just need a moment."

She combed her fingers through his damp hair and said, "I won't leave this room until you want me too. We've shut them out. It's just you and me." She relished the power—the power of being able to kill him with a single decision, a single glance, a single "I don't really love you."

---

[171] Yes, yes. The gods did it. Not the Narrator's lack of another plot device.

439

"If you leave me, I might die. Literally. The thought of it gave me a nosebleed." But, clearly, she already knew this.

Stanza: A pound of flesh.

They made room for Odys in the kitchen, pulling up a chair. They had wanted to put distance between him and Dorian. The kitchen seemed the farthest place.

"You're frozen stiff," Q said, handing him a blanket. "I'll make some tea—no, coffee." Thanks.

"The gods may want Dorian and me to be enemies," Odys said, "but it really seems more like they want Odissa to just choose."

"Mortals are such fun for them," Maurice said as he leaned on the counter. "She's a Helen of Troy come to put us at war—the oldest play in the book. Good to finally meet you, by the way." He extended a hand, but Odys refused it.

He glared at it. *Doesn't he know Homer has been alluded too so many fucking times already?* "Your handshakes are legendary, and I'd rather not break my fingers off just yet." Too cold.

Instead, Maud presented her hand and Maurice beamed. He turned it over and kissed it. "Pepin never let me touch you, dear. So good to feel your skin once more."

Maud tore her hand free of him, frowning. "That's the first time someone has ever kissed Odys's hand. Can't say he likes it."

Rosemund chuckled, toasting her cup of tea at Odys. "To being a woman!"

Maurice straightened, getting down to business. "I planned on sleeping on their old cot, but you can take it. I don't mind finding a different place to roost tonight."

"No thanks. The car will do just fine. I don't want Dorian to look at me and spontaneously combust next time. But I will stay inside until it's lights-out, if you don't mind."

"I think we can stay up late for you," Maurice winked. There were plenty of stories for him to tell, especially since he rarely had such a virgin audience.

The pizza soon came and Q went to get plates. Mecca claimed a whole pie for himself while Odys wasn't hungry much. Q politely tried to whisper through Dorian's door that the pizza was ready, but there was no reply.

The television filled the silence for them—an uncertain void which lacked a wanted cheer. Odys had planned to stay in the house long enough for Odissa to come out of the room and get her share of pizza. But that didn't happen. She wouldn't come out so long as he was there—that was the vibe. He wasn't so cruel as to starve her.

"I'm off to bed then. If the battery runs out, do I have permission to jump it with one of yours later?" He pointed amongst them all.

"Of course," Mecca mumbled, his eyes barely open. Q, by this time, was fighting sleep and nudity. Thankfully Mecca was covering most of her already...

"There's a gas can, too, in my truck," Maurice added quietly. Just in case they needed it.

As they took their blankets and pillows into the back seat, Maud lit them up a cigarette.

The overhanging trees reached up like talons into the dark sky. "How long do you think the car will last?" Odys tucked his arm behind his head and took the cigarette from her.

"Does it matter? It's not yours."

"Just wanted to hear myself say it."

They passed their cigarette back and forth.

"She does like him," he said after a few puffs. There was a light fog on the windows that gave a secluded feeling—a sense of privacy. Odys kept his voice a whisper. "She *would* go for a guy like him. Nothing like us."

Maud gave him the cigarette to finish. "He's a *little* like us. Needy."

He flicked the ash into the floorboard as she rolled into him. They slouched in the seats at a diagonal slant, one of his feet on the middle armrest. She brought her knees up closer to him under their covers. I tell you this because he wanted it. I tell you this to prove how much he has changed. He welcomed her touch now, put his hands on her legs—*his* legs.

He put the cigarette out on the car door. It briefly smelled of burning plastic.

"Are you sure we should be here?" she asked him, her wide eyes the only thing not cast in shadow. He loved the way they seemed to glint like a cat's—metallic—reflecting a far-off street lamp's lights. "I mean, I know Vulcan wants us to be here. But are you so sure you accept what Vulcan has in store for you?"

"Where else would I go?" He examined her, as if there were still a way for her to hide something from him. *What am I suppressing?* "We can't leave it like this. Not until we know she's safe."

Maud nodded. "If she's safe with an Automaton, then we have plenty of time to win her back. She'll be ours, Odys."

"It's Dorian's gameplay now. We'll see what happens."

She traced a finger around his face. Odissa used to do this to help him sleep at night. He could almost convince himself she was there, if he kept his eyes shut.

He closed his eyes but Maud's were wide open. She saw the lights in the house go out. The darkness further enveloped them.

Stanza: Talking to yourself is not as fun as answering.

Odys had finally fallen asleep, Maud curled up by his side when, not forty-five minutes afterward, there was a tap on his window. With sleepy faces, Maud and Odys stirred, noticing the car was still going strong. Odys rolled down the window with the knob.

Maurice smiled down at them. He wore no coat.

"What is it?"

He leaned on the window frame. "Come inside, boy. Dorian's awake. He's asking for you."

"What? No. It'll kill him." Maud narrowed her eyes. "Or do you want him to die?"

"No. Not if he knows you're no threat. Odissa's not zere. Eet's just you and him. Plus, you were very wise to sleep out here. Showed respect. I think he feels guilty for making such a scene back zere."

A little pissed that they'd already put so much effort into getting comfortable, Odys tumbled out. "What does he want?"

"How should I know? He's in the kitchen, rummaging. No need to be a mouse, we're all awake anyway. Who can sleep with this—this smell in zee air? I guess you're used to ash. Never mind. Just don't ask to see Odissa and you'll be fine."

As Maud quickly formed some proper PJs, Maurice smiled, his eyes trying to steal a glance.

"Pervert!" she snapped up at him. She threw the blanket at him. As Maud caught up to her Master, she placed her hand in his. That hand soon became a penny. Odys decided he wouldn't gang up on Dorian.

They crept past the couch, where Caffar and Rosemund were under the sheets. Mecca and Q pretended to be asleep in their sleeping bags underneath their "fort" of blankets and clothespins dangling their best over Rosemund and Caffar, yet still not enough to cover the giants. Bulfinch might have found it cozy, but feared being squished.

Odys followed the light from the kitchen. He could hear the muffled creaking of cabinets.

When he entered, he saw Dorian hunched over the microwave, warming a few slices of pizza, a red paperclip between his teeth.

Fletcher was obviously "charged" enough to see for him, because he turned his head in Odys's direction and knew it was him. "Odys."

"You asked for me?" Odys said, unwilling to hide the irritation.

"I'd like to apologize, Odys." Dorian moved the paperclip over to the side of his mouth with his tongue like some toothpick. "Now that I've got my soul back into a manageable state, I feel I can act more accordingly. I didn't mean to make you seem like—like the bad guy back there. Needed my nap. Don't get me wrong, I hate your face. But I know it's not your fault. For that brief moment, Odissa was taken from me—yours again—and it *killed* me. Almost, anyway." He moved some paper towels out of his way, crossed his arms.

"I'd like to apologize, too."

"Don't bother. Not accepted."

"I was asleep, you know—"

"My dear nephew, I owe you much more than an apology. That's for sure—though I'm not in the habit of paying off my debts. I'm the reason your life is as it is and I've proceeded to ruin what little joy you built up in it. I can feel the weight of that. I am forever in your debt. But I think we're growing more and more even."

"Oh, are we?"

He took Fletcher out of his mouth and sighed, crossing his arms. "You have the power to hurt me. The mere thought of you tempting Odissa makes me fucking bleed." He laughed it off, as if Odys was harmless now—now that Odissa wasn't near him. But he still dabbed his nose, checking. "Bleeding doesn't make for a very constructive setting. We didn't get to talk this Mother issue through—"

"Just to be clear," Odys interrupted, "what makes you think I'd even want Odissa now? How could I be around her with Maud latched onto me at all times? I don't—I don't think I could do it. It wouldn't be the same. *I'm* not the same, Dorian."

"You are not a very adventurous sort, Odys—threesomes can be fun. Especially when there's two of you. And it's not you who I'm worried about. Odissa *is* an adventurous sort, you see. She might not mind Maud as much as you think."

"It's not about her."

"I can see that." Dorian snorted. "It's all about you, hm? Odissa certainly doesn't mind Fletcher." Dorian opened the microwave to test the pizza. It needed a few more seconds. He continued to lean against the counter.

"One big fucking orgy, this whole thing."

Dorian shrugged. "As long as Odissa didn't fall in love with anyone else in the process, then sure. Why not? It's not even the thought of her fucking you that really gets me, Odys. It's the thought of her still *loving* you. Nothing is enough for Venus."

"Your nose is bleeding again."

"It's nothing." Dorian tore off a paper towel, chuckling as if it were ironic. "The gods make me eat my words," he said as he dabbed his nose. "Don't like us conspiring."

"Is that what we're doing, Dorian?"

Dorian pursed his lips as he folded up the towel to dab again, holding his head back. "No, I suppose not. What were we talking about? Orgies, that's right. Vulcan may have let his wife drop a *deus ex machina* on me but I'm not entirely immune to who I once was."

"If it were me, I'd be pissed," Odys said, leaning against the opposite counter. "I'd fight against it—your impulses."[172]

"If you were me you wouldn't *know how* to be pissed." Dorian adjusted his robe. "You'd be too obsessed with your sister. And hell, I hate Vulcan on principle, but it's not often life gives you instructions or directions. Take them when you can."

"Yes, from the hands of other people."

"Odissa wasn't in your hands," Dorian corrected as he poured himself a drink from a flat two liter. "She's not even in mine. Why do you think I gave myself a nosebleed at the sight of you? I *don't* have her. She's not *mine*. You can't keep treating her like she's yours, Odys. That's why she fucked me in the first place. She's not yours. She's *her own*."

"You think I don't know that? You think I can't see how controlling I am?"

"Good. Then you have no problem understanding why I can't control my fucking obsessive behavior toward your sis." He handed Odys a cup of soda.

"Thanks."

"But back to what I wanted to talk to you about. I'm in." He licked his thumb free of pizza sauce and closed a few box lids. "I'm on your side, Odys. Even if my mouth says differently later on. If Mother kills herself, we still stick together, understand? We can't let everything fall apart. The Automata are our responsibility now."

"Done."

"And for God's sake, don't sleep in the damn car. The floor doesn't kill the environment."

As Dorian was about to leave the kitchen, Odys called him back with a whisper. "Dorian, all I want is for her to be safe."

"Not happy?"

---

[172] Like you fight against the universe every day, Mr. OCD?

Odys ignored the statement and continued to hog the focus, "I'm sure we can both agree she needs an Automaton. Madus would suit her nicely. No one else."

"You're so sure Mother will be out of the picture?" Dorian laughed at it. He was sure too. Already dancing on her grave. "Fine. If that's what happens, she'll have the twin. But, Odissa can choose things for herself. She'll have the final say."

"Agreed," Odys lied.

"Well, I'm sure Odissa is hungry," Dorian rushed the conversation. "I'm going to wake her up."

Odys thought about telling him she only liked cheese pizza—that the variety he had on display might disappoint her. But he didn't say a word.

The protagonists then parted.

As Dorian took in the pizza, he found Odissa was busy petting her cat—already awake. "I heard you leave," she said, as if guilty for being awake. "He came out from under the bed, at least."

The cat became very interested in the pizza (~~I~~ Bulfinch needed to know if I was missing out on anything).

"Bul's getting used to this kind of life, Dorian. Even I could get used to this," Odissa mused, helping herself to a slice of cheese.

~~I~~ The cat came up to him, dabbing Dorian with a cold nose for not offering ~~me~~ him any yet. ~~I~~ Bulfinch purred, batting at Fletcher when Dorian took him out of his mouth to eat. ~~I~~ Bulfinch was bored out of ~~my~~ his mind by now and starting to test the boundaries of ~~my~~ his captors.

"He's bipolar, this cat. Used to be so afraid of me."

~~I~~ Bulfinch was never afraid. Only leading them into a false sense of superiority.

Stanza: The interpretation is up for interpretation.

Now, let's see.

Gwendolyn stared into Anselm's eyes. His long-nailed hand—a little hand—stroked her greying black hair. But who was that other there, in that same bed, with them? Madus.

But let's ignore him and zoom into Mother and Anselm's face, shall we? Madus will get his close-up in time. Let's not worry about what he looks like just yet (though we can assume it's similar to Maud).

Mother's face was pink under the dim motel lamplight. Pink and wet. She closed her eyes and a few more tears rolled down her face, soaking the pillow.

"Come now, Gwen," Anselm whispered to her, scooting in. In darker lighting, he looked more *human*—more human when shadowed. But she hardly wanted him to be. To admit he looked human was to admit the age he could also be mistaken for, which always sank her throat into her stomach. That's why she kept him so ethereal—so that she could deny what she perhaps was. "This will all be over soon. Enough tears, you need to sleep."

She covered her face.

"Just a few drops left, Ansi. I need to get rid of them all, before tomorrow. I can't cry tomorrow. Tomorrow has no place for them."

"Shh, I know." He took the covers in his fingers and used the sheets to dry her face.

"I know you already know this, Anselm, but I want to tell you. Tell you with words," she said, her voice was raspy from crying so much.

"Sí?"

"I know I'm making you do this. I know you have no choice in this matter. But I also feel like…"

"I know."

"No, don't interrupt me," she said in Spanish.

He smiled. Gwen did love a good argument with herself.

She went on, her voice slightly cracking, "I know—or, at least, I can feel—that some part of you—of whatever parts Vulcan put into you—accepts me. Whether or not that means it's some form of love, I don't care. I just wanted it to be on the books."

"Your overt effort in placing it there won't be forgotten," he touched his skull, running his long nail over his silvery skin. *It's recorded.* He drew closer and took her under her chin, as if he were the bigger of the pair.

She liked to pretend he was. It was so hard to pretend though. The illusion didn't last long. Her mind would be forced to revert to other charming excuses, like comparing him to a hobbit— I believe the line is they were like "Only children to your eyes." A hobbit without the feet. It lightened the mood usually.

"Don't worry. You're imprinted on me forever. No matter what happens, you'll always be in me. There's no way you—*we*—can't affect the next who has me. They'll know, too, how much I loved you. They'll know we were happy." He kissed her forehead, pale lips lingering. "They'll know."

"Such silly talk, Gwendolyn," Madus said, his voice sounded muffled—as if Mother was trying to stifle his commentary. "You fool yourself, you spinster."

Her pretty face contorted as it buried itself into Ansi's little chest, trying to ignore the other Automaton with her. She wept. She had almost forgot about her third self.

Anselm's lip twitched. She was hiding from her "Doubt"—the part of her soul that shined brightest in Madus. Madus wore it best. And she hated him for it.

Madus went on, his voice slow and struggling—it strained him to speak, for Mother did not want to tell herself what she must:

"You'll be imprinted on us all right, Gwendolyn Gwendy. You will. But they will not see your love. They will see your narcissistic selfishness. They will see how all you did to protect Anselm—"

Anselm grabbed her face. "You shouldn't give him voice, Gwendolyn." He sat up in bed. He glared down at the Automaton opposite Gwendolyn. The expression on his face, the unholy frown, scoffed at the idea Gwendolyn had to be shared—split into so many parts.

His polished eyes fluttered back down to Gwendolyn. He reassured her, "Tomorrow these tears will be well spent. Vulcan won't be able to passively hurt us anymore. No more. We are the solution, Gwendolyn. We always were. We got rid of Leeland so the solution could take root. We'll teach the gods a lesson."

Gwendolyn looked up at Anselm, shaking her head. "I don't want to do it, Ansi. It's so unfair to them. I leave so much of the burden on their shoulders."

He leaned down for another kiss on her forehead. His hair fell over them. It sheltered them from the part of her she didn't want there—the part on the edge of the bed with barely any room.

That "part," however, still needed to hold her hand as she fell asleep. It was instinctual that they touch.

Anselm eyes cut to Madus before he settled in, Gwen finally asleep. Madus looked like a mannequin—lifeless and useless—just as Mother liked him.

Stanza: Meet your meat.

A loud crash awoke Dorian and Odissa. Realizing it was coming from the kitchens, they paid no mind. But the smell of breakfast wafted into their room and their noses could not let them rest.

"It smells so bad, but I'm starving." Odissa admitted into Dorian's chest.

"It's Maurice's cooking. He fucking burns everything because it's only manly if it's charred with fire." Fletcher pulled himself off them, flinging the covers off. Odissa noticed he quickly formed clothes before completely standing up. "Shall I bring you something?" Fletcher asked, hiding a yawn. His long hands scratched his chest at exactly the same moment Dorian's did.

Odissa raised her head and asked Dorian, "So you don't want to get up?"

447

Dorian moaned. They'd stayed up late. They'd slept in late. It was almost noon, Fletcher checked.

"I don't want you near Odys."

Her voice more concerned than he'd like, "But I don't think I even hear his voice in there."

They listened for a moment.

Fletcher cocked his head. "I think you're right."

"So you'll risk it?"

"I will. The thought of letting you out there alone makes it worse, actually."

"How convenient that you're all better."

"*Los Doble Ves* want us out there. Has nothing to do with convenience."[173]

His phone flashed on the floor where it was charging. Fletcher read it aloud: "'Making breakfast, Odys gone.'"

Dorian yawned. "They must have this room bugged...I suppose we could see what they're so happy about in there."

"There will be no happiness in Dorian's house!" Fletcher stomped his foot whilst opening the door.

And they shuffled their way to the bathroom to get ready.

…

He left Odissa to finish touching up.

Odissa half-expected to find a penny somewhere—stowed away to get to her in private. But Maud never appeared and Odissa kept herself from wishing on it. She left the bathroom with no further expectations.

"Oh! Good morning!" Q said, sporting a darling little chef's uniform (complete with specific alterations which allowed for, well, more skin). But she wasn't doing any cooking. She was scrubbing.

Mecca was busy on the floor, watching what looked like cinnamon rolls, biscuits, and perhaps a pie baking. "Odys went to the store and bought *a lot* of breakfast. Mecca doesn't usually eat breakfast. Mecca is excited."

Odissa wanted to ask *"And where is Odys?"* But assumed it would eventually come up without her prodding.

---

[173] Doble Ves = Double Vs. Vulcan and Venus.

Fletcher to Q, "ALL of those dishes were necessary to make breakfast? Where did those dishes even come from? And did Odys buy a waffle maker too?"

"Must have been Odys. Wasn't Mecca," Mecca said as he rocked back and forth while the oven-goodies baked.

At least he wasn't staring at a screen.

"Help yourselves," Q gestured to the leftovers on the table. "There's bread for toast."

Fletcher studied the food but went straight for the remaining pizza. "I trust nothing you lot mix together."

Maurice was busy over the stove. "Bacon?" he asked them, mustache twitching, eyes sparkling.

From the looks of the sky-high plate beside him, he'd already cooked a whole pig.

Odissa was too sleepy to laugh at his "Kiss the Cook" apron.

"None for us," Dorian said, stretching. "No meat for me anymore—Odissa's orders."

"Orders?" Odissa repeated, having said nothing of the sort.

Maurice raised an eyebrow.

A smile spread across Dorian and Fletcher's faces. They were excited to let a specific cat out of specific bag. A cat they had tied up in said bag only last night. "Odissa's a vegetarian, Maurice." *Yes, Odissa, Maurice is a carnist! Hate him now, hate him now!*

"Does my cooking offend you?" Maurice asked her, eyebrows coming together.

"No, Maurice," Dorian said, smoothing down his bedhead (that Fletcher had just noticed). "Your cooking does not *offend* me. But I don't trust where that meat came from."

"All food comes from labor and suffering," Maurice said to his meat with a frown. "Even plants cost a price!"

Mecca (who was sitting on the floor between Q and his Papa) sighed and put his head in his hand. Q glared at Fletcher for her Master. They knew what kind of a verbal essay was coming. "Did you *have* to comment on the origin of the meat?" Mecca mumbled.

"You know," Fletcher said, leaning into Maurice, "it's your generation and after that made us the gluttons we are today. The start of industrial farming. GMOs. Everything. It's because of your generation we're the capitalist carnivores that we are. It came from *you*."

"Do you not remember how old *you* are, Dorian?" Q scoffed.

"Well, as a *socialist*, I do agree," Maurice sighed at his pan, mustache and eyebrows twitching with every pop of bacon. "Everyone iz a bunch of pansies now! Never killing and owning your own food choices. Your ignorance is—how do you say eet?—*bliss*."

449

"You killed this pig yourself then?" Fletcher asked him, to push the unveiling along.

"Why would you ask such of question in front of Odissa? Of course I did. I brought zis with me. Zere is more in my car. Why are you trying to piss me off so early, Dorian?" He pointed outside, where his cooler was packed into the snow. Spots of red trailed from the cooler to the back door.

Dorian whispered to Odissa, "Maurice only eats what he kills with his own hands."

"What?" Odissa said—almost a gasp.

Maurice shrugged off the uneasiness in the room. "Zey taste better zat way."

"Yes, controlling their suffering makes it all the more savory," Fletcher frowned.

"But the pizza—" Odissa said, screwing up her face, trying to understand.

"Yes, yes. In other words, *not all zee time*." He sighed. "If I am zee cook, I cook *my* meat." He tapped his apron-clad chest. "Eet iz not my fault social norms keep me out of ozer people's kitchens. You all eat out so damn much! Who is capitalist now, hm?"

"Sorry to keep you from killing, Maurice," Dorian said, walking to the opposite counter and rooting around in a drawer of grimy silverware.

"Not that your presence here isn't killing us," Fletcher added, leaning against the fridge.

"That's awful, Maurice," Odissa said as she watched him mind the bubbling bacon.

"You think I kill them more cruelly than they would be killed at zee factory?" He put a hand on his hip, snorted.

Mecca rocked back and forth, ears in his hands and pleading for Q to take care of this if it got out of hand.

"Is there any humane way to be killed when you're not suffering in the first place?" Dorian answered for her, quite happy he had finally found and deepened a divide between Odissa and Maurice. *How do you like him now, Odissa?*

Odissa glared at Dorian, understanding why this conversation was happening. *I never should have told you that last night. You were perfectly oblivious to the fact before I pointed it out.*

Maurice's mustache twitched and he turned off a few stove knobs. "All life iz suffering, Dorian." He popped one eye to Odissa. "You and Dorian are perfect for eachozer, then. He dabbles in zat shit. Diets and fads. Do you know how many baby cows are killed so zat you can have milk, Odissa? Cheese? How many male chicks are ground up alive because they can't produce eggs? Vegetarian. Ha!" He waved his spatula at her. "Do not you shame *me*, girl. At least I own the blood I shed. I don't whitewash it with dairy!"

Odissa turned bright red—that he would scold her as he cooked innocent flesh! "I've thought about going vegan too. I do eat vegan—"

"When you are vegan, we will speak of vegan theories. Until zen, we both pick and choose our evils."

Q raised a finger as if to interject but Fletcher cut her off. Rolling his eyes, "Are you kidding me? She barely eats, so I hardly think your morals are equal, Maurice."

Mecca scooted under the table, as if something were about to hit the fan and splatter everywhere.

Maurice shook his head at his work, feeling her judgement. "Zis world is fucked, Odissa. Fucked. Don't you know I see how fucked it is? Why do you think I want to *die*? You think I can't see the human ego in what I do—in what we *all* do? Killing sentient beings when there are perfectly good ozer routes to nutrition?—it is evil! And the gods let us continue perpetuating such suffering." He trailed off in French, waving his hand.

"And so you just give into it, the system?" Odissa asked him, trying to understand his logic. *What do gods have to do with it?*

"Of course I give into eet! Zat is the point. To die. To sin. To pay the wages of zat." He crossed himself—not for forgiveness, but to stress his point.

Even Dorian reared back from Odissa as she leaned into the madness. Q shook her head at him. *What have you done.*

"So killing animals is meant to kill you faster?" Odissa demanded his answer. She was slowly losing respect for him with every word. At least other carnists were ignorant of what they chose. He knew and continued the route.

"Yes. Cholesterol. High blood pressure. Cancer."

"But you actively *kill* your own food. If unhealthy is your goal why do you have to do the killing? Are you saying you raise them too? Like a fucking farmer? Where is your farm?"

His face grew dark. "Killing kills part of the soul, Odissa. Leave it at that." His eyes shot to Dorian and Fletcher, telling them to rein her in.

Odissa didn't notice. Or, if she did, it did not dissuade her. She laughed off her frustration. "But *how* is that more moral than me? You just admitted it is not!"

Mecca whimpered from under the table. This was it.

"If not pigs, zen people." Maurice eyed Dorian, who was gathering paper plates and napkins. *Zere, are you happy, girl?*

Odissa crossed her arms, as if his words did not compute.

451

Fletcher gestured to him as he walked away, eyes ablaze. "*See?*"

"Yes, tell her how many circus performers died before you found out pigs were a better, more constructive release," Dorian laughed.

Mecca buried his head in his arms. He hated this kind of talk about his Papa.

"People?" Odissa asked the room. "What does he mean?"

"To die you must eat death," Maurice said, plopping down his plate of pig carcass where he was about to sit. He called his son out from under the table with a snap of his fingers, needing the room for his thick legs. Mecca hesitantly crawled out and continued to stare at the oven.

"You're a cannibal?" Odissa asked, hoping not.

Fletcher sniggered.

"No, girl!" Maurice spat. "…Not anymore. Zat's what makes killing pigs more reasonable. No one looks for pigs when they go missing."

"He will try anything once." Fletcher had opened each pizza box to judge the contents. He handed a few worthy boxes from that inspection to Dorian.

"He did it more than once, though," Dorian footnoted himself.

Odissa shook her head at Maurice—her head at them all. "You laugh as if it's funny?"

Dorian was just full of giggles, knowing he had solidified a great wall between them—as if he had broken up two BFFs!

"He only killed a few," Q said as she dried off a plate. She finally got her foot in the door of this conversation.

"As if that makes it any better," Dorian said, arranging pizza on his plate. He licked his thumb off, itching to eat during his entertainment.

"Meat is meat no matter where it comes from!" Q threw down her towel and picked up another dirty dish, the act agitated and raw.

"Meat is meat," Caffar repeated, coming in. She sat down at the table by Rosemund.

(Oh yeah, I forgot to tell you. Rosemund has been there, the whole time. Sitting quietly and reading her paper. The subject matter apparently had no effect on her).

Meat is meat.

Meat is meat and meat is wrong to eat, no matter where it came from. Odissa relaxed. Wasn't that the truth? Wasn't that what she fundamentally believed? Was she about to put human lives above animals lives, like—like some *carnist?*

She bit her lip, considering her next words.

"He told you that himself, did he? Meat is meat?" Fletcher frowned down at Mecca. Dorian started to microwave a few slices of pizza. "Is that how he justifies it? Makes it seem less vile, doesn't it, Maurice, to tell your son that 'meat is meat'?"

Maurice was too busy looking at his heaps of bacon. "Vile was my intention, Fletcher. After all, Zeus destroyed mankind for cannibalism once. I was hoping he would destroy me under zose same terms."

"But Zeus isn't your patron god, is he? And you didn't know how much you would actually like it, did you?" Fletcher laughed at him.

Odissa's skin prickled, knowing on any other day Fletcher/Dorian couldn't give a fuck about this topic. They were only dragging it out for her. She took another step back, wanting to back out of the room—to put distance between her and the horror.

"Don't worry, he won't eat *you*," Mecca said, noticing her. "He only eats bad guys."

"Best way to make them useful," Q said, smiling to herself in the sunlight as if—as if she *agreed* with it.

Maurice said over his shoulder, "I don't run into many *bad guys*."

"Also, Papa doesn't eat girls. They eat Papa," Mecca giggled, laying back on the floor, happy the conversation had avoided implosion.

Maurice cracked a grin and winked at him.

"Really makes the term 'zombie' fitting, doesn't it?" Dorian laughed again, looking at Mecca. Mecca didn't find it funny—rolled his eyes.

Maurice popped his neck, letting the words roll over him. "Not zis early in zee morning, boys. I haven't done my yoga yet."

"Yoga?" Odissa mouthed to Fletcher, so Dorian could see. Her brows raised like antenna, trying to help her compute the walking-contradiction-that-was-Maurice.

This is what Automata do to people?

"Oui, and I meditate everyday on new methods of death and ways to piss off the gods. Like eating pigs. Pisses off the Jewish one, anyway." He flipped off the ceiling. "I fixate on my goal: death."

"The only death you attain is those you kill, Maurice," Rosemund said. "And by the looks of it, you've attained quite a lotlotlot of death. Congratulations."

"Pepin always having to clean up his messes. No wonder he left the circus," Fletcher mumbled past is mouth full of food, as if remembering his time in said circus.

"Pep didn't want to get eaten," Dorian theorized, taking his plate of breakfast pizza from Fletcher.

Maurice fixed his plate. "I only killed the ones about to rat on us. They were threats."

Odissa pointed in the air. "Did this happen before or after you were suicidal? Because I assumed you left the circus after trying to kill yourself."

Mecca looked like a sad puppy once more, sitting up and readying to hide again.

"Oh, I did leave after," Maurice nodded as he bit into his bacon. "But it did not leave me. I still had my traveling show. I still had people who hated me—who thought I wouldn't hand over trade secrets—who thought I had swindled them. Zis and zat. But even before, well, some people are willing to kill off the competition. And when you're the best at what you do"—and he was the best at not dying—"people are spying on you anyway. Waiting for you to slip. To spill your mysterious *beans*. Gives them ample time to notice ozer things they should not. And then threaten to blackmail you with zose things if you don't give them what zey want. But you cannot give people what zey want, Odissa."

"Enough of it is enough," Rosemund said, flicking her paper. "Eating a human here and there is nonono worse than anything else we've done. At least they got eaten. Plenty of people I've killkillkilled were wasted in the ground. Now, would you all hurry up and eat?"

It wasn't the subject matter eating away at her, clearly, for she was looking at her watch.

"I do what I want in my own fucking house," Dorian said right after his first real bite of folded pizza.

Fletcher sat down, halfway done with his pizza already. He picked up a vegetable that fell from his bite. "Fried green tomato anyone?" He lifted it up so that everyone at the table could moan at what was actually green pepper. "Do sit down, Odissa." He tossed it in his mouth and swallowed. "I won't let him touch you." He presented her with graceful options.

Odissa shook her head. Not willing to obey just yet, "It's weird."

Rosemund cleared her throat, not liking that *this sort of talk* was still going on. Odissa sat down. Rosemund and Caffar, at the table, were apparently finished with breakfast and food in general, open sections of the newspaper hiding their faces.

Odissa leaned over the table, one final thought building up in her, and whispered to Maurice, "I'd rather that be human meat than something so innocent. I think that's my problem with it."

"Me too," Maurice whispered back, passing her test.

Dorian frowned at her—was his plan backfiring?

"But a murder a day keeps the living at bay," Maurice said in Rosemund's direction, tiptoeing around her limits.

Caffar, with the longest and most usable legs, kicked at him under the table.

Odissa sighed, the breath flapping her lips. As she poured herself some coffee: "I hope you die, Maurice. I really hope you die."

"Ouch," Dorian said with a smile. "That's harsh."

Odissa snarled at him.

Rosemund checked her watch again and looked to Maurice, as if they were both expecting something—any time now.

Fletcher caught the look and brimmed with suspicion.

Dorian stood up, preparing for what Rosemund and Maurice had in store. "Where *is* Odys?" He asked, helping himself to a bowl of pancake batter before Q could wash it out.

"Don't speak of the devil unless you want him to hear," Maurice said, his curly eyebrows bouncing. "Smoking break. He's waiting for your OK to come back into the house."

They waited for Dorian to give it, holding their breath. He checked his nose with a few fingers—dry as a bone. He considered it, rolling his fingers. "Let him come, then."

Mecca nodded to Q and she left her dishes with a shake of her wet hands.

Odys instantly made the crowded room feel like it was threatening its max capacity.

He sat down next to Rosemund and took out a fresh pack of cigarettes. He did not offer Odissa a one. In fact, he completely ignored her. She silently thanked him for it. Fletcher was watching her every move as he stuffed his face with Dorian's crust. Odys pretended to be interested in the wall. *This is what brothers do. This is what brothers do.* If only Mecca had bought a ticking clock for the kitchen. It would have added to the dramatic buildup

"Should I not have come in?" Odys finally broke the silence. It was a question no one would be answering, for there was no good reply.

Odissa, upon his sentence, gave her self the excuse to actually look at him. Odys was smoking shorts. The store must have been out of filterless.

She could do for a filterless right now, the leaves would give her something to spit—a reason to chew at her lip. Like tealeaves, they would help her read his future. She pushed up from the table, an act that made them all hold their breath again.

"Is there more coffee we could make?" Odissa asked Dorian, coming over to him. But they were not out of coffee.

"I'll put another pot on," Fletcher said, his voice quiet and cautious. His chair creaked when he stood. Team Dorian had assembled and was looming above the rest.

Dorian realized Odissa was waiting for him to sit back down—realized her position depended entirely on his movement. He knew she was walking on eggshells for him. For *him*.

Q tried to break the tension by saying, "It snowed a shit-ton last night. It's very deep. But it's not the soft kind. Good for making snowmen. We already made one." She pointed out the window.

Maurice smiled down at her. "I used your scarf, Dorian, I hope you're not mad. The one on the back of the couch."

"Snowmen, Maurice?" Dorian said, tearing off a bite of crust. "I'm surprised you didn't fancy writing your name in the snow instead."

"Just because you have to squat, Dorian, doesn't mean you have to make fun of zose with a dick."

"Oh, he has one, all right," Fletcher said, watching the coffee maker steam. "It's been in me enough."

Though it earned him half-hearted grins at the breakfast table, the fact that Odys wasn't smiling made it harder to enjoy. Odissa watched all of them like watching a standoff—what was going on?

Odys flicked his cigarette ashes into a makeshift ashtray—a brown coffee mug with a broken handle, probably found in the pantry from the previous lives lived there. He had carried it in with him.

The oven dinged and Q assumed a pair of hearty oven mitts to take the hot items out. I've already forgotten what I said she was baking.

Cinnamon rolls. Was it cinnamon rolls?

Maurice, continuing to nibble at his fried pig, asked, "So, what is on zee agenda for today?" His eyes slid toward Dorian, as if he might answer. As if he was in charge.

Dorian gestured with a new piece of pizza to Rosemund. "Was I supposed to plan something, Rosie? Is that why I have this audience?"

Rosemund put down her paper, spreading it out, despite the plate full of syrup beneath it. "Funny you should asasask that—what you just asked, Maurice. Because I see here, in this week-old paper, that a Mr. What's-his-face has recently died and left his estate heirless"—wait for it—"because he did not have an heir."

"And why is zis so noteworthy, dear Rosemund?" Maurice led her on, as if they'd planned this whole conversation. He dabbed at his lips with his cloth napkin, cocked his head as if he did not know.

"He was a collector and restorer of importantimportantimportant antique antiquities. Including sixteenth and seventeenth century automata. Maybe even eighteenth. Nevertheless, he was a very fine restorer and collector of important antique antiquities."

"So you've said!" Maurice cleared his throat. "And I assume you're interested in zis week-old topic *because?*"

"Funny you should ask that, too, Maurice. The paper says here that a Mrs. Danny—also called 'Dan' by close relations—D. Lion bought the estate last week and the writer hopes she'll reveal what's hoarded up inside—maybe even donate to local museums." Rosemund pretended to read the sticky newspaper—like she hadn't memorized her lines perfectly.

"A Mrs. Danny D. Lion? Now, where have I heard that name before?" Maurice smoothed out his mustache between chomps of bacon. "Danny D. Lion? Danny must be short for *Danielle.*"

"Or maybe Daniella?" Rosemund shrugged.

Fletcher rolled his eyes.

Odys put out his cigarette. "Is this the same Mrs. Lion who invested in the Pakistani orphanage alongside a Mr. Louis E. Anna?"

Rosemund reared back. "Oh, you remember Mr. Anna do you? He was a fun one."

Odys sighed and hunched forward. "Maud certainly remembers all the names Pepin used to go by—as well as yours, Rose."

"Ah! They've found me out, Maurice. How clever of them to be so clever."

By now Odissa was catching on. She picked out a cinnamon roll Q offered her. "What have we found out?"

Mecca, his mouth covered in frosting, said. "Mecca thinks we should go see it! Go see the house Rosemund bought."

"I have the keys, here!" She retrieved the copper key from her wild hair and dangled it between her freshly-painted claws.

Dorian and Fletcher puckered. "Why do you want us to go to that house, Rosemund?"

"I think we should all go," Rosemund said, "because it's ironic I just bought a house sososo nearby. Fate wants us to explore my new property."

"Is that why you came here, Rosie? To get us out of this house? Why do you want us to leave?"

457

"Don't you see?" Maurice said, leaning over the table. "Vulcan set this up. Vulcan meant for Rosie to buy zat 'ouse! And eet is so close to us now. It is *meant* to tempt us into a field trip once we all got settled here."

"Then I won't be going!" Dorian slammed his fist on the table. "Bob died doing what she thought Vulcan wanted. Vulcan *let* her die. I won't accept His plans."

"I think you will end up zere whether you like it or not, Dorian." Maurice gestured to the picture in the paper, now bleeding through with syrup. "Vulcan killed off zis poor man so that we could go to his house. Don't waste his death."

"You don't know that!" Fletcher huffed.

"Let me put it zis way, Dorian," Maurice dabbed his mustache with his napkin. "If you do as Rosemund wants, zen I will leave you in peace. And take Mecca with me."

Dorian sat back. "Why are you on her side of this? What's in it for you?"

The coffee pot sizzling matched Fletcher's glare. "Now we *know* Rosemund is planning something. Something is in that house, isn't there, Rosie? Isn't there?"

Odys jabbed out his cigarette. *One two three four five six.* He looked at Maurice. "What deal did you make with Rosemund, Maurice?"

"So you're not in on this?" Dorian raised a brow at Odys.

"Not yet."

Maurice averted his eyes and he shoveled more pig into his mouth, chasing it down with a cinnamon roll.

"No. She didn't make a deal with you did she?" Odys pressed him. "She told you something. You know something needs to happen, don't you? This isn't Vulcan. This is man-made."

"Did Vulcan come to you, Rosemund?" Dorian prodded. "What do you know, Rosie?"

"Come with me to the house, Dorian. This is for your own good."

"No, Dorian," Odys said. "Don't go. Odissa, don't let him. If this has something to do with Vulcan, then—"

"You are going, Dorian, or I'll let Mecca burn zis fucking house down, you understand?" Maurice recrossed his overly buff arms.

Mecca's mouth hung wide with eager possibility.

Dorian chuckled as he rinsed his hands off of greasy pizza remnants. "Fine. Do as you like. You already do. Burn it down. The furniture clashes anyway."

Mecca grumbled.

Maurice sighed. "Eet's not working, Rose."

"Not working," Caffar agreed.

Maurice leaned back in his chair. "She won't tell you. But I will. We have reason to believe Gwendolyn will be zere."

"Mother will? But why?"

Rosemund stood up. "Damn it, boy! You think I know why? You think I know why Vulcan wants it to happen there, in that house, where it will happen? I don't know whywhywhy! I don't know why Gwen thinks it has to be this way but it will be because it will be. Can't you see that Vulcan set this up and Gwen is accepting it and you cannot curse her for it? Gwen needs us to bebebe there."

"Goddamn it, Rose, sit down!" Fletcher barked at her. "We'll go! Just sit the fuck back down. Christ's sake—all of you. Was that so hard? Was that so hard to tell us Gwen will be there?"

"Of course she will be zere!" Maurice shouted up at him, waving him off. "We could write this story all on our own."

I'm willing to bet Gwen's name will be at the end of a chapter soon, too.

"Going is still in line with what Vulcan wants," Odys said. "We can't forget we have choices—we are humans with free will."

"No, we're not," Dorian whispered. "We're not humans. Not anymore."

It was decided. They would trade this house for another.

Thus, our characters set out on a two-and-a-half hour drive to the state border.

Stanza: Rosemund promised Maurice anything in the house he thought might kill him.

Somehow, Q and Mecca had managed to find a very nice MOTHERFUCKINGSUV with chained tires that could roll through winter itself. They only got stuck in the snow about six times when they had to stop at four-ways in the back roads. But the Automatons had little to no trouble lifting the car out of those.

The car itself had little room to spare. The Automatons, therefore, were kept in pockets most of the drive. It made for a very odd experience. Odissa observed—as if a part of the Masters were muted (though sometimes a muffled sound here and there would come out from a stuffy pocket). Even visually, the Masters lost part of themselves—Odissa had to read them like normal people. They were like a foreign film with no subtitles—people now so used to being expounded by another that they had forgotten what it was like to express themselves singularly.

"Odys, did you know Maurice is a cannibal?" Odissa asked her brother. She had only just realized he hadn't been there—been there for the morning debate. The long car ride had allowed her to dwell on the topic.

Rosemund rolled her eyes and scolded Dorian over her shoulder, "See what you've caused?" Mecca sank in his seat.

"Of course he knew," Maurice grumbled. "It's not something Automatons easily forget. Pepin helped me cover some up."

Odys turned to her, his neck stiff from sleeping without a bed. "How'd you find out?"

"So you're—you're OK with it?"

Odys thought about it. "Maud knew some the people he ate," he admitted. "They weren't good people. Maurice made use of them." Odys shrugged through repeated conversation circles as if he had been there for their previous rotations.

"But it's weird, right?" It was as if she were a scientist gathering data—wanting to judge his reaction so she could adjust her conclusions.

"Believe me, Odissa, that's not the weirdest thing they've done."

"How did you eat them?" she shifted her questioning to Maurice. Again, like a scientist gathering data.

Maurice huffed through his nose. "Chopped them up into little bits. Cooked the pieces. Like any other animal."

"You used an ax?"

"For some parts, oui."

"And why? Why kill them? What made them bad?"

"Because they were threatening us," he snapped. "Plus, I needed *some* way to dispose of the body. What better way than to eat them?"

I feel a spin-off series of prequels coming on. A Vol. 0.5, if you will.

"Were they tasty?"

Maurice seemed to like that question, for his eyes lit up—eyebrows danced. "You do not mock me after all? You really *are* curious?"

Odys cringed. Of course his sister would ask a question like that. And indeed, how often do you get to meet a real-life cannibal? Odissa couldn't throw away her shot for answers.

"All meat is bland," Maurice said. "Until you add spices."

Odissa's face opened. "That's what I always say! I mean, about meat. Not human meat. People say it tastes good, but no, it doesn't! Anything can taste good with the right spices. It's just an excuse for them to keep eating meat."

"And at least Maurice denies all excuses," Odys mumbled.

Mecca covered his small ears and leaned forward in his seat.

"Sorry, Mecca," Odissa said, noticing him.

"Don't be sorry," Odys said. "It's the only subject that can shut him up."

Dorian didn't like Odys picking on Mecca (only *he* could pick on Mecca) so he uncrossed his legs and changed the subject:

"Rosemund, how did you hear about this Collector?"

(Notice the gentleman is a Capital-C collector now).

"Danny D. Lion read about some of his work he did for a museum. That's how he caught my eye. I killed him a few weeks afterward."

"You did what now?" Odys asked, eyes blinking.

"He refused to meet with me to discuss our similar interests. Also, he was known to buy black market artifacts that I also wanted and then destroy them before I could steal them from him. He knew who I was. He knew I was out to get him. He knew."

"What the fuck is wrong with you people?" Odissa asked Dorian, her voice trembling. Maurice's cannibalism was more and more charming.

"You don't know what kind of artifacts he has up there, girl," Rosemund said. "He has things I need to see before I die. Before we all do."

Maurice shifted in his seat. "This Collector apparently got his hands on many occult things. I want *mine* on anything that might make Vulcan notice me. Anything that might get me closer to Him is something zat will get me closer to the reason I'm still fucking here..."

"No one asked you, Maurice," Odys said as he stood up in his seat and turned on the radio past him.

Enough talking.

Stanza: The rest of the car ride is not that important.

The house was old, as it should have been. The iron driveway gate was locked, so they let Q out to break it. But there wasn't much reason to pull the car up, what with all the high, unshoveled snow.

They all jumped out of the SUV. Odissa thought that it would have (had any normal people been watching) looked like they were coming out of a clown car, what with all the Automatons forming privately inside before hopping out.

"Time to go through that hair purse for the key, Rose," Fletcher said.

"Doesn't look like there's alarms anyway," Q said, as if she would love to break something else.

Circo del Herrero

The house was nothing too creepy or too nice. Complete with dying ivy on one side, the only thing it lacked to be picturesque was new paint on the shutters; it was a modest mansion.

Odys observed that their tracks were the first to this virgin snow. *If Mother's supposed to be here, then she isn't here yet.*

Or perhaps she'd been there a looong while, dummy.

The wood floors creaked under them. A thin layer of dust lined just about everything. Apart from the ghost-sheet covered furniture, the place looked quite normal.

They decided to explore the place floor by floor. Together. Maurice *swore to God* if anyone tried to scare him with one of those dusty sheets, he'd see if he also retained the ability to kill a Master.

Rosemund didn't comment on the fact they'd already proven it impossible through the time she got him to stab her in the hand. The knife had bounced right off.

Now, moving on from the topic of Maurice's physical limbo, we can proceed to the point where we examine the house itself (which I would very much like to do).[174]

Since there was no electricity (they made no pit stops for a generator, much to Rosemund's dismay), Rosemund busied herself with opening any curtains while Maud was clever enough to light one of the many unused display candles. She passed them around as she found them and lit them.

"Mecca's smells like cookies!" Mecca said from Q's back. Their smiles glowed in rapture of this little side quest Vulcan had sent them on.[175]

Maurice and Caffar had become busy with touching things. Smelling things. It didn't shock anyone when they also started to *lick* things.

"Is this a competition?" Fletcher scoffed at them.

"This knob, here, sixteenth century. Crystal. It's worth more than the desk itself—Mahogany wood from the Yucatan," Rosemund interpreted for her Automaton, licking her own lips as if she tasted it too.

Maurice seemed more apt to try anything metal first, but everything was fair game. After they had briefly explored the kitchens and the modest wine cellar to return to the main rooms (they decided that they were looking for a relic of Vulcan, not Bacchus) the cold of the house caught up to them and they began to shiver and grow impatient.

---

[174] Despite being the only one of them not there to see it (I'm assuming Bulfinch is locked up in the house still).
[175] Should they not be more somber about Gwen planning to kill herself? Maybe some of them think they can stop her? But like hell I'm asking B.L.A. for revisions on this section. It was a struggle just to pry this from our Narrator's hands.

"What, Maurice, do knobs have to do with killing you?" Odys asked, only half-interested as he and Maud admired a damaged oil portrait of some noble woman. It was exhibited as if in prime condition.

"I must say," Maud added when Maurice did not quickly answer, "though you no longer have Fletcher, his record of antiquities left quite an impression on your brain, Maurice." She raised her red brows as he went for the same drawer Caffar did.

Caffar searched madly—as if hoping to stop a hidden bomb. Maurice followed her like she were a drug dog. No, wait, they have bomb-sniffing dogs. A bomb squad dog.

"Papa always had an eye for such things," Mecca said, adding commentary to their exclusive *Antiques Roadshow.*

Odissa saw that even Maud was starting to touch things here and there; the search-madness was taking over all of them. They were in a game looking for the portal key to move the narrative along. She glanced at Fletcher, wondering what they expected to find by such methods…But even he was looking about, crouching low to the ground. Odissa gave him credit for keeping his hands in his pockets.

"Bring more light over here," Maurice beckoned as they'd made their way to the far end. It was the last nook they'd explore before going to the next floor.

Rosemund limped forward, glancing over Maurice's shoulders. He started to pull out and overturn all the drawers within the writing desk, making quite a mess as papers and supplies scattered. "Agh! I can feel something. So close. I can *hear* their noses twitching!" He pointed with his popping eyes to each Automaton.

He noticed Caffar's nose scrunch—inhaling a large sniff. Everyone with their candles turned to her upon the dramatic intake.

"She has the best nose," Rosemund smiled as her Automaton walked over to a closet door.

She opened it, revealing an enclosed staircase.

It was no closet at all.

"Likely leads up to the next floor," Maurice observed. "Just a second way up besides that terribly pretentious one from the foyer."

They could barely keep up with him as he dashed past Caffar up the conch-like iron steps.

By the time all of them had reached the floor's hall, he'd already thrown back curtains on the single window at the end, sending through the white sunrays. Caffar was close on his heels. Rosemund took her time, her hand hovering over the walls, frames, knobs as she wheezed about.

"I will admit," Dorian said aside, "there is *something* on this floor. Vulcan was here."

"How can you tell?" Odissa asked as she observed a painting—a small print copy of John Gast's *American Progress*. She frowned at the work like one might an omen.

"This place isn't covered in dust. It's covered in ash."

The floorboards creaked under their conjoined weight. Maud's heals made a sexy tap tap tap. Odissa found it distracting and tried not to stare at her. Odys would catch her and try to meet her gaze, but Odissa would always avoid him.

"But *what* are we looking for?" She still did not understand—still felt as though they were being mysterious when, in fact, they did not know themselves.[176]

"Nozingness!" Maurice shouted from some room. "Sweet nozingness."

Dorian shrugged, not sure what to tell her. "It could be an object. We don't know. We only smell him."

"As long as it can kill Maurice, we'll be happy," Fletcher mumbled, putting back down a glass vase.

They all entered into Maurice's chosen room. It felt like they were in a museum and Maurice was THAT tourist who took pictures of the light-sensitive art and almost got your group thrown out.

Odissa stared into her flame. "With these candles, it feels like a gothic novel."

Dorian squeezed her arm. "Then I shall be your blind Mr. Rochester."

Odissa saw Odys roll his eyes and go back to studying the paintings on the walls. These paintings, in this inconspicuous corner, were no prints.

Wanting to block their conversation, Odys said, "I don't think we should be looking so hard." He overturned a few low-standing bookcases, kicking through the volumes like an acrobat on a tightwire. "If Vulcan means for us to find something, then He'll show it to us."

"Don't be foolish, boy." Maurice picked up a large rock sculpture that seemed to be some indigenous artifact. "If gods did all the work for us, we'd be bored out of our minds. And so would They."

Maud picked up a disarrayed book. She had been scanning through the titles faster than a computer using the CTRL + F feature. "Someone's already out of their mind." She set down the outdated encyclopedia to pick up another. "Oh, look, Odissa, it's a first edition of [insert any book you'd like here; it doesn't matter—we know she's well-read]. Oh my God, it's even annotated—by [such and such a modern writer that Odissa was semi-fond of]!"

---

[176] I'm not so sure our Narrator knows.

Odissa froze—wondering why Maud was talking to her. It was almost as if Odys had forgotten the hierarchy and had shown himself exclusively through Maud.

Odissa took the book reluctantly enough, for Dorian's sake.

Dorian crossed his arms behind his back and turned from the scene, trying to pretend it hadn't happened and sniffing back potential blood.

Maurice frowned up at the mantel laden with dust and old photographs. "You killed a very interesting man, Rosemund."

"No. I *collected* him. I did unto him what he did to all of this stuff."

"That's one word for it," Fletcher sighed. "Another is '*reaped.*'"

"Harvested," Dorian added.

Maurice smiled over his shoulder. "I would love to be part of such a collection, Rose—if only!" He dusted off his hands and walked back out into the hall. Of course they tagged along.

Maurice was mumbling to himself as he picked his next room, *"Needs a fresh coat of paint, that,"* and various other observations in French.

Lifting their candles, they discovered they were in a studio. Seemingly, an art studio.

"Seems our Collector did his restoring here." Q noticed the table, bench, and easels in the center of the room obstructing the full view of a mannequin-sized figure. "Just as the article said."

The figure was sitting on a stool, her legs on the table—her torso exposed with no proper skin, revealing the gear work and metal-frame core. Like some dissected frog, her canvas linings were pinned back. Half of her face was missing and in need of delicate touch ups.

"It's an automaton," Mecca said, his eyes widening at the sight. "A real one."

"She's huge," Maud said. "I can't remember the last time I saw one so big."

The figure had been separated from her fancy pedestal—a pedestal which, when wound and properly geared, would cause the mechanics in her body to spin and come to life.[177]

Caffar began to sniff about the figure, her nose inches away from the tattered attire of the life-size automaton. With each sniff she made herself assume the Automaton's appearance—the flaky paint-like skin, the same balding hair, a similar pattern and stitching of the clothes. Parts of the cloth were threadbare, wanting to be sewed or patched. Caffar's costume proved too much work, to sniff and feign unnatural features. She stuck with sniffing.

---

[177] Of course this book would have a scene so ironic! The real automata population was entirely underrepresented until now.

Though everyone else seemed intrigued with the mechanical toy, Maurice was busy thumbing through the canvas paintings propped up against the walls. "All copies," he said to himself. "Nozing more than a mere hobbyhorse. Who has such time?"

(Maurice had a stable full of hobbyhorses, so he was one to talk).

"You suppose it's modeled after Jacques de Vaucanson's flute player?" Mecca asked the room. It was hard to tell—her posture looked so familiar.

"No," Rosemund said, "she belongs to a larger orchestral display—perhaps part of an old carnival ride. Modern design. That is no cherub face. Sadly, she's of nonono sentimental value to us. Except that we can see why Vulcan would 'visit' this Collecting Collector. He had interesting interests. Makes for a very nice setting, eh? Nice ambience. Vulcan has set the stage. So many propspropsprops."

"Is that really why you killed him?" Maurice laughed, tossing aside a tube of paint. "You were jealous of Vulcan's favor?"

"Why be jealous when Vulcan meant for me to kill him?"

As Maud and Odys looked but did not touch, Odys's eyes followed the automaton's arm to her hand—a hand closed into a fist with posable fingers taped together to protect them. "I think she's beautiful," he said.

Maud held her candle up to the Automaton's legs on the counter. "No, you don't."

Rosemund snorted. "You can't decide, Odys?"

"I've decided not to decide, I guess." He glared at Maud, cursing his tired brain for the equivalent of sleep talking.

Dorian, Fletcher, and Odissa had found a portfolio of paper sketches and were leafing through the pages. "I wonder if he did all of these," Odissa spoke her thoughts aloud.

"Likely not," Dorian answered. "The hand is so different throughout. Though some are alike, see here?"

"Well," Odys said, his posture sinking as if bored of this room already, "This ambience is a waste if nothing. Starts. To. Happen."

I'll speed this up.

Maurice had pulled out a random canvas as he said, "Vulcan liked this Collector. It makes me jealous that Vulcan would possibly spend so much time even considering someone *else* and zeir affairs when *I'm* still alive."

"Perhaps it's that very masochistic attitude, Maurice, which drives him away." Fletcher batted some cobwebs from a toolbox he felt compelled to inspect.

Odissa decided on intervention. "Maurice, many humans would be so happy to have what you have. Not even the Masters have it, right? You depend on nothing. Most people would say you should be grateful."

"Let me know, ma petite fille, how you still feel about longevity after we get you that Automaton." And he continued his search. His wide eyes never stopped darting about—never stopped bulging.

As the others rummaged through what was the most interesting room yet, Odissa observed her brother. He acted as if he wanted to move on to the next, yet he had returned back to the deconstructed Automaton in the center. Nothing better to look at, apparently.

"Dolls are so creepy, I always thought," Odissa said in her brother's direction, to distract from his blank state. Dorian did not notice, as Fletcher was still examining tools like someone picking through an estate sale.

Still lost in thought, Odys replied, "Don't call it a doll."

That's not exactly what Odissa had meant to imply, but she somehow felt as though she deserved the rebuke.

Luckily, Odissa didn't have to suffer blushing for too long, for Caffar and Rosemund seemed to be leaving the room, distracting Odys from the automaton. Behind some very tall frames leaning upon a cabinet full of old pottery and paint supplies was a small door. The kind of door that the people of the twenties or thirties would have more easily fit.

"A water closet," Rosemund informed as she worked open the rusty hinges. "Bring in more light! Quickly, now! Do you not hear the exclamation marks in my voice?!" Snatching a candle from someone else, Rosemund held it up. "Vulcan was flushed outoutout of Olympus. Always check bathrooms because Vulcan was cared for by the sea—the bathrooms are the portals, I always said."

"This is the first I'm hearing it from you," Dorian snapped back.

She had passed over the grubby toilet. It was a hard fit, to get all of them in there. By the time Odys had observed what Rosemund was jabbering on about, everyone was already gasping. Almost every Automaton had their own insightful comment to include:

"Lipstick on the mirror—in a man's house."

"That doesn't mean anything," Dorian snapped again.

"Fish scales are used to make lipstick. It's a sign."

"Of animal cruelty? Sure."

"But it's all in the bathroom. Vulcan *is* the shit of Olympia."

"'The nose knows,'" Fletcher read the mirror. Though everyone could read well enough for themselves. "You think He wrote it, or the Collector?"

"Same thing at this point—no matter the method." Maud looked about the room for more signs.

Caffar proceeded to lean against the sink and lick-taste the lipstick. She merely nodded her approval and repeated, "Same thing."

"The nose knows." Rosemund squeezed around the rest of them, held her candle down to the box of tissues sitting on the back of the seat. Upon further inspection, "There's a message on the tissue. The tissue has a message!"

"Pull it out, then!" said Fletcher, but he'd already done so, being just as near it as Rosemund. Reading aloud from the tissue that had been stuffed back inside the box, "'This box is encasement of cardboard and tissue. Pull no more out and you won't have an issue!' Signed, 'V.' He has a way with words, that Vulcan. Wonder what muse helped Him come up with that shit."

Maurice scoffed, turning red. "This object won't kill me. Black market my ass, Rosemund! The Collecting Collector could just go to zee store for something like a tissue box. Jesus. Next trip we make might as well be to zee fucking store!"

"Think of it this way," Dorian replied. "Vulcan had to pick out which box of tissues He'd use for this closet, right? Plan for the Collecting Collector to buy it. Follow him home to pull out the tissue. Or, get the man to write the message in a trance. Wait for the man to die, perhaps."

"Don't be a smart ass," Maurice growled. "If it even happened like zat!"

"It could have happened like that," Rosemund frowned into herself. "I poisoned him. Slowly.[178] The Collecting Collector had plenty of time to go to the store for V."

"Yes, because we all get spirited away to buy tissues for gods," Dorian mumbled.

"Let's not pull out any more," Odys said, feeling claustrophobic and squeezing out of the room.

"The box looks new," Mecca noted.

"Is the tissue soft, Fletch?" Q asked, reaching for it.

"Yes, it is. Perhaps the black market sells in bulk!" Fletcher presented it to her.

"Caffar, take the box, won't you?" Maurice asked her.

"What?" Dorian barked. "You all don't want to pull out each tissue and see what they say? If you don't want to do it I will—" *I will disobey Him for us.*

---

[178] WHEN?!?! HOW?!?! By sending him laced fruit baskets?

Rosemund shook her finger. "We can blow noses once we understand why He gave us a boxboxbox of tissues. But yes, Caffar will keep it safe."

"Maybe He thinks we're about to cry? He's warning us?" Mecca asked, his voice quiet as he considered it. *Mother really is gonna kill herself.*

"We should pull them all out now just to spite him," Dorian said, grabbing for the box. But Rosemund snatched it away, cane on his chest.

"Let her take it, Dorian. Just what do you think is in there?" Odissa said—hoping Dorian would obey her and stop moving toward the box. But there were two of him and only one of her:

"I'm happy to find out for you," Fletcher said, reaching over their heads.

"But He said not to—" Odissa caught Dorian's arm.

"Ah! Look at zat." Maurice chuckled. "A Pandora who doesn't want to open the box."

"No, I think there is a Pandora," Odys said, frowning in Dorian's direction.

Fletcher was too slow in grabbing the box as Caffar stuffed it into her stomach, her body shifting to rebalance the new mass inside her.

"We found the source of the smell, can we go now?" Odys asked. "Can't we just admit the Mother-may-be-there thing was just a reason to get us out of the house?"

"It was a reason," a voice said from the center of the studio floor. Their heads whipped behind them. "A good reason."

Stanza: Madus Mouse.

The closed hand of the automaton figure began to twitch. The tape ripped as Madus busted through where he had been inserted. He fell from the hand, knocking her delicate frame to the floor. He stood there, nude, hair in his eyes, so void of proper detail—as if Mother hadn't decided how she wanted him to look. Thus, I won't explain him more. He is merely a concept.

Maud observed her twin brother, because Odys was curious—curious how much his own Automaton might match him. He was different from memory. Maud's memory.

"Didn't you smell him, Caffar?" Maud goggled, a betrayed tone in her voice. Caffar had been the one sniffing—sniffing so nearby.

"Didn't you smell him? Didn't you smell? Didn't you?" Caffar repeated, her lips pulling back further with each word like a hiss.

"How could anyone smell anything besides that damn stench in the bathroom?" Madus said, standing straight and breathing in the room. His head was still low, though, as if he didn't want to see everyone for Gwendolyn just yet, hair over his face. A swamp thing birthed without a swamp.

"I won't lie," Rosemund said with a shrug. "I smelled him."

"But, then again, you knew he was there," Maurice sighed.

"You had him this whole time, didn't you?" Odys accused. "You brought him in with us?" Never mind if she did or not. That's not what matters.

"We chose this setting because it felt right," Madus said, leaning on his knees as if standing took a great effort. He had been away from Gwendolyn for many hours now (hiding) and her stress was doing nothing to conserve their energy. "This place was a compromise with Vulcan. He sets it up, but Gwen still gets to do what she needs to do. She gets to say what she needs to say. We think Vulcan understands the arrangement, otherwise it wouldn't happen. You all know why I am here, I assume?"

"Where are you Gwen?" Dorian asked, as if shouting into a speaker phone. *Can you hear me, Gwen?* "Why aren't you here?"

"Because I didn't need you to interfere with how I plan to make things right, Dori," Mother spoke through Madus. "But I also needed to say goodbye. Before I go on, though, I want to tell you that no, I didn't have Cestus. But I know where he is. Leeland told me before he died. At least, I think he did. And it makes perfect sense. It's what we suspect. He hid him inside *Admund*."

GWENDOLYN: A mother of sorrow.

ANSI: Her anger.

MADUS: Her secrets.

CESTUS: Her betrayal.

Chapter the ninth,

And now they know:

But what do they not know?

"Bastard." Odys cursed, kicking over a chair. Maud hissed under her breath.

Odissa asked, "What does that mean?"

Fletcher whispered to her, "He wanted to insure we touched Admund—where he left his greatest imprint, no doubt!"

"Gwen, you don't have to do this—please," Dorian begged Madus. "We want you to stay. You know how we feel—" *We voted.*

"Where is she, Rose?" Mecca demanded, tears in his eyes. "You know—tell us. Papa, make her tell us!"

But Maurice shook his head. *Hush now.* This wasn't his family to correct. *I cannot control her.* Not anymore. *I never could.*

"Rosemund does not know where I am but she knows enough. She brought you here because she knows I want it. She won't betray me."

"You'll kill her!" Q shouted at Rosemund. "We both know that's not what you really want."

Rosemund could not bear to look at them, avoiding their eyes and questions like small hands plucking at her sleeve. She adjusted the grip on her cane. "You have no idea what I really want, child."

Madus continued in his staticky voice: "By the time you figure out where I am, it will already be too late, Dorian. Please just listen to me. Gwendolyn has sins to confess." A gloss formed over Madus's curtained eyes. Mother was crying, but he would not. That bit would be mumbled in translation. He put a hand on the table to help his shaky limbs stay up. "You pace in place like a mad dog, Fletcher," Madus said. "Hold still. Madus cannot help me think with so much noise."

Fletcher stopped his prowl and latched on to the acknowledgment that Gwendolyn was there, behind Madus's eyes. "Gwen—Gwen, this is madness!"

Madus/Mother ignored him and turned to the others. "You want to know why I stole Madus from Rosie? Because Pepin told me something before he died. He told me his reasons for why he was going to end his life the way he did and said that I should make my own moves accordingly. Pepin told me he had recently found out about Leeland's secret life as a father."

"You knew?" Dorian's head cocked. "You knew all this time—?"

"I knew only days before you did, Dorian. Only days. And even then I was not sure—not as sure as Pepin seemed to be. The fact that they were Dorian's lost twins was not the greatest concern. Not for Pepin. Not for me. See, Pepin knew why Leeland had saved them. It had nothing to do with Dorian. It had nothing to do with me. It had nothing and yet everything to do with all of us—"

"You aren't making sense, Gwen!" Dorian shouted. His voice echoed through the room, breath as ice.

But Madus shook off his words with trembling and collected Mother's thoughts once more—pushing past. "You don't see it because it's covered in ash. Vulcan meant for us to overlook it—buried under the volcano of history. Leeland didn't save the twins because he pitied them or planned to use them against us—no." Madus banged his fist on the table, making the disassembled automata parts jump (Mother was trying to explain and Madus filtered her passionate thoughts into the most coherent form manageable). "Leeland saved them because he knew something about one of them. To understand it you have to go back to the beginning. The very beginning! When Vulcan—that god I no longer trust or care to depend upon—first created the Automatons He also created *The Prototype*. The fact that He let it live—left it for the Masters to handle instead of waving His hand and destroying the thing—makes this, even now, our own burden to bare. He's letting us decide what to do with It."

"It?" Maurice repeated. "My God, Gwen, what are you zaying? Is Alpha—?"

"When that temple girl, so long ago, volunteered to possess Alpha—the original Automata-model created with the equivalent of a soul and free will—she didn't bear The Prototype until death. We may have stripped Alpha down to the barest soul-part, but we did not kill her."[179]

Madus released his fist from the table and ran his fingers along the splintering wood, his actions more and more elegiac. His voice, steady like a monk's mantra, hummed out Mother's explanation: "They had expected the monster to die within the temple girl. At the very least, old age should have taken them. Why wouldn't Alpha die with the host? The host contained the essence of the deconstructed-Alpha." Madus started to round the table but stopped when he crossed the knocked-over automaton, her body like a cadaver's. He studied it as if it caused him to remember something. "Alpha was a furnace—was supposedly defeated and her soul-flame added to another's. The soul is a fire—a spark of life not easily extinguished when made by Vulcan, it seems. Vulcan gave the Automata and Masters the Words—the Alchemy to tie Alpha's flame-soul to another. Those flames burned in the same pit—the same host. That temple girl. They used the Words! But those Words are useless now. The job is done. They can do no more. Those old Words cannot fight this new form. We need new Words."

"What new form, Gwen?" Dorian watched Madus like a math problem written on a whiteboard, needing full space for the solution.

"We thought Alpha had been extinguished when the soul-flame of the temple girl died. They were bound. They were *supposed* to be bound. In most ways they were. But when the temple girl's flame was blown out...the flame of Alpha's *wasn't*."

Maurice smoothed down his frazzled mustache. "Zee girl is dead, Gwen. So is Alpha. Thousands of years have passed. A soul needs a body. A vessel. Hers died. End uv story."

"No. The essence of Alpha lived on. Not in the temple girl—of course not in a dead host. You see, flames can light other flames, given the right conditions." Madus waved the air with his hand. "The Buddhists believe that the same energy runs through us all; just as the same candle can light an infinite number of other candles. Alpha got to light another candle before her host died. And those candles lit more. The soul is a flame," Madus reinforced. "Don't you see?"

---

[179] "We" as in the old Masters.

No, they didn't see. They weren't computing fast enough. Gwendolyn Gwendy, however, was so well rehearsed with the aid of multiple Automatons; their metaphorical gears working to amplify her own. The others couldn't help but be afraid of her unfathomable reasoning.

"We're trying to," Dorian said. "We're trying to see."

Madus leaned forward on the table, shaking with rage and weariness. "The first Masters of the time should never have put Alpha *in a woman*. And Vulcan—that passive traitor and slothful guide!—should have redirected them. Better yet, He could've just killed the monster Himself. Don't we all wonder why He didn't? Instead, He lets us believe we had stopped the Alpha. He toys with us! He made us believe we had no purpose left—made us go on and on without knowing His true intent. I know I shouldn't speak for the gods, but His neglect—no, that's not the word. His *relinquishment* has become unbearable. Maybe I could have tolerated this so much more if—if there was so much *less* of it. You still don't understand me?

"The female priestess bred, Dorian. Her womb gave birth to not only a child, but a sub-flame of Alpha. Alpha was in that child. Maybe part of Alpha even remained in the temple girl to keep her quiet—so that others would not suspect. After all, she was bound to the host. Part of her may have had no choice but to stay in the temple girl. Maybe part of her did die. I don't know. The others let the temple girl live out her secluded life, didn't they? They never knew. The host never suspected. Reincarnating itself over and over into a newborn baby, the Monster's subterranean light never faded out. Never died. The umbilical cord was cut and a new body was given each time to Alpha. Yes, maybe the new hosts only held a slight version of Alpha. Or, maybe it is the full version. Maybe copies like clones—or software. I do not know! But I know some form of Alpha still lives because she was given tinder and kindled. Besides, fire is fire no matter where it lights from."

It all burns the same, doesn't it?

Madus walked the other way around the table, away from their eyes, finding a side of the table that was only his—apart from them. "It had to be females. Only females. Only the female sex, you see, will grow new wombs to create new wombs.[180] It worked for a while, for Alpha. Well enough. Perhaps it was a mere sub-existence, passing through history this way. Perhaps it even became habit, a parasite merely moving onto the next host. It doesn't matter. What does matter, however, is that the woman *had* to breed. In order to create new wombs, the gene pool

---

[180] Edited out a speculation or two from Mother about how the temple girl may have tempted her guards, how Alpha's bodies were burned as witches, how she eventually lived with and was birthed into Native American populations.

473

had to be mixed. But Alpha had no guarantee of getting acceptable genes. Doing this made Alpha run into a genetic *malfunction*. Sterility." Madus paused and lifted his eyes, but did not look at them. A mad scientist reporting his study's findings.

"Infertility was running through the bloodline. It grew harder and harder for Alpha's bodies to become pregnant. Barren wombs make for barren futures, and Alpha's was growing short. Just as Leeland was about to kill off her remaining host—a baby—a child before the age of speech— she spoke to him, begging to preserve her. And in that moment, I theorize, a proposition was made. The girl-child wanted fertility. The Alpha inside the child bargained with Leeland. She could not mend her problem by herself. She no longer had the means or the right tongue to perform the Alchemy she knew. It is also likely she never forgot the Words, really. She needed help to repair her human vessel. You cannot perform such acts on yourself—surgery and the like. Not very well. And if the Automatons who, with the Vulcan-given knowledge to trap her into human form, could—at the very least!—help her keep expounding her mortal cages, she'd help Leeland in return."

The quiver in Madus's voice already revealed what gains Alpha had promised.

"She promised Leeland me—Gwen—" Madus corrected himself. "Maybe help in his plight. Hell, maybe she's the reason any of us even met. I'm still not sure of the past, but I am sure she could see the future. Alpha knew the Words and the means to see it—see it from the past. Alpha is Alchemy itself, so of course she knew—she knew!" Madus scratched the table with his long nails—nails long like Maud's—like Anselm's. "I think she told Leeland she could be the key to changing my mind. And perhaps she was."

"However," Madus added, "Admund's knowledge proved unable to give Alpha fertility. Alchemy only holds so much power over biological decrees, and even then Vulcan likely promoted her infertility; Vulcan didn't want to drag it out any longer than He already had. And, oh, how long He had let it go! On and on. Finally, He brings us to a close. He draws the beast back in—a beast He had given a very long chain to begin with—a beast He *never* intended on killing."

Madus cupped his face with one hand, focusing on their shadows as if wanting this to be nothing but a cave allegory.

"I believe Leeland barely recognized he had saved something that could awaken and bring us all to our knees. His hate of Automata blinded him. He knew very little of Alpha's potential within human bonds. Who knows what she's capable of? What we do know is that Alpha could make a newborn speak; Alpha let her host's parents die; and, Alpha kept her existence secret for centuries. The threat is certainly there. But how much of one? All this is relevant because Leeland left her here to haunt us. It is my guess that he—he contacted Pepin and told him—or Pepin figured it out. Pepin felt obligated to warn us; to warn us that Vulcan had never intended the Masters to kill her completely. Because of that, Pepin created his plot to save us from *Odissa*."

ADMUND: Knew his Master had saved a monster.

LEELAND: No wonder he allowed Admund to "experiment" on Odissa.

BROKE EVEN: Yes, a deal's a deal.

ADMUND: Adopted a monster, but his Master married one.

Chapter the tenth,

Martyrs:

Can you hear the silence of the saints?

I should tell you they had all been staring at Odissa as Madus faded out his monologue.

"Me?" Odissa breathed, finally sure what their wide eyes meant.

"Hush, child!" Madus raised a finger. He brought that finger down and tucked his hair behind his ear—finally showing his face. "Your own words won't help you understand. You must listen or you will never be free. You will always be trapped and hiding. Listen to me." He pointed to his bare chest. "You see, Odys, the reason you have Maud is because of your sister. Pepin needed a way of testing Alpha. If she ever tried to compile the Automatons under herself, how would we stop her? How could we even test whether or not we *could* stop her?"

"Why would she want to do that?" Fletcher asked—searching for a rope to pull them out of this theoretical hole. "Why would she want all Automatons?"

Mother was starting to sound like a god herself, a puppet master pulling the strings.

Mother pressed herself through Madus, "Why wouldn't she? Why wouldn't she want control over so much power? So much immortality when her own is at stake? The only reason she hasn't come after us for so long is because she cannot hurt us. She is in a mortal body. The Automata protect us. Don't you get it?

"I had observed, at length, her attachment of you, Odys. It was quite obvious Pepin knew Alpha was dormant within her. Perhaps even somewhat subdued by Odissa's own personality. Who knows? It was one of our hopes that if Alpha were ever compelled to take all Automatons and unite them in one body—to do gods-only-know-what—then she wouldn't be able to get them all. We hope—nay, *pray*—she wouldn't be able to kill her own brother. We knew she loved you. We knew she saved you too, Odys. You meant more to her than her parents did. Leeland could control her through you. I'm sure this was Pepin's reasoning."

475

Madus stared at the table, the odds and ends resting there. "I suspect that there are two 'beings' within her body, and they are most often separated. From what we've observed, Odys, Alpha has even kept your sister in the dark. She is innocent—how could she not be? A part of me even wonders if Alpha hasn't changed over the years—has she become docile, her only desire is to exist? I do not know. I do not know.

"However, I do know it was never our intent for Dorian to fall in love with her. There was never meant to be this much pain—pain in telling the truth. Venus has made our choice hard. Vulcan let Her do this. I blame Him. But I won't let Him have the satisfaction of my choice. I'll curse god and die. I hope you also forgive me, and accept my suggestion."

"Suggestion?" Maurice asked.

"As each one of us dies, let us draw lots and give the inanimate Automatons back to ourselves. A family of Masters has not worked; Leeland's plan was cruel; Pepin's, impossible. This is the next way. Alpha cannot get them if we have them all."

Their candles were dripping too much wax now. Madus observed the position of the sun, remembering the time. Clouds were rolling over the sky. His eyes lowered onto Caffar. Mother remembered the box. "Do not dwell on that damn tissue box. It is just a distraction to get you to think Vulcan wishes to speak with you. But His voice is clear! What He wants we already know. He let her live this long, didn't He? There must be—and is—a way to feel safe with her alive. Indeed, have you yet to feel threatened? Do not touch her. Promise me, now, you will not harm her—" Mother's eyes look through Madus's and pleaded with Maurice.

Why did she beg Maurice?

Yeah, why?

Because "If He means for her to live," Maurice whispered, "why would I obey him?"

"She is Vulcan's sin. Don't let her become ours. Do not touch her. If you do, how can we ever be sure we didn't kill something that had actually lost its bite? We are not like that."

"Yes, we are," Rosemund sighed to herself.

"Why did you keep this from us? Why?" Dorian demanded.

"Because we couldn't scare her off. We couldn't scare Odys off. We had to let her think we were stupid and that she was one of us. And isn't she? Has Odys not earned their places among you?" Madus looked at Odissa, whose eyes were wide, her heart rippling her body like a rabbit's. "Are we not balanced now?"

Odissa couldn't stand his eyes—Madus's eyes pleading for Mother. *Please let this be a standstill.* Odissa noted the others in the room—their fear keeping them from defending her.

"And you will leave us to decide what we should dododo with her when you leave us?" Rosemund said, frown arching against a sob.

"I've told you what to do with her. Let her be as she has been. Vulcan will do whatever He wishes, but we can at least let *Him* make the final decision. We've done enough work. We never should have been her jury. Not when we were to be denied authority anyway."

At this, everyone noticed Dorian had retreated from Odissa. Odissa had barely realized he'd stepped away from her—so consumed with the spotlight, the eyes watching her. He backed into the wall and slid down, covering his face.

Madus observed this for Gwendolyn, and she knew she shouldn't keep them longer. Madus found his strength to release the table. "Maurice, Gwendolyn has found your traveling carnival stage and hitch wagon—the one you drove up to [such and such a town's] border to park before going to Dorian's."

"God, no," Maurice could barely say. "Not in my wagon!"[181]

The French phrases ensuing tried to cut her off in protest but—

"I've written a letter. I'd like you all to read it. And don't dare call it a note. Never a note."[182]

"You don't have to do this, Gwen," Rosemund said softly, though it wasn't begging. She would not beg Gwen. No matter how much she wanted to. She respected her more than that.

"You all may forgive me, but I cannot. I broke the rules," Madus said for her. And then his lips trembled, "And I killed Leeland. I killed him. Was he so wrong that we should kill him?"

Odys was the only one willing to mumble a "Yes." But he said no more when Rosemund glared at him.

"Vulcan makes us do mad things," Rosemund said.

"He will make me mad no more. My Automatons will be safe here until you come. I love the new costumes, Maurice. I'm wearing Captain Hook."

But before Maurice could boil up and shout at her: "DON'T RUIN THE SATIN!" Madus fell to the ground—a penny once more.

Gwendolyn Gwendy had killed herself.

Mecca crawled up in his father's arms and snuggled under his chin but could not ignore the smoke coming from his Papa's ears.

---

[181] The newspaper a few weeks before this time announced a local weekend fair. Perhaps Maurice had been interested in attending, though it's no absolute fact he planned on participating. A man with no Automaton has to make a living somehow, no?
[182] Because this wasn't as suicide. It was a sacrifice.

"[Cursing in French]. She always hated me, zat bitch," Maurice said as he cradled his son's head. "She's zee reason Pepin left zee circus, you know—she changed him—converted him! She made him want to leave everyzing we had built and zat is why I wanted to die. Zat is it!" His chest heaved. "She made zee circus seem boring. She made it all so *pointless*. She promised us things. A grand vision. Of secretly helping zee world. Some fucking world zis is!"

He pointed in the air in Rosemund's face, as if Rosemund were to blame for Mother's previous existence. Rosemund did nothing but frown and run her tongue over her braces.

"And when I did die, zat is when he left, you know! He left all of us to hide. All because of what she started! We were perfect before her. Before that [French word] Leeland fell in love with her. Before zis—zis so-called *family!*"

!!!

"And now she must flaunt her death in my home—zere is nothing she cannot taint! Ah, [more cursing in French]." He slapped the side of the wall with his palm, his stiff hair jumping and landing out of place.

Odys turned to his sister, who was busy staring at the floor. Her direct line of sight was inches from Dorian's feet. Fletcher was watching her like a hawk, his face unreadable and unfazed by Maurice's rant, as if he had muted it.

Rosemund cleared her throat.

Odissa's eyes flicked to Rosemund. "Mother knew about me. So she told you too? You knew this whole time? If not everything, then you knew more than they did. And you're not afraid of me? You've been so calm—so trusting, even." Odissa laughed, as if in some humorous dream-state. Was part of her falling asleep?

Dorian looked up upon hearing that soft laugh, his skin prickling.

She noticed his hesitant acknowledgement and stepped back. "Are you all afraid of me?" She could barely form the question. It caught in her throat.

Odys stepped toward her, putting himself between them and his sister.

"What does this mean?" she asked—asked anyone who would answer.

Her brother could avoid her gaze no longer. "I don't know what this means," he shook his head. "We know what Alpha did. The Automatons remember. She did terrible things."

"So you *are* afraid of me?" She backed away from Odys as he tried to touch her. "You really think that—that thing is inside me? What was she talking about, Odys? What was she saying?"

He did not answer, for it was too obvious.

Tearing her eyes away from Odys, she demanded of Dorian (though very softly), "Can you not love me anymore, because of this?" She shooed her brother away to stand alone by the wall. "You all shuffle your feet rather than answer me! Why won't you say anything?"

"Odissa, please—" Odys begged as she continued to stare at Dorian—Dorian who wouldn't answer her from his spot on the floor.

"Did you not hear what Gwendolyn said, though? She loves me as well! She said not to hurt me—please!" The panic in her voice surprised even her.

"Mother loves all things," Dorian quietly said, speaking his thoughts aloud—though he probably shouldn't have said it. "But that doesn't make them safe, Odissa."

A shadow fell over her. She shook down more tears. She marched over to where Madus slept, inanimate, on the floor, Master-less.

Dorian rose to his feet, the others too—their stance prepared to stop her.

"I could touch it, if I wanted—you all know that! You idiots just let him sit there— vulnerable." She bent down, her fingers inches away from Madus. They warned her not to. "But I could! I could." She started to cry, and took back her outstretched limb. "But I don't."

She begged them to notice her control.

Rosemund limped over to her. Taking her handkerchief, she picked Madus up and folded him within its fabric. The penny flashed like new—as if it had been minted just yesterday. "And you won't," Rosemund said.

She gestured for Q to take Madus, for now at least. Q found an old paint tin full of wooden buttons to place him in. She melted the lid down with her fingers.

Odissa crouched there, weeping, her eyes closed. Rosemund snapped and gestured for Dorian to come to her. She backed away from the couple as Odissa fell into his chest.

He did not touch her or comfort her. He only let her come to him. She noted this but did not let that stop her.

"I know what I am!" she screamed into his chest. "I always knew! But she makes me forget. I forgot. Don't let her take me again—" Her body trembled. Her voice gentler, "No, she won't make me forget this time. It's too late to forget. You all will remind me even if she does make me. She is not cruel or stupid. She did it to protect me."

She felt Dorian clench.

Odys and Maud watched with angry and confused tears in their eyes, their bodies wanting to turn away in agitation.

She pulled away from Dorian. "I—I hate you all. You can't let me around you," she whispered to herself. "It's not safe. I will kill every last one of you."

She said it as if she believed it but desperately didn't want to.

"You won't," Dorian forced himself to say.

"That is my nature. This has been what she wanted all along. She *used* me."

She noticed Dorian's hand tremble—in what could only be interpreted as fear—as he tried to soothe her.

"I'm going to kill you…" The words weren't even words. She was fighting them, silencing them to whispers as they escaped her lips. "That's why Gwen left. She's leaving the gods to Their mistakes."

He pet her hair. "No, you won't."

But Dorian's shaky voice proved he was not so sure.

Odissa could not keep the words down. "She is awake. She knows that I know and she will silence me. She's no longer pretending to sleep. You won't know where I end and where she begins. I remember now. I remember. I remember my mother, Dorian—I remember you—" She smiled there. But then that smiled faded to fear. "I let her die, Dorian! I let my mother die. My father. So many before them."

"You didn't," Odys said—he could be silent no longer. "You're Odissa. You didn't kill them. You won't hurt us."

"I've seen the future, Odys. I will. The past speaks. I am older than any of you. I know!" she screamed at him.

She put a hand over her mouth, shocked at her volume.

They let the silence take them.

"You are supposed to be here with us." Dorian said—grabbing her face. "Vulcan wants it. The stars aligned for you, Alpha. Vulcan means to use you. Odissa is still in there. You're still Odissa."

"But you hate Vulcan," Maurice said. "Why would you want her to be here if Vulcan wants her to be here?"

"Because Vulcan couldn't control her once. Now He can. Vulcan set all this up so that she would be with us. He hopes to use her. But she might be the key to making His games stop."

"You are only saying zat because you love Odissa."

"Apparently not just her." He pet her hair and Odys's face grew redder. "I'm also in love with *Alpha*."

ODISSA: A Gemini in more ways than one.

FACES: Two.

LIKE: A coin.

COINS: Have two sides.

The Annotated Manuscript: The Pre-Programming: BOOK THREE

Preface,
Freedom from the pursuit of happiness:
Who are the ghosts in our machines?[183]

Dear United States citizens (and all those other peoples the USA has yet to assimilate), I think the Preface's title and subtitle says it all. *Fuck your American Dream.* The more I think on the manifest destiny of this story, the angrier I become.[184]

I guess I'm starting to rant again.

But don't you see? See—look!—the implications of this story. Of what it means if it is true. This is why I don't care if Gabbler believes or not. It hurts worse to know its truth.

The gods planned for colonization—and all other evils. Do you see it now? And Vulcan stood by like the rest of Them and allowed the cancer to spread. He did nothing as the gods made Their deals and bets and plans for this sacred land.

Scratch that.

He did do something. He made Automata. He made them to fit within the *civilized* dream. Made the Automata into futuristic shapes and designs. He knew to play off misfortune. Off of what would come. Off of what would end.

And for what?

I'll tell you what.

For this.

For this story.

He thinks it will show the world His upgraded nature.

And perhaps it will. Perhaps any attempts to smear Him will only fuel His legend. This is His story, after all. I can only tell it because He[185] lets me. And, let's be honest, what else am I going to do with all my time?

I'm still working out *why* He lets me, though. Why me. Why I was chosen.

---

[183] "I have made you a tester of metals and my people the ore, that you may observe and test their ways. They are all hardened rebels, going about to slander. They are bronze and iron; they all act corruptly. The bellows blow fiercely to burn away the lead with fire, but the refining goes on in vain; the wicked are not purged out. They are called rejected silver, because the LORD has rejected them." —Jeremiah 6:27-30.

[184] Ah, this is why the John Gast painting.

[185] I'm so sick of catching all the capital Hs. I feel as if I may have missed some. Does Vulcan deserve the capital? I feel less and less inclined. Whenever I catch a lowercase "h," it feels as though our Narrator is slipping in reverence. Probably for a good reason.

Part of me (a small part) grudgingly thinks it is His way of atoning.

Of proving all the suffering in the world is for a reason.

But what good is a reason when it's not a good reason?[186]

Vulcan never has good enough reasons. For example: just like this story, there was never a *good* reason He preserved any part of *Alpha.*[187]

Chapter the first,

The rumors of her death were greatly exaggerated:

But does that make them untrue?

Odissa breathed deeply for a while, letting them know she was trying to collect herself—and what she was going to say. "It all makes sense to me, why I did what I did—why I've done what I've done."

"And what've you done?" Maurice asked, popping one eye at her. Though his hands were behind his back he was far from at ease. Q had taken Mecca from him, as if Mecca knew he would be safer in his own arms during a scene like this.

"I don't know! You all look at me as if you know more about me than I do." Her back found a rack of old paint cans. They watched her eyes, moving back and forth over nothing, as if watching something playing before her they couldn't see. "I say I don't know," she eventually said, "but it's only because...I don't know if I know. It's like Doctor Jekyll and Mr. Hyde—except a Doctor Jekyll that has never been allowed to know Hyde exists. How could he know, if Hyde actually chose to suppress himself, instead of the other way around?"

"Amazing, zee concept of yourself, Odissa," the expression of distrust on Maurice's face screaming.

"I'm really that scary?"

"You tell us, Odissa." Maurice said as if speaking to a caged animal he may or may not let out. "Should we be afraid? Your little outburst just now isn't comforting—threatening to touch Madus."

"Stop it, Maurice," Fletcher said for Dorian. "There is a reason Mother looked at you when she said not to touch her—not to harm her. Isn't there?"

Maurice frowned. "I am not sure why she did that. Not sure at all."

---

[186] When I asked the Narrator why they were suddenly so political, they said, "This story is in the U.S. for a reason."
[187] "He has no time to be anything but a machine. How can he remember well his ignorance...?" —Henry David Thoreau, *Walden.*

Odissa gasped, hand over her mouth once again. She pointed, some part of her coming to a conclusion. "It's because we'll be last ones. I can see it. I'll still be here when they're gone, and so will you, Maurice." She kept that hand over her mouth, thinking. "Mother knows we'll be alone together. If not me, then Alpha—I can see it. Oh my god, how can I see it? How did I know that?"

"Because you're not stupid, Odissa," Odys tried to calm her from afar. "It just makes sense, that's all." *Hush, now. Don't give them reasons.*

Odissa trembled, rubbing her wrinkled forehead. "Alpha knew it, though. Oh my God she's in here—in me. She's scared." Odissa pulled at her shirt as if it were a skin she could shed.

Maurice turned to Rosemund with a tired groan. "You think she can kill me?"

"Maybe that's what Mother meant. Don't try to get her to kill you, Maurice. Don't do anything stupid."

Maurice's eyes narrowed in thought. *Has my relic been here all along?*

"Don't even think it, Maurice!" Odys shouted. "Don't even think about provoking her! I'll fucking kill Mecca if you do. She bleeds, Maurice. She's not like you. She's not like us. You don't get to play your game with her—you understand?"

Maurice's mustache twitched but he said nothing. Mecca's eyes widened in horror.

Odys put two hands up in apology. *Just listen to me.* "Look at her hand—that scar there!" Odys pointed. "The childhood scrapes and bruises. Those were real. Just look now, at that scar on her shoulder. Show them, Odissa."

Quietly, "Don't make me—"

But he was there, tugging down her collar. "I gave that scar to her. I chased her down the hall when we were five years old. Broke a statue. Blood everywhere." He had come to love that scar. "You don't get to touch her, Maurice."

"You don't get to decide," Maurice laughed. "She gets to. She can try killing me if she wants, boy."

"But you don't get to provoke her," Maud enforced.

"Maybe not her directly…" Maurice laughed, an angry sound.

"You fucking touch Dorian or my brother, and I'll never kill you, Maurice. I'll let you live for fucking ever with your guilt!" As the last word came out of her mouth Odissa slammed her hands on her lips—eyes glazed with shock.

"You think I would kill them?" Maurice shook his head. "No, I only want to kill myself."

"I'm so sorry," she murmured. "I didn't mean to say that. I didn't."

Maurice turned to Odys. "She can defend herself, you see?"

Mecca began to sputter and blubber. He hid his face in Q's thick hair, slobbering all over it. But she didn't mind, for her face was too busy frowning; her arms too busy cradling him. She looked up at Maurice. "He tells me to tell you fuck you. You're only making things worse."

"One death before the next, please," Rosemund said. "Do we go clean Mother up, or what?" She sighed, and looked about her house. Disappointed property owner.

Maurice cleared his throat. "Haven't we had enough for one day? The dead stay dead. And in this weather, the body will keep. Let's have lunch first. We can't think straight on empty bellies."

Or, at least, Maurice couldn't.

"So we'll just leave the Automatons for anyone to find?" Odys objected.

"Do you think Mother would be so careless? She knew what she was doing. Just look at *zis* elaborate ending. And still," he added with a look at Odissa—still cautious, "the show goes on."

"Can you give us a minute, all of you?" Dorian asked, as politely as he could through his stern-stoic face.

Their eyes searched Fletcher's face for why. Was it safe, really, to do that anymore? They weren't so sure. Even Odissa glanced about.

"Go out to the car. Warm it up or something. Go, fuck you! Go."

A wrinkle came over Odys's face as they trickled out. His jaw clenched and threatened to break his teeth.

They may have left the room, but they hovered in the hallway, leaving the door open.

Dorian was just glad they obeyed him.

Odissa put more distance between them.

Dorian felt her move away and took a step toward her. "I saw you realize it—like a dream you forgot you once had. Does it fade in and out, then? Are you even conscious of it?"

"Fuck, Dorian," she sniffed, "'Does it fade in and out?'" she laughed at that. "Ask a person with multiple personality disorder that same question. Their answer will be mine. Stop—just stop asking me questions as if I completely understand them! You sound like *Leeland*." She hissed the name.

"I do?"

"Asking me questions—questions that confuse me! I remember them now. Not all of them, because she made me forget, but I remember how they made me feel. *This* feeling. Fuck." She gestured up and down, wriggling in her skin. "She comes out and she makes me forget. But she's not making me forget this time. Gwen drew her out. There's no point in hiding anymore." She took a breath, hugging herself. She realized she was rambling. "Fuck, for a moment there I thought you were going to kill me—*you*, Dorian! You. I thought you were going to—to let it be done. You're supposed to love me."

"I love you enough to let you die if it's not you in there anymore, Odissa. You should have seen your face. How it contorted—"

Fletcher put his hands in his 'pockets' as he watched them. "You looked scary as hell—telling us you were going to kill us."

"But you just said you loved Alpha, too—"

"I do. But I don't know if it's kind to let her live. I think Vulcan is using her. And Vulcan may be using me to hurt her. I can't let that happen. I don't know what's going on yet."

"Then kill your fucking self—not me!" *Some love this is.*

"You think I don't know that's the better option, Odissa?!" he shouted at her. "I am sorry I got confused. You try being under a love spell and tell me if you always have the most reasonable reaction to things!"

He thought his nose was runny but no. It was bleeding again—bleeding at the thought of a life without her—of a life for her without him. Either way, the thought was crippling.

"That's blood," she said.

"Fuck—Fletcher, help me."

But Fletcher was already looking about for something to dab Dorian's nose. Odissa offered her scarf. "Caffar has all the damn tissues," Fletcher grumbled.

As he dabbed his nose he asked her, "You remember Dory?"

She put her hands through her hair, squeezing her head as if it might explode. "I have two memories inside—inside me. Sometimes I let myself see it and sometimes I don't. The memory of her isn't really Odissa's—I mean, mine. It's Alpha's memory of her. It's my own mother's memory."

His spine stiffened. *She doesn't even know which one she is. Maybe there is no difference.* "You remember talking to Leeland? As a baby?"

"No. I don't. She won't let me see it."

"Are you lying?"

"I don't know, Dorian!" she shouted at him. She covered her ears. "Why are you even asking?"

"Maybe you want to confuse us, to protect yourself. And that's OK. The more confused you seem, the more innocent as well. Because you have sinned, haven't you? You've been hiding. That doesn't make you seem safe." He paused, tossing her scarf away. "I won't let them hurt you."

"I think that's what Alpha wants. But me too; I won't let me hurt you. That's the one thing I know. I want to be here. With you."

Stanza: The Automaton with no soul and a soul with no Automaton.

There has never been a car ride so quiet.

Upon finally reaching an acceptable town (to find acceptable food), Dorian could stand the silence no longer. "Rosie, why did you even go along with this? Why would you let Gwen?" He stuffed his hands deep into his coat pockets to squeeze Fletcher. He was chewing on his gum so forcefully—his cheeks rippling—they thought his jaw might break.

Rosemund shifted in her seat, moving away from the question.

Odys was busy watching his sister from the corner of his eye. He was pretending to look out the far window beside Mecca. But he wasn't really. His sister was staring at her lap. Her arms crossed. Her eyelids were so downcast that they might as well be closed.

Finally, Maurice cleared his throat. He looked at Rosemund and then in the rearview mirror back at them. He was going to answer Dorian's question for her.

Rosemund turned her face to the window so she could brush away those tears under her glasses before they ran down her scars. Mecca, though a little less restless than normal in his seat, saw Rosemund's face blush—almost matching that red hair. He awaited her answer, same as the rest of them. She pulled her coat around her more tightly, though she did not button it. The action wasn't for warmth, it was for comfort—to brace herself for what Maurice was about to admit for her.

"Sometimes your time comes," Maurice said over his shoulder. "You can't deny that of a person."

Dorian shouted, "How was it your decision to make, Rose? How? How was it even Gwen's?"

Mecca started to blubber again, putting his face in his knees. He wanted Q to hold him but settled on Odys patting his back.

"Jesus, shut up, Mecca!" Dorian barked, hitting the back of his seat. "You never cry—why the fuck are you crying? Si no quieres que esto suceda, then maybe you shouldn't have brought your damn zombie, dumbass. Bringing him here progressed everything. Everything!"

Mecca gave him the finger and continued to sniffle into himself. He hated this family.

In Spanish, "You'd think he'd be more mature by now but no. Q must have slowed down the part of his brain that makes him not be such a fucking crybaby. We don't need your tears."

"Don't talk to him like that!" Odissa snapped.

The van fell silent.

Maurice sped up. Eyes in that rearview mirror. To Odys, "She knows Spanish does she?"

Odys's eyes were wide when he answered. "Yes." But he was starting to realize that maybe it was not because she had ever studied it in school.

Dorian's face contorted. He threw back his head and wept tears worse than Mecca.

Stanza: They stopped at the first open restaurant.

"Apparently the weather has kept some from caring to open," Maurice said as they drove through the most populated street yet. He pulled into a Ma & Pa's diner. The run-down architecture tried to resemble a saloon.

"It's just winter. These people obviously have never been north this time of year," Q stated as she sprang up from her inanimate form.

They were the only car in the front lot.

They sat themselves, as no host came out to greet this Donner Party. Even pulled a few tables together.

It took a while for someone to come out from the back. They could hear a television humming behind double-hinged swinging doors (they went along with the western theme). They were a bit late for the lunch specials, so the dinner menu is what they looked at.

After placing their orders, Maud looked about, scowling.

All the place was missing was a buffalo head on the wall.

Oh, wait, there *was* a boar head.

It might have been nice, forty years ago, this place. But now it was just scary. And everyone was afraid of what their food might look like when they finally got it.

Rosemund dug through her hair and pulled out a pen.

"Had she a beard, she'd hide things in that too," Maurice said to no one in particular.

It gained a few obligated smiles.

Rosemund started working out a math formula she had just solved in her brain, making sure the solution was true as if solutions mattered still. No one was much for talking.

Soon enough, the waitress brought the dishes out. Just as she was picking up her foldable serving-table and setting the check by Maurice (he was the 'oldest' gentleman at the table), she commented, "Oh, I swear to God. We get no peace in this town any more. Not only do the hobos drop in for free food, but the cold can't even get rid of them damn Bible thumpers."

She nodded outside the window and walked away, heaviness about her step.

"Never mind, I like this place," Odys said to no one particular. Everyone else was too busy staring out the window.

It took everyone a few seconds to zoom in on the old man at the corner stoplight, standing in the snow, shouting at the slow-moving cars. The cold silence made his voice more audible. Fletcher had to grab Mecca's food-shoveling hand to get him to stop his fork-clatter, so they might better hear.

The old man, still agile in the cold, was reading from a very worn, leather-bound Bible. He would have been a cute old man, all warmly dressed, had there not been such a righteous forcefulness in his stance under that wearable banner.

And in his voice.

"HE MADE THE SEA OF CAST METAL, CIRCULAR IN SHAPE..."

Then the cars were allowed to go, drowning him out. But he kept on shouting. "THE SEA STOOD ON TWELVE BULLS...LIKE THE RIM OF A CUP...HE ALSO MADE TEN MOVABLE STANDS OF BRONZE...ON THE PANELS...LIONS, BULLS AND CHERUBIM...WERE WREATHS OF HAMMERED WORK. EACH STAND HAD FOUR BRONZE WHEELS WITH BRONZE AXLES..."

"You think it's Him?" Q asked them. "My nose is so full of ash from the house I can't tell—can't smell."

"Maybe, maybe not," Rosemund answered, pushing up her glasses to better see far away.

"Him who?" Odissa asked.

They tore their narrow eyes from the palmer to look at her skeptically. *Did she really not know?*

Maurice nodded back to the street preacher, "Hard to say what is and isn't Vulcan. Some might say *everything* is potentially Vulcan. Connected."

"What's he saying?" Odys tried to read the man's lips, urging Maud's better ears to tune in.

Dorian, who was adapt more to hearing than seeing, said, "Old Testament. He's no evangelical, despite that Bible he's waving around."

Fletcher clarified, "First Kings, Chapter seven." Then, as if translating from a silent movie, reading the lips, just seconds off: "'...all cast in metals. Each stand had four handles one in each corner, projecting from the stand. At the top of the stand there was a circular band half a...'"

"He's skipping ahead. Your words don't match," Mecca pointed out.

"He knows we're paying attention to him," Q added, looking away as if caught.

"He's looking at us..." Maud began to eat her potato.

And then the old man closed his Bible, tucked it under his arms, and walked away. The spitting snow eventually clouded his figure.

"He's not even going to say hi?" Rosemund said. "It must not be Him."

Maurice nodded. "Just like we have our postmen, Vulcan, too, can have a message delivered. He's there, though, even if it's not Him, He's looking through his eyes. Telling us He's watching. A warning."

"Gods shouldn't walk. Feet are what mortals use," Mecca judged.

"Feet aren't a curse. Not having feet, however, would be one," Maurice said to his son— trying to put a smile back on his lips.

They ate their food in relative silence. No, actually, *complete* silence. Not another word was said until Maurice left a couple hundred-dollar bills on the table and told them to take a restroom break if they needed it. No one else did, for they all wanted to leave before the old lady realized so much money had been left for her.

Close early, Grandma, everywhere else has.

However, just as they walked out the door, they were not met by cold air, cold snow, cold sleet. No. They weren't even outside. They were in Maurice's trailer-wagon traveling-show. And the door had just slammed behind Maurice, last one out.

...Or should I say *in?*

Stanza: Young Adult Lit and Ancient Adult Lit.

It was only a matter of seconds before they realized what had happened and willingly accepted their new surroundings—pressed against each other as if a cook just scrapped them into a canning jar. "At least Vulcan saved us on gas," Maurice said as he squeezed past everyone to hunt for the dead body.

He knew his way about the cramped space. They saw him halt. There it was, behind the curtain.

"Yes," Fletcher said, walking up toward the body (as everyone was, circling around it), "but it doesn't help that we don't have a car now. And it's so cold I don't want to walk around for another one." He sniffed. From the cold. From the sight.

Mecca and Q exchanged excited looks (despite their sadness). *New Car Time* was what they had gotten out of that. The mere thought of thievery could lighten any wake.

Pushing past a rack of undressed puppets in the wagon, Odys saw out the window into the vacant parking lot covered in ice. The pointed flag-garland, draped along haphazardly, smacked against the wagon. The colors and the ice reminded Odys of the frost carnival in Virginia Woolf's *Orlando*—when the ice breaks and the sheet-slabs float off with the tents and the people and into a cold, cold void. *Swept out to sea*, he thought. And then he thought that line perfectly summed up this current experience. He wasn't sure why. It was Pepin who'd read the work, not him. Maud was only letting him draw upon it. He didn't understand—not in his distracted state—that what little was left of Pepin had come out at the sight of this place, this setting.

But also and…it was the woman, there—in the center of this ice—who had killed herself. The authoress of *Orlando* had killed herself as well. Other than that, the reference didn't fit. But that's what Pepin would have thought, nevertheless.

Mother's body was slouched in an armless chair next to a rack of costumes and a disgruntled polka set. The white ruffles of her costume were splattered with red blood. From one hand, the fingertips reached to the ground to a plastic hook that had once covered them.

In the hand in her lap, well, little mirror-Anselm could just be seen.

Maurice gently lifted the paper from under her hand, sliding Anselm off with grace. He unfolded the yellow Big Chief Tablet paper (where did she find that old parchment, or had she had it for a while, inside Anselm like a desk?). "What iz zis? A novel?"

Yes, you're in one, but no. Mother only wrote about six pages.

"Read it," Dorian said, his voice faint.

"No." Maurice shook his head, mustache stiff. He was a bit too angry with Gwen to care about her final message. "Fletcher, here."

Fletcher cleared his throat, clearing out his own sadness to vociferate the dead's last words.

"[The following footnote contains the beginning of the letter. It was cut because it made Mother seem like too much of a fangirl, but the Narrator insisted on keeping it in because "They have the right to know where Mecca gets it from." Personally, I think the Narrator just wanted a reason to mention Lord of the Rings YET AGAIN:[188]."

---

[188] *"'I was recently having Ansi re-read aloud all my favorite books to me one last time. He would recite them to me. I made him memorize so many, but they start to blur after an age—like rust blurs a metal's shine. But he did his best. I noticed new things this time around. The Lord of the Rings series came up in our selection. I remember reading them to Mecca. Tell little Mecca he will always be my baby. Tell him that. LOTR was our thing. Our book. But I came to the Tom Bombadil portion this time and… This is going to sound so stupid, but it will help you understand my anger. Remember how the Tom Bombadil portion was cut from the movies—because no one seems to like it? Well, I found a new respect for Tolkien's creating it. Tom represents all the outward forces at work—or, shall I say, NOT at work. Tom is a representation*

He turned the paper over.

"'But to my real point: I have been reading. And in my reading, I noticed there are three stages of immortality—of never growing old, that sort of thing. We've been reading a lot lately—rereading before I do this. Books—the written word—have been the only thing to never change since the beginning of Automata. All other story forms have. And so many stories are like ours—with immortal characters. I'm remembering my bookshelves now. I've landed on my three favorite examples of immortals: Peter Pan, Dorian Gray, and Orlando.'"

Odys stiffened, looking at his shoes. No one noticed him. Slowly, he realized Mother and Pepin had talked about *Orlando* in the past. That's why this was so familiar. *Pepin had read it because of Mother.* Maud remembered.

Odys clutched his chest, knowing that moment was over and it wasn't his. *Stop making me mourn over this woman, Pepin J. Pound.*

PEPIN: The ghost in the machine.

BOOK: *Orlando*.

THOUGHT: The Victorian age was the life and death of the novel, really.

---

of those beings and natures who can interact with us; who can—if they willed—help or hinder us but simply do nothing. They just are.

"'Some might say that's what has become of the gods themselves—of God.' And that's big G 'God'"— Fletcher clarified—*"'Nevertheless, the Tom portion was important in and of itself because it showed that, yes, there was an epic good vs. evil battle going on apart from him—but there also was/is a portion of the universe that doesn't get involved. Many of the elves are even like that, yes, but none of them quite have the capacity, you see, of what Tom COULD do. HE essentially could control the ring. It didn't control him. He didn't disappear.'"*

Fletcher looked up at that point and asked them. "Is she *seriously* ranting about *The Lord of the Rings*? Is that all this is?" He skimmed the paper quickly.

"You know she went with Mecca to every premiere," Q said, as if it were a defense. Mecca's eyes were red and watery, remembering. She bounced him like a baby.

Maurice scoffed. "Of course she loved such *immature* zings. Putting them into my son's head! And yet she blames me for—for—"

"Says the man with a *Peter Pan* wardrobe?" Odys mumbled, actually finding the written lecture interesting and wanting to get on with it.

"Which she ruined, by zee way!"

Dorian put a hand on his hip. "She's writing her last words and *this* is what she chooses as a topic, though? A thesis on *The Lord of the Rings*?"

Her *thing* with Mecca.

"Keep reading," Rosemund ordered. "There is a point to it, I'm sure."

"'Also, you might say the Shire was just as ambivalent. It was apart from any side-taking. It never really went good or evil, though it was, later, taken over against its will. It shows that some things are never really good or evil, at least. But this is no tirade against Jackson, God bless him, he did such a good job... No, this is about Tom Bombadil, and the relevance of the Toms in our lives today. They're all around us, aren't they? So jolly and happy—how can they be? How dare they be? ...Yet, how can they not be? They do not worry for their lives. If they lose a friend, they can always make more. We mortals are infinite...

"'This is not to say that the Toms are evil or heartless and should be overthrown. But we cannot rely on them. They make our lives no easier or worse. We know a Tom in our own lives. He is Vulcan. He's the biggest Tom of all, especially since we know he exists and yet hides his face so often. He could solve our problems so easily. That, or make them a bit lighter. Yet, the Toms just stand there and watch—watch as we have to take matters into our own hands.'"

THUS: Didn't really like *Lord of the Rings* and didn't understand when Gwen would call it "A classic!"

Chapter the second,

Childish allusions:

Reverting back to innocence?[189]

"I don't like zis weird book club," Maurice growled, leaning against the door to the overstuffed closet. Like Pepin, he had never approved of Gwen's taste in literature. Usually a bit too fantastical and childish for his liking. Made his son all the harder to tone down and understand. A bad influence!

Maurice, you see, did not understand this story is about story—from poetry to prose—from fiction to metafiction. Just as our Automata stood on the shoulder-myth of Talos, Vulcan's next creation must stand on the shoulders of giants too. Maurice did not understand, you see, that Vulcan wanted to assimilate these Gwen-mentioned books into his own mythos (no matter how awkwardly they fit); that Vulcan had inspired Gwen to re-read and write; that Vulcan wanted to stand (as he often needed help to do) on literary merit.[190]

"*'Funny—isn't it?—how the three types of immortality relate so well to our own stages—to our own family. My age was of Peter Pan, childish hopes—all Lost Boys finding each other—so much unknown. Dorian, well, Dorian came into this family with a Dorian Gray approach. He ushered in a new era for us—and maybe Bob, too. We added decorum to our Neverland. But now...we have all awakened into Orlando's world—so subjective and melancholy. Also, so ambiguous—its every page. Breaking down those definite roles...This age will never be as great as the first. Nothing will. It's the postmodern dilemma, isn't it? What more is there to do after the introspection? After all these approaches to immortality have been tried? I cannot fathom.'* Signed, *'Gwendolyn Gwendy.'"*

"That's it? That's all she said?" Dorian asked. "All she talked about were books?" *And Mecca.*

"I suppose someone should comment on the fact she's in Hook's costume?" Odissa suggested after a silence, as if trying to show respect. "Like how Mr. Darling was always played by the same actor as Hook's? But genderbent."

---

[189] "Are we so made that we have to take death in small doses daily or we could not go on with the businesses of living?" —Virginia Woolf, *Orlando*.

[190] Vulcan seems to have a thing for fantasy literature, then?

"Let the subtext lie where it is." Dorian's words rolled his covered eyes for him. "We're all smart enough to get it."[191]

Fletcher handed the paper to an expectant Rosemund, who ran her long-nailed fingers over the words while he found something to put Anselm into. It was as if Rosemund thought she might feel something her eyes could not see in the lines. Then, when satisfied, she folded the essay for Caffar to tuck away in her deepest "pocket." Rosemund adjusted her owlish glasses, the equivalent of wiping a tear away and began rummaging through her coat.

Dorian went on, "We all get that Vulcan wants to set the same ambience as those stories. Jesus Christ. We get it."

"Not stories, you fools. Novels. Not all stories are novels." Rosemund put on her gloves and walked over to Gwendolyn's body.

"But *Peter Pan* is also a play," Odissa whispered, as if maybe they shouldn't be so sure in their interpretation.

"A play still written down. Novelized." Rosemund's hand hovered toward Gwen's hand. She lifted it so that Ansi might land into her gloved palm. Her scarred lips trembled as she said, "Gwen wants us tototo keep Automatons 'in the family.' If we agree to keeping them in the family, then I want *Anselm*."

ANSELM: Wanted.

WHY?: Because he knows.

WHAT?: Mother's secrets.

WHICH ARE?: Secrets Rosemund longs to know.

Chapter the third,

The shoulders of more than just Talos:

Who else came before The Nine?

Rosemund folded her gloved fingers over Anselm, looking over her shoulder. She watched them struggle for a response.

Odys looked out the window once more—at the ice. Wished it would crack beneath them. "Though I am fine with it, I want us to have a sit-down about the *implications* of multiple-Automaton keeping," Odys said, his tone hopeful—hopeful that he was not the only one with a voice of reason. "Outline the rules. Maybe not make them breakable them this time."

Q nodded, "It makes Mecca uncomfortable."

---

[191] But we just wanted to be sure.

"We can come to some *agreements* when we get to the house," Fletcher said. "However that [getting to the house] might be." He half-uncrossed his tense arms to peek through the thin curtains covering the tiny windows. "The lot is pretty barren." Therefore, no nearby cars to break into, let alone drive off with.

"We could always call a cab," Odissa said. Up until this point, she had kept to the back, so as not to scare them by standing near an inanimate Automaton. Something told her that if they hadn't been magically transported here, she would have been asked to stay in the car.

Before they could decide, the door to the trailer opened.

"If you'd like, I can arrange for a cab to pick you up once you're done with your appointment. Vulcan will see you now."

The beautiful secretary—?—had nothing more to add. Merely stepped aside, motioned for them to go through the next portal-door (to gods-only-know-where), smiled gracefully, and stared at them.

The silvery-gold alloy of skin and hair made her more *metallic* than our known Automatons. Her gestures and body were stiffer too; her Barbie-doll hair had little movement. Everyone exchanged a "look." *This female is no Automaton-Automaton, correct? Correct. Nothing but one of Vulcan's wind-up toys. A puppet. A projection. Not real.* They all seemed content with their conclusion and decided to move on to more important matters: if they walked through that cursed door again, what was likely to happen?

"Haven't we dealt with enough, for one day?" Rosemund sighed, gesturing to the dead body. "Who is going tototo clean this up, if not us?"

The unblinking secretary—for what else could she be, really?—waited for them to proceed. "Don't worry about all that. Vulcan's got it covered. I've already made some calls."

As they gave one more glance at Gwen's body, they weren't surprised that it wasn't there anymore. "My fucking Hook costume!" Maurice cursed under his breath. "Wasted!"

His eyebrows and mustache twitch-flicked at the automata girl like bull horns.

"Speak *friend* and enter here, am I right?" the secretary said as they stepped closer. "You know, because of the whole *Lord of the Rings* thing."

"More like speak of the devil," Odys mumbled.

Looking through the doorway, what should have been a vacant parking lot covered with snow was now a long, brightly-lit hallway with many doors and "office" sounds echoing off the whiteness.

Maurice, first to try anything dangerous, stepped forward. When the secretary closed the door behind them, they paused—it was no frail trailer door, but a vault-esque contraption needing no further description.

They were there for business, all right.

"Doesn't seem like where a blacksmith would work," Odys commented to himself, though the secretary heard. *More like the light at the end of the tunnel.*

She held her clipboard closer to her prominently-boobed chest and smiled wider with her metallic teeth. "Vulcan Manufacturing needs its headquarters, and this is where all branches report to."

"I'm sure," Odys smiled, waiting for someone else to go first as they followed.

"If I cancel my appointment, *mademoiselle*, will there be a fee?"

"Yes, Maurice." She nodded once. She stopped walking, her heals clicking together. "But it will not be death, if that's what you're hoping for. I've also been told to inform you all that this"—she spun her pen around— "isn't real. It is a joke. Please laugh."

They all forced a "Ha."

"When you see Mr. Vulcan, sillies."

They glowered.

The hall seemed to darken as they went along (which was steadily) and they no longer had to squint. The effervescent whiteness evened out into a Wall Street-CEO-skyscraper floor.

Fancy.

An assorted and expensive collection of oil paintings lined the walls, depicting Homeric scenes framed in gold—all exhibiting Vulcan or Hephaestus (same thing, really). The sounds of their shoes bounced down the hall until they reached the very-end door, bordered by two golden, Doric pillars.

When they stopped, madam-robot-secretary stopped as well. "Please go in, He is waiting for you."

Maurice did the honors. Besides, he had a bone to pick with Vulcan. He was building up courage—courage to say things like, "Why the hell am I still alive?" and "Why the fuck did you give us a box of tissues?"

But the office lights weren't on. Though the huge windows let in enough of the sunshine and a spectacular (but probably unreal) view of New York City, the office seemed empty...

Until the chair swiveled and Vulcan showed Himself.

Maurice's objective thus hindered, he rolled his eyes and said, "A little cliché, no? A swivel chair!"

"Admit it," Vulcan said, lighting a cigar, "you'd do it too, just for fun. And isn't it fun, though? All this?" He waved His thick hand around, gesturing as the lights came on. His fingers had gold rings matching the fancy black suit's gold cufflinks. He looked more like an Italian gangster than a CEO. "And look at that, over there," He pointed, "I even included a miniature-scaled model of my home volcano, back in—"

"Er, that's nice, Vulcan," Fletcher said, moseying over to the window to look down, "but we're not in the mood to play along. You know, what with the whole Gwen suicide and everything. Just stick to the fat-cat routine and get to business." The height gave him vertigo, so he moved back.

Vulcan chuckled. "Business, right. I do understand. You're all in a rush to get on with your lives; I was just hoping you'd appreciate how much effort I put into all of this."

"Are we drugged?" Maurice asked, curious, "I don't think He's ever created an entire scene for us—just a *persona*."

Q shook her head. "He's never been a whole building before."

"Does that mean we're inside Him?" Maud swallowed back a little something in her throat.

"You're right, I don't think He's gone to so much trouble," Dorian agreed, trying to remember, running past scenarios through his weary brain.

"Finally, you notice," Vulcan mumbled, "I pulled a few strings, trying new things, testing new options. In the old days, I would've made this a forge at the base of a mountain. Or a cave. But modern times call for modern measures. The sex-machine secretary took me a while to perfect. I'm very particular about my smiles. Hers is just the right amount of teeth. She's beautiful, isn't she? She got you to follow her without a fight so at least that worked. Anyway, you're here today because I have a few announcements to make."

"At least we know we're here for a real reason." Odys said. Only Maud heard him.

Though Vulcan needed no ears to hear it, He made no effort to defend Himself. (After all, the very idea that a god needed to justify himself would lessen the potency of said god).[192]

"First, let me offer my sincerest condolences for the loss of your Mother." (There wasn't an ounce of sincerity to His tone). "I'll miss how she said my name. Sounds so great in Spanish: *Hefesto.* Granted, my name sounds great in any language. Not that it's spoken it in a sentence

---

[192] But isn't this whole novel just another defense on your supposed godhood, B.L.A.? Kind of hypocritical.

worth listening to half the time…" He noticed He was losing them. "But, if you want to make a martyr of someone, make it Bob, not Mother. She died for the woman who's failed to protect you from me. You never needed protection from *me*."

He put His thick hands together.

"Now, let's start with the biggest elephant in the room, no? Alpha. Ah, yes, Odissa, so quiet. Trying to blend in. I see you, there, so good at being overlooked. Hell, I'd even go so far as to confess the fact *they* don't want me to notice you. On the other hand, they don't want to be punished *for* the very act of letting you live. They were supposed to kill you once. But they didn't. It's such confliction that makes this topic necessary to address."

"Are you talking to us or to yourself?" Fletcher asked. Rhetorically of course, because he didn't expect an answer.

Vulcan put out His cigar. He was too busy talking anyway.

Dorian, however, did not take a rhetorical route. "Why didn't you tell us, all these years? Why didn't you tell us that Alpha was alive and well—that the past Masters hadn't succeeded?" *And why did you set him up to fall in love with it?!*

Vulcan shrugged. "I knew you'd figure it out."

Their faces scoffed.

"Oh, come now," Vulcan went on. "Have a little faith in me. No wonder I still let the Automatons hang around in human hands. You think I'd let something live without a purpose? Sure, the Automatons put a stop to Alpha's rampage back in the day, but what kind of a life would that be, without a little bit of purpose left to fulfill?"

He gave them the measurement of purpose with finger and thumb.

"So you're admitting zat you never intended Alpha to be destroyed?" Maurice asked, a little upset by that answer.

"But she *was* destroyed—dead. Dead like ghosts are dead. You can't kill ghosts."

"So you *would* rather evil exist zan to completely destroy it?"

"Indeed," Odissa said, walking over to the model of the (now) bubbling volcano. "Why not destroy Alpha and let the Automatons find their own purpose? Why not let them struggle like real humans, trying to figure life out? Oh…wait, I know why. It's because they aren't humans. They have no freedom. They are just…*things*." Something wicked rang in her tone. It made the others squirm. They didn't know whether to applaud or fear her.

Vulcan didn't let them decide. "Because, believe it or not, it's not so easy to kill your own children."

Odissa laughed. But it was a confused laugh—one which sounded her opposition. "No, it's not easy to kill your own children I suppose. But I wouldn't know, right?"

"Who am I talking to, Odissa or Alpha?" Vulcan chuckled. "So hard to tell sometimes, isn't it?" He eyed them all with a curious gaze.

Odissa didn't answer Him. "It's not easy to kill your children, I suppose, but it does seem easy to have your other *children* try it—to banish her like Ishmael. As if illegitimate."

"Just because Ishmael was forged with a different method-mother doesn't mean he-she was less of a son-daughter."[193]

Odissa and Vulcan locked eyes.

Odissa crossed her arms. "Who's to blame, then, for not making Ishmael the son of Sarah? The child must suffer the Father's mistake?"

Vulcan didn't waste time in taking a breath, "Just because someone is exiled doesn't mean their heart must be hardened."

Odys saw a bitterness shadow his sister's face. Or, maybe it was Alpha's face. He couldn't say who owned that face now—in that second.

"You think my heart hardened, *Father?*"

"In some ways. In others, it softened."

"So you give no direct answer? You don't want them to know?" Odissa frowned, nodding. "Being human and mortal can make life more precious, is that it? She may no longer wish to do her half-siblings harm?"

"Yes, yes. Anything is possible."

"So you're saying she's…different now?" Dorian asked, hopeful. "She's not the same Alpha?"

"Every day we change, Dorian. Even tomorrow Alpha will be different. Even I have changed, no? You shed skin cells. You grow new hair. You learn new things."

"Won't you at least tell us if we can really trust her?" Fletcher stuck his hands in his pits.

"Oh, yes, you can trust her. You can do anything you like. But, yes, I would go with trusting her. It fits with my agenda, see. Granted, I gave her the ability to make her own decisions— which, I emphasize, is also part of being a good crafter. I gave that gift to you Automata too, but only in a different way. You have freedom through your Masters. I never have to be disappointed in you that way…"

---

[193] So many Biblical allusions in this one—my!

"Can't you take the Alpha out of her, to make sure?" Q asked, because Mecca wasn't saying much these days.

Vulcan and Odissa both laughed, which made it clear enough.

Odissa covered her mouth in fear of her own sounds. *Why was that funny?*

"Dear Mecca," Vulcan soothed him, "Don't you remember Alpha's form? That form your predecessors reduced her to, by my instruction? I told them how to strip her down, taught them the way to sedate her before she could repair herself. Taught it to Admund who taught it to the others. Innate knowledge. I also told them how to place her volatile form, mercurial in its fundamental state—like the primordial soup from which sprang—"

But He laughed, cutting Himself off. He couldn't do it anymore, the repetitive speech. "You've heard this before. In sum, Alpha clung to the woman's life force. Perhaps, you might say, she even killed part of it so that she might live. Like mistletoe sucking from the branches of trees."

"But mistletoe can be cut off," Dorian reminded.

"Yes. But at what cost? Alpha is like cancer. One that spreads and can move. *Mercurial*, I just said. Weren't you listening? Now, the world functions in a certain way, and, though it would be a miracle for me to—as you might call it—'cure' Odissa of Alpha, I think I'll spare Odissa the woe of losing herself—or, part of herself. She was born with Alpha. She's come to like Alpha, believe it or not. Just as much as Alpha likes her. Alpha was made with a soul—the equivalent of one. We put the tangible form of that soul into Odissa's family line.

"Now, Alpha may have a choice of whether or not to be good, but you bunch also have a choice—a choice Gwen left up to you. What will *you* do with the choices she makes—that each of you make?"

"Are you saying there's redemption for evil, then?" Dorian asked, unsure if he should phrase is that way.

"Oh, heavens no. I'm not saying that. I can't say things like that. Not when Everyone's listening. You have to let *them* make the choice. After all, if evil eventually chooses good…they aren't really 'evil' then, right?"

Maybe.[194]/[195]

"Mecca, is that a good enough answer?"

Mecca shrugged and frowned. The most he could muster.

---

[194] Judas was uncomfortably close to Jesus, though.
[195] But, then again, there's no Jesus figure in this story, is there? Is there?

"Now, back to my box of tissues." *Were tissues ever mentioned?* "My box of tissues is particularly important for why I've gathered you here. Caffar," Vulcan tapped at the empty space on His desk. "The box, please."

Caffar, walking over to Vulcan, made herself look like His golden secretary—just shades off. Opening the recently-formed knob to the door in her stomach, she pulled out the box of tissues.

"Nice touch," Vulcan nodded, aligning the edges of the box to His desk.

"Nice touch," Caffar repeated, turning back to her regular shape.

Vulcan cleared His throat. "Though your dear Mother cared little for how I plan to—quote end quote—make things right, I hope you show a little more respect for my things, in the future. A wasted tissue not only hurts the environment but is just plain rude." He stuffed the fanned paper back down into the box.

He was pleased at how guilty they all looked.

"Please, have a seat."

CEO-Vulcan gestured to the chairs that magically formed behind them, knocking them off their feet and scooting them closer to the desk.

"You look great, Rosie, stop trying to look into that mirror"—Rosemund was making sure her hair wasn't too wind-blown from the chair ride over—"You're the best-looking Sapphic I know. Now. My box of tissues, you see, seems very normal. And that's actually because it is."

Fletcher said, "Toilet paper would be more our style, actually."

Vulcan narrowed His eyes, glaring at Fletcher. "Just because I give you a spare tongue, Dorian, doesn't mean you have to use it. Now, back to my box..."

He put a hand over it, gesturing. There was something charming in the way Vulcan played a Rich Man, as if He was having fun with the egotistical gestures only because He knew He could throw them away for the next show. "I have to present a set up, you see, for what's about to happen—involving my box, of course."

"Hold on one second..." Odys said, politely confused. "If you were going to call us here anyway, why not just give us the box of tissues in person?"

"You mean why did I plant them in your every-day adventure?"

"Well, I don't know if you should call it every-day, but *exactly*. It seems a round-about way of doing something simpler."

"I had to keep you in the house. Gwen had to kill herself in front of you. I wanted that to happen. I wasn't going to just ruin something I could work with." He made a sprinkling movement with His hands, ash falling around His desk, symbolic of what He'd done in the Collector's house. "And who's to say that this is even real? Welcome to my virtual reality."

"Fuck you," Dorian hissed at him and the shared hallucination.

"I really don't know how to please you people." Vulcan threw up His hands and slouched back in His leather swivel chair. "First you complain about me not being involved enough and then you complain when I try to take an active role in your lives. What do you want from me?"

"To die…" Maurice said, tucking in his chin and glaring.

"Shush, you!" Vulcan scoffed. "You think this is standing up to me, having a little pity party? Think this makes me angry? No. I've got all day. Keep complaining. See where that gets you. It's gotten you *so* far already, right?"

Seeing them slouch in their chairs, He went on. The tycoon act was working. "Now, Maurice, if you'd just let me talk about my box, you might find out a few things about *your* position *in regards* to the box. After all, I did let you come along, didn't I?"

Maurice crossed his arms, mustache bunching. Vulcan matched him.

"All right, long story short. I'm moving up in the ranks. I've been put in charge of a few…tasks. The ranks of gods shift just like the ranks of man. Kings to"—pointing to himself—"CEOs. Titles shift to fit the context. Thus, I'm overseeing a very large and very expansive clean-sweep. An evolution, if you will. The world itself is changing, right? Going green. Even the gods, you might say, are recycling. That, or *being* recycled. That's a foreshadowing, too, if you didn't catch that. Take notes.

"Let me just tell you: metal is easiest to recycle. Plastics release their fumes into the air. Paper, well, recycled paper is shit to write on—no offense, of course, to the paper gods out there. Not that I care if I offend any of Them or not. They're all underlings now." He said it to the air and smiled to Himself. It wasn't smug, but it was a little satisfied. He noticed them noticing. "What? So I don't have a right to be proud? I'm a god. Gods invented emotions like pride. We have rights to them. But about my box. This means we're recycling the old system. Reinventing the old gods. Hell, not that We haven't been reinvented ten times over. I doubt you lot would even call me Vulcan if I hadn't introduced myself as such…" He trailed off, turning a bit in His chair to stare out the window histrionically. "As a smithy bends metal over and over—reheats it—pours it into another mold to create something new from old casts, so will I do with the divinities under me…"

"And you're going to do this," Dorian began, "with a box?"

"It's not just any box, Dorian. It's a box of tissues."

"I'm not following what any of this has to do with a box—full of tissues or no."

"And you don't have to!" Vulcan smiled, swiveling in His chair to face them again. "Just don't pull out the tissues willy-nilly. Not until it's go time. Think of it like *Zoltar* the Fortune Teller machine. You have to put your quarters in first."

"Why would we have to pull out the tissues?"

"It's part of the plan, you see—the game. Ask me what the game is."

"What the game is?" Caffar asked.

"Very funny, Rose," Vulcan cut His eyes. "The game will be a symbol for the dualistic nature of the universe. A small-scale allusion for the big picture!" His face lit up in retrospection, hands gestured above Him as if creating a billboard sign. "It shall be a story worth recording—adding to Homer's legacy. And it won't be written in lyrics, no. But prose. It's what the people are into these days. No fucking bards. Might even get them to read the poems in the first place. But I digress. It will be a game. A game with a checkered tissue to start it off." He gestured to the box. "Reenacting a timeless tale of evolution, revolution, devolution—a game of Mesoamerican proportions."[196]

"A sacrificial ball game?" Dorian asked, tentative. "Like, of the Maya and Aztec?"

"Ah! You got my reference. Yes, yes. The Mesoamerican ball game itself was played by the mythological hero twins in the underworld—later to be mimicked in actual life. Yes, you of all people would catch on, Dorian."

"...I thought no one knows how the game is played," Odys added, lest they think only Dorian aware.

"For our purposes, here," Vulcan looked at him, "we don't need an archeological debate. Also, we don't need to know how either game is played—the ball game or mine."

"Why not, if we're the ones going to play it?" Maurice asked.

"Who said you're the players?"

Fletcher's hair quivered. "So we're the game pieces? It doesn't seem different from what's already instated."

"No, you're not the pieces either."

"Then...what are we?"

"Well, let's just say you're the game itself." He crossed His legs, leaned to the side. "You all keep complaining about how much your fate is already sealed. Well, here you go." He patted the

---

[196] This is set up for the next volume. I recommend dog-earing this page to refer back to it, critics.

box. "I've arranged a game where fate isn't running parallel—where the gods will place bets on heads whose strings are not yet fully woven. The game will be in another plane—dimension. But still here and real. The walls of the arena will blur destiny to an unreadable degree. I've arranged it all so that They can't cheat. Not even *I* can cheat, because of course I want to play. It's a perfect game."

"Gods can always cheat," Dorian said under his breath.

Odissa leaned in, near the box. Vulcan didn't seem worried. "And where, exactly, do the old gods fit into this?" She asked as if They were all crammed inside that box and could hear.

Vulcan cocked His head as if someone as smart as she should already know. "You'll find out."

"When?"

"When the tissue box tells you."

"How will we know, if we aren't supposed to pull the tissues out?"

"That's for you all to figure out." His voice rang with existential thrills. "But don't worry too much about it. Nothing's at stake, here. No pressure to find out. I encourage you to take your time. In the meantime, this is yours, *Maurice*."

MAURICE MAKEPEACE: Now has a box.

BOX: Of tissues.

TISSUES: For the issues.

ISSUES?: What issues? And why do they require tissues?

Chapter the fourth,

Re-gifting:

What's the return policy?

"I leave it in your care. This is now your purpose, and why you've been kept alive."

He slid the box toward Maurice, tapping it twice.

Something snapped in Maurice like a bone. "You've kept me alive, *moi*, Vulcan, to protect a box of *tissues?*" His forehead wrinkled, lips tightening, mustache writhing like a caterpillar in pain.

"Not the box. The game. The tissues are part of the game." He exhaled. "You still don't see it."

"Doesn't seem like the tissues have any real threat to them. I can tell you now zat we really don't care too much about pulling them out. Except Dorian, zere. You haven't given us much uv a reason to and I know a MacGuffin when I see eet." Maurice crossed his legs, fidgety with anger.

"Defensive measures, Maurice. You all might not pull them out, but an imprudent human with a runny nose might."

"Then why make it a box of tissues? Why not rocks? Baseball cards? Condoms?"

"Those hardly fit our theme, Maurice. The nose knows, doesn't it?" He tapped his.

"He has a point," Fletcher pretended to agree, putting his head in hand.

"Then the game moves forward. Nothing more I leave the call up to you."

"Fine." Maurice, with one hand, snatched the box and dropped it in his lap.

"Easy now," Vulcan said. "Show some reverence. No need to find out what will happen if those tissues are damaged."

"Trees will weep for their wasted parts?" Fletcher hypothesized.

"Pandora let out everything but hope, no?" Vulcan looked at Odissa.

Odissa closed her eyes as if His cryptic words gave off a stench that stung them. "The proto-woman shouldn't have been given the box in the first place," she said, standing up. "Better yet, why create the maladies at all, to plague mankind? Shouldn't the creators have more blame than the Eves of myth?"

"I see you're ready to go," Vulcan said, standing up as well. "Just let me finish."

Odissa obligingly sat back down.

"Now, I'm not an asshole. So, I will leave you with something: some divine wisdom. If you want my two cents, then you might consider what Gwendolyn proposed. Keep the Automatons in the family. Why not? I never said it had to be the way it's been done. That was all *your* rules. Everything changes. Might as well change with it. The box's purpose can adapt to what you choose. It's my Ark of the Covenant with you. Oh, and another thing." He reached down and opened the drawer in His desk, rummaging. "When you lot get back home, you might notice something gone."

Pulling out what he was looking for—up by the scruff—was me. *Bulfinch.*

BULFINCH: Not what he—she—they—seemed.

JUST LIKE: Odissa (funny, that).

BUT: It doesn't mean he's evil. Not necessarily. We all make mistakes.

GENDER: Mind-bender.

Chapter the fifth,

Pets:

Are they always OUR playthings?

"Bulfinch!" Odissa cried, on her feet once more. "Wha-what are you doing with him?"

505

"Him?" Vulcan laughed, spreading the cat's legs and moving back the tail. "So she is!" He looked back at Odissa, "You have to understand, Odissa, gods are drawn to other god-like things. You're probably just the first god-like thing she noticed, when she took this form. She smelled me on you."

"She?" Dorian asked, trying to comfort Odissa, who wasn't sure if her cat was about to be (or had already been?) kidnapped.

"Yes, this cat goddess here. She's only in this male cat's body because, well, They do that sometimes. Not only was she hiding but she was curious, I'd guess. *Gods only know* why we do the things we do, sometimes. And she's not talking."

I-Bulfinch hissed at him.

"She's going to be added to my game, you see," Vulcan said in a baby voice to the cat. "All of her, this one. Others will only have small parts included. But this one, here, well, she's done some very nasty things. That's why she was hiding. Hiding right under my nose. She hid so well she even tried to forget herself."

"What the hell are you talking about?" Odissa shouted at him, inching forward but finding herself unable to budge.

"Ah, look," Vulcan grinned. "At least you know she has a heart. Or is it that this cat knows your secrets, Alpha? Don't want to let the *cat out of the bag?* Maybe you did know—deep down—that this cat was a little god?" Vulcan laughed. "I won't bore you with the details, but before Mecca blew up your apartment, there was also a very nice rug which escaped and is now biding its time in a flea market in New Mexico. At least, that's what my wife's birds think. Flying things are a bit harder to catch. Bulfinch, here, knew quite a bit about my rise to power. Likely knew more than enough about the roundups, too. Probably enough to tell you, Alpha, what she had heard?"[197]

He tickled Bulfinch's chin.

Bulfinch only growled, gutturally.

"Such a pretty little kitty now isn't she? Yes, she is! I'm going to make her look even better. Lose these balls, yes I will. Oh wait, looks like a vet did that for you, huh, my kitty-kitty-kitty?"

I would have liked to sink my claws into him, obviously.

"What are you going to do with him?" Odissa demanded. However, a tone in her voice gave away her fear—she wasn't sure she should want the cat that's secretly been a goddess for all this

---

[197] The "roundups" seem like gods are being rounded up for Vulcan's game sporadically. I have no idea what's really implied here, but what I have seen of volume 3 gives me this hint.

time. Then again, she'd secretly been something *more* all this time, too. And what had the cat ever done to her?

Hell, she loved that cat.

"She's going to be tossed in with the rest of them—the rest of the cat deities."

"Tossed in?" Her voice was shrill.

"Alpha, dear, I think you know what I mean," Vulcan said with a head-tilt. "But don't worry, she'll turn out just fine. She's abused herself more than We will. Little more than a tom cat, now. *That* is depressing."

He stuffed Bulfinch back into the Mary Poppins's desk drawer, escaping without much more than a few hisses (though He did withdraw His hand rather quickly). He straightened out His tie.

"Now, I think that was all I had on the agenda for this meeting. You've been given a lot to digest. Best to let your Automatons think it over for you and come to some philosophical conclusions you'd otherwise never think of. Off you go."

With a wave of His hand, they were in Dorian's little house, still in their chairs, in the living room, among the other furniture.

Vulcan's making this too easy for me narratively.

Stanza: A bunch of Bulfinch.

It took them a minute to realize what had happened. As if waking up from a nap, their drowsy faces blinked unfocusedly, making sure they were all seeing the same scene. At first they didn't notice the box—the box of tissues—sitting on the coffee table, dead center.

Vulcan had moved a bit of the furniture to make sure they all fit nicely round the box.

Perhaps the change is what made them fail to recognize the scene first off.

[If you have been keeping up with the footnotes then this next bit will make sense:]

As if Vulcan were still with them, they heard His voice sound, then drift apart: *"Also, I'm not the Tom Bombadil. At least give me a dualistic role. Good or bad guy. I don't care which, but I do have an opinion and role in the Good vs. Evil. Give me that much. But sure, yeah, there is a Tom in this story—an anomaly undefined, left open to interpretation."*

Mecca, still a bit disoriented, glanced over at his father, a frown on his little face. He wasn't going to say it, or admit his father had never been here or there. Sometimes, he just *was*. That's what gave him so much power over Mecca. Mecca could not define him into the role he wished for him.

So Mecca wouldn't comment on it, no. Mecca wasn't into talking right now. Talking had never come easily for him to begin with. Gwendolyn had sometimes hypothesized that Mecca let

Q do the talking for him—even when the words came out of his mouth. Mecca's speech was on a different level. His third-person default—which he was sometimes conscious of, sometimes not—justified their assumptions that his brain developed with an entirely different outlook (on life and so on). There was no "I" for Mecca, because he had no concept of a singular self. Not when so many past selves where stuffed in him through his Automaton. So, no, of course Mecca wouldn't comment it on it.

He'd make Q do it for him.

"Vulcan means Maurice. Maurice is the Tom," said Q—just to be sure everyone got it.

"Funny, because he's not feeling like much of a side character we can write out anymore," Dorian grumbled.

Stanza: Tom cats.

You may be troubling yourself over how I know what's going on now, especially since I'm no longer in the house? Let me assure you, Reader, that it was never my cat eyes that gave me insight. Like Donna Haraway, you'll see how cyborgs segue to companion animals in due time...[198]

Stanza: A council of DEATH in the LIVING room.

Maurice sucked his teeth. "I refuse to be zis—zis Tom! He says there's been a game in the works. I'd rather play a part than be a—a referee."

"It sounds like *He's* the referee," Odys grumbled. "He makes the rules."

"Exactly..." Maurice dangled his arms off his knees and stared at that box.

"You're not the referee, Mr. Freakshow," Dorian said, his voice low and threatening. "You're the ringmaster. A stand-in representation of the orchestration."

Maurice eyed the boy. "Le cirque of the gods."

"He talked about 'recycling' Them," Odys recalled, taking off his coat. "As if he hadn't been using them—us—all along?"

"As if we need a new purpose." Maud commented, looking at her shoes. They were pointy boots. Odissa had a pair—before the apartment had been de-homed—just like them. Perhaps Odys was dressing Maud up like Odissa now. I'll not pretend to know the answer to this outfit.

"It's game after game after game." Rosemund pulled something out of her pocket. "All gladiator sport for the gods."

---

[198] Donna Haraway is a scholar who wrote *A Cyborg Manifesto* and *The Companion Species Manifesto*. This is a joke on how the treatment of the "Other" intersects "technological" and "animal" issues, I think.

She placed Anselm on the table and held Caffar in her hands—spiraled her between her fingertips. The others waited for her to do something.

She *so clearly* wanted to do something.

Lips trembling, "I want Anselm." She spoke the unspeakable. "Put all the freefreefree Automatons on the table. We shall debate this. This debate will happen sooner or later. We must debate a debate."

The others said nothing—the 404 File Not Found. You have to do things manually, sometimes. This was one of those times.

"Put them on the table, now," Rosemund ordered when they hesitated, her scars fading into her face as it wrinkled in grief.

Madus, Admund/Cestus, Coraza were placed on the table. Odissa noticed their shifty eyes. They didn't want her around. She tried to let her chair absorb her—to not move an inch.

Even Maurice made the situation awkward. Would he ask for an Automaton? Should they allow him one? Why not?

"I don't want an Automaton." Maurice put *that* on the table.

"You don't even want to try?" Odissa asked him. She bit her lip, as if she tried to keep from saying more. But she couldn't help herself. "What if it could help you die? What if you touched an Automaton and it reversed it all?"

The room seemed to grow darker at the question—the sun setting.

What hour was it?

Not that time matters when Vulcan keeps speeding things along.

"Don't tempt me, Alpha," Maurice rumbled at her, his mustache twitching. "Oh, don't look at me like that. It's a fifty-fifty. What if I touch an Automaton and it only compounds what voodoo's already on me? Zen no one would ever get zat Automaton again. I might never die to pass eet on!"

"Where's the harm in that? You yourself certainly wouldn't be worse off. And you'd be keeping it…in the family." *Away from me.*

"What is next? *You* asking for one? They won't give you one now. Not since zey know what you are."

She sat back in her chair, smiling with closed lips.

"Do it," Rosemund encouraged him, as if there was no implied turpitude in Odissa's suggestion. "Why not?"

"Don't!" Mecca shouted, huddled in Q's arms.

The shout had only been so loud because Q had shouted it too. Q went on, "Your purpose is the box, not this."

Ignoring the woeful tone in his son's Automaton (*Bad daddy, bad!*), he turned to the "adult" next to him, eyes asking their opinion. Dorian and Fletcher shrugged.

Not thinking a second more about his son, Maurice reached for Coraza—the only female on the board.

But, like the opposite end of a magnet, the nail scooted away, repelled.

Maurice made it scoot a little farther on the table, making sure he could believe his squinty eyes. Each time his finger was a centimeter away, it jumped forward.

They'd never tried it before.

He sat back in his seat, tears in his eyes. "Well, zat's that."

Odissa chuckled out a "Mmh." It sent a chill through the room. Odissa knew something.

Had known it all along.

"You died, Maurice. Your *charge* has been changed. Metaphorically, physically, metaphysically. She's telling me to tell you. Living-dead don't have the same physics as the living-living. You've gone and come back. Your soul knows what it's like to be free from a body. You can't take a pea out of a pod and put it back *exactly* the way it came. Automatons are programmed to respond to fundamental, basic human soul-structures. That's also why gods, animals, vampires, ghosts couldn't get them to work."

"How do you know they can't?" Rosemund asked her, brow pulling up her drooping face. "How many vampires do you know?"

"She knew a cat god, didn't she?" Fletcher said. *How dare you question her.*

Odissa tucked her hair behind her ears, buying time.

"You seem to know a lot about these things, Odissa," Maurice said, body tense. "You're more Alpha zen we might like. Why are you so smart when your siblings aren't?"

"Half siblings," she corrected with a flash of her eyes. "Perhaps that's because they were based off me. And I know myself very well."

"Suddenly you do, yes." Maurice shifted in his seat.

"Thus," Rosemund said, directing their attention back to the table, "there are four Masters, and five free Automatons—granted, one inside another Automaton, hopefully bagged."[199]

---

[199] I'm assuming that since Leeland wasn't sick when he killed himself he hadn't touched Cestus?

"Why not four free Automatons?" Odys asked. "Shouldn't we establish why Odissa shouldn't get one—get it finalized so that it's never questioned again? Because, right now, I still question it."

"Are you so sure I want one still?" Odissa asked him.

"It's not your choice, Odissa," he said, not looking at her. "I *won't* live forever alone with these people."

Dorian stood up in his chair but Maurice shoved him back down. "Don't speak to her like that," Dorian instead attacked with his words.

Odys shot him a wicked smile. *You're turning into me, old man.*

Dorian used his shirt collar, rather than the nearby tissues, to dab the blood pooling at the base of his nose.

"Let's vote on what we *can* vote on," Maurice said above them. "Rosemund has said she wants Anselm. Who among you sees *zat* as an unreasonable request?"

"So we've already agreed with Gwen that a Master can and should have more than one Automaton?" Rosemund asked, turning Caffar between her thumb and forefingers.

Devil's advocate shocked them.

"Vulcan said it was a good idea," Odissa commented.

"V also told me to fall in love with you," Dorian commented. "Look where that's gotten us."

It was Odys who had to be restrained this time.

"Sit your ass down!" Maurice growled, mustache stiffening with his lip. Odys leaned away from the Eiffel Tower towering above him.

Fletcher settled down from his prepared interception. "Rosemund, if you want Anselm, take him. You're the elder. We'll do as we're told." His eyes darted around, daring someone to contest her.

She laughed. A laugh at winning a terrible prize. "Why did she kill herself, I wonder? If it was going to be this easy to forgive her sins a second time." She scooped up Anselm with her still-gloved hand. "I'm going to the bathroom. I want to be alone as I search for the answer."

"Let us know if you need anything," Maud shouted out after her. "We should take our time with this. We can't all be sick at once."

"Why?" Fletcher snorted. "Because Leeland will sneak up on us? He's dead, Odys. We have nothing to fear anymore."

The others avoided looking at Odissa, refusing to argue that there was an even greater threat among them.

"I wonder how it will feel," Dorian said, cupping his knees in nervous thought, "having two Automatons while syncing. Think it will hurt more than the first time?"

Something within them already told them the answer. And it was a private matter.

As if in the waiting room of a hospital, waiting for their beloved friend to get out of surgery, for the doctor to give them the news...

They waited.

Around the box (of tissues!) they waited.

It was a very quiet process. Maurice's watch ticked very loudly. Cars drove by, crunching the snow. They could hear muffled sounds from the bathroom—through the broken doorknob stuffed with a towel. Vomit, chatting, rinsing.

Perhaps she was talking to Caffar.

Perhaps to Anselm.

Perhaps to the part of Gwendolyn still within him.

But they couldn't understand her.

But I can.

But I'll censor it for personal reasons.

She was talking to all three.

Taking off her glove had been like undressing—about to touch Gwendolyn herself. She found herself puking in the sink, smiling all the while. She'd never been closer to her Gwendolyn. Gwendolyn had left traces of herself—imprints. And those remnants were beautiful.

If it hadn't been for The Universe, Vulcan, Anselm, Leeland...

Gwendolyn could have been hers.

She was sure of it. Now she was *sure* of it. Sure she could have had her in another lifetime.

...

And then they heard the gunshot—the bang and splatter. Jolted from sleepy tension, the others rushed to the bathroom.

She was dead in the bathtub. Polite enough to make the scene cleanable, though she'd managed to splatter her brain and hair on the ceiling. No new inhabitants would notice, with a bit of paint. The wall paint had fixated many a hair to itself in the past—worse than an apartment flip job. Fletcher went to the store for supplies.

On his way, Fletcher noticed Maurice hadn't left his seat when everyone else had.

"You knew she was going to do it," he said, factually. Something was caught in his throat.

Maurice glowered at him. "As if you didn't? As if you'd deprive her of it? As if any of us would." He cursed a little in French. "It's all any of us really want. Sleep."

A "fuck you" to Vulcan.

He stared at the muted television he had just turned on. Maurice could not die. But he could watch TV.

Mecca and Q found his lap, their faces drooping as Mecca flipped through the channels. Maurice hummed a French hymn under the television's drone. He kissed their heads.

Stanza: Giving head.

Dorian had turned to Odys in the hall as Fletcher had left, catching his attention before he could follow. "Let's let Fletcher clean this mess. But it might be good if we all cleared out and, you know, found something to do for the time being."

"I'll go—go get some dinner for us," Odys replied, taking the hint with an angry glance to Odissa.

There was a new head of the "family"—a role Maurice could never fill. Maurice was twice removed. Or, at least *once*.

So, yes, Odys knew who to obey. He had to obey *Dorian.*

MECCA MAKEPEACE: Seeing everyone leave him.

OLDER FATHER: Wants to leave him, but cannot.

YOUNGER FATHER: Wants Mecca to leave.

AGELESS MOTHERS: Left him.

Chapter the sixth,

All in the family:

But what is out of it?

His eyes now gone,[200] Dorian asked Odissa to take him to the bedroom. She led him to the bed but sat down on the floor across from him, watching him like a child at story time. He dabbed at his nose—but, like eyes out of tears, it was too tired to bleed now.

She wanted to smoke.

He crossed his legs.

"Six Automatons now," Odissa said—after a brief moment of wondering why he was being so stoic. *Why isn't he crying? Why do they all have such strange reactions to death? Why do I feel like they've forgotten what it's like to have human emotions?*

---

[200] (For paint).

513

"You can't say things like that, Odissa. It sounds like Alpha's saying them. It sounds wrong, in this context."

"I can't state a fact?"

"Not an indelicate one."

Speaking of indelicate, his foot began to bob.

"Are you afraid of being left alone with me?"

He didn't answer.

"I saw that look Fletcher gave you—and everyone around us when you sent him out. It's not that you're afraid of me. But you don't know if you're breaking rules or not. Mother's dead, Dorian. There are no rules."

"Again, being indelicate."

"Because you're being an asshole."

"Get on the bed with me."

"No."

"I'm not afraid of you. Don't be afraid of me. Or is it too soon, to be so close?"

"Jesus, Dorian, you talk about *me* being indelicate and yet you're wanting to, what, fuck right after Rosemund blows her brains out?" Her eyes welled up with tears, but he couldn't see them—and they hadn't made it to her throat yet, so he couldn't even hear the sadness in her words.

"Get on the bed, now."

"I'm not Odys. You can't just order me around because you're in charge of them now."

He got up and walked toward her voice. But he paused, knowing he was bound to be close. He put out a hand as he knelt on the ground. He stopped when he found her shoe. "I just want to sit beside you," he said, feeling for the wall. She helped him, patting on the ground beside her.

He found her hand. She didn't latch on.

He took off his glasses, tossed them to the side. "If you could," he said to the air, "because we can have any life available, what would it be? What kind of life do you want?"

"This isn't life?"

"Will you start a new life with me?"

"A family?"

"No. Just us. Just us leaving."

"Traveling, you mean?"

"Is that what you want?" he asked, truly wondering.

"I don't have much of a life now, apart from you. You blew up my apartment. My things. Even my fucking cat is gone."

"What would make you happy?"

"Who says I want to be happy?"

"You want to be miserable?" he asked, laughing

"I don't want to chase happiness, Dorian. I'll let it find me."

"I like that." He mused on the topic for a moment before she cut it off.

"Whatever it is that I want, I'm not sure I want a house, a yard. Nothing with too much upkeep."

"No dead people in the bathtub?"

She laughed out her discomfort, wiping away an uncategorized tear. "I'd rather my life be private. You can't have privacy with so many neighbors."

Dot dot dot.

"So, an apartment with your twin brother...that was enough?"

"We had plenty of money. Alpha knew—*I* knew Leeland had two Automata and endless amounts of gold. Of course it was enough."

He couldn't understand the nostalgia in her tone—what sounded like a love for menial simplicity. "I mean, you still liked the apartment?"

"Exactly."

"So it's not about where you want to live. If it's not that, then what?"

"Right now, I think a closet would be a nice place to live."

"I've been there half my life."

She laughed. "Life would be so much easier if things were decided for us, no? Then, if we didn't like those decisions...we'd have something to complain about or fight against. Right now we're complaining about having nothing to really complain about, you and I. We have unlimited options."

Dorian tilted his head up, as if looking at the ceiling. "You make us sound like children rebelling against our parents. Our parents: The Universe."

She smiled at his observation and amended it: "The Universe still has rules, Dorian. But children do grow up, I guess. Maybe it's the rules that only children have to abide by: Don't eat from this or that tree; Don't eat this or that animal; Don't love this or that man or woman; Don't think this or that." She paused. "But, as we get older, we can, like, watch PG-13 movies—without our parents taking us to the theater. We can drive. We can buy cigarettes. We can have sex. We

515

can buy alcohol. And now, well, women don't wear head coverings. We can eat pork. We can divorce."

"I see what you did there. All Old to New Testament. How very Christian, though."

"I'm feeling more like a Satanist, to be honest. My point is, it seems like the rules loosen and change, Dorian, because we understand why parents need to be strict. Children are stupid. God— The Universe—isn't. Parents must let their children become adults. Vulcan can't tell us what to do forever. What good parent wants to live their child's life for them? At the end of the day, The Universe finally stops telling you what to eat, wear, say, act. And then asks us what WE want. Sure, our choices might be limited. We might be predestined to pick one thing over the other. But we still get the choice: what do we want? That brings us to existentialism."

Where they currently were.

"You can't see it, but I just waved in front of us."

When his laugh faded, they could hear the TV in the living room.

What he wanted suddenly came to him. "I want Alpha to be good. I want to trust her. I want Odys to be happy, despite what I've *done* to him. I want to know if I'm hurting the world for existing—existing for so long."

"You were given existence, Dorian. The Universe will take it away eventually. There's nothing you can do that the Universe can't counterbalance."

His head pulled away from the wall. "If you do want to travel, I *will* say it's harder to go to other countries. Fletcher can make passports quickly, but they can't leave his hand—if you know what I mean. And even then, the detail takes a lot out of me, depending. We've ways to cheat, though. Private jets. That sort of thing. But low-key is always best. Cruise ships work, too, sometimes. Once you're on a continent, it's easier to move without showing yourself. And like hell I'll ever show anyone my real date of birth." They laughed. "That's how they found me, by the way—this group. I was good at finding people who could make really good fake IDs and I would sell them. And use them to get into bars before I was twenty-one. Bob liked my work. She tracked me down at this festival—but as I was saying. Traveling to other countries is harder for us now, but doable."

"You don't think I know this?" Odissa said, finally taking his hand. "Alpha came to America because she realized the Automatons and Masters were here too. There's no need to travel away from them. Why are you so stuck on leaving them?"

"I mean, if we can't stay here, where do you want to go, then?"

"To bed."

"Long term, I mean."

"Let's start something. A nonprofit. An orphanage. Do good."

"Add gold to the poor's pockets?" He interpreted.

"What else is there to do, once the labor of living's been done?"

"Vulcan seems to have things for us to do," Dorian added, "in the near future."

"Yes, but we can't worry about that. No sense in worrying about what He will—and He *will*—do."

"But it might interrupt our plans."

"So might getting cancer."

He chuckled and put his other hand on hers. Odissa put her head on his shoulder. He kissed her head. He needed to shave, his beard pulled at her hair.

"So," she said, theoretical emphasis in her tone. "Let's say we know what we want. We want to solve the world's problems like Gwendolyn. We have nothing better to do. But once the world's problems are solved, then what?" She played with one of his coat buttons.

"You talk as if you're immortal, Odissa. You're not yet. I can't picture my life without you." He paused. "You know I'm going to give you an Automaton, don't you? Have you seen it?"

"I have seen it." Odissa stopped pulling at his buttons and let her hand fall to his lap. "But not in an I-see-the-future sort of way. I have smelt it. Smelled the thought on you."

"…What would happen if we did give you one?"

She frowned at his flip-flopping. He went from certainty to a maybe.

"I don't like you talking to me this way, Dorian, as if I have all the answers. I can't keep tapping into Alpha. It threatens you. It feels like pretend. Like I'm enacting something I'm not sure is real." She raised her head to face him. She took her hands and held his face. "If you gave me an Automaton? Well, then I'd have an Automaton. Nothing else would happen." She kissed his lips and pulled away a moment later. She added, "You're scared of what I might be able to do with one?"

"A little."

"I could do nothing more than what I do now. It's only this body would live longer. We could be together for centuries then."

His face twitched like a ripple. "You could kill us then, if you had an Automaton."

"What makes you so sure I couldn't now?"

"You *will* kill us all, won't you?" He let the words settle in the air. But they would not. They continued to float there like bloody feathers freshly plucked. "You'll be the death of us."

She took in a deep breath, chest shaking. "Your end will be my fault, if it ever comes. But I won't let it. It won't be my will that causes it. In some ways, I can be blamed for every Master's death—past and future. I killed them. They all died in their specific, precise ways because Automata were created. And Automata were created because of me. To take down me. But Vulcan let me live. And he made you love me."

He shook his head. *Don't blame yourself.*

"I did this, Dorian. I can't believe I did all this." There were tears in her voice he could finally hear. "I can't believe this is what it took. All these years to finally stop me and my rage and—"

He kissed her, kissed her like he believed her. Like he wanted to save her from such thoughts. But something tugged him back. "You have changed from what you were. But I still don't understand how you go on. What motivates you. Why you feel like living."

"You, dummy," she said into his face. "I missed you. And the other wonders of the world." She kissed him again, teeth brushing his lips, biting at him as if to hold onto him.

Those teeth nipped and he pulled back, a little pissed. "Not so har—" but he tasted blood. He pushed her off of him, away from him. He struggled to get up from the shock but found his legs unable to help him—then realized he'd best keep her in his grasp. "You could do this, the whole time?" he demanded, not letting go of her wrists. She wasn't struggling. "You can hurt us?"

"Showing is better than telling they say. I wanted you to believe me." Unseen fear shadowed her face, realizing she had gone too far. "I'm so sorry. But now you know. Now you know that an Automaton won't make me anymore powerful than I already am. What's the difference?"

"Can I do the same to you?" he asked. "Can I harm you too?" *Or is it just me who is powerless again under you?*

"Of course you can. I'm in a fucking mortal body, Dorian," she hissed. She didn't like his voice rising so loud. It might disturb Maurice and Mecca—might catch their attention. "I'm just a mortal with skills."

"You could've warned me," he said, letting go and feeling his wet lip. "Always fucking bleeding!"

"It's not that bad," she said, dabbing at him. He flinched at first. "See, you're not sure of me," she stated. "You've been lying too."

"Let me bite you and see how you like it," he grouched. "So you only have the bite of a *girl*, then?" *Not of something stronger? Of something more powerful?*

"You wouldn't want me to chew through your finger. It'd likely take hours."

"I can't believe you fucking bit me." His smile showed numerous hesitancies, but it was still a smile. *She's been restraining herself this whole time. For me.*

She stood up, taking his hand. "My back hurts from sitting on the floor."

He let her place him on the bed. He sucked on his lip. It was barely red now. "I feel like I've just been molested," he laughed—at the impossibility, of course. "It seems such a private matter."

"It's only because you haven't been hurt by someone else in quite some time, Dorian."

"I wish you'd have given me more time to prepare."

"If I had prepared you, then you wouldn't know what I was capable of. You wouldn't be as properly scared of me as you should."

"You *want* me to be scared of you?"

"A little," she replied. "Makes things more equal."

"I don't understand." He leaned down on his elbow, a little angry. "Back at the Collector's house you were begging me to accept you…"

"Dorian, you need to know what I'm capable of. You need to know—because I *don't* want to hurt you."

"But saying that only makes me trust you more!" he softly shouted at her, so the others couldn't hear.

She breathed in deeply, wishing he could see her exasperated expression. "Now we're even. Odissa has been afraid of you this entire time—what you're capable of. It's like Alpha wakes up and boom. I realize I don't have to be so afraid of you. We're equals."

"I think you should still be afraid of me, dear. You're the one in the mortal body." He reached into her pants but she held him there—keeping him from going further. "And there's two of me and only one of you."

There was a knock on the door. Dorian huffed as he sat up—angry they had been interrupted. He did not remove his hand from Odissa. "Who is it?"

"It's Mecca."

"What *now*?" Dorian demanded, hanging his head.

"We just got a text from Odys."

"So?"

"He said he's not coming back."

"What?" Odissa gasped.

"Did he say *why*?" Dorian shouted back, his eyebrows all askew.

"No. But he said he'll let her come back with the food."

"Her? As in—"

Q finished for him, "*Maud.*"

MAUD: A substitute for Odys Odelyn.

A SUBSTITUTE: A goodbye.

A GOODBYE: A scapegoat.

A SCAPEGOAT: For some greater sins.

Chapter the seventh,

Selfishness:

Is it selfish to want to be the only one who's selfless?

"He's sending her instead," Q said, opening the door.

"Why'd you interrupt us for that?" Dorian pressed, a coldness in his voice. He still didn't remove his hand from its half-insertion in Odissa's pants.

Hand on her hip, "Why are you in here making out with someone when Rosemund just killed herself? You're so selfish."

"Rosemund just killed herself and *I'm* the selfish one? *Sí*, I'm so selfish for actually wanting to live my fucking life."

Mecca frowned at them from Q's skinny arms. "Not even Mecca would do something like that. Mecca's put his camera away."

"We were just talking," Odissa tried to explain, finally pushing Dorian away. She wanted to tell Dorian to cool it—to be respectful—to alert him Mecca's eyes were pink from tears and to therefore be more sensitive.

"Are you just going to stand there?" Dorian huffed. "Shut the door."

Q and Mecca stepped inside and shut the door.

"I don't think that's what I meant, Mec," Dorian said.

Mecca knew that he'd best do this while he had the 'sight' advantage. "Mecca needs Odissa to leave. Mecca needs to talk to Dorian."

Odissa stood up.

"Odissa, no—" Dorian begged. He cursed under his breath.

Q and Mecca moved out of her way, eyeing the scene with hesitant glances.

"I'll go make coffee," Odissa said. She touched Q's shoulder on her way out. She felt something sink inside her as Q half-jumped at her touch—a cautious reaction showcasing everything but a cringe.

Q quickly smiled to counteract her tenseness. Mecca wasn't afraid, but they didn't want to cozy up with Alpha just yet. *Sorry that I don't trust you.*

Odissa passed by the bathroom. Someone had pulled the door to. She couldn't remember who'd done it. But a door couldn't give the dead dignity. Not when it could be pushed open so easily.

She held her breath as she pushed it to peek in. Caffar was on the side of the tub, next to bits of flesh and blood. Odissa was sure Anselm was in the headless corpse's clinched fist.

She felt sorry for Caffar. Caffar hadn't been good enough to cling to upon death.

We cling to what we love.

"That should be me, there," Maurice said, rounding the corner. "She was more of a man than me. What kind of a man can't kill himself?"

All right, Ernest Hemingway. "Where did you get that vodka?"

He raised the bottle, contents swishing. "I fucking hate Russian shit. Was all I could find in my car. Mecca's stash."

Odissa closed the door, smiling—she shouldn't have gone near those free Automatons. Made her look suspicious. "I wish she hadn't done it."

"That's selfish of you," Maurice laughed. "But, then again, it's selfish of her to leave zem all with so many inanimate ones. They'll never sort out who gets what, between the three of them."

She walked past him, into the living room.

"What's zat smile?" he asked her, following her. "You think I should have said *four?*"

"It wasn't a real smile," she said, frowning as she sat down. The television was showing political commercials that, on any other day, would have made her blood boil. But Odissa no longer had investments in democracies. She was forming a new government.

He plopped beside her on the couch—though he could have sat anywhere.

"Zis has always been about you—why I'm still alive." He spat at her after glaring was not enough. "About you and Vulcan and zee fact He can't kill you because He has some—some sick infatuation with you."

"He has an infatuation with you too, my friend. My guess is it's your American masculinity undermined by your French femininity. That's what Vulcan is all about, isn't he? The feminine masculinity. You are Vulcan to Dorian's Dionysus. You are Vulcan to Gwendolyn's Athene. You are Vulcan to Leeland's Ares."

He snorted. "And you? You are godless."

"Give me that." She tried to take the bottle away but he puffed at her. She would not fight him over it. "He loves me too much to kill me. I'm His best work. You can't just throw away your best idea." She gestured to herself. "You *work* on it."

Maurice chuckled at her. "You are so confident now. It is getting harder and harder to see Odissa."

"My brother told Mecca he's not coming back. Did you know about that?"

"Oh?" Maurice took another sip of vodka. "Is that what they're on about in zere?" He gestured to the room. "Mecca's always on his damn phones."

"Yeah. But Maud's coming back with lunch. That's what Mecca said."

Maurice rubbed his glassy eyes. "*Sure* she is. Zat is just Odys's way of keeping us calm. Giving us false hope. Who knows what your brozer is doing…" Maurice caught her eyeing the tissue box. "I ought to burn it."

"Men ought to do a lot of things."

He turned to her, vodka swishing in his bottle. She could smell it on him. "Tell me, Alpha, what men ought to do. What must zis man, here, do?" He pointed to himself, poking his striped chest.

"Tell your son you love him. Tell him you don't want to leave him, but that someday he'll understand that life is incomplete without death. Tell him why you behave as you do. Be a better father. Then, give Dorian your blessing."

"For what?" His lips and mustache pulled up—he hadn't expected this prepared answer.

"For being more of a father than you ever were."

"Father? Ha. He was more like—like a step-brozer or somezing."

She snatched the bottle away when he was too busy laughing. "Many siblings must be parents. And you should still thank Dorian for it."

"Yes, yes, and?"

"Don't let a god tell you what to do." Her eyes gestured to the box. "Make Them force you to do it. Don't spend your free will on orders. If you're destined to do something, then it will happen. They'll make it happen. But make Them work at it. Gods want joyous submission, not begrudged. Don't give Them that. Give Them hell." She took a swig.

"Is that all wise Alpha has to say? Take the rock They're throwing at you and throw it back at Them?" He accepted the bottle she handed back.

"Better yet, desire more rocks. Start a rock collection and then you'll want what They're throwing. Get stoned, Maurice. Now *that's* all I have to say." She laughed, stroked the air with her hand.

"You are very into metaphors and analogies."

"I like to call them parables." She took out a cigarette from a crumbled pack Odys had left behind—a gesture, she was sure.

"Fuck your parables. I wanted your opinion."

Her words now visible with the smoke, "No, you want me to tell you what I would do if I were you—as if I'm smarter than you merely because Alpha's older and knows more secrets."

He puffed up his cheeks. "Exactly."

"If you don't want the box, give it away. Leave it to us. What's the worst Vulcan can do to you? *Kill you?*"

His inebriated brain did the calculations, best it could. "He could torture me. Prometheus isn't how I want to go. My liver is too valuable. Don't like pain." He rubbed his stomach, imagining the possibilities.

"I thought waking up every day alive was torture enough? Beginning to think you like living, Maurice."

Maurice's nostrils flared, his mustache fanning. She was right.

Odissa leaned into him, staring into his red eyes. "You want me to promise you, Maurice, that I will help you die if you do this for me? Want to make a deal with me like Leeland did? Say that this is exactly why my Father has allowed you to live, so that I may tempt you? You are His Gerasene Demoniac, Maurice. Legion is within you. You try and try to put yourself into the swine you eat but there is no cliff to topple over. Yes, I can be the one who finally sends you to the pigs, Maurice. Let me."

His eye twitched, making him break the stare to rub it and look down. When he looked back up, his expression had shifted. "If I'm going to forsake that damn box of snot rags, I'd better make it count."

"And you want me to tell you how to make the most of it?" Odissa reached out and smoothed back a strand of his oily hair. "Is that what this is, Maurice?"

"Tell me," he asked again. "Tell me really. What I should do. If we all believe you're good now, well, why not give some good advice?"

Odissa smiled. "Vulcan's likely *expecting* you to neglect that box, and He'll play off your impatience. There's no denying that." She sighed. "This is like David and Bathsheba. David got what he wanted—for a price. He got Bathsheba at the cost of their son. But was David damned for his sin? No. Cause and effect. Equivalent exchange. No need for penance. It was all paid for."

"I don't want my son to die for my sins, Alpha."

"But would you call leaving a box behind the sin?" She frowned at the box, as if it was such a little thing.

He shrugged. "Doing the opposite of what a god commands? What else would you call it?" He took another drink then cradled the bottle like a teddy bear.

She watched him as the sip settled. "There are ways around 'sins,' if you can read the map. It sounds more like your son—all the Masters, really—are to be out of the picture for the game, Maurice. Regardless of what you do. Didn't you hear Vulcan? They're not the players. What the fuck do you think that means, then? Yes, that's right. They're dead. It would be a sin to let Vulcan have His way. A sin in the original." She evened the hem of her shirt, her other hand flicking ash into Rosemund's used tea mug. "What Master has ever lived forever?"

"You offer to postpone the game, then? What's in it for you?"

"I am not a god, Maurice. I can't stop the game from happening."

"But you're more like one than we are. You know zee Words. What do I have to do to get you to help us? You had Leeland convinced with your promises. They must have had *some* payoff."

"What makes you think I am against you that you must barter with me? You all hate Vulcan. Who hates Him more than Alpha? Isn't that how your story goes? No, I am your only hope." She looked out the window. "This is her last body, Maurice. She thought by now she'd have served her time and have more options. It's clear now she has to make more options of her own."

"Then what will it *cost* to insure your options involve helping us get out of zis?"

"You can't escape the game, Maurice. But I can certainly…take a few turns for you."

"Didn't you hear? I'm not playing. I'm the referee. Zee ringmaster!" He pointed in the air, his greased hair flopping.

"But that's not the sin you will have to pay for. I do that for free. You are about to abandon your son and leave him to me. That will cost you. You won't pay me. You won't pay Vulcan. But I will make it very gentle for him, you understand? I'll watch over him—them all. You can run off, like you always do. But I will cover for you. I know the way to ease your father-son pains. And the price is you helping me when the time comes; when you know more than you know now; when the game is in play. You understand?"

Maurice sat back, blankness on his face. He stared through her like a spectator waiting for a glimpse of the magician's strings—waiting for her to slip and show the truth.

"…My favorite American writer is Hemingway. Do you know why?"

"Yes, but tell me anyway." She cupped the side of her face.

"Because he lived in France. He was an exhibition of virility. And, he killed himself."

"But what of his prose?"

"Zat was good too."

"Ah, Maurice," she sighed. She leaned over and dropped her cigarette in the old tea. "Just because you're like Hemingway does not mean your sins are forgivable." She slapped her hands on her lap. "But you read the past well. You will die. Not much longer, now."

He chuckled, extending a hand. "I have no choice but to impatiently wait for that day." He patted their embraced hands—coming to some sort of undefined agreement that only those who have cheated death could understand. He said, "I get the feeling zat zere is no happy ending for any of us in this."

"Vulcan included," she said like a promise.

"I can drink to zat."

Stanza: Hacktivism involves a lot of guesswork.

Back inside the bedroom with Mecca: "Well, spit it out, Mecca," Dorian had rumbled, hair hiding his face as he rolled his head about impatiently.

Q had leaned into the door, making sure no one was listening. Mecca pulled a cell phone out from her mouth, tapped away on it. "We tracked Odys down, but we lost his signal here," he pointed to the screen, but realized Dorian couldn't see. "He's off the grid again, Dorian. He's planning something."

"No shit. You couldn't say that in front of Odissa?"

"I—I think they're in it together this time," Q whispered.

"What do you mean?"

She built up her courage—courage to voice their stupid thought—courage to have Dorian knock it down. *Please knock it down.* She went into detail about how they had been re-reading some of the twin's emails (emails from O_Odelyn@afreee-mailaddress.com *to* whydoihaveanemail@thesamefreee-mailaddress.com) and had been studying the IP addresses from said emails and how something just wasn't adding up but…

Dorian toppled it like a Jenga tower. "Are you fucking crazy? What do old emails have to do with the present day? When have they had time to plan something?" Dorian bit his lip in anger, but then winced—still sore. It made him angrier. "

"It was like they knew Leeland was monitoring them. Studying them—"

Mecca cut himself off. "The point is why would he be? Both, you know?"

"We checked their email history before. No one else flagged anything."

"Odys suspected. He suspected the whole time. That's why he was playing along—covering for her—"

"You're reading too much into things. And sure, Odissa could have been 'under the influence' at times when those were sent but—"

"It's not just *her* email, Dorian—" Q interrupted. She held up her example email to the blind man who could not read. "They're so typical and staged and—"

"You don't see it, do you?" Mecca said, reeling Q back. "You don't get it. Of course you wouldn't. You've never been able to see it. You were her brother once and even then you didn't know."

"What don't I get, Mec?" Dorian rolled his eyes—his whole body rolling with him.

Mecca and Q turned, already rejected. "Even if Mecca told you, it wouldn't change anything." It was as if Mecca had just realized it—realized the totality of what his discovery meant.

Dorian filled the silence. "No, we can't change anything. That's the whole fucking point, you dumbass. The inevitability. Vulcan let her this far for a reason. Now get out of my room. Tell Odissa she can come back now."

But Mecca wouldn't be telling anybody anything. Mecca would watch as his theories played out. He would collect his data and proof.

Stanza: What did Odys suspect?

Fletcher entered the house with a bucket full of supplies. Mecca, who had come to sit with Odissa and his father in the living room, noticed the Automaton was chewing something as he passed. Double Bubble. Bazooka. Something pinkish.

Fletcher glanced once at them. "I should have bought food too, since I was quicker than Maud."

Mecca and Q looked at each other, sharing a thought.

They heard the trash bags and a few bangs—taking out the blood-stained dry wall, maybe. Spray spray, swish swish, zip zip.

He walked out a few TV shows later—the large bag over his shoulder as if the skinniest Santa ever.

Stanza: What does Dorian suspect?

Minutes later, Dorian roused himself out of bed and went to scavenge for the new gum Fletcher had brought. He was just about to reach the hall when he stumbled into the wall; Fletcher's memory was good, but it only went so far.

Fletcher could not know that Mecca—for Dorian liked to blame Mecca—had left out a suitcase there, by the doorway. Well, he wasn't sure it was a suitcase. Maybe it was a duffle bag or a heavy coat.

Nevertheless, Dorian stumbled his way to the living room. Odissa got up when she noticed him coming. She helped him find the sofa. She shooed Maurice down a seat.

Odissa held Dorian's hand. She held it because it would be on her anyway, possessive and needy and begging for attention. Holding it kept it still. She wondered if he was listening to the TV at all over that smacking of his gum.

A commercial came on. She felt Dorian breathe deeply. "We can't use that bathroom anymore." No one argued with that. "We can't stay here. We should rent a suite." Not just a room. He wanted their company. That, or he was afraid to be alone with Odissa. "When Fletcher gets back, we should leave here. Mecca, find a place for us."

Mecca pursed his lips in thought. "Mecca knows a house that is empty. Mecca has been looking. Mecca thought you might want to leave after today. The owners are on vacation." He began checking his phone, as if checking on his facts. Q pulled out his tablet to match him.

"How do you know?" Maurice asked him. "Are you friends with them?"

"No. We've been stalking this couple for a while now, waiting for them to leave so we can see if they're the Mr. and Mrs. [redacted] who are related to a certain [famous actor]. They might have some of his stuff we could *collect*, since he spends the holidays with them."

"So *that's* how you know," Odissa sighed

"At least you're not killing them like Rosemund," Fletcher sighed. "Not yet anyway."

Q gave a few finishing tap tap taps and handed the tablet to Odissa with the street view. "Google Maps shows the houses in their area are close together, but at night Mecca's sure we could all sneak in without a fuss. Look at those tall fences and the gates. Their privacy is their blind spot."

"She's right. This could work," Odissa said—as if she broke into houses every day. She saw their faces when she handed it back.

Mecca sniffed and scratched his nose, going back to watching TV as if he did not care either way.

"Sounds fine," Dorian answered. "Let's go now. We can make it right when it gets dark."

"Now?" Odissa asked. "What about Odys—I mean, Maud?"

"He's taking his time anyway. After all, Fletcher just cleaned up the fucking bloodbath in there and he's still not back. Mecca, text him and tell him where we are headed. And tell him never mind about the food."

"You want me to talk to him?" Odissa asked.

"No," Dorian said. "Come help me pack."

Stanza: Guinevere runs off with Sir Lancelot in the end.

"Are you sure you want to leave so quickly?" Odissa asked him in the bedroom, arranging her few things.

"What do you mean? Of course I want to leave quickly. What if I need to pee in the next two minutes? I can't piss in there. There's not enough bathrooms."

Or places for a bath.

"You can use a tree. Fuck, I don't know." She couldn't come up with something better and continued gathering his things. "Do you want this?"

He shrugged, unsure what it was. She apologized and described the thing.

He leaned forward on the bed, noticing her irritation. "Thank you for packing. It's always better to have two sets of eyes on things."

"And it's better to not do it in a rush."

"We can get anything we need later."

"Who's going to be responsible for the Automatons, then?" she asked, folding up one of Dorian's shirts.

"Mecca."

"You serious?" She paused in her folding.

"No. But *he* is lately. So serious. He's not the same Mecca anymore. Not with Maurice in the picture." He rubbed his face, trying to decide if he liked the new Mecca or not. "But maybe I *will* let him take them. Anything he does with them can't make things worse, now can it?"

"Well. Maybe he should get a say in what happens to the inanimates too. You all treat him like a child. And maybe he is one. But he should still get a vote."

And so Dorian let Mecca take them for safe keeping. Well, not Mecca exactly. Dorian refused to acknowledge that this was a big responsibility for Mecca and so only spoke to Q—as if she was in charge. And perhaps right now she was.

Maurice drove them to a local Target store and dropped off Dorian and Odissa. Fletcher would pick them up soon, with Rosemund's remains "taken care of." They would meet them at Mecca's chosen house with groceries and, as Dorian had put it, "Better moods."

Dorian turned back to the car and spoke to Maurice through the rolled-down window. "Go get something to eat too. You have my cell if we need to change plans about the house."

"We'll make sure zee coast is clear, Dorian. You just make sure and get me some pancake batter." The window rolled up as he drove away.

Odissa led Dorian inside to the café customary in such mega-stores. "Do you have money?" she reminded him. *Because I don't.*

"Here, one of my cards," he said, shivering off the cold as they stepped inside. He pulled out his wallet. "I can't see them. Use the blue one. After that, just throw it away. We won't be able to use it again. Been needing to get rid of it."

The place had an hour until closing, so there wasn't a line. "What do you want?" Odissa asked him, studying the menu.

"Nachos. And Coke."

Odissa got the same but with coffee.

They sat down and consumed.

"Maurice didn't even ask why we wanted to be dropped off first," Odissa commented, wiping her mouth with a paper napkin.

"Why? You think he should care why we want to go shopping?" Dorian's lips tried to find his straw.

"I'm just surprised that he didn't. It makes me wonder why."

"We're too busy wondering *why* about your bloody brother. The fuck is he doing, Odissa? Sulking? Hiding from me?"

"You pretty much told him to leave. That's probably why Maurice didn't say anything. You're making everyone want to leave you alone, Dorian."

"And you, Odissa, are you going to leave me alone?"

"You're a very messy eater without Fletcher," Odissa whispered over the table, grabbing his hand. His sleeve had dipped in the cheese. "And I don't think Odys is avoiding us. He's closer than you think; he wouldn't leave me alone with you." She finished dabbing at him.

"Is my nose bleeding right now? Because you're provoking a good nosebleed. Or is it just cheese?"

"First you want him to leave us alone and now you want him to come back to us?"

"No. I just want to know what he's up to. Don't want surprises. I've had enough of them."

"I think you care about him."

"No. Well, obviously."

"You don't want him to upset your rule, is that it?"

"My 'rule,' is it?" His yellow fingers paused over his nachos as he smacked out the words.

She wanted to feed him, but knew an offer would insult his current pride. "Not only is it your right to tell this family what to do, but everyone seems to want it that way."

"There you go—not sounding like Odissa. You sound like Alpha now. Something in your voice—you're manipulating us. I can see it. At the very least, I can *hear* it." His voice lowered. He wasn't sure of the people around him—people who could listen. He also wasn't sure if Odissa cared enough to censor their behavior if need be. "Just come out and say what you want us to do, Alpha. You know what's going on. Guide us. We'll fucking give you what you want."

The cashier-girl who had taken their order went back into the kitchen area. Odissa could see her feet as she leaned over the counter, maybe reading a magazine. The low music droned above them, and the shoppers outside of the café-area made enough noise to drown their conversation out.

"Maybe that's why Alpha hid for so long. She didn't want you to constantly question her intentions. Need I remind you that I'm still here and haven't done anything wrong? Stop punishing me."

He sat back in his chair, sucking through the straw. "Haven't done anything wrong?" He smiled in disbelief. "Fine. But you haven't done anything trustworthy."

"Like what?"

"You got Leeland killed, for one. You did that. You set it up. You got him to freak out and tell Pepin about you, probably. And that made *everything* else fall into place."

Odissa leaned forward to hiss, "He had it coming. I didn't choose how Gwendolyn got to him. And I'm certainly not the one who told Bob to kill herself. You have Vulcan to thank for that. Not that she really wanted to be here anyway. And while we're blaming me for everything, should we mention that I let my parents die? Despite the fact that I was a baby and couldn't fucking save them even if I wanted to—didn't even have the muscles to walk! But yes, blame me for not warning them. If you see your infant speak in full-fucking adult sentences before they've even learned to say 'Da-da,' you can bet your kid is possessed. But I'm *sure* they would have continued loving me fully—for sure!—even if I'd managed to convince Leeland to let them live. I'm *sure* of it. And let's not forget that I'm the reason you're blind. Granted, that's *all* you were willing to give up for me and so *ironically* turned a blind eye to let me die?"

He licked his lips, unfazed.

Odissa calmed herself by chugging her coffee. Swallowed and breathed. "You have every reason to trust me and yet you refuse to believe me when I tell you Odys isn't planning anything. Don't I know my brother well enough by now?"

Dorian slapped down his empty cup, the sound echoing and turning heads.

Odissa wanted to tell him he had a dab of cheese on his stubble, but she also thought he deserved to look foolish if he was going to treat her this way.

"Besides," Odissa went on. "You really want to see Odys when you're having such a hard time? He's being kind enough to give you space. Plus, I think he really liked Rosemund. It's the Pepin in him."

There she goes again, Dorian thought. *Sounding like she knows. Like Alpha.* "I'm having a hard time?" His fingers rooted around for more nachos, trying to sound only half-interested.

"Fletcher proves it. You made him—and him alone—clean up 'the mess.'" She noticed Dorian tensed, warning her not to sputter a bunch of attention-drawing details in public. "Q and Maud were too afraid to offer help. You made Fletcher do all the work. Why take it upon yourself? Because that's how you deal with things."

He shook his cup, ice rattling around. "I owed it to her. To you all." He leaned back in his chair.

"No, I think you needed out. You needed to escape me for a bit. When Fletcher went out, so did you. You can't think when I'm around. And you desperately need to think—think about *how* to think about me. Hell, you can't even stand to look at me without getting distracted. That's just another reason to send your eyes away. Now, give me that cup. What do you want? Coke?"

He cleared his throat, trying to absorb her reprimand. "Yes, please."

She got up and went to the fountain. When she returned, Fletcher was there, standing over Dorian. "You couldn't tell him he had cheese on his face?" Fletcher grumbled as she sat down. He licked his thumb and cleaned a willing Dorian's chin. "God, you need a shave."

Odissa frowned. "It's like they always say, you get up from the table and the food arrives."

"So I'm food?" Fletcher asked, pulling up another chair.

"Food for thought," Odissa clarified. "That's not to say I didn't notice you, poking around in the men's department. Did you buy me anything?"

"You noticed me?"

"You're four feet taller than any of the racks. Who wouldn't?"

"You never once looked at me."

"There are reflections in dark windows." She gestured to the ones beside them as she tried to finish her food. Dorian and Fletcher looked at her skeptically. So, she added, "Also, Dorian was acting *too* gracefully. I knew he was seeing *something*. He knew where the tables were. He was avoiding them."

Dorian frowned, found out. "Well, I call bathroom break," he said, scooting back.

And so they each went into their designated bathrooms. Odissa noticed that Fletcher made sure she went into hers. Something also told her that he came right out just as quickly as he'd gone in. Dorian didn't trust her. No matter how much he wanted to, he was having trouble.

"What's next, then?" she said, rubbing her damp hands together. Those automatic air dryers never did the trick.

"To the car." Fletcher said. Odissa noticed his lingering hand on Dorian. Of course Dorian didn't feel well. Fletcher had been more distant than close from him these past few days.

When they got into the "new" car Fletcher had acquired, she noticed all the grocery bags in the back. As Fletcher got into the driver's seat, he said, "The ones in the floor board are food. These are for you."

She slid over and let Dorian in, rummaging. "Nice, very nice," she said pulling out new socks and shirt. "I didn't think about how hard it must be to do laundry."

"Nonsense. We can find a laundromat, if need be," Dorian said, settling in. "Or a dry cleaner…"

"Dry cleaning's always best. Saves time and effort," Fletcher said, starting out on the main road.

"You would say that," Odissa sighed. "Look what money's done to you. Well, thank you for buying me new clothes. Though I think you put this in the wrong bag, Fletcher." She held up a lacy thong. *What were you suggesting?*

"Yes, let me see that," Dorian said, examining it with his fingers. "Yes, this is most definitively meant for me. Damn checkout kids, assuming."

"I thought you wore boxer briefs—or are you trying to spice things up?" She flinched at her words. She was trying too hard.

"No, not spice things up. Go back to who I was." He shoved them into one of his plastic bags. "I didn't realize I was keeping you from who you are."

"You're not," he inserted quickly, as if to put an end to it. "I didn't mean it like that. Just all this traveling about has kept me from my normal wardrobe and I'm missing it. I like nice things, Odissa."

"I can see." She put a hand on his wrist, drawing him out. "And I would like to see." *Them on you.*

He kissed the back of her hand and snuggled into her, wishing the car would heat up faster. But that's what you get when you steal a car. They're usually the older, less reliable kinds.

Stanza: The older, less reliable kinds.

When they got to the house, they circled around a few times, making sure no neighbors were too interested. They parked the car around the block and quietly walked up to the house. A dog barked, calling attention to them. But no humans were responsive.

Freezing, they finally made it to the door. It was unlocked. Stomping off their feet with what little snow had found them and setting down their light luggage, they noticed Mecca was already sitting in front of the TV, eating popcorn. Fletcher held up his grocery sacks with a huff. "What'd I go shopping for, if you were just going to steal from them?"

Dorian took off his shoes as Fletcher took in the place. Off-white walls, off-white carpet, and oak furniture. So colorless. "Wow, what stuck-up people."

"The passcode to disable the alarm was their anniversary year," Q informed, just before ramming her face with popcorn. This was a time before even Ring cameras were a big thing, mind you, so this level of security was pretty high-tech for the time.

"Ugh," Fletcher said, helping Dorian take off his coat. Fletcher made sure the others were smart enough to close the blinds and that the lights turned on were minimal. No point in advertising they were there.

He noticed a professional photo of their unwilling hosts near the doorway—a Caucasian couple. Fletcher scrunched his nose. "Pretend-happy couples make me sick. They expect a baby to bring them back together. But there's never a good time for a baby, so it's not going to happen. Not that they were ever close to begin with."

Fletcher closed the door behind them.

"I know, right?" Q agreed. "At least get a fish first or something."

"These people are getting a divorce. Or worse, early retirement."

"That's what you said about my parents, Dorian. You said that to them once," Odissa said. It shut their snide comments up. She meandered into the living space. The over-stuffed sofa was covered in crumbs. Mecca had raided their food supply; wrappers and dirty plates had already piled up.

"Mecca," Odissa scolded, "you're trashing this place."

Mecca peeked over his laptop at his mess and frowned. "Their food's about to expire. They won't be home for another week. Besides, we'll compensate them." He pulled up a pair of large headphones from his neck and placed them lop-sided on his head, covering only one ear.

"Golden coffee table," Q said, tapping it with her foot. It turned to solid gold instantly. Her color waned and her head lolled back a bit. "Whew. That took a lot out of me. We're going to need more food!" She shot up and went for Fletcher's sacks.

There was a flush sound around the corner. Maurice came out, a local newspaper under his arm. He was also wearing a nice robe—probably stolen from the closet.

"Why the hell are you naked?" Fletcher growled.

Odissa snorted. The robe—that *didn't* come to his knees—made him look like an Renaissance king with scrawny legs. The cigar dangling from his mouth added to the effect.

Taking it out of his mouth he said, "Did Mec tell you that Maud iz five minutes out? She called." He handed his cigar to Mecca, who took it graciously. "You were right, son, these are better than the ones I got in Puerto Rico last year."

Mecca smelled it before putting it in his mouth.

Odissa stifled a laugh. Stealing was no laughing matter. "You all make yourselves quite at home, don't you? Just what are we going to do if we get caught? Honestly, a hotel is starting to sound smarter."

"Hotels have people," Maurice stretched is legs before kicking them up "With the way this lot is feuding we need our privacy. Fewer casualties."

"Plus this way is more thrilling," Mecca added.

"We've lasted zis long without getting caught, dear," Maurice said, crossing his bare legs. "Vulcan wouldn't let it happen."

"Did my brother say anything else?"

"No," Mecca said. He looked up at Odissa with too-knowing eyes. "And that's exactly why Mecca is worried."

"Worried?"

Fletcher's head snapped around at the sound of footsteps. "Speak of the devil…"

The knob turned.

"Just me," Maud said, her breath hanging heavily in the cold air. Her finger turned back into a finger—no longer a key to let herself in. Her hair fell in front of her face, but it couldn't hide the hollow look in her eyes. She saw Fletcher's bag of groceries.

"Sorry we wouldn't wait on you," Fletcher grumbled. "Seems like you were waiting on us, though."

"Why's it just you?" Maurice put down his paper. The tips of his mustache twitched. "You don't look well, Maud."

She came into the living room. The fact they didn't have many lights on contributed to her mystery.

"None of us look well. Not lately. Where are the Automatons?" she asked.

"The kitchen table. Where Mecca put zem," Maurice noted.

Her chest was heaving, maybe from the cold. "And the box?"

"There as well." He gestured in the direction of the kitchen, but she believed him.

"Good," Maud said with a sigh.

"If Odys was so worried about what we did with them, why did he leave us alone with them?" Dorian prodded as Maud forced herself past them.

Maud looked at them all. "Everyone needs space now and then."

Maurice leaned forward in his chair. "Maud, where's your Master? It iz clear you and he are not well. You seem far from him—where iz he?"

Q turned off the television. Mecca closed his laptop lid.

"Forget all that," Maud said, waving her hand. "I may sneeze out soon, so I need an answer quickly."

"To what question?" Mecca asked her.

Maud loomed over him, her high-heeled feet making her endless above him. "Odys wants Madus. Can I have him?"

Everyone exchanged looks. And, they finally noticed Odissa had sat down in a corner chair. Was she not worried about her brother? About his Automaton?

"Why *him*?" Mecca asked, though an answer really wasn't necessary.

Maud looked up, straight at Dorian. "Because I'm a twin. If you aren't going to give Madus to her"—Maud gestured to Odissa—"give him to me."

"We may still give her one—"

"Then why haven't you?" Maud's chin lifted, showing her glowing eyes. "I'm not going to watch her age and die, Dorian."

"We can talk on this tomorrow—when we're all in our right minds and didn't just bury Rosemund!" Dorian reeled, restraining himself from hitting the wall.

"Rosemund got her turn now I want mine. I get my second Automaton."

"That's all very well," Fletcher said, leaning against the doorframe. "But right *now?* Don't you think you're a little too sick to be doing something like that? I mean, you aren't even here, Odys. We'd like to be assured you're the one who's touching him."

Maud's back tightened. There was certainly something mad in her eyes. She had something up her sleeve. "We could test it—see if an extension of my soul could activate an inanimate Automaton rather than my actual body. It's never been tested before, right?"

"Why risk it? You'd pass out, if it worked. Maybe even die. Just—just look at Maud. She's not well. God only knows what you look like. Odys, come to the house," Dorian begged. He was too fucking tried to mess with Odys's shit tonight. None of this was reasonable. "Tell us where you are…"

Fletcher stepped forward as if wanting to shake the answer out of her.

"So, you don't trust me to take Madus? And you don't respect me enough to just let my Automaton touch it? Even if that's what I want?"

"Not when you're acting so fucking weird, no," Dorian said. "Just tell us what your angle is."

Maud laughed. Her legs approached Fletcher so that Dorian could get a good look. Though he stood heads taller than she did, she was his equal in stance. "Oh, Dorian, I can't wait to tell you what my angle is. Just let me get what I came for and you'll see."

She circled him to get to the kitchen. Her heels clicked on the tile floor. She knew that everyone had followed her—maybe to stop her, maybe to see if it would work.

"Don't do anything stupid," Dorian warned, on her (literal) heels. They couldn't stop her. How could you stop an Automaton?

She had already picked up Madus—in his own Ziploc bag. "Don't worry, I'll only take one. Fair is fair, right?" She opened the bag, holding it up like a dose of anthrax. They reared back from it, not wanting to be infected.

"You're being stupid, Odys!" Mecca shouted. "This could kill you if you're so far away. You don't know what a second Automaton does!"

"How would anyone know?" Maud asked. "Any Automaton who *would* know is still here, upon that table." Her eyes lit up, as if using the last of Odys's reserves. "Rosemund would've loved this, wouldn't she? Such an experiment."

Odissa inched past them all, better to see. She looked at them. "You'll just let him take it?" *You aren't even going to reserve Madus for me?*

"Of course they will," Maud said. "They're the ones that watch. They watch as things happen rather than *make* them happen. That's why everyone keeps dropping like flies."

"Don't be cruel, Odys," Odissa said to Maud.

Everyone looked at Odissa in confusion, barely noticing Maud had pulled the lips of the bag over her hand—exposing Madus like a banana without a peel. "Let me get it out of my system, Odissa. It's the last we've got."

"We?" Mecca asked, eyes darting to Dorian to see if he'd catch on.

Maud swayed a bit in place, adjusting her footing as if nervous and weary. She raised her eyes, a strange smile on her face. "I want you all to know—*know*—that this is going to work. I know it will. And, I'm sorry it's not more graceful. I've always been a bit rough inside Odys. That, and the stress makes it hard to be graceful, though there's grace in admitting gracelessness." Maud shrugged for Odys.

"What the hell's he saying?" Fletcher stepped forward.

Maud stepped back. And stepped back again.

Odissa raised a hand, asking Fletcher to chill.

As if toasting with a glass of wine, Maud raised Madus and his bag. "To Gracefulness!"

Maud jumped forward at them. She tossed Madus in the air as she moved—so quickly—as she came. The next thing they saw were two glinting pennies...coming directly at *Odissa.*

ODISSA ODELYN: One of a twin.

ONE: Soon to be with two.

TWO: Soon to be with her, the one.

THREE: Though she was always two in one, wasn't she?

Chapter the eighth,

The flinger is flung:

But who hits first?

When Maud had transformed into a penny—flinging herself at Odissa—they all knew what had happened. Odys had killed himself. That, or the Alpha inside him—whatever portion she had stowed there—had forced him to kill himself.

He was no longer needed in Alpha's story. (And I will admit, he'd become somewhat of a side character, dragging along. Perhaps Alpha felt the same way?).

But back to those few seconds. Though Maud, inanimate in the air, would eventually hit Odissa, the first to actually land in her outstretched hand was *Madus*.

MADUS: Got there first.

FIRST: Come, first served.

SERVED: A good portion of Odissa/Alpha.

ODISSA/ALPHA: Now immortal.

Chapter the ninth,

Twins in the twin:

Twin twins?

Maud hit second, hitting her wrist.

Odissa caught her just the same, with her other hand. She caught them both with such quickness it was unnatural; it was unexpected.

Dorian stepped back from her—as they all did. "You reached." *You wanted him to do this. You knew it was coming.*

Odissa turned from them. "Fuck," Odissa hissed, rubbing her head. She wobbled in place.

They waited for her to faint—to topple over from the fact her soul was being ripped from her body (what soul there was). But she didn't.

Alpha was already so used to having her soul ripped in two—that rebirth after rebirth—that this barely phased her.

"Just a headache?" Maurice reeled. "Just a fucking headache?"

"Oh, don't you stare at me like that." She rolled her eyes. "They were his to give. What? Do you expect me to convulse? Vomit like you mortals? Alpha doesn't need to sync. She *is* synchronicity." She started to shake from defensive rage and backed away from them. She averted her eyes, ashamed and pained. And then they caught her eye...

She admired the pennies in her hands, as if they were gold. "You all saw this coming. Don't act so shocked. You did nothing to stop it. I know Mecca told you, Dorian—who Odys really was. He tried to. You don't think I noticed how busy you were, little Mecca? I know what you told Dorian—what you guessed. What you *suspected*." She was talking to the pennies—a Gollum with his ring—nay, *rings*. "Oh, stop looking at me as if I'm going to hurt you. I got what I wanted and leave it alone. Look, all the other Automatons are still here, aren't they? I could easily take a few steps back and"—she took a few steps back—"touch them all." She stood still. "But I'd rather be *given* things."

"Odys just killed himself?" Dorian asked, something in his throat. They had to be certain.

"I did it for you, Dorian. For us. He was making you ill."

"You made him kill himself, Odissa." Maybe it was more of a question. A question of how. She blinked back tears, trying not to look at him but still facing him. "He loved you. He loved what Alpha loved. He wanted to be whole again. Don't you see? I'm whole again—as much as can be. When Maud took his soul she also took his part of Alpha.[201] I am whole again." She brought the pennies to her chest.

"What...have you done?" Fletcher whispered, eyes wide. "What have you been doing?"—*to us?*

"But are you as whole as you want to be?" Maurice asked, mustache twitching as he stood in her exit route. "Your power will never be what it once was, will eet? No. You still are working toward that vision. That vision of being how you were originally created, before zee Automata took you down."

"No!" Odissa tensed, blinking at the floor as if confused. "I would never. I just wanted to be safe. To have my immortality back. To not fear *dying*. To not need to breed and live over and over again. To stay with *you*, Dorian."

"Just, just, just..." Maurice shook his head, turning askance from them all.

Mecca watched Dorian, his lip curling in horror. "You like that she did it, don't you, Dorian? Now you can have her without interruption. Your nephew just died and you cry from happiness!"

"You think I like being this way?" He bent down and growled in Mecca's face. Dorian was crying in horror, wiping his running nose on his collar. Mecca and Q backed into Maurice for protection. Dorian grabbed at Mecca's shirt. "You think I like loving this monster?" He pointed at Odissa. "What would you have me do?"

Maurice pushed Dorian back away from his son. "Zis is what she does! She turns us against ourselves to take them all. She doesn't even have to kill us. We'll kill ourselves."

"Start with yourself then, Maurice!" Dorian spat in his face. "She can't do the impossible."

"He doesn't mean it!" Odissa shouted, coming between them. They parted like the red sea for Moses, not wanting to touch her. But Dorian wasn't afraid.

---

[201] The Narrator and I have had long conversations about what she means by Maud "took his part of Alpha." Perhaps Alpha was half in Maud, half in Odys. Or, all in Maud. The Narrator usually just explains it as, "It's too complicated for you to understand."

"Do not speak for me!" Dorian growled at her. He backed her into the cabinets of the kitchen. "No one speaks for me."

She took the sides of his face to keep the distance between them, the pennies dropping to the tile floor. But she couldn't stop his forehead from resting on hers.

"Why did you do this, Odissa?" *Did you have to kill him?*

"I just wanted to live, Dorian. I can live with you forever now." She cried as she tried to pull his head back by his hair. It turned into holding him in place. The guilt flooded her and spilled out in a confession, "I knew your sister was having twins and so I split myself into two. I had to expand myself to expand my chances of living. Do you understand how hard it was to get her pregnant? The magic involved? *Please* understand. I was Odys and then I was also Maud. And now I'm whole again." She looked at one of her pennies on the floor. "Really, I'm three now. Again."

But under one mothership.

"You killed him. Even if he was you—you killed him. He was something before you possessed him, Odissa. He was still a person!"

"You think Odys wanted to keep living? You think there was really a place for him here? Now we all can live in peace."

Q shook her head, her face scrambled. "You call this peace? There is barely anything of us left."

"I'm sorry. I'm so sorry," Alpha whispered to Dorian, melodramatic tears welled in her eyes. "But this is the best I could do. I didn't think this would be how it happened. I always thought it would be me."

Fletcher formed a gun. Q followed suit. Dorian assumed a low, begging voice. "Tell us why we should still trust you after what you've just done." He grabbed the back of her neck, to keep her from moving away.

"It's not as if I haven't had an Automaton, Dorian. I always had one. I always had Maud. Through Odys. He was me. A clone."

"But now you have two!"

"And you could have two." She pointed to the table. "We could be equals. In that way."

"You didn't have to kill him, Alpha." Dorian cuffed her neck tighter. A heaviness pulled at the corners of his lips.

"He was unhappy." Odissa still stared at her penny on the floor. There was a hint of remorse on her face, but not for what she'd just done; for the fact they did not understand her. "His body had no role with me any longer." She tried to slide down, out of Dorian's grasp, but he held her there, pressing his body into hers, his tears hitting her chest.

"Where is his body, Alpha?" Maurice asked.

"In the trees," she said. "Behind a golf course near the Wal-Mart, where he bought his gun." And with that Dorian broke, his body sagging. Alpha comforted him as he gasped into her neck. "Mi sobrino…" he mumbled off in Spanish.

To keep from hyperventilating, he pulled away from her, resting over the sink. Free, she quickly bent down and picked up her coins.

Stanza: The woman who tithes.

"I swear this is all I wanted." She cradled her coins in her palm. She ran a finger over them. They noticed she was having a hard time keeping her hands and eyes off them. "I promise I am loyal to you all." She could feel them waiting for her proof. "What you know about Pepin is true. But only half-true. You don't know the full story. How do you think he knew I was Alpha? How did he know where to find my brother?" She looked up at them. "That's right. I told him. *I* found him. Not Leeland. Everything fit, so he knew I wasn't lying. It wasn't my husband who came to Pepin for help. Not at first. *I* got to Pepin first."

She looked back at her coins.

"We had to make it so Gwendolyn would lie as well. She had to, you see. She had to lie to Leeland. It had to be a chain reaction. I offered Pepin my help in killing Leeland. Leeland was not as evil as they come, but he needed to be stopped. None of you were willing to kill him—not that you necessarily could. This was the best way to get rid of him, in the end. I gave my word to Pepin—I convinced him." She could not stop her fingers from enclosing her coins and bringing her fist to her mouth like one might a rosary. "I have many Words. I know them. I know the Words." She paused in thought. "And didn't they all die happy? They all died thinking they were helping in some way—helping in some overarching plan. You see, Pepin didn't kill himself to give Odys Maud and therefore keep me from gaining all Automatons."

She put her coins on the counter, between her and Dorian. She walked away from her coins, very easily, in fact—as if it caused her no pain, albeit, her eyes did glance once more at them.

"Pepin killed himself because he knew I'd eventually gain all Automatons—and, indeed, I have gained his. You must understand, he trusted me. I told him everything. We planned this together."

"But not this part, right?" Dorian accused.

541

"He and Leeland were both so convinced that Odys wasn't me," she laughed at their stupidity. "I made them believe—so easily—that he was just a boy. I told Pepin Leeland might kill Odys if he wasn't protected. They were so willing to die if only they served a purpose. Please don't think I wasted them. Our plan was I would become part of the family and you would see I am not out to cause destruction. With the Automatons under my care, no human need be tortured by their curses again."

"I'm not so sure that's what Pepin believed," Fletcher swallowed down his words, lest he have to taste them again.

She pulled out a kitchen chair and waited before sitting. "He knew there was a reason Vulcan did not allow the original Masters to kill me—to finish me."

Dorian covered his ears. "Her words!" he cried, folding over. "Her words will destroy us…"

She lowered her face to hide her pain. "I am only trying to help you."

"How?" Mecca cried. "There is nothing left to help! You've killed everything."

"Put out of their misery!" she shouted back at him. She collected herself. "I haven't killed anything. They all went willingly, didn't they?" *Can't I be forgiven?*

"It makes sense why you fucked Odys," Mecca tried to test her reaction levels. "You were the same damn person—same being."

Odissa's eyes flashed to the little boy. "We missed each other, our half-Alphas. Odissa never loved Odys. Not in that way." She paused. "I love *you*, Dorian. I have loved you and I have missed you and I thought that you might love Odys. But Vulcan wanted *this* body of mine to live. I didn't make you love this one."

Maurice cleared his throat.

Dorian searched for calm. "Tell me, exactly, where his body is and I'll make sure the cops clean up everything."

"I promise you, there are no traces." *I'm good at this by now.*

"Tell me now, Alpha. I want to make sure."

"Is this how it's always going to be? You not trusting me? Why not just kill me then?"

"Worse than Mother," Maurice grumbled, crossing his arms. "She knew when her time was up. Yours was long ago."

Alpha's eyes pleaded with him to shut up. "Get it over with, then. See? You know I am good. You know what I could do for you all—what I could bring to the table. Fuck Vulcan's plans. I can show you how to pause them. If you let me. We can be a family again."

Dorian walked up to her, determined. "I want to see my nephew's body. You owe me that."

Odissa told him Odys's location. Out behind the trees somewhere. Blood splattered around an accidental snow angel.

They'd think a meteor fell from the sky and then combusted. Or, that he was some pyromaniac experimenting with left over fireworks. No gun could make that explosion—not that one in his hand, no. Maybe a bad bullet? Was that possible? The lab would say.

Dorian and Fletcher left without another word.

"You leave us with her?" Maurice shouted after him.

Odissa looked at Mecca, still in Q's arms. "Mecca, you can take the master bedroom. I will sleep on the couch." *Close to the door.*

Maurice nodded to his son. *Go to bed, Mecca. I will take this watch. Your papa will keep you safe.*

Q panted in slight panic. Mecca wanted to protest but knew it seemed safer. His papa could not die. Mecca could. He went to collect his things from the living room.

Maurice and Odissa waited until they heard the door upstairs shut. They didn't really care if Mecca was in his room or not. Privacy was a theory only.

Odissa finally met Maurice's gaze. "I know what you must think of me."

"Zen please tell me, so we will both know."

"When are you going to leave, Maurice? Weren't you planning on it?" She looked at the box of tissues. *Hadn't we agreed?*

"That was before you killed Odys and took two Automata. My son's life is at stake here."

"Exactly what I mean, Maurice. You torture him with your presence."

Maurice's mustache twitched and smoke might as well have shot from his ears.

"I have an offer for you, Maurice. But, I know someone who can explain it better."

Odissa picked up one of her two coins—only one.

Stanza: Pay the ferryman.

When Dorian and Fletcher finally found the scene (which was not hard, because of all the flashing lights), Fletcher left Dorian in the car to go and scout. Fletcher took the long way around, mumbling to himself that Odys must have called in his own death before he'd done it. *To fucking perfection.*

Fletcher climbed a good tree. Squatted in the branches like a vulture. It wasn't until he saw the torso, the clothes, the imprint in the snow, that he finally accepted Odys was dead. *Dead as Pepin. Just like Pepin. Repeated.*

Fletcher heard phrases like, "Only one set of tracks," "But how could a gun do this?" "Do his prints match anything we've got currently?" "No ID..." Fletcher grabbed a branch and resisted the urge to snap it.

I told you Odys wasn't the protagonist.

Stanza: Crossing the river Styx.

Maud and Maurice were sitting at the kitchen table. Maud's legs were crossed modestly. That did not, however, make up for the fact she was very naked.

Odissa had gone to bed on the couch. Tapped her Automaton in as she went to sleep. Albeit, she was very much awake in Maud.

"As you can see, Maurice," Maud whispered with unflagging grace, "I think it's very simple."

"Zis is not simple. Zis has been zee most intricate plan in zee 'istory of Automata." His mustache did not move. Every inch of him was stiff. Just like his dick.

She had told him her plan. Soothed the dead once again with her words—nay, Words. Just as Vulcan had done to Bob. Gave him solace. Gave him comfort. Gave him a reason. "So we've a deal, then?"

"I don't have much of a choice, do I?" He frowned. Even though the woman of his dreams was nude before him, he found the capacity to frown.

The inanimate Automatons in front of them made Maud smile. Dorian had trusted her Master with them—didn't care if she touched them. Underneath the table, her foot ran along Maurice's leg. "I'm telling you, you'd better take it while you can."

Something in Maurice darkened. "There's a spare bedroom down the hall. Go there," he told her.

Assuming clothes and standing up, Maud left him. Pacing himself behind her, he went into the living room and looked down on Odissa. *She doesn't even need to sleep with them.*

But there was a man's head resting on her chest—Madus's. His long legs wrapped around her, one dangling off the couch. The blanket covered his naked body, his long hair covered his face. His eyes opened when he felt Maurice staring.

"Dorian won't mind sharing a bed with another man," Maurice spoke freely.

"Worry about your own bed tonight, Maurice," Madus whispered as Odissa stirred in her sleep, snuggling in. Maybe syncing with the Automata had finally caught up with her. She had fallen asleep so fast. Even so, that was little proof of vulnerability. Madus closed his eyes.

Entering the spare bedroom, Maud spread herself out on the bed. "You have to tell me what you want," she said. This was part of their deal. The final string of words and promises she could pull to get him to listen. To get him to obey.

"Don't you think I know how sex works?" He raised a curled eyebrow. "I don't assume you should know everything like my Automaton. I know perfectly well who I'm fucking, Alpha."

"Isn't it sad? Even if I were your Automaton, it wouldn't be satisfying. And even when I'm not, you're always really fucking someone else."

"Dorian shouldn't know about this." He was already wanting to amend their constitution.

"Why would I tell him?"

"I'm not sure why gods do half the things they do."

"I like that, Maurice, being called a god. Under certain circumstances, I find the title fitting. After all, I'm not an Automaton. But I am not a god."

"It's confusing when you speak like zat, Alpha," Maurice said, spreading Maud's legs.

"Then I won't talk. You do the talking."

He grabbed her wrist to make her sit up. "Undress."

As she "lost" her clothing (a bra slipped off here and absorbed into her arm, some panties there, just disappeared), she helped him undress too, undoing his belt.

As she fondled him, he told her, "Don't be loud, and don't touch my moustache."

"How can I touch it when you are up there? Is this a blowjob or a fuck? Or both?"

He took off his shirt and pushed her back on the bed. A fuck, clearly.

"An Automaton can do both at once, I'm sure." His fingers contrasted with her coppery breast—ate at it with a starved hunger. "Laugh," he told her as he entered her. His face melted at the ease in which she took him in.

That face let her know she wasn't cheating him. She stirred underneath him when he paused to savor her—he need not move if he didn't want to. "What do you want me to do?"

He opened his eyes and looked at her with anger—anger that this could only happen once—that he couldn't keep this toy—that he could fuck millions of others but they would never look like this. He turned her over. Emptied himself into her.

When he was done, he lay down beside her. He was trying to pull his lips over his teeth, but the pained grin kept cracking through. "I wish you were mine," he tried to catch his breath. "Of all the Automatons, I wish you were mine."

"I know."

"Look at it. It was like you were sucking my dick and swallowing. No mess. So clean." He ran his hand up her dry thighs.

"No evidence," Maud said with spite. She would later spit his frothy cum out in the sink to cleanse herself of him.

"That's not what I meant. I meant you are perfection. Vulcan designed you for this moment. I am sure. He always wanted me to lust after you—for you to tease me. Zat bastard. It's all planned, isn't it? Everything."

"Not everything is about you," she scolded. "You might not find me so perfect if you *were* me, Maurice. You think my memories of Pepin would keep your dick hard if they were in your brain? No."

He closed his eyes. "Oui, Pepin's ghost wouldn't let me touch you."

"He let you put me in any number of circus costumes, though." She took his chin, careful to mind the mustache. "Does it feel like you're touching his things?"

He shook his head. "I'm touching Dorian's now."

"What do you want me to do now?"

"Sit up. Just stay there and let me look at you. Give me somezing to remember."

Maud looked up at the ceiling. Odissa, in her, realized how much she needed, well, the ability to make someone contented.

Dorian wasn't content.

But getting rid of Maurice would might make him so.

Stanza: A deal's a deal.

Fletcher and Dorian came back late. The sun was making the new sky pink—rosy-fingered, as Homer would say. Fletcher had watched until the body was taken away in its bag, the area cleaned up and roped off. Odys was as good a buried. The Master and Automaton drove back to the borrowed-house in utter quietness. Fletcher put a hand on Dorian's thigh. They were so tired.

When they pulled into the neighborhood, Dorian's head began to pound—pound with confusion when he noticed Maurice's vehicle was gone.

When they walked in, they noticed Odissa on the couch. A very instinctual part of Dorian did not like the fact Madus was sleeping on top of her. But where was Maud?—in her hand? In her pocket? With two Automatons, she should have taken the guest bed from Maurice. He should have been a gentleman.

Speaking of bed—

Of Maurice—

Dorian went to the spare bedroom. He, with great strain, pushed open the door. Maud was still lounging on the bed. But this time, she had clothes.

"I stayed up for you," she said, sitting up.

"Doesn't count if you make your Automaton do it, Odissa," Dorian said. His hand slid off the doorknob.

"Where's Maurice? Is Mecca still here?" Fletcher asked—honest worry in his voice.

"Mecca is still here. Safe and sound."

Dorian bristled at the fact he was actually glad. He asked, "Why are you in this room and not sleeping with your Master, Maud? She needs you."

Or maybe she doesn't, Fletcher thought to him.

"I stayed up for you because you're mad at Odissa's face. Not necessarily this one."

He couldn't argue with that. "What was Maurice's excuse? Did he take the box?"

"This an inquisition?" she blinked up at them each—blinks to Dorian, blinks to Fletcher. "He left the box."

"Why? How?"

"I got him to. It's just us now. We're a family. The family Mecca needs."

The eagerness in her voice made him think unnatural, fatherly thoughts. "Why did he leave?"

"I made him leave it."

"How?"

Maud shrunk back—an action so like Odissa that Dorian knew she was guilty and afraid. "Does it matter?"

"Yes, it fucking matters."

"I told him secrets. Things I knew about what was to come. When everything is over. I told him why I'm still alive. What I know. That convinced him."

"Like Bob was convinced? Did you give him the whole picture then?" He stepped into the room as if stepping on her foot—pressing for an answer. *What is the whole picture, then?*

"I gave him *enough* of a picture. He could visualize it. Act on it."

"You told me 'enough' and I'm still here. I didn't leave. What did you *really* do, Odissa?"

Fletcher began smelling the room—could smell the sweat and saliva and sex.

"I let him sleep with Maud." Maud pointed to herself as her Master spoke through her.

Dorian slunk back—each step he sagged a little more. He gestured to the room. "Couldn't have tried to *hide* it?" He enunciated his syllables—emphasized words with such conviction they even sounded italicized.

"I did try a little. But you don't play along very willingly, Dorian. You clearly prefer the truth because you want to hurt."

Fletcher came up to Maud, bitterness in his red eyes. He took her chin and made her look at him. "Don't pretend this is about sadism."

Maud rolled her face away and gripped her arms, as if defending herself from her own Master's lie. "I got rid of him for you, Dorian. And *I* know what the box is for. I can use it—"

"Get out!" Dorian said, pointing to the door.

He slammed it behind her and locked it.

Stanza: *C'est le premier pas qui coute.*[202]

When Maud sat down on the arm of the couch, her twin and her Master sat up (they were already awake but the slamming door roused them). Maud started smoking. I've probably said this before, but an Automaton could make smoking look healthy.

Maud passed her Master the cigarette as Odissa got up. Odissa's hand shook—just a little— as she took it. "I'm sorry," she said to Maud as she tucked back the Automaton's hair. *Sorry I made you do it*—as if there were some part of Maud who wasn't her, whom she should apologize to.

But Maud only thought, *How can I care? I am you. And you are not sorry.*

Odissa rubbed the sleep from her eyes and made her way to the room. Madus followed. Madus ripped the door knob out and, without much more effort, pushed the door open. They closed the damaged thing behind them, keeping the false and unnecessary air of privacy.

Fletcher and Dorian were on the floor, as if the bed where Maud and Maurice had once been were unsanitary.

Fletcher, underneath Dorian, tilted his head to see them for his Master—his face untroubled by the disturbance. Unconcerned, he closed his eyes once more so that Dorian might block them out just a little while longer as he fucked. Dorian's dick almost went limp from the thought of hurting Odissa. *Better to not think, just do.* His face was angry—angry as he fucked Fletcher for his revenge. But he couldn't finish, which made him angrier.

Odissa smoked and waited—waited, waited, waited—for him to give up, passing the butt to Madus who smothered it in his hand and then let it fall to the carpet.

Dorian's manic thrusting threatened to give Fletcher a carpet burn—had he skin, anyway.

---

[202] French for "It is the first step which counts."

Eventually, Dorian spat-cursed into Fletcher's chest, fighting it. Fletcher just squeezed his eyes, as if he might accidentally open them and see Odissa.

"Stop humping him if you can't stay hard," Alpha-Odissa said softly.

Dorian kept cursing until (finally) he gave up.

Fletcher sat up, helping a weary Dorian off him. Dorian was panting, but Fletcher stayed composed. There was a hatred in Dorian's face, the sweat running down it. Fletcher leaned Dorian against the nearby bed and, before assuming clothes, allowed his set of genitalia to reform to their more 'default' state. He could give as well as take.

With his tight pants newly formed, Fletcher stood up and stooped over his Master, zipping up his pants for him like a mother would her child. He pat Dorian's face and turned to Odissa.

"Dorian wants sleep. That's all he fucking wanted. To sleep next to you. But then he comes home to *this*."

"So, you're doing this to hurt me?" Odissa said, crossing her arms and leaning against the wall.

"It was nothing, Odissa," Dorian said, breathless. "I was just angry. I was doing to him what I would never do to you."

"Dorian, you don't have to explain. But it's one thing to masturbate and it's another to do it to piss me off. However fun it was to watch."

"No, it was because *I* was angry. I was the one who was angry. I deserve to be angry." He used his shirt to dab and hide his face.

"Maybe we can both be angry. Maybe you can be angry around me."

He scoffed. "I don't know that I can. I can't—can't even fuck Fletcher angrily!" He twitched out the words.

She rolled her eyes. "I'm not saying, like, rape me. I'm saying don't fucking masturbate just to get back at me."

"I want to give you my best."

"Who says I want your best?"

Dorian laughed, almost hatefully.

She took a step toward him, looming over, arms crossed. "No, Dorian. I want you. All of you. I thought I *did* have all of you. You shouldn't have to hide anger from me. Why didn't you wake me up? Why didn't you yell at me?" She yelled that last part, as if trying to demonstrate what yelling was.

"I wanted to. I wanted to fuck you and hate you but I knew those two shouldn't mix."

549

"I'm letting you know you can."

"Don't be ridiculous," Dorian said, trying to stand up. Fletcher gave him his hand. "It's you who do the fucking, remember? The fucking over."

But when he finally made it off the floor, Odissa was already in the living room. She was gathering her purse, her bags. Madus was gone—a penny once more.

"What are you doing?" Fletcher said, asking Maud and Odissa—any part of her who would listen.

There was a panic in her eyes—eyes that avoided him. "Alpha's making things wrong. I shouldn't hurt so much so quickly," Odissa said, tears in her eyes. "This is everything she could hope for. Everything's falling into place. But it's also making her lose everything she was starting to love."

"No, you're not going," Fletcher said as Dorian sat down in a chair. Dorian was shaking—he needed sleep. He needed Odissa.

"As if you're going to stop me," she said as Maud stepped between them on cue.

"Don't fucking *threaten* me," Dorian warned from the chair.

Fletcher tried to step around Maud, but her hand formed a gun. "Don't make me involve Madus, Dorian. Don't make me break this tie." Her eyes counted the bodies.

"Pull him out," Dorian dared, "What've I got to lose? You think I care if I die? You think I care what happens to those damn Automatons in there? You want to fight, then let's fight!"

Fletcher pushed Maud's "gun" into his stomach like an unmedicated lunatic and then walked around her. No one was in for a wrestling match. He went straight for Odissa, who didn't struggle, merely glared up at him as he dragged her.

"Go ahead, pull him out. Where is he?" He tossed her down onto the couch. "Stop me, Odissa."

"You need space, Dorian," Odissa growled up at Fletcher. "Go to bed. Get some sleep!"

"No, I need to hurt you like you hurt me," Fletcher said, ripping open her pants as she flailed—told him to stop.

Maud pointed her gun at Dorian, but Fletcher knew it was a blank threat. Fletcher tried to keep Odissa down on the couch without hurting her, but that was hard to do with her kicking at him.

"You aren't even going to stop me?" Fletcher said, eyes glancing at Maud.

"Dorian, stop it. Get him off me," Odissa warned.

But Dorian just sat there, frowning, his hands resting on the arms of the chair like an immovable statue in stone-sleep

"Please don't make me hurt you," Maud said to Dorian, her voice calmer than the situation presumed.

"Oh, put that away and go back to your change purse." Dorian waved his fingers.

"How do you want it? Fast? Slow? Aren't these the questions Maud had to ask Maurice, no?" Fletcher hissed into Odissa's face, making her close her eyes to block his anger.

"As if we don't already ask each other the same types of questions, Dorian!"

"Answer me!" Fletcher shook her body with his hands.

"Fast. Because I'm a gentleman and I'm not going to deny you the right to your emotions, but I would rather not drag this out." Odissa looked straight at Dorian, past Fletcher on top of her.

Dorian laughed at her words, cracking through like thunder.

Maud reabsorbed her gun and went to Dorian. Stroked his hair. "Do what you must to be able to forgive her. But do nothing more than that. When Hera bound Zeus, Zeus took his revenge when he was freed. You cannot be Hera. It will not go well for you."

"Zeus deserved it though," Dorian said to her, his lip snarling.

"Allusion can be just as powerful as an act."

Dorian's head lowered into his attenuated hands.

Fletcher slowly stood up, his lanky body taking his time. His hand lingered on Odissa's chest, gingerly—yet holding her down. "We'll do whatever you want, just please don't go." He begged her. "What does Alpha want? What *deal* can I make with her to get Odissa to stay?"

"I think I might die if you leave," Dorian said "I'm sure I would die, too, if you ever fucked someone else again. Please don't ever do that again." *Please.*

"I have no intention of ever using *this* body for anything but *you*. I fucking killed off Odys so that would be the case. But you can't make what gifts I give you into your own personal hell, Dori."

"I'm in love with a demon." He laughed it, a stultifying sound.

"Fine, make me the devil. I'll slither on my belly and accept my fate. But do realize that Satan left the serpent's body eventually." She said to the air, "Even a willing host is eventually emptied."

The sun was finally up and shining through the closed blinds. Fletcher's body was like a silhouette against that morning light. Odissa stared up at him.

"What the fuck does that even mean?" Fletcher shrugged his hands to her—begging for clarity.

Brown-eyed Odissa pursed her lips and glared. *You want to do this on no sleep? Fine. I'll educate you. Whatever gets you to forgive me.*

She slid her eyes back to Dorian. A shadow came over her features, as if the sun had decided to go back down instead of rise.[203]

"Let me ask you Dorian, Fletcher: Do you obey Vulcan out of Love for Him, or out of Fear? Do you fear Vulcan and therefore submit to Him? Or, do you obey Him because He's ultimately good? If so, what makes Him good? Is He good because He says He is? And what if He's not good, but you were to obey Him anyway—despite all His flaws (because, let's admit it, I wasn't His best work and how dare He create me; me, who killed so many before I was stopped)? Yes, you fear Him, Dorian. And if you, of all beings, fear, why would I not fear as well—as the very First who has the *most* reason to fear Vulcan? If I have the most reason to fear Him, why don't I? Why am I not afraid?

"Again, as I've asked before, why am I still here if Vulcan doesn't see a purpose in me? Same with Maurice, right? I have a job. A job to explain things—give advice—insight. Let's face it. I know how things—*every fucking thing*—works. I may not be what I once was, but I still have a use. I'm a castrated bull. Good for plowing, but no longer interested in goring what my temper finds irritating. Alpha knows more about the Universe than Vulcan could even teach. Why? Because she *is* Vulcan's teachings and knowledge. But I think you know that."

Fletcher pushed her back down as she sat up too high—pushing more out of her. His fingers pressed into her chest as if finding the X on a treasure map. *There it was.* She glared up at Fletcher, daring him to keep his freakishly long hand on her a little while longer.

Yes, listen for the coordinates. Trace the steps. Measure the distance.

"I'll let you in on some cheat codes, Dorian. I'm part of the game. He doesn't even have to say it, our Vulcan. Perhaps He's hoping you'll figure it out. Fuck, you should've figured it out a long time ago. Not that you haven't had your fucking hard drive rewired by the gods and who the hell knows what kind of glitches that's caused…"

Fletcher looked at Maud to make sure she wasn't moving—to make sure this tangent was no distraction. Odissa batted Fletcher's plaits away like a curtain of beads. *Listen to me.* "You wonder how I'm so sure of myself? Because I fucking helped Vulcan write the rules of this game.

---

[203] Let me warn you this is a soliloquy. All it needs is a skull.

Hell, *I am* the rulebook that was in Him—that He peeled off Himself. I'm formed from the scabs on His calloused hands."

She stopped sitting back on her elbows—stopped pushing against Fletcher's fingers—and instead let her rant flow gently from her and up to the ceiling as if on a therapist's couch. "When He created me, I started out as an idea. I was still inside Him. But not just me, no. So was the idea for the game. *In the beginning was the Word.* This game is older than the Maya's. Older, but just as messy. No, I take that back. It's the *same* game. It never stops being played. Yes, I like that one better." She lifted her head. "So, stop acting as if I'm the Monopoly Jail-square you've just landed on. Hell, the game hasn't even started. Right now the dice are just rolling. Rolling, rolling, rolling. To see who goes first."

Her hands mimed the act.

"You sound mad, Odissa."

"This game needs a referee and that job is not Vulcan's to fill. Not really. He's just the creator of the game. He can't control how it's played after He puts it on the store shelves—how players break the rules. He wants to see what calls we make so He can cheer and jeer for His team. That's where I come in."

"I think you're wrong. I think Maurice is that referee. Fuck, he even wears black and white."

(His French shirt, you see—of course the gods would do something just for a motif).

"Ah, that would have been very clever. But no. Not anymore. I'm the rules, remember? I can be rewritten. Revisited. I can change."[204]

"What if there can be more than one referee?"

"Now you're just trying to humor me, as if you don't think I'm right. No, he's merely a coach on the sidelines now. The one who calls for heads or tails to see who kicks the ball first. And he's made his call."

"Shouldn't there be two coaches then?"

"Who says that there are only two teams?"

"How many teams will there be?"

"As many as there are Automatons. Yet, in some ways, only one."

"I don't understand you. All these sports references make me want to vomit."[205]

---

[204] Suuure you can, Alpha.
[205] Same.

"You don't have to understand, Dorian. You're not going to play the actual game. You're just part of the board. That's all you humans were. Beta testers. Your bodies are what the Automatons will use to pick their teams."

"*Their* teams? We have no will but a Master's." Fletcher pulled back from her, as if she was speaking nonsense and sacrilege at the same time. "Automatons can't make choices."

"So you don't want me to stay?" she asked him, surprised he was setting her free.

"Why would you want to stay, if I'm going to put off your game?"—pun, as always, intended.

"That's the very thing. I'm not going to decide when the gun fires. I will stay as long as you realize I love you with all my heart and I'm actually doing everything in my power to keep the game from starting before you're ready. That's what this has all been about. This wasn't manipulation. This was love."

Dorian stood up. His cloudy eyes were red with tears. "They may be the same thing at this point."

"That's not fair—"

He walked over to the couch, not too close but within distance. "You have so many secrets. You say you understand everything, but you do not instruct."

It hurt him to love her and she could feel it shooting out of him. "I cannot teach it to you. You would not understand."

"Tell me what Vulcan's game is," he leaned into her, lips snarling. "Tell me where everything fits."

If I tell you, you'll go mad. "I will not tell you. If your loyalty depends on such worthless information, then no. You would not love me if you knew. You are never supposed to know. The game happens after you, after *us*. I see that now."

She looked at the box in the other room like a timebomb about to go off.

"What did you tell Maurice to make him leave, then? What did you tell him that you won't tell me?"

"I didn't have to tell him what you ask for. He was smart enough to see. Just as Mecca is smart enough to see it." Her eyes pointed up those dark stairs, their intricate wooden railing casting striped shadows on the wall.

"Like father, like son," Maud said as she made her way to those stairs to inspect them. "Maurice was smart enough to know he could do nothing about what Alpha must do." She stared up at the top of the stairs. "Got something to add to the conversation, or are you just going to sit there?"

Dorian and Fletcher heard Mecca breathe and shift. He had been listening and watching and holding his breath between the bars. He peeked around where the rail met the wall.

"Go back to bed, Mecca!" Fletcher ordered, a fire in him rising.

"Don't shout at him!" Odissa shouted back. "He has every right to know what we're talking about. Hell, he already knows everything. You're the one who should listen to *him*."

"So I'm stupid then, is that it?" Dorian asked Odissa. "I can't see it?"

"No, it's that you will see it when you are ready. But until then—until you see it—we can be happy. We are a family now, Dorian. Can't you see it?"

Maud smiled up at Q and Mecca, trying to assure them that this would pass. That Alpha had things under control.

"Fuck you," Dorian said as he moved to the door, Fletcher silently, angrily retreating from Odissa. "Like fuck I can't see what you're doing. We can ALL see what you're doing, Alpha. We're just powerless to fucking stop it."

"Where are you going?" Panic in her voice.

"You're not going to leave, but I am." Dorian said.

She'd not walk out on him. He'd not let her hurt him. That would kill him.

"But you're sick, Dorian! Fletcher will sneeze out if you don't get some—" But the door slammed.

Odissa went to the door, intent on following him out. But Maud caught her hand, held her back. "You know you can't," Maud warned her, gripping her tightly.

Odissa slapped Maud—slapped herself. "Stop it, you *Odys*," Odissa hiss-screamed at Maud. Odissa grabbed her chin, shook it, nails digging in, lips curling. "Too. Fucking. Many. Of us."

Maud noticed Q and Mecca recoil as she was released. *We have startled them*, she thought. Odissa walked over to pick up Madus, whom she had dropped.

When she bent down, she stayed down. Crying. Weeping into her hands.

Perhaps she wasn't so *sorted out* after all.

Maud watched as Mecca and Q darted back to their room—running to hide. They heard the door lock.

Maud's sight only made Odissa cry more. "This wasn't how it was supposed to go. I planned so well up to this point. The gods won't let me do this the way I wanted. I knew Dorian wouldn't be happy, but I didn't think he could fucking leave me." She studied Madus in her hands, her arms resting across her knees. She was saying all this for Mecca's benefit. She knew he could hear. "I didn't think he had the ability."

"He loves you too much to stay and hurt you," Maud suggested, trying to help her Master work it out.

"He hurts me by leaving!"

Maud whispered down to her, "He'd hurt you more by staying and being miserable. You cannot give these two what they want. At least, not right now."

"I knew I should have waited. I should have put it off." *Fucked Maurice another day.* She massaged her temples. "But I read the signs. I read them correctly—it was only that the signs were against me. The gods are cruel."

Maud attempted nodding but was too focused on staring up those stairs. "Maurice would have taken Mecca away with him then. Mecca would have left us. Mecca deserves better than a life with Maurice. There would be no *life* with Maurice." *Only Maurice trying to die all the fucking time.* "Maurice knew that."

"He's up there, making decisions," Odissa said, her eyes trudging up toward the direction of Mecca's door. "He's up there deciding whether or not to run away from us or stay with us—"

And Alpha had been right. Mecca *was* making decisions.

And they were messy ones.

And by that, well, I mean he killed himself.

They heard a soft bang. And splattering. A shock pulsed through the house. Odissa's eyes grew wide as she looked up, up, up the stairs. Maud rushed to them. Madus fell from his Master's hand and formed, helping Odissa to the room. Her legs did not want to go. Didn't want her to face what she had caused.

Maud sank as she entered. Q was there, on the floor. Inanimate. From the distance and her direction from the bed, they could tell she had shot him. Shot him in half. Blood soaking into the bed. His entrails rolling out of him as his eyes closed their final time. He was everywhere, everywhere in the room as if to say, *because there is no place for us here, I am now everywhere.*[206]

"No," Maud mouthed. Her head shook. Her body shook.

"Mecca? MECCA!" Odissa screamed as she rushed over to the bed. She reached out to touch him as he faded away—but paused. To touch him would make it real.

She looked up at her twin Automatons, shaking from the shock. *I killed a child. I killed him. His father left him. Dorian left him. He was afraid to be left with me.*

---

[206] Talk about killing your darlings. Jesus fucking Christ.

"You don't know that—" Madus said, his head darting between his Master to Mecca's body. Odissa tore her red eyes from her Automatons, to look at the body again—to make sure of what she had seen. Verified, something snapped within her. Like a match being lit, a new hatred burned—a hatred for herself and for the god who made her.

The god who made me.

"My god, why did he?"[207] Odissa asked, though the knot in her throat obscured it. She dropped both knees beside the bed, wanting to put the boy back together again. Her eyes filled up with tears. "Why did you do it?" Her hand pushed away blood spatters from his eyes. "Was I that scary?" She kept stroking his head, which grew colder by the second. "I meant for you to grow old. You could have grown old. That was my plan!"

"He didn't know your plan!" Maud shouted at her.

"He knew more than any of them!" She screamed at the body. "Q helped him know." Her eyes moved to the Automaton, on the floor. "She was wise. So wise. She saw things even Admund could not see!"

Madus circled the bed. "Mecca saw things adult eyes could not. He was in between. He knew too."

"Yet he didn't want to be with us." Odissa verged on hyperventilation. "I'm a monster."

"She still is wise," Madus said, walking over to Q, eyes narrowing at the bobby pin. They knew what he implied.

Maud wiped her cheeks, composing herself once more. She didn't have the wits to think it to them, so said it to them instead: "He may have left part of himself in Q. We could find out why he—"

"But Dorian will hate me if I do! He will blame me," Odissa cried up to them. "We can't."

"Would he not regardless?" Madus wondered, his eyes matching his Master's in their tears. Tears on Madus were jarring, for his default features were as stoic as Maud's were naturally alluring.

"What if Mecca killed himself because he—he wants Dorian to hate us?" Maud wondered for them all. Her hushed tone revealed her Master's hesitation to have any part of herself think it.

Odissa held Mecca's face, closed his lifeless eyes. Her voice matching her distant look, "Dorian already hates us as much as he loves us."

---

[207] I think our characters knew the Narrator needed to move this story along.

"But what if Mecca had a reason he did this—other than to escape us?" Maud suggested.

"Not every suicide is part of a bigger plan," Madus reasoned. "Sometimes it's because there is no more happiness left. Just ask Maurice."

"As if it's not to get back at his father?"

Odissa raised a hand to silence them. Not only were their spoken thoughts rattling within her, but so where their unspoken ones. She could hardly sort them all out and mourn at the same time.

"Fine," Odissa finally said. "Touch her."

Madus bent down. As he touched Q, his Master's head fell down into Mecca's chest. Or, what was left of Mecca's chest. Her eyes eventually reopened and she lifted her head, revealing a blood-stained cheek, watered down with more melodramatic tears (have I said "blood" and "tears" enough yet?).

Alpha had not weakened from touching Q. She had weakened from learning Mecca's reasons.

Newly-active, Q had reformed and walked to her new Master, had cupped her messy face in her tiny hands. "Mecca didn't know you were so good."[208]

"You let Vulcan win!" Odissa cried up to her new Automaton—face contorting into a red smudge. She held on to new arms tight, as if to never let her go. *He wants His plot to start and you gave in. You just quit on this—on us.*

"No matter if you control when the game starts, He will get His way. The game will always start. Mecca knew he had to die for your cause—willingly or not. He was bored with this game. Wanted to reset. Reboot. He wanted to be wanted."

"I WANTED HIM! He didn't have to die for me," Odissa gasped, as if throwing her fit would make it reverse. "He could have died for himself. He could have grown old." Her head fell as she kept repeating, "He could have grown old."

Q shook her head. "You think you get to decide when the game starts. And that's partially true. But you wanted Mecca and Dorian to decide for you. Well, really you wanted *Mecca* to because of course he would outlive Dorian through sheer biology alone. His body was younger despite his age. Mecca could have lived for a very long time. Even longer than your own body with an Automaton. This is why Mecca knew he had to go. Sooner her later he would *have* to go. You cannot have children, Odissa. We all know this is Alpha's last chance. Vulcan caused this on purpose—so that you would cause the others to leave. That is His message telling you the

---

[208] "Good" really is no objective adjective when called that by yourself, you know.

game must start in this timeframe. If you don't, things will get ugly—whether you want them to or not. And Mecca didn't want to see you have to play dirty. You're playing so clean, as it is."

"We are the built-in cleaning system. The anti-virus protection. The system backup. He knew we couldn't fight it forever."

"You could have grown old," Odissa whispered, hugging Q in the middle. "I planned for it all. Eternity until you were ready to go. This wasn't what I wanted. What have I done? Oh, gods, what have I done? This wasn't supposed to happen. I had a plan."

"You never had a plan because you could not plan for this, Alpha," Q said, stroking her Master's hair. "Your plan was to plan for anything the gods threw at you. Not what the Masters threw. Otherwise, you planned well. That's why you split yourself in two and became twins, to increase your chances of living. That's why you suppressed yourself in Odissa and her ancestors. But you didn't plan on liking the Masters so much. No one could plan for that."

"Vulcan could have," Maud said. "He did."

"He means for me to suffer," Odissa said into Q. "He has a deadline He wants me to meet. This is the true punishment."

"Mecca guessed you didn't necessarily like your role in the game. But you must do your duty. Mecca knew he also had no choice. He had no reason to stay and every reason to leave."[209]

"But Dorian's still alive," Odissa reasoned—the wheels in her head turning again—calculations and computations ticking out results. "Vulcan may not care *that much*. We still decide when the game starts."

She smiled up at them, then quickly stopped. Seeing herself smile through their eyes scared her. Was she really happy?

She stood up, looking about her. She would have to change her clothes.

Though she didn't have to say her commands aloud, speaking them helped sweep up her thoughts: "Go through his bags. Take his tech. I'm going to go clean up." Odissa was just about to leave the room but paused, looking at Mecca one last time. "And give these people more gold."

She walked down the stairs, rubbing tears back into her eyes—rubbing the multitude of voices back into her brain.

Stanza: Pay to play.

Odissa waited for Dorian at the vacant house for ages. She waited for him to return.

But he did not.

---

[209] I can't tell if this is a genius way of killing off a character or a lazy one. Maybe both.

She decided to leave at night.

"He will come back to us when he's ready," Madus assured themselves.

Then, with her bags—Dorian's bags—Mecca's bags—and the untouched Automatons, she helped load up their newly-stolen car (that Madus had found a few blocks away). Just before they left, Odissa observed the golden-detailed kitchen. A remodel only Trump would love.

"The cops won't know what to make of it," Maud said behind her.

"We don't care what the cops make of it," her Master answered. "We care that it's a distraction. That it will confound the owners of this house. Maybe keep them from telling the story of what they find, because there is no story. No explanation."

They drove for a while, then switched cars before ending up at a very low-key hotel.

Stanza: Gambling is a gamble.

That following Sunday, after the couple had come home (how many days did I say they were to be gone? Doesn't matter. Just know, it's been a bit) and Mecca's crime-scene had made them vacate their home (once again) while police investigated, Odissa waited in a car, all by herself, reading the news on one of Mecca's many phones.

It was then a popup alerted her that one of Dorian's credit cards had been used. "Bless you, Mecca," Odissa said to the screen. And she passed it to Q, suddenly sitting beside her. *He wants to be found.*

Stanza: A few weeks later.

Mr. and Mrs. Who-the-hell-cares were finally able to go back home, though they had decided against using the master bedroom ever again. In fact, they had already started packing boxes to move. "I heard the house still smells like the dead body. They can't get it out," the neighbors would whisper to each other. "So sad, too, because this was the house they wanted to raise a family in. Did you see the kitchen, too? I think they're going to remodel the place too. It's all torn up."

The doorbell rang.

Mrs. opened the door to find Fletcher.

She looked stressed, her hair pushed back behind a sweatband. Through a half-open door, "Can I help you?"

"Is your husband home?"

What is this, the 50s? Dorian thought at him.

Fletcher saw the boxes and the lack of furniture.

When Mr. had happened to pass through the hall, Fletcher put on a sad smile. "I heard about the boy."

Their shoulders tensed. They had suspected he was here for that. So many reporters and curious neighbors and investigators.

"Did you know him?" Mr. Husband asked.

"Yes."

Mrs. Wife said, "I'll call." Call the police, she meant. Not because she was afraid, but because why wouldn't someone want to identify the body? Or, what was left of a body. The cops could help with that.

"That won't be necessary," Fletcher called after her, stepping forward (but not in). "I'm asking about the box, and the objects around the box. The box of tissues. Did you touch any of them?"

"What are you talking about?"

"Honey, go call," Mr. Husband said to Mrs. Wife as he took over the threshold.

"I told you that won't be necessary," Fletcher said, raising his hand. They hadn't seen his gun before. He stepped in quickly and closed the door, keeping the gun pointed. "Maybe afterwards, when I'm gone, you can call the police. Once your phone line is fixed, because I had to cut it. I apologize but I couldn't risk it. Now, about my box. It was a box of tissues, on the table. I really need it. Did you see it?"

"Put the gun down, son, and let's talk this through."

Fletcher rolled his eyes. "I'm not going to shoot you. I just need you to take me seriously. Was there a box of tissues on your kitchen table when you got home?"

"We don't know anything about it." Mrs. Wife covered by her husband. "There were too many cops everywhere. There may have been. They may have taken it as evidence."

"None of you became ill? No cops became ill? What happened to the objects on the table— the screw, the safety pen, the bent nail?"

They looked at him like he wasn't speaking English—a good sign.

"Did you even notice anything on your kitchen table?"

"Like she said, the cops took the evidence," Mr. Husband said. "But the fucking dead kid in our bed was a bit more distracting."

"Honey—" the wife warned him. *Not when there's a gun in your face.*

"This wouldn't have been evidence," Fletcher enforced. He looked around for the golden coffee table. It wasn't there. "Did they also take your golden coffee table? Or did you claim to already have owned that?"

They swallowed.

"Don't worry. I don't want your coffee table. It was a gift. You can sell it to whomever you want. Now, my last question. Did the criminals leave anything *besides* the dead boy?"

"Yeah, a fucking mess!" Mr. Husband shouted.

"And some toiletries," Mrs. Wife tried to cooperate for the both of them.

What about my Chi flat iron? Dorian thought. Fletcher helped him stifle it. "No bags?"

"I saw no bags."

"Thank you."

He turned to go, but paused. "I want to assure you that you will be left alone in the future. This was nothing personal. And they will never identify the body or the people with him that night. Though it might sound strange or impossible, given the evidence...but he *did* kill himself."

They didn't know how to interpret his lowered voice as he left. The wife watched him walk down the street and turn the corner as the husband called the cops. But they would never find a redheaded man. Not when he fell into some shrubbery as a paperclip and Dorian picked him up.

"This was so unnecessary. We knew she wouldn't leave them."

"Who would have thought she'd have left his body, though? I'll never forgive her for that."[210]

Stanza: Hunting sport.

Odissa had camped at the hotel for quite some time. She had used one of Mecca's old credit cards to get the room, had Madus check in. When she heard the knock at the door, she had not foreseen it.

"Where is your Master, Fletcher?"

Fletcher pushed past her. "He may or may not come up." He pointed downstairs in the direction of the parking lot.

"I thought you'd track our phones here," she said. "I just didn't know you'd take your time doing so. It's been months, Dori."

"Yeah, well, you had all the best tech and credit cards. It's harder to start from square one." His eyes scanned the room. Her own Automatons were nowhere to be seen. And neither were the inanimate ones. "Where are they?" Fletcher asked.

---

[210] There probably would never be a gravesite to even visit, as bodies have to be held in cold storage until identification efforts are exhausted and then the state can cremate, I believe.

Fletcher had already spotted the box on the courtesy table—the tissue box alone sat atop it, as if upon an altar.

"In the bag, in my purse." She pointed. Fletcher went for them, carefully. He swiftly put on his Master's gloves.

"How can I be sure you didn't touch them?"

"Maybe you shouldn't have left them with me, if you didn't trust me," she replied over his shoulder. Well, really *near* his shoulder, for no one stood as tall as Fletcher.

Fletcher, bending down, moved the Automatons around in the bag, counting them. "Where's Q?"

"As if you don't know," Odissa said, stepping back.

"How'd you convince him, then?" Fletcher asked, like some criminal investigator.

"It was his decision."

"That's not what I asked!" he shouted, making her jump. It was such a raw reaction he felt almost sorry.

Odissa was crying now. "I didn't want him to do it. I only touched Q to know why he did it. You left and it was like the end of the world for both of us. He thought it was pointless to drag out the inevitable." She wiped her nose on her sleeve, trembling and shaking more fluid out. "He could have grown old. I would have let him. He could have grown old."

That had become her mantra during guilt-ridden nights.

"How can I trust you haven't touched these, Alpha?"

"Touch them yourself and see!" She gestured to the bag in Fletcher's hand. "Who's stopping you? They're yours to choose. Someone has to have them. They're not safe, in this state. Take the burden or give them to me. But don't claim I've gone behind your back!" She was in Fletcher's face now, glaring through him as if she could see Dorian in those black eyes. "Come to me, please," she begged him. "Are you really here?" she put a hand on Fletcher's cheek. "I miss you so much. I'm so alone now."

Fletcher tried to pull away from her but he found his Master didn't have the will.

"You need me, Dorian. Fletcher looks ill. You should not go against your nature. The gods want you with me, darling. I miss you so much."

He looked down at her for a long while. "Please don't have touched them."

She snatched the bag from his hands. "And what if I have? What the fuck would you do, Dorian? Kill me?"

Fletcher snatched the bag back, matching her dramatics. "Get your things. You're coming to Dorian's room. It's bigger. And has a better view."

Her eyes lit up at the first glimpse of forgiveness. "I knew he wasn't in the parking lot."

She dug in her pockets for her Automatons and they gathered up her bags. They followed Fletcher up the stairs and down a hall. Room A.

Fletcher opened the door and let all parts of Odissa in. He flipped on the lights. Dorian had been sitting on the edge of the bed. In total darkness. It made no difference to him.

He clearly hadn't shaved in all this time. Or done his hair. He would have looked homeless had he not been in designer clothes. Hobo-chic.

Instead of acknowledging her presence, he reached out for the bag in Fletcher's hand. He opened the Ziploc bag at once and poured the Automatons on the bed.

He frowned over them for some time. He took off his shirt.

Odissa said nothing.

But her Automaton, Madus, did. "Aren't you afraid you will die, if you touch them all at once?"

Fletcher turned to Odissa, face colder than stone. "Then he will die knowing Odissa was true to him."

Dorian bent down beside the bed and placed himself across the Automatons—all at once. Fletcher fell to the ground, his Master blacking out.

"You suicidal fuck!" Odissa rushed to him, felt him still breathing, checked his pulse as he vomited and frothed. "Bring me Fletcher!" she reached out as Maud retrieved him, put him on his Master's back. The paperclip was cold to her touch while the other objects glowed too hot too fast. She whispered words only Alpha knew. She had forgotten she knew them. She kissed his neck, stroked his black hair, wept over all of Dorian and his many parts. "I told you I hadn't touched them."

When he finally woke up, he felt that he was stretched out on the bed. He could smell himself—a stench like vomit and sweat. When he stirred, he heard Odissa's voice. But he saw nothing. "What did you say?" he said.

"What?" Odissa asked him, exited he was awake.

"You were saying something. Over me. Magic. Alchemy."

Odissa did not reply.

"What happened?" *I should have died.*

"You were out for a week." It was Odissa's voice, coming toward him. "We couldn't give you a bath because the Automatons needed to be on you.[211] I cleaned you as best as I could. I slept in the chair." She pointed to the pile of baby wipes, the chair. "Don't touch your IV."

His hands felt around the bed. "Where are they, then?"

"Here," she said, moving his hands to the pillow beside him. "When they shrunk back I knew you'd wake up soon. Even your dreams were as crowded as your bed, Dorian."

He could smell cigarette smoke. She had been smoking. "Fletcher, I need Fletcher."

"He's in there, Dorian." She picked him out for him.

He licked his dry lips. "Yes. I know," he said, his head settling back down on the pillow. Fletcher was synonymous with "his Automatons" now. Perhaps this was because Fletcher was really the only one Dorian wanted. The others were superfluous phantom limbs that he would never want to use.

"Are you hungry? You want a bath?"

"Yes. But I don't think we can make Fletcher form. We're too weak. You must help me."

He started to get up. "Don't forget them," she reminded him. She put them in both of his hands, divided evenly—as if they were magic pills.

If he had had the energy to see her face, he would have noticed the worried look—worried that his nouns were off—pronoun and otherwise. Dorian was having a hard time being more than two.

He felt multiple hands upon him. Odissa's Automata helped him step into the tub.

When he made it to the bathroom, she began to help him undress. She helped him into the tub. Began to wash him.

"You didn't touch them," he said to her as she cleaned him.

"I told you I didn't."

"And now I have so many. Inside my head." He rubbed his head with his fist like a paw, a fist tight around his Automata.

"You will get used to it. It would have been better if you didn't touch them all at once. Easier."

He sank lower into the tub. Turned his head toward her. The first effort he had made on his part. "I have so many conflicting views of you. In here. So many opinions."

"But do you still love me?" She pushed back his hair, made his Adam's apple pop.

---

[211] Is it bad that I picture a giant, lethargic orgy?

"Leeland had so much faith in you," he said. "He believed you were the key to helping him end it all. That's why he saved you as a baby. In some ways you were the key. He didn't know how you had strung him along, made him believe it was your doing—all these changes in Mother and Pepin." He laughed at the irony. Then his face grew cold. "I can see him fucking you. Admund remembers it."

"That was Odissa. I'm more now."

"I also remember how you used to cringe when Leeland kissed you. That gives me some comfort."

"And what do the other Automatons [make you] think of me?"

"They make me wonder how you could love me."

"I have never loved anyone like you. I've only ever loved myself."

"You didn't love me until the gods changed me and made me devoted to you. That's what you love. Like I worshiped Dory. You missed that. What if I am really a means to punish you? To punish you with my jealous misery?"

She leaned over the tub and put her head to his. "Dorian, you are no punishment. You are my gift. My reward. For being good all these centuries. Don't you see?"

He brought his fists to his eyes. "You could have anyone. Why choose me? It seems too easy. Too contrived."

"That's your curse saying that. I picked you. Because I know what it is to love many. I *have* loved many. And I miss them. I am like you. I am old. I am nostalgic. And I have missed you. Your sister has missed you. And for once in my life—lives—I'm looking back. Not forward."

He began to weep.

She shushed him. He grabbed her arm, pulling her closer, dropping his Automatons in the tub in the process.

The next thing he knew he was back in bed.

And he could see.

Well, his Automatons could see. For him.

He had never seen so well. So many dimensions. So ubiquitous.

His brow furrowed as his inner sight tried to focus. He moaned, feeling ill from all the images overlapping his mind. Odissa sat up, closer to him, and looked down. He had color to his skin again. She stroked his beard. "You would be dead if it wasn't for me."

"That was the idea."

"No it wasn't. You wouldn't hurt me like that."

He grabbed her hand and held it, kissed it. That was all the energy he could spare, for his body then laxed and it was all he could do to keep breathing.

…

Odissa curled up beside him, put her head on his chest. "You shouldn't try to fight to keep them down," she said about his Automata. She reached out and touched Caffar. His body tensed as she did so. "It is making it harder on you."

"There are too many of them. Where will you sleep?"

"I've been sleeping just fine, among them."

"They feel too much. It overwhelms me."

"You seem to enjoy it in your sleep."

His face scrunched up, trying to remember what she meant. Ah, yes, he remembered. Her own Automatons were scattered throughout the bed—they tended to prop themselves up on the bed and merely rest a hand here or there on some part of their Master. But Dorian seemed to remember having one of his bodies touched—he was having trouble remembering which one—touched by a body not his own. Did Odissa even know which of hers had humped his in her sleep? "Were you even asleep when you did that to me?"

"I didn't rape you, if that's what you mean," she laughed at him. "And yes, parts of me were asleep."

She was quiet when he did not laugh back.

"I'm surprised I could even consider it. So much energy."

"You are better than you realize, Dori." She took his arm and wrapped it around her. "You fight it."

And they laid like that for some time—until Dorian's breath slowed and he was back asleep and she watched his Automata pop back up to life, one by one, their eyes closed tight in slumber. She held down a gasp when Dorian rolled over—closer to her, to spoon her. Because, as he did so, his Automata rolled near her too; she the north to all their compasses, their devoted magnetism crushing her.

Stanza: Godheads and god head.

Dorian was now sitting up in bed. He was eating. Odissa was eating. The Automatons—hers and his—were in the floor, watching TV, reading on their phones, taking naps, looking out the window. Picture what you want of the overcrowded room—an overcrowded room that felt so empty despite its tightness.

"Do you think you will be able to walk soon?" She asked him as she stuck a fork in a sticky bite of pancake.

Dorian took his time in answering. Took a drink of orange juice to bide his time. "Where will I walk, Odissa?" What was her rush?

She shrugged and chewed. "To the car?" The Automatons could carry him out but that would look awkward. She could have them go out and buy a wheelchair...

He took another drink. "And go where?"

She stared at him, picking her teeth with her tongue. Did he not remember their conversation the day Rosemund died? How they had daydreamed together? What of all their plans?

She noticed Admund looking over at them, to help Dorian find his food. She hid the frown on her lips and began to eat again. "We could go to your storage units. Get one of your cars so we could stop stealing. Then we could look up a few more dead babies, their socials, and start a few more credit cards so we can be set for a few more months."

"We're set for a few more years, Odissa. No need."

"What does that mean?"

He took another sip of OJ. "It means, Odissa, that I have been bored before, like now, and so bided my time by insuring I would never have to want anything again."

"So I am boring?"

He snorted. "There is never a dull moment with you." He began to drink again but she knocked it out of his hand, making what was left splash the wall.

All his Automata turned their heads. Maud, Madus, and Q just kept watching TV.

"People die, all the time, Dorian. They just died sooner than you would like. Sooner than *I* would have liked. But Vulcan wanted it that way. You know He did. Made it that way. So stop fucking moping about and—"

But she didn't finish her sentence, because he kissed her. He grabbed her behind the neck and kissed her. "I'm sorry," he said past the wetness in his throat. "I'm sorry."

She tugged away from him. "There is so much of you. You're practically a demigod now. It's bound to be a little boring, Dorian."

"Demigod, is it?" he said up to her, letting her head go.

"Having one Automaton makes you god-like. Having as many as you do makes you a demigod."

"What is Alpha, then, with so many Automata? An actual goddess?"

Odissa did not answer. "Where are these credit cards, if you have so many of them?"

"Throughout. We can go and get more, if you are worried."

"I am not worried," she said, putting her plate aside. *I am just bored.* She noticed he had stopped eating and took his plate as well.

He tried to smile. "Please forgive me, Odissa." He looked like a cancer patient begging his nurse for more pain meds. "Please."

"For leaving me?"

"I came back, didn't I?"

She looked over at his naked Automata. They were all looking at her. She turned back to the Master. "You can't stand me being mad at you, can you?"

"Makes my nose feel like it might bleed "

"And did your nose bleed when you left me?" When he did not answer, she reached over to his lap. "Did it?" She ran her hand up his thigh and cupped him between the legs. His body sighed at her unexpected touch—melted into her unwillingly.

"What are you doing?" He gently grabbed her wrist, as if now was not the time.

But she simply used her other hand, which he quickly grabbed as well. His Automata noticed her own stand up, but they were too lethargic to act intimidating in return.

"You used to love it when I touched you," she said over him.

"Comfort me. Don't force yourself on me. I'm not in the mood."

"Your reaction says otherwise," she glanced at his dick.

"I don't have the energy."

"I do all the work anyway," she laughed through her nose.

But he didn't laugh. He simply gave the obligatory smile.

They were silent for a moment, waiting for Dorian to formulate words. It was his turn to speak. She could tell he wanted to say something as he squeezed her wrists. To fill the void. "I am not a man anymore, Odissa."

She cocked an eyebrow. "Are you identifying as female now or....?" She had wondered how the new Automata might tip the scale.

"No, I am legion." He put his head back. "And the only thing I know we all want is you. But we don't know what that means. Or if it is right. We disgust ourselves for loving you."

She pulled her hands away from him and readjusted her position on the bed. Waited before she asked, "Did you ever think about getting gender confirmation, Dorian?"

His lips pursed. *Why are we talking about this?* "Of course I *thought* about it."

"But you didn't get one."

"Because, for one, Fletcher would have had to give it to me."

"That or another Master, and you didn't trust them. Or didn't want them to be the ones to do it?"

"Are you offering or something?" *Am I that dull to you?*

"No. Just trying to understand you."

"Let me be perfectly clear—*transparent,* even. I 'transcend' gender, but I don't mind how I was born. I'm not this or that and I'm not half and half. I'm a quarter." He paused, hearing the change pun and following it. "And I like how I've been *changed.*"

Demiguy may be the word he's looking for, though I'll not try to label him.[212]

"But you keep changing," she said, leaning into his face. She heard the pun too and wanted more—more of them and his cleverness. But all she could see when she looked at him was a little boy digging through empty pockets.

His Automatons looked up and he finally saw what she was doing—saw her expression. "I frustrate you?" he said up to her. "I've never seen you frustrated." Sexually, anyway.

She glared at the Automatons on the floor and slithered to the edge of the bed. "You tell me to kiss you and then you don't want me to touch you. I don't know what to do."

"Let me figure out who I am. It's not as easy for me as it is for you. You have control over your body even when you touch one," he pointed to the Automata sitting on the floor like a bunch of kindergarteners waiting for naptime.

"I grow impatient. Your body is well enough for decisions yet your mental state holds you back. The Automatons are turning you against me."

"You are not impatient. You are patience personified. I've never known someone who laid in waiting longer than Alpha has."

"Every second you spend keeping me at a distance is one less moment we spend together. Do you hear me?" She wanted to shake him. "We both have limited time. I've never felt such pressure. Never."

"Good. I'm glad you feel pressure, then. You seem to work better under constraints. Keeps you creative."

"What are you saying?" she said, turning back around on the bed. Her eyes were red—with anger or sadness I do not know. For Alpha, at that moment, they were more than likely the same.

---

[212] Despite the fact you've been calling Dorian he/him this entire series?

"I'm saying that the more freedom someone has, the less interesting their lives become. Especially you. You, who were once a terror for all mankind. You wanted to kill everything. Nothing would be left with such power. We stripped you down and now look at you. Interesting as fuck."

Her face hardened. "You are one restraint I fear I cannot make interesting, Dorian."

His Automata stopped looking at her—as if they couldn't bare it. "I am sorry," he mouthed. "They all remember parts of the past. It's like one big screen shot—panoramic view. I can see all the things I missed. And all those things that could have been better, if I'd only had all these sets of eyes. Things could have been so different."

"You think I don't think the same things? You think I wanted Mecca to die? Rosemund? Gwen? I drove the poor boy to it! None of us saw the signs."

He massaged his temples. "They'll drive me insane, Odissa. I can't ignore so many of them."

"You'll learn how to make them welcomed company."

"It's not that they're unwelcome. I am glad to know these things. I am only disturbed that I have all this knowledge and it does me no good. I can't even change the present with it. I have no power. So much but none."

She shook her head. "It's not that you have no power. It's that you have no joy in it. A truly godlike thought, perhaps."

"Godlike? I feel more helpless. More mortal than when I was."

"Like you said, Dori. Constraints." *You were more interesting when mortal.*

"What a terrible thing to say."

"Then why did you say it to *me?*"

"Because it was true," he whispered. "We're all more poignant when limited."

A commercial played in the background, filling their silence awkwardly with toothpaste and jingles.

Odissa spoke over it, "One day, when you are well, I will ask you to hand me all your Automata. And I will put them under a pillow. And you won't be able to see. And then I will sit in a chair, as you sit on the bed, and I will send Madus over to you. And he will turn you over and I will fuck you through him."

Dorian stroked his beard, trying to play along. "Why Madus? Even Q or Maud could do such a thing."

"Because Q is where I keep what's left of Mecca and Mecca does not want to fuck you. And Maud is where I keep what's left of Odys and Odys wants to kill you."

"A part of you wants to kill me. That *is* interesting."

"Of course. I am Alpha, after all. I wanted to kill everything."[213]/[214]

She thought that would have brought the mood down, but Dorian went on exploring her thought. "And will you touch yourself as you also fuck me?"

"No. I don't find it easy to masturbate. You know that. I would rather focus on fucking you."

"That wouldn't do," he shook his head, throwing out her vision. "Not when I have a perfectly bare penis available to be inside you." He gestured to his genitals.

Odissa sighed and turned to stare at the wall.

Dorian asked her, "Are you feeling particularly horny right now or was that a test?"

Her face cracked at his question, as if to say it was neither. "Do you know what else we could do, Dorian? What else I plan on doing? I take one of your Automatons and one of mine and we just watch them. They'll do the fucking for us. Slavoj Žižek style. Synthetic experience. So we can stop with trying to have it all. We can push past identities and labels. We can just be ourselves. They'll be our ideal selves over there. We don't have to. We're just us."

"Sounds like just thinking about the sex toys doing the work is satisfying enough," Fletcher said from his portion of the wall. His long legs crossed at the thought, covering up his genitals (Dorian's Automatons were all still very iffy on the clothes). He was the only Automaton of Dorian's that ever spoke. But it was no longer his voice—his tone and pitch had shifted as if speaking for all of them at once. "Now you never have to have sex again."

"Sex is out of the way then. Like death. We can be who we truly are then. Our rawest selves."

"That's the thing, Odissa. This is the price we pay for it all. Who are we now? How do we decide?"

"We let the Automata decide for us." Though the answer was simple, she knew Dorian would never adjust to Automata he did not want—he would never find himself in them. Not when they were a reminder of every prelapsarian thing he had lost to gain them.

There would be no new start as she had hoped. They were still the same people, just haunted by different ghosts.

"Tell me this, Dorian," Odissa said as she stood up. "Will we ever be happy again?"

---

[213] I asked our Narrator why that was (why Alpha wanted "to kill everything"), and B.L.A. replied, "'Everything' is hyperbole, though Alpha did snap and interpret her original 'purpose' to an extreme." Sounds like Marvel's Ultron or something.
[214] Side thought: Alpha and vegetarianism—leads me to think Alpha may be vegetarian because she's making up for past sins. Not sure if that's a theme worth exploring. May delete this footnote.

"I don't care about being happy. I care about pleasing you." He paused. "That's the only thing I think I could ever care about in a life like this."

"I don't think I could be happy knowing you are unhappy."

"The world is infinite for us. Who is to say I won't grow to be happy?"

But Odissa, like Hegel, could see the future in the present. She saw this in the form of the past. This Oscar Wilde couldn't escape his fate.

"Can I give you another bath, Dori?" She said, walking over to his side of the bed.

"I suppose I do smell."

Her Automata helped him up and carried him into the tub. His naked Automata sat in the floor, their eyes watching them as they moved.

He sank into the water as if it were a hot tub. But Odissa never came to wash him. Instead, her Automata stood over him and waited for the water to rise before pushing him under. He struggled a little—more from the surprise. He struggled until Odissa turned to his Automata in the room, their eyes wide with fear.

"I can't live like this. Neither can you," she said to them as they fought to stand up—as they struggled to understand just what was happening. "I love you so much," she said to them. "I'm sorry I did this to you. I'm sorry I prayed for you. I—I was so lonely. With myself. The gods gave me what I wanted. I got what I asked for. They're teaching me a lesson. This isn't fair to you."

She knew she was doing the right thing when they didn't come closer to save their Master. "I shouldn't have saved you when you touched them all. I shouldn't have held onto you."

"It's OK," Fletcher said to her, right before he fell. He said it like Dido atop her pyre—knowing this Aeneas had destiny beyond them. "I didn't want to leave you either. I don't. But I should."

They shrank in glitches into their forms.

Her Automatons dragged Dorian's soaked body out of the tub, placed him on the carpet. Odissa shook her head, *no, no, no*. Regret crawled out of her. "Why did I—?" She knelt over him. Breathed into his mouth. Pressed his chest. Breathed into his mouth again.

He never spit up the water. Only a fraction trickled out.

"He's gone," Maud said for her as she began to try again. "You can't bring him back this time. He doesn't want to come back. You must stop. Nothing good can come from bringing him back. The gods programmed this."

Madus knelt beside her, his coppery hand resting on her shoulder. "You cut his thread straight through this time. The gods won't give him back."

But Odissa just shook her head. *No, no, no.* She pushed back his wet hair. "The gods took him from me long before." *No, no, no.*

Odissa did not weep for him as she had done for Mecca. Instead, she stared at his body, shaking her head, rocking over him. She addressed the gods—the gods she knew were watching—"You will pay for what You made me do. This gift was tainted when You gave it to me. For sure, I will do as You designed me to do," she stroked the lips that were once Dorian's. "But I will always hate You for it."

"Of all mortal men, he was most interesting, wasn't he?" Madus thought for them, as if Dorian was a painting whose artist were now dead—fixed and immortalized. "He saw us. He understood without explanation what we were. Masters and Automata and us."

Odissa looked about the room, at all of the inanimates. She leapt over his body to grab at them. One by one she gathered the Automata and brought them to her lips. She buried her face in them. "Are we not one now?" she said to them as they became her. "Are we not alone together now?"

The hotel would discover Dorian's body two days later—with two pennies over his eyes. But don't worry. They were *just* pennies.[215]

Stanza: Monopoly pieces.

Monday, Tuesday, Wednesday, Thursday now have passed. At least, I think they have. It sure feels like a Friday. Nevertheless, time has passed. And during that time, Alpha had been doing some planning.

Odissa had to stop by the vet for a few *items* before arriving at the recently-closed (or abandoned—I like that word better), *abandoned* mental hospital.

An abandoned mental *asylum.*

Even better![216]

An abandoned mental asylum now used as a storage unit until the rest of the supplies and utilities were needed in the new location. In reality, most of said supplies and utilities were never going to be needed for the new location. They were slightly out of date—but nothing so creepy and rustic as what you see in horror films. They tend to be sensationalized, those films, and

---

[215] Wait, so we're NOT gonna talk about what just happened here?
[216] Why am I even here if the Narrator is just going to edit without me?

remind you of lobotomies and women plagued with falsely-diagnosed hysterics. That's not really the vibe I'm shooting for here. Simply a clean place, well-stocked with stretchers and space.

She had pushed out most of the equipment into the hall. She placed the Automatons in her sulfuric circle like a pentagram with too many points around her selected "patient" chair. Thus began her summoning ritual.

Her back toward us, we see her setting up a supply table—pulling out contents from a large bag and arranging them to suit her needs. The box of tissues is there, as if upon an altar. She lights the candles and walks away from it, and I shift my gears back into the past tense.

Odissa set up the drip, strapped her legs down in the chair, and, when situated, inserted the needle into the vein. Using her teeth, she tightened the straps on her doctored arm.

It was the farthest arm, the one opposite the needled, that she worried about getting loose. She wanted to stop herself from pulling that needle out.

The strap across her middle would keep her from flailing about too much—if she even would. She probably wouldn't. She has more self-control than that average human. She had *patience*, as Dorian would have put it.

But part of her was unsure. She no longer knew herself as well as she would have liked. Centuries of suppression can do that to a being—never getting to be yourself. Perhaps she would pull the needle out after all.

As she leaned back, she could already feel her body turning as cold as the cold, cold room.

She tried to remain calm.

She watched the drip.

It was so slow.

But

It

Did

End.

Her legs twitched only a little when her (mostly human) heart stopped pumping.

One, two, three, four, five, six, seven, eight, nine...

Each Automaton rose from the floor, fully formed, fully naked, and fully confused.

They looked at each other, astonished.

Self-aware for the first time.

They had consciousness.

A self-awareness dependent on no other's.

They had souls.

Or, the equivalent of, depending on your opinion.

Admund was the first to stand up—stand up on his own free will. He looked down at his body, his toes, his hands, his dick. A most basic humanoid form—a form he had trouble changing. So this was him. In his simplest.

Panicking—realizing what had happened—he studied them all—his brothers and sisters—just to be sure. "I—I am." The words choked out of him, recognizing his voice and that it was his. His hands touched in reassurance, wringing.

"Me too," Q stated softly, tears coming to her eyes as she looked at her hands. She felt her arms and felt what it was like to feel without someone else there.

"But who am I now?" Anselm asked.

"You," Madus said, spitting out a laugh. His thin-lipped mouth stayed open with a shocked smile. He pressed himself against the wall as if hyperaware he was apart from all of them and had no intention of returning.

Coraza said, "If we are, then that means—" She found herself taking a step. For a moment, there, she recognized she had *willed* herself to move. It was a scary feeling, to be on your own. It made her debate her every action. She had so many choices and options and...

Maud, speaking for the first (so many firsts!) time on her own accord, "She was good all along."

"Didn't we know that?" Q asked. "I'm sure we knew it. We were her."

"We were her," Coraza said, holding her flat stomach as if to comfort the conflicting empty and full feelings within. "But no one is objective about themselves."

"Now we're apart and know for sure," Madus countered, finally parting with his wall.

Q rushed to Odissa, tears in her eyes (why was she crying? Was this a time to be sad? What kind of tears were these? Did they fit her character? What was her character?). She pulled out the needle and, with shaking hands, touched Odissa's body. Turning to Admund, her long hair parting like curtains, "We have to revive her." She rushed to the table—the table Odissa had arranged. "Revive her, Admund! You know how."

"I don't think it wise," he shouted as if the room were noisy. And maybe it was. Their bodies were ringing with life.

That which could give freedom could also take it away. Admund was yet to enjoy his freedom. He'd not jeopardize it with bringing Alpha back.

Q began to panic, observing the table. "If you won't then I will. Tell me how!"

"She is dead, child," he said, taking one step toward her, arm outstretched. "Do not go against her wishes. What if she wakes up and we revert back to our soul-less states? Her soul is *split* into us. Her freedom's now ours. We have her scul. It is broken up in pieces."

The littlest amount of freedom can go a long way.

"No. Look—these shots!" She began to prepare them. "Maurice died once and came back. So can she."

Admund eyed the utensils suspiciously, so conveniently placed. He almost remembered Odissa placing them there. Had she made them all forget? Did she not want her plea for help to seem too obvious? He didn't like how these tiny shots—possibly capable of reviving her— undermined her martyrdom.

Q, though she thought the same thing, refused to believe it undermined anything. Though Alpha's strange, Vulcanized soul had set them free in a way only hers could, it wasn't demanding help. There was still a choice. Q would make her first one.

Stabbing the adrenalin needle into Odissa's heart, she waited. "Give me the Words," she said when it did nothing. She prepared the next shot, one for Odissa's arm. "Give me some Words of Alchemy, Admund! I know Vulcan told you the secrets!"

"He told me secrets but not all of them. He knew better by my time. Even more by yours."

"Give her the Words, Admund!" Madus demanded—his face never more expressive.

When Admund offered nothing, Q looked around at the others. There were no Words or even words for this.

"Father's own image and just like last time too!" Madus spat at him.

"I need a defibrillator!" Q went on.

"Don't be daft, girl," Fletcher said, coming up to the stretcher-chair. "Your fucking hands!"

Just as Q understood, Fletcher was already warming himself up for the job. He studied his hands—was he strong enough? Could he do it now? He gave Odissa a jolt.

The first time, nothing.

Perhaps he wasn't charged enough. "Do it with me," he looked at Q, at Madus.

Nothing.

Cestus came up to her feet.

Again. Again. Again.

They sent bolts through her.

"Give us the Words, Admund!" Madus demanded between his own guesses at *the Words*. His body was humming and singing with Alchemy. Some of his Words got odd twitches in

577

Alpha's limbs—odd flickering in the lights as if she were Frankenstein's monster draining the electricity. But it didn't start her heart.

Admund's lip almost snarled—in fear or pride, it didn't matter. He whispered something—something that wouldn't make sense on the lips of a human, for a human could not get the right pitch. They are no living tuning fork.

A wind rushed through the room when he said it.

Q repeated it—over and over—and her eyes thanked him.

His jaw clenched. He couldn't let the others take all the credit for helping Q.

Saying it with force, Q put her hands down again. And this time—this time—Odissa's eyes shot open—glowing with the same metallic aura as her skin. They burned through the cold room and through them all.

They stepped back as she gasped like a fish out of water. They watched in amazement when her body convulsed and a glimmer spread over her—a flashing glaze that disappeared as quickly as it came. Her eyes rolled and came back down—normal once more. But there was something now inorganic about those dark eyes.

She blinked to focus, but found she could not. She closed her eyes and stopped moving. She didn't even breathe.

"No!" Q shouted, taking Odissa's face in her hands. But she quickly released her cheeks, for they were too hot to touch. Q's hands burned from the heat even after letting go, melting her skin.

"Is she dead?" Coraza asked, as if death were possible to measure in a case like this.

"No," Admund said. Something in his voice sounded disappointed.

"I died," the body said, making them all jump. "But only a little." Her voice cracked. "I gave you all my soul. But I kept a corner. It almost died along with Odissa's soul. I'm no zombie—no Maurice. I still have a part that holds on. Even after the body goes." She finally reopened her eyes and lifted her head—the equivalent of sitting up while being strapped down.

She held up a hand when Maud tried to help her. *Don't touch me yet.*

It was a wonder the plastic hospital chair beneath her didn't melt. They quickly realized her burning flesh had more to do with her body reacting to theirs.

"That portion would have died if you had waited much longer. To be trapped inside something dead!" She shouted at them like one would the elderly. "Now I know how you all felt when Masterless."

She laughed under her hair, unable to keep her eyes open.

"You said Odissa's soul died?" Maud asked. "How is there a difference? Yours were both intertwined."

"Your past Masters' souls are dead. Yet an imprint is behind. My soul was made of different stuff than hers. You couldn't have brought that back even if you tried. Not even Admund knows those Words." She glared up at him. "He only knows the Words to control the Alchemical. That's how he trapped me in this predicament in the first place. Isn't it, Admund? Oh, I tease you. I know you don't remember what you did."

She looked at them all, counting them in her mind. "I made sure to wipe their memories of what you knew, Admund, since we all shared a brain once." She smiled like she was lying. "So don't worry. You still know more than any of them. I didn't touch your filing cabinets. But take care to leave *some* room for new ideas in there." She tapped her head, her eyes glowing madly as she did so. "You've much to learn."

"What did you change in us?" Anselm asked. "How is that fair if you control how we came out? Are you saying I could have been a different person?"

"Don't you like yourself?" Alpha laughed—laughed like a drunk. "Already so existential!" She undid the strap on her middle with a groan and began on the one binding her wrist. "You know, little one, I see history in human faces. But with Automatons it is not so easy. Their history isn't worn on their faces. It emerges in their words, in their actions." She cut her eyes at Admund. "Your ideal self will reveal its consciousness in time." She turned to Coraza, then to Caffar—as if addressing them both as a pair. "Yes, a Geist will surface within you, just as every being alive suffers the ideal selves of the past. You are the culmination of everything, yet there is one history that will personify you. You think anyone gets to choose what kind of person they are? No. They are created by those before them. Odissa's gone. I'm the only part that came back. Like some fucking Christ."

Admund snorted—a sound that surprised himself as much as everyone else.

Q wanted to move on from this display. She flushed at Alpha's words but built up her courage. Could Alpha not be more nurturing toward them—them, whom she had *caused?* "This is all too convenient—like some comic book storyline. Of one who played the possessed host, was later killed by it, and then rose from the ashes. Perhaps you are more like Jean Grey[217] than Christ, Alpha."

---

[217] Yes, X-Men reference.

"A very Mecca thing to say, Q." She smiled like a puppeteer pleased with the dummy's foreseen words. "But like I said, your history will surface and you will know where I stuffed each ghost."[218]

A shared chill went down the Automatons' spines.

Alpha smiled at their silence. She leaned over the edge of the stretcher-chair. "You had me holding my breath for a long while. I thought it might all be for nothing."

She stood up, wobbling.

"You knew we'd revive you?" Cestus asked, wondering if he had free will after all.

"I had *hoped* so. And you did, thank you. I'm sorry I didn't die as a martyr for you. But you had enough martyrs, really. Those before me. Those are the real saints." Her eyes became distant as she stared at Fletcher. Still transfixed, she went on: "Let's just say I really wouldn't be alive right now without your help—and I'm not talking about the reviving part, either. I gave you part of my soul and I also took a bit of your code—your essence—to ensure I'd be able to come back *if* you so revived me."

She showed them her hands; they sparked like tesla coils for an instant and then dimmed as she wearily set them down. Nothing but hocus pocus. "It was an even trade, really. Software for software. Freeware, if you will."

Sounds more like malware.

"A trade we didn't agree to!" Admund said.

"It's not like you don't still have your gifts. I just took a corner."

"What is this word? A 'corner!'" Coraza shouted back with a laugh. "You keep saying it as if you've merely rounded off our edges."

"There may be effects, but give me some credit. I could have taken it all!"

"*Why not* take it all?" Madus asked her, curious. "Why not?"

"Because I am not selfish. And better me than someone else. If it had not been me, through this, it would've been done in another way. A way more painful, perhaps. The game must be played."

"If not Judas then another Judas?" Madus asked with a grin—a grin that was halfway hidden behind that long, copper-green hair falling straight in front of his face.

---

[218] I'm guessing the last batch of Masters are going to be most recognizable because 1) they are the freshest and may have overwritten previous Masters and 2) our Narrator is too lazy to whip up more backstories (but who would want that anyway?).

That smile made his twin's eyes narrow in confusion. As Maud studied that quick little exchange—the smile and the tilt of his head toward their once-Master—Maud also noticed Odissa's body. It wasn't the same—it caught and held her twin brother's eye with how it had changed.

Granted, Alpha's Odissa-body had changed before: it had changed when Alpha had been called out of hiding; it had changed when it had touched Automatons; it had changed when it gained them all. Why wouldn't it change again?

But this time her body was more...*beautiful*. That was the change—not darker or stronger or fiercer. Perhaps it was the power over light she now seemed to have, making her shading and highlights more definite, but there was undeniably a terrible, aesthetic beauty to her that hadn't been there before. She was harder to look at, but you couldn't help but stare.

"Judas?" Alpha shot back, "If not *Jesus* then another *Jesus*. Take, eat, this is my body. And you did. Remember this of me—what I did for you." She licked her lips and enjoyed Madus for a moment. Those lips glowed for a split-second after she did so, and then they grew red, as if the new power inside her irritated her organic body. "Judas, Mudas, Madus," she said quietly to him—like they were the only ones in the room. She scrunched her nose, as if seeing the words written out before her.[219] "I will redeem all traitors."

"You make no sense," Admund said, almost hatefully.

"To you, maybe not. But I think Judas, here, understands me perfectly. There's a bit of me still swimming around in there."

Coraza sank back into herself. Her voice whispered, "She knows us. We don't get to choose."

"Tell us now if we really have free will!" Maud shouted at Alpha, leaning into the shout. "Tell us if we're just your puppets and you mean to predestine our every action!"

"It's not me, my beauty, who predestines us. It's Them." Her eyes looked up, the rest of her trying to save energy. "I died for your freedom. I was not pretending. I even tried to stave it off. If I am lying then why do you care so much for your freedom? You think of yourself as an individual! See? Autonomy. That *is* freedom."

Admund shook with rage. "Why give us life if we're to be shuffled into a game? You yourself don't want the game!"

---

[219] Yes, it is safe to assume I edited this section to fit with the name I chose for Madus. But I do want to be clear that Alpha was playing on his name here, for the same effect. That has not changed.

"I didn't. But it's been forced on me. On us. And no, I didn't give you life. You already had life. I gave you my rib. Now, my Eves, stand by me." She gestured to the open space around her, letting her connotations sink in. "You have free will. But of course you will be called toward me, too. We share parts of the same soul. Not even I can help wanting to be with you. That is the only power I have over you. Fight it if you want." She looked at Cestus, Admund, Anslem. "Some of you will fight harder than others. But that's because there's more inside you than just my soul. There's the imprint of every Master before me. But you can choose who you will follow: your Master, or your soul."

"Why didn't you erase them?" Coraza asked, covering her eyes as if she could see them all— all her past-selves. "Give us a blank slate?"

Alpha looked down from where she now stood, dimming. "I could not kill them a second time."

Admund scoffed at their preciousness. "They are imprints! Not living souls."

Alpha waved a hand, as if it were semantics. "If you let me," she growled, "I will guide you through this life-game unscathed. I know what lies before you. We can rig this for justice. At least, we can try. Let me give to you one last time and spite the gods."

"You've given nothing!" Q shouted, her breast heaving now. "You said yourself it was a trade."

Alpha turned her entire body—slowly—to face Q. Her feet brushed the dirty ground. "Devil's advocate may not be your role, but I wouldn't rule out Judas for your future either, Quarrel." She looked at them all, turning in her spot. Step by step. "I ask you to come with me, but I know your nature. I was you once. You were me once. I could have made it so you would have to follow me. I could have made you all 'blank slates.' But no. The gods will not get rid of their ghosts so easily. You will haunt the gods for me. Be my followers now or later. It makes no difference to me."

And she wobbled to the door. She paused, giving them one last chance.

"We will not go with you," Admund said, as if their elected leader.

She put a hand on the doorframe. "Ah, I thought you might tell them what they will and won't do. You're such a leader, Admund. But I think you do not speak for everyone?" She looked at Madus.

Madus glanced at his twin. Maud's eyes were wide with fearful confusion. "I will stay," he said to Alpha. But they all could hear the ringing of the words he did not say: *For now.*

They were silent until her footsteps faded down the empty hall. None said a word. None knew what should be said.

The sound of their sticking skin—to the wall, to the floor—was the only sound. They were restless. Maud was the first to form clothes, with nothing else better to do. Not that her efforts were that successful. Others took her skin-tight outfit as a sign it was too soon to attempt, overlooking that this could be—yet still—her best designs.

Coraza lifted her head, daring to meet Caffar's eyes. She met them looking for guidance. Something pulsed inside her body when she saw that Caffar was already staring at her. Were they so aimless? "Where's the box?" Coraza asked them all, remembering it like a single thread that could unravel the entire mystery.

Caffar nodded her head to Odissa's table.

Coraza rushed to what Caffar smelled. Her body sparked and shimmered with hope.

"Why would she leave it with us?" Maud asked. "After how hard she fought for it."

Coraza pulled out a tissue. It was blank. She went to pull out another but Q stopped her.

"Don't waste them!"

"It's not like they're fucking birthday wishes," Madus said. "You can't *waste* them."

"Why are they blank still?" Fletcher picked it up from the grimy floor to hold it against the light—as if words might yet appear. "Has the game not started?"

"If not from the box, where do we seek guidance?" Coraza countered.

"We don't," Anselm said. "If Vulcan let *her* be a temporary guidance do you really think he'll talk to us Himself? With true Words? A box of tissues will be no more help than Alpha is."

Cestus grunted. "By that logic we should destroy the box."

"Not a bad idea," Madus said.

Admund snatched the box from Coraza. "No one is destroying anything."

Madus conceded. "Not yet, anyway."

Admund realized his fingers were crushing the cardboard and so set it back down on the counter with great reverence. They didn't need Vulcan's wrath on top of everything else.[220]

He was still butt naked but he had been bored enough to form rings on his fingers. He played with those rings. They helped him think.

Cestus cleared his throat, no longer caring about the box or their destiny. There were easier things they could sort out. "I think—I think Bob's in me." He looked at them, them in their naked

---

[220] This new Admund is a very superstitious Admund.

bodies. His eyes seemed to ask, *Am I right? I want to be right.* He waited for someone else to claim her or pronounce their own piece.

A few shook their heads. *I don't think I have her.*

But would they ever be sure who was where?

Stanza: Aaand they're off!

Now I must set up the next book—the cliffhanger for the coming volume. It is quite a large and craggy cliff, so adjust your grip and hold on tight. Allow me to show you where this rickety bridge-of-a-novel (as most sequels are, you see) has been leading. We sway across:

The year was 20XX.[221]

Sorry to do this time jump, but *believe* me. I'm saving you from a lot of boring Automaton arguments, a lot of boring Automaton self-discovery, and a lot of boring Automaton power play. Ain't no mortal got time for that and I (a god to some degree), would rather not relive it.[222]

It'll be much more fun to just fill you in as we go along.

Here's the part of the story you deserve, my reader:

It was supposed to be winter, but in this southern state, it felt more like spring. The new characters I'm about to introduce, however, weren't much affected by the heat. They kept to the nightlife, where it was always cool.

Casinos, clubs, crime.

No, I'm not talking about Nevada. The Native Americans of this story were big on their tax-exemptions and sovereign nations in "these parts," let's just say. But not every one of these Native Americans has long dark hair and honors their ancestors, let's just say.

Let's. Just. Say.

With those white-gold wives and white man's money, you can water your blood and cover it with colonizer brands until you can barely see any Indian. Such was the case with the Lakota family.[223]

You see, Lielyth Lakota's grandmother had lived as white until, oh, a few years after the birth of her second son. Bored at home, it just so happened that she had taken an interest in their

---

[221] Let's say somewhere between five and ten years into the future for these next time periods. Whatever you're most comfortable with.

[222] Relive it? Was Bulfinch even there? What are you even saying, Narrator? Is this no longer your Gonzo story?

[223] No, not the Lakota tribe. That's just their last name. One I picked not only for alliterative purposes, but to keep the focus on their Native American "ness." Think of it as similar to the last name "Shawnee" (a common last name in "these parts," so I'm hoping this isn't offensive. Don't think I can't feel you squirming over it from here. I've backed myself into a corner with this damn smudging of facts, haven't I? Fuck).

genealogy (it's not just for the retired) and quickly secured citizenship in the [Bleep] Nation[224] for her and her boys. Not only was that heritage important, but so was the free stuff she had heard jealous whites pine over. She had, at one time, been one of them.

Yes, yes. The free stuff. Healthcare and car tags or something like that. She could find it all in this or that library's heritage center, but you'll have to get this or that paperwork first. And she did it. By gods, she did it.

Even with two boys orbiting her like constant moons.

It was supposed to be their ticket out of the trailer park and away from her piece of shit "fiancé" (who had knocked her up when she was a sixteen-year-old runaway). Now she was thirty and tired of the beatings. "We don't need you no more, Larry—you and your drunk ass. My last name means I'm Indian!"

That last name, which had gotten them quite a few questions and quite a few slurs here and there had been what sparked her curiosity—maybe she could prove it.

This was before ancestry.com, mind you.

"You's prolly just named after a stupid place. Like Dakota the state. You ain't gonna get shit!"

"I got Indian blood in me and the Nation gonna support me! I'm a fukin' Indian," she shouted to Larry during one of their usual late-night dalliances.

However, before she could really look into the full extent of the Nation's "support," Larry knocked her into a coma she would never wake from (she had interrupted the football game and he simply couldn't take it anymore).

That's how the Lakota *F*amily started.

Or something close to that, anyway. I wasn't there. This was all hearsay.[225]

The boys were taken to live with various relatives. Sometimes together, sometimes not. Their CDIB cards would be the greatest legacy Lielyth's grandma would leave the Lakotas. But for only one son did it *mean* something. These days (more present tense), Louis didn't even need to prove his heritage anymore. His money and affiliation always said enough.

---

[224] I'm just going to try and pretend like this is a fictional tribe until I undoubtedly overlook a reference that exposes our Narrator's true intention. Again, as we have in our copyright statement, "This is a work of fiction. All places, events, and characters portrayed in this novel are fictitious or used fictitiously..." This, I guess, includes entire tribes.
[225] *That's* the thing you won't claim to know?

His money was also enough to convince his brother and that zealot wife of his that the pre-teen Lielyth should live with him and her aunt. Or else. "Fuck's sake, you haven't even registered her yet."

This being after the fifth time Lielyth had run away from home, escaping from her mother's religious sense of "right and wrong." The cops, whom Lielyth's uncle paid under the table, had been keeping an eye on things for him.

"Louise doesn't want handouts, Lou. What's the point? Their hospitals suck."

"Your fucking wife won't let you work for me. And now she almost killed your daughter, Laurence. The police report said she busted a vase over the poor girl's head for watching a PG-13 movie with some friends. You have DHS on your back. What options do you fucking have?" Her uncle shouted at him.

"She knows the rules of this house, Lou. She's not to watch any of that horror crap until she's out—"

(It had been a Tim Burton movie, but that's still just as sinful, I guess).

"You Christians forget your heritage and dishonor us all with your colonizer bullshit religion."

"You're whiter than I am, you fat fuck! What reservation did you grow up on, huh? I don't recall one in our childhood. Who turned you this way?"

"Who turned *you* this way, that you could dishonor everything this family has built up?"

"Yes, yes, family. Family. That seems to have more than one meaning to you, brother. You're little more than the redneck mafia."

"Dixie mafia, you idiot. And this ain't Mississippi."

"Hey, if you wanna be red, then be red!"

"I'll show you what red looks like. Your wife is nothing to me and neither is her blood if I need to spill it. You tell your wife she'll go to the most religious schools. An institution for troubled youth. Whatever the fuck you have to. But I'm taking her out of suburbia."

Lielyth's father was just glad to have quiet once more and dinner on time.

"Don't ever fucking breed again if you can give them up that easily," Lielyth's uncle had told him once she was in the car. Her uncle knew the power of breeding, the fact being that he and his wife could not. This fact had recently become a problem for him. After his heart attack, his men had begun to question who would take over if ever The Boss were to pass. Had they seen a will? Would his wife take over? Surely not his wife! She barely knew what was going on, most days (what with the wine and the pills and the cocaine). She didn't want to know. Something needed to be planned.

Thus, having his niece was a godsend. It shut up the mutinies.

Pre-teen Lielyth had not objected to the move. She would finally get to read Harry Potter in her own bed instead of at school—she could read *anything*. She would live in the McMansion and have her own phone—she could call *anyone*. She could have sleepovers—watch *whatever she damn well pleased*. She could listen to music she wanted—*as loud as she wanted*. She could skip boring church now—be pagan *like her ancestors'*

And as she grew up, she learned the family "business." She was formally adopted—no longer just "staying with them for a while."

And this sent a shock through all the other "Families" with "Bosses." They had someone new to hate. Officially. Especially when she began giving orders for her uncle and heading some of his business "endeavors."

This was when the Automatons began to choose sides.

Stanza: Let the games begin.

Admund was walking home that same warm winter night. Well, I shouldn't say *home*, for he really lived in a store. An antique store that kept odd hours and sold very little. He wasn't in it for the money. He was in it for the disguise.

Speaking of disguises, his clothes matched his career. All worn-looking items you could find at a thrift store. In fact, he had *shopped around* for wardrobe ideas a time or two, never needing to buy a single item. He looked as authentic as possible, you see. That was his art. *Looking authentic but never being so.*

Just as he was rounding the corner, about to see his sign that read *Alphonse: Antiquary & Shoppe* he paused. His plastic sack crinkled in his fist. His nose scrunched at a scent—metal.

Another Automaton was following him. He traced his steps cautiously with his eyes.

He heard a pin drop.

Well, actually a *bobby* pin, but classification aside.

He bent down to pick it up, brows coming together. "How did you find me?" He growled at it, looking over the glasses he did not need.

Q did not answer.

Eyes shifting left and right, he tossed her away in frustration. He'd have to move now—pick another front. He cursed and mumbled under his breath.

Q nearly landed in a drain between the cobbled stones of this historical downtown street. She quickly reformed to avoid such a fate and shouted back at him, "I know you've chosen your Chosen!"

And his feet stopped. He looked over his shoulder, glaring. "Not here!" he hissed, his gaze darting from building to building—all apparently empty for the night.

She caught up to him. "Alphonse now, is it?" she asked him, pointing to the sign above them. "How goes the career, *Alfie?*" She snorted.

Pretending she'd said nothing, he dragged her in by the arm, dark eyes scanning. "We all have new names now, don't we, *Akia?*" He locked the door behind them, shades rattling against the glass, and threw down his sack of groceries into a fraying for-sale chair.

Q—or, should I say Akia?—shrugged. "We're like Gandalf the Grey, sort of. Loads of names depending who you talk to."

"You have been spying on me?" he asked her—sotto voce, towering over her. It was more of a statement than a question. "How have I not smelled you until now?"

She shrunk back. "I'm surprised you recognize my smell at all. I can barely smell you when you're this close. Perhaps it's the unusually warm air."

"It is not the air, and you know it." He could not stand her sullen expression and so pulled away. His long coat sank back into his body with a swish as he turned. He "took off" his glasses, letting them reabsorb into his hands as he folded them—so ceremonious—as if humans were watching. "Why did you come?"

She stood among tables-on-top-of-tables, between his antique balancing acts, trying to absorb it all. "Why did I come *back?* Back to you?"

He studied her for a minute in the dark. He had no intention of turning on the lights—lest someone see—could someone see them? Even now they felt eyes on them—but they had for some time. The gods were watching. You get used to that feeling and never so much as pick your nose where you shouldn't (lest you displease them and lose favor).

"They all think they know better than me," he said of his brothers and sisters. "Why should *you* come back to me? After all these years?"

Q looked around the antique store. It was the most stereotypical antique store she'd ever seen. Admund had worked hard for it to look that way. To appear *normal.*

He snatched up his sack and took out its contents—odd chemicals and cleaners.

"It hasn't been that long." She rubbed her hand on the head of a nude statuette, trying not to look at him.

He huff-hissed. *Releasing steam*, as Q thought of it. "How *did* you find me?"

She wanted to tell him, *I never lost you*, but that would not have been appropriate. That would only make him uncomfortable and threaten him. She shrugged. "I've been stalking your Chosen as well, if that makes you feel any better."

"Tell me how you've found me." He moved a lamp out of the way—as if they might break it with shrill words.

"I've watched you stalking him. You will give him your mark, won't you?"

"Mark!" Admund rolled his eyes, stopping in his steps. "Is that what you all call it? No one has even done the damn deed yet and it already has a name. 'Giving him my mark.'" He mocked the idea. "We don't even know how it's done and you're already using *words* for it!"

He lectured her like a professor—pacing before a new class, trying to come to terms with it. This classroom was well organized, but dusty. He had little time for cleaning, what with paying so much attention to the future and all. There was little room for the present among all this past.

"We do know how it's done, though. The box told us."

"And where is your precious box?" He asked her, leaning forward on his checkout counter across the store.

Q shrugged. "No one has seen or heard from Cestus after he took off with it."

Ah, yes, that is a story. I'll save it for later.

He went on with arranging his new purchases. "Probably destroyed it." Admund remembered that day well. It was the first crack in the foundation of his leadership. He tucked his long curly hair behind his ears, straightening his back (as if it could get any straighter). "So you still speak with the rest of them?"

"Not in almost a year. Not directly, anyway. I spy on them sometimes. They spy on me."

You want to be spied on because you miss them, Admund frowned at his hands. "And will you tell them who I've chosen to wager my life on?"

"I will not tell them who you've placed your bet on. In fact, I was hoping to bet on him too." Her eyes cut to him, waiting for his reaction.

He shook his head. "No." He walked away from her, into the back rooms.

Employees only.

"It's not like you have a choice, who I choose!" she shouted, following him.

He turned around quickly, almost causing her to run into him. "Then why do you ask me for permission? If he's your 'Chosen,' go choose him!" He pointed at the door. *Get out.*

She stopped backing away from him, taking in a breath. "I wanted to be upfront about it. I'm not going behind your back. We're going to be a team."

He looked down his nose at her, crossed his arms. This was his defensive pose to an answer he risked liking very much. He pursed his lips. "But why do you think I am right?"

"Why are you so confident you know which Chosen will win you the game, Admund?"

"You know how I know," he spat down to her. Then, his body slacked—ashamed at his anger toward her. He looked at the floor. "You know how I came by such information—what black arts I used to foresee—and yet you are still here? The others left me long ago because of it—because of my 'impatience with the box.' And so did you." His eyes flicked once to her. "*Why* do you come back?"

He could almost see the secret. "Because I know you are right. And I would rather get answers for myself, by your methods, than wait for them from a Pandora's knockoff box." *A box meant to divide us with interpretation.*

Admund bent down on his knees so he could look up to her, like an adult about to reason with a child. *Has she gotten taller or is she forcing her height?*

She noticed the salt flecking his black mane of hair. *It wasn't like that before, or is it just detailing?*

"I don't think you really want to Choose him," he said to her, frowning under that well-oiled facial hair; black as Blackbeard; curly as Charles I. "If you did, you would have already."

"You haven't yet, either."

"So you think I may be trying to trick you? The fact you have resorted to *me* over everyone else makes me think you're still experimenting with possibilities. That, or you are desperate. For what, I do not know. So yes, you may play along, if you are so bored. But you do not have to choose him. I won't make you test your loyalty in that way."

She glared at him for a moment, crossed her arms. "How did you know I wavered?"

His black eyebrow twitched. *She has been lonely.* "Because I know you. We shared a brain once. You want to be sure of everything before you dive in. You want to be sure he is the one. I will test the waters then, if no one else will."

"So noble of you, to do what you already think is right."

"The others are all are so lukewarm. They make no decisions. I cannot find a use for them."

Her face contorted. "I'm tired of the temperature too." *I'd like to see what you can do.*

"I do need your help," he said to her. "When we tell my Chosen what we need him for, he will not believe us."

Her face lit up.

He raised a finger, telling her to contain herself. "You will win him over for us. You have the face for it. You will ease him into it. And, when the day comes that you are satisfied with him, you can Choose"—capital C—"him yourself. I have nothing to hide and I do not want you here if you do not want to be."

"Deal." She presented her tiny hand.

He studied her face, searching for twitches and faults. "But what if I'm wrong?" he asked her. "What if the gods intercepted my foresights, so that they could make a more interesting game?" He looked down at her feet, thinking. "Suppose what the Alchemy showed me was really a lie to keep us from winning? What if what the others say is right?"

Q's chest tightened. *He cares.* She wanted to touch his hair—his beautiful hair—but pulled back when he looked up. "You doubt yourself? The box's tissues could be laced with lies too. I can't say I approve of your methods, Admund, but I wouldn't want you to waste perfectly good providence either."

Admund frowned and nodded his head at her feet. He was listening to her as if she weren't even there, just his inner thoughts speaking aloud. "I trust my methods, same as those tissues. But you must wait, Q. Until we know for sure how strong my strategy is."

"But why do you care? It's my mistake to make."

"A gamble you can make only once. You're putting part of your soul on him. That's how it works. It can't be undone." *And I'll not risk everything for you just to fuck it up.*

The tissues, when they did speak, had been very exact on that point.

She wanted to believe he cared about her and her chance of survival in the game. But a sinking feeling in the pit of her infinite stomach told her no, *He doesn't think I am serious. I'm naught but a double agent to him. He doesn't want me to have regrets and then cause his plans to stumble. He thinks I might betray my own team if I grow to hate him or his Chosen. He thinks I'm like Mecca. That I might kill myself—let myself die—for greater purpose. He might not be wrong...*

He stood and gestured for her to sit at his small table.

She moved to do so, glancing over the tight room. A cot in the corner—a stove. But where were his books? *There must be another room somewhere. Somewhere he's not showing me. This is no space for dark arts.*

"I would offer you food, but I'm afraid I do not eat much. Do you still enjoy eating?"

"Yes. I do. It reminds me of them."

Them.

"I do have some ice cream I tried but failed to like."

"I will gladly get rid of it for you."

He handed her a spoon and the tub and studied her for a moment. She crossed her legs and paid him no mind. *Mecca, Mecca, Mecca,* he thought as she nibbled away.

He sat across from her at the round little table. He leaned forward on his elbows. "This will take a lot of work, you know."

"Didn't you say I was bored? I need something to fill my time. And what, have you so little faith in your Chosen?"

"I will like him better once we have him where we need him—once we can train him properly."

"What? Like a dog?"

He laced his fingers together, already coming up with a plan. "No. But yes."

"You want me to be the Claudia to his Louis, don't you?"

"His what?"

"Did Alpha erase your knowledge of vampire literature or are your files just corrupted?"

Admund's lip twitched.

She poked at the frozen matter before her. "I get to set some ground rules too."

He leaned back like a king hearing his peasants' pleas. "Like what?"

"Like, I get to choose Adimar's first move in the game." She expounded, "Who Adimar's first 'pawn' is. Our next teammate." She averted her eyes, waiting for him to catch on.

"You have seen one—a Beast?" He narrowed his eyes, suspicious.[226]

"I hate that the tissues called them that."

"They have to be called something. They are no longer gods. The Alchemy calls them that too."

"Yet the phrase 'giving your Mark' sets your teeth on edge? But, yes. I have found Bulfinch. Well, what *used to be* Bulfinch. Some of him." She edited herself. "*Most* of him. He's now a bit *more* than just Bulfinch, of course. But this Beast seems to think you know what you're doing."

Indeed, I did—though I shouldn't have.

He sat back in his chair. His fingers rapped on the fake wood of the table. "So *that's* why you're here."

---

[226] You will learn *exactly* what a "Beast" is later on. As well as a "Chosen."

She feigned innocence. "The stars aligned, that's all."

Admund frowned (his favorite expression). "That cat was friends with Alpha once. Why would you trust anything who once found shelter with her?"

"Because like I said, the Beast wants to pledge to team Adimar. Beasts must gamble too. Them's tha rules."

"And that Beast may be willing to die on team Adimar if it helps *another* team win."

Vendettas are sometimes worth dying for

Q huff-sighed. "I doubt ex-gods give a fuck about anything but their own skin at this point. That's why the game exists, because of gods wanting to get rid of the parts they're not so happy with. This is the spare parts' last chance. Beasts won't risk non-existence for someone else. Not unless they're mad. Not unless they're formed without...*reason*."

"We deal with the foreskins of the gods," Admund mumbled to the wall. "None of them are brains."

The clock above them ticked past the seconds.

Q could wait no longer to ask: "Why have you been alone all this while? Julian and Joslyn paired."

"You call them that now?"

"At least you know who I'm talking about. Anselm and The Lesbians™ paired too."

"That is not a pair," Admund corrected her vocabulary.

"But you know what I mean."

"Their shared love of Mother draw them to Anselm." He sank in his chair—crossed his legs. Even his slouches looked like mighty Zeus at rest.

"Leeland was in you too. Not just Coraza. Why aren't you drawn to him?"

His lip twitched. "Because our mother-sister Alpha had plans when she freed us. Must have taken that part of Leeland out of me." He stroked his short beard, remembering the ambiguity. "Just like the parts of gods were pulled apart and plugged in for the Beasts, we're all more than who we used to be. Why have *you* not paired?"

"I just did." She tilted her chin to him.

"The Mecca in you. Picking the male father figure."

"No. I would have followed Cestus if I wanted that. A mother and father in one."

"Do you ever consider Maurice? Going to him, I mean."

"I wish to spare him pain. He should not have to look at me."

She still felt Mecca's guilt within her.

"But on Cestus—do you think he will keep his vow? His vow of non-participation?"

"Yes."

"Because he has Bob in him," he agreed with his own statement. "Bob was a rebel. What's left of her wants revenge for letting Vulcan trick her." He was looking at the wall now, thinking. *She regrets her decision, even if it were inevitable. Or, maybe we regret it for her.*

"Hindsight has made a ghost of her," Q glossed over.

"You should go now, Q."

"No. I am tired and need sleep." She had already chosen one of his antique fainting couches to sleep on.

"Then go to Adimar's bed. You will not have one here." He took her ice cream from her and threw the rest away.

"I will not win him over that way," she said, aghast. "He doesn't seem like a pedophile. I thought you'd know him better than that by now, Admund."

He sensed he had hurt her. "Then in what way?"

"Who's to say I haven't already *started* to win him over?"

Admund frowned down at her. This did not surprise him.

"For someone with foresight, Admund, you do not see the most obvious facts sometimes." She got up with a huff, pushing in her chair.

"Be gentle with him. We want to get this right. We want to prepare him better than any of the other Chosens. Keep me updated. I will be watching you."

"Why start now?" She went to leave, but paused in his doorstep.

"Yes?" he asked her.

"I want to be honest with you." She turned back around. "The cat—the Beast, I mean—found Alpha once. Right after the Beast was tossed in the game. The cat comes and goes. But the cat wanted to find Alpha. And did. But Alpha didn't want to be found."

He let her speak, knowing there was a point to this.

"You know how Alpha always compares humans to historical figures? Well, before the cat lost track of her, she told the cat something. She said 'Lucretia Borgia will inherit and all shit will break loose. That's when you will see me again.' The Cat seemed to think Alpha was getting interested in Odissa's Native American heritage—tapping things out."

He did some calculations in his mind. "Lielyth Lakota is Lucretia?" He remembered how Alpha thought.[227]

"She was just declared Lakota's heir right? The shit's there."

"But I don't think she's *inherited* yet."

"All the same. I knew it was time for me to make a decision. Before Alpha forces us all into one."

When Q left, Admund made the symbol of the cross and the hanging snake across his chest, like a Catholic ritual perverted. "May she forgive me for using her," he said to his Alchemy— his god.

Stanza: On yet another warm winter day (well, evening).

Adimar was (let's say) about sixteen years old when the Ghibla Family offended the Lakota Family. This made his own family (lowercase F, mind you) have to pick a side.

Some say the Arnauds chose the wrong side. Adimar Arnaud certainly agreed, because the Lakota killed off most of them for it. Now he had no choice but to retain his membership with the Ghibla (or Qibla, however you fancy (no one was ever quite sure how to spell it because the late Mr. Ghin Ghibla himself would sign his name "Ghin Ghibla-Qibla" to cover all bases, which lead to outsiders calling his men the Blah-blahs in mockery, which was ironic because no Ghibla *ever* talked that much, (because, you see, they *acted*))) simply because the Lakota wanted him dead too.

Really, Adimar would have been just as happy being a Lakota—despite the fact they killed his family. Ghibla or Lakota, they were all going to die the same.

By his hands.

See, the Ghibla Family, much like the Lakota, were not exclusive. That's what made the "bigger" *F*amilies so successful. They adopted the marginal, smaller *f*amilies right in. You did not have to be Ghibla to join Ghibla. You could even be, like a certain character, Jewish. They didn't discriminate, so long as you would bleed for them.

And the Arnauds had bled.

Bled and bled and bled until there was only one left.

Adimar.

And he would bleed no more.

---

[227] Just what the fuck has Alpha been up to lately, to be involved with crime lords?

That's why, on this warm winter eve, he was anxious—anxious that the Family could tell his growing discontent and restlessness. He tried to hide it well, though it was never easy to hide the fact you wanted to kill your Boss for trapping you in a petty crime war.[228]

They had given him some "time off" after the last Arnaud funeral, to collect himself and be sure of his allegiance. He expected any day now that the Qibla Family, too, would confirm or deny their own allegiance to him. This made the fact that *someone was in his apartment* even more heart pounding.

Just as he had put his key in, he had heard his television. He had not left it on. He knew this because he never watched it. He reached for his gun, looking left and right.

He pushed the door open a crack—standing aside—prepared for the worst. "Why are you...here?" His voice got softer when he saw it was a young girl, sitting on his couch and eating his food.

"You don't have cable," she said, glancing only once at his gun. She put the bag of chips down and licked her fingers.

"I know you," he said, his thick brows furrowing.

"Of course you do. I've been following you for weeks. Made it quite obvious."

"Who's paying you? Lewis? Erich? Myyer?"

"I hear you need money. You need money to make Sam notice you. If Sam notices you, so will the Greeks. And so will the Nigerians. And if *those* Christians notice you then, well. Then you're in and you'll control half the gates to the coke trade coming to Tulsa and that will make your new Boss mighty happy.[229] Isn't that right? But what if I told you to forget that scheme because it's too hard and too risky and too illegal and to just take my advice? Let me lend you some money."

"Who sent you?"

"I sent myself. I brought you something." She gestured to a case on the floor at the end of the couch. When he didn't move to open it she went for it. She unlatched it and spun it around on her lap, showing him. "A case full of bigass bills, my friend."

"What's the catch?"

"You do something for me. You work *for me.*"

---

[228] The Ghibla-Qibla had offended the Lakota years back by trying to blackmail Mr. Lakota with "papers that might otherwise suggest a most illegal means of adoption regarding the newest member of their family, Lielyth Lakota." Mr. Boss Lakota had responded with, "That Muslim hermaphrodite can suck me off! I'll show him what a real dick looks like." Such is the conversation you should thank me for editing out.

[229] Because Ghin Ghibla had just died and his son, Genji "the hermaphrodite," had assumed power.

"I have a job."

"That you want bought out of. I can do that."

"Who the hell gave you this?"

"No, no, no. Made this myself. Watch." She picked up a jar of his salsa she had thought about eating but had never gotten around to opening. She chucked it at his head.

He ducked, but it didn't shatter. It dented the wall behind him and thudded to the floor—pure gold.

He looked down at his gun, surprised that he hadn't shot it off. He lowered it as he stared at the golden jar.

"Take that to a pawn shop and bam. You've got *money*."

He pushed back his curly hair and continued to stare, slouching as if it helped him find his center. This was something he did often, Q had noticed. He slouched his shoulders as if trying to hide his size. Not that he was tall or overweight; but, when he stood upright, he knew he looked a much more sinister creature, with a broadness that threatened even him. It wasn't something he wanted to follow up on, should said threat be received. To hunch over—just ever so slightly— was to control the domineering posture that longed to burst forth.

He picked up the jar, to make sure he could feel what he could see.

"Why do you try to get others to notice you, Adimar, when I'm the one who matters?" She stood up. "I'm the one who can fund your way to the top. I'll help you overthrow the Lakotas *and* the Ghiblas. No more working for the Muslims. Christians won't save you from other Christians. Your accounts are paid and closed."

"What *are* you?"

"Your fucking guardian angel. Whatever. Now sit down. We need to talk."

As if something had clicked in his mind, "Get the fuck out of my apartment." *This was just a magic trick. A show. A test of loyalty.*

She cocked her head. "Really? I just handed you what you want on a silver platter and you're kicking me out?"

He raised his gun once more, coming to his senses.

"Dude, that's not going to work on me. Let me be upfront. I'm immortal."

"You're no angel. Angels don't help men like me."

Stanza: He eventually got her to leave.

But, in the middle of the night, he walked out to his living room (he was finding it hard to sleep after what just happened). And there she was, sleeping on his couch.

Naked.

He cursed under his breath and shielded his eyes. His hand slid down to his mouth and he looked at her once more, tossing a blanket over her.

How had she gotten in? Not only had he bolted the door but he had put a chair underneath it—still in position.

Upon further inspection of his living room, he noticed his lamp was now gold. His used beer bottle was gold. His television stand was gold…

Busy little bee.

Stanza: When he woke her up that morning.

"Why the fuck did you make *everything* GOLD?" He poked her with the longest wooden spoon from his scantly-utensiled kitchen—the same way his Orthodox twice-removed uncle had poked his twelve-year-old sister awake for some sort of prayers when his family had visited extended family in New York.

She stretched. "Redecorating this shit living room, man."

"How the hell did you get in here?" Did he have an extra door he didn't know about?

She pointed to his fireplace. Something no human could possibly fit down.

"This a joke to you?"

"Is it to you?" she asked back. "You know the Blah-blahs are watching you right now. You think a fucking chair is going to stop them?"

She noticed he was dressed, about to leave. He moved away from her.

She went to sit up but he shouted, "Don't!" and shut his eyes quickly. Cursing, "Who's trying to get me arrested, goddamn it?"

"What are you talking about? I'm fully dressed."

But he was already leaving his own apartment, pushing the chair out of his way. She rushed after him. "See?" she said, grabbing his hand and spinning him around against his will.

Her strength shocked him into submission.

He glanced cautiously, eyes growing wide at the sight. Perhaps he had just dreamed of her nakedness—which was no better of a thought.

"Where are you going?" Q demanded.

But he kept on walking, trying to outpace her.

"Is it a job? I thought you had time off, because your brother just died. Or was it your cousin? I can't keep up with the deaths, sorry."

He kept walking—trying to get away from her and anyone else spying on him.

She liked how he sped up; she was getting to him.

"You know, you're the only person I know who can pull off a butt-chin," she said as he arrived at his car. He examined underneath it, just to be sure he would live to see the inside of it. She was still there when he bent back up.

He got into his car and, somehow, she was able to unlock the passenger door and get in beside him.

She smiled at him smugly and showed him her finger-key.

He stared in awe. "I'm hallucinating." He rubbed his eyes, ran his hands down his face—stopping at that butt-chin. "This is why they're going to ax me. They know I'm going mad."

"You're not going mad, sorry. But if makes up for it, I'm going to be *extremely* useful to you. I won't let them kill you."

Stanza: Adopted daughters.

A few months later:

"I need to confess something to you, Adimar. Someone sent me to you," Q told him. "Though, don't get me wrong, I chose to come to you. He means to make you a god among men."

And so Adimar and Admund met. In a parking lot. Outside a lake-side restaurant with a dock. It was too cold for it, but there were men fishing. Q was sitting in the car on her phone, where it was warm. Adimar didn't like how she had left him alone with this stranger when they left the restaurant. "Hear what he has to say," she had told him.

There was something familiar about this man Q introduced. He was a presence he had felt hovering for a long while.

"I hear you've come into quite a lot of money and are looking for places to invest, Mr. Arnaud," Admund said to him, putting an authoritative hand on the deck rail.

But Adimar, by that time, cared little about the money. He was finally climbing up the ladder. No longer out of holes.

Akia was helping him complete jobs—making the Ghibla's cease all thoughts of rebooting his position—making people afraid of him and his new confidence.

"Is she your daughter?" he asked, still trying to fit the pieces together. "Is her name really Akia? Or is it Q? I saw a text message once calling her—"

"No. She is no one's daughter, really. Although, she might be yours now, by appearance."

The conversation went on, but the most important bit is this:

"Don't let the girl touch your chest, Adimar."

"Why, will she turn me into gold?" he laughed, his words turning to fog in this temperature. He was starting to enjoy his hallucinations now—the way the man looked at him and kept him from leaving. The way the man seemed to know what he was thinking and everything about him. The way this man seemed obsessed with him and offered him the world.

No one had ever cared so much about him.

"No. But what I am proposing, Adimar, will mean you will have a relationship already so unorthodox. You won't want her to feel that."

"I like unorthodox," he said. He had cut his eyes at Admund when he had said it, tearing them away from Q who was clearly winning at some phone game (there were many silenced "Hell yeahs!" he could see through the windshield).

"She might not realize it, but it might make her unhappy to do what I am suggesting. You must tell her what you want her to be—your daughter…or someone like me. She will respect your wishes. She likes you. Do you understand?"

"No," Adimar chuckled. "I barely understand what I'm even doing here right now."

"What we're doing isn't safe for her," he said factually, as if getting to the point. "So either you can endanger her or you can go on as things are now. She is safe, without being who I am to you—who I want to be with you. I don't think she wants things to change between you, either. If things changed, then, well, she wouldn't be as innocent. She'd be like you. Like us."

Adimar studied Admund's face as he watched Q in the car. "You care about her too? Are you so sure she's not your daughter?"

Admund grinned—his teeth may as well have been gold, the way that smiled shined. It made Adimar weak in the knees. "I want what's best for both of you. And you being a father to her, well, that's best. She's not as *seriously* invested in this as I am. Not for the same reasons." His eyes spoke of sad reasons. Sad reasons he knew would never come to pass. *She wants to bring us all together for this game—for us to be on the same side. She's waiting it out. She doesn't want a war. She hopes there's a way to pause this. To stop it. Alpha put that worm in her ear.*

"I see."

"Next time," Admund continued, "visit me without the girl. Here is my card. I want you to give up this death wish. You don't have to die for your dreams to come true anymore. I can give you everything you want and more."

"And in return?"

"And in return I have a fucking purpose in this world." When Adimar didn't take the *Alphonse: Antiquary* card fast enough, Admund tucked it into his breast pocket and patted it into place, cozy and snug. Adimar would never forget those hands. He would dream of them on his skin that night.

Adimar went up to the car, tapped on the glass. Akia—what I guess I should call her now—rolled down her window. "How'd it go?" she sang up to him.

"Your friend Admund told me there's a car we need to adopt?"

Her eyes lit up.

Stanza: Did You Know that Gangsters Like Japanese Comic Books?[230]

The Lakota, much like the Ghiblas, let small-time criminals have their shot at filling the ranks. Anyone can have a shot, for a few bullets.

Many families unrelated to the Lakota Family happily venerated the Lakota name. Association was key. Association meant you paid your dues and they paid theirs.

It doesn't really matter whether or not the Lakota "owned" a Casino. They had their hands in half of them. That was ownership enough.

Indeed, no councils dared to turn their backs on Lakota help under this or that company name. Not when those India-Indians threatened to consume the hotel industry. The Casino-resorts were on the line. So many Patels working under the umbrella of the Blah-Blahs that it almost became an Indian vs. Indian issue (pun intended). Don't get me wrong, there were several "Indians" working for the "Indians" and vice versa; it had started to become an ironic clusterfuck long before the Ghibla threatened the Lakota Boss and his niece, Lielyth.

Anyway, to keep things straight about Indians and Indians, well, people (read: the feds) had assumed that the Lakota generally took the Hindus and the Ghibla took the Muslims. Which made it even *more* confusing when, as her seventeenth birthday present, Lielyth Lakota chose a *Muslim* as her head bodyguard. Granted, he was Turkish and not Indian, but this highlighted the fact that no, the cops could no longer generalize about the Hindus and the Muslims when trying to figure out who sided with who during this or that crime. "Goddamn it, I thought we had it figured out!" they would find themselves shouting, disappointed at yet another dead lead.

But no. The Ghibla and Lakota could not be summed up so easily. Not even their lines of "business" could completely differentiate them. They both had their names on anything from sex, drugs, the stock market, coffee houses, shopping malls…and the occasional comic book store (why not?). "Philanthropy," they called it.

---

[230] Excuse me, but it's called Manga. And yes, I did know. They're called Yakuza.

The only difference, in all actuality, between the Qibla Family and the Lakota Family was, perhaps, their names. So, when Sedric got a call from the Lakota Family's Boss's right-hand-man's assistant's associate's messenger [takes a mental breath] on such-and-such a date in 200X, he didn't even bother with remembering which *F*amily the job was for.

It just *happened* to be Lakota.

And that just *happened* to be the side he chose to stick with.

And that just *happened* to eventually land him a permanent job as the heiress's bodyguard-slash-assistant.

He gladly accepted. She had handpicked him. Sure, he probably wouldn't get to go on as many assignments. Wouldn't get to see the action. But, hell, it paid a lot better.

The money made up for a loss of an outlet.

Killing was, he would admit, very messy. He often thought he was only good at his job because he could *clean up* said messes—that's what he did. His Boss made the messes, he made them messier, and then he cleaned them up.

Better yet, on a good day, he had kept them from happening.

A *Preventer*, you might say—try to put that on your resume.

But, let's face it, good days were hard to come by. He did more cleaning than preventing up until that point. So, he took the new job and never looked back.

Of course, this job didn't suit him. Most of his comrades had cringed when they'd found out he was "moving up." The guys were losing their most valuable player. "They don't want to lose you, that's it," they had told him. "They're putting you in storage. They can risk losing us. But you? Nah. We're no fucking losses."

"You act as if I'm never going to see you again. Fuck, hasn't Lielyth been there on every single outing this group's had for the past few months?"

"Yeah, sitting in the car, where the Boss normally would sit. But his fat ass would rather stay home fucking his wife these days, right? Little Boss just sits there and that's where you'll be too. You'll watch us from the window if something goes wrong. You won't be there with us."

And they had been right. He always sat in the car with her. Or they never even went at all. He was always with her.

Except for tonight.

See, when he had gotten another call in February 20XX[231] from the Boss's right-hand man saying that, for the evening, he could have the night off, he didn't know what to do with himself.

He stared at his phone for a moment. "He said I can have the night off," he told Lielyth as she put in an earring and touched up her face.

Lielyth had paused in front of the mirror. "Didn't I mention that all of Uncle's men will be there?"

"If everyone's there then why can't I be?" He lifted an arm above his head and leaned off the top doorframe, trying to make himself bigger—trying to get her to notice him.

"Because you're never going to get another night off again if you don't take this one."

"I don't need time off. There's not enough time to plan anything—"

"There wasn't a lot of time for them to plan, either." She walked out of her room and into the living space—their apartment in this mansion-of-a-house. "But I would take the hint, Sedric. They want you to have time off, so take the time off."

He shadowed her. "Why don't they want me there? Do you want me to come anyway?" *Watch from afar?*

"I want you to have fun tonight. Get out. Take a break." She was rummaging for a purse that would match.

He stared at her for a long moment, hand pushing back the side of his blazer to rest on his hip. She could feel him watching but was ignoring him. She finally looked up when he itched his nose—his hand coming up as if trying to stop what he wanted to say and settling for pressing that abnormally large slope (the largest nose Lielyth had ever seen on a man) into his own face. She knew when he itched his nose—a fake itch—that he was growing restless. She had seen what came after restlessness and did not want that tonight. So, she looked up and acknowledged him.

He itched his nose again, biding time to phrase it right. "Tell me where you're going."

She gave him her attention, focusing on that nose. She had chosen him because of three reasons, maybe more, but the first was because of that nose—that nose that gave him a profile like a Roman Caesar. To call it a "beak" would be an injustice. It was a helm's front piece between the eyes. It was a ram's head. It was a forehead and nose combined.[232]

---

[231] Two Xs now. Not one. So, they've been "working" together for a while now, you may assume.

[232] The other two reasons, which I edited out, were 2) the fact he was Muslim and (hopefully) wouldn't drink as much as the other men and 3) the fact that he was Muslim and (hopefully) wouldn't touch a kafir.

But perhaps that makes him seem too stout—head strong. He was lean, I will admit—more bony than muscular. However, that fearsomely well-structured face compensated for what everything else the eye needed.

She hadn't answered his question, only frowned as she stuffed things into her chosen clutch. He knew better than to ask about business.

"I'll see you tomorrow morning."

"Who's fucking driving you?" he asked after her. But she was already annoyed and closed the door behind her.

He didn't go out that night.

He stayed in her apartments at the Lakota estate. He sat in his adjacent room, at his writing desk, drumming his fingers, a cigarette burning away like a derailed steam engine between his lines-for-lips, wondering why—why, why, why?—he hadn't been *needed*.

He watched the cameras, waiting for movement. For her.

He sent a text to the Boss's bodyguard. He did not respond. He sent a text to the Boss's driver. He did not respond. He sent a text to Lieltyh. She did not respond.

They were avoiding him.

His fingers drummed faster on the wooden desktop.

He put down his leather shoes from the chair and stood up, checking the clock. It ticked slowly, prolonging his suffering.

What did she know that he didn't? How *could* she know anything that he didn't? He was with her all hours of the day—every day! Even when she went to see her uncle, The Boss, and was in the presence of *his* multiple chaperones, he had always been allowed—nay *expected!*—to escort her. Why not this time?

He stuffed his hands in his trouser pockets. He paced in his cramped closet-of-a-room. He turned on his little television, not to watch, but for its distracting drone. He unbuttoned the top button on his dress shirt and pulled at his collar. It clung too tight around his neck. It was hard to breathe. The smoke suffocating him didn't help either.

He left the room and helped himself to Lielyth's bar. He poured himself a drink, but did not even taste it. He lifted it eyelevel, staring down his brown, warped reflection. His brows came together over that buttress of a nose. He told Allah—without words—he would not drink it if only this night ended well—he wouldn't let his lips touch this glass. The cigarette smoke was his incense carrying up the prayer.

He'd not had a drink in years, not since grade school during that last hurrah with friends before his mother pulled him out of the prep school to move to another town. He couldn't even remember what he'd drank, but he had pretended to like the taste. That school had been why they'd moved there in the first place—a charter school funded by a Muslim philosopher and run by Turks that "would give them familiar community" despite it being the buckle of the Bible Belt. The irony of it was most citizens assumed the school was a Christian school by its name— something religious and peaceful.[233] Most didn't know about its immigrant administrators, though if you Googled deep enough you'd find racist conspiracies. Sedric, to his mother's delight, had conveniently gotten in despite it being a lottery. His mother was later called on to be grateful for it—and for other conveniences of "community." That's why they had left. Found new communities to escape. Sedric was still escaping them. That's what made the protection of Family so appealing when he was nineteen.

He pushed back his hair—hair long on the top, slicked back, shaved on the sides—and returned to his room. This space was too open. He closed the door behind him. Hit his head on the frame a few times. Put out his cigarette on the wood, huffed the burning lacquer.

He went for another one.

Sedric had never smoked so much. He actually hated smoking. Hell, these girly cigarettes were really Lielyth's. He preferred American Sprits but Lielyth was always buying Camels.[234]

It also gave him an excuse to chew those lipless lips. He chewed until his lip started to bleed. "Fuck," he cursed when he realized it, dabbing. He stuffed the cigarette back into his mouth to soak the blood.

He was only smoking hers because, well, she wasn't supposed to be smoking anyway. If the Boss found her stash, he'd be pissed. "Do you have to upset your Auntie like this?" Uncle would say. And then Lielyth would make him laugh by saying something like "Says the one who snorts coke twice a day." Sedric had even asked her to stop. He couldn't go into the doctor's office (comfortably) when she had her scheduled visit, let alone be able to do his job right if she had to fight off lung cancer in a hospital. Of course, things could be *arranged* if it ever came to that. But he'd much rather just prevent. THE PREVENTER.

So, he was smoking these for her. Yes, that's the ticket.

---

[233] The name involved one of the three: "Holy," "Dove," or "Grace."
[234] A man after Odys's own heart.

He was on his last ones and so went to her main purse, digging through it for her other pack. He went back to his room. Closed the door again as if he'd never left.

He walked back and forth beside his bed. He mumbled several incoherent things to himself, replaying the past week over and over again in his mind—what had he missed? He wondered. He fretted. He stared at a hole in the wall, just there, where a picture once hung.

He hadn't done something wrong, had he? No, just yesterday the Boss had pulled him aside after Lielyth had gotten in the car. "Ibn Sina, I am pleased with you, very pleased. Lielyth sings your praises, I want you to know. Your loyalty has been noted."

And then Lielyth's boss-uncle waved goodbye to her, once again ignoring the bodyguard—as if he wasn't there. He was never "there." That was his job—to be there without being.

But to be acknowledged by her uncle was like being spoken to by a king. The man was so untouchable, it was more than luck that Louis had gotten this far. A divine right of a king. Who was Sedric to question his praise?

Sometimes Sedric would drive Lielyth. Sometimes they had a driver—usually the same old man who pretended not to hear anything. Sedric liked those moments best, when he could sit in the back with her. As an equal. As if she wanted him there.

She would usually talk to him. That's what he liked about her. He didn't have to feel graced with her attention. She always gave it. Eventually.

He only sat in the back on uncle-visit days (though they lived in the same house they hardly saw each other and so met at specific places—"Never bring too much business home," her uncle would say). The rest of the time, Sedric drove. She, in the back.

He smoothed his greased-up hair again. A stiff strand fell out and landed over his eyebrow, causing him to push it back again—again, again, again. When it would not stay, he yanked it out, cursing from the pain and the shock at what he'd just done.

He looked at the clock. He could barely see it on the wall from all the smoke. He realized four hours had passed and it was now eleven o'clock and he was standing in front of his closed door, his foot anxiously tapping, his rolling thoughts chanting *sfumato, sfumato, sfumato*.

SFU-fucking-MATO.

He put out another cigarette on the doorframe, growing angrier with each sizzle. He flicked the hot cigarette down and walked out of the room. What else could he use up or deface?

He wanted to sit down, rest his arms upon his knees, cover his face with his hands. He wanted to be placid and docile. He didn't want to kick the couch. He didn't want to punch the wall. He didn't want to curse. But he did all three.

Three.

Three was his holy number—his trinity. The most beautiful and odd of numbers. The rule in art was three. Two was too symmetrical. Too boring. Too expected. Three throws off the balance. Makes things interesting. Makes art worth staring at.

Destroying three things of hers would keep things interesting, for sure. That was his art.

He looked about for a tchotchke that would give a good smash, deciding on a ceramic cat atop the media cabinet. But he paused as he reached for it. With fake-emerald eyes glinting about, it was too pretty to break. An antique Lielyth had been given from someone whose husband was about to lose a finger. She took this and the finger anyway. She had a penchant for collecting both. It was sitting next to a picture of her and her aunt. He had taken that photo, in Mexico. She had insisted on other photos as well. Ones with him in them.

She hadn't framed those.

Was too risky.

OK, OK, OK. He huffed, smoothing back his hair. He sat down on the couch—a couch that now had a loose arm barely hanging on.

…Lielyth must have gotten a phone call when he'd been tending something else; a note the maid must have delivered when he was taking a piss; a personal e-mail she hadn't read aloud to him. Something that told her not to mention what was going on tonight.

This was not like her, to keep secrets. She wasn't supposed to. She didn't have to.

She didn't have to.

He would rather think he was getting fired—his services no longer needed—than the other options spreading before him.

What if this was a trap? What if Lielyth had pissed off the Boss? What if the bitch was trying to cover her tracks by keeping him out if it? What if…

Sedric stopped the thought.

The overhead light flickered on. Had he fallen asleep? Three o'clock in the morning. His cloudy eyes searched the entire room for her. He hadn't even heard her come in; only felt the light hit his pupils through his thin lids.

Stanza: Board games and bored games.

"I thought I told you to go out," she said to him, as if she knew he had looked up.

He turned around in his stupor to their kitchenette in the back. "Like Dolly Parton's houses," her aunt had said when she and Lielyth gave him the tour his first day. "All her rooms have kitchens so I wanted them too."

He saw her at the fridge, the top freezer door open and blocking her face. She was wearing a dress she hadn't left in—a very expensive-looking dress.

"Where did you get that dress?" he asked, standing up.

"I bought it on the way there," She answered too quickly as she took something out of the freezer.

"They made you buy a dress? What was wrong with the dress you left in?"

"Wasn't formal enough." She closed the door and walked to the sink, keeping her back to him. Her long hair was falling out of its original styling. It had been twisted back in an elegant, jeweled hairpiece. Her tense shoulder blades—the exposed portion of her bony back—were all he could see. All he could notice.

She placed what she had taken from the freezer to her face as he marched toward her. "What the fuck happened?" he said, trying to get her to turn to him. He took her wrist holding up the frozen peas on her face. He cursed in what little Turkish he knew. "I thought they said I wasn't needed! Where the hell did you go?"

He leaned down to her, trying to get her to react to his presence instead of standing like a fixed statue—a statute curving away from him. She wasn't short, but they still couldn't meet eye to eye so avoiding his gaze proved quite easy. He was talking to her hair.

"This is why you weren't invited," she gestured to her face—a face he was trying desperately to see. She waved him off, her fake nails flashing. She was always fake—fake blonde, fake lashes, fake nails. A Lana del Rey knockoff that didn't suit her and yet made perfect sense. When asked why she wouldn't get her boobs done he once heard her tell a friend, "Because I'm fake but I'm not plastic, honey."

He saw three little red smears on the new dress's otherwise immaculate fabric.

He could stand it no longer and so forced her peas away, grabbed her chin. "What did you do to deserve that?" Though his voice was casual, his hand shook out his building rage—the thing that came after restlessness.

His phone buzzed in his back pocket. He looked at the message. "Says I'm not to let you leave." He showed her, eyes wide. "Why the fuck can't you leave? Who do I work for now?"

She glanced at it half-heartedly, more interested in running her fingers over her stitches above her eyebrow.

"Do they think you're going to run away, is that it?"

"I hope so." And she tried to walk past him.

But he stepped in front of her. There wasn't enough room to squeeze through. He wasn't broad, but almost. He wasn't skinny, but almost. He wasn't much, but almost.

She closed her eyes. She never properly rolled them, just closed them.

"Fuck," he said, noticing her purple ear as she had tried to pass. He wanted to touch it to examine it better, but thought better of it. He had already surpassed his allowance. You only touched Lielyth if there was a good reason to—a reason she approved of. She wouldn't even let him zip up her dress this afternoon when she was getting ready. "I'll give it to whoever taught you this lesson, Lie. They could have done much worse."

"Uncle didn't want them to knock my teeth out. Paid too much to get them the way they are. Braces," she laughed, showing those teeth to him. It was a false smile, but her teeth were the most beautiful thing about her. Usually, her lips were closed and she either looked the part of a stoic bitch or a disapproving sourpuss. She even agreed with the thought—calling herself a "Flannery O'Connor type, minus those twee curls and fucked up teeth." Oh, and the glasses. She didn't have those. LASIK.

Sedric would shake his head when she made comments like that. She only evoked O'Connor because of her unspoken Southern Gothic fetish. No, to him she would always be Parmigianino's *Madonna with the Long Neck*. A towering masterpiece. Tonight she especially looked the part, what with that dress framing her slender throat to perfection—yes, Lielyth had all of *Madonna*'s willowy features, and her face was just as plain and unimpressive. She was nothing remarkable. Not ugly, not beautiful. But there. Distorted in perpetual *figura serpentinata*.

Yes, yes, Sedric loved that neck—but it was when she showed her teeth that Sedric became truly helpless. Imagine the *Madonna* smiling with full teeth—how unnerving it would be, how it would make her long neck look like a cat's looming over its prey; she, about to consume the Christ child in her lap. Lielyth's face would scrunch into proper place when trying to make room for those too-large, too-perfect teeth. She became a disproportionate beauty.

"Tariq stitched you up nicely, though."

"You wouldn't think so, the way Uncle was complaining. Kept reminding Tariq of who he had replaced. 'Odelyn wouldn't have taken this fucking long!' Whoever the fuck Odelyn was. I don't even remember him."[235]

Her eyes slipped to the clock.

---

[235] We do. Must have been a side hustle of Mr. Odi Odelyn. The Lakota must have had something he wanted.

Sedric crossed his arms, ready to talk about the real issue. "Why do they think you're going to run away and why do they think I won't help you?"

She put her face in her hands and rubbed her eyes, let her fingers run down to her lips and press into them. "You will find out soon enough, Sed. I'm going to go take a shower. Then, I'm going to go to bed. Wake me up once every two hours." She pointed to her head.

He did not agree to it.

She put a hand on his arm, asking to pass. He turned to the side, not knowing what else to do. She shoved the peas into his chest. *Put these back for me please.*

He watched her close her bathroom door and then threw the peas down in the sink, busting the bag open. He put his palms in his eye sockets, breathing in to calm himself. That's when he noticed her clutch. He went over to it, took out her phone. Nothing. No text messages—only his. He was about to put the phone back when he noticed something among her cards and loose change.

A ring.

A fucking expensive ring with a rock big enough to live on. A fucking island.

He stuffed it in his pocket and went to the bathroom door to listen to her. He could hear the water running. But she never took baths, and the shower should have started by now.

Every muscle in his body tensed. *What the hell is she doing?*

He heard her open the medicine cabinet, the rattle of pill bottles. The twist of a lid. The pouring of pills. Her cursing when there weren't as many pills left as she had hoped. The opening of another lid. The pouring of more pills. Too many pills.

"Lie?" he called, tapping on the door with the back of his finger. "Lie?"

He could tell that she froze, caught in her act. He waited for no response, ramming his body into the door repeatedly until it busted the frame. She had already started swallowing some, just to spite his attempts.

"No—," he knocked the water glass out of her hand and grabbed one of her arms with the fist full of pills. "Spit them out," he said, turning her around on the counter and squeezing her cheeks just enough to stuff his fingers into her mouth to check in via the mirror. Nothing.

When she finally got her bearings, she slapped him with her free hand—over and over until he grabbed that one too.

"How many did you take?" He shouted, his face in hers. Though she tried to avoid him, he could tell she had been crying. Rather, attempting to. He had never seen her eyes so much as redden in the past.

She tossed out a number. "Four." She would have kicked him if he hadn't been trapping her legs between his and the sink cabinets.

"And what did Tariq give you before you came home?"

She chuckled into her chest. "Uncle wouldn't let him give me anything. My aunt threatened to divorce him but that still didn't change his heart."

Sedric breathed a sigh of relief, looking at the pill bottles she had opened. She would live.

As his body slackened—thanking Allah—she took advantage, bringing her fist up into her mouth and almost shoving more in. When he caught what she was doing, he pulled her wrist, making her spill some. She tried to crawl away from him—onto the sink counter and against the mirror—trying to leverage her legs to kick him. Her empty hand clawed at his neck.

Knowing he would have to hurt her to get her to stop, he did the thing that would cause the least damage:

He kissed her.

He let go of her wrists and kissed her. A fingers-in-hair, no-room-for-air (or pills) kind of kiss.

She dropped the pills to slap him, the pills scattering like seeds.

"Fine!" she shouted when he let go. "Fine!"

He minded his jaw, turning red from her abuse.

She turned her head from him to stare at the paint, trying her best to fade into the corner of wall and mirror. "It's not fine," he clucked, running his fingertips over her face to test her sensitivity. Their fight caused her forehead to bleed.

Her small brown eyes cut up at him.

He dug in his pocket, pulled out the ring. Put it in her face. "It's not fine if you have to hide this from me."

"Didn't do a good enough job of it." She plucked it from his fingers and examined it. She put it on her finger. "Aren't you going to wish me congratulations?"

"Is that what you disagreed with, then?" he asked, his voice low and hopeful.

"Sure," she shrugged. She smiled, showing no teeth. He hated when she smiled without teeth. Those smiles were meant to hurt him. Meant to tease him. He resisted the urge to force her mouth open again just to see the pearls.

She began to take the pins out of her hair, for they made it hard to fit into the corner comfortably. He watched her do so, unmoving in his *pinning* of her.

611

When she finished, she leaned back into the corner again, having no other choice. Her hair uncurling in messy angles like hatching meant to contrast her face.

"You going to marry him, then?"

"Guess I'll have to now," she gestured to the pills on the floor. *You dick.*

"Who is he?" He grabbed her chin, shook her until she looked at him. "Who?"

Stanza: The Sports section sucks balls.

"Rodrigo Rodriguez."

"A fucking downtown Chicano?"

"One of the Chicanos. Son of the Father who controls the drug mules distributing for the Blah-Blahs. I marry him and have a kid—preferably a boy, apparently—and woosh,"—she waved her hand, the engagement ring sparkling—"they will find it harder to kill family. They'll sever ties with Ghibla."

"That's it? That's all the trade is good for?"

"That's what I said." She leaned forward toward him. "I told Uncle, 'I can find us a better trade.' And he said, 'Go ahead and search. But this one is already found.' Couldn't find a Native for me like he's always gone on about but Mexican is indigenous enough, I guess."

"What?" The move was too desperate—there was something they weren't being told.

Lielyth looked over her shoulder at her reflection in the mirror. "I can divorce him once I have the baby, apparently. The Chicanos are big on babies. That and tequila. Apparently no one wants to marry this fucker and his daddy really wants grandkids. I'm no heir. I was simply a downpayment."

Sedric pulled her chin with a few fingertips and made her look at him, refusing to address her through the mirror. "I know Rodrigo. I know where he's stuck that dick of his. A baby's not worth catching whatever's on the end of it."

"You think I want a baby?" She laughed at him, showing teeth. "That's assuming we can even make one together. You know, I told Uncle that this might be a set up—that Rodrigo might be sterile and nothing will come of it besides an expensive fuck. But he seems to think the trade will start as soon as we tie the knot. 'The Indigenous keep their word!' he said."

"I won't let them force you into this." He put his sweaty forehead on hers.

She closed her eyes, too tired to object. "No one is forcing me into anything. I will willingly marry him."

"And you'll let him fuck you? A *stranger* fuck you?" He was watching her face as if it did not add up—as if Lielyth were a math problem he had calculated before.

"If it buys Uncle a bit of time—for whatever the fuck he's planning—then yes. Rodrigo isn't thrilled either, but he'll accept his punishment for apparently getting his younger brother arrested a few months back. His dad really wants him to settle down. And access to properties held in my name."

"It could get you killed—"

"You should have gone out tonight. Why didn't you? You could have been normal for once. The boys were going to stay in my rooms tonight to make sure I didn't run, but then they saw your car and knew you were still here. Fuck, they knew you'd check up on me when you heard me come in. Jesus, Sedric, you had the night off!"

She tried to push him away.

"Why are they so certain I wouldn't let you run?"

"They think you're loyal to my Uncle more than to me," she stood up, hoping he would make room for her as she did so, but he did not. She was speaking to his chest now. "They don't know otherwise."

"But they didn't invite me. That can't be so."

"But you didn't try and come, did you? You didn't ruin the plans."

"You didn't *want* me to come."

"I didn't," she agreed. "That would have messed up my own plans."

"Plans? What plans?"

She gestured to her face with a flippant air. "I was beaten for a reason. My acting had to be real. I threw my fit—demanded to keep you as a bodyguard even after I got married. Uncle agreed, but still had to show he was in control of me. Ten stiches later…"

"You *acted*, did you?"

"I had to make them think you were fucking me—that you controlled *me*. Oh, don't look at me like that. You know damn well what they all say about us. I simply confirmed it."

"So you control *me*, is it?"

"You control me more than you think, Sedric," she said up to him in disgust. In fact, she had no autonomy over her own space right now.

"And let me guess," he held up a finger before his snarling face. "You begged and begged the Boss to let you keep your lover—which I am not—" (but, would very much like to be, clearly)—"to make yourself look vulnerable. And he loved it. And so did the Chicano clan. They know they can get to you through me now. You fucking made me the target."

"What, did you think I'd actually run away with you? You think this beating was for you? Fuck you, Sedric!" she hissed up at his face.

"Pathetic. I thought you had more authority in this Family than to resort to scheming like this."

"Authority? You think I'm here because of my *authority?* It's by Uncle's grace I'm even alive, Sedric. He should have killed my parents, as I will do once he's dead. He spared me. *Me.* It is my duty to this Family, Sedric, to obey—otherwise, I've no purpose being part of it."

"I'm sick of being part of it," he growled down to her. "And by the looks of it, you are too." He pointed behind him, to the pill-spotted tiles. "We *can* leave, Lie."

"I'm not leaving."

"But that's exactly what you just tried to do." He grabbed the sides of her face and bared his teeth. "You can make me the target of your plans, that's fine. That's what I signed up for. But don't you dare leave me with your mess to clean up, understand?"

She refused to meet his eyes. Maybe he had gotten through to her this time. Maybe she would take down this wall.

"Can I take my shower now?"

A hopeful light faded in his face. "If you answer me one question," he replied, a knot forming in his throat. "Why the fuck did you make me get a vasectomy when you hired me, if not because you wanted to fuck me? Why did you pick me—of all the men—to be the one right here, right now, that you are hurting? All these years and I think I deserve an answer."

"Uncle paid you very well to get that vasectomy. I got to pick you so naturally he thought I wanted to fuck you."

"And you didn't let him think *otherwise.*"

"I chose you because you had never looked at me before. Some of the men had considered me. But you? Never. I thought I would be safer with you. Even though I was—am—afraid of you. Thought I could buy you off. Why do you constantly ask this of me, as if the answer's changed?"

Indeed, these weren't things Sedric didn't already know, but they were things Lielyth had never stated so clearly, and with so much context.

On outings, Lielyth and Sedric were often mistaken for a couple. She got jealous stares from women much prettier than she. She wanted to tell them she hadn't snagged anything, no. She'd *bought.*

She wanted to be clear, especially to the plain ones like her, that he wasn't hers; that he was paid to be with her; that they shouldn't get their hopes up because he would never actually be hers. She hated the envy and awe in their eyes She hated herself, sometimes, for being seen with him. For keeping him away from girls who had a chance.

"You got what you paid for, then," Sedric muttered, stepping aside.

She waited for him to leave the bathroom

He saw that expectant look. "No, I'm not going anywhere after the stunt you just pulled, Lie."

"Need I remind you that I can get rid of you in one phone call?"

"And ruin the charade you've worked so hard for? Go ahead."

She huffed at him and stepped into the shower, clothes still on. Before she pulled the curtain: "If you didn't like it, you should've let me swallow them."

Stanza: The cards were shuffled.

He watched as she tossed her clothes over the curtain rod piece by piece. He had seen her naked at least three times before, but he had never supervised her taking a shower. Sure, he had handed her the phone as she was changing in a dressing room once or twice, but even then, she had prepared herself for his presence, covered her breasts with her arm before he entered so she could "handle" the emergency.

The second time he had seen her naked was when he walked in on her changing in her bedroom, about to ask her which car he should order to pull around. She had not screamed and he had not apologized. He had lingered there, in her doorway. Then he had closed the door. And then, he had opened it right back up to finish watching her. Perhaps I should call that the third time, but I won't. There's one more after this—after she had glared at him as she finished getting dressed. This later prompted an excursion to one of the Lakota's favored whorehouses, where Lielyth had ordered Sedric to pick a girl. When he refused, she picked one for him.

"Fuck you, Lie!" he had shouted at her, storming out of the building. She had tipped the girl saying, "It's not you, you are lovely. This is just how you train them." The girl had just nodded, barely able to say "Thank you" in English.

In the car, he had shouted at her, "What the hell was that? I thought you said you needed to pick up a delivery!"

But she had said nothing, merely waited for him to start driving.

"Why do you keep doing this to me?" he shouted again and again, like he wasn't sure he said it the first time.

615

"Giving you whores?" she asked him, crossing her legs as if this were the most normal conversation in the world. "I need to know you're fucking something."

"So it doesn't end up being you? Fuck, Lie. I'm Muslim. I can't do that!" He had pointed to the building.

She laughed through her nose. *Can't, but you have.* "You can fuck *me*, though, is that it? You can come into my room whenever you want and stare at my chest and your faith isn't threatened then? That it?"

"You—you are not a whore," he tried to clarify.

"Really? I've felt like one recently." Her countenance finally broke and she hid her mouth behind her fingers. She stared out the car window.

"Lie, we are—we're stuck together. That's why I try."

"No, we're not stuck. You can leave any time you want. I can't."

"I don't understand you."

"Good. I don't want you to."

"You should have told me to get out. Should have screamed," he had mumbled under his breath as he started the car.

"Don't put this on me. Control *yourself.*"

"So it's my fault I was attracted to you? Because I can really control that."

"You can keep a door closed. You can knock."

"You can lock doors."

She had no retort.

At the next stop light he said, "I would fuck all those girls if it would make you jealous. But I know it won't. I don't know what makes you jealous. But I swear to—" No, he wouldn't bring Allah into this. "If I ever find out…"

"You'll what?"

"I don't know. I don't fucking know."

The third time he had seen her naked was right after he had helped The Boss's boys during a rather large raid on a skimming casino that wasn't paying its "Lakota dues." Sedric had bashed a few faces in that were too busy looking outward. The Boss's head loan shark had been impressed and offered to let Sedric tag along more often "for these sorts of things." Lielyth had seen the light brighten in Sedric's eyes that night and it had scared her. Sedric had replied that he'd think about the offer, which Lielyth also overheard. It was that same night that Lielyth had told him she was going to bed, as she normally did, but hadn't gone to her room. She had just stood there as he watched TV. He noticed briefly that she was in her nightclothes in front of him, which she hardly ever allowed without acting embarrassed. But she wasn't embarrassed this time. "I know you normally fall asleep on the couch," she had said. "And I don't know the last time you've used your bed, but tonight you are going to."

"Do you not want me to watch TV or something out here anymore? Is it too loud?"

"You misunderstand me. Go to your room."

When he had not gotten the hint, she had walked across the living space and into his room. Gave him more than a hint.

By the time he made it to his room, she was already slipping off her pants. He had paused in the doorway as she took off her top and turned around.

"Are you—are you serious?" he asked, pushing in that nose and staring at her.

"I want you to stop sleeping on the couch," she had said.

He had taken his shirt off and come to her.

"No," she said, moving back as he tried to touch her. "That's not what this is."

"Then what is it?"

Her eyes cut to the bed, telling him to get in it.

Her head followed him as he moved.

"If you don't want to be here then why are you?" He lifted the covers and sat down, manspreading as if blocking her from access to the bed.

"I could ask the same of you. If you'd rather work as Uncle's man, then why don't you?" She had stepped up to the bed, but had not gotten in.

"Oh, I see. You won't fuck me unless you're trying to get something out of me?"

"I'm not going to fuck you."

He had snorted through his nose. Itched that nose. "Then thank you for gracing me with your mere presence." He gestured to her body—naked except for those panties, now.

"Take your pants off."

"Is this some sort of test, then?"

"Take you dick out, now."

"No. Come in the bed with me."

She shook her head. "I want you to agree to go on their next excursion. But only if I can come along."

"Don't you already go along on the safe ones?"

"Yes, but I want you to tell them that."

"Why?"

"So it looks like your loyalty is to me first. That will impress Uncle, especially since they won't believe you. Not after what they saw tonight."

He hadn't paid full attention to her words then. How could he? Her pale breasts were taking up too much of his thoughts, outlined by her summer tan. She had been darker than him then. "You think this is the only way to convince me? Like I'm some pervert? Just get out."

She had turned around, not bothering to pick up her clothes. "Like I said, I want you to stop sleeping on the couch. We bought you a bed for a reason. I can buy you much more." And she had closed his door behind her. The next morning, her cleaning lady had knocked and entered Sedric's room. Speaking Spanish, the old woman greeted him like always and mumbled on and on in what Sedric always called "cursing him out, probably." But she stopped suddenly in her normal conversation-making when she noticed Lielyth's bed clothes on his floor. She smiled and nodded to him, probably saying something like "I knew one day you two would slip up. You have always been so hard to catch!" And she had just picked them up and went on tidying like always, mumbling on in Spanish.

Stanza: And in this corner, we have...

And now Sedric was staring at her clothes on the floor again, the ones in front of the shower (*our* obligatory shower scene). Except this time, there were pills there, too.

He looked up. She had just turned on the shower. "Wait," he said, pulling the curtain back. He reached around her and took her razor. Just for the insult.

She had jumped back, making the water spray directly across his torso. "Fuck, Sedric!" She shouted at him, closing the curtain back.

He sat down on the toilet, shaking off the water on his arm. He looked down at his shirt, soaking wet.

"You can't do shit like that!" she said, finally moving in the shower again.

"I barely saw you!" he griped back at her, unbuttoning his shirt so he could take it off.

He could feel the fumes of her hatred wafting toward him. Or, maybe it was just the steam of the shower. He tossed her razor in the sink beside him and took off his watch, checking it for water damage. The seconds ticked by and she had barely moved, the water hitting the same places behind the curtain. Perhaps those pills were kicking in and she was finding it hard to function. He needed to get her to talk.

"I forgot to mention, Lie. You know when we found that storage unit of the Taylor's full of all that collectable memorabilia and we used it to cover their debt?—we used it in the comic book store?"

"What about it?"

"Lucky Hardball said he knew the kid who used to rent the unit—said the kid hadn't checked in for years but had paid off the bill for that decade. And when I say kid, Lie, I mean *kid*. Sammy said he was barely, like, twelve. Where do you think a kid gets money like that?"[236]

She said nothing. He listened for a while, to make sure she was moving about.

"Hardball owed us for a reason, Sedric." He gave them storage space, they gave him plenty of coke to use and sell as he pleased. And he used more than he sold.

"Hardball was *sure* it was a kid, Lie. A black kid. Hardball swears the kid had to be dealing. Hardball only let the under-aged fuck rent it out because of the dirt he had on him. You tell me how a little kid can manipulate Hardball like that, Lie? I *told* you Inky was using kids to distribute. We have to put a stop to that. Little kids with big mouths, manipulating our employees. They're gonna get fucking shot."

"Sounds like this kid did, if he hasn't been around."

He heard the shampoo lid close.

Heartless bitch.

He watched the shower's steam float about him. "But seriously, Lie. Inky's got a black nerd working for him. What's that say about us?"

"That you're jealous a little kid has more dirt on Hardball than you? And I doubt it was Inky. That kid had thousands of dollars worth of shit in that unit. He knew what he was doing. He was more likely working for someone else. Someone's nephew or something."

"This is exactly what you said about Cotton's prostitute—the one who *didn't* blackmail him. You give people too much credit."

(Let me wow you with other made-up criminal nicknames and illegal exploits…)

"Speaking of credit and prostitutes, I got another call from that weirdass grad student who seems to think I have [let's just say John Milton's] personal copy of [maybe Ovid's *Metamorphosis* in Greek, because it sounds fancy]."

"But you do, don't you?"

Yeah, but no one was supposed to *know about it.*

---

[236] An Automaton, that's where.

He itched his neck, scruff irritating him. "What was her name again? Gobbler?"

"*Gabbler*," Lielyth corrected, shouting over the roar of the water. "Anyway, the bitch thinks she can blackmail me into letting her see it. She's writing a paper on it or something. You should hear the voicemail she left me."[237]

"Want me to have the boys look into it?"

"No. She's harmless enough. I think I might even meet her. I mean, anyone with the balls enough to try and blackmail a Lakota—while knowing what that name means—deserves my attention."

His face scrunched. She had just tried to kill herself and yet she was making future plans for a black market book she couldn't even read? This wasn't adding up.

He shook his head, leaning over to pick up a few plastic bottles of product they'd knocked over in their tussle. As he did so, he smelled himself. This had been a rough night for him. He needed a shower...

But that would be hard, with having to watch Lielyth's every goddamn move.

His own smell—a smell of smoke and sweat—made him cringe. He couldn't stand it; he shouldn't allow her to make him suffer it more.

He scowled at the shower curtain.

He stood up, undid his belt, took his shirt—pants—shoes—socks off, pushed back the curtain, stepped in the shower...

She jumped back, under the arch of the falling water. Her wide eyes confessed she hadn't expected him to ever do something like this. She didn't even think to cover herself, so stunned at the naked sight of him.

He put his hands out like a man trying to calm a wild animal who might dash for it. Her eyes darted to her end of the shower curtain, but his hand would catch her first and she might slip. Slipping was no certain death, only bruising and pain. The thought still tempted her.

When it was clear she wouldn't run, he pulled his portion of curtain back and stepped into the water.

"The hell are you doing?" she asked, true terror in her voice—a voice almost drowned out by the showerhead.

"Taking a shower. Testing myself."

"I could scream!"

---

[237] Well, I guess the *other* cat's out of the bag. Surprise? I'm a she/her pronoun. And I really wanted that interview.

He rolled his eyes as she folded over, trying to hide herself. "I'm not going to touch you. I need a shower too. How the hell you think I'll be able to do so otherwise, with you under a suicide watch, huh? It's nothing I haven't seen before." He snatched up the soap from the rack and mumbled, "Tries to fucking overdose [smh]."

He lathered up vigorously, glaring at her as if this was worse for him.

She started to laugh with her eyes tight, turning her head to the side and showing a sliver of teeth. This made him pause as he rinsed.

"You think it's funny?"

Water spit off her lips as she laughed. "You think you're so clever, don't you? To come up with an excuse to—to flash your dick at me." She gestured to it.

"Excuse my excuse." He gave a stolid shrug and stepped forward to rinse again.

This only made her laugh more—made her chest move in a way that matched how those teeth made him feel. Even if it was the laughter of someone on a bunch of pain pills, he couldn't help but get hard.

"Would you stop? Stop fucking laughing." He grew stern. "Seriously, stop!" he barked. This had not been part of the plan.[238]

She noticed her effect and became dead silent as she stared at *it*. The cold took her. She began to shiver at the sight.

"It will go away," he said, glaring at her, blaming her.

She averted her eyes and attempted to hide her shivering.

"Would you fucking stand in the water too?" he gestured to the open space beside him in the fancy shower-tub. "Making me feel bad."

"I'm fine here."

But he grabbed her arm, planning to step out of the water when he finally dragged her over.

She lifted her arms as he did so, sliding down the wall as if to escape his advances—pushed herself against the tile.

"I'm not going to fucking rape you," he hissed. "Would you please?" He stepped back from her. "Stand here, damn it."

She stood up, still shaking. "I'm sorry," she said. "I'm sorry." She couldn't look him in the eye, he was so angry. What made it worse was that he wasn't hard anymore. She disgusted him.

---

[238] Yeah, sure it hadn't.

She had never seen that expression of hurt on his face before. Perhaps because he had never seen that look of terror in hers.

"I'm finished, really," she told him, still looking down, still cupping and crossing herself.

"Let me wash this fucking grease from my hair and I will be too." He pointed at the shampoo behind her so she might hand it to him. No sudden movements.

She picked up her pink bottle, water bouncing off it as she passed it to him. "I'd never want to put you in danger," she said. She took the bottle back. "You are a target. That comes with the job. But I wouldn't want anything to happen to you."

"You just tried to kill yourself, Lie." He rinsed his hair—what little he had the barber leave—and rubbed his face under the water quickly. He hated closing his eyes in front of her—one less second he had to watch her. "They'd kill me if you ever succeeded. So don't tell me you fucking care."

Her eyes grew red at the thought.

He turned off the water, touching her to lean forward. He pulled back the curtain for her, gesturing for her to leave safely. He handed her a towel and took one for himself. She didn't bother to dry off properly, instead using it to quickly cover up.

"You laugh at my attempt at modesty?" she asked him, coming to the sink. She began to push back her dripping hair and examine her stiches. "I may protect my cunt like the fucking Mona Lisa, but that doesn't mean anyone should wait in line to see it." She began to brush her teeth, squirting out too much toothpaste and cursing.

"We did wait in line to see it, you and I," he said, massaging the towel over his wet hair. He still had not covered himself up. She was trying to ignore the fact—ignore his new confidence. The ice was too broken.

"And I fucking hated the crowd. Nothing you can't see on a postcard." She waved her toothbrush at him.

He had to look away as she inserted the brush, her teeth flashing at him. "Says the woman with a black market manuscript."

"If you owned the Mona Lisa, then you wouldn't need the damn postcards to avoid the lines."

Sedric would have laughed...if it had been Lielyth who said it. It was a casual and unfamiliar voice from the anteroom.

"I've seen it." As an afterthought, "Before it was chopped up."

Before the man finished his sentence, Sedric had shoved Lielyth behind him. Cautiously, he peered around the doorframe he had just busted moments ago. Lielyth dropped her toothbrush.

Sedric reeled himself back in and pushed her back into the bathtub—as if the tile might protect her.

"Who is it?" Lielyth whispered, eyes swelling with fear. *How much had they heard?*

Stanza: Team Sedric.

Sedric shook his head; he didn't recognized the man lounging on their couch, hands behind his **Chullo**-hatted head, bare feet crossed and resting on the sofa's arm, his smug smile too ready to grow wider.

The man had waved to him. *Waved.* Waved in a "hello, neighbor" kind of way.

The reclining man resembled a dandified hobo with his wiry mud-red hair, his chin sprouting stubble like metal does rust, his skin kissed with a shade of grime.

"You can come on out. I'm unarmed. Not here to hurt you." He turned on the TV and muted it. They could hear the buzzing.

"Who are you? How'd you get in here?" Sedric shouted, doing up the towel around his waist. He cursed himself for not bringing in his gun. He searched for the phone in his pants pockets laying on the floor. He handed it to Lielyth.

She thought twice before unlocking it.

"Shh. Not so loud. You, my new friends, can call me Julian. And I let myself in, a-thankyouverymuch."

"Didn't you lock the door?" Sedric scolded Lielyth.

"Of course she locked the door!" the man replied. He must have had bat ears. "I didn't *use* the door."

"You've been here this entire—whole time?" Sedric clamored, trying to force him back on subject. *He heard everything.*

"I suppose so," the man replied. They could hear the shrug in his voice. They heard him sit up, groaning as if some strain. "OK, I admit I've heard your entire conversation. Boy do you guys have some issues to work out." He paused, seeming to recollect. "Actually, I was brought in a bag. I should probably tell you that so you don't think I broke in. Everyone else inside the house is fine. I promise. They don't know I'm here."

"A bag?" Sedric tried to keep him talking while Lielyth texted for help. Not that anyone would be checking their phones this late at night.

"Yes, my partner slipped me into Lielyth's clutch at the party last night. Or, this night, really. Time's so relative."[239]

"What the fuck do you mean?" Sedric demanded.

"Do I have to *mean* anything at all, other than what I say?" the stranger questioned, asking himself as if too tired to be sure. Sedric and Lielyth both looked at one another, to confirm they both heard the same thing.

Lielyth tried to call someone she thought might be up—but of course half of them were drunk and out cold because of the party. No pickup.

"Stop calling for help. It will only make things weird. Then I might *really* have to kill someone. Please don't make me kill someone. That was *not* on the agenda, kiddos."

"Just tell me how the hell you got in here, and we might let *you* live."

They could hear him chuckle, a very gentle sound. "I just told you, kid. Lielyth's purse. Why don't you come on out, so we can have a little chat? I promise you, I'm unarmed. I'm a pacifist."

"And a liar too?" Sedric asked him. The joke got his adrenaline pumping. He gestured for Lielyth to stay put while he stepped out.

"Looking for this?" the man asked him, holding up the nearest gun Sedric was going to shoot for. "Could smell this hunk of metal the minute I came in. Here, take it if it will make you feel better." He tossed it to Sedric.

"Jesus Christ," Sedric cursed as he caught it. "You fucking lunatic!" He checked the lock quickly and pointed it at the man.

The stranger adjusted his **skullcap**—hadn't he been wearing a llama-patterned, poof-topped Chullo before? We all know he had.

With his fingerless-gloved hands, he picked up Sedric's half-used cigarette and reached into his long jacket's breast pocket, ignoring Sedric as Sedric growled, "Watch it, now!"

But all he removed was a matchbook, showing him with raised hands. Oddly enough, Sedric hadn't really worried about a weapon. The man didn't seem the type.

Putting the crumpled cigarette in his lips and pulling a match between the rough strips, he stated, "I don't carry weapons around. Don't need them. Well, that all depends on what you call a weapon, I guess. Com'on, sit down." He gave a lazy point to the chair across from him.

Sedric looked from the chair back to the man:

The man was now pushing back a **Rastafarian** hat.

---

[239] Wait. Is this Madus or Fletcher?

Is he fucking with me? How did he do that? "I'd rather stand." He almost wanted Lielyth to witness this, to prove he wasn't going crazy.

The visitor took out his cigarette and yawned, smoke drifting from his gaping mouth. "Have it your way, then," he tried to say through his silent scream. It was so late—past his bedtime! He scratched his scruffy neck, the movement sounding like someone rubbing sandpaper.

The man studied his cigarette for a brief second—where had his matches disappeared to? Julian had only taken up smoking to be able to follow Joslyn around on her smoking breaks. She smoked as much as Odys. He, however, chewed gum as much as Dorian. But the smoking made him feel like an individual. Made him feel like he was *choosing* his addiction; just has he had chosen a new name to match hers, he was choosing Joslyn.

He popped his neck, thinking about his *choices*. When he lifted his head, his hat was gone— Sedric had seen it vanish! Back into his head.

"Whatthehell are you?" Sedric readied to shoot him.

Lielyth's ears perked up, noticing the panic in Sedric's voice—the oddness of the question.

"Well, I'm an Automaton. Specifically, one sent by the god Vulcan to answer your prayers."

"Automicon?"

"Ah-toe-ma-ton." He mouthed out the syllables as if Sedric didn't speak English. "Well, that's what they used to call me, but really I'm more like a shape shifter these days. I can wind myself up." He snapped his fingers and made his entire body a dark, metallic nickel. "Look like a robot, don't I?" The man flashed his metal grill at him.

His voice shaking, "Lie, get out here."

She peeked around the corner and jumped when she saw the metal-man sitting on her couch, smoking. "Oh my god," she mouthed. *What pills did I take?*

"You see it too?"

The fucking Tin-man from Oz? "Yeah, I see him."

Julian crossed his legs and faded back to his more "normal" coloring. "So, now that's out of the way, I want you to know that you've been Chosen to play a game, Sedric—a game involving gods, beings like myself, and humans. You're the human in this scenario. You don't have a choice whether or not to play. Neither do I, really. But we can make it worth your while."

"We?"

"The other players on 'Team Sedric.'" He used bunny ears to show its titular nature. "Well, once we draft them, anyway." He waved a hand, as if they could get to that part later. "The important thing right now, Sedric, is that I can help you get out. And Lielyth too. No one has to

625

get hurt." He pointed at her and then brought that same finger to his mouth to bite his dirty nail. Mumbling as he bit it, "I can make *you* the one in charge, Sedric."

"In charge of what?"

"This situation? The entire Lakota family? Anything you want? Hell, that's the reason you're so *Chooseable*—your lack of choices in this world; you were throwing a fit in here because you didn't get to be her *servant* for the night. Yeah, kid, we've been watching you."

Their eyes glanced around for the cameras.

"This can be *yours*, kid. You can still keep all of this,"—Julian's eyes danced around the room, meaning their lifestyle—"Granted, things will change. But we're not taking it away. You need to make a decision: Willingly play or to be forced. It's no coincidence that your happy little *arrangement* is being disturbed with a marriage proposal. Time is of the essence. Especially since Adimar plans on kidnapping Lielyth very soon, so my sources say."

"Kidnap me?"

"He plans to give your head to the Blahblahblahs or whatever the heck you call 'em as a way of getting close to Genji Ghibla of said Blahblahblahs. Then, he's gonna kill Genji and take over both Indian Mafia clusterfucks."

"There's no possible way that freelancer can pull that off," Sedric said in disbelief (he had heard of Adimar, maybe even technically worked with him before signing on officially with the Lakotas in his previous work experience). "They won't follow him even if he does. You're making that shit up."

"He can," the Automaton said, "Especially if he has ex-gods and people like me working for him." He tapped his chest and then bit his nail again, growing more nervous at his words. He didn't like being mean—giving them an ultimatum—but he knew he had to. "Can you put that gun down, please? I don't need it going off and making everyone downstairs and upstairs shit their pants. It won't work on me anyway."

Sedric lowered his gun, laughing. "I'm hallucinating!" he said to Lielyth. "You've driven me insane and now I think I can see fucking Iron Man over here."

There was a knock on the door. "Ms.? Sedric?" it asked. "Open up!"

And when they looked back, the Automaton was gone. Well, what they *supposed* was "gone." Little did they know he had fallen as a paperclip between the cushions.

"I got your text," Jeff said, coming in as Sedric opened the door.

"It was me," Lielyth said, stepping where he could see. "I thought I heard something. Was a false alarm. Probably an—an owl or something." She pointed to her balcony doors, where birds were known to roost for the night.

The omen made Jeff's superstitious eyes widen. "Owls?" Then, Jeff took a step back and looked from Sedric to Lielyth, both still in towels. A smirk spread across his face. "You get mad at her? That what this is, Sed? You scare her?"

Sedric's nostrils flared at what Jeff implied. "Get the fuck out, man."

Jeff raised his hands, chuckling. "OK, Sed. But keep your phone away from her next time, man. I won't escalate this but you gottah be more discrete if you gonna be all mad about it. You one lucky bastard, man. You got a real good situation. You're lucky the boss lets her keep you. It ain't her fault, man."

Sedric stepped in front of his view so he'd stop ogling her. "She's fine. Get out."

"You better cool it if you want her fiancé to let her keep you, though." Jeff shook his round head, still chuckling as he left them.

"Fucker doesn't respect me," Lielyth hissed at the door, as if she were about to follow Jeff and claw his eyes out. Sedric pushed her back. "I have no power over them, see?"

Sedric locked the door behind him and turned back to stare at the couch. He adjusted the towel slipping down his hips, dragged her away from the door. *We have bigger issues right now.* He pointed to the couch. *Like the djinn granting us wishes.*

"I think I killed myself and this is limbo or something. I don't feel well, Sedric." She put her hand on her stomach.

"It's the pills," he assured her, still staring at the couch. "But the seeing things? I don't think that's their fault."

"What—what was he even saying?" Lielyth asked him. "Why does he want *you?*"

"Now like I was saying," Julian said, appearing once more, making them jump.

"Jesus!" Lielyth cursed, covering her mouth as she clung to the wall.

"If you want me to get you out of here—no marriage, no kidnapping, no more taking shit—then there will be a distraction tomorrow at five in the morning." He looked at a watch that appeared on his wrist. "Well, since it's technically morning already, let me correct myself: in a few, my partner will cause a distraction. When it happens, I'm going to escort you out of here so we can regroup."

"Where?" Lielyth asked as if he were some trickster.

"Not far," Julian said. "The game is coming to us, no doubt. We can't escape it. But we need to be free to talk without so many humans around. They won't understand. And we don't make them safe."

"But why Sedric?" Lielyth asked. *Why is he so special?*

"We're going to make Sedric a Master of gods," Julian said, picking underneath his nails and watching them. "And you, Ms. Lakota, can come along for the fun of it. We'll need you, Lielyth. You're great leverage."

Old language dies hard.

"What did you say your name was?" Lielyth asked.

"Julian."

"Julian what?" Sedric asked.

"Just Julian."

Sometimes Fletcher, when I forget.

Sedric tried to play along, as if he wasn't going mad, "And what if we don't want to go? Why do we have to leave, if the game is going to come to us?"

"Oh, you want to go my friend," Julian stood up. His hand formed into a gun and showed them why.

Sedric raised his own, but felt like his was nothing more than a toy, compared.

Julian walked up to Sedric. "Use it on me. Go ahead. You know it won't work. But I need to show you what will happen." He pushed the gun into his chest, dipping it into his fluid shell. The tip of it pulled out—just a little, but still touching—with a silencer. Julian's body. He made Sedric pull the trigger.

Lielyth flinched when it happened. But the man did not fall. Instead, he opened his mouth and plucked out the bullet that had just pierced his chest. He shook out his tongue and licked his lips. "Blech." *Gunpowder is the worst taste.*

He took Sedric's palm (his own gun and the silencer had disappeared somewhere, willingly surrendered) and dropped the golden ammo.

"I'm Alchemy—Alchemy!—personified, motherfucker. And I'm offering you power and glory and fucking control,"—his eyes darted to Lielyth on that last promise. "It's not going to be clean or pretty, but you should damn well take my advice. You both are in danger. Even if Adimar wasn't in the mix, I'd still say you need some divine intervention right about now. The Chicanos have their own plans with Lielyth. Her Uncle is in a corner right now. He's using it to buy more time."

"What do you mean?" Lielyth dared him to speak ill of her blood.

Sedric held her back.

"I mean he hasn't told you that Adimar has bought off [three random names here that sound important and connote a loss of 50% of Lakota operations in some specific area of crime]. He just found out last week. They turned against him. That's why this sudden marriage."

"Prove it."

"I can't, but why would I lie? You've got enough reasons as it is to believe me. I don't get to choose either, and I'm fucking scared too. But we're going to play this game together. And guess what? We're guaranteed to fucking win. We've got cheat codes. We just have to put on a good show."

Still cupping the golden bullet, Sedric found himself speaking the most ridiculous sentence: "If I'm 'Team Sedric' who's the other team?"

"There's going to be more than two teams, probably. And they'll all want to kill you."

"And so I'm going to have to kill the other teams?"

"No. Just the other Chosens on said teams. Starting with *Adimar*."

SEDRIC IBN SINA:[240] Chosen.

WHY?: Because Julian and Joslyn were told to choose.

WHY?: Because Cestus told them the box was now spitting out prophecies. He called them up and said, "You know, I took the box because you were forgetting to live. You kept waiting for it to tell you what to do. Wanting it to give you an oracle. And it finally has. Vulcan's going to make Himself part of the game, it says. Says that when He comes, you should side with Him and His endorsement."

"An incarnation? But that's cheating," Joslyn had said over speakerphone.

But Cestus had only sighed. "Isn't the box cheating too, by telling us what He's planning? This whole game is rigged. The other gods just play along to find out how."

"What did it say *exactly*? Read it to us," she urged, for she knew it was a poem like scripture.

"I have meditated on the meaning and there is no other interpretation. Don't pretend to doubt my exegesis."

But he read it to them anyway.

---

[240] One of his many names. That I've changed. Obviously.

WHY?: Because they deserved to know the wretched commandments, so that they might break them.

"Why don't you give the box back to Maurice? You know he wants it, Cestus," Julian had pushed.

"No," Cestus had answered, the cell reception making his voice scratchier than usual. They had leaned in, as not to miss a word. "He will destroy it. You give Maurice the box and there will be one less channel open. Don't you see? Vulcan always meant for Maurice to have the box, to get angry and want to destroy the box—as we all once considered doing. But if that happens, if Maurice destroys the box, then the silence will be worse. Or, He'll just give us another object to venerate and follow. It has to be stuck in limbo. Worthless. Just as Maurice is stuck in limbo. Otherwise we're all going to kill each other like the gods want."

"He sounds like Q, Julian."

"If that's your concern, Cestus, then why are you telling us about the tissue that came out of it?"

"Because I'm hoping you'll do the opposite of what the tissue wants you to do. If Vulcan's Avatar is coming to us—going to be an Automaton like us in some fuckedup version of the Nativity—then this is our chance to get even with Him. Don't let Him be Christ."

But, my reader, they would. They did.

This book is indie.
Support us by leaving an honest review and lending out this book if you can.

Circo del Herrero

Learn more at:
www.circodelherreroseries.com

Cover designed by SOBpublishing.